MARY POPPINS

COLLECTION

BY P. L. TRAVERS

ILLUSTRATED BY MARY SHEPARD

HOUGHTON MIFFLIN HARCOURT
Boston   New York

Manufactured in the United States
DOC 10 9 8 7
4500684158

BY P. L. TRAVERS

CONTENTS

FOREWORD

Mary Poppins, the Disney film starring Julie Andrews, burst onto American movie screens in 1964. I was ten. Yes, I loved it. But I loved the books more. The movie is sunny and as sweet as a spoonful of sugar. The books, though, show glimmers of a far more mysterious and even dangerous world. For thirty years before the nanny began to sing on the screen, she stalked the pages of these books with ferocity, vanity, and power.

There can be few other characters in literature who are as well known and cryptic as Mary Poppins. Frankenstein's monster, perhaps. The Yahweh voice in the story of Job. Like them, Mary Poppins is an eternal conundrum. And no one can ever forget the domestic servant who makes magic, the goddess in disguise as a governess who takes every second Thursday off.

I moved to England in 1990. I was trying to find the nerve to begin an adult novel to be called *Wicked*. It would be about a mysterious, powerful woman. But I felt daunted, weighed down by fears of my own hubris. Then, somehow I learned that P. L. Travers, the creator of Mary Poppins, lived in London. I wrote and asked if I could come visit. I got an answer back within a day or two, written in a quavery hand. I might come for tea on Tuesday week.

The day arrived. I took the Tube to Sloane Square and headed west on the King's Road. Travers's home was on a short street that branched off to the left. The neighborhood had been laid out in the eighteenth century, I suspect; the houses were small but pretty, and lined up right next to one another. I skulked up and down the block, getting up my nerve. (I had read interviews; P. L. Travers seemed to be fierce.) I noticed that brass stars were embedded in the sidewalk, which in England is called the pavement. I remember them as about the size of a small child's palm with outstretched fingers. They gave me courage.

I found the address and pressed on the bell. A harried-looking aide, a woman of a certain age, let me in and said without fanfare, "You'll find *her* in the reception room."

I pushed through the door into a shadowy parlor that hadn't been fluffed up recently. An old woman slumped in an upholstered chair set back from the window. "Miss Travers?" I ventured. "P. L. Travers?" As if this bright-eyed, gnarled creature might be someone else.

"The electric mains are through the swinging door to the kitchen," she said. She thought I was the man who came to read the meters.

I said, "I am a devoted fan."

"No doubt," she said, "but the mains aren't in this

room; they're through the passage." She pointed as if I might not be very bright, then observed, "You have *books* with you."

"Your books," I said. "I love them."

I had with me one of the Mary Poppins books, and a Christmas story named *The Fox at the Manger,* and an old essay called "Aunt Sass," which P. L. Travers had had privately printed for friends and family. I showed them to her. She wasn't surprised that the meter man might be conversant with the ephemera of her career.

The disgruntled aide sloughed in with some tea and digestive biscuits. "Well, you're here, you might as well stay," allowed P. L. Travers. She seemed not to remember that she had invited me. Or was she only pretending in order to set me on edge? I perched on a stool and sipped weak Typhoo tea and told her what Mary Poppins had meant to me as a child.

It was clear to me within moments that the great P. L. Travers might be easily tired; she was about ninety-three. She was unable to leave her chair without assistance. Her dancing days were over. But I stayed the hour. She suffered me a little less than gladly, and sniffed a lot.

I told her I loved the chapter about the two newborn babies speaking the language of the birds, but then growing older and forgetting it. She pouted at that but didn't comment. Growing older and forgetting are habits of the elderly too.

I told her there were stars in the pavement outside her house. She looked down at her own opened hands.

I asked her if she ever read her own books. She leaned forward. "Well, I do glance at the Mary Poppins stories now and then." Full of hesitations and static, hers was an interesting, querulous, theatrical voice. "And I do not know where they came from. It is hard to believe I wrote them. I am so very old now that I do not remember how the stories turn out. They unfold for me with novelty and mystery, and I turn the pages to find out what happens."

"And how do they seem to you?"

"Do you know," she said, settling back in her chair, "I find them de-*light*-ful."

Then I asked her where in London the Banks family lived.

She glared at me as if I were an idiot. "They aren't *real*," she said. "They don't exist. They are imaginary. The meter is waiting for your attention. Through there."

"Yes, I realize the Bankses are characters in a book. What I mean is, where in London would we expect to find a Cherry Tree Lane? I know it is a made-up street, but London is full of neighborhoods. What neighborhood do you picture Cherry Tree Lane to be? Hampstead? Pimlico? Maida Vale?"

She mused, and then said—slowly, ruminatively— "Somewhere . . . between the stars in the pavement . . . and World's End."

World's End is the name of an intersection toward the western end of the King's Road. For a long time I thought it was named World's End because prisoners and debtors being exiled from England to Australia left from there. I'm not able to verify this theory today; maybe I heard it from Travers herself, that cartographer, that exile. That mythmaker.

But how like P. L. Travers, I thought, to answer a question about geography with a poetic puzzle. Of course the place that Mary Poppins showed up was somewhere between the stars and World's End. Of *course*.

Sometimes people from worlds apart come together for an hour, and for an hour learn to speak each other's language, before they forget it again.

She signed my books for me with a flourish. I left shortly thereafter. She hadn't had her electric mains properly read that day. But I felt I had stood within a few square feet of the power source of Mary Poppins, and I had not exploded or disappeared or floated up to the ceiling.

I had, however, become a little lighter. I remembered what magic there is in storytelling. As I hurried back to the Tube, back to my own work, my feet fairly danced on the stars.

Gregory Maguire

Inside a little curly frame was a painting of Mary Poppins

MARY POPPINS

TO MY MOTHER 1875–1928

CONTENTS

ILLUSTRATIONS

Also insets and tailpieces

CHAPTER ONE

EAST WIND

If you want to find Cherry-Tree Lane all you have to do is ask the Policeman at the cross-roads. He will push his helmet slightly to one side, scratch his head thoughtfully, and then he will point his huge white-gloved finger and say: "First to your right, second to your left, sharp right again, and you're there. Good-morning."

And sure enough, if you follow his directions exactly, you *will* be there — right in the middle of Cherry-Tree Lane, where the houses run down one side and the Park runs down the other and the cherry-trees go dancing right down the middle.

If you are looking for Number Seventeen — and it is more than likely that you will be, for this book is all about that particular house — you will very soon find it. To begin with, it is the smallest house in the Lane. And besides that, it is the only one that is rather dilapidated and needs a coat of paint. But Mr. Banks, who owns it, said to Mrs. Banks that she could have either a nice, clean, comfortable house or four children. But not both, for he couldn't afford it.

And after Mrs. Banks had given the matter some consideration she came to the conclusion that she would rather have Jane, who was the eldest, and Michael, who came next, and John and Barbara, who were Twins and came last of all. So it was settled, and that was how the Banks family came to live at Number Seventeen, with Mrs. Brill to cook for them, and Ellen to lay the tables, and Robertson Ay to cut the lawn and clean the knives and polish the shoes and, as Mr. Banks always said, "to waste his time and my money."

And, of course, besides these there was Katie Nanna, who doesn't really deserve to come into the book at all because, at the time I am speaking of, she had just left Number Seventeen.

"Without by your leave or a word of warning. And what am I to do?" said Mrs. Banks.

"Advertise, my dear," said Mr. Banks, putting on his shoes. "And I wish Robertson Ay would go without a word of warning, for he has again polished one boot and left the other untouched. I shall look very lopsided."

"That," said Mrs. Banks, "is not of the least importance. You haven't told me what I'm to do about Katie Nanna."

"I don't see how you can do anything about her since she has disappeared," replied Mr. Banks, "But if it were me — I mean I — well, I should get somebody to put in the *Morning Paper* the news that Jane and Michael and John and Barbara Banks (to say nothing of their Mother) require the best possible Nannie at the lowest possible wage and at once. Then I should wait and watch for the Nannies to queue up outside the front gate, and I should get very cross with them for holding up the traffic and making it necessary for me to give the policeman a shilling for putting him to so much trouble. Now I must be off. Whew, it's as cold as the North Pole. Which way is the wind blowing?"

And as he said that, Mr. Banks popped his head out of the window and looked down the Lane to Admiral Boom's house at the corner. This was the grandest house in the Lane, and the Lane was very proud of it because it was built exactly like a ship. There was a flagstaff in the garden, and on the roof was a gilt weathercock shaped like a telescope.

"Ha!" said Mr. Banks, drawing in his head very quickly. "Admiral's telescope says East Wind. I thought as much. There is frost in my bones. I shall wear two overcoats." And he kissed his wife absent-mindedly on one side of her nose and waved to the children and went away to the City.

Now, the City was a place where Mr. Banks went every day — except Sundays, of course, and Bank Holidays — and while he was there he sat on a large chair in front of a large desk and made money. All day long he

worked, cutting out pennies and shillings and half-crowns
and threepenny-bits. And he brought them home with
him in his little black bag. Sometimes he would give some
to Jane and Michael for their money-boxes, and when he
couldn't spare any he would say, "The Bank is broken,"
and they would know he hadn't made much money that
day.

Well, Mr. Banks went off with his black bag, and Mrs.
Banks went into the drawing-room and sat there all day
long writing letters to the papers and begging them to
send some Nannies to her at once as she was waiting; and
upstairs in the Nursery, Jane and Michael watched at the

window and wondered who would come. They were glad
Katie Nanna had gone, for they had never liked her. She
was old and fat and smelt of barley-water. Anything, they
thought, would be better than Katie Nanna — if not *much*
better.

When the afternoon began to die away behind the Park,
Mrs. Brill and Ellen came to give them their supper and to
bath the Twins. And after supper Jane and Michael sat at
the window watching for Mr. Banks to come home, and
listening to the sound of the East Wind blowing through
the naked branches of the cherry-trees in the Lane. The
trees themselves, turning and bending in the half light,
looked as though they had gone mad and were dancing
their roots out of the ground.

"There he is!" said Michael, pointing suddenly to a
shape that banged heavily against the gate. Jane peered
through the gathering darkness.

"That's not Daddy," she said. "It's somebody else."

Then the shape, tossed and bent under the wind, lifted
the latch of the gate, and they could see that it belonged
to a woman, who was holding her hat on with one hand
and carrying a bag in the other. As they watched, Jane and
Michael saw a curious thing happen. As soon as the shape
was inside the gate the wind seemed to catch her up into
the air and fling her at the house. It was as though it had
flung her first at the gate, waited for her to open it, and
then had lifted and thrown her, bag and all, at the front

door. The watching children heard a terrific bang, and as she landed the whole house shook.

"How funny! I've never seen that happen before," said Michael.

"Let's go and see who it is!" said Jane, and taking Michael's arm she drew him away from the window, through the Nursery and out on to the landing. From there they always had a good view of anything that happened in the front hall.

Presently they saw their Mother coming out of the drawing-room with a visitor following her. Jane and Michael could see that the newcomer had shiny black hair — "Rather like a wooden Dutch doll," whispered Jane. And that she was thin, with large feet and hands, and small, rather peering blue eyes.

"You'll find that they are very nice children," Mrs. Banks was saying.

Michael's elbow gave a sharp dig at Jane's ribs.

"And that they give no trouble at all," continued Mrs. Banks uncertainly, as if she herself didn't really believe what she was saying. They heard the visitor sniff as though *she* didn't either.

"Now, about references ——" Mrs. Banks went on.

"Oh, I make it a rule never to give references," said the other firmly. Mrs. Banks stared.

"But I thought it was usual," she said. "I mean — I understood people always did."

Holding her hat on with one hand and carrying a bag in the other

"A very old-fashioned idea, to *my* mind," Jane and Michael heard the stern voice say. "*Very* old-fashioned. *Quite* out of date, as you might say."

Now, if there was one thing Mrs. Banks did not like, it was to be thought old-fashioned. She just couldn't bear it. So she said quickly:

"Very well, then. We won't bother about them. I only asked, of course, in case *you* — er — required it. The nursery is upstairs —— " And she led the way towards the staircase, talking all the time, without stopping once. And because she was doing that Mrs. Banks did not notice what was happening behind her, but Jane and Michael, watching from the top landing, had an excellent view of the extraordinary thing the visitor now did.

Certainly she followed Mrs. Banks upstairs, but not in the usual way. With her large bag in her hands she slid gracefully *up* the banisters, and arrived at the landing at the same time as Mrs. Banks. Such a thing, Jane and Michael knew, had never been done before. Down, of course, for they had often done it themselves. But up — never! They gazed curiously at the strange new visitor.

"Well, that's all settled, then." A sigh of relief came from the children's Mother.

"Quite. As long as *I'm* satisfied," said the other, wiping her nose with a large red and white bandanna handkerchief.

"Why, children," said Mrs. Banks, noticing them suddenly, "what are you doing there? This is your new nurse, Mary Poppins. Jane, Michael, say how do you do! And these" — she waved her hand at the babies in their cots — "are the Twins."

Mary Poppins regarded them steadily, looking from one to the other as though she were making up her mind whether she liked them or not.

"Will we do?" said Michael.

"Michael, don't be naughty," said his Mother.

Mary Poppins continued to regard the four children searchingly. Then, with a long, loud sniff that seemed to indicate that she had made up her mind, she said:

"I'll take the position."

"For all the world," as Mrs. Banks said to her husband later, "as though she were doing us a signal honour."

"Perhaps she is," said Mr. Banks, putting his nose round the corner of the newspaper for a moment and then withdrawing it very quickly.

When their Mother had gone, Jane and Michael edged towards Mary Poppins, who stood, still as a post, with her hands folded in front of her.

"How did you come?" Jane asked. "It looked just as if the wind blew you here."

"It did," said Mary Poppins briefly. And she proceeded to unwind her muffler from her neck and to take off her hat, which she hung on one of the bedposts.

As it did not seem as though Mary Poppins were going to say any more — though she sniffed a great deal — Jane, too, remained silent. But when she bent down to undo her bag, Michael could not restrain himself.

"What a funny bag!" he said, pinching it with his fingers.

"Carpet," said Mary Poppins, putting her key in the lock.

"To carry carpets in, you mean?"

"No. Made of."

"Oh," said Michael. "I see." But he didn't — quite.

By this time the bag was open, and Jane and Michael were more than surprised to find it was completely empty.

"Why," said Jane, "there's nothing in it!"

"What do you mean — nothing?" demanded Mary Poppins, drawing herself up and looking as though she had been insulted. "Nothing in it, did you say?"

And with that she took out from the empty bag a starched white apron and tied it round her waist. Next she unpacked a large cake of Sunlight Soap, a toothbrush, a packet of hairpins, a bottle of scent, a small folding armchair and a box of throat lozenges.

Jane and Michael stared.

"But I *saw*," whispered Michael. "It *was* empty."

"Hush!" said Jane, as Mary Poppins took out a large bottle labelled "One Tea-Spoon to be Taken at Bed-Time."

A spoon was attached to the neck of the bottle, and into this Mary Poppins poured a dark crimson fluid.

"Is that your medicine?" enquired Michael, looking very interested.

"No, yours," said Mary Poppins, holding out the spoon to him. Michael stared. He wrinkled up his nose. He began to protest.

"I don't want it. I don't need it. I won't!"

But Mary Poppins's eyes were fixed upon him, and Michael suddenly discovered that you could not look at Mary Poppins and disobey her. There was something strange and extraordinary about her — something that was frightening and at the same time most exciting. The spoon came nearer. He held his breath, shut his eyes and gulped. A delicious taste ran round his mouth. He turned his tongue in it. He swallowed, and a happy smile ran round his face.

"Strawberry ice," he said ecstatically. "More, more, more!"

But Mary Poppins, her face as stern as before, was pouring out a dose for Jane. It ran into the spoon, silvery, greeny, yellowy. Jane tasted it.

"Lime-juice cordial," she said, sliding her tongue deliciously over her lips. But when she saw Mary Poppins moving towards the Twins with the bottle Jane rushed at her.

"Oh, no — please. They're too young. It wouldn't be good for them. Please!"

Mary Poppins, however, took no notice, but with a warning, terrible glance at Jane, tipped the spoon towards

John's mouth. He lapped at it eagerly, and by the few drops that were spilt on his bib, Jane and Michael could tell that the substance in the spoon this time was milk. Then Barbara had her share, and she gurgled and licked the spoon twice.

Mary Poppins then poured out another dose and solemnly took it herself.

"Rum punch," she said, smacking her lips and corking the bottle.

Jane's eyes and Michael's popped with astonishment, but they were not given much time to wonder, for Mary Poppins, having put the miraculous bottle on the mantelpiece, turned to them.

"Now," she said, "spit-spot into bed." And she began to undress them. They noticed that whereas buttons and hooks had needed all sorts of coaxing from Katie Nanna, for Mary Poppins they flew apart almost at a look. In less than a minute they found themselves in bed and watching, by the dim light from the night-light, the rest of Mary Poppins's unpacking being performed.

From the carpet bag she took out seven flannel nightgowns, four cotton ones, a pair of boots, a set of dominoes, two bathing-caps and a postcard album. Last of all came a folding camp-bedstead with blankets and eiderdown complete, and this she set down between John's cot and Barbara's.

Jane and Michael sat hugging themselves and watching. It was all so surprising that they could find nothing to say. But they knew, both of them, that something strange and wonderful had happened at Number Seventeen, Cherry-Tree Lane.

Mary Poppins, slipping one of the flannel nightgowns over her head, began to undress underneath it as though it were a tent. Michael, charmed by this strange new arrival, unable to keep silent any longer, called to her.

"Mary Poppins," he cried, "you'll never leave us, will you?"

There was no reply from under the nightgown. Michael could not bear it.

"You won't leave us, will you?" he called anxiously.

Mary Poppins's head came out of the top of the nightgown. She looked very fierce.

"One word more from that direction," she said threateningly, "and I'll call the Policeman."

"I was only saying," began Michael, meekly, "that we hoped you wouldn't be going away soon——" He stopped, feeling very red and confused.

Mary Poppins stared from him to Jane in silence. Then she sniffed.

"I'll stay till the wind changes," she said shortly, and she blew out her candle and got into bed.

"That's all right," said Michael, half to himself and half to Jane. But Jane wasn't listening. She was thinking about all that had happened, and wondering. . . .

And that is how Mary Poppins came to live at Number
Seventeen, Cherry-Tree Lane. And although they sometimes found themselves wishing for the quieter, more
ordinary days when Katie Nanna ruled the household,
everybody, on the whole, was glad of Mary Poppins's
arrival. Mr. Banks was glad because, as she arrived by
herself and did not hold up the traffic, he had not had to
tip the Policeman. Mrs. Banks was glad because she was
able to tell everybody that *her* children's nurse was so
fashionable that she didn't believe in giving references.
Mrs. Brill and Ellen were glad because they could drink
strong cups of tea all day in the kitchen and no longer
needed to preside at nursery suppers. Robertson Ay was
glad, too, because Mary Poppins had only one pair of
shoes, and those she polished herself.

But nobody ever knew what Mary Poppins felt about
it, for Mary Poppins never told anybody anything. . . .

CHAPTER
Two

THE DAY OUT

very third Thursday," said Mrs. Banks. "Two till five."

Mary Poppins eyed her sternly. "The best people, ma'am," she said, "give every *second* Thursday, and one till six. And those I shall take or———" Mary Poppins paused, and Mrs. Banks knew what the pause meant. It meant that if she didn't get what she wanted Mary Poppins would not stay.

"Very well, very well," said Mrs. Banks hurriedly, though she wished Mary Poppins did not know so very much more about the best people than she did herself.

So Mary Poppins put on her white gloves and tucked her umbrella under her arm — not because it was raining but because it had such a beautiful handle that she couldn't possibly leave it at home. How could you leave your umbrella behind if it had a parrot's head for a handle? Besides, Mary Poppins was very vain and liked to look her best. Indeed, she was quite sure that she never looked anything else.

Jane waved to her from the Nursery window.

"Where are you going?" she called.

"Kindly close that window," replied Mary Poppins, and Jane's head hurriedly disappeared inside the Nursery.

Mary Poppins walked down the garden path and opened the gate. Once outside in the Lane, she set off walking very quickly as if she were afraid the afternoon would run away from her if she didn't keep up with it. At the corner she turned to the right and then to the left, nodded haughtily to the Policeman, who said it was a nice day, and by that time she felt that her Day Out had begun.

She stopped beside an empty motor-car in order to put her hat straight with the help of the wind-screen, in which it was reflected, then she smoothed down her frock and tucked her umbrella more securely under her arm so that the handle, or rather the parrot, could be seen by everybody. After these preparations she went forward to meet the Match-Man.

Now, the Match-Man had two professions. He not only sold matches like any ordinary match-man, but he drew pavement pictures as well. He did these things turn-about according to the weather. If it was wet, he sold matches because the rain would have washed away his pictures if he had painted them. If it was fine, he was on his knees all day, making pictures in coloured chalks on the side-walks, and doing them so quickly that often you would find he had painted up one side of a street and down the

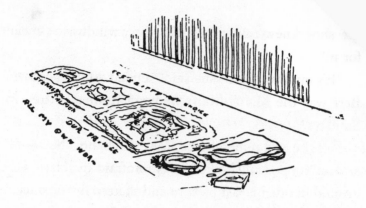

other almost before you'd had time to come round the corner.

On this particular day, which was fine but cold, he was painting. He was in the act of adding a picture of two bananas, an apple, and a head of Queen Elizabeth to a long string of others, when Mary Poppins walked up to him, tip-toeing so as to surprise him.

"Hey!" called Mary Poppins softly.

He went on putting brown stripes on a banana and brown curls on Queen Elizabeth's head.

"Ahem!" said Mary Poppins, with a ladylike cough.

He turned with a start and saw her.

"Mary!" he cried, and you could tell by the way he cried it that Mary Poppins was a very important person in his life.

Mary Poppins looked down at her feet and rubbed the toe of one shoe along the pavement two or three times. Then she smiled at the shoe in such a way that quite well that the smile wasn't meant

y, Bert," she said. "Didn't you remember?"

Match-Man's name — Herbert Alfred for Sundays.

"Of course I remembered, Mary," he said, "but ——" and he stopped and looked sadly into his cap. It lay on the ground beside his last picture and there was tuppence in it. He picked it up and jingled the pennies.

"That all you got, Bert?" said Mary Poppins, and she said it so brightly you could hardly tell she was disappointed at all.

"That's the lot," he said. "Business is bad today. You'd think anybody'd be glad to pay to see that, wouldn't you?" And he nodded his head at Queen Elizabeth. "Well — that's how it is, Mary," he sighed. "Can't take you to tea today, I'm afraid."

Mary Poppins thought of the raspberry-jam-cakes they always had on her Day Out, and she was just going to sigh, when she saw the Match-Man's face. So, very cleverly, she turned the sigh into a smile — a good one with both ends turned up — and said:

"That's all right, Bert. Don't you mind. I'd much rather not go to tea. A stodgy meal, I call it — really."

And that, when you think how very much she liked raspberry-jam-cakes, was rather nice of Mary Poppins.

The Match-Man apparently thought so, too, for he

took her white-gloved hand in his and squeezed it hard. Then together they walked down the row of pictures.

"Now, *there's* one you've never seen before!" said the Match-Man proudly, pointing to a painting of a mountain covered with snow and its slopes simply littered with grasshoppers sitting on gigantic roses.

This time Mary Poppins could indulge in a sigh without hurting his feelings.

"Oh, Bert," she said, "that's a fair treat!" And by the way she said it she made him feel that by rights the picture should have been in the Royal Academy, which is a large room where people hang the pictures they have painted. Everybody comes to see them, and when they have looked at them for a very long time, everybody says to everybody else: "The idea — my dear!"

The next picture Mary Poppins and the Match-Man came to was even better. It was the country — all trees and grass and a little bit of blue sea in the distance, and something that looked like Margate in the background.

"My word!" said Mary Poppins admiringly, stooping so that she could see it better. "Why, Bert, whatever is the matter?"

For the Match-Man had caught hold of her other hand now, and was looking very excited.

"Mary," he said, "I got an idea! A real *idea*. Why don't we go there — right now — this very day? Both together, into the picture. Eh, Mary?" And still holding her hands he drew her right out of the street, away from the iron railings and the lamp-posts, into the very middle of the picture. Pff! There they were, right inside it!

How green it was there and how quiet, and what soft crisp grass under their feet! They could hardly believe it was true, and yet here were green branches huskily rattling on their hats as they bent beneath them, and little coloured flowers curling round their shoes. They stared at each other, and each noticed that the other had changed. To Mary Poppins the Match-Man seemed to have bought himself an entirely new suit of clothes, for he was now wearing a bright green-and-red striped coat and white flannel trousers and, best of all, a new straw hat. He looked unusually clean, as though he had been polished.

"Why, Bert, you look fine!" she cried in an admiring voice.

Bert could not say anything for a moment, for his mouth had fallen open and he was staring at her with round eyes. Then he gulped and said: "Golly!"

That was all. But he said it in such a way and stared so steadily and so delightedly at her that she took a little mirror out of her bag and looked at herself in it.

She, too, she discovered, had changed. Round her shoulders hung a cloak of lovely artificial silk with watery patterns all over it, and the tickling feeling at the back of her neck came, the mirror told her, from a long curly feather that swept down from the brim of her hat. Her best shoes had disappeared, and in their place were others much finer and with large diamond buckles shining upon them. She was still wearing the white gloves and carrying the umbrella.

"My goodness," said Mary Poppins, "I *am* having a Day Out!"

So, still admiring themselves and each other, they moved on together through the little wood, till presently they came upon a little open space filled with sunlight. And there on a green table was Afternoon-Tea!

A pile of raspberry-jam-cakes as high as Mary Poppins's waist stood in the centre, and beside it tea was boiling in a big brass urn. Best of all, there were two plates of whelks and two pins to pick them out with.

"Strike me pink!" said Mary Poppins. That was what she always said when she was pleased.

"Golly!" said the Match-Man. And that was *his* particular phrase.

"Won't you sit down, Moddom?" enquired a voice, and they turned to find a tall man in a black coat coming out of the wood with a table-napkin over his arm.

Mary Poppins, thoroughly surprised, sat down with a plop upon one of the little green chairs that stood round the table. The Match-Man, staring, collapsed on to another.

"I'm the Waiter, you know!" explained the man in the black coat.

"Oh! But I didn't see you in the picture," said Mary Poppins.

"Ah, I was behind the tree," explained the Waiter.

"Won't you sit down?" said Mary Poppins, politely.

"Waiters never sit down, Moddom," said the man, but he seemed pleased at being asked.

"Your whelks, Mister!" he said, pushing a plate of them over to the Match-Man. "*And* your Pin!" He dusted the pin on his napkin and handed it to the Match-Man.

They began upon the afternoon-tea, and the Waiter stood beside them to see they had everything they needed.

"We're having them after all," said Mary Poppins in a loud whisper, as she began on the heap of raspberry-jam-cakes.

"Golly!" agreed the Match-Man, helping himself to two of the largest.

"Tea?" said the Waiter, filling a large cup for each of them from the urn.

They drank it and had two cups more each, and then, for luck, they finished the pile of raspberry-jam-cakes. After that they got up and brushed the crumbs off.

"There is Nothing to Pay," said the Waiter, before they had time to ask for the bill. "It is a Pleasure. You will find the Merry-go-Round just over there!" And he waved his hand to a little gap in the trees, where Mary Poppins and the Match-Man could see several wooden horses whirling round on a stand.

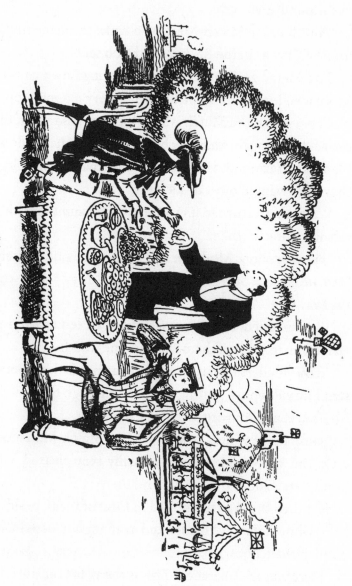

"I'm the Waiter, you know!"

"That's funny," said she. "I don't remember seeing that in the picture, either."

"Ah," said the Match-Man, who hadn't remembered it himself, "it was in the Background, you see!"

The Merry-go-Round was just slowing down as they approached it. They leapt upon it, Mary Poppins on a black horse and the Match-Man on a grey. And when the music started again and they began to move, they rode all the way to Yarmouth and back, because that was the place they both wanted most to see.

When they returned it was nearly dark and the Waiter was watching for them.

"I'm very sorry, Moddom and Mister," he said politely, "but we close at Seven. Rules, you know. May I show you the Way Out?"

They nodded as he flourished his table-napkin and walked on in front of them through the wood.

"It's a wonderful picture you've drawn this time, Bert," said Mary Poppins, putting her hand through the Match-Man's arm and drawing her cloak about her.

"Well, I did my best, Mary," said the Match-Man modestly. But you could see he was really very pleased with himself indeed.

Just then the Waiter stopped in front of them, beside a large white doorway that looked as though it were made of thick chalk lines.

"Here you are!" he said. "This is the Way Out."

"Good-bye, and thank you," said Mary Poppins, shaking his hand.

"Moddom, good-bye!" said the Waiter, bowing so low that his head knocked against his knees.

He nodded to the Match-Man, who cocked his head on one side and closed one eye at the Waiter, which was his way of bidding him farewell. Then Mary Poppins stepped through the white doorway and the Match-Man followed her.

And as they went, the feather dropped from her hat and the silk cloak from her shoulders and the diamonds from her shoes. The bright clothes of the Match-Man faded, and his straw hat turned into his old ragged cap again. Mary Poppins turned and looked at him, and she knew at once what had happened. Standing on the pavement she gazed at him for a long minute, and then her glance explored the wood behind him for the Waiter. But the Waiter was nowhere to be seen. There was nobody in the picture. Nothing moved there. Even the Merry-go-Round had disappeared. Only the still trees and the grass and the unmoving little patch of sea remained.

But Mary Poppins and the Match-Man smiled at one another. They knew, you see, what lay behind the trees. . . .

When she came back from her Day Out, Jane and Michael came running to meet her.

"Where have you been?" they asked her.

"In Fairyland," said Mary Poppins.

"Did you see Cinderella?" said Jane.

"Huh, Cinderella? Not me," said Mary Poppins, contemptuously. "Cinderella, indeed!"

"Or Robinson Crusoe?" asked Michael.

"Robinson Crusoe — pooh!" said Mary Poppins rudely.

"Then how could you have been there? It couldn't have been *our* Fairyland!"

Mary Poppins gave a superior sniff.

"Don't you know," she said pityingly, "that everybody's got a Fairyland of their own?"

And with another sniff she went upstairs to take off her white gloves and put the umbrella away.

CHAPTER THREE

LAUGHING GAS

Are you quite sure he will be at home?" said Jane, as they got off the Bus, she and Michael and Mary Poppins.

"Would my Uncle ask me to bring you to tea if he intended to go out, I'd like to know?" said Mary Poppins, who was evidently very offended by the question. She was wearing her blue coat with the silver buttons and the blue hat to match, and on the days when she wore these it was the easiest thing in the world to offend her.

All three of them were on the way to pay a visit to Mary Poppins's uncle, Mr. Wigg, and Jane and Michael had looked forward to the trip for so long that they were more than half afraid that Mr. Wigg might not be in, after all.

"Why is he called Mr. Wigg — does he wear one?" asked Michael, hurrying along beside Mary Poppins.

"He is called Mr. Wigg because Mr. Wigg is his name. And he doesn't wear one. He is bald," said Mary Poppins. "And if I have any more questions we will just go Back Home." And she sniffed her usual sniff of displeasure.

Jane and Michael looked at each other and frowned. And the frown meant: "Don't let's ask her anything else or we'll never get there."

Mary Poppins put her hat straight at the Tobacconist's Shop at the corner. It had one of those curious windows where there seem to be three of you instead of one, so that if you look long enough at them you begin to feel you are not yourself but a whole crowd of somebody else. Mary Poppins sighed with pleasure, however, when she saw three of herself, each wearing a blue coat with silver buttons and a blue hat to match. She thought it was such a lovely sight that she wished there had been a dozen of her or even thirty. The more Mary Poppins the better.

"Come along," she said sternly, as though they had kept *her* waiting. Then they turned the corner and pulled the bell of Number Three, Robertson Road. Jane and Michael could hear it faintly echoing from a long way away and they knew that in one minute, or two at the most, they would be having tea with Mary Poppins's uncle, Mr. Wigg, for the first time ever.

"If he's in, of course," Jane said to Michael in a whisper.

At that moment the door flew open and a thin, watery-looking lady appeared.

"Is he in?" said Michael quickly.

"I'll thank you," said Mary Poppins, giving him a terrible glance, "to let *me* do the talking."

"How do you do, Mrs. Wigg," said Jane politely.

"Mrs. Wigg!" said the thin lady, in a voice even thinner than herself. "How dare you call me Mrs. Wigg! No, thank you! I'm plain Miss Persimmon *and* proud of it. Mrs. Wigg indeed!" She seemed to be quite upset, and they thought Mr. Wigg must be a very odd person if Miss Persimmon was so glad not to be Mrs. Wigg.

"Straight up and first door on the landing," said Miss Persimmon, and she went hurrying away down the passage saying: "Mrs. Wigg indeed!" to herself in a high, thin, outraged voice.

Jane and Michael followed Mary Poppins upstairs. Mary Poppins knocked at the door.

"Come in! Come in! And welcome!" called a loud, cheery voice from inside. Jane's heart was pitter-pattering with excitement.

"He *is* in!" she signalled to Michael with a look.

Mary Poppins opened the door and pushed them in front of her. A large cheerful room lay before them. At one end of it a fire was burning brightly and in the centre stood an enormous table laid for tea — four cups and saucers, piles of bread and butter, crumpets, coconut cakes and a large plum cake with pink icing.

"Well, this is indeed a Pleasure," a huge voice greeted them, and Jane and Michael looked round for its owner. He was nowhere to be seen. The room appeared to be quite empty. Then they heard Mary Poppins saying crossly:

"Oh, Uncle Albert — not *again?* It's not your birthday, is it?"

And as she spoke she looked up at the ceiling. Jane and Michael looked up too and to their surprise saw a round, fat, bald man who was hanging in the air without holding on to anything. Indeed, he appeared to be *sitting* on the air, for his legs were crossed and he had just put down the newspaper which he had been reading when they came in.

"My dear," said Mr. Wigg, smiling down at the children, and looking apologetically at Mary Poppins, "I'm very sorry, but I'm afraid it *is* my birthday."

"Tch, tch, tch!" said Mary Poppins.

"I only remembered last night and there was no time then to send you a postcard asking you to come another day. Very distressing, isn't it?" he said, looking down at Jane and Michael.

"I can see you're rather surprised," said Mr. Wigg. And, indeed, their mouths were so wide open with astonishment that Mr. Wigg, if he had been a little smaller, might almost have fallen into one of them.

"I'd better explain, I think," Mr. Wigg went on calmly. "You see, it's this way. I'm a cheerful sort of man and very disposed to laughter. You wouldn't believe, either of you, the number of things that strike me as being funny. I can laugh at pretty nearly everything, I can."

And with that Mr. Wigg began to bob up and down, shaking with laughter at the thought of his own cheerfulness.

"Uncle Albert!" said Mary Poppins, and Mr. Wigg stopped laughing with a jerk.

"Oh, beg pardon, my dear. Where was I? Oh, yes. Well, the funny thing about me is — all right, Mary, I won't laugh if I can help it! — that whenever my birthday falls on a Friday, well, it's all up with me. Absolutely U.P.," said Mr. Wigg.

"But why —— ?" began Jane.

"But how —— ?" began Michael.

"Well, you see, if I laugh on that particular day I become so filled with Laughing Gas that I simply can't keep on the ground. Even if I smile it happens. The first funny thought, and I'm up like a balloon. And until I can think of something serious I can't get down again." Mr. Wigg began to chuckle at that, but he caught sight of Mary Poppins's face and stopped the chuckle, and continued:

"It's awkward, of course, but not unpleasant. Never happens to either of you, I suppose?"

Jane and Michael shook their heads.

"No, I thought not. It seems to be my own special habit. Once, after I'd been to the Circus the night before, I laughed so much that — would you believe it? — I was up here for a whole twelve hours, and couldn't get down till the last stroke of midnight. Then, of course, I came down with a flop because it was Saturday and not my birthday any more. It's rather odd, isn't it? Not to say funny?

"And now here it is Friday again and my birthday, and you two and Mary P. to visit me. Oh, Lordy, Lordy, don't make me laugh, I beg of you ——" But although Jane and Michael had done nothing very amusing, except to stare at him in astonishment, Mr. Wigg began to laugh again loudly, and as he laughed he went bouncing and bobbing about in the air, with the newspaper rattling in his hand and his spectacles half on and half off his nose.

He looked so comic, floundering in the air like a great human bubble, clutching at the ceiling sometimes and sometimes at the gas-bracket as he passed it, that Jane and Michael, though they were trying hard to be polite, just couldn't help doing what they did. They laughed. *And* they laughed. They shut their mouths tight to prevent the laughter escaping, but that didn't do any good. And presently they were rolling over and over on the floor, squealing and shrieking with laughter.

"Really!" said Mary Poppins. "Really, *such* behaviour!"

"I can't help it, I can't help it!" shrieked Michael as he rolled into the fender. "It's so terribly funny. Oh, Jane, *isn't* it funny?"

Jane did not reply, for a curious thing was happening to her. As she laughed she felt herself growing lighter and lighter, just as though she were being pumped full of air. It was a curious and delicious feeling and it made her want to laugh all the more. And then suddenly, with a bouncing bound, she felt herself jumping through the air. Michael, to his astonishment, saw her go soaring up through the room. With a little bump her head touched the ceiling

and then she went bouncing along it till she reached Mr.
Wigg.

"Well!" said Mr. Wigg, looking very surprised indeed.
"Don't tell me it's *your* birthday, too?" Jane shook her
head.

"It's not? Then this Laughing Gas must be catching!
Hi — whoa there, look out for the mantelpiece!" This was
to Michael, who had suddenly risen from the floor and
was swooping through the air, roaring with laughter, and
just grazing the china ornaments on the mantelpiece as
he passed. He landed with a bounce right on Mr. Wigg's
knee.

"How do you do," said Mr. Wigg, heartily shaking Michael by the hand. "I call this really friendly of
you — bless my soul, I do! To come up to me since I
couldn't come down to you — eh?" And then he and
Michael looked at each other and flung back their heads
and simply howled with laughter.

"I say," said Mr. Wigg to Jane, as he wiped his eyes.
"You'll be thinking I have the worst manners in the world.
You're standing and you ought to be sitting — a nice
young lady like you. I'm afraid I can't offer you a chair up
here, but I think you'll find the air quite comfortable to
sit on. I do."

Jane tried it and found she could sit down quite comfortably on the air. She took off her hat and laid it down
beside her and it hung there in space without any support
at all.

"That's right," said Mr. Wigg. Then he turned and looked down at Mary Poppins.

"Well, Mary, we're fixed. And now I can enquire about *you*, my dear. I must say, I am very glad to welcome you and my two young friends here today — why, Mary, you're frowning. I'm afraid you don't approve of — er — all this."

He waved his hand at Jane and Michael, and said hurriedly:

"I apologise, Mary, my dear. But you know how it is with me. Still, I must say I never thought my two young friends here would catch it, really I didn't, Mary! I suppose I should have asked them for another day or tried to think of something sad or something ——"

"Well, I must say," said Mary Poppins primly, "that I have never in my life seen such a sight. And at your age, Uncle ——"

"Mary Poppins, Mary Poppins, do come up!" interrupted Michael. "Think of something funny and you'll find it's quite easy."

"Ah, now do, Mary!" said Mr. Wigg persuasively.

"We're lonely up here without you!" said Jane, and held out her arms towards Mary Poppins. "*Do* think of something funny!"

"Ah, *she* doesn't need to," said Mr. Wigg sighing. "She can come up if she wants to, even without laughing — and she knows it." And he looked mysteriously and secretly at Mary Poppins as she stood down there on the hearth-rug.

"Well," said Mary Poppins, "it's all very silly and un-dignified, but, since you're all up there and don't seem able to get down, I suppose I'd better come up, too."

With that, to the surprise of Jane and Michael, she put her hands down at her sides and without a laugh, without even the faintest glimmer of a smile, she shot up through the air and sat down beside Jane.

"How many times, I should like to know," she said snappily, "have I told you to take off your coat when you come into a hot room?" And she unbuttoned Jane's coat and laid it neatly on the air beside the hat.

"That's right, Mary, that's right," said Mr. Wigg con-tentedly, as he leant down and put his spectacles on the mantelpiece. "Now we're all comfortable —— "

"There's comfort *and* comfort," sniffed Mary Poppins.

"And we can have tea," Mr. Wigg went on, apparently not noticing her remark. And then a startled look came over his face.

"My goodness!" he said. "How dreadful! I've just re-alised — that table's down there and we're up here. What *are* we going to do? We're here and it's there. It's an aw-ful tragedy — awful! But oh, it's terribly comic!" And he hid his face in his handkerchief and laughed loudly into it. Jane and Michael, though they did not want to miss the crumpets and the cakes, couldn't help laughing too, because Mr. Wigg's mirth was so infectious.

Mr. Wigg dried his eyes.

"There's only one thing for it," he said. "We must think of something serious. Something sad, very sad. And then we shall be able to get down. Now — one, two, three! Something *very* sad, mind you!"

They thought and thought, with their chins on their hands.

Michael thought of school, and that one day he would have to go there. But even that seemed funny today and he had to laugh.

Jane thought: "I shall be grown up in another fourteen years!" But that didn't sound sad at all but quite nice and rather funny. She could not help smiling at the thought of herself grown up, with long skirts and a hand-bag.

"There was my poor old Aunt Emily," thought Mr. Wigg out loud. "She was run over by an omnibus. Sad. Very sad. Unbearably sad. Poor Aunt Emily. But they saved her umbrella. That was funny, wasn't it?" And before he knew where he was, he was heaving and trembling and bursting with laughter at the thought of Aunt Emily's umbrella.

"It's no good," he said, blowing his nose. "I give it up. And my young friends here seem to be no better at sadness than I am. Mary, can't *you* do something? We want our tea."

To this day Jane and Michael cannot be sure of what happened then. All they know for certain is that, as soon as Mr. Wigg had appealed to Mary Poppins, the table be-

low began to wriggle on its legs. Presently it was swaying dangerously, and then with a rattle of china and with
cakes lurching off their plates on to the cloth, the table
came soaring through the room, gave one graceful turn,
and landed beside them so that Mr. Wigg was at its head.

"Good girl!" said Mr. Wigg, smiling proudly upon her.
"I knew you'd fix something. Now, will you take the foot
of the table and pour out, Mary? And the guests on either
side of me. That's the idea," he said, as Michael ran bobbing through the air and sat down on Mr. Wigg's right.
Jane was at his left hand. There they were, all together, up
in the air and the table between them. Not a single piece
of bread-and-butter or a lump of sugar had been left behind.

Mr. Wigg smiled contentedly.

"It is usual, I think, to begin with bread-and-butter," he
said to Jane and Michael, "but as it's my birthday we will
begin the wrong way — which I always think is the *right*
way — with the Cake!"

And he cut a large slice for everybody.

"More tea?" he said to Jane. But before she had time to
reply there was a quick, sharp knock at the door.

"Come in!" called Mr. Wigg.

The door opened, and there stood Miss Persimmon
with a jug of hot water on a tray.

"I thought, Mr. Wigg," she began, looking searchingly round the room, "you'd be wanting some more

hot——Well, I never! I simply *never!*" she said, as she caught sight of them all seated on the air round the table. "Such goings on I never did see. In all my born days I never saw such. I'm sure, Mr. Wigg, I always knew *you* were a bit odd. But I've closed my eyes to it — being as how you paid your rent regular. But such behaviour as this — having tea in the air with your guests — Mr. Wigg, sir, I'm astonished at you! It's that undignified, and for a gentleman of your age — I never did——"

"But perhaps you will, Miss Persimmon!" said Michael.

There they were, all together, up in the air

"Will what?" said Miss Persimmon haughtily.

"Catch the Laughing Gas, as we did," said Michael.

Miss Persimmon flung back her head scornfully.

"I hope, young man," she retorted, "I have more respect for myself than to go bouncing about in the air like a rubber ball on the end of a bat. I'll stay on my own feet, thank you, or my name's not Amy Persimmon, and — oh dear, oh *dear*, my goodness, oh *DEAR* — what *is* the matter? I can't walk, I'm going, I — oh, help, *HELP!*"

For Miss Persimmon, quite against her will, was off the ground and was stumbling through the air, rolling from side to side like a very thin barrel, balancing the tray in her hand. She was almost weeping with distress as she arrived at the table and put down her jug of hot water.

"Thank you," said Mary Poppins in a calm, very polite voice. Then Miss Persimmon turned and went wafting down again, murmuring as she went: "So undignified — and me a well-behaved, steady-going woman. I must see a doctor——"

When she touched the floor she ran hurriedly out of

the room, wringing her hands, and not giving a single glance backwards.

"So undignified!" they heard her moaning as she shut the door behind her.

"Her name can't be Amy Persimmon, because she *didn't* stay on her own feet!" whispered Jane to Michael.

But Mr. Wigg was looking at Mary Poppins — a curious look, half-amused, half-accusing.

"Mary, Mary, you shouldn't — bless my soul, you shouldn't, Mary. The poor old body will never get over it. But, oh, my Goodness, didn't she look funny waddling through the air — my Gracious Goodness, but didn't she?"

And he and Jane and Michael were off again, rolling about the air, clutching their sides and gasping with laughter at the thought of how funny Miss Persimmon had looked.

"Oh dear!" said Michael. "Don't make me laugh any more. I can't stand it! I shall break!"

"Oh, oh, oh!" cried Jane, as she gasped for breath, with her hand over her heart.

"Oh, my Gracious, Glorious, Galumphing Goodness!" roared Mr. Wigg, dabbing his eyes with the tail of his coat because he couldn't find his handkerchief.

"IT IS TIME TO GO HOME." Mary Poppins's voice sounded above the roars of laughter like a trumpet.

And suddenly, with a rush, Jane and Michael and Mr. Wigg came down. They landed on the floor with a huge bump, all together. The thought that they would have to go home was the first sad thought of the afternoon, and the moment it was in their minds the Laughing Gas went out of them.

Jane and Michael sighed as they watched Mary Poppins come slowly down the air, carrying Jane's coat and hat.

Mr. Wigg sighed, too. A great, long, heavy sigh.

"Well, isn't that a pity?" he said soberly. "It's very sad that you've got to go home. I never enjoyed an afternoon so much — did you?"

"Never," said Michael sadly, feeling how dull it was to be down on the earth again with no Laughing Gas inside him.

"Never, never," said Jane, as she stood on tip-toe and kissed Mr. Wigg's withered-apple cheeks. "Never, never, never, never . . . !"

They sat on either side of Mary Poppins going home in the Bus. They were both very quiet, thinking over the lovely afternoon. Presently Michael said sleepily to Mary Poppins:

"How often does your Uncle get like that?"

"Like what?" said Mary Poppins sharply, as though Michael had deliberately said something to offend her.

"Well — all bouncy and boundy and laughing and going up in the air."

"Up in the air?" Mary Poppins's voice was high and angry. "What do you mean, pray, up in the air?"

Jane tried to explain.

Crept closer to her and fell asleep

"Michael means — is your Uncle often full of Laughing Gas, and does he often go rolling and bobbing about on the ceiling when —— "

"Rolling and bobbing! What an idea! Rolling and bobbing on the ceiling! You'll be telling me next he's a balloon!" Mary Poppins gave an offended sniff.

"But he did!" said Michael. "We saw him."

"What, roll and bob? How dare you! I'll have you know that my uncle is a sober, honest, hard-working man, and you'll be kind enough to speak of him respectfully. And don't bite your Bus ticket! Roll and bob, indeed — the idea!"

Michael and Jane looked across Mary Poppins at each other. They said nothing, for they had learnt that it was better not to argue with Mary Poppins, no matter how odd anything seemed.

But the look that passed between them said: "Is it true or isn't it? About Mr. Wigg. Is Mary Poppins right or are we?"

But there was nobody to give them the right answer.

The Bus roared on, wildly lurching and bounding.

Mary Poppins sat between them, offended and silent, and presently, because they were very tired, they crept closer to her and leant up against her sides and fell asleep, still wondering. . . .

CHAPTER FOUR

MISS LARK'S ANDREW

iss Lark lived Next Door.

But before we go any further I must tell you what Next Door looked like. It was a very grand house, by far the grandest in Cherry-Tree Lane. Even Admiral Boom had been known to envy Miss Lark her wonderful house, though his own had ship's funnels instead of chimneys and a flagstaff in the front garden. Over and over again the inhabitants of the Lane heard him say, as he rolled past Miss Lark's mansion: "Blast my gizzard! What does *she* want with a house like that?"

And the reason of Admiral Boom's jealousy was that Miss Lark had two gates. One was for Miss Lark's friends and relations, and the other for the Butcher and the Baker and the Milkman.

Once the Baker made a mistake and came in through the gate reserved for the friends and relations, and Miss Lark was so angry that she said she wouldn't have any more bread ever.

But in the end she had to forgive the Baker because he

was the only one in the neighbourhood who made those little flat rolls with the curly twists of crust on the top. She never really liked him very much after that, however, and when he came he pulled his hat far down over his eyes so that Miss Lark might think he was somebody else. But she never did.

Jane and Michael always knew when Miss Lark was in the garden or coming along the Lane, because she wore so many brooches and necklaces and earrings that she jingled and jangled just like a brass band. And, whenever she met them, she always said the same thing:

"Good-morning!" (or "Good-afternoon!" if it happened to be after luncheon), "and how are *we* today?"

And Jane and Michael were never quite sure whether Miss Lark was asking how *they* were, or how she and Andrew were.

So they just replied: "Good-afternoon!" (or, of course, "Good-morning!" if it was before luncheon).

All day long, no matter where the children were, they could hear Miss Lark calling, in a very loud voice, things like:

"Andrew, where are you?" or

"Andrew, you mustn't go out without your overcoat!" or

"Andrew, come to Mother!"

And, if you didn't know, you would think that Andrew must be a little boy. Indeed, Jane thought that Miss Lark thought that Andrew *was* a little boy. But Andrew wasn't.

He was a dog — one of those small, silky, fluffy dogs that look like a fur necklet, until they begin to bark. But, of course, when they do that you *know* that they're dogs. No fur necklet ever made a noise like that.

Now, Andrew led such a luxurious life that you might have thought he was the Shah of Persia in disguise. He slept on a silk pillow in Miss Lark's room; he went by car to the Hairdresser's twice a week to be shampooed; he had cream for every meal and sometimes oysters, and he possessed four overcoats with checks and stripes in different colours. Andrew's ordinary days were filled with the kind of things most people have only on birthdays. And when Andrew himself had a birthday he had *two* candles on his cake for every year, instead of only one.

The effect of all this was to make Andrew very much disliked in the neighbourhood. People used to laugh heartily when they saw Andrew sitting up in the back seat of Miss Lark's car on the way to the Hairdresser's, with the fur rug over his knees and his best coat on. And on the day when Miss Lark bought him two pairs of small leather boots so that he could go out in the Park wet or fine, everybody in the Lane came down to their front gates to watch him go by and to smile secretly behind their hands.

"Pooh!" said Michael, as they were watching Andrew one day through the fence that separated Number Seventeen from Next Door. "Pooh, he's a ninkypoop!"

"How do you know?" asked Jane, very interested.

"I know because I heard Daddy call him one this morning!" said Michael, and he laughed at Andrew very rudely.

"He is *not* a nincompoop," said Mary Poppins. "And that is that."

And Mary Poppins was right. Andrew wasn't a nincompoop, as you will very soon see.

You must not think he did not respect Miss Lark. He did. He was even fond of her in a mild sort of way. He couldn't help having a kindly feeling for somebody who had been so good to him ever since he was a puppy, even if she *did* kiss him rather too often. But there was no doubt about it that the life Andrew led bored him to distraction. He would have given half his fortune, if he had one, for a nice piece of raw, red meat, instead of the usual breast of chicken or scrambled eggs with asparagus.

For in his secret, innermost heart, Andrew longed to be a common dog. He never passed his pedigree (which hung on the wall in Miss Lark's drawing-room) without a shudder of shame. And many a time he wished he'd never had a father, nor a grandfather, nor a great-grandfather, if Miss Lark was going to make such a fuss of it.

It was this desire of his to *be* a common dog that made Andrew choose common dogs for his friends. And whenever he got the chance, he would run down to the front gate and sit there watching for them, so that he could exchange a few common remarks. But Miss Lark, when she discovered him, would be sure to call out:

"Andrew, Andrew, come in, my darling! Come away from those dreadful street arabs!"

And of course Andrew would *have* to come in, or Miss Lark would shame him by coming out and *bringing* him in. And Andrew would blush and hurry up the steps so that his friends should not hear her calling him her Precious, her Joy, her Little Lump of Sugar.

Andrew's most special friend was more than common, he was a Byword. He was half an Airedale and half a Retriever and the worst half of both. Whenever there was a fight in the road he would be sure to be in the thick of it; he was always getting into trouble with the Postman or the Policeman, and there was nothing he loved better than sniffing about in drains or garbage tins. He was, in fact, the talk of the whole street, and more than one person had been heard to say thankfully that they were glad he was not *their* dog.

But Andrew loved him and was continually on the watch for him. Sometimes they had only time to exchange a sniff in the Park, but on luckier occasions — though these were very rare — they would have long talks at the gate. From his friend, Andrew heard all the town gossip, and you could see by the rude way in which the other dog laughed as he told it, that it wasn't very complimentary.

Then suddenly Miss Lark's voice would be heard calling from a window, and the other dog would get up, loll out his tongue at Miss Lark, wink at Andrew and wander off, waving his hindquarters as he went just to show that *he* didn't care.

Andrew, of course, was never allowed outside the gate unless he went with Miss Lark for a walk in the Park, or with one of the maids to have his toes manicured.

Imagine, then, the surprise of Jane and Michael when they saw Andrew, all alone, careering past them through the Park, with his ears back and his tail up as though he were on the track of a tiger.

Mary Poppins pulled the perambulator up with a jerk, in case Andrew, in his wild flight, should upset it and the Twins. And Jane and Michael screamed at him as he passed.

"Hi, Andrew! Where's your overcoat?" cried Michael, trying to make a high, windy voice like Miss Lark's.

"Andrew, you naughty little boy!" said Jane, and her voice, because she was a girl, was much more like Miss Lark's.

But Andrew just looked at them both very haughtily and barked sharply in the direction of Mary Poppins.

"Yap-yap!" said Andrew several times very quickly.

"Let me see. I think it's the first on your right and second house on the left-hand side," said Mary Poppins.

"Yap?" said Andrew.

"No — no garden. Only a back-yard. Gate's usually open."

Andrew barked again.

"I'm not sure," said Mary Poppins. "But I should think so. Generally goes home at tea-time."

Andrew flung back his head and set off again at a gallop.

Jane's eyes and Michael's were round as saucers with surprise.

"What was he saying?" they demanded breathlessly, both together.

"Just passing the time of day!" said Mary Poppins, and shut her mouth tightly as though she did not intend any more words to escape from it. John and Barbara gurgled from their perambulator.

"He wasn't!" said Michael.

"He *couldn't* have been!" said Jane.

"Well, you know best, of course. *As* usual," said Mary Poppins haughtily.

"He must have been asking you where somebody lived, I'm sure he must —— " Michael began.

"Well, if you know, why bother to ask me?" said Mary Poppins sniffing. "*I'm* no dictionary."

"Oh, Michael," said Jane, "she'll never tell us if you talk like that. Mary Poppins, do say what Andrew was saying to you, *please.*"

"Ask *him. He* knows — Mr. Know-All!" said Mary Poppins, nodding her head scornfully at Michael.

"Oh no, I don't. I promise I don't, Mary Poppins. Do tell."

"Half-past three. Tea-time," said Mary Poppins, and she wheeled the perambulator round and shut her mouth tight again as though it were a trapdoor. She did not say another word all the way home.

Jane dropped behind with Michael.

"It's your fault!" she said. "Now we'll never know."

"I don't care!" said Michael, and he began to push his scooter very quickly. "I don't want to know."

But he did want to know very badly indeed. And, as it turned out, he and Jane and everybody else knew all about it before tea-time.

Just as they were about to cross the road to their own house, they heard loud cries coming from Next Door, and there they saw a curious sight. Miss Lark's two maids were rushing wildly about the garden, looking under bushes and up into the trees as people do who have lost their most valuable possession. And there was Robertson Ay, from Number Seventeen, busily wasting his time by poking at the gravel on Miss Lark's path with a broom as though he expected to find the missing treasure under a pebble. Miss Lark herself was running about in her garden, waving her arms and calling: "Andrew, Andrew! Oh, he's lost. My darling boy is lost! We must send for the Police. I must see the Prime Minister. Andrew is lost! Oh dear! oh dear!"

"Oh, poor Miss Lark!" said Jane, hurrying across the road. She could not help feeling sorry because Miss Lark looked so upset.

But it was Michael who really comforted Miss Lark. Just as he was going in at the gate of Number Seventeen, he looked down the Lane and there he saw —

"Why, there's Andrew, Miss Lark. See, down there — just turning Admiral Boom's corner!"

"Where, where? Show me!" said Miss Lark breathlessly, and she peered in the direction in which Michael was pointing.

Miss Lark was running about in her garden

And there, sure enough, *was* Andrew, walking as slowly and as casually as though nothing in the world was the
matter; and beside him waltzed a huge dog that seemed to
be half an Airedale and half a Retriever, and the worst half
of both.

"Oh, what a relief!" said Miss Lark, sighing loudly.
"What a load off my mind!"

Mary Poppins and the children waited in the Lane
outside Miss Lark's gate, Miss Lark herself and her two
maids leant over the fence, Robertson Ay, resting from
his labours, propped himself up with his broom-han-
dle, and all of them watched in silence the return of
Andrew.

He and his friend marched sedately up to the group,
whisking their tails jauntily and keeping their ears well
cocked, and you could tell by the look in Andrew's eye
that, whatever he meant, he meant business.

"That dreadful dog!" said Miss Lark, looking at
Andrew's companion.

"Shoo! Shoo! Go home!" she cried.

But the dog just sat down on the pavement and
scratched his right ear with his left leg and yawned.

"Go away! Go home! Shoo, I say!" said Miss Lark, waving her arms angrily at the dog.

"And you, Andrew," she went on, "come indoors this
minute! Going out like that — all alone and without your
overcoat. I am very displeased with you!"

Andrew barked lazily, but did not move.

"What do you mean, Andrew? Come in at once!" said Miss Lark.

Andrew barked again.

"He says," put in Mary Poppins, "that he's not coming in."

Miss Lark turned and regarded her haughtily. "How do *you* know what my dog says, may I ask? Of course he will come in."

Andrew, however, merely shook his head and gave one or two low growls.

"He won't," said Mary Poppins. "Not unless his friend comes, too."

"Stuff and nonsense," said Miss Lark crossly. "That *can't* be what he says. As if I could have a great hulking mongrel like that inside my gate."

Andrew yapped three or four times.

"He says he means it," said Mary Poppins. "And what's more, he'll go and live with his friend unless his friend is allowed to come and live with him."

"Oh, Andrew, you can't — you can't, really — after all I've done for you and everything!" Miss Lark was nearly weeping.

Andrew barked and turned away. The other dog got up.

"Oh, he *does* mean it!" cried Miss Lark. "I see he does. He is going away." She sobbed a moment into her handkerchief, then she blew her nose and said:

"Very well, then, Andrew. I give in. This — this common dog can stay. On condition, of course, that he sleeps in the coal-cellar."

Another yap from Andrew.

"He insists, ma'am, that that won't do. His friend must have a silk cushion just like his and sleep in your room too. Otherwise he will go and sleep in the coal-cellar with his friend," said Mary Poppins.

"Andrew, how could you?" moaned Miss Lark. "I shall never consent to such a thing."

Andrew looked as though he were preparing to depart. So did the other dog.

"Oh, he's leaving me!" shrieked Miss Lark. "Very well, then, Andrew. It will be as you wish. He *shall* sleep in my room. But I shall never be the same again, never, never. Such a common dog!"

She wiped her streaming eyes and went on:

"I should never have thought it of you, Andrew. But I'll say no more, no matter what I think. And this — er — creature — I shall call Waif or Stray or —— "

At that the other dog looked at Miss Lark very indignantly, and Andrew barked loudly.

"They say you must call him Willoughby and nothing else," said Mary Poppins. "Willoughby being his name."

"Willoughby! What a name! Worse and worse!" said Miss Lark despairingly. "What is he saying now?" For Andrew was barking again.

"He says that if he comes back you are never to

make him wear overcoats or go to the Hairdresser's again — that's his last word," said Mary Poppins.

There was a pause.

"Very well," said Miss Lark at last. "But I warn you, Andrew, if you catch your death of cold — don't blame me!"

And with that she turned and walked haughtily up the steps, sniffing away the last of her tears.

Andrew cocked his head towards Willoughby as if to say: "Come on!" and the two of them waltzed side by side slowly up the garden path, waving their tails like banners, and followed Miss Lark into the house.

"He isn't a ninkypoop after all, you see," said Jane, as they went upstairs to the nursery and Tea.

"No," agreed Michael. "But how do you think Mary Poppins knew?"

"I don't know," said Jane. "And she'll never, never tell us. I am sure of that . . ."

CHAPTER FIVE

THE DANCING COW

Jane, with her head tied up in Mary Poppins's bandanna handkerchief, was in bed with earache.

"What does it feel like?" Michael wanted to know.

"Like guns going off inside my head," said Jane.

"Cannons?"

"No, pop-guns."

"Oh," said Michael. And he almost wished he could have earache, too. It sounded so exciting.

"Shall I tell you a story out of one of the books?" said Michael, going to the bookshelf.

"No. I just couldn't bear it," said Jane, holding her ear with her hand.

"Well, shall I sit at the window and tell you what is happening outside?"

"Yes, do," said Jane.

So Michael sat all the afternoon on the window-seat telling her everything that occurred in the Lane. And sometimes his accounts were very dull and sometimes very exciting.

"There's Admiral Boom!" he said once. "He has come out of his gate and is hurrying down the Lane. Here he comes. His nose is redder than ever and he's wearing a top-hat. Now he is passing Next Door ——"

"Is he saying 'Blast my gizzard!'?" enquired Jane.

"I can't hear. I expect so. There's Miss Lark's second housemaid in Miss Lark's garden. And Robertson Ay is in *our* garden, sweeping up the leaves and looking at her over the fence. He is sitting down now, having a rest."

"He has a weak heart," said Jane.

"How do you know?"

"He told me. He said his doctor said he was to do as little as possible. And I heard Daddy say if Robertson Ay does what his doctor told him to he'll sack him. Oh, how it bangs and *bangs!*" said Jane, clutching her ear again.

"Hull*oh!*" said Michael excitedly from the window.

"What is it?" cried Jane, sitting up. "Do tell me."

"A very extraordinary thing. There's a cow down in the Lane," said Michael, jumping up and down on the window-seat.

"A cow? A real cow — right in the middle of a town? How funny! Mary Poppins," said Jane, "there's a cow in the Lane, Michael says."

"Yes, and it's walking very slowly, putting its head over every gate and looking round as though it had lost something."

"I *wish* I could see it," said Jane mournfully.

"Look!" said Michael, pointing downwards as Mary Poppins came to the window. "A cow. Isn't that funny?"

Mary Poppins gave a quick, sharp glance down into the Lane. She started with surprise.

"Certainly not," she said, turning to Jane and Michael. "It's not funny at all. I know that cow. She was a great friend of my Mother's and I'll thank you to speak politely of her." She smoothed her apron and looked at them both very severely.

"Have you known her long?" enquired Michael gently, hoping that if he was particularly polite he would hear something more about the cow.

"Since before she saw the King," said Mary Poppins.

"And when was that?" asked Jane, in a soft encouraging voice.

Mary Poppins stared into space, her eyes fixed upon something that they could not see. Jane and Michael held their breath, waiting.

"It was long ago," said Mary Poppins, in a brooding, story-telling voice. She paused, as though she were remembering events that happened hundreds of years before that time. Then she went on dreamily, still gazing into the middle of the room, but without seeing anything.

The Red Cow — that's the name she went by. And very important and prosperous she was, too (so my Mother said). She lived in the best field in the whole district — a large one full of buttercups the size of saucers and dandelions rather larger than brooms. The field was all primrose-colour and gold with the buttercups and dandelions standing up in it like soldiers. Every time she ate the head off one soldier, another grew up in its place, with a green military coat and a yellow busby.

She had lived there always — she often told my Mother that she couldn't remember the time when she hadn't lived in that field. Her world was bounded by green hedges and the sky and she knew nothing of what lay beyond these.

The Red Cow was very respectable, she always behaved like a perfect lady and she knew What was What. To her a thing was either black or white — there was no question of it being grey or perhaps pink. People were good or they were bad — there was nothing in between. Dandelions were either sweet or sour — there were never any moderately nice ones.

She led a very busy life. Her mornings were taken up in giving lessons to the Red Calf, her daughter, and in the afternoon she taught the little one deportment and mooing and all the things a really well brought up calf should know. Then they had their supper, and the Red Cow showed the Red Calf how to select a good blade of grass from a bad one; and when her child had gone to sleep at night she would go into a corner of the field and chew the cud and think her own quiet thoughts.

All her days were exactly the same. One Red Calf grew up and went away and another came in its place. And it was natural that the Red Cow should imagine that her life would always be the same as it always had been — indeed, she felt that she could ask for nothing better than for all her days to be alike till she came to the end of them.

But at the very moment she was thinking these thoughts, adventure, as she afterwards told my Mother, was stalking her. It came upon her one night when the stars themselves looked like dandelions in the sky and the moon a great daisy among the stars.

On this night, long after the Red Calf was asleep, the Red Cow stood up suddenly and began to dance. She danced wildly and beautifully and in perfect time, though she had no music to go by. Sometimes it was a polka, sometimes a Highland Fling and sometimes a special dance that she made up out of her own head. And in between these dances she would curtsey and make sweeping bows and knock her head against the dandelions.

"Dear me!" said the Red Cow to herself, as she began on a Sailor's Hornpipe. "What an extraordinary thing! I always thought dancing improper, but it can't be since I myself am dancing. For I am a model cow."

And she went on dancing, and thoroughly enjoying herself. At last, however, she grew tired and decided that she had danced enough and that she would go to sleep. But, to her great surprise, she found that she could not stop dancing. When she went to lie down beside the Red Calf, her legs would not let her. They went on capering and prancing and, of course, carrying her with them. Round and round the field she went, leaping and waltzing and stepping on tip-toe.

"Dear me!" she murmured at intervals with a ladylike accent. "How very peculiar!" But she couldn't stop.

In the morning she was still dancing and the Red Calf had to take its breakfast of dandelions all by itself because the Red Cow could not remain still enough to eat.

All through the day she danced, up and down the meadow and round and round the meadow, with the Red Calf mooing piteously behind her. When the second night came, and she was still at it and still could not stop, she grew very worried. And at the end of a week of dancing she was nearly distracted.

"I must go and see the King about it," she decided, shaking her head.

So she kissed her Red Calf and told it to be good. Then she turned and danced out of the meadow and went to tell the King.

She danced all the way, snatching little sprays of green food from the hedges as she went, and every eye that saw her stared with astonishment. But none of them were more astonished than the Red Cow herself.

At last she came to the Palace where the King lived. She pulled the bell-rope with her mouth, and when the gate opened she danced through it and up the broad garden path till she came to the flight of steps that led to the King's throne.

Upon this the King was sitting, busily making a new set of Laws. His Secretary was writing them down in a little red note-book, one after another, as the King thought of them. There were Courtiers and Ladies-in-Waiting everywhere, all very gorgeously dressed and all talking at once.

"How many have I made today?" asked the King, turning to the Secretary. The Secretary counted the Laws he had written down in the red note-book.

"Seventy-two, your Majesty," he said, bowing low and taking care not to trip over his quill pen, which was a very large one.

"H'm. Not bad for an hour's work," said the King, looking very pleased with himself. "That's enough for today." He stood up and arranged his ermine cloak very tastefully.

"Order my coach. I must go to the Barber's," he said magnificently.

It was then that he noticed the Red Cow approaching. He sat down again and took up his sceptre.

"What have we here, ho?" he demanded, as the Red Cow danced to the foot of the steps.

"A Cow, your Majesty!" she answered simply.

"I can see *that*," said the King. "I still have my eyesight. But what do you want? Be quick, because I have an appointment with the Barber at ten. He won't wait for me longer than that and I *must* have my hair cut. And for goodness' sake stop jigging and jagging about like that!" he added irritably. "It makes me quite giddy."

"Quite giddy!" echoed all the Courtiers, staring.

"That's just my trouble, your Majesty. I *can't* stop!" said the Red Cow piteously.

"Can't stop? Nonsense!" said the King furiously. "Stop at *once!* I, the King, command you!"

"Stop at once! The King commands you!" cried all the Courtiers.

The Red Cow made a great effort. She tried so hard to stop dancing that every muscle and every rib stood out like mountain ranges all over her. But it was no good. She just went on dancing at the foot of the King's steps.

"I *have* tried, your Majesty. And I can't. I've been dancing now for seven days running. And I've had no sleep. And very little to eat. A white-thorn spray or two — that's all. So I've come to ask your advice."

"H'm — very curious," said the King, pushing the crown on one side and scratching his head.

"Very curious," said the Courtiers, scratching their heads, too.

"What does it feel like?" asked the King.

"What have we here, ho?"

"Funny," said the Red Cow. "And yet," she paused, as if choosing her words, "it's rather a pleasant feeling, too. As if laughter were running up and down inside me."

"*Extraordinary,*" said the King, and he put his chin on his hand and stared at the Red Cow, pondering on what was the best thing to do.

Suddenly he sprang to his feet and said:

"Good gracious!"

"What is it?" cried all the Courtiers.

"Why, don't you see?" said the King, getting very excited and dropping his sceptre. "What an idiot I was not to have noticed it before. And what idiots *you* were!" He turned furiously upon the Courtiers. "Don't you see that there's a fallen star caught on her horn?"

"So there is!" cried the Courtiers, as they all suddenly noticed the star for the first time. And as they looked it seemed to them that the star grew brighter.

"That's what's wrong!" said the King. "Now, you Courtiers had better pull it off so that this — er — lady can stop dancing and have some breakfast. It's the star, madam, that is making you dance," he said to the Red Cow. "Now, come along, you!"

And he motioned to the Chief Courtier, who presented himself smartly before the Red Cow and began to tug at the star. It would not come off. The Chief Courtier was joined by one after another of the other Courtiers, until at last there was a long chain of them, each holding the man in front of him by the waist, and a tug-of-war began between the Courtiers and the star.

"Mind my head!" entreated the Red Cow.

"Pull harder!" roared the King.

They pulled harder. They pulled until their faces were red as raspberries. They pulled till they could pull no longer and all fell back, one on top of the other. The star did not move. It remained firmly fixed to the horn.

"Tch, tch, tch!" said the King. "Secretary, look in the Encyclopædia and see what it says about cows with stars on their horns."

The Secretary knelt down and began to crawl under the throne. Presently he emerged, carrying a large green book which was always kept there in case the King wanted to know anything.

He turned the pages.

"There's nothing at all, your Majesty, except the story of the Cow Who Jumped Over the Moon, and you know all about that."

The King rubbed his chin, because that helped him to think.

He sighed irritably and looked at the Red Cow.

"All I can say," he said, "is that you'd better try that too."

"Try what?" said the Red Cow.

"Jumping over the moon. It might have an effect. Worth trying, anyway."

"Me?" said the Red Cow, with an outraged stare.

"Yes, you — who else?" said the King impatiently. He was anxious to get to the Barber's.

"Sire," said the Red Cow, "I beg you to remember that I am a decent, respectable animal and have been taught from my infancy that jumping was no occupation for a lady."

The King stood up and shook his sceptre at her.

"Madam," he said, "you came here for my advice and I have given it to you. Do you want to go on dancing for ever? Do you want to go hungry for ever? Do you want to go sleepless for ever?"

The Red Cow thought of the lush sweet taste of dandelions. She thought of meadow grass and how soft it was to lie on. She thought of her weary capering legs and how nice it would be to rest them. And she said to herself: "Perhaps, just for once, it wouldn't matter and nobody — except the King — need know."

"How high do you suppose it is?" she said aloud as she danced.

The King looked up at the Moon.

"At least a mile, I should think," said he.

The Red Cow nodded. She thought so, too. For a moment she considered, and then she made up her mind.

"I never thought that I should come to this, your Majesty. Jumping — and over the moon at that. But — I'll try it," she said and curtseyed gracefully to the throne.

"Good," said the King pleasantly, realising that he would be in time for the Barber, after all. "Follow me!"

He led the way into the garden, and the Red Cow and the Courtiers followed him.

"Now," said the King, when he reached the open lawn, "when I blow the whistle — jump!"

He took a large golden whistle from his waistcoat pocket and blew into it lightly to make sure there was no dust in it.

The Red Cow danced at attention.

"Now — one!" said the King.

"Two!"

"Three!"

Then he blew the whistle.

The Red Cow, drawing in her breath, gave one huge tremendous jump and the earth fell away beneath her. She could see the figures of the King and the Courtiers growing smaller and smaller until they disappeared below. She herself shot upwards through the sky, with the stars spinning around her like great golden plates, and presently, in blinding light, she felt the cold rays of the moon upon her. She shut her eyes as she went over it, and as the dazzling gleam passed behind her and she bent her head towards the earth again, she felt the star slip down her horn. With a great rush it fell off and went rolling down the sky. And it seemed to her that as it disappeared into the darkness great chords of music came from it and echoed through the air.

In another minute the Red Cow had landed on the earth again. To her great surprise she found that she was not in the King's garden but in her own dandelion field.

And she had stopped dancing! Her feet were as steady as though they were made of stone and she walked as sedately as any other respectable cow. Quietly and serenely she moved across the field, beheading her golden soldiers as she went to greet the Red Calf.

"I'm so glad you're back!" said the Red Calf. "I've been *so* lonely."

The Red Cow kissed it and fell to munching the meadow. It was her first good meal for a week. And by the time her hunger was satisfied she had eaten up several regiments. After that she felt better. She soon began to live her life just exactly as she had lived it before.

At first she enjoyed her quiet regular habits very much, and was glad to be able to eat her breakfast without dancing and to lie down in the grass and sleep at night instead of curtseying to the moon until the morning.

But after a little she began to feel uncomfortable and dissatisfied. Her dandelion field and her Red Calf were all very well, but she wanted something else and she couldn't think what it was. At last she realised that she was missing her star. She had grown so used to dancing and to the happy feeling the star had given her that she wanted to do a Sailor's Hornpipe and to have the star on her horn again.

She fretted, she lost her appetite, her temper was atrocious. And she frequently burst into tears for no reason at all. Eventually, she went to my Mother and told her the whole story and asked her advice.

"Good gracious, my dear!" my Mother said to her. "You don't suppose that only one star ever fell out of the sky! Billions fall every night, I'm told. But they fall in different places, of course. You can't expect two stars to drop in the same field in one lifetime."

"Then, you think — if I moved about a bit —— ?" the Red Cow began, a happy eager look coming into her eyes.

"If it were me," said my Mother, "I'd go and look for one."

"I will," said the Red Cow joyously, "I will indeed."

Mary Poppins paused.

"And that, I suppose, is why she was walking down Cherry-Tree Lane," Jane prompted gently.

"Yes," whispered Michael, "she was looking for her star."

Mary Poppins sat up with a little start. The intent look had gone from her eyes and the stillness from her body.

"Come down from that window at once, sir!" she said crossly. "I am going to turn on the lights." And she hurried across the landing to the electric light switch.

"Michael!" said Jane in a careful whisper. "Just have one look and see if the cow's still there."

Hurriedly Michael peered out through the gathering dusk.

"Quickly!" said Jane. "Mary Poppins will be back in one minute. Can you see her?"

"No-o-o," said Michael, staring out. "Not a sign of her. She's gone."

"I do hope she finds it!" said Jane, thinking of the Red Cow roaming through the world looking for a star to stick on her horn.

"So do I," said Michael as, at the sound of Mary Poppins's returning footsteps, he hurriedly pulled down the blind. . . .

CHAPTER SIX

BAD TUESDAY

(Revised version)

I t was not very long afterwards that Michael woke up one morning with a curious feeling inside him. He knew, the moment he opened his eyes, that something was wrong but he was not quite sure what it was.

"What is today, Mary Poppins?" he enquired, pushing the bedclothes away from him.

"Tuesday," said Mary Poppins. "Go and turn on your bath. Hurry!" she said, as he made no effort to move. He turned over and pulled the bedclothes up over his head and the curious feeling increased.

"What did I say?" said Mary Poppins in that cold, clear voice that was always a Warning.

Michael knew now what was happening to him. He knew he was going to be naughty.

"I won't," he said slowly, his voice muffled by the blanket.

Mary Poppins twitched the clothes from his hand and looked down upon him.

"I WON'T."

He waited, wondering what she would do and was surprised when, without a word, she went into the bathroom and turned on the tap herself. He took his towel and went slowly in as she came out. And for the first time in his life Michael entirely bathed himself. He knew by this that he was in disgrace, and he purposely neglected to wash behind his ears.

"Shall I let out the water?" he enquired in the rudest voice he had.

There was no reply.

"Pooh, I don't care!" said Michael, and the hot heavy weight that was within him swelled and grew larger. "I *don't* care!"

He dressed himself then, putting on his best clothes, that he knew were only for Sunday. And after that he went downstairs, kicking the banisters with his feet — a thing he knew he should not do as it waked up everybody else in the house. On the stairs he met Ellen, the housemaid, and as he passed her he knocked the hot-water jug out of her hand.

"Well, you *are* a clumsy," said Ellen, as she bent down to mop up the water. "That was for your father's shaving."

"I meant to," said Michael calmly.

Ellen's red face went quite white with surprise.

"*Meant* to? You *meant* — well, then, you're a very bad heathen boy, and I'll tell your Ma, so I will —— "

"Do," said Michael, and he went on down the stairs.

Well, that was the beginning of it. Throughout the rest of the day nothing went right with him. The hot, heavy feeling inside him made him do the most awful things, and as soon as he'd done them he felt extraordinarily pleased and glad and thought out some more at once.

In the kitchen Mrs. Brill, the cook, was making scones.

"No, Master Michael," she said, "you *can't* scrape out the basin. It's not empty yet."

And at that he let out his foot and kicked Mrs. Brill very hard on the shin, so that she dropped the rolling-pin and screamed aloud.

"You kicked Mrs. Brill? Kind Mrs. Brill? I'm ashamed

of you," said his Mother a few minutes later when Mrs. Brill had told her the whole story. "You must beg her pardon at once. Say you're sorry, Michael!"

"But I'm not sorry. I'm glad. Her legs are too fat," he said, and before they could catch him he ran away up the area steps and into the garden. There he purposely bumped into Robertson Ay, who was sound asleep on top of one of the best rock plants, and Robertson Ay was very angry.

"I'll tell your Pa!" he said threateningly.

"And I'll tell him you haven't cleaned the shoes this morning," said Michael, and was a little astonished at himself. It was his habit and Jane's always to protect Robertson Ay, because they loved him and didn't want to lose him.

But he was not astonished long, for he had begun to wonder what he could do next. And it was no time before he thought of something.

Through the bars of the fence he could see Miss Lark's Andrew daintily sniffing at the Next Door lawn and choosing for himself the best blades of grass. He called softly to Andrew and gave him a biscuit out of his own pocket, and while Andrew was munching it he tied Andrew's tail to the fence with a piece of string. Then he ran away with Miss Lark's angry, outraged voice screaming in his ears, and his body almost bursting with the exciting weight of that heavy thing inside him.

The door of his Father's study stood open — for Ellen had just been dusting the books. So Michael did a forbidden thing. He went in, sat down at his Father's desk, and with his Father's pen began to scribble on the blotter. Suddenly his elbow, knocking against the inkpot, upset it, and the chair and the desk and the quill pen and his own best clothes were covered with great spreading stains of blue ink. It looked dreadful, and fear of what would happen to him stirred within Michael. But, in spite of that, he didn't care — he didn't feel the least bit sorry.

"That child must be ill," said Mrs. Banks, when she was told by Ellen — who suddenly returned and discovered him — of the latest adventure. "Michael, you shall have some syrup of figs."

"I'm not ill. I'm weller than you," said Michael rudely.

"Then you're simply naughty," said his Mother. "And you shall be punished."

And, sure enough, five minutes later, Michael found himself standing in his stained clothes in a corner of the nursery, facing the wall.

Jane tried to speak to him when Mary Poppins was not looking, but he would not answer, and put out his tongue at her. When John and Barbara crawled along the floor and each took hold of one of his shoes and gurgled, he just pushed them roughly away. And all the time he was enjoying his badness, hugging it to him as though it were a friend, and not caring a bit.

〜

"I *hate* being good," he said aloud to himself, as he trailed after Mary Poppins and Jane and the perambulator on the afternoon walk to the Park.

"Don't dawdle," said Mary Poppins, looking back at him.

But he went on dawdling and dragging the sides of his shoes along the pavement in order to scratch the leather.

Suddenly Mary Poppins turned and faced him, one hand on the handle of the perambulator.

"You," she began, "got out of bed the wrong side this morning."

"I didn't," said Michael. "There is no wrong side to my bed."

"Every bed has a right and a wrong side," said Mary Poppins, primly.

"Not mine — it's next the wall."

"That makes no difference. It's still a side," scoffed Mary Poppins.

"Well, is the wrong side the left side or is the wrong side the right side? Because I got out on the right side, so how can it be wrong?"

"Both sides were the wrong side, this morning, Mr. Smarty!"

"But it has only one, and if I got out the right side —— " he argued.

"One word more from you —— " began Mary Poppins, and she said it in such a peculiarly threatening voice that even Michael felt a little nervous. "One more word and I'll —— "

She did not say what she would do, but he quickened his pace.

"Pull yourself together, Michael," said Jane in a whisper.

"You shut up," he said, but so low that Mary Poppins could not hear.

"Now, Sir," said Mary Poppins. "Off you go — in front of me, please. I'm not going to have you stravaiging behind any longer. You'll oblige me by going on ahead." She pushed him in front of her. "And," she continued, "there's a shiny thing sparkling on the path just along there. I'll thank you to go and pick it up and bring it to me. Somebody's dropped their tiara, perhaps."

Against his will, but because he didn't dare not to, Michael looked in the direction in which she was pointing. Yes — there *was* something shining on the path. From that distance it looked very interesting and its sparkling rays of light seemed to beckon him. He walked on, swaggering a little, going as slowly as he dared and pretending that he didn't really want to see what it was.

He reached the spot and, stooping, picked up the shining thing. It was a small round sort of box with a glass top and on the glass an arrow marked. Inside, a round disc that seemed to be covered with letters swung gently as he moved the box.

Jane ran up and looked at it over his shoulder.

"What is it, Michael?" she asked.

"I won't tell you," said Michael, though he didn't know himself.

"Mary Poppins, what is it?" demanded Jane, as the perambulator drew up beside them. Mary Poppins took the little box from Michael's hand.

"It's mine," he said jealously.

"No, mine," said Mary Poppins. "I saw it first."

"But I picked it up." He tried to snatch it from her hand, but she gave him such a look that his hand fell to his side.

She tilted the round thing backwards and forwards, and in the sunlight the disc and its letters went careering madly inside the box.

"What's it for?" asked Jane.

"To go round the world with," said Mary Poppins.

"Pooh!" said Michael. "You go round the world in a ship, or an aeroplane. *I* know that. The box thing wouldn't take you round the world."

"Oh, indeed — wouldn't it?" said Mary Poppins, with a curious I-know-better-than-you expression on her face. "You just watch!"

And holding the compass in her hand she turned towards the entrance of the Park and said the word "North!"

The letters slid round the arrow, dancing giddily. Suddenly the atmosphere seemed to grow bitterly cold, and the wind became so icy that Jane and Michael shut their eyes against it. When they opened them the

The compass

Park had entirely disappeared—not a tree nor a green-painted seat nor an asphalt footpath was in sight. Instead, they were surrounded by great boulders of blue ice and beneath their feet snow lay thickly frosted upon the ground.

"Oh, oh!" cried Jane, shivering with cold and surprise, and she rushed to cover the Twins with their perambulator rug. "What *has* happened to us?"

Mary Poppins sniffed. She had no time to reply, however, for at that moment a white furry head peered cautiously round a boulder. Then, a huge Polar Bear leapt out and, standing on his hind legs, proceeded to hug Mary Poppins.

"I was afraid you might be trappers," he said. "Welcome to the North Pole, all of you."

He put out a long pink tongue, rough and warm as a bath towel, and gently licked the children's cheeks.

They trembled. Did Polar Bears eat children, they wondered?

"You're shivering!" the Bear said kindly. "That's because you need something to eat. Make yourselves comfortable on this iceberg." He waved a paw at a block of ice. "Now, what would you like? Cod? Shrimps? Just something to keep the wolf from the door."

"I'm afraid we can't stay," Mary Poppins broke in. "We're on our way round the world."

"Well, do let me get you a little snack. It won't take me a jiffy."

He sprang into the blue-green water and came up with a herring. "I wish you could have stayed for a chat." He tucked the fish into Mary Poppins's hand. "I long for a bit of gossip."

"Another time perhaps," she said. "And thank you for the fish."

"South!" she said to the compass.

It seemed to Jane and Michael then that the world was spinning round them. As they felt the air getting soft and warm, they found themselves in a leafy jungle from which came a noisy sound of squawking.

"Welcome!" shrieked a large Hyacinth Macaw who was perched on a branch with outstretched wings. "You're just the person we need, Mary Poppins. My wife's off gadding, and I'm left to sit on the eggs. Do take a turn, there's a good girl. I need a little rest."

He lifted a spread wing cautiously, disclosing a nest with two white eggs.

"Alas, this is just a passing visit. We're on our way round the world."

"Gracious, what a journey! Well, stay for a little moment so that I can get some sleep. If you can look after all those creatures" — he nodded at the children — "you can keep two small eggs warm. Do, Mary Poppins! And I'll get you some bananas instead of that wriggling fish."

"It was a present," said Mary Poppins.

"Well, well, keep it if you must. But what madness to go gallivanting round the world when you could stay and bring up our nestlings. Why should *we* spend our time sitting when you could do it as well?"

"Better, you mean!" sniffed Mary Poppins.

Then, to Jane and Michael's disappointment — they would dearly have liked some tropical fruit — she shook her head decisively and said, "East!"

Again the world went spinning round them — or were they spinning round the world? And then, whichever it was ceased.

They found themselves in a grassy clearing surrounded by bamboo trees. Green paperlike leaves rustled in the breeze. And above that quiet swishing they could hear a steady rhythmic sound — a snore, or was it a purr?

Glancing round, they beheld a large furry shape — black with blotches of white, or was it white with blotches of black? They could not really be sure.

Jane and Michael gazed at each other. Was it a dream from which they would wake? Or were they seeing, of all things, a Panda! And a Panda in its own home and not behind bars in a zoo.

The dream, if it was a dream, drew a long breath.

"Whoever it is, please go away. I rest in the afternoon."

The voice was as furry as the rest of him.

"Very well, then, we *will* go away. And then perhaps" — Mary Poppins's voice was at its most priggish — "you'll be sorry you missed us."

The Panda opened one black eye. "Oh, it's you, my dear girl," he said sleepily. "Why not have let me know you were coming? Difficult though it would have been, for *you* I would have stayed awake." The furry shape yawned and stretched itself. "Ah well, I'll have to make a home for you all. There wouldn't be enough room in mine." He nodded at a neat shelter made of leaves and bamboo sticks. "But," he added, eying the herring, "I will not allow that scaly seathing under any roof of mine. Fishes are far too fishy for me."

"We shall not be staying," Mary Poppins assured him. "We're taking a little trip round the world and just looked in for a moment."

"What nonsense!" The Panda gave an enormous yawn. "Traipsing wildly round the world when you could stay here with me. Never mind, my dear Mary, you always do what you want to do, however absurd and foolish. Pluck a few young bamboo shoots. They'll sustain you till you get home. And you two" — he nodded at Jane and Michael — "tickle me gently behind the ears. That always sends me to sleep."

Eagerly they sat down beside him and stroked the silky fur. Never again — they were sure of it — would they have the chance of stroking a Panda.

The furry shape settled itself, and as they stroked, the snore — or the purr — began its rhythm.

"He's asleep," said Mary Poppins softly. "We mustn't wake him again." She beckoned to the children, and as they came on tip-toe towards her, she gave a flick of her wrist. And the compass, apparently, understood, for the spinning began again.

Hills and lakes, mountains and forests went waltzing round them to unheard music. Then again the world was still, as if it had never moved.

This time they found themselves on a long white shore, with wavelets lapping and curling against it.

And immediately before them was a cloud of whirling,

swirling sand from which came a series of grunts. Then slowly the cloud settled, disclosing a large black and grey Dolphin with a young one at her side.

"Is that you, Amelia?" called Mary Poppins.

The Dolphin blew some sand from her nose and gave a start of surprise. "Well, of all people, it's Mary Poppins! You're just in time to share our sand-bath. Nothing like a sand-bath for cleansing the fins and the tail."

"I had a bath this morning, thank you!"

"Well, what about those young ones, dear? Couldn't they do with a bit of scouring?"

"They have no fins and tails," said Mary Poppins, much to the children's disappointment. They would have liked a roll in the sand.

"Well, what on earth or sea are you doing here?" Amelia demanded briskly.

"Oh, just going round the world, you know," Mary Poppins said airily, as though going round the world was a thing you did every day.

"Well, it's a treat for Froggie and me — isn't it, Froggie?" Amelia butted him with her nose, and the young Dolphin gave a friendly squeak.

"I call him Froggie because he so often strays away — just like the Frog that would a-wooing go, whether his mother would let him or no. Don't you, Froggie?" His answer was another squeak.

"Well, now for a meal. What would you like?" Amelia

grinned at Jane and Michael, displaying a splendid array of teeth. "There's cockles and mussels alive, alive-O. And the seaweed here is excellent."

"Thank you kindly, I'm sure, Amelia. But we have to be home in half a minute." Mary Poppins laid a firm hand on the handle of the perambulator.

Amelia was clearly disappointed.

"Whatever kind of visit is that? Hullo and goodbye in the same breath. Next time you must stay for tea, and we'll all sit together on a rock and sing a song to the moon. Eh, Froggie?"

Froggie squeaked.

"That will be lovely," said Mary Poppins, and Jane and Michael echoed her words. They had never yet sat on a rock and sung a song to the moon.

"Well, au revoir, one and all. By the way, Mary, my dear, were you going to take that herring with you?"

Amelia greedily eyed the fish, which, fearing the worst was about to happen, made itself as limp as it could in Mary Poppins's hand.

"No. I am planning to throw it back to the sea!" The herring gasped with relief.

"A very proper decision, Mary." Amelia toothily smiled. "We get so few of them in these parts, and they make a delicious meal. Why don't we race for it, Froggie and me? When you say 'Go!', we'll start swimming and see who gets it first."

Mary Poppins held the fish aloft.

"Ready! Steady! Go!" she cried.

And as if it were bird rather than fish, the herring swooped up and splashed into the sea.

The Dolphins were after it in a second, two dark striving shapes rippling through the water.

Jane and Michael could hardly breathe. Which would win the prize? Or would the prize escape?

"Froggie! Froggie! Froggie!" yelled Michael. If the herring had to be caught and eaten, he wanted Froggie to win.

"F-r-o-g-g-i-e!" The wind and sea both cried the name, but Michael's voice was the stronger.

"What *do* you think you're doing, Michael?" Mary Poppins sounded ferocious.

He glanced at her for a moment and turned again to the sea.

But the sea was not there. Nothing but a neat green lawn; Jane, agog, beside him; the Twins in the perambulator; and Mary Poppins pushing it in the middle of the Park.

"Jumping up and down and shouting! Making a nuisance of yourself. One would think you had done enough for one day. Step along at once, please!"

"Round the world and back in a minute — what a wonderful box!" said Jane.

"It's a *compass*. Not a box. And it's mine," said Michael. "I found it. Give it to me!"

"*My* compass, thank you," said Mary Poppins, as she slipped it into her pocket.

He looked as if he would like to kill her. But he shrugged his shoulders and stalked off taking no notice of anyone.

The burning weight still hung heavily within him. After the adventure with the compass it seemed to grow worse, and towards the evening he grew naughtier and naughtier. He pinched the Twins when Mary Poppins was not looking, and when they cried he said in a falsely kind voice:

"Why, darlings, what *is* the matter?"

But Mary Poppins was not deceived by it.

"You've got something coming to *you!*" she said significantly. But the burning thing inside him would not let him care. He just shrugged his shoulders and pulled Jane's hair. And after that he went to the supper table and upset his bread-and-milk.

"And that," said Mary Poppins, "is the end. Such deliberate naughtiness I never saw. In all my born days I never did, and that's a fact. Off you go! Straight into bed with you and not another word!" He had never seen her look so terrible.

But still he didn't care.

He went into the Night-nursery and undressed. No, he didn't care. He was bad, and if they didn't look out he'd be worse. He didn't care. He hated everybody. If they weren't careful he would run away and join a circus. There! Off went a button. Good — there would be fewer to do up in the morning. And another! All the better. Nothing in all the world could ever make him feel sorry. He would get into bed without brushing his hair or his teeth — certainly without saying his prayers.

He was just about to get into bed and, indeed, had one foot already in it, when he noticed the compass lying on the top of the chest of drawers.

Very slowly he withdrew his foot and tip-toed across the room. He knew now what he would do. He would take the compass and spin it and go round the world. And they'd never find him again. And it would serve them right. Without making a sound he lifted a chair and put it against the chest of drawers. Then he climbed up on it and took the compass in his hand.

He moved it.

"North, South, East, West!" he said very quickly, in case anybody should come in before he got well away.

A noise behind the chair startled him and he turned round guiltily, expecting to see Mary Poppins. But instead, there were four gigantic figures bearing down upon him — the bear with his fangs showing, the Macaw fiercely flapping his wings, the Panda with his fur on end, the Dolphin thrusting out her snout. From all quarters of the room they were rushing upon him, their shadows huge on the ceiling. No longer kind and friendly, they were now full of revenge. Their terrible angry faces loomed nearer. He could feel their hot breath on his face.

"Oh! Oh!" Michael dropped the compass. "Mary Poppins, help me!" he screamed and shut his eyes in terror.

And then something enveloped him. The great creatures and their greater shadows, with a mingled roar or squawk of triumph, flung themselves upon him. What was it that held him, soft and warm, in its smothering embrace? The Polar Bear's fur coat? The Macaw's feathers? The Panda's fur he had stroked so gently? The mother Dolphin's flipper? And what was he — or it might be she — planning to do to him? If only he had been good — if only!

"Mary Poppins!" he wailed, as he felt himself carried through the air and set down in something still softer.

"Oh, dear Mary Poppins!"

"All right, all right. I'm not deaf, I'm thankful to say — no need to shout," he heard her saying calmly.

He opened one eye. He could see no sign of the four gigantic figures of the compass. He opened the other eye to make sure. No — not a glint of any of them. He sat up. He looked round the room. There was nothing there.

Then he discovered that the soft thing that was round him was his own blanket, and the soft thing he was lying on was his own bed. And oh, the heavy burning thing that had been inside him all day had melted and disappeared. He felt peaceful and happy, and as if he would like to give everybody he knew a birthday present.

"What — what happened?" he said rather anxiously to Mary Poppins.

"I told you that was my compass, didn't I? Be kind enough not to touch my things, *if* you please," was all she said as she stooped and picked up the compass and put it in her pocket. Then she began to fold the clothes that he had thrown down on the floor.

"Shall I do it?" he said.

"No, thank you."

He watched her go into the next room, and presently she returned and put something warm into his hands. It was a cup of milk.

Michael sipped it, tasting every drop several times with his tongue, making it last as long as possible so that Mary Poppins should stay beside him.

She stood there without saying a word, watching the milk slowly disappear. He could smell her crackling white apron and the faint flavour of toast that always hung about her so deliciously. But try as he would, he could not make the milk last for ever, and presently, with a sigh of regret, he handed her the empty cup and slipped down into the bed. He had never known it to be so comfortable, he thought. And he thought, too, how warm he was and how happy he felt and how lucky he was to be alive.

"Isn't it a funny thing, Mary Poppins," he said drowsily. "I've been so very naughty and I feel so very good."

"Humph!" said Mary Poppins as she tucked him in and went away to wash up the supper things. . . .

CHAPTER SEVEN

THE BIRD WOMAN

erhaps she won't be there," said Michael.

"Yes, she will," said Jane. "She's always there for ever and ever."

They were walking up Ludgate Hill on the way to pay a visit to Mr. Banks in the City. For he had said that morning to Mrs. Banks:

"My dear, if it doesn't rain I think Jane and Michael might call for me at the Office today — that is, if you are agreeable. I have a feeling I should like to be taken out to Tea and Shortbread Fingers and it's not often I have a Treat."

And Mrs. Banks had said she would think about it.

But all day long, though Jane and Michael had watched her anxiously, she had not seemed to be thinking about it at all. From the things she said, she was thinking about the Laundry Bill and Michael's new overcoat and where was Aunt Flossie's address, and why did that wretched Mrs. Jackson ask her to tea on the second Thursday of the month when she knew that was the very day Mrs. Banks had to go to the Dentist's?

Suddenly, when they felt quite sure she would never think about Mr. Banks's treat, she said:

"Now, children, don't stand staring at me like that. Get your things on. You are going to the City to have tea with your Father. Had you forgotten?"

As if they could have forgotten! For it was not as though it were only the Tea that mattered. There was also the Bird Woman, and she herself was the best of all Treats.

That is why they were walking up Ludgate Hill and feeling very excited.

Mary Poppins walked between them, wearing her new hat and looking very distinguished. Every now and then she would look into the shop window just to make sure the hat was still there and that the pink roses on it had not turned into common flowers like marigolds.

Every time she stopped to make sure, Jane and Michael would sigh, but they did not dare say anything for fear she would spend even longer looking at herself in the windows, and turning this way and that to see which attitude was the most becoming.

But at last they came to St. Paul's Cathedral, which was built a long time ago by a man with a bird's name. Wren it was, but he was no relation to Jenny. That is why so many birds live near Sir Christopher Wren's Cathedral, which also belongs to St. Paul, and that is why the Bird Woman lives there, too.

"There she is!" cried Michael suddenly, and he danced on his toes with excitement.

Sir Christopher Wren's Cathedral

"Don't point," said Mary Poppins, giving a last glance at the pink roses in the window of a carpet-shop.

"She's saying it! She's saying it!" cried Jane, holding tight to herself for fear she would break in two with delight.

And she *was* saying it. The Bird Woman was there and she was saying it.

"Feed the Birds, Tuppence a Bag! Feed the Birds, Tuppence a Bag! Feed the Birds, Feed the Birds, Tuppence a Bag, Tuppence a Bag!" Over and over again, the same thing, in a high chanting voice that made the words seem like a song.

And as she said it she held out little bags of bread-crumbs to the passers-by.

All round her flew the birds, circling and leaping and swooping and rising. Mary Poppins always called them "sparrers," because, she said conceitedly, all birds were alike to her. But Jane and Michael knew that they were not sparrows, but doves and pigeons. There were fussy and chatty grey doves like Grandmothers; and brown, rough-voiced pigeons like Uncles; and greeny, cackling, no-I've-no-money-today pigeons like Fathers. And the silly, anxious, soft blue doves were like Mothers. That's what Jane and Michael thought, anyway.

They flew round and round the head of the Bird Woman as the children approached, and then, as though to tease her, they suddenly rushed away through the air and sat on the top of St. Paul's, laughing and turning their heads away and pretending they didn't know her.

It was Michael's turn to buy a bag. Jane had bought one last time. He walked up to the Bird Woman and held out four halfpennies.

"*Feed* the Birds, Tuppence a Bag!" said the Bird Woman, as she put a bag of crumbs into his hand and tucked the money away into the folds of her huge black skirt.

"Why don't you have penny bags?" said Michael. "Then I could buy two."

"Feed the Birds, *Tuppence* a Bag!" said the Bird Woman, and Michael knew it was no good asking her any more questions. He and Jane had often tried, but all she could say, and all she had ever been able to say was, "Feed the Birds, Tuppence a Bag!" Just as a cuckoo can only say "Cuckoo," no matter what questions you ask him.

Jane and Michael and Mary Poppins spread the crumbs in a circle on the ground, and presently, one by one at first, and then in twos and threes, the birds came down from St. Paul's.

"Dainty David," said Mary Poppins with a sniff, as one bird picked up a crumb and dropped it again from its beak.

But the other birds swarmed upon the food, pushing and scrambling and shouting. At last there wasn't a crumb left, for it is not really polite for a pigeon or a dove to leave anything on the plate. When they were quite certain that the meal was finished the birds rose with one grand, fluttering movement and flew round the Bird Woman's head, copying in their own language the words she said. One of them sat on her hat and pretended he was a decoration for the crown. And another of them mistook Mary Poppins's new hat for a rose garden and pecked off a flower.

"You sparrer!" cried Mary Poppins, and shook her umbrella at him. The pigeon, very offended, flew back to the Bird Woman and, to pay out Mary Poppins, stuck the rose in the ribbon of the Bird Woman's hat.

"You ought to be in a pie — that's where *you* ought to be," said Mary Poppins to him very angrily. Then she called to Jane and Michael.

"Time to go," she said, and flung a parting glance of fury at the pigeon. But he only laughed and flicked his tail and turned his back on her.

"Good-bye," said Michael to the Bird Woman.

"Feed the Birds," she replied, smiling.

"Good-bye," said Jane.

"Tuppence a Bag!" said the Bird Woman and waved her hand.

They left her then, walking one on either side of Mary Poppins.

"What happens when *everybody* goes away — like us?" said Michael to Jane.

He knew quite well what happened, but it was the proper thing to ask Jane because the story was really hers.

So Jane told him and he added the bits she had forgotten.

"At night when everybody goes to bed——" began Jane.

"And the stars come out," added Michael.

"Yes, and even if they don't — all the birds come down from the top of St. Paul's and run very carefully all over the ground just to see there are no crumbs left, and to tidy it up for the morning. And when they have done that——"

"You've forgotten the baths."

"Oh, yes — they bath themselves and comb their wings with their claws. And when they have done that they fly

three times round the head of the Bird Woman and then they settle."

"Do they sit on her shoulders?"

"Yes, and on her hat."

"And on her basket with the bags in it?"

"Yes, and some on her knee. Then she smooths down the head-feathers of each one in turn and tells it to be a good bird —— "

"In the bird language?"

"Yes. And when they are all sleepy and don't want to stay awake any longer, she spreads out her skirts, as a mother hen spreads out her wings, and the birds go creep, creep, creeping underneath. And as soon as the last one is under she settles down over them, making little brooding, nesting noises and they sleep there till the morning."

Michael sighed happily. He loved the story and was never tired of hearing it.

"And it's all quite true, isn't it?" he said, just as he always did.

"No," said Mary Poppins, who always said "No."

"Yes," said Jane, who always knew everything. . . .

CHAPTER EIGHT

MRS. CORRY

wo pounds of sausages — Best Pork," said Mary Poppins. "And at once, please. We're in a hurry."

The Butcher, who wore a large blue-and-white striped apron, was a fat and friendly man. He was also large and red and rather like one of his own sausages. He leant upon his chopping-block and gazed admiringly at Mary Poppins. Then he winked pleasantly at Jane and Michael.

"In a Nurry?" he said to Mary Poppins. "Well, that's a pity. I'd hoped you'd dropped in for a bit of a chat. We Butchers, you know, like a bit of company. And we don't often get the chance of talking to a nice, handsome young lady like you——" He broke off suddenly, for he had caught sight of Mary Poppins's face. The expression on it was awful. And the Butcher found himself wishing there was a trapdoor in the floor of his shop that would open and swallow him up.

"Oh, well——" he said, blushing even redder than

usual. "If you're in a Nurry, of course. Two pounds, did you say? Best Pork? Right you are!"

And he hurriedly hooked down a long string of the sausages that were festooned across the shop. He cut off a length — about three-quarters of a yard — wound it into a sort of garland, and wrapped it up first in white and then in brown paper. He pushed the parcel across the chopping-block.

"*AND* the next?" he said hopefully, still blushing.

"There will be *no* next," said Mary Poppins, with a haughty sniff. And she took the sausages and turned the perambulator round very quickly, and wheeled it out of the shop in such a way that the Butcher knew he had mortally offended her. But she glanced at the window as she went so that she could see how her new shoes looked reflected in it. They were bright brown kid with two buttons, very smart.

Jane and Michael trailed after her, wondering when she would have come to the end of her shopping-list but, because of the look on her face, not daring to ask her.

Mary Poppins gazed up and down the street as if deep in thought, and then, suddenly making up her mind, she snapped:

"Fishmonger!" and turned the perambulator in at the shop next to the Butcher's.

"One Dover Sole, pound and a half of Halibut, pint of Prawns and a Lobster," said Mary Poppins, talking so quickly that only somebody used to taking such orders could possibly have understood her.

The Fishmonger, unlike the Butcher, was a long thin man, so thin that he seemed to have no front to him but only two sides. And he looked so sad that you felt he had either just been weeping or was just going to. Jane said that this was due to some secret sorrow that had haunted him since his youth, and Michael thought that the Fishmonger's Mother must have fed him entirely on bread and water when he was a baby, and that he had never forgotten it.

"Anything else?" said the Fishmonger hopelessly, in a voice that suggested he was quite sure there wouldn't be.

"Not today," said Mary Poppins.

The Fishmonger shook his head sadly and did not look at all surprised. He had known all along there would be nothing else.

Sniffing gently, he tied up the parcel and dropped it into the perambulator.

"Bad weather," he observed, wiping his eye with his hand. "Don't believe we're going to get any summer at all — not that we ever did, of course. *You* don't look too blooming," he said to Mary Poppins. "But then, nobody does —— "

Mary Poppins tossed her head.

"Speak for yourself," she said crossly, and flounced to the door, pushing the perambulator so fiercely that it bumped into a bag of oysters.

"The idea!" Jane and Michael heard her say as she glanced down at her shoes. Not looking too blooming in her new brown kid shoes with two buttons — the idea! That was what they heard her thinking.

Outside on the pavement she paused, looking at her list and ticking off what she had bought. Michael stood first on one leg and then on the other.

"Mary Poppins, are we *never* going home?" he said crossly.

Mary Poppins turned and regarded him with something like disgust.

"That," she said briefly, "is as it may be." And Michael, watching her fold up her list, wished he had not spoken.

"*You* can go home, if you like," she said haughtily. "*We* are going to buy the gingerbread."

Michael's face fell. If only he had managed to say nothing! He hadn't known that Gingerbread was at the end of the list.

"That's your way," said Mary Poppins shortly, pointing in the direction of Cherry-Tree Lane. "If you don't get lost," she added as an afterthought.

"Oh no, Mary Poppins, *please,* no! I didn't mean it, really. I — oh — Mary Poppins, please —— " cried Michael.

"Do let him come, Mary Poppins!" said Jane. "I'll push the perambulator if only you'll let him come."

Mary Poppins sniffed. "If it wasn't Friday," she said darkly to Michael, "you'd go home in a twink — an absolute Twink!"

She moved onwards, pushing John and Barbara. Jane and Michael knew that she had relented, and followed wondering what a Twink was. Suddenly Jane noticed that they were going in the wrong direction.

"But, Mary Poppins, I thought you said ginger-bread — this isn't the way to Green, Brown and Johnson's, where we always get it —— " she began, and stopped because of Mary Poppins's face.

"Am I doing the shopping or are you?" Mary Poppins enquired.

"You," said Jane, in a very small voice.

"Oh, really? I thought it was the other way round," said Mary Poppins with a scornful laugh.

She gave the perambulator a little twist with her hand and it turned a corner and drew up suddenly. Jane and Michael, stopping abruptly behind it, found themselves outside the most curious shop they had ever seen. It was very small and very dingy. Faded loops of coloured paper hung in the windows, and on the shelves were shabby little boxes of Sherbet, old Liquorice Sticks, and very withered, very hard Apples-on-a-stick. There was a small dark doorway between the windows, and through this Mary Poppins propelled the perambulator while Jane and Michael followed at her heels.

Inside the shop they could dimly see the glass-topped counter that ran round three sides of it. And in a case under the glass were rows and rows of dark, dry gingerbread, each slab so studded with gilt stars that the shop itself seemed to be faintly lit by them. Jane and Michael glanced round to find out what kind of a person was to serve them, and were very surprised when Mary Poppins called out:

"Fannie! Annie! Where are you?" Her voice seemed to echo back to them from each dark wall of the shop.

And as she called, two of the largest people the children had ever seen rose from behind the counter and shook hands with Mary Poppins. The huge women then leant down over the counter and said, "How de do?" in voices as large as themselves, and shook hands with Jane and Michael.

"How do you do, Miss —— ?" Michael paused, wondering which of the large ladies was which.

"Fannie's my name," said one of them. "My rheumatism is about the same; thank you for asking." She spoke very mournfully, as though she were unused to such a courteous greeting.

"It's a lovely day —— " began Jane politely to the other sister, who kept Jane's hand imprisoned for almost a minute in her huge clasp.

"I'm Annie," she informed them miserably. "And handsome is as handsome does."

Jane and Michael thought that both the sisters had a very odd way of expressing themselves, but they had not time to be surprised for long, for Miss Fannie and Miss

Annie were reaching out their long arms to the perambulator. Each shook hands solemnly with one of the Twins,
who were so astonished that they began to cry.

"Now, now, now, now! What's this, what's this?" A
high, thin, crackly little voice came from the back of the
shop. At the sound of it the expression on the faces of
Miss Fannie and Miss Annie, sad before, became even
sadder. They seemed frightened and ill at ease, and
somehow Jane and Michael realised that the two huge
sisters were wishing that they were much smaller and
less conspicuous.

. "What's all this I hear?" cried the curious high little
voice, coming nearer. And presently, round the corner of
the glass case the owner of it appeared. She was as small
as her voice and as crackly, and to the children she seemed
to be older than anything in the world, with her wispy
hair and her sticklike legs and her wizened, wrinkled little face. But in spite of this she ran towards them as lightly
and as gaily as though she were still a young girl.

"Now, now, now — well, I do declare! Bless me if
it isn't Mary Poppins, with John and Barbara Banks.
What — Jane and Michael, too? Well, isn't this a nice surprise for me? I assure you I haven't been so surprised since
Christopher Columbus discovered America — truly I
haven't!"

She smiled delightedly as she came to greet them,
and her feet made little dancing movements inside the

tiny elastic-sided boots. She ran to the perambulator and rocked it gently, crooking her thin, twisted, old fingers at John and Barbara until they stopped crying and began to laugh.

"That's better!" she said, cackling gaily. Then she did a very odd thing. She broke off two of her fingers and gave one each to John and Barbara. And the oddest part of it was that in the space left by the broken-off fingers two new ones grew at once. Jane and Michael clearly saw it happen.

"Only Barley-Sugar — can't possibly hurt 'em," the old lady said to Mary Poppins.

"Anything *you* give them, Mrs. Corry, could only do

them good," said Mary Poppins with most surprising courtesy.

"What a pity," Michael couldn't help saying, "they weren't Peppermint Bars."

"Well, they are, sometimes," said Mrs. Corry gleefully, "and very good they taste, too. I often nibble 'em myself, if I can't sleep at night. Splendid for the digestion."

"What will they be next time?" asked Jane, looking at Mrs. Corry's fingers with interest.

"Aha!" said Mrs. Corry. "That's just the question. I never know from day to day what they will be. I take the chance, my dear, as I heard William the Conqueror say to his Mother when she advised him not to go conquering England."

"You must be *very* old!" said Jane, sighing enviously, and wondering if she would ever be able to remember what Mrs. Corry remembered.

Mrs. Corry flung back her wispy little head and shrieked with laughter.

"Old!" she said. "Why, I'm quite a chicken compared to my Grandmother. Now, there's an old woman *if* you like. Still, I go back a good way. I remember the time when they were making this world, anyway, and I was well out of my teens then. My goodness, that *was* a to-do, I can tell you!"

She broke off suddenly, screwing up her little eyes at the children.

"But, deary me — here am I running on and on and

you not being served! I suppose, my dear" — she turned
to Mary Poppins, whom she appeared to know very
well — "I suppose you've all come for some Gingerbread?"

"That's right, Mrs. Corry," said Mary Poppins politely.

"Good. Have Fannie and Annie given you any?" She
looked at Jane and Michael as she said this.

Jane shook her head. Two hushed voices came from behind the counter.

"No, Mother," said Miss Fannie meekly.

"We were just going to, Mother ——" began Miss
Annie in a frightened whisper.

At that Mrs. Corry drew herself up to her full height
and regarded her gigantic daughters furiously. Then she
said in a soft, fierce, terrifying voice:

"Just going to? Oh, *indeed!* That is *very* interesting.
And who, may I ask, Annie, gave you permission to give
away *my* gingerbread —— ?"

"Nobody, Mother. And I didn't give it away. I only
thought ——"

"You only thought! That is *very* kind of you. But I will
thank you not to think. *I* can do all the thinking that is
necessary here!" said Mrs. Corry in her soft, terrible voice.
Then she burst into a harsh cackle of laughter.

"Look at her! Just look at her! Cowardy-custard! Cry-
baby!" she shrieked, pointing her knotty finger at her
daughter.

Jane and Michael turned and saw a large tear coursing down Miss Annie's huge, sad face, but they did not like to say anything, for, in spite of her tininess, Mrs. Corry made them feel rather small and frightened. But as soon as Mrs. Corry looked the other way Jane seized the opportunity to offer Miss Annie her handkerchief. The huge tear completely drenched it, and Miss Annie, with a grateful look, wrung it out before she returned it to Jane.

"And you, Fannie — did *you* think, too, I wonder?" The high little voice was now directed at the other daughter.

"No, Mother," said Miss Fannie trembling.

"Humph! Just as well for you! Open that case!"

With frightened, fumbling fingers, Miss Fannie opened the glass case.

"Now, my darlings," said Mrs. Corry in quite a different voice. She smiled and beckoned so sweetly to Jane and Michael that they were ashamed of having been frightened of her, and felt that she must be very nice after all. "Won't you come and take your pick, my lambs? It's a special recipe today — one I got from Alfred the Great. He was a very good cook, I remember, though he did once burn the cakes. How many?"

Jane and Michael looked at Mary Poppins.

"Four each," she said. "That's twelve. One dozen."

"I'll make it a Baker's Dozen — take thirteen," said Mrs. Corry cheerfully.

So Jane and Michael chose thirteen slabs of gingerbread, each with its gilt paper star. Their arms were piled up with the delicious dark cakes. Michael could not resist nibbling a corner of one of them.

"Good?" squeaked Mrs. Corry, and when he nodded she picked up her skirts and did a few steps of the Highland Fling for pure pleasure.

"Hooray, hooray, splendid, hooray!" she cried in her shrill little voice. Then she came to a standstill and her face grew serious.

"But remember — I'm not *giving* them away. I must be paid. The price is threepence for each of you."

Mary Poppins opened her purse and took out three threepenny-bits. She gave one each to Jane and Michael.

"Now," said Mrs. Corry. "Stick 'em on my coat! That's where they all go."

They looked closely at her long black coat. And sure enough they found it was studded with threepenny-bits as a Coster's coat is with pearl buttons.

"Come along. Stick 'em on!" repeated Mrs. Corry, rubbing her hands with pleasant expectation. "You'll find they won't drop off."

Mary Poppins stepped forward and pressed her three-penny-bit against the collar of Mrs. Corry's coat.

To the surprise of Jane and Michael, it stuck.

Then they put theirs on — Jane's on the right shoulder and Michael's on the front hem. Theirs stuck, too.

"How very extraordinary," said Jane.

"Not at all, my dear," said Mrs. Corry chuckling. "Or rather, not so extraordinary as other things I could mention." And she winked largely at Mary Poppins.

"I'm afraid we must be off now, Mrs. Corry," said Mary Poppins. "There is Baked Custard for lunch, and I must be home in time to make it. That Mrs. Brill —— "

"A poor cook?" enquired Mrs. Corry interrupting.

"Poor!" said Mary Poppins contemptuously. "*That's* not the word."

"Ah!" Mrs. Corry put her finger alongside her nose and looked very wise. Then she said:

"Well, my dear Miss Poppins, it has been a very pleasant visit and I am sure my girls have enjoyed it as much as I have." She nodded in the direction of her two large mournful daughters. "And you'll come again soon, won't you, with Jane and Michael and the Babies? Now, are you sure you can carry the Gingerbread?" she continued, turning to Michael and Jane.

They nodded. Mrs. Corry drew closer to them, with a curious, important, inquisitive look on her face.

"I wonder," she said dreamily, "what you will do with the paper stars?"

"Oh, we'll keep them," said Jane. "We always do."

"Ah — you keep them! And I wonder *where* you keep them?" Mrs. Corry's eyes were half closed and she looked more inquisitive than ever.

"Well," Jane began. "Mine are all under my handkerchiefs in the top left-hand drawer and —— "

"Mine are in a shoe-box on the bottom shelf of the wardrobe," said Michael.

"Top left-hand drawer and shoe-box in the wardrobe," said Mrs. Corry thoughtfully, as though she were committing the words to memory. Then she gave Mary Poppins a long look and nodded her head slightly. Mary Poppins nodded slightly in return. It seemed as if some secret had passed between them.

"Well," said Mrs. Corry brightly, "that is very interesting. You don't know how glad I am to know you keep your stars. I shall remember that. You see, I remember everything — even what Guy Fawkes had for dinner every second Sunday. And now, good-bye. Come again soon. Come again so-o-o-o-n!"

Mrs. Corry's voice seemed to be growing fainter and fading away, and presently, without being quite aware of what had happened, Jane and Michael found themselves on the pavement, walking behind Mary Poppins, who was again examining her list.

They turned and looked behind them.

"Why, Jane," said Michael with surprise, "it's not there!"

"So I see," said Jane, staring and staring.

And they were right. The shop was *not* there. It had entirely disappeared.

"How odd!" said Jane.

"Isn't it?" said Michael. "But the Gingerbread is very good."

And they were so busy biting their Gingerbread into different shapes — a man, a flower, a teapot — that they quite forgot how *very* odd it was.

They remembered it again at night, however, when the lights were out and they were both supposed to be sound asleep.

"Jane, Jane!" whispered Michael. "I hear someone tiptoeing on the stairs — listen!"

"Sssh!" hissed Jane from her bed, for she, too, had heard the footsteps.

Presently the door opened with a little click and somebody came into the room. It was Mary Poppins, dressed in hat and coat all ready to go out.

She moved about the room softly with quick secret movements. Jane and Michael watched her through half-closed eyes without stirring.

First she went to the chest of drawers, opened a drawer and shut it again after a moment. Then, on tiptoe, she went to the wardrobe, opened it, bent down and put something in or took something out (they couldn't tell which). Snap! The wardrobe door shut quickly and Mary Poppins hurried from the room.

Michael sat up in bed.

"What was she doing?" he said to Jane in a loud whisper.

"I don't know. Perhaps she'd forgotten her gloves or her shoes or —— " Jane broke off suddenly. "Michael, listen!"

He listened. From down below — in the garden, it seemed — they could hear several voices whispering together, very earnestly and excitedly.

With a quick movement Jane got out of bed and beckoned Michael. They crept on bare feet to the window and looked down.

There, outside in the Lane, stood a tiny form and two gigantic figures.

"Mrs. Corry and Miss Fannie and Miss Annie," said Jane in a whisper.

And so indeed it was. It was a curious group. Mrs. Corry was looking through the bars of the gate of Number Seventeen, Miss Fannie had two long ladders balanced on one huge shoulder, while Miss Annie appeared to be carrying in one hand a large pail of something that looked like glue and in the other an enormous paint-brush.

From where they stood, hidden by the curtain, Jane and Michael could distinctly hear their voices.

"She's late!" Mrs. Corry was saying crossly and anxiously.

"Perhaps," Miss Fannie began timidly, settling the ladders more firmly on her shoulder, "one of the children is ill and she couldn't —— "

"Get away in time," said Miss Annie, nervously completing her sister's sentence.

"Silence!" said Mrs. Corry fiercely, and Jane and Michael distinctly heard her whisper something about "great galumphing giraffes," and they knew she was referring to her unfortunate daughters.

"Hist!" said Mrs. Corry suddenly, listening with her head on one side, like a small bird.

There was the sound of the front door being quietly opened and shut again, and the creak of footsteps on the path. Mrs. Corry smiled and waved her hand as Mary Poppins came to meet them, carrying a market basket on her arm, and in the basket was something that seemed to give out a faint, mysterious light.

"Come along, come along, we must hurry! We haven't much time," said Mrs. Corry, taking Mary Poppins by the arm. "Look lively, you two!" And she moved off, followed by Miss Fannie and Miss Annie, who were obviously trying to look as lively as possible but not succeeding very well. They tramped heavily after their Mother and Mary Poppins, bending under their loads.

Jane and Michael saw all four of them go down Cherry-Tree Lane, and then they turned a little to the left and went up the hill. When they got to the top of the hill, where there were no houses but only grass and clover, they stopped.

Miss Annie put down her pail of glue, and Miss Fannie swung the ladders from her shoulder and steadied them until both stood in an upright position. Then she held one and Miss Annie the other.

"What on earth are they going to do?" said Michael, gaping.

But there was no need for Jane to reply, for he could see for himself what was happening.

As soon as Miss Fannie and Miss Annie had so fixed the ladders that they seemed to be standing with one end on the earth and the other leaning on the sky, Mrs. Corry picked up her skirts and the paint-brush in one hand and the pail of glue in the other. Then she set her foot on the lowest rung of one of the ladders and began to climb it. Mary Poppins, carrying her basket, climbed the other.

Then Jane and Michael saw a most amazing sight. As soon as she arrived at the top of her ladder, Mrs. Corry dipped her brush into the glue and began slapping the sticky substance against the sky. And Mary Poppins, when this had been done, took something shiny from her basket and fixed it to the glue. When she took her hand away they saw that she was sticking the Gingerbread Stars to the sky. As each one was placed in position it began to twinkle furiously, sending out rays of sparkling golden light.

"They're ours!" said Michael breathlessly. "They're our stars. She thought we were asleep and came in and took them!"

But Jane was silent. She was watching Mrs. Corry splashing the glue on the sky and Mary Poppins sticking on the stars and Miss Fannie and Miss Annie moving the ladders to a new position as the spaces in the sky became filled up.

At last it was over. Mary Poppins shook out her basket and showed Mrs. Corry that there was nothing left in it.

One end on the earth and the other leaning on the sky

Then they came down from the ladders and the procession started down the hill again, Miss Fannie shouldering the ladders, Miss Annie jangling her empty pail of glue. At the corner they stood talking for a moment; then Mary Poppins shook hands with them all and hurried up the Lane again. Mrs. Corry, dancing lightly in her elastic-sided boots and holding her skirts daintily with her hands, disappeared in the other direction with her huge daughters stumping noisily behind her.

The garden-gate clicked. Footsteps creaked on the path. The front door opened and shut with a soft clanging sound. Presently they heard Mary Poppins come quietly up the stairs, tip-toe past the nursery and go on into the room where she slept with John and Barbara.

As the sound of her footsteps died away, Jane and Michael looked at each other. Then without a word they went together to the top left-hand drawer and looked.

There was nothing there but a pile of Jane's handkerchiefs.

"I told you so," said Michael.

Next they went to the wardrobe and looked into the shoe-box. It was empty.

"But how? But why?" said Michael, sitting down on the edge of his bed and staring at Jane.

Jane said nothing. She just sat beside him with her arms round her knees and thought and thought and thought. At last she shook back her hair and stretched herself and stood up.

"What *I* want to know," she said, "is this: Are the stars gold paper or is the gold paper stars?"

There was no reply to her question and she did not expect one. She knew that only somebody very much wiser than Michael could give her the right answer. . . .

CHAPTER NINE

JOHN AND BARBARA'S STORY

Jane and Michael had gone off to a party, wearing their best clothes and looking, as Ellen the housemaid said when she saw them, "just like a shop window."

All the afternoon the house was very quiet and still, as though it were thinking its own thoughts, or dreaming perhaps.

Down in the kitchen Mrs. Brill was reading the paper with her spectacles perched on her nose. Robertson Ay was sitting in the garden busily doing nothing. Mrs. Banks was on the drawing-room sofa with her feet up. And the house stood very quietly around them all, dreaming its own dreams, or thinking perhaps.

Upstairs in the nursery Mary Poppins was airing the clothes by the fire, and the sunlight poured in at the window, flickering on the white walls, dancing over the cots where the babies were lying.

"I say, move over! You're right in my eyes," said John in a loud voice.

"Sorry!" said the sunlight. "But I can't help it. I've got to get across this room somehow. Orders is orders. I must move from East to West in a day and my way lies through this Nursery. Sorry! Shut your eyes and you won't notice me."

The gold shaft of sunlight lengthened across the room. It was obviously moving as quickly as it could in order to oblige John.

"How soft, how sweet you are! I love you," said Barbara, holding out her hands to its shining warmth.

"Good girl," said the sunlight approvingly, and moved up over her cheeks and into her hair with a light, caressing movement. "Do you like the feel of me?" it said, as though it loved being praised.

"Dee-licious!" said Barbara, with a happy sigh.

"Chatter, chatter, chatter! I never heard such a place for chatter. There's always somebody talking in this room," said a shrill voice at the window.

John and Barbara looked up.

It was the Starling who lived on the top of the chimney.

"I like that," said Mary Poppins, turning round quickly. "What about yourself? All day long — yes, and half the night, too, on the roofs and telegraph poles. Roaring and screaming and shouting — you'd talk the leg off a chair, you would. Worse than any sparrer, and that's the truth."

The Starling cocked his head on one side and looked down at her from his perch on the window-frame.

"Well," he said, "I have my business to attend to. Consultations, discussions, arguments, bargaining. And that, of course, necessitates a certain amount of — er — quiet conversation —— "

"Quiet!" exclaimed John, laughing heartily.

"And I wasn't talking to you, young man," said the Starling, hopping down on to the window-sill. "And *you* needn't talk — anyway. I heard you for several hours on end last Saturday week. Goodness, I thought you'd never stop — you kept me awake all night."

"That wasn't talking," said John. "I was —— " He paused. "I mean, I had a pain."

"Humph!" said the Starling, and hopped on to the railing of Barbara's cot. He sidled along it until he came to the head of the cot. Then he said in a soft, wheedling voice:

"Well, Barbara B., anything for the old fellow today, eh?"

Barbara pulled herself into a sitting position by holding on to one of the bars of her cot.

"There's the other half of my arrowroot biscuit," she said, and held it out in her round, fat fist.

The Starling swooped down, plucked it out of her

hand and flew back to the window-sill. He began nibbling it greedily.

"Thank you!" said Mary Poppins, meaningly, but the Starling was too busy eating to notice the rebuke.

"I said 'Thank you!'" said Mary Poppins a little louder. The Starling looked up.

"Eh — what? Oh, get along, girl, get along. I've no time for such frills and furbelows." And he gobbled up the last of his biscuit.

The room was very quiet.

John, drowsing in the sunlight, put the toes of his right foot into his mouth and ran them along the place where his teeth were just beginning to come through.

"Why do you bother to do that?" said Barbara, in her soft, amused voice that seemed always to be full of laughter. "There's nobody to see you."

"I know," said John, playing a tune on his toes. "But I like to keep in practice. It *does* so amuse the Grown-ups. Did you notice that Aunt Flossie nearly went mad with delight when I did it yesterday? 'The Darling, the Clever, the Marvel, the Creature!' — didn't you hear her saying all that?" And John threw his foot from him and roared with laughter as he thought of Aunt Flossie.

"She liked my trick, too," said Barbara complacently. "I took off both my socks and she said I was so sweet she would like to eat me. Isn't it funny — when *I* say I'd like to eat something I really mean it. Biscuits and Rusks and the knobs of beds and so on. But Grown-ups never mean what they say, it seems to me. She couldn't have *really* wanted to eat me, could she?"

"No. It's only the idiotic way they have of talking," said John. "I don't believe I'll ever understand Grown-ups. They all seem so stupid. And even Jane and Michael are stupid sometimes."

"Um," agreed Barbara, thoughtfully pulling off her socks and putting them on again.

"For instance," John went on, "they don't understand a single thing we say. But, worse than that, they don't understand what *other* things say. Why, only last Monday I heard Jane remark that she wished she knew what language the Wind spoke."

"I know," said Barbara. "It's astonishing. And Michael always insists — haven't you heard him? — that the Starling says 'Wee-Twe — ee — ee!' He seems not to know that the Starling says nothing of the kind, but speaks exactly the same language as we do. Of course, one doesn't expect Mother and Father to know about it — they don't know *anything*, though they *are* such darlings — but you'd think Jane and Michael would —— "

"They did once," said Mary Poppins, folding up one of Jane's nightgowns.

"What?" said John and Barbara together in very surprised voices. "Really? You mean they understood the Starling and the Wind and —— "

"And what the trees say and the language of the sun-light and the stars — of course they did! *Once,*" said Mary Poppins.

"But — but how is it that they've forgotten it all?" said John, wrinkling up his forehead and trying to understand.

"Aha!" said the Starling knowingly, looking up from the remains of his biscuit. "Wouldn't you like to know?"

"Because they've grown older," explained Mary Poppins. "Barbara, put on your socks at once, please."

"That's a silly reason," said John, looking sternly at her.

"It's the true one, then," Mary Poppins said, tying Barbara's socks firmly round her ankles.

"Well, it's Jane and Michael who are silly," John continued. "I know *I* shan't forget when *I* get older."

"Nor I," said Barbara, contentedly sucking her finger.

"Yes, you will," said Mary Poppins firmly.

The Twins sat up and looked at her.

"Huh!" said the Starling contemptuously. "Look at 'em! They think they're the World's Wonders. Little miracles — I *don't* think! Of course you'll forget — same as Jane and Michael."

"We *won't,*" said the Twins, looking at the Starling as if they would like to murder him.

The Starling jeered.

"I say you will," he insisted. "It isn't your fault, of course," he added more kindly. "You'll forget because you just can't help it. There never was a human being

"Huh!" said the Starling. "Look at 'em!"

that remembered after the age of one — at the very latest — except, of course, Her." And he jerked his head over his shoulder at Mary Poppins.

"But why can she remember and not us?" said John.

"A-a-a-h! She's different. She's the Great Exception. Can't go by *her*," said the Starling, grinning at them both.

John and Barbara were silent.

The Starling went on explaining.

"She's something special, you see. Not in the matter of looks, of course. One of my own day-old chicks is handsomer than Mary P. ever was ——"

"Here, you impertinence!" said Mary Poppins crossly, making a dart at him and flicking her apron in his direction. But the Starling leapt aside and flew up to the window-frame, whistling wickedly, well out of reach.

"Thought you had me that time, didn't you?" he jeered and shook his wing-feathers at her.

Mary Poppins snorted.

The sunlight moved on through the room, drawing its long gold shaft after it. Outside a light wind had sprung up and was whispering gently to the cherry-trees in the Lane.

"Listen, listen, the wind's talking," said John, tilting his head on one side. "Do you really mean we won't be able to hear *that* when we're older, Mary Poppins?"

"You'll hear all right," said Mary Poppins, "but you won't understand." At that Barbara began to weep gently. There were tears in John's eyes, too. "Well, it can't be helped. It's how things happen," said Mary Poppins sensibly.

"Look at them, just look at them!" jeered the Starling. "Crying fit to kill themselves! Why, a starling in the egg's got more sense. Look at them!"

For John and Barbara were now crying piteously in their cots — long-drawn sobs of deep unhappiness.

Suddenly the door opened and in came Mrs. Banks.

"I thought I heard the babies," she said. Then she ran to the Twins. "What is it, my darlings? Oh, my Treasures, my Sweets, my Love-birds, what is it? Why are they crying so, Mary Poppins? They've been so quiet all the afternoon — not a sound out of them. What can be the matter?"

"Yes, ma'am. No, ma'am. I expect they're getting their teeth, ma'am," said Mary Poppins, deliberately not looking in the direction of the Starling.

"Oh, of course — that must be it," said Mrs. Banks brightly.

"I don't want teeth if they make me forget all the things I like best," wailed John, tossing about in his cot.

"Neither do I," wept Barbara, burying her face in her pillow.

"My poor ones, my pets — it will be all right when the naughty old teeth come through," said Mrs. Banks soothingly, going from one cot to another.

"You don't understand!" roared John furiously. "I don't *want* teeth."

"It won't be all right, it will be all *wrong!*" wailed Barbara to her pillow.

"Yes — yes. There — there. Mother knows — Mother understands. It will be all right when the teeth come through," crooned Mrs. Banks tenderly.

A faint noise came from the window. It was the Starling hurriedly swallowing a laugh. Mary Poppins gave him one look. That sobered him, and he continued to regard the scene without the hint of a smile.

Mrs. Banks was patting her children gently, first one and then the other, and murmuring words that were meant to be reassuring. Suddenly John stopped crying. He had very good manners, and he was fond of his Mother and re-membered what was due to her. It was not *her* fault, poor woman, that she always said the wrong thing. It was just, he reflected, that she did not understand. So, to show that he forgave her, he turned over on his back, and very dole-fully, sniffing back his tears, he picked up his right foot in both hands and ran his toes along his open mouth.

"Clever One, oh, Clever One," said his Mother admir-ingly. He did it again and she was very pleased.

Then Barbara, not to be outdone in courtesy, came out of her pillow and with her tears still wet on her face, sat up and plucked off both her socks.

"Wonderful Girl," said Mrs. Banks proudly, and kissed her.

"There, you see, Mary Poppins! They're quite good again. I can always comfort them. Quite good, quite good," said Mrs. Banks, as though she were singing a lullaby. "And the teeth will soon be through."

"Yes, ma'am," said Mary Poppins quietly; and smiling to the Twins, Mrs. Banks went out and closed the door.

The moment she had disappeared the Starling burst into a peal of rude laughter.

"Excuse me smiling!" he cried. "But really — I can't help it. What a scene! *What* a scene!"

John took no notice of him. He pushed his face through the bars of his cot and called softly and fiercely to Barbara:

"I *won't* be like the others. I tell you I won't. They," he jerked his head towards the Starling and Mary Poppins, "can say what they like. I'll never forget, *never!*"

Mary Poppins smiled, a secret, I-know-better-than-you sort of smile, all to herself.

"Nor I," answered Barbara. "Ever."

"Bless my tail-feathers — listen to them!" shrieked the Starling, as he put his wings on his hips and roared with mirth. "As if they could help forgetting! Why, in a month or two — three at the *most* — they won't even know what my name is — silly cuckoos! Silly, half-grown, featherless cuckoos! Ha! Ha! Ha!" And with another loud peal of laughter he spread his speckled wings and flew out of the window. . . .

It was not very long afterwards that the teeth, after much trouble, came through as all teeth must, and the Twins had their first birthday.

The day after the birthday party the Starling, who had been away on holiday at Bournemouth, came back to Number Seventeen, Cherry-Tree Lane.

"Hullo, hullo, hullo! Here we are again!" he screamed joyfully, landing with a little wobble upon the window-sill.

"Well, how's the girl?" he enquired cheekily of Mary Poppins, cocking his little head on one side and regarding her with bright, amused, twinkling eyes.

"None the better for *your* asking," said Mary Poppins, tossing her head.

The Starling laughed.

"Same old Mary P.," he said. "No change out of *you!* How are the other ones — the cuckoos?" he asked, and looked across at Barbara's cot.

"Well, Barbarina," he began in his soft, wheedling voice, "anything for the old fellow today?"

"Be-lah-belah-belah-belah!" said Barbara, crooning gently as she continued to eat her arrowroot biscuit.

The Starling, with a start of surprise, hopped a little nearer.

"I said," he repeated more distinctly, "is there anything for the old fellow today, Barbie dear?"

"Ba-loo — ba-loo — ba-loo," murmured Barbara, staring at the ceiling as she swallowed the last sweet crumb.

The Starling stared at her.

"Ha!" he said suddenly, and turned and looked enquiringly at Mary Poppins. Her quiet glance met his in a long look.

Then with a darting movement the Starling flew over to John's cot and alighted on the rail. John had a large woolly lamb hugged close in his arms.

"What's my name? What's my name? What's my name?" cried the Starling in a shrill anxious voice.

"Er-umph!" said John, opening his mouth and putting the leg of the woolly lamb into it.

With a little shake of the head the Starling turned away.

"So — it's happened," he said quietly to Mary Poppins. She nodded.

The Starling gazed dejectedly for a moment at the Twins. Then he shrugged his speckled shoulders.

"Oh, well —— I knew it would. Always told 'em so. But they wouldn't believe it." He remained silent for a little while, staring into the cots. Then he shook himself vigorously.

"Well, well. I must be off. Back to my chimney. It will

need a spring-cleaning, I'll be bound." He flew on to the window-sill and paused, looking back over his shoulder.

"It'll seem funny without them, though. Always liked talking to them — so I did. I shall miss them."

He brushed his wing quickly across his eyes.

"Crying?" jeered Mary Poppins. The Starling drew himself up.

"Crying? Certainly not. I have — er — a slight cold, caught on my return journey — that's all. Yes, a slight cold. Nothing serious." He darted up to the window-pane, brushed down his breast-feathers with his beak and then, "Cheerio!" he said perkily, and spread his wings and was gone. . . .

CHAPTER TEN

FULL MOON

ll day long Mary Poppins had been in a hurry, and when she was in a hurry she was always cross.

Everything Jane did was bad, everything Michael did was worse. She even snapped at the Twins.

Jane and Michael kept out of her way as much as possible, for they knew that there were times when it was better not to be seen or heard by Mary Poppins.

"I wish we were invisible," said Michael, when Mary Poppins had told him that the very sight of him was more than any self-respecting person could be expected to stand.

"We shall be," said Jane, "if we go behind the sofa. We can count the money in our money-boxes, and she may be better after she's had her supper."

So they did that.

"Sixpence and four pennies — that's tenpence, and a halfpenny and a threepenny-bit," said Jane, counting up quickly.

"Four pennies and three farthings and — and that's all," sighed Michael, putting his money in a little heap.

"That'll do nicely for the poor-box," said Mary Poppins, looking over the arm of the sofa and sniffing.

"Oh no," said Michael reproachfully. "It's for myself. I'm saving."

"Huh — for one of those aeryoplanes, I suppose!" said Mary Poppins scornfully.

"No, for an elephant — a private one for myself, like Lizzie at the Zoo. I could take you for rides then," said Michael, half-looking and half-not-looking at her to see how she would take it.

"Humph," said Mary Poppins, "what an idea!" But they could see she was not quite so cross as before.

"I wonder," said Michael thoughtfully, "what happens in the Zoo at night, when everybody's gone home?"

"Care killed a cat," snapped Mary Poppins.

"I wasn't *caring,* I was only wondering," corrected Michael. "Do *you* know?" he enquired of Mary Poppins, who was whisking the crumbs off the table in double-quick time.

"One more question from you — and spit-spot, to bed you go!" she said, and began to tidy the Nursery so busily that she looked more like a whirlwind in a cap and apron than a human being.

"It's no good asking her. She knows everything, but she never tells," said Jane.

"What's the good of knowing if you don't tell anyone?" grumbled Michael, but he said it under his breath so that Mary Poppins couldn't hear. . . .

Jane and Michael could never remember having been put to bed so quickly as they were that night. Mary Poppins blew out the light very early, and went away as hurriedly as though all the winds of the world were blowing behind her.

It seemed to them that they had been there no time, however, when they heard a low voice whispering at the door.

"Hurry, Jane and Michael!" said the voice. "Get some things on and hurry!"

They jumped out of their beds, surprised and startled.

"Come on," said Jane. "Something's happening." And she began to rummage for some clothes in the darkness.

"Hurry!" called the voice again.

"Oh dear, all I can find is my sailor hat and a pair of gloves!" said Michael, running round the room pulling at drawers and feeling along shelves.

"Those'll do. Put them on. It isn't cold. Come on."

Jane herself had only been able to find a little coat of John's, but she squeezed her arms into it and opened the door. There was nobody there, but they seemed to hear something hurrying away down the stairs. Jane and Michael followed. Whatever it was, or whoever it was, kept continually in front of them. They never saw it, but they had the distinct sensation of being led on and on by something that constantly beckoned them to follow. Presently they were in the Lane, their slippers making a soft hissing noise on the pavement as they scurried along.

"Hurry!" urged the voice again from a near-by corner, but when they turned it they could still see nothing. They began to run, hand in hand, following the voice down streets, through alley-ways, under arches and across Parks until, panting and breathless, they were brought to a standstill beside a large turnstile in a wall.

"Here you are!" said the voice.

"Where?" called Michael to it. But there was no reply. Jane moved towards the turnstile, dragging Michael by the hand.

"Look!" she said. "Don't you see where we are? It's the Zoo!"

A very bright full moon was shining in the sky and by its light Michael examined the iron grating and looked through the bars. Of course! How silly of him not to have known it was the Zoo!

"But how shall we get in?" he said. "We've no money."

"That's all right!" said a deep, gruff voice from within. "Special Visitors allowed in free tonight. Push the wheel, please!"

Jane and Michael pushed and were through the turnstile in a second.

"Here's your ticket," the gruff voice said, and looking

up, they found that it came from a huge Brown Bear who was wearing a coat with brass buttons and a peaked cap on his head. In his paw were two pink tickets which he held out to the children.

"But we usually *give* tickets," said Jane.

"Usual is as usual does. Tonight you receive them," said the Bear, smiling.

Michael had been regarding him closely.

"I remember you," he said to the Bear. "I once gave you a tin of golden syrup."

"You did," said the Bear. "And you forgot to take the lid off. Do you know, I was more than ten days working at that lid? Be more careful in the future."

"But why aren't you in your cage? Are you always out at night?" said Michael.

"No — only when the Birthday falls on a Full Moon. But — you must excuse me. I must attend to the gate." And the Bear turned away and began to spin the handle of the turnstile again.

Jane and Michael, holding their tickets, walked on into the Zoo grounds. In the light of the full moon every tree and flower and shrub was visible, and they could see the houses and cages quite clearly.

"There seems to be a lot going on," observed Michael.

And, indeed, there was. Animals were running about in all the paths, sometimes accompanied by birds and sometimes alone. Two wolves ran past the children, talking eagerly to a very tall stork who was tip-toeing between them with dainty, delicate movements. Jane and Michael distinctly caught the words "Birthday" and "Full Moon" as they went by.

In the distance three camels were strolling along side by side, and not far away a beaver and an American vulture were deep in conversation. And they all seemed to the children to be discussing the same subject.

"Whose Birthday is it, I wonder?" said Michael, but Jane was moving ahead, gazing at a curious sight.

Just by the Elephant Stand a very large, very fat old gentleman was walking up and down on all fours, and on his back, on two small parallel seats, were eight monkeys going for a ride.

"Why, it's all upside down!" exclaimed Jane.

The old gentleman gave her an angry look as he went past.

"Upside down!" he snorted. "Me! Upside down? Certainly not. Gross insult!" The eight monkeys laughed rudely.

"Oh, please — I didn't mean you — but the whole thing," explained Jane, hurrying after him to apologise. "On ordinary days the animals carry human beings and now there's a human being carrying the animals. That's what I meant."

But the old gentleman, shuffling and panting, insisted that he had been insulted, and hurried away with the monkeys screaming on his back.

Jane saw it was no good following him, so she took
Michael's hand and moved onwards. They were startled
when a voice, almost at their feet, hailed them.

"Come on, you two! In you come. Let's see *you* dive
for a bit of orange-peel you don't want." It was a bitter, angry voice, and looking down they saw that it came from a
small black Seal who was leering at them from a moonlit
pool of water.

"Come on, now — and see how *you* like it!" he said.

"But — but we can't swim!" said Michael.

"Can't help that!" said the Seal. "You should have
thought of that before. Nobody ever bothers to find out
whether *I* can swim or not. Eh, what? What's that?"

He spoke the last question to another Seal who had
emerged from the water and was whispering in his ear.

"Who?" said the first Seal. "Speak up!"

The second Seal whispered again. Jane caught the
words "Special Visitors — Friends of —— " and then no
more. The first Seal seemed disappointed, but he said politely enough to Jane and Michael:

"Oh, beg pardon. Pleased to meet you. Beg pardon."
And he held out his flipper and shook hands limply with
them both.

"Look where you're going, can't you?" he shouted, as
something bumped into Jane. She turned quickly and
gave a little frightened start as she beheld an enormous
Lion. The eyes of the Lion brightened as he saw her.

"Oh, I say —— " he began. "I didn't know it was you!

This place is so crowded tonight and I'm in such a hurry to see the humans fed I'm afraid I didn't look where I was going. Coming along? You oughtn't to miss it, you know——"

"Perhaps," said Jane politely, "you'd show us the way." She was a little uncertain of the Lion, but he seemed kindly enough. "And after all," she thought, "everything is topsy-turvy tonight."

"Dee-lighted!" said the Lion in rather a mincing voice, and he offered her his arm. She took it, but to be on the safe side she kept Michael beside her. He was such a round, fat little boy, and after all, she thought, lions are lions——

"Does my mane look nice?" asked the Lion as they moved off. "I had it curled for the occasion."

Jane looked at it. She could see that it had been carefully oiled and combed into ringlets.

"Very," she said. "But — isn't it rather odd for a lion to care about such things? I thought——"

"What! My dear young lady, the Lion, as you know, is the King of the Beasts. He has to remember his position. And I, personally, am not likely to forget it. I believe a lion should *always* look his best no matter where he is. This way."

And with a graceful wave of his forepaw he pointed towards the Big Cat House and ushered them in at the entrance.

Jane and Michael caught their breaths at the sight that

met their eyes. The great hall was thronged with animals.
Some were leaning over the long bar that separated them
from the cages, some were standing on the seats that
rose in tiers opposite. There were panthers and leopards,
wolves, tigers and antelopes; monkeys and hedgehogs,
wombats, mountain goats and giraffes; and an enormous
group composed entirely of kittiwakes and vultures.

"Splendid, isn't it?" said the Lion proudly. "Just like the
dear old jungle days. But come along — we must get good
places."

And he pushed his way through the crowd crying,
"Gangway, gangway!" and dragging Jane and Michael after him. Presently, through a little clearing in the middle
of the hall, they were able to get a glimpse of the cages.

"Why," said Michael, opening his mouth very wide,
"they're full of human beings!"

And they were.

In one cage two large, middle-aged gentlemen in top-
hats and striped trousers were prowling up and down,
anxiously gazing through the bars as though they were
waiting for something.

Children of all shapes and sizes, from babies in long
clothes upwards, were scrambling about in another cage.
The animals outside regarded these with great interest and some of them tried to make the babies laugh by
thrusting their paws or their tails in through the bars. A
giraffe stretched his long neck out over the heads of the

other animals and let a little boy in a sailor-suit tickle its nose.

In a third cage three elderly ladies in raincoats and galoshes were imprisoned. One of them was knitting, but the other two were standing near the bars shouting at the animals and poking at them with their umbrellas.

"Nasty brutes. Go away. I want my tea!" screamed one of them.

"Isn't she funny?" said several of the animals, and they laughed loudly at her.

"Jane — look!" said Michael, pointing to the cage at the end of the row. "Isn't that —— ?"

"Admiral Boom!" said Jane, looking very surprised.

And Admiral Boom it was. He was ramping up and

down in his cage, coughing, and blowing his nose, and spluttering with rage.

"Blast my gizzard! All hands to the Pump! Land, ho! Heave away there! Blast my gizzard!" shouted the Admiral. Every time he came near the bars a tiger prodded him gently with a stick and this made Admiral Boom swear dreadfully.

"But how did they all get in there?" Jane asked the Lion.

"Lost," said the Lion. "Or rather, left behind. These are the people who've dawdled and been left inside when the gates were shut. Got to put 'em somewhere, so we keep 'em here. He's dangerous — that one there! Nearly did for his keeper not long ago. Don't go near him!" And he pointed at Admiral Boom.

"Stand back, please, stand back! Don't crush! Make way, please!" Jane and Michael could hear several voices crying these words loudly.

"Ah — now they're going to be fed!" said the Lion, excitedly pressing forward into the crowd. "Here come the keepers."

Four Brown Bears, each wearing a peaked cap, were trundling trolleys of food along the little corridor that separated the animals from the cages.

"Stand back, there!" they said, whenever an animal got in the way. Then they opened a small door in each cage and thrust the food through on pronged forks.

Jane and Michael had a good view of what was happening, through a gap between a panther and a dingo. Bottles of milk were being thrown in to the babies, who made soft little grabs with their hands and clutched them greedily. The older children snatched sponge-cakes and dough-nuts from the forks and began to eat ravenously. Plates of thin bread-and-butter and wholemeal scones were provided for the ladies in galoshes, and the gentlemen in top-hats had lamb cutlets and custard in glasses. These, as they received their food, took it away into a corner, spread handkerchiefs over their striped trousers and began to eat.

Presently, as the keepers passed down the line of cages, a great commotion was heard.

"Blast my vitals — call that a meal? A skimpy lit-tle round of beef and a couple of cabbages! What — no Yorkshire pudding? Outrageous! Up with the anchor! And where's my port? Port, I say! Heave her over! Below there, where's the Admiral's port?"

"Listen to him! He's turned nasty. I tell you, he's not safe — that one," said the Lion.

Jane and Michael did not need to be told whom he meant. They knew Admiral Boom's language too well.

"Well," said the Lion, as the noise in the hall grew less uproarious. "That appears to be the end. And I'm afraid, if you'll excuse me, I must be getting along. See you later at the Grand Chain, I hope. I'll look out for you." And, lead-ing them to the door, he took his leave of them, sidling away, swinging his curled mane, his golden body dappled with moonlight and shadow.

"Oh, please —— " Jane called after him. But he was out of hearing.

"I wanted to ask him if they'd ever get out. The poor humans! Why, it might have been John and Barbara — or any of us." She turned to Michael, but found that he was no longer by her side. He had moved away along one of the paths and, running after him, she found him talking to a Penguin who was standing in the middle of the path with a large copy-book under one wing and an enormous pencil under the other. He was biting the end of it thoughtfully as she approached.

"I can't think," she heard Michael saying, apparently in answer to a question.

The Penguin turned to Jane. "Perhaps *you* can tell me," he said. "Now, what rhymes with Mary? I can't use 'contrary' because that has been done before and one must be original. If you're going to say 'fairy,' don't. I've thought of that already, but as it's not a bit like her, it won't do."

"Hairy," said Michael brightly.

"H'm. Not poetic enough," observed the Penguin.

"What about 'wary'?" said Jane.

"Well —— " The Penguin appeared to be considering it. "It's not *very* good, is it?" he said forlornly. "I'm afraid I'll have to give it up. You see, I was trying to write a poem for the Birthday. I thought it would be so nice if I began:

"O Mary, Mary —— "

and then I couldn't get any further. It's very annoying. They expect something learned from a penguin, and I don't want to disappoint them. Well, well — you mustn't keep me. I must get on with it." And with that he hurried away, biting his pencil and bending over his copy-book.

"This is all very confusing," said Jane. "Whose birthday is it, I wonder?"

"Now, come along, you two, come along. You want to pay your respects, I suppose, it being the Birthday and all!" said a voice behind them, and turning, they saw the Brown Bear who had given them their tickets at the gate.

"Oh, of course!" said Jane, thinking that was the safest thing to say, but not knowing in the least whom they were to pay their respects to.

The Brown Bear put an arm round each of them and propelled them along the path. They could feel his warm soft fur brushing against their bodies and hear the rumblings his voice made in his stomach as he talked.

"Here we are, *here* we are!" said the Brown Bear, stopping before a small house whose windows were all so brightly lit that if it hadn't been a moonlight night you would have thought the sun was shining. The Bear opened the door and gently pushed the two children through it.

The light dazzled them at first, but their eyes soon became accustomed to it and they saw that they were in the Snake House. All the cages were open and the snakes were out — some curled lazily into great scaly knots, others slipping gently about the floor. And in the middle of the snakes, on a log that had evidently been brought from one of the cages, sat Mary Poppins. Jane and Michael could hardly believe their eyes.

"Coupla birthday guests, ma'am," announced the Brown Bear respectfully. The snakes turned their heads enquiringly towards the children. Mary Poppins did not move. But she spoke.

"And where's your overcoat, may I ask?" she demanded, looking crossly but without surprise at Michael.

"And *your* hat and gloves?" she snapped, turning to Jane.

But before either of them had time to reply there was a stir in the Snake House.

"Hsssst! Hssst!"

The snakes, with a soft hissing sound, were rising up on end and bowing to something behind Jane and Michael. The Brown Bear took off his peaked cap. And slowly Mary Poppins, too, stood up.

"My dear child. My very dear child!" said a small, delicate, hissing voice. And out from the largest of the cages there came, with slow, soft, winding movements, a Hamadryad. He slid in graceful curves past the bowing snakes and the Brown Bear, towards Mary Poppins. And when he reached her, he raised the front half of his long golden body, and, thrusting upwards his scaly golden hood, daintily kissed her, first on one cheek and then on the other.

"So!" he hissed softly. "This is very pleasant — very pleasant, indeed. It is long since your Birthday fell on a Full Moon, my dear." He turned his head.

"Be seated, friends!" he said, bowing graciously to the other snakes who, at that word, slid reverently to the floor again, coiled themselves up, and gazed steadily at the Hamadryad and Mary Poppins.

The Hamadryad turned then to Jane and Michael, and with a little shiver they saw that his face was smaller and more wizened than anything they had ever seen. They took a step forward, for his curious deep eyes seemed to draw them towards him. Long and narrow they were, with a dark sleepy look in them, and in the middle of that dark sleepiness a wakeful light glittered like a jewel.

"And who, may I ask, are these?" he said in his soft, terrifying voice, looking at the children enquiringly.

"Miss Jane Banks and Master Michael Banks, at your service," said the Brown Bear gruffly, as though he were half afraid. "*Her* friends."

"Ah, *her* friends. Then they are welcome. My dears, pray be seated."

Jane and Michael, feeling somehow that they were in the presence of a King — as they had not felt when they met the Lion — with difficulty drew their eyes from that compelling gaze and looked round for something to sit on. The Brown Bear provided this by squatting down himself and offering them each a furry knee.

Jane said, in a whisper: "He talks as though he were a great lord."

"He *is*. He's the lord of our world — the wisest and most terrible of us all," said the Brown Bear softly and reverently.

The Hamadryad smiled, a long, slow, secret smile, and turned to Mary Poppins.

"Cousin," he began, gently hissing.

"Is she *really* his cousin?" whispered Michael.

"First cousin once removed — on the mother's side," returned the Brown Bear, whispering the information behind his paw. "But, listen now. He's going to give the Birthday Present."

"Cousin," repeated the Hamadryad, "it is long since your Birthday fell on the Full Moon and long since we have been able to celebrate the event as we celebrate it tonight. I have, therefore, had time to give the question of your Birthday Present some consideration. And I have decided" — he paused, and there was no sound in the Snake House but the sound of many creatures all holding their breath — "that I cannot do better than give you one of my own skins."

"Indeed, cousin, it is too kind of you —— " began Mary Poppins, but the Hamadryad held up his hood for silence.

"Not at all. Not at all. You know that I change my skin from time to time and that one more or less means little to me. Am I not —— ?" he paused and looked round him.

"The Lord of the Jungle," hissed all the snakes in unison, as though the question and the answer were part of a well-known ceremony.

The Hamadryad nodded. "So," he said, "what seems good to me will seem so to you. It is a small enough gift, dear Mary, but it may serve for a belt or a pair of shoes, even a hat-band —— these things always come in useful, you know."

And with that he began to sway gently from side to side, and it seemed to Jane and Michael as they watched that little waves were running up his body from the tail to the head. Suddenly he gave a long, twisting, corkscrew leap and his golden outer skin lay on the floor, and in its place he was wearing a new coat of shining silver.

"Wait!" said the Hamadryad, as Mary Poppins bent to pick up the skin. "I will write a Greeting upon it." And he ran his tail very quickly along his thrown skin, deftly bent the golden sheath into a circle, and diving his head through this as though it were a crown, offered it graciously to Mary Poppins. She took it, bowing.

"I just can't thank you enough —— " she began, and paused. She was evidently very pleased, for she kept running the skin backwards and forwards through her fingers and looking at it admiringly.

"Don't try," said the Hamadryad. "Hsst!" he went on, and spread out his hood as though he were listening with it. "Do I not hear the signal for the Grand Chain?"

Everybody listened. A bell was ringing and a deep gruff voice could be heard coming nearer and nearer, crying out:

"Grand Chain, Grand Chain! Everybody to the centre for the Grand Chain and Finale. Come along, come along. Stand ready for the Grand Chain!"

"I thought so," said the Hamadryad, smiling. "You must be off, my dear. They'll be waiting for you to take your place in the centre. Farewell, till your next Birthday." And he raised himself as he had done before and lightly saluted Mary Poppins on both cheeks.

"Hurry away!" said the Hamadryad. "I will take care of your young friends."

Jane and Michael felt the Brown Bear moving under them and they stood up. Past their feet they could feel all the snakes slipping and writhing as they hurried from the Snake House. Mary Poppins bowed towards the Hamadryad very ceremoniously, and without a backward glance at the children went running towards the huge green square in the centre of the Zoo.

"You may leave us," said the Hamadryad to the Brown Bear who, after bowing humbly, ran off with his cap in his hand to where all the other animals were congregating round Mary Poppins.

"Will you go with me?" said the Hamadryad kindly to Jane and Michael. And without waiting for them to reply he slid between them, and with a movement of his hood directed them to walk one on either side of him.

"It has begun," he said, hissing with pleasure.

And from the loud cries that were now coming from the Green, the children could guess that he meant the Grand Chain. As they drew nearer they could hear the animals singing and shouting, and presently they saw leopards and lions, beavers, camels, bears, cranes, antelopes and many others all forming themselves into a ring round Mary Poppins. Then the animals began to move, wildly crying their Jungle songs, prancing in and out of the ring, and exchanging hand and wing as they went as dancers do in the Grand Chain of the Lancers.

A little piping voice rose high above the rest:

> "Oh, Mary Mary,
>   She's my Dearie,
>   She's my Dear-i-o!"

And they saw the Penguin come dancing by, waving his short wings and singing lustily. He caught sight of them, bowed to the Hamadryad, and called out:

"I got it — did you hear me singing it? It's not perfect, of course. 'Dearie' does not rhyme *exactly* with Mary. But it'll do, it'll do!" and he skipped off and offered his wing to a leopard.

Forming themselves into a ring round Mary Poppins

Jane and Michael watched the dance, the Hamadryad secret and still between them. As their friend the Lion, dancing past, bent down to take the wing of a Brazilian Pheasant in his paw, Jane shyly tried to put her feelings into words.

"I thought, Sir——" she began and stopped, feeling confused, and not sure whether she ought to say it or not.

"Speak, my child!" said the Hamadryad. "You thought?"

"Well—that lions and birds, and tigers and little animals——"

The Hamadryad helped her. "You thought that they were natural enemies, that the lion could not meet a bird without eating it, nor the tiger the hare—eh?"

Jane blushed and nodded.

"Ah—you may be right. It is possible. But not on the Birthday," said the Hamadryad. "Tonight the small are free from the great and the great protect the small. Even I——" he paused and seemed to be thinking deeply, "even I can meet a Barnacle Goose without any thought of dinner—on this occasion. And after all," he went on, flicking his terrible little forked tongue in and out as he spoke, "it may be that to eat and be eaten are the same thing in the end. My wisdom tells me that this is probably so. We are all made of the same stuff, remember, we of the Jungle, you of the City. The same substance composes us — the tree overhead, the stone beneath us, the bird, the beast, the star — we are all one, all moving to the same end. Remember that when you no longer remember me, my child."

"But how can tree be stone? A bird is not me. Jane is not a tiger," said Michael stoutly.

"You think not?" said the Hamadryad's hissing voice. "Look!" and he nodded his head towards the moving mass of creatures before them. Birds and animals were now swaying together, closely encircling Mary Poppins, who was rocking lightly from side to side. Backwards and forwards went the swaying crowd, keeping time together, swinging like the pendulum of a clock. Even the trees were bending and lifting gently, and the moon seemed to be rocking in the sky as a ship rocks on the sea.

"Bird and beast and stone and star — we are all one, all one —— " murmured the Hamadryad, softly folding his hood about him as he himself swayed between the children.

"Child and serpent, star and stone — all one."

The hissing voice grew softer. The cries of the swaying animals dwindled and became fainter. Jane and Michael, as they listened, felt themselves gently rocking too, or as if they were being rocked. . . .

Soft, shaded light fell on their faces.

"Asleep and dreaming — both of them," said a whispering voice. Was it the voice of the Hamadryad, or their Mother's voice as she tucked them in, on her usual nightly round of the Nursery?

"Good." Was that the Brown Bear gruffly speaking, or Mr. Banks?

Jane and Michael, rocking and swaying, could not tell . . . could not tell. . . .

"I had such a strange dream last night," said Jane, as she sprinkled sugar over her porridge at breakfast. "I dreamed we were at the Zoo and it was Mary Poppins's birthday, and instead of animals in the cages there were human beings, and all the animals were outside ——"

"Why, that's *my* dream. *I* dreamed that, too," said Michael, looking very surprised.

"We can't both have dreamed the same thing," said Jane. "Are you sure? Do you remember the Lion who curled his mane and the Seal who wanted us to ——"

"Dive for orange-peel?" said Michael. "Of course I do! And the babies inside the cage, and the Penguin who couldn't find a rhyme and the Hamadryad ——"

"Then it couldn't have been a dream at all," said Jane emphatically. "It must have been *true*. And if it was ——" She looked curiously at Mary Poppins, who was boiling the milk.

"Mary Poppins," she said, "could Michael and I have dreamed the same dream?"

"You and your dreams!" said Mary Poppins, sniffing. "Eat your porridge, please, or you will have no buttered toast."

But Jane would not be put off. She *had* to know.

"Mary Poppins," she said, looking very hard at her, "were you at the Zoo last night?"

Mary Poppins's eyes popped.

"At the Zoo? In the middle of the night? Me? A quiet, orderly person who knows that early to bed, early to rise makes a man healthy, wealthy and wise?"

"But *were* you?" Jane persisted.

"I have all I need of Zoos in this nursery, thank you," said Mary Poppins, uppishly. "Hyenas, orangoutangs, all of you. Sit up straight, and no more nonsense."

Jane poured out her milk.

"Then it must have been a dream," she said, "after all."

But Michael was staring, open-mouthed, at Mary Poppins, who was now making toast at the fire.

"Jane," he said in a shrill whisper, "Jane, look!" He pointed, and Jane, too, saw what he was looking at.

Round her waist Mary Poppins was wearing a belt made of golden scaly snake-skin, and on it was written in curving, snaky writing:

"A Present From the Zoo."

CHAPTER
ELEVEN

CHRISTMAS SHOPPING

I smell snow" said Jane, as they got out of the Bus.
"I smell Christmas trees," said Michael.
"I smell fried fish," said Mary Poppins.

And then there was no time to smell anything else, for the Bus had stopped outside the Largest Shop in the World, and they were all going into it to do their Christmas shopping.

"May we look at the windows first?" said Michael, hopping excitedly on one leg.

"I don't mind," said Mary Poppins with surprising mildness. Not that Jane and Michael were *really* very surprised, for they knew that the thing Mary Poppins liked doing best of all was looking in shop windows. They knew, too, that while they saw toys and books and hollyboughs and plum cakes, Mary Poppins saw nothing but herself reflected there.

"Look, aeroplanes!" said Michael, as they stopped before a window in which toy aeroplanes were careering through the air on wires.

"And look there!" said Jane. "Two tiny black babies in one cradle — are they chocolate, do you think, or china?"

"Just look at *you!*" said Mary Poppins to herself, particularly noticing how nice her new gloves with the fur

tops looked. They were the first pair she had ever had, and she thought she would never grow tired of looking at them in the shop windows with her hands inside them. And having examined the reflection of the gloves she went carefully over her whole person — coat, hat, scarf and shoes, with herself inside — and she thought that, on the whole, she had never seen anybody looking quite so smart and distinguished.

But the winter afternoons, she knew, were short, and they had to be home by tea-time. So with a sigh she wrenched herself away from her glorious reflection.

"Now we will go in," she said, and annoyed Jane and Michael very much by lingering at the Haberdashery counter and taking great trouble over the choice of a reel of black cotton.

"The Toy Department," Michael reminded her, "is in *that* direction."

"I know, thank you. Don't point," she said, and paid her bill with aggravating slowness.

But at last they found themselves alongside Father Christmas, who went to the greatest trouble in helping them choose their presents.

"That will do nicely for Daddy," said Michael, selecting a clockwork train with special signals. "I will take care of it for him when he goes to the City."

"I think I will get this for Mother," said Jane, pushing a small doll's perambulator which, she felt sure, her Mother had always wanted. "Perhaps she will lend it to me sometimes."

After that, Michael chose a packet of hairpins for each of the Twins and a Meccano set for his Mother, a mechanical beetle for Robertson Ay, a pair of spectacles for Ellen whose eyesight was perfectly good, and some bootlaces for Mrs. Brill who always wore slippers.

Jane, after some hesitation, eventually decided that a white dickey would be just the thing for Mr. Banks, and she bought *Robinson Crusoe* for the Twins to read when they grew up.

"Until they are old enough, I can read it myself," she said. "I am sure they will lend it to me."

Mary Poppins then had a great argument with Father Christmas over a cake of soap.

"Why not Lifebuoy?" said Father Christmas, trying to be helpful and looking anxiously at Mary Poppins, for she was being rather snappy.

"I prefer Vinolia," she said haughtily, and she bought a cake of that.

"My goodness," she said, smoothing the fur on her right-hand glove. "I wouldn't half like a cup of tea!"

"Would you quarter like it, though?" asked Michael.

"There is no call for you to be funny," said Mary Poppins, in such a voice that Michael felt that, indeed, there wasn't.

"And it is time to go home."

There! She had said the very words they had been hoping she wouldn't say. That was so like Mary Poppins.

"Just five minutes longer," pleaded Jane.

"Ah do, Mary Poppins! You look so nice in your new gloves," said Michael wilily.

But Mary Poppins, though she appreciated the remark, was not taken in by it.

"No," she said, and closed her mouth with a snap and stalked towards the doorway.

"Oh, dear!" said Michael to himself, as he followed her, staggering under the weight of his parcels. "If only she would say 'Yes' for once!"

But Mary Poppins hurried on and they had to go with her. Behind them Father Christmas was waving his hand, and the Fairy Queen on the Christmas tree and all the other dolls were smiling sadly and saying, "Take me home, somebody!" and the aeroplanes were all beating their wings and saying in bird-like voices, "Let me fly! Ah, do let me fly!"

Jane and Michael hurried away, closing their ears to those enchanting voices, and feeling that the time in the Toy Department had been unreasonably and cruelly short.

And then, just as they came towards the shop entrance, the adventure happened.

They were just about to spin the glass door and go out, when they saw coming towards it from the pavement the running, flickering figure of a child.

"Look!" said Jane and Michael both together.

"My gracious, goodness, glory me!" exclaimed Mary Poppins, and stood still.

And well she might, for the child had practically no clothes on, only a light wispy strip of blue stuff that looked as though she had torn it from the sky to wrap round her naked body.

It was evident that she did not know much about spinning doors, for she went round and round inside it, pushing it so that it should spin faster and laughing as it caught her and sent her whirling round and round. Then suddenly, with a quick little movement she freed herself, sprang away from it and landed inside the shop.

She paused on tip-toe, turning her head this way and

that as though she were looking for someone. Then, with a start of pleasure, she caught sight of Jane and Michael and Mary Poppins as they stood, half-hidden behind an enormous fir-tree, and ran towards them joyously.

"Ah, *there* you are! Thank you for waiting. I'm afraid I'm a little late," said the child, stretching out her bright arms to Jane and Michael. "Now," she cocked her head on one side, "aren't you glad to see me? Say yes, say yes!"

"Yes," said Jane smiling, for nobody, she felt, could help being glad to see anyone so bright and happy. "But who are you?" she enquired curiously.

"What is your name?" said Michael, gazing at her.

"Who am I? What is my name? Don't say you don't know me? Oh, surely, surely——" The child seemed very surprised and a little disappointed. She turned suddenly to Mary Poppins and pointed her finger.

"*She* knows me. Don't you? I'm sure you know me!"

There was a curious look on Mary Poppins's face. Jane and Michael could see blue fires in her eyes as though they reflected the blue of the child's dress and her brightness.

"Does it — does it," she whispered, "begin with an M?"

The child hopped on one leg delightedly.

"Of course it does — and you know it. M-A-I-A. I'm Maia." She turned to Jane and Michael.

"*Now* you recognise me, don't you? I'm the second of the Pleiades. Electra — she's the eldest — couldn't come because she's minding Merope. Merope's the baby, and the other five of us come in between — all girls. Our Mother was very disappointed at first not to have a boy, but now she doesn't mind."

The child danced a few steps and burst out again in her excited little voice:

"Oh, Jane! Oh, Michael — I've often watched you from the sky, and now I'm actually talking to you. There is nothing about you I don't know. Michael doesn't like having his hair brushed, and Jane has a thrush's egg in a jam-jar on the mantelpiece. And your Father is going bald on the top. I like him. It was he who first introduced us — don't you remember? He said one evening last summer:

" 'Look, there are the Pleiades. Seven stars all together, the smallest in the sky. But there is one of them you can't see.'

"He meant Merope, of course. She's still too young to stay up all night. She's such a baby that she has to go to bed very early. Some of them up there call us the Little Sisters, and sometimes we are called the Seven Doves, but Orion calls us 'You girls' and takes us hunting with him."

"But what are you doing here?" demanded Michael, still very surprised.

Maia laughed. "Ask Mary Poppins. I am sure she knows."

"Tell us, Mary Poppins," said Jane.

"Well," said Mary Poppins snappily, "I suppose you

two aren't the only ones in the world that want to go shopping at Christmas ——"

"That's it," squealed Maia delightedly. "She's quite
right. I've come down to buy toys for them all. We can't
get away very often, you know, because we're so busy
making and storing up the Spring Rains. That's the special job of the Pleiades. However, we drew lots and I won.
Wasn't it lucky?"

She hugged herself happily.

"Now, come on. I can't stay very long. And you must
come back and help me choose."

And dancing about them, running now to one and
now to another, she shepherded them back to the Toy
Department. As they went the crowds of shoppers stood
and stared at them and dropped their parcels with astonishment.

"So cold for her. What can her parents be thinking of!"
said the Mothers, with voices that were suddenly soft and
gentle.

"I mean to say ——!" said the Fathers. "It shouldn't
be allowed. Must write to *The Times* about it." And their
voices were unnaturally gruff and gritty.

The shop-walkers behaved curiously, too. As the little
group passed they bowed to Maia as though she were a
Queen.

But none of them — not Jane, nor Michael, nor Mary
Poppins, nor Maia — noticed nor heard anything extraor-

dinary. They were too busy with their own extraordinary adventure.

"Here we are!" said Maia, as she pranced into the Toy Department. "Now, what shall we choose?"

An Assistant, with a start, bowed respectfully as soon as he saw her.

"I want something for each of my sisters — six of them. You must help me, please," said Maia, smiling at him.

"Certainly, madam," said the Assistant agreeably.

"First — my eldest sister," said Maia. "She's very domestic. What about that little stove with the silver saucepans? Yes. And that striped broom. We are so troubled with star-dust, and she will love having that to sweep it up with."

The Assistant began wrapping the things in coloured paper.

"Now for Taygete. She likes dancing. Don't you think, Jane, a skipping-rope would be just the thing for her? You'll tie them carefully, won't you?" she said to the Assistant. "I have a long way to go."

She fluttered on among the toys, never standing still for a moment, but walking with a light quicksilver step, as though she were still twinkling in the sky.

Mary Poppins and Jane and Michael could not take their eyes off her as she flickered from one of them to another asking their advice.

"Then there's Alcyone. She's difficult. She's so quiet

and thoughtful and never seems to want anything. A book, do you think, Mary Poppins? What is this Family — the *Swiss-Robinsons*? I think she would like that. And if she doesn't, she can look at the pictures. Wrap it up!"

She handed the book to the Assistant.

"I know what Celæno wants," she went on. "A hoop. She can bowl it across the sky in the day-time and make a circle of it to spin about her at night. She'll love that red and blue one." The Assistant bowed again and began to wrap up the hoop.

"Now there are only the two little ones left. Michael, what would you advise for Sterope?"

"What about a top?" said Michael, giving the question his earnest consideration.

"A humming-top? *What* a good idea! She will love to watch it go waltzing and singing down the sky. And what do you think for Merope, the baby, Jane?"

"John and Barbara," said Jane shyly, "have rubber ducks!"

Maia gave a delighted squeak and hugged herself.

"Oh, Jane, how wise you are! I should never have thought of that. A rubber duck for Merope, please — a blue one with yellow eyes."

The Assistant tied up the parcels, while Maia ran round him, pushing at the paper, giving a tug to the string to make sure that it was firmly knotted.

"That's right," she said. "You see, I mustn't drop anything."

Michael, who had been staring steadily at her ever since she first appeared, turned and said in a loud whisper to Mary Poppins:

"But she has no purse. Who will pay for the toys?"

"None of your business," snapped Mary Poppins. "And it's rude to whisper." But she began to fumble busily in her pocket.

"What did you say?" demanded Maia with round, surprised eyes. "Pay? Nobody will pay. There is nothing to pay — is there?"

She turned her shining gaze upon the Assistant.

"Nothing at all, madam," he assured her, as he put the parcels into her arms and bowed again.

"I thought not. You see," she said, turning to Michael, "the whole point of Christmas is that things should be *given* away, isn't it? Besides, what could I pay with? We have no money up there." And she laughed at the mere suggestion of such a thing.

"Now we must go," she went on, taking Michael's arm. "We must all go home. It's very late, and I heard your Mother telling you that you must be home in time for tea. Besides, I must get back, too. Come." And drawing Michael and Jane and Mary Poppins after her, she led the way through the shop and out by the spinning door.

Outside the entrance Jane suddenly said:

"But there's no present for *her*. She's bought something for all the others and nothing for herself. Maia has no Christmas present." And she began to search hurriedly through the parcels she was carrying, to see what she could spare for Maia.

Mary Poppins gave a quick glance into the window beside her. She saw herself shining back at her, very smart, very interesting, her hat on straight, her coat nicely pressed and her new gloves just completing the whole effect.

"You be quiet," she said to Jane in her snappiest voice. At the same time she whipped off her new gloves and thrust one on to each of Maia's hands.

"There!" she said gruffly. "It's cold today. You'll be glad of them."

Maia looked at the gloves, hanging very large and almost empty upon her hands. She said nothing, but moving close to Mary Poppins she reached up her spare arm and put it round Mary Poppins's neck and kissed her. A long look passed between them, and they smiled as people smile who understand each other. Maia turned then, and with her hand lightly touched the cheeks of Jane and Michael. And for a moment they all stood in a ring at the windy corner gazing at each other as though they were enchanted.

"I've been so happy," said Maia softly, breaking the silence. "Don't forget me, will you?"

" 'Ere! Come down! We can't 'ave this kind of thing!"

They shook their heads.

"Good-bye," said Maia.

"Good-bye," said the others, though it was the last thing they wanted to say.

Then Maia, standing poised on tip-toe, lifted up her arms and sprang into the air. She began to walk up it, step by step, climbing ever higher, as though there were invisible stairs cut into the grey sky. She waved to them as she went, and the three of them waved back.

"What on earth is happening?" somebody said close by.

"But it's not possible!" said another voice.

"Preposterous!" cried a third. For a crowd was gathering to witness the extraordinary sight of Maia returning home.

A Policeman pushed his way through the throng, scattering the people with his truncheon.

"Naow, naow. Wot's all this? A Naccident or wot?"

He looked up, his gaze following that of the rest of the crowd.

"'Ere!" he called angrily, shaking his fist at Maia. "Come down! Wot you doing up there? 'Olding up the traffic and all. Come down! We can't 'ave this kind of thing — not in a public place. 'Tisn't natural!"

Far away they heard Maia laughing and saw something bright dangling from her arm. It was the skipping-rope. After all, the parcel had come undone.

For a moment longer they saw her prancing up the airy stair, and then a bank of cloud hid her from their eyes. They knew she was behind it, though, because of the brightness that shone about its thick dark edge.

"Well, I'm jiggered!" said the Policeman, staring upwards, and scratching his head under its helmet.

"And well you might be!" said Mary Poppins, with such a ferocious snap that anyone else might have thought she was really cross with the Policeman. But Jane and Michael were not taken in by that snap. For they could see in Mary Poppins's eyes something that, if she were anybody else but Mary Poppins, might have been described as tears. . . .

"Could we have imagined it?" said Michael, when they got home and told the story to their Mother.

"Perhaps," said Mrs. Banks. "We imagine strange and lovely things, my darling."

"But what about Mary Poppins's gloves?" said Jane. "We saw her give them away to Maia. And she's not wearing them now. So it must be true!"

"What, Mary Poppins!" exclaimed Mrs. Banks. "Your best fur-topped gloves! You gave them away!"

Mary Poppins sniffed.

"My gloves are my gloves and I do what I like with them!" she said haughtily.

And she straightened her hat and went down to the Kitchen to have her tea. . . .

CHAPTER TWELVE

WEST WIND

I t was the first day of Spring.

Jane and Michael knew this at once, because they heard Mr. Banks singing in his bath, and there was only one day in the year when he did that.

They always remembered that particular morning. For one thing, it was the first time they were allowed to come downstairs for breakfast, and for another Mr. Banks lost his black bag. So that the day began with two extraordinary happenings.

"Where is my *BAG?*" shouted Mr. Banks, turning round and round in the hall like a dog chasing its tail.

And everybody else began running round and round too — Ellen and Mrs. Brill and the children. Even Robertson Ay made a special effort and turned round twice. At last Mr. Banks discovered the bag himself in his study, and he rushed into the hall with it, holding it aloft.

"Now," he said, as though he were delivering a sermon, "my bag is always kept in one place. Here. On the umbrella-stand. Who put it in the study?" he roared.

"You did, my dear, when you took the Income Tax papers out of it last night," said Mrs. Banks.

Mr. Banks gave her such a hurt look that she wished she had been less tactless and had said she had put it there herself.

"Humph — Urrumph!" he said, blowing his nose very hard and taking his overcoat from its peg. He walked with it to the front door.

"Hullo," he said more cheerfully, "the Parrot Tulips are in bud!" He went into the garden and sniffed the air. "H'm, wind's in the West, I think." He looked down towards Admiral Boom's house where the telescope weathercock swung. "I thought so," he said. "Westerly weather. Bright and balmy. I won't take an overcoat."

And with that he picked up his bag and his bowler hat and hurried away to the City.

"Did you hear what he said?" Michael grabbed Jane's arm.

She nodded. "The wind's in the West," she said slowly.

Neither of them said any more, but there was a thought in each of their minds that they wished was not there.

They forgot it soon, however, for everything seemed to be as it always was, and the Spring sunlight lit up the house so beautifully that nobody remembered it needed a coat of paint and new wall-papers. On the contrary, they all found themselves thinking that it was the best house in Cherry-Tree Lane.

But trouble began after luncheon.

Jane had gone down to dig in the garden with Robertson Ay. She had just sown a row of radish-seed when she heard a great commotion in the Nursery and the sound of hurrying footsteps on the stairs. Presently Michael appeared, very red in the face and panting loudly.

"Look, Jane, look!" he cried, and held out his hand. Within it lay Mary Poppins's compass, with the disc frantically swinging round the arrow as it trembled in Michael's shaking hand.

"The compass?" said Jane, and looked at him questioningly.

Michael suddenly burst into tears.

"She gave it to me," he wept. "She said I could have it all for myself now. Oh, oh, there must be something wrong! What is going to happen? She has never given me anything before."

"Perhaps she was only being nice," said Jane to soothe him, but in her heart she felt as disturbed as Michael was. She knew very well that Mary Poppins never wasted time in being nice.

And yet, strange to say, during that afternoon Mary Poppins never said a cross word. Indeed, she hardly said a word at all. She seemed to be thinking very deeply, and when they asked questions she answered them in a faraway voice. At last Michael could bear it no longer.

"Oh, do be cross, Mary Poppins! Do be cross again!

It is not like you. Oh, I feel so anxious." And indeed, his heart felt heavy with the thought that something, he did not quite know what, was about to happen at Number Seventeen, Cherry-Tree Lane.

"Trouble trouble and it will trouble you!" retorted Mary Poppins crossly, in her usual voice.

And immediately he felt a little better.

"Perhaps it's only a feeling," he said to Jane. "Perhaps everything is all right and I'm just imagining — don't you think so, Jane?"

"Probably," said Jane slowly. But she was thinking hard and her heart felt tight in her body.

The wind grew wilder towards evening, and blew in little gusts about the house. It went puffing and whistling down the chimneys, slipping in through the cracks under the windows, turning the Nursery carpet up at the corners.

Mary Poppins gave them their supper and cleared away the things, stacking them neatly and methodically. Then she tidied up the Nursery and put the kettle on the hob.

"There!" she said, glancing round the room to see that everything was all right. She was silent for a minute. Then she put one hand lightly on Michael's head and the other on Jane's shoulder.

"Now," she said, "I am just going to take the shoes down for Robertson Ay to clean. Behave yourselves, please, till

I come back." She went out and shut the door quietly behind her.

Suddenly, as she went, they both felt they must run after her, but something seemed to stop them. They remained quiet, with their elbows on the table waiting for her to come back. Each was trying to reassure the other without saying anything.

"How silly we are," said Jane presently. "Everything's all right." But she knew that she said it more to comfort Michael than because she thought it was true.

The Nursery clock ticked loudly from the mantelpiece. The fire flickered and crackled and slowly died down. They still sat there at the table, waiting.

At last Michael said uneasily: "She's been gone a very long time, hasn't she?"

The wind whistled and cried about the house as if in reply. The clock went on ticking its solemn double note.

Suddenly the silence was broken by the sound of the front door shutting with a loud bang.

"Michael!" said Jane, starting up.

"Jane!" said Michael, with a white, anxious look on his face.

They listened. Then they ran quickly to the window and looked out.

Down below, just outside the front door, stood Mary Poppins, dressed in her coat and hat, with her carpet bag in one hand and her umbrella in the other. The wind was

blowing wildly about her, tugging at her skirt, tilting her hat rakishly to one side. But it seemed to Jane and Michael that she did not mind, for she smiled as though she and the wind understood each other.

She paused for a moment on the step and glanced back towards the front door. Then with a quick movement she opened the umbrella, though it was not raining, and thrust it over her head.

The wind, with a wild cry, slipped under the umbrella, pressing it upwards as though trying to force it out of Mary Poppins's hand. But she held on tightly, and that, apparently, was what the wind wanted her to do, for presently it lifted the umbrella higher into the air and Mary Poppins from the ground. It carried her lightly so that her toes just grazed along the garden path. Then it lifted her over the front gate and swept her upwards towards the branches of the cherry-trees in the Lane.

"She's going, Jane, she's going!" cried Michael, weeping.

"Quick!" cried Jane. "Let us get the Twins. They must see the last of her." She had no doubt now, nor had Michael, that Mary Poppins had gone for good because the wind had changed.

They each seized a Twin and rushed back to the window.

Mary Poppins was in the upper air now, floating away over the cherry-trees and the roofs of the houses, holding tightly to the umbrella with one hand and to the carpet bag with the other.

The Twins began to cry quietly.

With their free hands Jane and Michael opened the window and made one last effort to stay Mary Poppins's flight.

"Mary Poppins!" they cried. "Mary Poppins, come back!"

But she either did not hear or deliberately took no notice. For she went sailing on and on, up into the cloudy, whistling air, till at last she was wafted away over the hill and the children could see nothing but the trees bending and moaning under the wild west wind. . . .

"She did what she said she would, anyway. She stayed till the wind changed," said Jane, sighing and turning sadly from the window. She took John to his cot and put him into it. Michael said nothing, but as he brought Barbara back and tucked her into bed he was sniffing uncomfortably.

"I wonder," said Jane, "if we'll ever see her again?"

Suddenly they heard voices on the stairs.

"Children, children!" Mrs. Banks was calling as she opened the door. "Children—I am very cross. Mary Poppins has left us ——"

"Yes," said Jane and Michael.

"You knew, then?" said Mrs. Banks, rather surprised. "Did she tell you she was going?"

They shook their heads, and Mrs. Banks went on:

"It's outrageous. One minute here and gone the next. Not even an apology. Simply said, 'I'm going!' and off she went. Anything more preposterous, more thoughtless, more discourteous —— What is it, Michael?" She broke off crossly, for Michael had grasped her skirt in his hands and was shaking her. "What *is* it, child?"

"Did she say she'd come back?" he cried, nearly knocking his Mother over. "Tell me — did she?"

"You will *not* behave like a Red Indian, Michael," she said, loosening his hold. "I don't remember *what* she

Floating away over the roofs of the houses

said, except that she was going. But I certainly shan't have her back if she does want to come. Leaving me high and dry with nobody to help me and without a word of notice."

"Oh, Mother!" said Jane reproachfully.

"You are a very cruel woman," said Michael, clenching his fist, as though at any minute he would have to strike her.

"Children! I'm ashamed of you — really I am! To want back anybody who has treated your Mother so badly. I'm utterly shocked."

Jane burst into tears.

"Mary Poppins is the only person I want in the world!" Michael wailed, and flung himself on to the floor.

"Really, children, really! I don't understand you. Do be good, I beg of you. There's nobody to look after you tonight. I have to go out to dinner and it's Ellen's Day Off. I shall have to send Mrs. Brill up." And she kissed them absentmindedly, and went away with an anxious little line on her forehead. . . .

"Well, if I ever did! Her going away and leaving you poor dear children in the lurch like that," said Mrs. Brill, a moment later, bustling in and setting to work on them.

"A heart of stone, that's what that girl had *and* no mistake, or my name's not Clara Brill. Always keeping herself to herself, too, and not even a lace handkerchief or a hatpin to remember her by. Get up, will you please, Master Michael!" Mrs. Brill went on, panting heavily.

"How we stood her so long, I *don't* know — with her airs and graces and all. What a lot of buttons, Miss Jane! Stand still, do now, and let me undress you, Master Michael. Plain she was, too, nothing much to look at. Indeed, all things considered, I don't know that we won't be better off, after all. Now, Miss Jane, where's your nightgown — why, what's this under your pillow —— ?"

Mrs. Brill had drawn out a small nobbly parcel.

"What is it? Give it to me — give it," said Jane, trembling with excitement, and she took it from Mrs. Brill's hands very quickly. Michael came and stood near her and watched her undo the string and tear away the brown paper. Mrs. Brill, without waiting to see what emerged from the package, went in to the Twins.

The last wrapping fell to the floor and the thing that was in the parcel lay in Jane's hand.

"It's her picture," she said in a whisper, looking closely at it.

And it was!

Inside a little curly frame was a painting of Mary Poppins, and underneath it was written, "Mary Poppins by Bert."

"That's the Match-Man — he did it," said Michael, and took it in his hand so that he could have a better look.

Jane found suddenly that there was a letter attached to the painting. She unfolded it carefully. It ran:

> DEAR JANE,
> Michael had the compass so the picture is for you. Au revoir.
>   MARY POPPINS

She read it out loud till she came to the words she couldn't understand.

"Mrs. Brill!" she called. "What does 'au revoir' mean?"

"Au revore, dearie?" shrieked Mrs. Brill from the next room. "Why, doesn't it mean — let me see, I'm not up in these foreign tongues — doesn't it mean 'God bless you'? No. No, I'm wrong. I think, Miss Jane dear, it means To Meet Again."

Jane and Michael looked at each other. Joy and understanding shone in their eyes. They knew what Mary Poppins meant.

Michael gave a long sigh of relief. "That's all right," he said shakily. "She always does what she says she will." He turned away.

"Michael, are you crying?" Jane asked.

He twisted his head and tried to smile at her.

"No, I am not," he said. "It is only my eyes."

She pushed him gently towards his bed, and as he

got in she slipped the portrait of Mary Poppins into his
hand — hurriedly, in case she should regret it.

"You have it for tonight, darling," whispered Jane, and
she tucked him in just as Mary Poppins used to do. . . .

"They saw before them their own pictured faces"

MARY
POPPINS
COMES
BACK

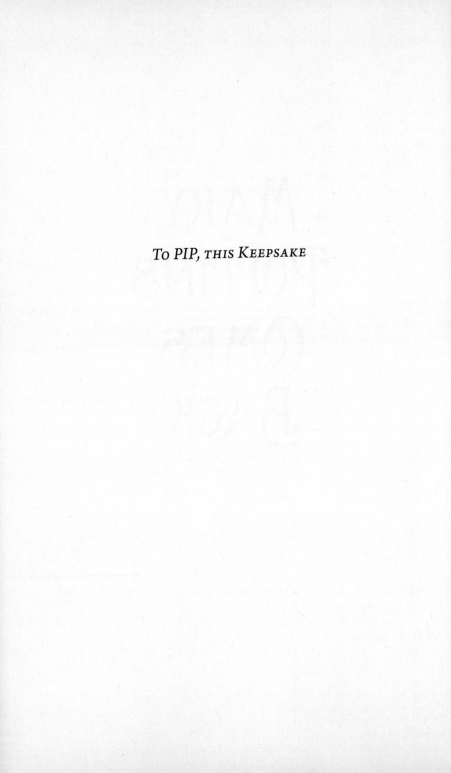

To Pip, this Keepsake

CONTENTS

ILLUSTRATIONS

Also insets and tailpieces

CHAPTER ONE

THE KITE

It was one of those mornings when everything looks very neat and bright and shiny, as though the world had been tidied up overnight.

In Cherry-Tree Lane the houses blinked as their blinds went up, and the thin shadows of the cherry-trees fell in dark stripes across the sunlight. But there was no sound anywhere, except for the tingling of the Ice Cream Man's bell as he wheeled his cart up and down.

"STOP ME AND BUY ONE"

said the placard in front of the cart. And presently a Sweep came round the corner of the Lane and held up his black sweepy hand.

The Ice Cream Man went tingling up to him.

"Penny one," said the Sweep. And he stood leaning on his bundle of brushes as he licked out the Ice Cream with the tip of his tongue. When it was all gone he gently wrapped the cone in his handkerchief and put it in his pocket.

"Don't you eat cones?" said the Ice Cream Man, very surprised.

"No. I collect them!" said the Sweep. And he picked up his brushes and went in through Admiral Boom's front gate because there was no Tradesman's Entrance.

The Ice Cream Man wheeled his cart up the Lane again and tingled, and the stripes of shadow and sunlight fell on him as he went.

"Never knew it so quiet before!" he murmured, gazing from right to left, and looking out for customers.

At that very moment a loud voice sounded from Number Seventeen. The Ice Cream Man cycled hurriedly up to the gate, hoping for an order.

"I won't stand it! I simply will not stand any more!" shouted Mr. Banks, striding angrily from the front door to the foot of the stairs and back again.

"What is it?" said Mrs. Banks anxiously, hurrying out of the dining-room. "And what is that you are kicking up and down the hall?"

Mr. Banks lunged out with his foot and something black flew half-way up the stairs.

"My hat!" he said between his teeth. "My Best Bowler Hat!"

He ran up the stairs and kicked it down again. It spun for a moment on the tiles and fell at Mrs. Banks' feet.

"Is anything wrong with it?" said Mrs. Banks, nervously. But to herself she wondered whether there was not something wrong with Mr. Banks.

"Look and see!" he roared at her.

Trembling, Mrs. Banks stooped and picked up the hat. It was covered with large, shiny, sticky patches and she noticed it had a peculiar smell.

She sniffed at the brim.

"It smells like boot-polish," she said.

"It *is* boot-polish," retorted Mr. Banks. "Robertson Ay has brushed my hat with the boot-brush — in fact, he has polished it."

Mrs. Banks' mouth fell with horror.

"I don't know what's come over this house," Mr. Banks went on. "Nothing ever goes right — hasn't for ages! Shaving water too hot, breakfast coffee too cold. And now — this!"

He snatched his hat from Mrs. Banks and caught up his bag.

"I am going!" he said. "And I don't know that I shall ever come back. I shall probably take a long sea-voyage."

Then he clapped the hat on his head, banged the front door behind him and went through the gate so quickly that he knocked over the Ice Cream Man, who had been listening to the conversation with interest.

"It's your own fault!" he said crossly. "You'd no right to be there!" And he went striding off towards the City, his polished hat shining like a jewel in the sun.

The Ice Cream Man got up carefully and, finding there

were no bones broken, he sat down on the kerb, and made it up to himself by eating a large Ice Cream. . . .

"Oh, dear!" said Mrs. Banks as she heard the gate slam. "It is quite true. Nothing *does* go right nowadays. First one thing and then another. Ever since Mary Poppins left without a Word of Warning everything has gone wrong."

She sat down at the foot of the stairs and took out her handkerchief and cried into it.

And as she cried, she thought of all that had happened since that day when Mary Poppins had so suddenly and so strangely disappeared.

"Here one night and gone the next — most upsetting!" said Mrs. Banks gulping.

Nurse Green had arrived soon after and had left at the end of a week because Michael had spat at her. She was followed by Nurse Brown who went out for a walk one day and never came back. And it was not until later that

they discovered that all the silver spoons had gone with her.

And after Nurse Brown came Miss Quigley, the Governess, who had to be asked to leave because she played scales for three hours every morning before breakfast and Mr. Banks did not care for music.

"And then," sobbed Mrs. Banks to her handkerchief, "there was Jane's attack of measles, and the bath-room geyser bursting and the Cherry-Trees ruined by frost and —— "

"If you please, m'm —— !" Mrs. Banks looked up to find Mrs. Brill, the cook, at her side.

"The kitchen flue's on fire!" said Mrs. Brill gloomily.

"Oh, dear. What next?" cried Mrs. Banks. "You must tell Robertson Ay to put it out. Where is he?"

"Asleep, m'm, in the broom-cupboard. And when that boy's asleep, nothing'll wake him — not if it's an Earthquake, or a regiment of Tom-toms," said Mrs. Brill, as she followed Mrs. Banks down the kitchen stairs.

Between them they managed to put out the fire but that was not the end of Mrs. Banks' troubles.

She had no sooner finished luncheon than a crash, followed by a loud thud, was heard from upstairs.

"What is it now?" Mrs. Banks rushed out to see what had happened.

"Oh, my leg, my leg!" cried Ellen, the housemaid.

She sat on the stairs, surrounded by broken china, groaning loudly.

"What is the matter with it?" said Mrs. Banks sharply.

"Broken!" said Ellen dismally, leaning against the banisters.

"Nonsense, Ellen! You've sprained your ankle, that's all!"

But Ellen only groaned again.

"My leg is broken! What will I do?" she wailed, over and over again.

At that moment the shrill cries of the Twins sounded from the nursery. They were fighting for the possession of a blue celluloid duck. Their screams rose thinly above the voices of Jane and Michael, who were painting pictures on the wall and arguing as to whether a green horse should have a purple or a red tail. And through this uproar there sounded, like the steady beat of a drum, the groans of Ellen the housemaid. "My leg is broken! What shall I do?"

"This," said Mrs. Banks, rushing upstairs, "is the Last Straw!"

She helped Ellen to bed and put a cold water bandage round her ankle. Then she went up to the Nursery.

Jane and Michael rushed at her.

"It should have a red tail, shouldn't it?" demanded Michael.

"Oh, Mother! Don't let him be so stupid. No horse has a red tail, has it?"

"Well, what horse has a purple tail? Tell me that!" he screamed.

"*My* duck!" shrieked John, snatching the duck from Barbara.

"Mine, mine, mine!" cried Barbara, snatching it back again.

"Children! Children!" Mrs. Banks was wringing her hands in despair. "Be quiet or I shall Go Mad!"

There was silence for a moment as they stared at her with interest. Would she really? They wondered. And what would she be like if she did?

"Now," said Mrs. Banks. "I will *not* have this behaviour. Poor Ellen has hurt her ankle, so there is nobody to look after you. You must all go into the Park and play there till Tea-time. Jane and Michael, you must look after the little ones. John, let Barbara have the duck now and you can have it when you go to bed. Michael, you may take your new kite. Now, get your hats, all of you!"

"But I want to finish my horse ——" began Michael crossly.

"Why must we go to the Park?" complained Jane. "There's nothing to do there!"

"Because," said Mrs. Banks, "I *must* have peace. And if you will go quietly and be good children there will be cocoanut cakes for tea."

And before they had time to break out again, she had put on their hats and was hurrying them down the stairs.

"Look both ways!" she called as they went through the gate, Jane pushing the Twins in the perambulator and Michael carrying his kite.

They looked to the right. There was nothing coming.

They looked to the left. Nobody there but the Ice Cream Man who was jingling his bell at the end of the Lane.

Jane hurried across.

Michael trailed after her.

"I hate this life," he said miserably to his kite. "Everything always goes wrong always."

Jane pushed the perambulator as far as the Lake.

"Now," she said, "give me the duck!"

The Twins shrieked and clutched it at either end. Jane uncurled their fingers.

"Look!" she said, throwing the duck into the Lake. "Look, darlings, it's going to India!"

The duck drifted off across the water. The Twins stared at it and sobbed.

Jane ran round the Lake and caught it and sent it off again.

"Now," she said brightly, "it's off to Southampton!"

The Twins did not appear to be amused.

"Now to New York!" They wept harder than ever.

Jane flung out her hands. "Michael, what *are* we to do with them? If we give it to them they'll fight over it and if we don't they'll go on crying."

"I'll fly the Kite for them," said Michael. "Look, children, look!"

He held up the beautiful green-and-yellow Kite and began to unwind the string. The Twins eyed it tearfully and without interest. He lifted the Kite above his head and ran a little way. It flapped along the air for a moment and then collapsed hollowly on the grass.

"Try again!" said Jane encouragingly.

"You hold it up while I run," said Michael.

This time the Kite rose a little higher. But, as it floated, its long tasselled tail caught in the branches of a lime tree and the Kite dangled limply among the leaves.

The Twins howled lustily.

"Oh, dear!" said Jane. "Nothing goes right nowadays."

"Hullo, hullo, hullo! What's all this?" said a voice behind them.

They turned and saw the Park Keeper, looking very smart in his uniform and peaked cap. He was prodding up stray pieces of paper with the sharp end of his walking stick.

Jane pointed to the lime tree. The Keeper looked up. His face became very stern.

"Now, now, you're breaking the rules! We don't allow Litter here, you know — not on the ground nor in the trees neither. This won't do at all!"

"It isn't litter. It's a Kite," said Michael.

A mild, soft, foolish look came over the Keeper's face. He went up to the lime tree.

"A Kite? So it is. And I haven't flown a Kite since I was a boy!" He sprang up into the tree and came down holding the Kite tenderly under his arm.

"Now," he said excitedly, "we'll wind her up and give her a run and away she'll go!" He put out his hand for the winding-stick.

Michael clutched it firmly.

"Thank you, but I want to fly it myself."

"Well, but you'll let me help, won't you?" said the Keeper humbly. "Seeing as I got it down and I haven't flown a Kite since I was a boy?"

"All right," said Michael, for he didn't want to seem unkind.

"Oh, thank you, thank you!" cried the Keeper gratefully. "Now, I take the Kite and walk ten paces down the green. And when I say 'Go!', you run. See!"

The Keeper walked away, counting his steps out loud.

"Eight, nine, ten."

He turned and raised the Kite above his head. "Go!"

Michael began to run.

"Let her out!" roared the Keeper.

Behind him Michael heard a soft flapping noise. There was a tug at the string as the winding-stick turned in his hand.

"She's afloat!" cried the Keeper.

Michael looked back. The Kite was sailing through the air, plunging steadily upwards. Higher and higher it dived, a tiny wisp of green-and-yellow bounding away into the blue. The Keeper's eyes were popping.

"I never saw such a Kite. Not even when I was a boy," he murmured, staring upwards.

A light cloud came up over the sun and puffed across the sky.

"It's coming towards the Kite," said Jane in an excited whisper.

Up and up went the tossing tail, darting through the air until it seemed but a faint dark speck on the sky. The cloud moved slowly towards it. Nearer, nearer!

"Gone!" said Michael, as the speck disappeared behind the thin grey screen.

Jane gave a little sigh. The Twins sat quietly in the perambulator. A curious stillness was upon them all. The taut string running up from Michael's hand seemed to link them all to the cloud, and the earth to the sky. They waited, holding their breaths, for the Kite to appear again.

Suddenly Jane could bear it no longer.

"Michael," she cried, "Pull it in! Pull it in!"

She laid her hand upon the tugging, quivering string.

Michael turned the stick and gave a long, strong pull. The string remained taut and steady. He pulled again, puffing and panting.

"I can't," he said. "It won't come."

"I'll help!" said Jane. "Now — pull!"

But, hard as they tugged, the string would not give and the Kite remained hidden behind the cloud.

"Let me!" said the Keeper importantly. "When I was a boy we did it this way."

And he put his hand on the string just above Jane's and gave it a short, sharp jerk. It seemed to give a little.

"Now — all together — pull!" he yelled.

The Keeper tossed off his hat, and, planting their feet firmly on the grass, Jane and Michael pulled with all their might.

"It's coming!" panted Michael.

Suddenly the string slackened and a small whirling shape shot through the grey cloud and came floating down.

"Wind her up!" the Keeper spluttered, glancing at Michael.

But the string was already winding round the stick of its own accord.

Down, down came the Kite, turning over and over in the air, wildly dancing at the end of the jerking string.

Jane gave a little gasp.

"Something's happened!" she cried. "That's not our Kite. It's quite a different one!"

They stared.

It was quite true. The Kite was no longer green-and-yellow. It had turned colour and was now navy-blue. Down it came, tossing and bounding.

Suddenly Michael gave a shout.

"Jane! Jane! It isn't a Kite at all. It looks like — oh, it looks like —— "

"Wind, Michael, wind quickly!" gasped Jane. "I can hardly wait!"

For now, above the tallest trees, the shape at the end of the string was clearly visible. There was no sign of the green-and-yellow Kite, but in its place danced a figure that seemed at once strange and familiar, a figure wearing a blue coat with silver buttons and a straw hat trimmed with daisies. Tucked under its arm was an umbrella with a parrot's head for a handle, a brown carpet bag dangled from one hand while the other held firmly to the end of the shortening string.

"Ah!" Jane gave a shout of triumph. "It *is* she!"

"I knew it!" cried Michael, his hands trembling on the winding-stick.

"Lumme!" said the Park Keeper, blinking. "Lumme!"

On sailed the curious figure, its feet neatly clearing the tops of the trees. They could see the face now and the well-known features — coal black hair, bright blue eyes and nose turned upwards like the nose of a Dutch doll. As the last length of string wound itself round the stick the figure drifted down between the lime trees and alighted primly upon the grass.

In a flash Michael dropped the stick. Away he bounded, with Jane at his heels.

"Mary Poppins, Mary Poppins!" they cried, and flung themselves upon her.

Behind them the Twins were crowing like cocks in the morning and the Park Keeper was opening and shutting his mouth as though he would like to say something but could not find the words.

On sailed the curious figure, its feet neatly clearing the tops of the trees

"At last! At last! At last!" shouted Michael wildly, clutching at her arm, her bag, her umbrella — anything, so long as he might touch her and feel that she was really true.

"We knew you'd come back! We found the letter that said *au revoir!*" cried Jane, flinging her arms round the waist of the blue overcoat.

A satisfied smile flickered for a moment over Mary Poppins' face — up from the mouth, over the turned-up nose, into the blue eyes. But it died away swiftly.

"I'll thank you to remember," she remarked, disengaging herself from their hands, "that this is a Public Park and not a Bear Garden. Such goings on! I might as well be at the Zoo. And where, may I ask, are your gloves?"

They fell back, fumbling in their pockets.

"Humph! Put them on, please!"

Trembling with excitement and delight, Jane and Michael stuffed their hands into the gloves and put on their hats.

Mary Poppins moved towards the perambulator. The Twins cooed happily as she strapped them in more securely and straightened the rug. Then she glanced round.

"Who put that duck in the pond?" she demanded, in that stern, haughty voice they knew so well.

"I did," said Jane. "For the Twins. He was going to New York."

"Well, take him out, then!" said Mary Poppins. "He is

not going to New York — wherever that is — but Home to Tea."

And, slinging her carpet bag over the handle of the perambulator, she began to push the Twins towards the gate.

The Park Keeper, suddenly finding his voice, blocked her way.

"See here," he said, staring. "I shall have to report this. It's against the Regulations. Coming down out of the sky, like that. And where from, I'd like to know, where from?"

He broke off, for Mary Poppins was eyeing him up and down in a way that made him feel he would rather be somewhere else.

"If I was a Park Keeper," she remarked, primly, "I should put on my cap and button my coat. Excuse me."

And, haughtily waving him aside, she pushed past with the perambulator.

Blushing, the Keeper bent to pick up his hat. When he looked up again Mary Poppins and the children had disappeared through the gate of Number Seventeen Cherry-Tree Lane.

He stared at the path. Then he stared up at the sky and down at the path again.

He took off his hat, scratched his head, and put it on again.

"I never saw such a thing!" he said, shakily "Not even when I was a boy!"

And he went away muttering and looking very upset.

~~~

"Why, it's Mary Poppins!" said Mrs. Banks, as they came into the hall. "Where did *you* come from? Out of the blue?"

"Yes," began Michael joyfully, "she came down on the end —— "

He stopped short for Mary Poppins had fixed him with one of her terrible looks.

"I found them in the Park, ma'am," she said, turning to Mrs. Banks, "so I brought them home!"

"Have you come to stay, then?"

"For the present, ma'am."

"But, Mary Poppins, last time you were here you left me without a Word of Warning. How do I know you won't do it again?"

"You don't, ma'am," replied Mary Poppins, calmly.

Mrs. Banks looked rather taken aback.

"But — but will you, do you think?" she asked uncertainly.

"I couldn't say, ma'am, I'm sure."

"Oh!" said Mrs. Banks, because, at the moment, she couldn't think of anything else.

And before she had recovered from her surprise, Mary Poppins had taken her carpet bag and was hurrying the children upstairs.

Mrs. Banks, gazing after them, heard the Nursery door shut quietly. Then with a sigh of relief she ran to the telephone.

"Mary Poppins has come back!" she said happily, into the receiver.

"Has she, indeed?" said Mr. Banks at the other end. "Then perhaps I will, too."

And he rang off.

Upstairs Mary Poppins was taking off her overcoat. She hung it on a hook behind the Night-Nursery door. Then she removed her hat and placed it neatly on one of the bed-posts.

Jane and Michael watched the familiar movements. Everything about her was just as it had always been. They could hardly believe she had ever been away.

Mary Poppins bent down and opened the carpet bag.

It was quite empty except for a large Thermometer.

"What's that for?" asked Jane curiously.

"You," said Mary Poppins.

"But I'm not ill," Jane protested. "It's two months since I had measles."

"Open!" said Mary Poppins in a voice that made Jane shut her eyes very quickly and open her mouth. The Thermometer slipped in.

"I want to know how you've been behaving since I went away," remarked Mary Poppins sternly. Then she took out the Thermometer and held it up to the light.

"Careless, thoughtless and untidy," she read out.

Jane stared.

"Humph!" said Mary Poppins, and thrust the Thermometer into Michael's mouth. He kept his lips tightly pressed upon it until she plucked it out and read.

"A very noisy, mischievous, troublesome little boy."

"I'm not," he said angrily.

For answer she thrust the Thermometer under his nose and he spelt out the large red letters.

"A-V-E-R-Y-N-O-I-S——"

"You see?" said Mary Poppins looking at him triumphantly. She opened John's mouth and popped in the Thermometer.

"Peevish and Excitable." That was John's temperature.

And when Barbara's was taken Mary Poppins read out the two words, "Thoroughly spoilt."

"Humph!" she snorted. "It's about time I came back!"

Then she popped it quickly in her own mouth, left it there for a moment, and took it out.

"A very excellent and worthy person, thoroughly reliable in every particular."

A pleased and conceited smile lit up her face as she read her temperature aloud.

"I thought so," she said, priggishly. "Now — Tea and Bed!"

It seemed to them no more than a minute before they had drunk their milk and eaten their cocoanut cakes and were in and out of the bath. As usual, everything that Mary Poppins did had the speed of electricity. Hooks and eyes rushed apart, buttons darted eagerly out of their holes, sponge and soap ran up and down like lightning, and towels dried with one rub.

Mary Poppins walked along the row of beds tucking them all in. Her starched white apron crackled and she smelt deliciously of newly made toast.

When she came to Michael's bed she bent down, and rummaged under it for a minute. Then she carefully drew out her camp-bedstead with her possessions laid upon it in neat piles. The cake of Sunlight-soap, the toothbrush, the packet of hairpins, the bottle of scent, the small folding arm-chair and the box of throat lozenges. Also the seven flannel nightgowns, the four cotton ones, the boots, the dominoes, the two bathing-caps and the postcard album.

Jane and Michael sat up and stared.

"Where did they come from?" demanded Michael. "I've been under my bed simply hundreds of times and I know they weren't there before."

Mary Poppins did not reply. She had begun to undress.

Jane and Michael exchanged glances. They knew it was no good asking, because Mary Poppins never explained anything.

She slipped off her starched white collar and fumbled at the clip of a chain round her neck.

"What's inside that?" enquired Michael, gazing at a small gold locket that hung on the end of the chain.

"A portrait."

"Whose?"

"You'll know when the time comes — not before," she snapped.

"When will the time come?"

"When I go."

They stared at her with startled eyes.

"But, Mary Poppins," cried Jane, "you won't ever leave us again, will you? Oh, say you won't!"

Mary Poppins glared at her.

"A nice life I'd have," she remarked, "if I spent all my days with *you!*"

"But you will stay?" persisted Jane eagerly.

Mary Poppins tossed the locket up and down on her palm.

"I'll stay till the chain breaks," she said briefly.

And popping a cotton nightgown over her head, she began to undress beneath it.

"That's all right," Michael whispered across to Jane. "I noticed the chain and it's a very strong one!"

He nodded to her reassuringly. They curled up in their beds and lay watching Mary Poppins as she moved mysteriously beneath the tent of her nightgown. And they thought of her first arrival at Cherry-Tree Lane and all the strange and astonishing things that happened afterwards; of how she had flown away on her umbrella when the wind changed; of the long weary days without her and her marvellous descent from the sky this afternoon.

Suddenly Michael remembered something.

"My Kite!" he said, sitting up in bed. "I forgot all about it! Where's my Kite?"

Mary Poppins' head came up through the neck of the nightgown.

"Kite?" she said crossly. "Which Kite? What Kite?"

"My green-and-yellow Kite with the tassels. The one you came down on, at the end of the string."

Mary Poppins stared at him. He could not tell if she was more astonished than angry, but she looked as if she was both.

And her voice when she spoke, was more awful than her look.

"Did I understand you to say that —— " she repeated the words slowly, between her teeth — "that I came down from somewhere and on the end of a string?"

"But — you did!" faltered Michael. "To-day. Out of a cloud. We saw you."

"On the end of a string? Like a monkey or a spinning-top? Me, Michael Banks?"

Mary Poppins, in her fury, seemed to have grown to twice her usual size. She hovered over him in her night-gown, huge and angry, waiting for him to reply.

He clutched the bedclothes for support.

"Don't say any more, Michael!" Jane whispered warn-ingly across from her bed. But he had gone too far now to stop.

"Then — where's my Kite?" he said recklessly. "If you

didn't come down — er, in the way I said — where's my Kite? It's not on the end of the string."

"O-ho? And I am, I suppose?" she enquired with a scoffing laugh.

He saw then that it was no good going on. He could not explain. He would have to give it up.

"N — no," he said, in a thin, small voice. "No, Mary Poppins."

She turned and snapped out the electric light.

"Your manners," she remarked tartly, "have not improved since I went away! On the end of a string, indeed! I have never been so insulted in my life. Never!"

And with a furious sweep of her arm, she turned down her bed and flounced into it, pulling the blankets tight over her head.

Michael lay very quiet, still holding his bedclothes tightly.

"She did, though, didn't she? We saw her." He whispered presently to Jane.

But Jane did not answer. Instead, she pointed towards the Night-Nursery door.

Michael lifted his head cautiously.

Behind the door, on a hook, hung Mary Poppins' overcoat, its silver buttons gleaming in the glow of the nightlight. And dangling from the pocket were a row of paper tassels, the tassels of a green-and-yellow Kite.

They gazed at it for a long time.

Then they nodded across to each other. They knew

there was nothing to be said, for there were things about Mary Poppins they would never understand. But — she was back again. That was all that mattered. The even sound of her breathing came floating across from the camp-bed. They felt peaceful and happy and complete.

"I don't mind, Jane, if it has a purple tail," hissed Michael presently.

"No, Michael!" said Jane. "I really think a red would be better."

After that there was no sound in the nursery but the sound of five people breathing very quietly. . . .

"P-p! P-p!" went Mr. Banks' pipe.

"Click-click!" went Mrs. Banks' knitting needles.

Mr. Banks put his feet up on the study mantelpiece and snored a little.

After a while Mrs. Banks spoke.

"Do you still think of taking a long sea-voyage?" she asked.

"Er — I don't think so. I am rather a bad sailor. And my hat's all right now. I had the whole of it polished by the shoe-black at the corner and it looks as good as new. Even better. Besides, now that Mary Poppins is back, my shaving water will be just the right temperature."

Mrs. Banks smiled to herself and went on knitting.

She felt very glad that Mr. Banks was such a bad sailor and that Mary Poppins had come back.

Down in the Kitchen, Mrs. Brill was putting a fresh bandage round Ellen's ankle.

"I never thought much of her when she was here!" said Mrs. Brill, "but I must say that this has been a different house since this afternoon. As quiet as a Sunday and as neat as ninepence. I'm not sorry she's back."

"Neither am I, indeed!" said Ellen thankfully.

"And neither am I," thought Robertson Ay, listening to the conversation through the wall of the broom-cupboard. "Now I shall have a little peace."

He settled himself comfortably on the upturned coal-scuttle and fell asleep again with his head against a broom.

But what Mary Poppins thought about it nobody ever knew for she kept her thoughts to herself and never told anyone anything. . . .

CHAPTER TWO

MISS ANDREW'S LARK

t was Saturday afternoon.

In the hall of Number Seventeen Cherry-Tree Lane, Mr. Banks was busy tapping the barometer and telling Mrs. Banks what the weather was going to do.

"Moderate South wind; average temperature; local thunder; sea slight," he said. "Further outlook unsettled. Hullo — what's that?"

He broke off as a bumping, jumping, thumping noise sounded overhead.

Round the bend in the staircase Michael appeared, looking very bad-tempered and sulky as he bumped heavily down. Behind him with a Twin on each arm came Mary Poppins, pushing her knee into his back and sending him with a sharp thud from one stair to the next. Jane followed, carrying the hats.

"Well begun is half done. Down you go, please!" Mary Poppins was saying tartly.

Mr. Banks turned from the barometer and looked up as they appeared.

"Well, what's the matter with you?" he demanded.

"I don't *want* to go for a walk! I want to play with my new engine," said Michael, gulping as Mary Poppins' knee jerked him one stair lower.

"Nonsense, darling!" said Mrs. Banks. "Of course you do. Walking makes such long, strong legs."

"But I like short legs best," grumbled Michael, stumbling heavily down another stair.

"When *I* was a little boy," said Mr. Banks, "I loved going for walks. I used to walk with my Governess down to the second lamp-post and back every day. And I *never* grumbled."

Michael stood still on his stair and looked doubtfully at Mr. Banks.

"Were you *ever* a little boy?" he said, very surprised.

Mr. Banks seemed quite hurt.

"Of course I was. A sweet little boy with long yellow curls, velvet breeches and button-up boots."

"I can hardly believe it," said Michael, hurrying down the stairs of his own accord and staring up at Mr. Banks.

He simply could not imagine his Father as a little boy. It seemed to him impossible that Mr. Banks had ever been anything but six feet high, middle-aged and rather bald.

"What was the name of your Governess?" asked Jane, running downstairs after Michael. "And was she nice?"

"She was called Miss Andrew and she was a Holy Terror!"

"Hush!" said Mrs. Banks, reproachfully.

"I mean—" Mr. Banks corrected himself, "she was—er—very strict. And always right. And she loved putting everybody else in the wrong and making them feel like a worm. That's what Miss Andrew was like!"

Mr. Banks mopped his brow at the mere memory of his Governess.

Ting! Ting! Ting!

The front door bell pealed and echoed through the house.

Mr. Banks went to the door and opened it. On the step, looking very important, stood the Telegraph Boy.

"Urgent Telegram. Name of Banks. Any answer?" He handed over an orange-coloured envelope.

"If it's good news I'll give you sixpence," said Mr. Banks as he tore open the Telegram and read the message. His face grew pale.

"No answer," he said shortly.

"And no sixpence?"

"Certainly not!" said Mr. Banks bitterly. The Telegraph Boy gave him a reproachful look and went sorrowfully away.

"Oh, what is it?" asked Mrs. Banks, realising the news must be very bad. "Is somebody ill?"

"Worse than that," said Mr. Banks miserably.

"Have we lost all our money?" By this time Mrs. Banks, too, was pale and very anxious.

"Worse still! Didn't the barometer say thunder? And further outlook Unsettled? Listen!"

He smoothed out the telegram and read aloud —

"Coming to stay with you for a month.
 Arriving this afternoon three o'clock.
 Please light fire in bedroom.
                                EUPHEMIA ANDREW."

"Andrew? Why, that's the same name as your Governess!" said Jane.

"It *is* my Governess," said Mr. Banks, striding up and down and running his hands nervously through what was left of his hair. "Her other name is Euphemia. And she's coming to-day at three!"

He groaned loudly.

"But I don't call that bad news," said Mrs. Banks, feeling very relieved. "It will mean getting the spare room ready, of course, but I don't mind. I shall like having the dear old soul —— "

"Dear old soul!" roared Mr. Banks. "You don't know what you're talking about. Dear old — my jumping godfathers, wait till you see her, that's all. Just wait till you see her!"

He seized his hat and waterproof.

"But, my dear!" cried Mrs. Banks, "you must be here to meet her. It looks so rude! Where are you going?"

"Anywhere. Everywhere. Tell her I'm dead!" he replied bitterly. And he hurried away from the house looking very nervous and depressed.

"My goodness, Michael, what *can* she be like?" said Jane.

"Curiosity killed the Cat," said Mary Poppins. "Put your hats on, please!"

She settled the Twins into the perambulator and pushed it down the garden path. Jane and Michael followed her out into the Lane.

"Where are we going to-day, Mary Poppins?"

"Across the Park and along the Thirty-Nine bus route, up the High Street and over the Bridge and home through the Railway Arch!" she snapped.

"If we do that we'll be walking all night," whispered Michael, dropping behind with Jane. "And we'll miss Miss Andrew."

"She's going to stay for a month," Jane reminded him.

"But I want to see her arrive," he complained, dragging his feet and shuffling along the pavement.

"Step along, please," said Mary Poppins, briskly. "I might as well be taking a stroll with a couple of snails as you two!"

But when they caught up with her she kept them waiting for quite five minutes outside a fried-fish shop while she looked at herself in the window.

She was wearing her new white blouse with the pink

spots and her face, as she beheld herself reflected back
from the piles of fried whiting, had a pleased and satisfied air. She pushed back her coat a little so that more
of the blouse was visible, and she thought that, on the
whole, she had never seen Mary Poppins look nicer.
Even the fried fish, with their fried tails curled into
their mouths, seemed to gaze at her with round admiring eyes.

Mary Poppins gave a little conceited nod to her reflection and hurried on. They had passed the High Street
now and were crossing the Bridge. Soon they came to the
Railway Arch and Jane and Michael sprang eagerly ahead
of the perambulator and ran all the way until they turned
the corner of Cherry-Tree Lane.

"There's a cab," cried Michael excitedly. "That must be
Miss Andrew's."

They stood still at the corner waiting for Mary Poppins and watching for Miss Andrew.

A Taxi-cab, moving slowly down the Lane, drew up at the gate of Number Seventeen. It groaned and rattled as the engine stopped. And this was not surprising for from wheel to roof it was heavily weighted with luggage. You could hardly see the cab itself for the trunks on the roof and the trunks at the back and the trunks on either side.

Suit-cases and hampers could be seen half in and half out of the windows. Hat-boxes were strapped to the steps and two large Gladstone bags appeared to be sitting in the Driver's seat.

Presently the Driver himself emerged from under them. He climbed out carefully as though he were descending a steep mountain, and opened the door.

A boot-box came bounding out, followed by a large brown-paper parcel and after these came an umbrella and a walking stick tied together with string. Last of all a small weighing-machine clattered down from the rack, knocking the Taxi-man down.

"Be careful! Be careful!" a huge, trumpeting voice shouted from inside the Taxi. "This is valuable luggage!"

"And I'm a valuable driver!" retorted the Taxi-man, picking himself up and rubbing his ankle. "You seem to 'ave forgotten that, 'aven't you?"

"Make way, please, make way! I'm coming out!" called the huge voice again.

And at that moment there appeared on the step of the cab the largest foot the children had ever seen. It was followed by the rest of Miss Andrew.

A large coat with a fur collar was wrapped about her, a man's felt hat was perched on her head and from the hat floated a long grey veil.

The children crept cautiously along by the fence, gazing with interest at the huge figure, with its beaked nose, grim mouth and small eyes that peered angrily from behind glasses. They were almost deafened by her voice as she argued with the Taxi-man.

"Four and threepence!" she was saying. "Preposterous! I could go half-way round the world for that amount. I shan't pay it! And I shall report you to the Police."

The Taxi-man shrugged his shoulders. "That's the fare," he said calmly. "If you can read, you can read it on the meter. You can't go driving in a Taxi for love, you know, not with this luggage."

Miss Andrew snorted and, diving her hand into her large pocket took out a very small purse. She handed over a coin. The Taxi-man looked at it, turned it over and over in his hand as if he thought it a curiosity. Then he laughed rudely.

"This for the Driver?" he remarked sarcastically.

"Certainly not. It's your fare. I don't approve of tips," said Miss Andrew.

"You wouldn't," said the Taxi-man, staring at her.

And to himself he remarked — "Enough luggage to fill 'arf the Park and she doesn't approve of tips — the 'Arpy!"

But Miss Andrew did not hear him. The children had arrived at the gate and she turned to greet them, her feet ringing on the pavement and the veil flowing out behind her.

"Well?" she said gruffly, smiling a thin smile. "I don't suppose you know who *I* am?"

"Oh, yes we do!" said Michael. He spoke in his friendliest voice for he was very glad to meet Miss Andrew. "You're the Holy Terror!"

A dark purple flush rose up from Miss Andrew's neck and flooded her face.

"You are a very rude, impertinent boy. I shall report you to your Father!"

Michael looked surprised. "I didn't mean to be rude," he began. "It was Daddy who said —— "

"Tut! Silence! Don't dare to argue with me!" said Miss Andrew. She turned to Jane.

"And you're Jane, I suppose? H'm. I never cared for the name."

"How do you do?" said Jane, politely, but secretly thinking she did not care much for the name Euphemia.

"That dress is much too short!" trumpeted Miss Andrew, "and you ought to be wearing stockings. Little girls in my day never had bare legs. I shall speak to your Mother."

"I don't like stockings," said Jane. "I only wear them in the Winter."

"Don't be impudent. Children should be seen and not heard!" said Miss Andrew.

She leaned over the perambulator and with her huge hand, pinched the Twins' cheeks in greeting.

John and Barbara began to cry.

"Tut! What manners!" exclaimed Miss Andrew. "Brimstone and treacle — that's what they need!" she went on, turning to Mary Poppins. "No well-brought-up child cries like that. Brimstone and treacle. And plenty of it. Don't forget!"

"Thank you, ma'am," said Mary Poppins with icy politeness. "But I bring the children up in my own way and take advice from nobody"

Miss Andrew stared. She looked as if she could not believe her ears.

Mary Poppins stared back, calm and unafraid.

"Young woman!" said Miss Andrew, drawing herself up. "You forget yourself. How dare you answer me like that! I shall take steps to have you removed from this establishment! Mark my words!"

She flung open the gate and strode up the path, furiously swinging the circular object under the checked cloth, and saying "Tut-tut!" over and over again.

Mrs. Banks came running out to meet her.

"Welcome, Miss Andrew, welcome!" she said politely.

"How kind of you to pay us a visit. Such an unexpected pleasure. I hope you had a good journey."

"Most unpleasant. I never enjoy travelling," said Miss Andrew. She glanced with an angry, peering eye round the garden.

"Disgracefully untidy!" she remarked disgustedly. "Take my advice and dig up those things —— " she pointed to the sunflowers, "and plant evergreens. Much less trouble. Saves time *and* money. And looks neater. Better still, no garden at all. Just a plain cement courtyard."

"But," protested Mrs. Banks gently, "I like flowers best!"

"Ridiculous! Stuff and nonsense! You are a silly woman. And your children are very rude — especially the boy."

"Oh, Michael — I *am* surprised! Were you rude to Miss Andrew? You must apologise at once." Mrs. Banks was getting very nervous and flustered.

"No, Mother, I wasn't. I only —— " He began to explain but Miss Andrew's loud voice interrupted.

"He was most insulting," she insisted. "He must go to a boarding-school at once. And the girl must have a Governess. I shall choose one myself. And as for the young person you have looking after them —— " she nodded in the direction of Mary Poppins, "you must dismiss her this instant. She is impertinent, incapable and totally unreliable."

Mrs. Banks was plainly horrified.

"Oh, surely you are mistaken, Miss Andrew! We think she is such a treasure."

"You know nothing about it. I am *never* mistaken. Dismiss her!"

Miss Andrew swept on up the path.

Mrs. Banks hurried behind her looking very worried and upset.

"I — er — hope we shall be able to make you comfortable, Miss Andrew!" she said, politely. But she was beginning to feel rather doubtful.

"H'm. It's not much of a house," replied Miss Andrew. "And it's in a shocking condition — peeling everywhere and most dilapidated. You must send for a carpenter. And when were these steps whitewashed? They're very dirty."

Mrs. Banks bit her lip. Miss Andrew was turning her lovely, comfortable house into something mean and shabby, and it made her feel very unhappy.

"I'll have them done to-morrow," she said meekly.

"Why not to-day?" demanded Miss Andrew. "No time like the present. And why paint your door white? Dark brown — that's the proper colour for a door. Cheaper, and doesn't show the dirt. Just look at those spots!"

And putting down the circular object, she began to point out the marks on the front door.

"There! There! There! Everywhere! Most disreputable!"

"I'll see to it immediately," said Mrs. Banks faintly. "Won't you come upstairs now to your room?"

Miss Andrew stamped into the hall after her.

"I hope there is a fire in it."

"Oh, yes. A good one. This way, Miss Andrew. Robertson Ay will bring up your luggage."

"Well, tell him to be careful. The trunks are full of medicine bottles. I have to take care of my health!" Miss Andrew moved towards the stairs. She glanced round the hall.

"This wall needs re-papering. I shall speak to George about it. And why, I should like to know, wasn't he here to meet me? Very rude of him. His manners, I see, have not improved!"

The voice grew a little fainter as Miss Andrew followed Mrs. Banks upstairs. Far away the children could hear their Mother's gentle voice, meekly agreeing to do whatever Miss Andrew wished.

Michael turned to Jane.

"Who is George?" he asked.

"Daddy."

"But his name is Mr. Banks."

"Yes, but his other name is George."

Michael sighed.

"A month is an awfully long time, Jane, isn't it?"

"Yes — four weeks and a bit," said Jane, feeling that a month with Miss Andrew would seem more like a year.

Michael edged closer to her.

"I say——" he began in an anxious whisper. "She can't really make them send Mary Poppins away, can she?"

"No, I don't think so. But she's very odd. I don't wonder Daddy went out."

"Odd!"

The word sounded behind them like an explosion.

They turned. Mary Poppins was gazing after Miss Andrew with a look that could have killed her.

"Odd!" she repeated with a long-drawn sniff. "*That's* not the word for her. Humph! I don't know how to bring up children, don't I? I'm impertinent, incapable, and to-tally unreliable, am I? We'll see about that!"

Jane and Michael were used to threats from Mary Poppins but to-day there was a note in her voice they had never heard before. They stared at her in silence, wondering what was going to happen.

A tiny sound, partly a sigh and partly a whistle, fell on the air.

"What was that?" said Jane quickly.

The sound came again, a little louder this time. Mary Poppins cocked her head and listened.

Again a faint chirping seemed to come from the door-step.

"Ah!" cried Mary Poppins, triumphantly. "I might have known it!"

And with a sudden movement, she sprang at the circular object Miss Andrew had left behind and tweaked off the cover.

Beneath it was a brass bird-cage, very neat and shiny. And sitting at one end of the perch, huddled between his wings, was a small light-brown bird. He blinked a little as the afternoon light streamed down upon his head. Then he gazed solemnly about him with a round dark eye. His glance fell upon Mary Poppins and with a start of recognition he opened his beak and gave a sad, throaty little cheep. Jane and Michael had never heard such a miserable sound.

"Did she, indeed? Tch, tch, tch! You don't say!" said Mary Poppins nodding her head sympathetically.

"Chirp-irrup!" said the bird, shrugging its wings dejectedly.

"What? Two years? In that cage? Shame on her!" said Mary Poppins to the bird, her face flushing with anger.

The children stared. The bird was speaking in no language they knew and yet here was Mary Poppins carrying on an intelligent conversation with him as though she understood.

"What is it saying —— " Michael began.

"Sh!" said Jane, pinching his arm to make him keep quiet.

They stared at the bird in silence. Presently he hopped a little way along the perch towards Mary Poppins and sang a note or two in a low questioning voice.

Mary Poppins nodded. "Yes — of course I know that field. Was that where she caught you?"

The bird nodded. Then he sang a quick trilling phrase that sounded like a question.

Mary Poppins thought for a moment. "Well," she said. "It's not very far. You could do it in about an hour. Flying South from here."

The bird seemed pleased. He danced a little on his perch and flapped his wings excitedly. Then his song broke out again, a stream of round, clear notes, as he looked imploringly at Mary Poppins.

She turned her head and glanced cautiously up the stairs.

"*Will* I? What do *you* think? Didn't you hear her call me a Young Person? Me!" She sniffed disgustedly.

The bird's shoulders shook as though he were laughing.

Mary Poppins bent down.

"What are you going to do, Mary Poppins?" cried Michael, unable to contain himself any longer. "What kind of a bird is that?"

"A lark," said Mary Poppins, briefly, turning the handle of the little door. "You're seeing a lark in a cage for the first time — and the last!"

And as she said that the door of the cage swung open. The Lark, flapping his wings, swooped out with a shrill cry and alighted on Mary Poppins' shoulder.

"Humph!" she said, turning her head. "That's an improvement, I should think?"

"Chirr-up!" agreed the Lark, nodding.

"Well, you'd better be off," Mary Poppins warned him. "She'll be back in a minute."

At that the Lark burst into a stream of running notes, flicking its wings at her and bowing his head again and again.

"There, there!" said Mary Poppins, gruffly. "Don't thank me. I was glad to do it. I couldn't see a Lark in a cage! Besides, you heard what she called me!"

The Lark tossed back his head and fluttered his wings. He seemed to be laughing heartily. Then he cocked his head on one side and listened.

"Oh, I quite forgot!" came a trumpeting voice from upstairs. "I left Caruso outside. On those dirty steps. I must go and get him."

Miss Andrew's heavy tread sounded on the stairs.

"What?" she called back in reply to some question of Mrs. Banks. "Oh, he's my lark, my lark, Caruso! I call him that because he used to be such a beautiful singer. What? No, he doesn't sing at all now, not since I trapped him in the field and put him in a cage. I can't think why."

The voice was coming nearer, growing louder as it approached.

"Certainly not!" it called back to Mrs. Banks. "I will fetch him myself. I wouldn't trust one of those impudent children with him. Your banisters want polishing. They should be done at once."

Tramp-tramp. Tramp-tramp. Miss Andrew's steps sounded through the hall.

"Here she comes!" hissed Mary Poppins. "Be off with you!" She gave her shoulder a little shake.

"Quickly!" cried Michael anxiously.

"Oh, hurry!" said Jane.

The Twins waved their hands.

With a quick movement the Lark bent his head and pulled out one of his wing feathers with his beak.

"Chirr-chirr-chirr-irrup!" he sang and stuck the feather into the ribbon of Mary Poppins' hat. Then he spread his wings and swept into the air.

At the same moment Miss Andrew appeared in the doorway.

"What?" she shouted, when she saw Jane and Michael and the Twins. "Not gone up to bed yet? This will never do. All well-brought-up children —— " she looked balefully at Mary Poppins, "should be in bed by five o'clock. I shall certainly speak to your Father."

She glanced round.

"Now, let me see. Where did I leave my —— " She broke off suddenly. The uncovered cage, with its open door, stood at her feet. She stared down at it as though she were unable to believe her eyes.

"Why? When? Where? What? Who?" she spluttered. Then she found her full voice.

"Who took off that cover?" she thundered. The children trembled at the sound.

"Who opened that cage?"

There was no reply.

"*Where is my Lark?*"

Still there was silence as Miss Andrew stared from one child to another. At last her gaze fell accusingly upon Mary Poppins.

"You did it!" she cried, pointing her large finger. "I can tell by the look on your face! How dare you! I shall see

that you leave this house to-night — bag and baggage!
You impudent, impertinent, worthless ——"

Chirp-irrup!

From the air came a little trill of laughter. Miss Andrew
looked up. The Lark was lightly balancing on his wings
just above the sunflowers.

"Ah, Caruso — there you are!" cried Miss Andrew.
"Now come along! Don't keep me waiting. Come back to
your nice, clean cage, Caruso, and let me shut the door!"

But the Lark just hung in the air and went into peals
of laughter, flinging back his head and clapping his wings
against his sides.

Miss Andrew bent and picked up the cage and held it
above her head.

"Caruso — what did I say? Come back at once!" she
commanded, swinging the cage towards him. But he
swooped past it and brushed against Mary Poppins' hat.

"Chirp-irrup!" he said, as he sped by.

"All right," said Mary Poppins, nodding in reply.

"Caruso, did you hear me?" cried Miss Andrew. But
now there was a hint of dismay in her loud voice. She put
down the cage and tried to catch the Lark with her hands.
But he dodged and flickered past her, and with a lift of his
wings, dived higher into the air.

A babble of notes streamed down to Mary Poppins.

"Ready!" she called back.

And then a strange thing happened.

Mary Poppins fixed her eyes upon Miss Andrew and

Miss Andrew, suddenly spell-bound by that strange dark gaze, began to tremble on her feet. She gave a little gasp, staggered uncertainly forward and with a thundering rush she dashed towards the cage. Then — was it that Miss Andrew grew smaller or the cage larger? Jane and Michael could not be sure. All they knew for certain was that the cage door shut to with a little click and closed upon Miss Andrew.

"Oh! Oh! Oh!" she cried, as the Lark swooped down and seized the cage by the handle.

"What am I doing? Where am I going?" Miss Andrew shouted as the cage swept into the air.

"I have no room to move! I can hardly breathe!" she cried.

"Neither could he!" said Mary Poppins quietly.

Miss Andrew rattled at the bars of the cage.

"Open the door! Open the door! Let me out, I say! Let me out!"

"Humph! Not likely," said Mary Poppins in a low, scoffing voice.

On and on went the Lark, climbing higher and higher and singing as he went. And the heavy cage, with Miss Andrew inside it, lurched after him, swaying dangerously as it swung from his claw.

Above the clear song of the Lark they heard Miss Andrew hammering at the bars and crying:

"I who was Well-Brought-Up! I who was Always Right! I who was Never Mistaken. That I should come to this!"

Mary Poppins gave a curious, quiet little laugh.

The Lark looked very small now, but still he circled upwards, singing loudly and triumphantly. And still Miss Andrew and her cage circled heavily after him, rocking from side to side, like a ship in a storm.

"Let me out, I say! Let me out!" Her voice came screaming down.

Suddenly the Lark changed his direction. His song ceased for a moment as he darted sideways. Then it began again, wild and clear, as shaking the ring of the cage from his foot, he flew towards the South.

"He's off!" said Mary Poppins.

"Where?" cried Jane and Michael.

"Home — to his meadows," she replied, gazing upwards.

"But he's dropped the cage!" said Michael, staring.

And well he might stare, for the cage was now hurtling downwards, lurching and tumbling, end over end. They could clearly see Miss Andrew, now standing on her head and now on her feet as the cage turned through the air. Down, down, it came, heavy as a stone, and landed with a plop on the top step.

With a fierce movement, Miss Andrew tore open the door. And it seemed to Jane and Michael as she came out that she was as large as ever and even more frightful.

For a moment she stood there, panting, unable to speak, her face purplier than before.

"How dare you!" she said in a throaty whisper, point-

"Let me out, I say! Let me out!"

ing a trembling finger at Mary Poppins. And Jane and Michael saw that her eyes were no longer angry and scornful, but full of terror.

"You — you — — " stammered Miss Andrew huskily, "you cruel, disrespectful, unkind, wicked, wilful girl — how could you, how could you?"

Mary Poppins fixed her with a look. From half-closed eyes, she gazed revengefully at Miss Andrew for a long moment.

"You said I didn't know how to bring up children," she said, speaking slowly and distinctly.

Miss Andrew shrank back, trembling with fear.

"I — I apologise," she said, gulping.

"That I was impudent, incapable, and totally unreliable," said the quiet, implacable voice.

Miss Andrew cowered beneath the steady gaze.

"It was a mistake. I — I'm sorry," she stammered.

"That I was a Young Person!" continued Mary Poppins, remorselessly.

"I take it back," panted Miss Andrew. "All of it. Only let me go. I ask nothing more." She clasped her hands and gazed at Mary Poppins, imploringly.

"I can't stay here," she whispered. "No, no! Not here! I beg you to let me go!"

Mary Poppins gazed at her, long and thoughtfully. Then with a little outward movement of her hand, "Go!" she said.

Miss Andrew gave a gasp of relief. "Oh, thank you! Thank you!" Still keeping her eyes fixed on Mary Poppins she staggered backwards down the steps, then she turned and went stumbling unevenly down the garden path.

The Taxi-man, who all this time had been unloading the luggage, was starting up his engine and preparing to depart.

Miss Andrew held up a trembling hand.

"Wait!" she cried brokenly. "Wait for me. You shall have a ten shilling note for yourself if you will drive me away at once."

The man stared at her.

"I mean it!" she said urgently. "See," she fumbled fever-ishly in her pocket, "here it is. Take it — and drive on!"

Miss Andrew tottered into the cab and collapsed upon the seat.

The Taxi-man, still gaping, closed the door upon her.

Then he began hurriedly re-loading the luggage. Robertson Ay had fallen asleep across a pile of trunks, but the Taxi-man did not stop to wake him. He swept him off on to the path and finished the work himself.

"Looks as though the 'ol' girl 'ad 'ad a shock! I never saw anybody take on so. Never!" he murmured to himself as he drove off.

But what kind of a shock it was the Taxi-man did not know and, if he lived to be a hundred, could not possibly guess. . . .

"Where is Miss Andrew?" said Mrs. Banks, hurrying to the front door in search of the visitor.

"Gone," said Michael.

"What do you mean — gone?" Mrs. Banks looked very surprised.

"She didn't seem to want to stay," said Jane.

Mrs. Banks frowned.

"What does this mean, Mary Poppins?" she de-manded.

"I couldn't say, m'm, I'm sure," said Mary Poppins, calmly, as though the matter did not interest her. She glanced down at her new blouse and smoothed out a crease.

Mrs. Banks looked from one to the other and shook her head.

"How very extraordinary! I can't understand it."

Just then the garden-gate opened and shut with a quiet little click. Mr. Banks came tip-toeing up the path. He hesitated and waited nervously on one foot as they all turned towards him.

"Well? Has she come?" he said anxiously, in a loud whisper.

"She has come and gone," said Mrs. Banks.

Mr. Banks stared.

"Gone? Do you mean — really gone? Miss Andrew?"

Mrs. Banks nodded.

"Oh, joy, joy!" cried Mr. Banks, and seizing the skirts of his waterproof in both hands he proceeded to dance the Highland Fling in the middle of the path. He stopped suddenly.

"But how? When? Why?" he asked.

"Just now — in a taxi. Because the children were rude to her, I suppose. She complained to me about them. I simply can't think of any other reason. Can you, Mary Poppins?"

"No, m'm, I can't," said Mary Poppins, brushing a speck of dust off her blouse with great care.

Mr. Banks turned to Jane and Michael with a sorrowful look on his face.

"You were rude to Miss Andrew? My Governess? That

dear old soul? I'm ashamed of you both — thoroughly ashamed." He spoke sternly, but there was a laughing twinkle in his eyes.

"I'm a most unfortunate man," he went on, putting his hands into his pockets. "Here am I slaving day in and day out to bring you up properly, and how do you repay me? By being rude to Miss Andrew! It's shameful! It's outrageous. I don't know that I shall ever be able to forgive you. But —— " he continued, taking two sixpences out of his pocket and solemnly offering one to each of them, "I shall do my best to forget!"

He turned away smiling.

"Hullo!" he remarked, stumbling against the birdcage. "Where did this come from? Whose is it?"

Jane and Michael and Mary Poppins were silent.

"Well, never mind," said Mr. Banks. "It's mine now. I shall keep it in the garden and train my sweet-peas over it."

And he went off, carrying the bird-cage and whistling very happily. . . .

"Well," said Mary Poppins, sternly, as she followed them into the Nursery. "This is nice goings on, I must say. You behaving so rudely to your Father's guest."

"But we weren't rude," Michael protested. "I only said she was a Holy Terror and he called her that himself."

"Sending her away like that when she'd only just come — don't you call that rude?" demanded Mary Poppins.

"But we didn't," said Jane. "It was you —— "

"*I* was rude to your Father's guest?" Mary Poppins, with her hands on her hips, eyed Jane furiously "Do you dare to stand there and tell me that?"

"No, no! You weren't rude, but —— "

"I should think not, indeed," retorted Mary Poppins, taking off her hat and unfolding her apron. "*I* was properly brought up!" she added sniffing, as she began to undress the Twins.

Michael sighed. He knew it was no use arguing with Mary Poppins.

He glanced at Jane. She was turning her sixpence over and over in her hand.

"Michael!" she said. "I've been thinking."

"What?"

"Daddy gave us these because he thought *we* sent Miss Andrew away."

"I know."

"And we didn't. It was Mary Poppins!"

Michael shuffled his feet.

"Then you think —— " he began uneasily, hoping she didn't mean what he thought she meant.

"Yes, I do," said Jane nodding.

"But — but I wanted to spend mine."

"So did I. But it wouldn't be fair. They're hers really."

Michael thought about it for a long time. Then he sighed.

"All right," he said regretfully and took his sixpence out of his pocket.

They went together to Mary Poppins.

Jane held out the coins.

"Here you are!" she said, breathlessly, "we think you should have them."

Mary Poppins took the sixpences and turned them over and over on her palm — heads first and then tails. Then her eye caught theirs and it seemed to them that her look plunged right down inside them and *saw* what they were thinking. For a long time she stood there, staring down into their thoughts.

"Humph!" she said at last, slipping the sixpences into her apron pocket. "Take care of the pennies and the pounds will take care of themselves."

"I expect you'll find them very useful," said Michael, gazing sadly at the pocket.

"I expect I shall," she retorted tartly, as she went to turn on the bath. . . .

CHAPTER THREE

BAD WEDNESDAY

ick-tack! Tick-tock!

The pendulum of the Nursery clock swung backwards and forwards like an old lady nodding her head.

Tick-tack! Tick-tock!

Then the clock stopped ticking and began to whir and growl, quietly at first and then more loudly, as though it were in pain. And as it whirred it shook so violently that the whole mantelpiece trembled. The empty marmalade jar hopped and shook and shivered; John's hair-brush, left there overnight, danced in its bristles; the Royal Doulton Bowl that Mrs. Banks' Great-Aunt Caroline had given her as a Christening Present slipped sideways, so that the three little boys who were playing horses inside it stood on their painted heads.

And after all that, just when it seemed as if the clock must burst, it began to strike.

One! Two! Three! Four! Five! Six! Seven!

On the last stroke Jane woke up.

The sun was streaming in through a gap in the curtains and falling in gold stripes upon her quilt. Jane sat up and looked round the Nursery. No sound came from Michael's bed. The Twins in their cots were sucking their thumbs and breathing deeply.

"I'm the only one awake," she said, feeling very pleased. "Everybody in the world is asleep except me. I can lie here all by myself and think and think and think."

And she drew her knees up to her chin and curled into the bed as though she were settling down into a nest.

"Now I am a bird!" she said to herself. "I have just laid

seven lovely white eggs and I am sitting with my wings over them, brooding. Cluck-cluck! Cluck-cluck!"

She made a small broody noise in her throat.

"And after a long time, say half an hour, there will be a little cheep, and a little tap and the shells will crack. Then, out will pop seven little chicks, three yellow, two brown and two —— "

"Time to get up!"

Mary Poppins, appearing suddenly from nowhere, tweaked the bedclothes from Jane's shoulders.

"Oh, no, NO!" grumbled Jane, pulling them up again.

She felt very cross with Mary Poppins for rushing in and spoiling everything.

"I don't want to get up!" she said, turning her face into the pillow.

"Oh, indeed?" Mary Poppins said calmly, as though the remark had no interest for her. She pulled the bedclothes right off the bed and Jane found herself standing on the floor.

"Oh, dear," she grumbled, "why do I always have to get up first?"

"You're the eldest — that's why." Mary Poppins pushed her towards the bath-room.

"But I don't *want* to be the eldest. Why can't Michael be the eldest sometimes?"

"Because you were born first — see?"

"Well, I didn't ask to be. I'm tired of being born first. I wanted to think."

"You can think when you're brushing your teeth."

"Not the same thoughts."

"Well, nobody wants to think the same thoughts all the time!"

"I do."

Mary Poppins gave her a quick, black look.

"That's enough, thank you!" And from the tone in her voice Jane knew she meant what she said.

Mary Poppins hurried away to wake Michael.

Jane put down her toothbrush and sat on the edge of the bath.

"It's not fair," she grumbled, kicking the linoleum with her toes. "Making me do all the horrid things just because I'm the eldest! I won't brush my teeth!"

Immediately she felt surprised at herself. She was usually quite glad to be older than Michael and the Twins. It made her feel rather superior and much more important. But to-day — what was the matter with to-day that she felt so cross and peevish?

"If Michael had been born first I'd have had time to hatch out my eggs!" She grumbled to herself, feeling that the day had begun badly.

Unfortunately, instead of getting better, it grew worse.

At breakfast Mary Poppins discovered there was only enough Puffed Rice for three.

"Well, Jane must have Porridge," she said, setting out the plates and sniffing angrily for she did not like making Porridge. There were always too many lumps in it.

"But why?" complained Jane. "I want Puffed Rice."

Mary Poppins darted a fierce look at her.

"Because you're the eldest!"

There it was again! That hateful word. She kicked the leg of her chair under the table, hoping she was scratching off the varnish, and ate her porridge as slowly as she dared. She turned it round and round in her mouth swallowing as little as possible. It would serve everybody right if she starved to death. Then they'd be sorry!

"What is to-day?" enquired Michael cheerfully, scraping up the last of his Puffed Rice.

"Wednesday," said Mary Poppins. "Leave the pattern on the plate, please!"

"Then it's to-day we're going to tea with Miss Lark!"

"*If* you're good," said Mary Poppins darkly, as though she did not believe such a thing was possible.

But Michael was in a cheerful mood and took no notice.

"Wednesday!" he shouted, banging his spoon on the table. "That's the day Jane was born. Wednesday's child is full of woe. That's why she has to have porridge instead of rice," he said naughtily.

Jane frowned and kicked at him under the table. But he swung his legs aside and laughed.

"Monday's child is fair of face, Tuesday's child is full of grace!" He chanted. "That's true, too. The Twins are full of grace and they were born on a Tuesday. And I'm Monday — fair of face."

Jane laughed scornfully.

"I am," he insisted. "I heard Mrs. Brill say so. She told Ellen I was as handsome as half-a-crown."

"Well, that's not very handsome," said Jane. "Besides, your nose turns up."

Michael looked at her reproachfully. And again Jane felt surprised at herself. At any other time she would have agreed with him, for she thought Michael a very good-looking little boy. But now she said cruelly,

"Yes, and your toes turn in. Bandy-legs! Bandy-legs!"

Michael rushed at her.

"That will be enough from you!" said Mary Poppins, looking angrily at Jane. "And if any body in this house is a beauty it's —— " She paused and glanced with a satisfied smile at her own reflection in the mirror.

"Who?" demanded Michael and Jane together.

"Nobody of the name of Banks!" retorted Mary Poppins. "So there!"

Michael looked across at Jane as he always did when Mary Poppins made one of her curious remarks. But though she felt his look she pretended not to notice. She turned away and took her paint-box from the toy-cupboard.

"Won't you play trains?" asked Michael, trying to be friendly.

"No, I won't. I want to be by myself."

"Well, darlings, and how are you all this morning?"

Mrs. Banks came running into the room and kissed them hurriedly. She was always so busy that she never had time to walk.

"Michael," she said, "you must have some new slippers — your toes are coming out at the top. Mary Poppins, John's curls will *have* to come off, I'm afraid. Barbara, my pet, don't suck your thumb! Jane, run downstairs and ask Mrs. Brill not to ice the plum cake, I want a plain one."

There they were again, breaking into her day! As soon as she began to do anything they made her stop and do something else.

"Oh, Mother, must I? Why can't Michael?"

Mrs. Banks looked surprised.

"But I thought you liked helping! And Michael always forgets the message. Besides, you're the eldest. Run along."

She went downstairs as slowly as she could. She hoped she would be so late with the message that Mrs. Brill would have already iced the cake.

And all the time she felt astonished at the way she was behaving. It was as if there was another person inside her — somebody with a very bad temper and an ugly face — who was making her feel cross.

She gave the message to Mrs. Brill and was disappointed to find that she was in plenty of time.

"Well, that'll save a penn'orth of trouble anyway," Mrs. Brill remarked.

"And, Dearie," she went on, "you might just slip out into the garden and tell that Robertson he hasn't done the knives. My legs are bad and they're my only pair."

"I can't. I'm busy."

It was Mrs. Brill's turn to look surprised.

"Ah, be a kind girl, then — it's all I can do to stand, let alone walk!"

Jane sighed. Why couldn't they leave her alone? She kicked the kitchen door shut and dawdled out into the garden.

Robertson Ay was asleep on the path with his head on the watering-can. His lank hair rose and fell as he snored. It was Robertson Ay's special gift that he could sleep anywhere and at any time. In fact, he preferred sleeping to waking. And, usually, whenever they could, Jane and Michael prevented him from being found out. But to-day was different. The bad-tempered person inside her didn't care a bit what happened to Robertson Ay.

"I hate everybody!" she said, and rapped sharply on the watering-can.

Robertson Ay sat up with a start.

"Help! Murder! Fire!" he cried, waving his arms wildly.

Then he rubbed his eyes and saw Jane.

"Oh, it's only you!" he said, in a disappointed voice as if he had hoped for something more exciting.

"You're to go and do the knives at once," she ordered.

Robertson Ay got slowly to his feet and shook himself.

"Ah," he said sadly, "it's always something. If it's not one thing, it's another. I ought to be resting. I never get a moment's peace."

"Yes, you do!" said Jane cruelly. "You get nothing but peace. You're always asleep."

A hurt, reproachful look came over Robertson Ay's face, and at any other time it would have made her feel ashamed. But to-day she wasn't a bit sorry.

"Saying such things!" said Robertson Ay sadly. "And you the eldest and all. I wouldn't have thought it — not if I'd done nothing but think for the rest of my life."

And he gave her a sorrowful glance and shuffled slowly away to the kitchen.

She wondered if he would ever forgive her. And, as if in reply, the sulky creature inside her said, "I don't care if he doesn't!"

She tossed her head and went slowly back to the Nursery dragging her sticky hands along the fresh white wall because she had always been told not to.

Mary Poppins was flicking her feather duster round the furniture.

"Off to a funeral?" she enquired as Jane appeared.

Jane looked sulky and did not answer.

"I know somebody who's looking for Trouble. And he that seeks shall find!"

"I don't care!"

"Don't Care was made care! Don't Care was hung!" jeered Mary Poppins, putting the duster away.

"And now —— " she looked warningly at Jane. "I am going to have my dinner. You are to look after the little ones and if I hear One Word —— " She did not finish the sentence but she gave a long threatening sniff as she went out of the room.

John and Barbara ran to Jane and caught her hands. But she uncurled their fingers and crossly pushed them away.

"I wish I were an only child," she said bitterly.

"Why don't you run away," suggested Michael. "Somebody might adopt you."

Jane looked up, startled and surprised.

"But you'd miss me!"

"No, I wouldn't," he said stoutly. "Not if you're always going to be cross. Besides, then I could have your paint-box."

"No, you couldn't," she said jealously. "I'd take it with me."

And, just to show him that the paint-box was hers and not his, she got out the brushes and the painting-book and spread them on the floor.

"Paint the clock," said Michael helpfully.

"No."

"Well, the Royal Doulton Bowl."

Jane glanced up. The three little boys were racing over the field inside the green rim of the bowl. At any other time she would have liked to paint them but today she was not going to be pleasant or obliging.

"I won't. I will paint what *I* want."

And she began to make a picture of herself, quite alone, brooding over her eggs.

Michael and John and Barbara sat on the floor watching.

Jane was so interested in her eggs that she almost forgot her bad temper.

Michael leaned forward. "Why not put in a hen — just there!"

He pointed to a spare white patch, brushing against John with his arm. Over went John, falling sideways and upsetting the cup with his foot. The coloured water splashed out and flooded the picture.

With a cry Jane sprang to her feet.

"Oh, I can't bear it. You great Clumsy! You've spoilt everything!"

And, rushing at Michael, she punched him so violently that he, too, toppled over and crashed down on top of John. A squeal of pain and terror broke from the Twins, and above their cries rose Michael's voice wailing "My head is broken! What shall I do? My head is broken!" over and over again.

"I don't care, I don't care!" shouted Jane. "You wouldn't leave me alone and you've spoilt my picture. I hate you, I hate you, I hate —— !"

The door burst open.

Mary Poppins surveyed the scene with furious eyes.

"What did I say to you?" she enquired of Jane in a voice so quiet that it was terrible. "That if I heard One Word — and now look what I find! A nice party you'll have at Miss Lark's, I *don't* think! Not one step will you go out of this room this afternoon or I'm a Chinaman."

"I don't *want* to go. I'd rather stay here." Jane put her hands behind her back and sauntered away. She did not feel a bit sorry.

"Very good."

Mary Poppins' voice was gentle but there was something very frightening in it.

Jane watched her dressing the others for the party. And when they were ready Mary Poppins took her best hat out of a brown-paper bag and set it on her head at a very smart angle. She clipped her gold locket round her neck and over it wound the red-and-white checked scarf Mrs. Banks had given her. At one end was stitched a white label marked with a large M.P., and Mary Poppins smiled at herself in the mirror as she tucked the label out of sight.

Then she took her parrot-handled umbrella from the cupboard, popped it under her arm and hurried the little ones down the stairs.

"Now you'll have time to think!" she remarked tartly, and, with a loud sniff, shut the door behind her.

For a long time Jane sat staring in front of her. She tried to think about her seven eggs. But somehow they didn't interest her any more.

What were they doing now, at Miss Lark's? she wondered. Playing with Miss Lark's dogs, perhaps, and listening to Miss Lark telling them that Andrew had a wonderful pedigree but that Willoughby was half an Airedale and half a Retriever and the worst half of both. And presently they would all, even the dogs, have chocolate biscuits and walnut cake for tea.

"Oh, dear!"

The thought of all she was missing stirred angrily inside Jane and when she remembered it was all her own fault she felt crosser than ever.

Tick-tack! Tick-tock! said the clock loudly.

"Oh, be quiet!" cried Jane furiously, and picking up her paint-box she hurled it across the room.

It crashed against the glass face of the clock and, glancing off, clattered down upon the Royal Doulton Bowl.

Crrrrrrack! The Bowl toppled sideways against the clock.

Oh! Oh! What had she done?

Jane shut her eyes, not daring to look and see.

"I say — that hurt!"

A clear reproachful voice sounded in the room.

Jane started and opened her eyes.

"Jane!" said the voice again. "That was my knee!"

She turned her head quickly. There was nobody in the room.

She ran to the door and opened it. Still nobody!

Then somebody laughed.

"Here, silly!" said the voice again. "Up here!"

She looked up at the mantelpiece. Beside the clock lay the Royal Doulton Bowl with a large crack running right across it and, to her surprise, Jane saw that one of the painted boys had dropped the reins and was bending down holding his knee with both hands. The other two had turned and were looking at him sympathetically.

"But —— " began Jane, half to herself and half to the unknown voice. "I don't understand." The boy in the Bowl lifted his head and smiled at her.

"Don't you? No, I suppose you don't. I've noticed that

you and Michael often don't understand the simplest
things — do they?"

He turned, laughing, to his brothers.

"No," said one of them, "not even how to keep the
Twins quiet!"

"Nor the proper way to draw bird's eggs — she's made
them all wriggly," said the other.

"How do you know about the Twins — and the eggs?"
said Jane, flushing.

"Gracious!" said the first boy. "You don't think we
could have watched you all this time without knowing
everything that happens in this room! We can't see into
the Night-Nursery, of course, or the bathroom. What coloured tiles has it?"

"Pink," said Jane.

"Ours has blue-and-white. Would you like to see it?"

Jane hesitated. She hardly knew what to reply, she was
so astonished.

"Do come! William and Everard will be *your* horses,
if you like, and I'll carry the whip and run alongside. I'm
Valentine, in case you don't know. We're Triplets. And, of
course, there's Christina."

"Where's Christina?" Jane searched the Bowl. But she
saw only the green meadow and a little wood of alders and
Valentine, William and Everard standing together.

"Come and see!" said Valentine persuasively, holding
out his hand. "Why should the others have all the fun?
You come with us — into the Bowl!"

That decided her. She would show Michael that he and the Twins were not the only ones who could go to a party. She would make them jealous and sorry for treating her so badly.

"All right," she said, putting out her hand. "I'll come!"

Valentine's hand closed round her wrist and pulled her towards the Bowl. And, suddenly, she was no longer in the cool Day-Nursery but out in a wide sunlit meadow, and instead of the ragged nursery carpet, a springing turf of grass and daisies was spread beneath her feet.

"Hooray!" said Valentine, William and Everard, dancing round her. She noticed that Valentine was limping.

"Oh," said Jane. "I forgot! Your knee!"

He smiled at her. "Never mind. It was the crack that did it. I know you didn't mean to hurt me!"

Jane took out her handkerchief and bound it round his knee.

"That's better!" he said politely, and put the reins into her hand.

William and Everard, tossing their heads and snorting, flew off across the meadow with Jane jingling the reins behind them.

Beside her, one foot heavy and one foot light, because of his knee, ran Valentine.

And as he ran, he sang —

> "My love, thou art a nosegay sweet.
>   My sweetest flower I prove thee;

And pleased I pin thee to my breast,
    And dearly I do love thee!"

William and Everard's voices came in with the chorus,

"And deeeee-arly I do lo-o-ove thee!"

Jane thought it was rather an old-fashioned song, but then, everything about the Triplets was old-fashioned — their long hair, their strange clothes and their polite way of speaking.

"It *is* odd!" she thought to herself, but she also thought that this was better than being at Miss Lark's, and that Michael would envy her when she told him all about it.

On ran the horses, tugging Jane after them, drawing her away and away from the Nursery.

Presently she pulled up, panting, and looked back over the tracks their feet had made in the grass. Behind her, at the other side of the meadow, she could see the outer rim of the Bowl. It seemed small and very far away. And something inside her warned her that it was time to turn back.

"I must go now," she said, dropping the jingling reins.

"Oh, no, no!" cried the Triplets, closing round her.

And now something in their voices made her feel uneasy.

"They'll miss me at home. I'm afraid I must go," she said quickly.

"It's quite early!" protested Valentine. "They'll still be at Miss Lark's. Come on. I'll show you my paint-box."

Jane was tempted.

"Has it got Chinese White?" she enquired. For Chinese White was just what her own paint-box lacked.

"Yes, in a silver tube. Come!"

Against her will Jane allowed him to draw her onwards. She thought she would just have one look at the paint-box and then hurry back. She would not even ask to be allowed to use it.

"But where is your house? It isn't in the Bowl!"

"Of course it is! But you can't see it because it's behind the wood. Come on!"

They were drawing her now under dark alder boughs. The dead leaves cracked under their feet and every now and then a pigeon swooped from branch to branch with a loud clapping of wings. William showed Jane a robin's nest in a pile of twigs, and Everard broke off a spray of leaves and twined it round her head. But in spite of their friendliness Jane was shy and nervous and she felt very glad when they reached the end of the wood.

"Here it is!" said Valentine, waving his hand.

And she saw rising before her a huge stone house covered with ivy. It was older than any house she had ever seen and it seemed to lean towards her threateningly. On either side of the steps a stone lion crouched, as if waiting the moment to spring.

Jane shivered as the shadow of the house fell upon her.

"I can't stay long——" she said, uneasily. "It's getting late."

"Just five minutes!" pleaded Valentine, drawing her into the hall.

Their feet rang hollowly on the stone floor. There was no sign of any human being. Except for herself and the Triplets the house seemed deserted. A cold wind swept whistling along the corridor.

"Christina! Christina!" called Valentine, pulling Jane up the stairs. "Here she is!"

His cry went echoing round the house and every wall seemed to call back frighteningly.

"HERE SHE IS!"

There was a sound of running feet and a door burst open. A little girl, slightly taller than the Triplets and dressed in an old-fashioned, flowery dress, rushed out and flung herself upon Jane.

"At last, at last!" she cried triumphantly. "The boys have been watching for you for ages! But they couldn't catch you before — you were always so happy!"

"Catch me?" said Jane. "I don't understand!"

She was beginning to be frightened and to wish she had never come with Valentine into the Bowl.

"Great-Grandfather will explain," said Christina,

laughing curiously. She drew Jane across the landing and through the door.

"Heh! Heh! Heh! What's this?" demanded a thin, cracked voice.

Jane stared and drew back against Christina. For at the far end of the room, on a seat by the fire, sat a figure that filled her with terror. The firelight flickered over a very old man, so old that he looked more like a shadow than a human being. From his thin mouth a thin grey beard straggled and, though he wore a smoking cap, Jane could see that he was as bald as an egg. He was dressed in a long old-fashioned dressing-gown of faded silk, and a pair of embroidered slippers hung on his thin feet.

"So!" said the shadowy figure, taking a long curved pipe from his mouth. "Jane has arrived at last."

He rose and came towards her smiling frighteningly, his eyes burning in their sockets with a bright steely fire.

"I hope you had a good journey, my dear!" he croaked. And drawing Jane to him with a bony hand he kissed her cheek. At the touch of his grey beard Jane started back with a cry.

"Heh! Heh! Heh!" He laughed his cackling, terrifying laugh.

"She came through the alder wood with the boys, Great-Grandfather," said Christina.

"Ah? How did they catch her?"

"She was cross at being the eldest. So she threw her paint-box at the Bowl and cracked Val's knee."

"So!" the horrible old voice whistled. "It was temper, was it? Well, well——" he laughed thinly, "now you'll be the youngest, my dear! My youngest Great-Granddaughter. But I shan't allow any tempers here! Heh! Heh! Heh! Oh, dear, no. Well, come along and sit by the fire. Will you take tea or cherry-wine?"

"No, no!" Jane burst out. "I'm afraid there's been a mistake. I must go home now. I live at Number Seventeen Cherry-Tree Lane."

"Used to, you mean," corrected Val triumphantly. "You live here now."

"But you don't understand!" Jane said desperately. "I don't want to live here. I want to go home."

"Nonsense!" croaked the Great-Grandfather. "Number Seventeen is a horrible place, mean and stuffy and modern. Besides you're not happy there. Heh! Heh! Heh! I know what it's like being the eldest — all the work and none of the fun. Heh! Heh! But here——" he waved his pipe, "here you'll be the Spoilt One, the Darling, the Treasure, and never go back any more!"

"Never!" echoed William and Everard dancing round her.

"Oh, I must. I will!" Jane cried, the tears springing to her eyes.

The Great-Grandfather smiled his horrible toothless smile.

"Do you think we will let you go?" he enquired, his bright eyes burning. "You cracked our Bowl. You must take the consequences. Christina, Valentine, William and Everard want you for their youngest sister. I want you for my youngest Great-Grandchild. Besides, you owe us something. You hurt Valentine's knee."

"I will make up to him. I will give him my paintbox."

"He has one."

"My hoop."

"He has out-grown hoops."

"Well——" faltered Jane. "I will marry him when I grow up."

The Great-Grandfather cackled with laughter.

Jane turned imploringly to Valentine. He shook his head.

"I'm afraid it's too late for that," he said sadly. "I grew up long ago."

"Then why, then what—oh, I don't understand. Where am I?" cried Jane, gazing about her in terror.

"Far from home, my child, far from home," croaked the Great-Grandfather. "You are back in the Past—back where Christina and the boys were young sixty years ago!"

Through her tears Jane saw his old eyes burning fiercely.

"Then—how can I get home?" she whispered.

"You cannot. You will stay here. There is no other place for you. You are back in the Past, remember! The Twins and Michael, even your Father and Mother, are not yet

"Do you think we will let you go?" he enquired

born; Number Seventeen is not even built. You cannot go home!"

"No, no!" cried Jane. "It's not true! It can't be!" Her heart was thumping inside her. Never to see Michael again, nor the Twins, nor her Father and Mother and Mary Poppins!

And suddenly she began to shout, lifting her voice so that it echoed wildly through the stone corridors.

"Mary Poppins! I'm sorry I was cross! Oh, Mary Poppins, help me, help me!"

"Quick! Hold her close! Surround her!"

She heard the Great-Grandfather's sharp command. She felt the four children pressing close about her.

She shut her eyes tight. "Mary Poppins!" she cried again, "Mary Poppins!"

A hand caught hers and pulled her away from the circling arms of Christina, Valentine, William and Everard.

"Heh! Heh! Heh!"

The Great-Grandfather's cackling laugh echoed through the room. The grasp on her hand tightened and she felt herself being drawn away. She dared not look for fear of those frightening eyes but she pulled fiercely against the tugging hand.

"Heh! Heh! Heh!"

The laugh sounded again and the hand drew her on, down stone stairs and echoing corridors.

She had no hope now. Behind her the voices of

Christina and the Triplets faded away. No help would come from them.

She stumbled desperately after the flying footsteps and felt, though her eyes were closed, dark shadows above her head and damp earth under her feet.

What was happening to her? Where, oh, where was she going? If only she hadn't been so cross — if only!

The strong hand pulled her onwards and presently she felt the warmth of sunlight on her cheeks and sharp grass scratched her legs as she was dragged along. Then suddenly a pair of arms, like bands of iron, closed about her, lifted her up and swung her through the air.

"Oh, help, help!" She cried, frantically twisting and turning against those arms. She would not give in without a struggle, she would kick and kick and kick and ——

"I'll thank you to remember," said a familiar voice in her ear, "that this is my best skirt and it has to last me the Summer!"

Jane opened her eyes. A pair of fierce blue eyes looked steadily into hers.

The arms that folded her so closely were Mary Poppins' arms and the legs she was kicking so furiously were the legs of Mary Poppins.

"Oh!" she faltered. "It was *you!* I thought you hadn't heard me, Mary Poppins! I thought I should be kept there forever. I thought —— "

"Some people," remarked Mary Poppins, putting her

gently down, "think a great deal too much. Of that I'm sure. Wipe your face, please!"

She thrust her blue handkerchief into Jane's hand and began to get the Nursery ready for the evening.

Jane watched her, drying her tear-stained face on the large blue handkerchief. She glanced round the well-known room. There were the ragged carpet and the toy-cupboard and Mary Poppins' arm-chair. At the sight of them she felt safe and warm and comforted. She listened to the familiar sounds as Mary Poppins went about her work, and her terror died away. A tide of happiness swept over her.

"It couldn't have been I who was cross!" she said wonderingly to herself. "It must have been somebody else."

Mary Poppins went to a drawer and took out the Twins' clean nightgowns.

Jane ran to her.

"Shall I air them, Mary Poppins?"

Mary Poppins sniffed.

"Don't trouble, thank you. You're much too busy, I'm sure! I'll get Michael to help me when he comes up."

Jane blushed.

"Please let me," she said. "I like helping. Besides I'm the eldest."

Mary Poppins put her hands on her hips and regarded Jane thoughtfully for a moment.

"Humph!" she said at last. "Don't burn them, then! I've enough holes to mend as it is."

And she handed Jane the nightgowns.

"But it couldn't *really* have happened!" scoffed Michael a little later when he heard of Jane's adventure. "You'd be much too big for the Bowl."

She thought for a moment. Somehow, as she told the story, it did seem rather impossible.

"I suppose it couldn't," she admitted. "But it seemed quite real at the time."

"I expect you just thought it. You're always thinking things." He felt rather superior because he himself didn't ever think at all.

"You two and your thoughts!" said Mary Poppins crossly, pushing them aside as she dumped the Twins into their cots.

"And now," she snapped, when John and Barbara were safely tucked in, "perhaps I shall have a moment to myself."

She took the pins out of her hat and thrust it back into its brown-paper bag. She unclipped the locket and put it carefully away in a drawer. Then she slipped off her coat, shook it out, and hung it on the peg behind the door.

"Why, where's your new scarf?" said Jane. "Have you lost it?"

"She couldn't have," said Michael. "She had it on when she came home. I saw it."

Mary Poppins turned on them.

"Be good enough to mind your own affairs," she said snappily, "and let me mind mine!"

"I only wanted to help ——" Jane began.

"I can help myself, thank you!" said Mary Poppins, sniffing.

Jane turned to exchange looks with Michael. But this time it was he who took no notice. He was staring at the mantelpiece as if he could not believe his eyes.

"What is it, Michael?"

"You didn't just think it, after all!" he whispered, pointing.

Jane looked up at the mantelpiece. There lay the Royal Doulton Bowl with the crack running right across it. There were the meadow grasses and the wood of alders. And there were the three little boys playing horses, two in front and one running behind with the whip.

But — around the leg of the driver was knotted a small white handkerchief and, sprawling across the grass, as though someone had dropped it as they ran, was a red-

and-white checked scarf. At one end of it was stitched a
large white label bearing the initials ——

M.P.

"So that's where she lost it!" said Michael, nodding his head wisely. "Shall we tell her we've found it?"

Jane glanced round. Mary Poppins was buttoning on her apron and looking as if the whole world had insulted her.

"Better not," she said, softly. "I expect she knows."

For a moment Jane stood there, gazing at the cracked Bowl, the knotted handkerchief and the scarf.

Then with a wild rush she ran across the room and flung herself upon the starched white figure.

"Oh," she cried, "oh, Mary Poppins! I'll never be naughty again."

A faint smile twinkled at the corners of Mary Poppins' mouth as she smoothed out the creases from her apron.

"Humph!" was all she said. . . .

CHAPTER FOUR

TOPSY-TURVY

eep close to me, please!" said Mary Poppins, stepping out of the Bus and putting up her umbrella, for it was raining heavily.

Jane and Michael scrambled out after her.

"If I keep close to you the drips from your umbrella run down my neck," complained Michael.

"Don't blame me, then, if you get lost and have to ask a Policeman!" snapped Mary Poppins, as she neatly avoided a puddle.

She paused outside the Chemist's shop at the corner so that she could see herself reflected in the three gigantic bottles in the window. She could see a Green Mary Poppins, a Blue Mary Poppins and a Red Mary Poppins all at once. And each one of them was carrying a brand-new leather hand-bag with brass knobs on it.

Mary Poppins looked at herself in the three bottles and smiled a pleased and satisfied smile. She spent some minutes changing the hand-bag from her right hand to her left, trying it in every possible position to see how it looked best. Then she decided that, after all, it was most effective when tucked under her arm. So she left it there.

Jane and Michael stood beside her, not daring to say anything but glancing across at each other and sighing inside themselves. And from two points of her parrot-handled umbrella the rain trickled uncomfortably down the backs of their necks.

"Now then — don't keep me waiting!" said Mary Poppins crossly, turning away from the Green, Blue and Red reflections of herself. Jane and Michael exchanged glances. Jane signalled to Michael to keep quiet. She shook her head and made a face at him. But he burst out ——

"We weren't. It was you keeping us waiting ——!"

"Silence!"

Michael did not dare to say any more. He and Jane trudged along, one on either side of Mary Poppins. Sometimes they had to run to keep up with her long, swift strides. And sometimes they had to wait about, standing first on one leg and then on the other, while she peered into a window to make sure the hand-bag looked as nice as she thought it did.

The rain poured down, dancing from the top of the umbrella on to Jane's and Michael's hats. Under her arm Jane carried the Royal Doulton Bowl wrapped carefully in two pieces of paper. They were taking it to Mary Poppins' cousin, Mr. Turvy, whose business, she had told Mrs. Banks, was mending things.

"Well," Mrs. Banks had said, rather doubtfully, "I hope he will do it satisfactorily, for until it is mended I shall not be able to look my Great-Aunt Caroline in the face."

Great-Aunt Caroline had given Mrs. Banks the bowl when Mrs. Banks was only three, and it was well-known that if it were broken Great-Aunt Caroline would make one of her famous scenes.

"Members of *my* family, ma'am," Mary Poppins had retorted with a sniff, "*always* give satisfaction."

And she had looked so fierce that Mrs. Banks felt quite uncomfortable and had to sit down and ring for a cup of tea.

Swish!

There was Jane, right in the middle of a puddle.

"Look where you're going, please!" snapped Mary Poppins, shaking her umbrella and tossing the drips over Jane and Michael. "This rain is enough to break your heart."

"If it did, could Mr. Turvy mend it?" enquired Michael. He was interested to know if Mr. Turvy could mend all broken things or only certain kinds. "Could he, Mary Poppins?"

"One more word," said Mary Poppins, "and Back Home you go!"

"I only asked," said Michael sulkily.

"Then don't!"

Mary Poppins, with an angry sniff, turned the corner smartly and, opening an old iron gate, knocked at the door of a small tumble-down building.

"Tap-tap-tappity-tap!" The sound of the knocker echoed hollowly through the house.

"Oh, dear," Jane whispered to Michael, "how awful if he's out!"

But at that moment heavy footsteps were heard tramping towards them, and with a loud rattle the door opened.

A round, red-faced woman, looking more like two apples placed one on top of the other than a human being, stood in the doorway. Her straight hair was scraped into a knob at the top of her head and her thin mouth had a cross and peevish expression.

"Well!" she said, staring. "It's you or I'm a Dutchman!"

She did not seem particularly pleased to see Mary Poppins. Nor did Mary Poppins seem particularly pleased to see her.

"Is Mr. Turvy in?" she enquired, without taking any notice of the round woman's remark.

"Well," said the round woman in an unfriendly voice, "I wouldn't be certain. He may be or he may not. It's all a matter of how you look at it."

Mary Poppins stepped through the door and peered about her.

"That's his hat, isn't it?" she demanded, pointing to an old felt hat that hung on a peg in the hall.

"Well, it is, of course — in a manner of speaking." The round woman admitted the fact unwillingly.

"Then he's in," said Mary Poppins. "No member of *my* family ever goes out without a hat. They're much too respectable."

"Well, all I can tell you is what he said to me this morning," said the round woman. "'Miss Tartlet,' he said, 'I may be in this afternoon and I may not. It is quite impossible to tell.' That's what he said. But you'd better go up and see for yourself. I'm not a mountaineer."

The round woman glanced down at her round body and shook her head. Jane and Michael could easily understand that a person of her size and shape would not want to climb up and down Mr. Turvy's narrow rickety stairs very often.

Mary Poppins sniffed.

"Follow me, please!" she snapped the words at Jane and Michael, and they ran after her up the creaking stairs.

Miss Tartlet stood in the hall watching them with a superior smile on her face.

At the top landing Mary Poppins knocked on the door with the head of her umbrella. There was no reply. She knocked again — louder this time. Still there was no answer.

"Cousin Arthur!" she called through the key-hole. "Cousin Arthur, are you in?"

"No, I'm out!" came a far-away voice from within.

"How can he be out? I can hear him!" whispered Michael to Jane.

"Cousin Arthur!" Mary Poppins rattled the door-handle. "I know you're in."

"No, no, I'm not," came the far-away voice. "I'm out, I tell you. It's the Second Monday!"

"Oh, dear — I'd forgotten!" said Mary Poppins, and with an angry movement she turned the handle and flung open the door.

At first all that Jane and Michael could see was a large

room that appeared to be quite empty except for a carpenter's bench at one end. Piled upon this was a curious collection of articles — china dogs with no noses, wooden horses that had lost their tails, chipped plates, broken dolls, knives without handles, stools with only two legs — everything in the world, it seemed, that could possibly want mending.

Round the walls of the room were shelves reaching from floor to ceiling and these, too, were crowded with cracked china, broken glass and shattered toys.

But there was no sign anywhere of a human being.

"Oh," said Jane in a disappointed voice. "He *is* out, after all!"

But Mary Poppins had darted across the room to the window.

"Come in at once, Arthur! Out in the rain like that, and you with bronchitis the winter before last!"

And to their amazement Jane and Michael saw her grasp a long leg that hung across the window-sill and pull in from the outer air a tall, thin, sad-looking man with a long drooping moustache.

"You ought to be ashamed of yourself," said Mary Poppins crossly, keeping a firm hold of Mr. Turvy with one hand while she shut the window with the other. "We've brought you some important work to do and here you are behaving like this."

"Well, I can't help it," said Mr. Turvy apologetically,

mopping his sad eyes with a large handkerchief. "I told you it was the Second Monday."

"What does that mean?" asked Michael, staring at Mr. Turvy with interest.

"Ah," said Mr. Turvy turning to him and shaking him limply by the hand. "It's kind of you to enquire. Very kind. I do appreciate it, really." He paused to wipe his eyes again. "You see," he went on, "it's this way. On the Second Monday of the month everything goes wrong with me."

"What kind of things?" asked Jane, feeling very sorry for Mr. Turvy but also very curious.

"Well, take to-day!" said Mr. Turvy. "This happens to be the Second Monday of the month. And because I want to be in — having so much work to do — I'm automatically out. And if I wanted to be out, sure enough, I'd be in."

"I see," said Jane, though she really found it very difficult to understand. "So that's why —— ?"

"Yes," Mr. Turvy nodded. "I heard you coming up the stairs and I did so long to be in. So, of course, as soon as that happened — there I was — out! And I'd be out still if Mary Poppins weren't holding on to me." He sighed heavily.

"Of course, it's not like this all the time. Only between the hours of three and six — but even then it can be very awkward."

"I'm sure it can," said Jane sympathetically.

"And it's not as if it was only In and Out ——" Mr. Turvy went on miserably. "It's other things, too. If I try to go up stairs, I find myself running down. I have only to turn to the right and I find myself going to the left. And I never set off for the West without immediately finding myself in the East."

Mr. Turvy blew his nose.

"And worst of all," he continued, his eyes filling again with tears, "my whole nature alters. To look at me now, you'd hardly believe I was really a happy and satisfied sort of person — would you?"

And, indeed, Mr. Turvy looked so melancholy and distressed that it seemed quite impossible he could ever have been cheerful and contented.

"But why? Why?" demanded Michael, staring up at him.

Mr. Turvy shook his head sadly.

"Ah!" he said solemnly. "I should have been a girl."

Jane and Michael stared at him and then at each other. What *could* he mean?

"You see," Mr. Turvy explained, "my Mother wanted a girl and it turned out, when I arrived, that I was a boy. So I went wrong right from the beginning — from the day I was born you might say. And that was the Second Monday of the month."

Mr. Turvy began to weep again, sobbing gently into his handkerchief.

Jane patted his hand kindly.

He seemed pleased, though he did not smile.

"And, of course," he went on, "it's very bad for my work. Look up there!"

He pointed to one of the larger shelves on which were standing a row of hearts in different colours and sizes, each one cracked or chipped or entirely broken.

"Now, those," said Mr. Turvy, "are wanted in a great hurry. You don't know how cross people get if I don't send their hearts back quickly. They make more fuss about them than anything else. And I simply daren't touch them till after six o'clock. They'd be ruined — like those things!"

He nodded to another shelf. Jane and Michael looked and saw that it was piled high with things that had been wrongly mended. A china shepherdess had been separated from her china shepherd and her arms were glued about the neck of a brass lion; a toy sailor whom somebody had wrenched from his boat, was firmly stuck to a willow-pattern plate; and in the boat, with his trunk curled round the mast and fixed there with sticking-plaster, was a grey-flannel elephant. Broken saucers were riveted together the wrong way of the pattern and the leg of a wooden horse was firmly attached to a silver Christening mug.

"You see?" said Mr. Turvy hopelessly, with a wave of his hand.

Jane and Michael nodded. They felt very, very sorry for Mr. Turvy.

"Well, never mind that now," Mary Poppins broke in impatiently. "What is important is this Bowl. We've brought it to be mended."

She took the Bowl from Jane and, still holding Mr. Turvy with one hand, she undid the string with the other.

"H'm," said Mr. Turvy. "Royal Doulton. A bad crack. Looks as though somebody had thrown something at it."

Jane felt herself blushing as he said that.

"Still," he went on, "if it were any other day, I could mend it. But to-day —— " he hesitated.

"Nonsense, it's quite simple. You've only to put a rivet here — and here — and here!"

Mary Poppins pointed to the crack and as she did so she dropped Mr. Turvy's hand.

Immediately he went spinning through the air, turning over and over like a Catherine wheel.

"Oh!" cried Mr. Turvy. "Why did you let go? Poor me, I'm off again!"

"Quick — shut the door!" cried Mary Poppins. And Jane and Michael rushed across the room and closed the door just before Mr. Turvy reached it. He banged against it and bounced away again, turning gracefully, with a very sad look on his face, through the air.

Suddenly he stopped but in a very curious position.

Instead of being right-side up he was upside down and standing on his head.

"Dear, dear!" said Mr. Turvy, giving a fierce kick with his feet, "Dear, dear!"

But his feet would not go down to the floor. They remained waving gently in the air.

"Well," Mr. Turvy remarked in his melancholy voice. "I suppose I should be glad it's no worse. This is certainly better — though not *much* better — than hanging outside in the rain with nothing to sit on and no overcoat. You see," he looked at Jane and Michael, "I want so much to be right-side up and so — just my luck! — I'm upside down. Well, well, never mind. I ought to be used to it by now. I've had forty-five years of it. Give me the Bowl."

Michael ran and took the Bowl from Mary Poppins and put it on the floor by Mr. Turvy's head. And as he did so he felt a curious thing happening to him. The floor seemed to be pushing his feet away from it and tilting them into the air.

"Oh!" he cried. "I feel so funny. Something most extraordinary is happening to me!"

For by now he, too, was turning Catherine wheels through the air, and flying up and down the room until he landed head-first on the floor beside Mr. Turvy.

"Strike me pink!" said Mr. Turvy in a surprised voice, looking at Michael out of the corner of his eye. "I never knew it was catching. You, too? Well, of all the — Hi! Hi, I say! Steady there! You'll knock the goods off the shelves, if you're not careful, and I shall be charged for breakages. What *are* you doing?"

He was now addressing Jane whose feet had suddenly swept off the carpet and were turning above her head in the giddiest manner. Over and over she went — first her head and then her feet in the air — until at last she came down on the other side of Mr. Turvy and found herself standing on her head.

"You know," said Mr. Turvy staring at her solemnly. "This is all very odd. I never knew it to happen to any one else before. Upon my word, I never did. I do hope you don't mind."

Jane laughed, turning her head towards him and waving her legs in the air.

"Not a bit, thank you. I've always wanted to stand on my head and I've never been able to do it before. It's very comfortable."

"H'm," said Mr. Turvy dolefully. "I'm glad somebody likes it. I can't say *I* feel like that."

"I do," said Michael. "I wish I could stay like this all my life. Everything looks so nice and different."

And, indeed, everything *was* different. From their strange position on the floor Jane and Michael could see that the articles on the carpenter's bench were all upside down — china dogs, broken dolls, wooden stools — all standing on their heads.

"Look!" whispered Jane to Michael. He turned his head as much as he could. And there, creeping out of a hole in the wainscoting, came a small mouse. It skipped, head over heels, into the middle of the room and, turning upside down, balanced daintily on its nose in front of them.

They watched it for a moment, very surprised. Then Michael suddenly said,

"Jane, look out of the window!"

She turned her head carefully for it was rather difficult and saw to her astonishment that everything outside the room, as well as everything in it, was different. Out in the street the houses were standing on their heads, their chimneys on the pavement and their doorsteps in the air and out of the doorsteps came little curls of smoke. In the distance a church had turned turtle and was balancing rather top-heavily on the point of its steeple. And the rain, which had always seemed to them to come down from the sky, was pouring up from the earth in a steady soaking shower.

"Oh," said Jane. "How beautifully strange it all is! It's like being in another world. I'm so glad we came to-day."

"Well," said Mr. Turvy, mournfully, "you're very kind, I must say. You do know how to make allowances. Now, what about this Bowl?"

He stretched out his hand to take it but at that moment the Bowl gave a little skip and turned upside down. And it did it so quickly and so funnily that Jane and Michael could not help laughing.

"This," said Mr. Turvy miserably, "is no laughing matter for me, I assure you. I shall have to put the rivets in wrong way up — and if they show, they show. I can't help it."

And taking his tools out of his pocket he mended the Bowl, weeping quietly as he worked.

"Humph!" said Mary Poppins, stooping to pick it up. "Well, that's done. And now we'll be going."

At that Mr. Turvy began to sob pitifully.

"That's right, leave me!" he said bitterly. "Don't stay and help me keep my mind off my misery. Don't hold out a friendly hand. I'm not worth it. I'd hoped you might all favour me by accepting some refreshment. There's a plum cake in a tin up there on the top shelf. But, there — I'd no right to expect it. You've your own lives to live and I shouldn't ask you to stay and brighten mine. This isn't my lucky day ——"

He fumbled for his pocket-handkerchief.

"Well ——" began Mary Poppins, pausing in the middle of buttoning her gloves.

"Oh, do stay, Mary Poppins, do!" cried Jane and Michael together, dancing eagerly on their heads.

"You could reach the cake if you stood on a chair!" said Jane, helpfully.

Mr. Turvy laughed for the first time. It was rather a melancholy sound, but still, it *was* a laugh.

"*She'll* need no chair!" he said, gloomily chuckling in his throat. "She'll get what she wants and in the way she wants it — *she* will."

And at that moment, before the children's astonished eyes, Mary Poppins did a curious thing. She raised herself stiffly on her toes and balanced there for a moment. Then, very slowly, and in a most dignified manner she turned seven Catherine wheels through the air. Over and over, her skirts clinging neatly about her ankles, her hat set tidily on her head, she wheeled up to the top of the shelf, took the cake and wheeled down again, landing neatly on her head in front of Mr. Turvy and the children.

"Hooray! Hooray! Hooray!" shouted Michael delightedly. But from the floor Mary Poppins gave him such a look that he rather wished he had remained quiet and said nothing.

"Thank you, Mary," said Mr. Turvy sadly, not seeming at all surprised.

"There!" snapped Mary Poppins. "That's the last thing I shall do for you to-day."

She put the cake-tin down in front of Mr. Turvy.

Immediately, with a little wobbly roll, it turned upside down. And each time Mr. Turvy turned it right-side up it turned over again.

"Ah," he said despairingly, "I might have known it! Nothing is right to-day — not even the cake-tin. We shall have to cut it open from the bottom. I'll just ask —— "

And he stumbled on his head to the door and shouted through the crack between it and the floor.

"Miss Tartlet! Miss Tartlet! I'm so sorry to trouble you, but could you — would you — do you mind bringing a tin-opener?"

Far away downstairs Miss Tartlet's voice could be heard grimly protesting.

"Tush!" said a loud croaky voice inside the room. "Tush and nonsense! Don't bother the woman! Let Polly do it! Pretty Polly! Clever Polly!"

Mary Poppins landed neatly on her head
in front of Mr. Turvy and the children

Turning their heads, Jane and Michael were surprised to see that the voice came from Mary Poppins' parrot-headed umbrella, which was at that moment Catherine-wheeling towards the cake. It landed head-downwards on the tin and in two seconds had cut a large hole in it with its beak.

"There!" squawked the parrot-head conceitedly, "Polly did it! Handsome Polly!" And a happy self-satisfied smile spread over its beak as it settled head-downwards on the floor beside Mary Poppins.

"Well, that's very kind, *very* kind," said Mr. Turvy in his gloomy voice, as the dark crust of the cake became visible.

He took a knife out of his pocket and cut a slice. He started violently, and peered at the cake more closely. Then he looked reproachfully at Mary Poppins.

"This is your doing, Mary! Don't deny it. That cake, when the tin was last open, was a plum cake and now —— "

"Sponge is much more digestible," said Mary Poppins, primly. "Eat slowly please. You're not starving savages!" she snapped, passing a small slice each to Jane and Michael.

"That's all very well," grumbled Mr. Turvy bitterly, eating his slice in two bites. "But I do like a plum or two, I must admit. Ah, well, this is not my lucky day!" He broke off as somebody rapped loudly on the door. "Come in!" called Mr. Turvy.

Miss Tartlet, looking, if anything, rounder than ever and panting from her climb up the stairs, burst into the room.

"The tin-opener, Mr. Turvy——" she began grimly. Then she paused and stared.

"My!" she said, opening her mouth very wide and letting the tin-opener slip from her hand. "Of all the sights I ever did see this is the one I wouldn't have expected!"

She took a step forward, gazing at the four pairs of waving feet with an expression of deep disgust.

"Upside down — the lot of you — like flies on a ceiling! And you supposed to be respectable human creatures. This is no place for a lady of *my* standing. I shall leave the house this instant, Mr. Turvy. Please note that!"

She flounced angrily towards the door.

But even as she went her great billowing skirts blew against her round legs and lifted her from the floor.

A look of agonised astonishment spread over her face. She flung out her hands wildly.

"Mr. Turvy! Mr. Turvy, Sir! Catch me! Hold me down! Help! Help!" cried Miss Tartlet as she, too, began a sweeping Catherine wheel.

"Oh, oh, the world's turning turtle! What shall I do? Help! Help!" she shrieked, as she went over again.

But as she turned a curious change came over her. Her round face lost its peevish expression and began to shine with smiles. And Jane and Michael, with a start of surprise, saw her straight hair crinkle into a mass of little curls and ringlets as she whirled and twirled through the room. When she spoke again her gruff voice was as sweet as honeysuckle.

"What can be happening to me?" cried Miss Tartlet's new voice. "I feel like a ball! A bouncing ball! Or perhaps a balloon! Or a cherry tart!" She broke into a peal of happy laughter.

"Dear me, how cheerful I am!" she trilled, turning and circling through the air. "I never enjoyed my life before but now I feel I shall never stop. It's the loveliest sensation. I shall write home to my sister about it, to my cousins and uncles and aunts. I shall tell them that the only proper way to live is upside down, upside down, upside down ——"

And, chanting happily, Miss Tartlet went whirling round and round. Jane and Michael watched her with delight and Mr. Turvy watched her with surprise, for he had never known Miss Tartlet to be anything but peevish and unfriendly.

"Very odd! Very odd!" said Mr. Turvy to himself, shaking his head as he stood on it.

Another knock sounded at the door.

"Anyone here name of Turvy?" enquired a voice, and the Post Man appeared in the doorway holding a letter. He stood staring at the sight that met his eyes.

"Holy smoke!" he remarked, pushing his cap to the

back of his head. "I must-a come to the wrong place. I'm looking for a decent quiet gentleman called Turvy. I've got a letter for him. Besides, I promised my wife I'd be home early and I've broken my word and I thought —— "

"Ha!" said Mr. Turvy from the floor. "A broken promise is one of the things I can't mend. Not my line. Sorry!"

The Post Man stared down at him.

"Am I dreaming or am I not?" he muttered. "It seems to me I've got into a whirling, twirling, skirling company of lunatics!"

"Give me the letter, dear Post Man! Give the letter to Topsy Tartlet and turn upside down with me. Mr. Turvy, you see, is engaged!"

Miss Tartlet, wheeling towards the Post Man, took his hand in hers. And as she touched him his feet slithered off the floor into the air. Then away they went, the Post Man and Miss Tartlet, hand in hand and over and over, like a pair of bouncing footballs. "How lovely it is!" cried Miss Tartlet happily. "Oh, Post Man dear, we're seeing life for the first time. And such a pleasant view of it! Over we go! Isn't it wonderful?"

"Yes!" shouted Jane and Michael, as they joined the wheeling dance of the Post Man and Miss Tartlet.

And presently Mr. Turvy, too, joined in, awkwardly turning and tossing through the air. Mary Poppins and her umbrella followed, going over and over evenly and neatly and with the utmost dignity. There they all were, spinning and wheeling, with the world going up and down outside and the happy cries of Miss Tartlet echoing through the room.

> "The whole of the Town
> Is Upside Down!"

she sang, bouncing and bounding.

And up on the shelves the cracked and broken hearts twirled and spun like tops, the shepherdess and her lion waltzed gracefully together, the grey-flannel elephant stood on his trunk in the boat and kicked his feet in the air, and the toy sailor danced a hornpipe, not on his feet but his head, which bobbed about the willow-pattern plate very gracefully.

"How happy I am!" cried Jane as she careered across the room.

"How happy *I* am!" cried Michael, turning somersaults in the air.

Mr. Turvy mopped his eyes with his handkerchief as he bounced off the window-pane.

Mary Poppins and her umbrella said nothing but just sailed calmly round, head-downwards.

"How happy we *all* are!" cried Miss Tartlet.

But the Post Man had now found his tongue and he did not agree with her.

"'Ere!" he shouted, turning again. "'Elp! 'Elp! Where

am I? Who am I? What am I? I don't know at all. I'm lost! Oh, 'elp!"

But nobody helped him, and firmly held in Miss Tartlet's grasp he was whirled on.

"Always lived a quiet life — I have!" he moaned. "Behaved like a decent citizen, too. Oh, what'll my wife say! And 'ow shall I get 'ome? 'Elp! Fire! Thieves!"

And making a great effort, he wrenched his hand violently from Miss Tartlet's. He dropped the letter into the cake-tin and went wheeling out of the door and down the stairs, head over heels, crying loudly —

"I'll have the law on them! I'll call the Police! I'll speak to the Post Master General!"

His voice died away as he went bounding further down the stairs.

"Ping, ping, ping, ping, ping, ping!"

The clock outside in the Square sounded six.

And at the same moment Jane's and Michael's feet came down to the floor with a thud and they stood up feeling rather giddy.

Mary Poppins gracefully turned right-side up, looking as smart and tidy as a figure in a shop window.

The Umbrella wheeled over and stood on its point.

Mr. Turvy, with a great tossing of legs, scrambled to his feet.

The hearts on the shelf stood still and steady and no movement came from the shepherdess or the lion, or the grey-flannel elephant or the toy sailor. To look at them you would never have guessed that a moment before they had all been dancing on their heads.

Only Miss Tartlet went whirling on, round and round the room, feet over head, laughing happily and singing her song.

> "The whole of the Town
> Is Upside down,
> Upside down,
> Upside down!"

she chanted joyfully.

"Miss Tartlet! Miss Tartlet!" cried Mr. Turvy, running

towards her, a strange light in his eyes. He took her arm as she wheeled past and held it tightly until she stood up on her feet beside him.

"*What* did you say your name was?" said Mr. Turvy, panting with excitement.

Miss Tartlet actually blushed. She looked at him shyly.

"Why, Tartlet, sir. Topsy Tartlet!"

Mr. Turvy took her hand.

"Then will you marry me, Miss Tartlet, and be Topsy Turvy? It would make up to me for so much. And you seem to have become so happy that perhaps you will be kind enough to overlook my Second Mondays."

"Overlook them, Mr. Turvy? Why, they will be my Greatest Treats," said Miss Tartlet. "I have seen the world upside down to-day and I have got a New Point of View. I assure you I shall look forward to the Second Mondays all the month!"

She laughed shyly and gave Mr. Turvy her other hand. And Mr. Turvy, Jane and Michael were glad to see, laughed too.

"It's after six o'clock, so I suppose he can be himself again!" whispered Michael to Jane.

Jane did not answer. She was watching the Mouse. It was no longer standing on its nose but hurrying away to its hole with a large crumb of cake in its mouth.

Mary Poppins picked up the Royal Doulton Bowl and proceeded to wrap it up.

"Pick up your handkerchiefs, please — and straighten your hats," she snapped.

"And now —— " she took her umbrella and tucked her new bag under her arm.

"Oh, we're not going yet, are we, Mary Poppins?" said Michael.

"If *you* are in the habit of staying out all night, I am not," she remarked, pushing him towards the door.

"Must you go, really?" said Mr. Turvy. But he seemed to be saying it out of mere politeness. He had eyes only for Miss Tartlet.

But Miss Tartlet herself came up to them, smiling radiantly and tossing her curls.

"Come again," she said, giving a hand to each of them. "Now, do. Mr. Turvy and I —— " she looked down shyly and blushed — "will be in to tea every Second Monday — won't we, Arthur?"

"Well," said Mr. Turvy, "we'll be in if we're not out — I'm sure of that!" And he laughed and Jane and Michael laughed.

And he and Miss Tartlet stood at the top of the stairs waving good-bye to Mary Poppins and the children, Miss Tartlet blushing happily and Mr. Turvy holding Miss Tartlet's hand and looking very proud and pompous. . . .

"I didn't know it was as easy as that," said Michael to Jane as they splashed through the rain, under Mary Popping' umbrella.

"What was?" said Jane.

"Standing on my head. I shall practise it when I get home."

"I wish *we* could have Second Mondays," said Jane dreamily.

"Get in, please!" said Mary Poppins, shutting her umbrella and pushing the children up the winding stairs of the bus.

They sat together in the seat behind her, talking quietly about all that had happened that afternoon.

Mary Poppins turned and glared at them.

"It is rude to whisper," she said fiercely. "And sit up straight. You're not flour-bags!"

They were quiet for a few minutes. Mary Poppins, half-turning in her seat, watched them with angry eyes.

"What a funny family you've got," Michael remarked to her, trying to make conversation.

Her head went up with a jerk.

"Funny? What do you mean, pray — funny?"

"Well — odd. Mr. Turvy turning Catherine wheels and standing on his head —— "

Mary Poppins stared at him as though she could not believe her ears.

"Did I understand you to say," she began, speaking her words as though she were biting them, "that my cousin turned a Catherine wheel? And stood on —— "

"But he did," protested Michael nervously. "We saw him."

"On his head? A relation of mine on his head? And turning about like a firework display?" Mary Poppins seemed hardly able to repeat the dreadful statement. She glared at Michael.

"Now this —— " she began, and he shrank back in terror from her wild darting eyes. "This is the Last Straw. First you are impudent to me and then you insult my relations. It would take very little more — Very Little More — to make me give notice. So — I warn you!"

And with that she bounced round on her seat and sat with her back to them. And even from the back she looked angrier than they had ever seen her.

Michael leaned forward.

"I — I apologise," he said.

There was no answer from the seat in front.

"I'm sorry, Mary Poppins!"

"Humph!"

"*Very* sorry!"

"And well you might be!" she retorted, staring straight ahead of her.

Michael leant towards Jane.

"But it was true — what I said. Wasn't it?" he whispered.

Jane shook her head and put her finger to her lip. She was staring at Mary Poppins' hat. And presently, when she

was sure that Mary Poppins was not looking, she pointed
to the brim.

There, gleaming on the black shiny straw, was a scattering of crumbs, yellow crumbs from a sponge-cake, the
kind of thing you would expect to find on the hat of a person who had stood on their head to have tea.

Michael gazed at the crumbs for a moment. Then he
turned and nodded understandingly to Jane.

They sat there, jogging up and down as the bus rumbled homewards. Mary Poppins' back, erect and angry,
was like a silent warning. They dared not speak to her.
But every time the bus turned a corner they saw the
crumbs turning Catherine wheels on the shining brim of
her hat. . . .

CHAPTER FIVE

THE NEW ONE

ut *why* must we go for a walk with Ellen?" grumbled Michael, slamming the gate. "I don't like her. Her nose is too red."

"Sh!" said Jane. "She'll hear you."

Ellen, who was wheeling the perambulator, turned round.

"You're a cruel, unkind boy, Master Michael. I'm only doing my duty, I'm sure! It's no pleasure to me to be going for a walk in this heat — so there!"

She blew her red nose on a green handkerchief.

"Then why do you go?" Michael demanded.

"Because Mary Poppins is busy. So come along, there's a good boy, and I'll buy you a pennorth of peppermints."

"I don't want peppermints," muttered Michael. "I want Mary Poppins."

Plop-plop. Plop-plop. Ellen's feet marched slowly and heavily along the Lane.

"I can see a rainbow through every chink of my hat," said Jane.

"I can't," said Michael crossly. "I can only see my silk lining."

Ellen stopped at the corner, looking anxiously for traffic.

"Want any help?" enquired the Policeman, sauntering up to her.

"Well," said Ellen, blushing, "if you could take us across the road, I'd be much obliged. What with a bad cold, and four children to look after, I don't know if I'm on my head or my feet." She blew her nose again.

"But you *must* know! You've only got to look!" said Michael thinking how Perfectly Awful Ellen was.

But the Policeman apparently thought differently for he took Ellen's arm with one hand, and the handle of the perambulator with the other, and led her across the street as tenderly as though she were a bride.

"Ever get a day off?" he enquired, looking interestedly into Ellen's red face.

"Well," said Ellen. "Half-days, so to speak. Every second Saturday." She blew her nose nervously.

"Funny," said the Policeman. "Those are *my* days, too. And I'm usually just around here at two o'clock in the afternoon."

"Oh!" said Ellen, opening her mouth very wide.

"So!" said the Policeman, nodding at her politely.

"Well, I'll see," said Ellen. "Good-bye."

And she went trudging on, looking back occasionally to see if the Policeman was still looking.

And he always was.

"Mary Poppins never needs a policeman," complained Michael. "What *can* she be busy about?"

"Something important is happening at home," said Jane. "I'm sure of it."

"How do you know?"

"I've got an empty, waiting sort of feeling inside."

"Pooh!" said Michael. "I expect you're hungry! Can't we go faster, Ellen, and get it over?"

"That boy," said Ellen to the Park railing, "has a heart of stone. No, we can't, Master Michael, because of my feet."

"What's the matter with them?"

"They will only go so fast and no faster."

"Oh, *dear* Mary Poppins!" said Michael bitterly.

He went sighing after the perambulator. Jane walked beside him counting rainbows through her hat.

Ellen's slow feet tramped steadily onward. One-two. One-two. Plop-plop. Plop-plop....

And away behind them in Cherry-Tree Lane the important thing was happening.

From the outside, Number Seventeen looked as peaceful and sleepy as all the other houses. But behind the drawn blinds there was such a stir and bustle that, if it hadn't been Summer-time, a passerby might have thought the people in the house were Spring-cleaning or getting ready for Christmas.

But the house itself stood blinking in the sunshine, taking no notice. After all, it thought to itself, I have seen such bustlings often before and shall probably see them many times again, so why should *I* bother about it?

And just then, the front door was flung open by Mrs. Brill, and Doctor Simpson hurried out. Mrs. Brill stood dancing on her toes as she watched him go down the garden path, swinging his little brown bag. Then she hurried to the Pantry and called excitedly——

"Where are you, Robertson? Come along, if you're coming!"

She scuttled up the stairs two at a time with Robertson Ay yawning and stretching, behind her.

"Sh!" hissed Mrs. Brill. "Sh!"

She put her finger to her lips and tip-toed to Mrs. Banks' door.

"Tch, tch! You can't see nothing but the wardrobe," she complained, as she bent to look through the keyhole. "The wardrobe and a bit of the winder."

But the next moment she started violently.

"My Glory-goodness!" she shrieked, as the door burst open suddenly, and she fell back against Robertson Ay.

For there, framed against the light, stood Mary Poppins, looking very stern and suspicious. In her arms she carried, with great care, something that looked like a bundle of blankets.

"Well!" said Mrs. Brill, breathlessly. "If it isn't you! I was just polishing the door-knob, putting a shine on it, so to say, as you came out."

Mary Poppins looked at the knob. It was very dirty.

"Polishing the key-hole is what *I* should have said!" she remarked tartly.

But Mrs. Brill took no notice. She was gazing tenderly at the bundle. With her large red hand she drew aside a fold of one of the blankets, and a satisfied smile spread over her face.

"Ah!" she cooed. "Ah, the Lamb! Ah, the Duck! Ah, the Trinket! And as good as a week of Sundays, I'll be bound!"

Robertson Ay yawned again and stared at the bundle with his mouth slightly open.

"Another pair of shoes to clean!" he said mournfully, leaning against the banisters for support.

"Mind you don't drop it, now!" said Mrs. Brill anxiously, as Mary Poppins brushed past her.

Mary Poppins glanced at them both contemptuously.

"If I were *some* people," she remarked acidly, "I'd mind my own business!"

And she folded the blanket over the bundle again and went upstairs to the Nursery.

"Excuse me, please! Excuse me!" Mr. Banks came rushing up the stairs, nearly knocking Mrs. Brill over as he hurried into Mrs. Banks' bedroom.

"Well!" he said, sitting down at the foot of the bed, "This is all very awkward. Very awkward indeed. I don't know that I can afford it. I hadn't bargained for five."

"I'm so sorry!" said Mrs. Banks, smiling at him happily.

"You're not sorry, not a bit. In fact you're very pleased

and conceited about it. And there's no reason to be. It's a very small one."

"I like them that way," said Mrs. Banks. "Besides, it will grow."

"Yes, unfortunately!" he replied bitterly. "And I shall have to buy it shoes and clothes and a tricycle. Yes, and send it to school and give it a Good Start in Life. A very expensive proceeding. And then, after all that, when I'm an old man sitting by the fire, it will go away and leave me. You hadn't thought of that, I suppose?"

"No," said Mrs. Banks, trying to look sorry but not succeeding. "I hadn't."

"I thought not. Well, there it is. But, I warn you, I shall not be able to afford to have the bathroom re-tiled."

"Don't worry about that," said Mrs. Banks comfortingly. "I really like the old tiles best."

"Then you're a very stupid woman. That's all I have to say."

And Mr. Banks went away, muttering and blustering through the house. But when he got outside the front door, he flung back his shoulders, and pushed out his chest, and put a large cigar into his mouth. And soon after that he was heard telling Admiral Boom the news in a voice that was very loud and conceited and boastful. . . .

Mary Poppins stooped over the new cradle between John's and Barbara's cots and laid the bundle of blankets carefully in it.

"Here you are at last! Bless my beak and tail feathers —— I thought you were never coming! Which is it?" cried a croaking voice from the window.

Mary Poppins looked up.

The Starling who lived on the top of the Chimney was hopping excitedly on the window-sill.

"A girl. Annabel," said Mary Poppins shortly. "And I'll thank you to be a little quieter. Squawking and croaking there like a packet of Magpies!"

But the Starling was not listening. He was turning somersaults on the window-sill, clapping his wings wildly together each time his head came up.

"What a treat!" he panted, when at last he stood up straight. "What a TREAT! Oh, I could sing!"

"You couldn't. Not if you tried till Doomsday!" scoffed Mary Poppins.

But the Starling was too happy to care.

"A girl!" he shrieked, dancing on his toes. "I've had three broods this season and — would you believe it? — every one of them boys. But Annabel will make up to me for that!"

He hopped a little along the sill. "Annabel!" he burst out again, "That's a nice name! I had an Aunt called Annabel. Used to live in Admiral Boom's chimney and died, poor thing, of eating green apples and grapes. I warned her, I warned her! But she wouldn't believe me! So, of course ——"

"Will you be quiet!" demanded Mary Poppins, making a dive at him with her apron.

"I will not!" he shouted, dodging neatly. "This is no time for silence. I'm going to spread the news."

He swooped out of the window.

"Back in five minutes!" he screamed at her over his shoulder, as he darted away.

Mary Poppins moved quietly about the Nursery, putting Annabel's new clothes in a neat pile.

The Sunlight, slipping in at the window, crept across the room and up to the cradle.

"Open your eyes!" it said softly. "And I'll put a shine on them!"

The coverlet of the cradle trembled. Annabel opened her eyes.

"Good girl!" said the Sunlight. "They're blue, I see. My favourite colour! There! You won't find a brighter pair of eyes anywhere!"

It slipped lightly out of Annabel's eyes and down the side of the cradle.

"Thank you very much!" said Annabel politely.

A warm Breeze stirred the muslin flounces at her head.

"Curls or straight?" it whispered, dropping into the cradle beside her.

"Oh, curls, please!" said Annabel softly.

"It does save trouble, doesn't it?" agreed the Breeze. And it moved over her head, carefully turning up the feathery edges of her hair, before it fluttered off across the room.

"Here we are! Here we are!"

A harsh voice shrilled from the window. The Starling had returned to the sill. And behind him, wobbling uncertainly as he alighted, came a very young bird.

Mary Poppins moved towards them threateningly.

"Now you be off!" she said angrily. "I'll have no sparrers littering up this Nursery ——"

But the Starling, with the young one at his side, brushed haughtily past her.

"Kindly remember, Mary Poppins," he said icily, "that *all* my families are properly brought up. Littering, indeed!"

He alighted neatly on the edge of the cradle and steadied the Fledgling beside him.

The young bird stared about him with round, inquisitive eyes. The Starling hopped along to the pillow.

"Annabel, dear," he began, in a husky, wheedling voice, "I'm very partial to a nice, crisp, crunchy piece of Arrowroot Biscuit." His eyes twinkled greedily. "You haven't one about you, I suppose?"

The curled head stirred on the pillow.

"No? Well, you're young yet for biscuits, perhaps. Your sister Barbara — nice girl, she was, very generous and pleasant — always remembered me. So if, in the future, *you* could spare the old fellow a crumb or two ——"

"Of course I will," said Annabel from the folds of the blanket.

"Good girl!" croaked the Starling approvingly. He cocked his head on one side and gazed at her with his round bright eye. "I hope," he remarked politely, "you are not too tired after your journey."

Annabel shook her head.

"Where has she come from — out of an egg?" cheeped the Fledgling suddenly.

"Huh-huh!" scoffed Mary Poppins. "Do you think she's a sparrer?"

The Starling gave her a pained and haughty look.

"Well, what is she, then? And where did she come from?" cried the Fledgling shrilly, flapping his short wings and staring down at the cradle.

"*You* tell him, Annabel!" the Starling croaked.

Annabel moved her hands inside the blanket.

"I am earth and air and fire and water," she said softly. "I come from the Dark where all things have their beginning."

"Ah, such dark!" said the Starling softly, bending his head to his breast.

"It was dark in the egg, too," the Fledgling cheeped.

"I come from the sea and its tides," Annabel went on. "I come from the sky and its stars, I come from the sun and its brightness —— "

"Ah, so bright!" said the Starling, nodding.

"And I come from the forests of earth."

As if in a dream, Mary Poppins rocked the cradle — to-and-fro, to-and-fro with a steady swinging movement.

"Yes?" whispered the Fledgling.

"Slowly I moved at first," said Annabel, "always sleeping and dreaming. I remembered all I had been and I thought of all I shall be. And when I had dreamed my dream I awoke and came swiftly."

She paused for a moment, her blue eyes full of memories.

"And then?" prompted the Fledgling.

"I heard the stars singing as I came and I felt warm wings about me. I passed the beasts of the jungle and came through the dark, deep waters. It was a long journey."

Annabel was silent.

The Fledgling stared at her with his bright inquisitive eyes.

Mary Poppins' hand lay quietly on the side of the cradle. She had stopped rocking.

"A long journey, indeed!" said the Starling softly, lifting his head from his breast. "And, ah, so soon forgotten!"

Annabel stirred under the quilt.

"No!" she said confidently. "I'll never forget."

"Stuff and Nonsense! Beaks and Claws! Of course you will! By the time the week's out you won't remember a word of it — what you are or where you came from!"

Inside her flannel petticoat Annabel was kicking furiously.

"I will! I will! How could I forget?"

"Because they all do!" jeered the Starling harshly. "Every silly human except — " he nodded his head at Mary Poppins — "her! She's Different, she's the Oddity, she's the Misfit —— "

"You Sparrer!" cried Mary Poppins, making a dart at him.

But with a rude laugh he swept his Fledgling off the edge of the cradle and flew with him to the window-sill.

"Tipped you last!" he said cheekily, as he brushed by. "Hullo, what's that?"

There was a chorus of voices outside on the landing and a clatter of feet on the stairs.

"I don't believe you! I won't believe you!" cried Annabel wildly.

And at that moment Jane and Michael and the Twins burst into the room.

"Mrs. Brill says you've got something to show us!" said Jane, flinging off her hat.

"What is it?" demanded Michael, gazing round the room.

"Show me! Me, too!" shrieked the Twins.

Mary Poppins glared at them. "Is this a decent nursery or the Zoological gardens?" she enquired angrily. "Answer me that!"

"The Zoo — er — I mean —— " Michael broke off hurriedly for he had caught Mary Poppins' eye. "I mean a Nursery," he said lamely.

"Oh, look, Michael, look!" Jane cried excitedly. "I told you something important was happening! It's a New Baby! Oh, Mary Poppins, can I have it to keep?"

Mary Poppins, with a furious glance at them all, stooped and lifted Annabel out of the cradle and sat down with her in the old arm-chair.

"Gently, please, gently!" she warned, as they crowded about her. "This is a baby, not a battle-ship!"

"A boy-baby?" asked Michael.

"No, a girl — Annabel."

Michael and Annabel stared at each other. He put his finger into her hand and she clutched it tightly.

"My doll!" said John, pushing up against Mary Poppins' knee.

"My rabbit!" said Barbara, tugging at Annabel's shawl.

She sat down in the old arm-chair

"Oh!" breathed Jane, touching the hair that the wind had curled. "How very small and sweet. Like a star. Where *did* you come from, Annabel?"

Very pleased to be asked, Annabel began her story again.

"I came from the Dark —— " she recited softly.

Jane laughed. "Such funny little sounds!" she cried. "I wish she could talk and tell us."

Annabel stared.

"But I *am* telling you," she protested, kicking.

"Ha-ha!" shrieked the Starling rudely from the window. "What did I say? Excuse me laughing!"

The Fledgling giggled behind his wing.

"Perhaps she came from a Toy-Shop," said Michael.

Annabel, with a furious movement, flung his finger from her.

"Don't be silly!" said Jane. "Doctor Simpson must have brought her in his little brown bag!"

"Was I right or was I wrong?" The Starling's old dark eyes gleamed tauntingly at Annabel.

"Tell me that!" he jeered, flapping his wings in triumph.

But for answer Annabel turned her face against Mary Poppins' apron and wept. Her first cries, thin and lonely, rang piercingly through the house.

"There! There!" said the Starling gruffly. "Don't take on! It can't be helped. You're only a human child after all. But next time, perhaps, you'll believe your Betters! Elders and Betters! Elders and Betters!" he screamed, prancing conceitedly up and down.

"Michael, take my feather duster please, and sweep those birds off the sill!" said Mary Poppins ominously.

A squawk of amusement came from the Starling.

"We can sweep ourselves off, Mary Poppins, thank you! We were just going, anyway! Come along, Boy!"

And with a loud clucking chuckle he flicked the Fledgling over the sill and swooped with him through the window. . . .

In a very short time, Annabel settled down comfortably to life in Cherry-Tree Lane. She enjoyed being the centre of attraction and was always pleased when somebody leant over her cradle and said how pretty she was, or how good or sweet-tempered.

"Do go on admiring me!" she would say, smiling. "I like it so much!"

And then they would hasten to tell her how curly her hair was and how blue her eyes, and Annabel would smile in such a satisfied way that they would cry, "How intelligent she is! You would almost think she understood!"

But *that* always annoyed her and she would turn away in disgust at their foolishness. Which was silly because when she was disgusted she looked so charming that they became more foolish than ever.

She was a week old before the Starling returned. Mary Poppins, in the dim glow of the night-light, was gently rocking the cradle when he appeared.

"Back again?" snapped Mary Poppins, watching him prance in. "You're as bad as a bad penny!" She gave a long disgusted sniff.

"I've been busy!" said the Starling. "Have to keep my affairs in order. And this isn't the *only* Nursery I have to look after, you know!" His beady black eyes twinkled wickedly.

"Humph!" she said shortly, "I'm sorry for the others!"

He chuckled and shook his head.

"Nobody like her!" he remarked chirpily to the blind-tassel. "Nobody like her! She's got an answer for everything!" He cocked his head towards the cradle. "Well, how are things? Annabel asleep?"

"No thanks to you, if she is!" said Mary Poppins.

The Starling ignored the remark. He hopped to the end of the sill.

"I'll keep watch," he said, in a whisper. "You go down and get a cup of tea!"

Mary Poppins stood up.

"Mind you don't wake her, then!"

The Starling laughed pityingly.

"My dear girl, I have in my time brought up at least twenty broods of fledglings. I don't need to be told how to look after a mere baby."

"Humph!" Mary Poppins walked to the cupboard and very pointedly put the biscuit-tin under her arm before she went out and shut the door.

The Starling marched up and down the windowsill,

backwards and forwards, with his wing-tips under his
tail-feathers.

There was a small stir in the cradle. Annabel opened
her eyes.

"Hullo!" she said. "I was wanting to see you."

"Ha!" said the Starling, swooping across to her.

"There's something I wanted to remember," said
Annabel frowning, "and I thought you might remind me."

He started. His dark eye glittered.

"How does it go?" he said softly. "Like this?"

And he began in a husky whisper — "I am earth and
air and fire and water — — "

"No, no!" said Annabel impatiently. "Of course it
doesn't."

"Well," said the Starling anxiously. "Was it about your
journey? You came from the sea and its tides, you came
from the sky and — — "

"Oh, don't be so *silly!*" cried Annabel. "The only journey I ever took was to the Park and back again this morning. No, no — it was something *important*. Something
beginning with B."

She crowed suddenly.

"I've got it!" she cried. "It's Biscuit. Half an Arrowroot
Biscuit on the mantelpiece. Michael left it there after tea!"

"Is that all?" said the Starling sadly.

"Yes, of course," Annabel said fretfully. "Isn't it enough?
I thought you'd be glad of a nice piece of biscuit!"

"So I am, so I am!" said the Starling hastily. "But — — "

She turned her head on the pillow and closed her eyes.

"Don't talk any more now, please!" she said. "I want to go to sleep."

The Starling glanced across at the mantelpiece, and down again at Annabel.

"Biscuits!" he said, shaking his head. "Alas, Annabel, alas!"

Mary Poppins came in quietly and closed the door.

"Did she wake?" she said in a whisper.

The Starling nodded.

"Only for a minute," he said sadly. "But it was long enough."

Mary Poppins' eyes questioned him.

"She's forgotten," he said, with a catch in his croak. "She's forgotten it all. I knew she would. But, ah, my dear, what a pity!"

"Humph!"

Mary Poppins moved quietly about the Nursery, putting the toys away. She glanced at the Starling. He was standing on the window-sill with his back to her, and his speckled shoulders were heaving.

"Caught another cold?" she remarked sarcastically.

He wheeled around.

"Certainly not! It's — ahem — the night air. Rather chilly, you know. Makes the eyes water. Well — I must be off!"

He waddled unsteadily to the edge of the sill. "I'm

getting old," he croaked sadly. "That's what it is! Not so young as we were. Eh, Mary Poppins?"

"I don't know about *you* —— " Mary Poppins drew herself up haughtily. "But I'm *quite* as young as I was, thank you!"

"Ah," said the Starling, shaking his head. "You're a Wonder. An absolute, Marvellous, Wonderful Wonder!" His round eye twinkled wickedly.

"I don't think!" he called back rudely, as he dived out of the window.

"Impudent Sparrer!" she shouted after him and shut the window with a bang. . . .

CHAPTER
SIX

ROBERTSON AY'S STORY

Step along, please!" said Mary Poppins, pushing the perambulator, with the Twins at one end of it and Annabel at the other, towards her favourite seat in the Park.

It was a green one, quite near the Lake, and she chose it because she could bend sideways, every now and again, and see her own reflection in the water. The sight of her face gleaming between two water-lilies always gave her a pleasant feeling of satisfaction and contentment.

Michael trudged behind.

"We're always stepping along," he grumbled to Jane in a whisper, taking care that Mary Poppins did not hear him, "but we never seem to get anywhere."

Mary Poppins turned round and glared at him.

"Put your hat on straight!"

Michael tilted his hat over his eyes. It had "H.M.S. Trumpeter" printed on the band and he thought it suited him very well.

But Mary Poppins was looking with contempt at them both.

"Humph!" she said. "You two look a picture, I must say! Stravaiging along like a couple of tortoises and no polish on your shoes."

"Well, it's Robertson Ay's Half-day," said Jane. "I suppose he didn't have time to do them before he went out."

"Tch, tch! Lazy, idle, Good-for-nothing — that's what he is. Always was and always will be!" Mary Poppins said, savagely pushing the perambulator up against her own green seat.

She lifted out the Twins, and tucked the shawl tightly around Annabel. She glanced at her sunlit reflection in the Lake and smiled in a superior way, straightening the new bow of ribbon at her neck. Then she took her bag of knitting from the perambulator.

"How do you know he's always been idle?" asked Jane. "Did you know Robertson Ay before you came here?"

"Ask no questions and you'll be told no lies!" said Mary Poppins priggishly, as she began to cast on stitches for a woolen vest for John.

"She never tells us *anything!*" Michael grumbled.

"I know!" sighed Jane.

But very soon they forgot about Robertson Ay and began to play Mr.-and-Mrs.-Banks-and-Their-Two-Children. Then they became Red Indians with John and Barbara for Squaws. And after that they changed into Tight-Rope-Walkers with the back of the green seat for a rope.

"Mind my hat — *if* you please!" said Mary Poppins. It was a brown one with a pigeon's feather stuck into the ribbon.

Michael went carefully, foot over foot, along the back of the seat. When he got to the end he took off his hat and waved it.

"Jane," he cried, "I'm the King of the Castle and you're the —— "

"Stop, Michael!" she interrupted and pointed across the Lake. "Look over there!"

Along the path at the edge of the Lake came a tall, slim figure, curiously dressed. He wore stockings of red striped with yellow, a red-and-yellow tunic scalloped at the edges, and on his head was a large-brimmed red-and-yellow hat with a high peaked crown.

Jane and Michael watched with interest as he came towards them, moving with a lazy swaggering step, his hands in his pockets and his hat pulled down over his eyes.

He was whistling loudly and as he drew nearer they saw that the peaks of his tunic, and the brim of his hat, were edged with little bells that jingled musically as he moved. He was the strangest person they had ever seen and yet — there was something about him that seemed familiar.

"I think I've seen him before," said Jane, frowning and trying to remember.

"So have I. But I can't think where." Michael balanced on the back of the seat and stared.

Whistling and jingling, the curious figure slouched up to Mary Poppins and leaned against the perambulator.

"Day, Mary!" he said, putting a finger lazily to the brim of his hat. "And how are you keeping?"

Mary Poppins looked up from her knitting.

"None the better for your asking," she said, with a loud sniff.

Jane and Michael could not see the man's face for the brim of his hat was well pulled down, but from the way the bells jingled they knew he was laughing.

"Busy as usual, I see!" he remarked, glancing at the

knitting. "But then, you always were, even at Court. If you weren't dusting the Throne you'd be making the King's bed, and if you weren't doing that you were polishing the Crown Jewels. I never knew such a one for work!"

"Well, it's more than anyone could say for you," said Mary Poppins crossly.

"Ah," laughed the Stranger, "that's just where you're wrong! I'm always busy. Doing nothing takes a great deal of time! All the time, in fact!"

Mary Poppins pursed up her lips and made no reply.

The Stranger gave an amused chuckle. "Well, I must be getting along." He said. "See you again some day!"

He brushed a finger along the bells of his hat and sauntered lazily away, whistling as he went.

Jane and Michael watched until he was out of sight.

"The Dirty Rascal!"

Mary Poppins' voice rapped out behind them, and they turned to find that she, too, was staring after the Stranger.

"Who was that man, Mary Poppins?" asked Michael, bouncing excitedly up and down on the seat.

"I've just told you," she snapped. "You said you were the King of the Castle — and you're not, not by any means! But that's the Dirty Rascal."

"You mean the one in the Nursery Rhyme?" demanded Jane breathlessly.

"But Nursery Rhymes aren't true, are they?" protested Michael. "And if they are, who *is* the King of the Castle."

"Hush!" said Jane, laying her hand on his arm.

Mary Poppins had put down her knitting and was gazing out across the Lake with a far-away look in her eyes.

Jane and Michael sat very still hoping, if they made no sound, she would tell them the whole story. The Twins huddled together at one end of the perambulator, solemnly staring at Mary Poppins. Annabel, at the other end, was sound asleep.

"The King of the Castle," began Mary Poppins, folding her hands over her ball of wool and gazing right through the children as though they were not there. "The King of the Castle lived in a country so far away that most people have never heard of it. Think as far as you can, and it's even further than that; think as high as you can, and it's higher than that; think as deep as you can, and it's even deeper.

"And," she said, "if I were to tell you how rich he was we'd be sitting here till next year and still be only halfway through the list of his treasures. He was enormously, preposterously, extravagantly rich. In fact, there was only one thing in the whole world that he did not possess.

"And that thing was wisdom."

And so Mary Poppins went on ———

His land was full of gold mines, his people were polite and prosperous and generally splenderiferous. He had a good wife and four fat children — or perhaps it was five. He never could remember the exact number because his memory was so bad.

His Castle was made of silver and granite and his coffers were full of gold and the diamonds in his crown were as big as duck's eggs.

He had many marvellous cities and sailing-ships at sea. And for his right-hand-man he had a Lord High Chancellor who knew exactly What was What and What was Not and advised the King accordingly.

But the King had no wisdom. He was utterly and absolutely foolish and, what was more, he knew it! Indeed, he could hardly help knowing it, for everybody, from the Queen and the Lord High Chancellor downwards, was constantly reminding him of the fact. Even bus-conductors and engine-drivers and the people who served in shops could hardly refrain from letting the King know *they* knew he had no wisdom. They didn't dislike him, they merely felt a contempt for him.

It was not the King's fault that he was so stupid. He had tried and tried to learn wisdom ever since he was a boy. But, in the middle of his lessons, even when he was grown up, he would suddenly burst into tears and, wiping his eyes on his ermine train, would cry ——

"I know I shall never be any good at it — never! So why nag at me?"

But still his teachers continued to make the effort. Professors came from all over the world to try to teach the King of the Castle something — even if it was only Twice-Times-Two or C-A-T cat. But none of them had the slightest effect on him.

Then the Queen had an idea.

"Let us," she said to the Lord High Chancellor, "offer a reward to the Professor who can teach the King a little wisdom! And if, at the end of a month, he has not succeeded, his head shall be cut off and spiked on the Castle gates as a warning to other Professors of what will happen if they fail."

And, as most of them were rather poor and the reward was a large money-prize, the Professors kept on coming and failing and losing hope, and also their heads. And the spikes of the Castle gates became rather crowded.

Things went from bad to worse. And at last the Queen said to the King——

"Ethelbert," (That was the King's private name) "I really think you had better leave the government of the Kingdom to me and the Lord High Chancellor, as we both know a good deal about everything!"

"But that wouldn't be fair!" said the King, protesting. "After all, it's my Kingdom!"

However, he gave in at last because he knew she was cleverer than he. But he so much resented being ordered about in his own Castle and having to use the bent sceptre because he always chewed the knob of the best one, that he went on receiving the Professors and trying to learn wisdom and weeping when he found he couldn't. He wept for their sakes as well as his own for it made him unhappy to see their heads on the gate.

Each new Professor arrived full of hope and assurance and began with some question that the last had not asked.

"What are six and seven, Your Majesty?" enquired a young and handsome Professor who had come from a great distance.

And the King, trying his hardest, thought for a moment. Then he leant forward eagerly and answered——

"Why, twelve, of course!"

"Tch, tch, tch!" said the Lord High Chancellor, standing behind the King's Chair.

The Professor groaned.

"Six and seven are *thirteen*, Your Majesty!"

"Oh, I'm *so* sorry! Try another question, please, Professor! I am sure I shall get the next one right."

"Well, then, what are five and eight?"

"Um — er — let me see! Don't tell me, it's just at the tip of my tongue. Yes! Five and eight are eleven!"

"Tch, tch, tch!" said the Lord High Chancellor.

"THIRTEEN," cried the young Professor hopelessly.

"But, my dear fellow, you just said that six and seven were thirteen, so how can five and eight be? There aren't two thirteens, surely?"

But the young Professor only shook his head and loosened his collar and went dejectedly away with the Executioner.

"*Is* there more than one thirteen, then?" asked the King nervously.

The Lord High Chancellor turned away in disgust.

"I'm sorry," said the King to himself. "I liked his face so much. It's a pity it has to go on the gate."

And after that he worked very hard at his Arithmetic, hoping that when the next Professor came, he would be able to give the right answers.

He would sit at the top of the Castle steps, just by the draw-bridge, with a book of Multiplication Tables on his knees, saying them over to himself. And while he was looking at the book everything went well but when he shut his eyes and tried to remember them everything went wrong.

"Seven ones are seven, seven twos are thirty-three, seven threes are forty-five ——" he began one day. And when he found he was wrong he threw the book away in disgust and buried his head in his cloak.

"It's no good, it's no good! I shall never be wise!" he cried in despair.

Then, because he could not go on weeping for ever, he wiped his eyes and leant back in his golden chair. And as he did that he gave a little start of surprise. For a stranger had pushed past the sentry at the gate and was walking up the path that led to the Castle.

"Hullo," said the King, "who are you?" For he had no memory for faces.

"Well, if it comes to that," replied the Stranger, "Who are *you*?"

"I'm the King of the Castle," said the King, picking up the bent sceptre and trying to look important.

"And I'm the Dirty Rascal," was the reply.

The King opened his eyes wide with astonishment.

"Are you really, though? That's interesting! I'm very pleased to meet you. Do you know seven times seven?"

"No. Why should I?"

At that the King gave a great cry of delight and, running down the steps, embraced the Stranger.

"At last, at last!" cried the King, "I have found a friend. You shall live with me! What is mine shall be yours! We shall spend our lives together!"

"But, Ethelbert," protested the Queen, "this is only a Common Person. You cannot have him here."

"Your Majesty," said the Lord High Chancellor, sternly, "IT WOULD NOT DO."

But for once the King defied him.

"It will do very nicely!" he said royally. "Who is King here — you or I?"

"Well, of course, in a manner of speaking, *you* are, as it were, Your Majesty, but —— "

"Very well. Put this man in cap and bells and he can be my Fool!"

"Fool!" cried the Queen, wringing her hands. "Do we need any more of these?"

But the King did not answer. He flung his arm round the Stranger's neck and the two went dancing to the Castle door.

"You first!" said the King politely.

"No, you!" said the Stranger.

"Both together, then!" said the King generously, and they went in side by side.

And from that day the King made no attempt to learn his lessons. He made a pile of all his books and burnt them in the courtyard while he and his new friend danced round it singing —

> "I'm the King of the Castle,
>   And you're the Dirty Rascal!"

"Is that the only song you can sing?" asked the Fool one day.

"Yes, I'm afraid it is!" said the King, rather sadly. "Do you know any others?"

"Oh, dear, yes!" said the Fool. And he sang sweetly.

> "Bright, bright
>   Bee in your flight,
>   Drop down some Honey
>   For Supper tonight!"

and

> "Sweet and low, over the Snow,
>   The lolloping, scalloping Lobsters go.
>   Did you know?"

and

> "Boys and Girls, come out to play
>   Over the Hills and Far Away,
>   The Sheep's in the Meadow, the Cow's in
>   the Stall,
>   And down will come Baby, Cradle and
>   All!"

"Lovely!" cried the King, clapping his hands. "Now, listen! I've just thought of one myself! It goes like this —

"All dogs — Tiddle-de-um!
Hate frogs — Tiddle-di-do!"

"H'm," said the Fool. "Not bad!"

"Wait a minute!" said the King. "I've thought of another! And I think it's a better one. Listen, carefully!"

And he sang —

"Pluck me a Flower,
And catch me a Star,
And braize them in Butter
And Treacle and Tar.
    Tra-la!
How delicious they are!"

"Bravo!" cried the Fool. "Let's sing it together!"

And he and the King went dancing through the Castle chanting the King's two songs, one after the other, to a very special tune.

And when they were tired of singing they fell together in a heap in the main corridor and there went to sleep.

"He gets worse and worse!" said the Queen to the Lord High Chancellor, "What *are* we to do?"

"I have just heard," replied the Lord High Chancellor, "that the wisest man in the kingdom, the Chief of all the Professors, is coming to-morrow. Perhaps he will help us!"

And the next day the Chief Professor arrived, walking

smartly up the path to the Castle carrying a little black bag. It was raining slightly but the whole court had gathered at the top of the steps to welcome him.

"Has he got his wisdom in that little bag, do you think?" whispered the King. But the Fool, who was playing knuckle-bones beside the throne, only smiled and went on tossing.

"Now, if Your Majesty pleases," said the Chief Professor, in a business-like voice, "let us take Arithmetic first. Can Your Majesty answer this? If two Men and a Boy were wheeling a Barrow over a Clover-field in the middle of February, how many Legs would they have between them?"

The King gazed at him for a moment, rubbing his sceptre against his cheek.

The Fool tossed a knuckle-bone and caught it neatly on the back of his wrist.

"Does it matter?" said the King, smiling pleasantly.

The Chief Professor started violently and looked at the King in astonishment.

"As a matter of fact," he said quietly, "it doesn't. But I will ask your Majesty another question. How deep is the sea?"

"Deep enough to sail a ship on."

Again the Chief Professor started and his long beard quivered. He was smiling.

"What is the difference, Majesty, between a star and a stone, a bird and a man?"

"How deep is the sea?"

"No difference at all, Professor. A stone is a star that shines not. A man is a bird without wings."

The Chief Professor drew nearer, and gazed wonderingly at the King.

"What is the best thing in the world?" he asked quietly.

"Doing nothing," answered the King, waving his bent sceptre.

"Oh, dear, oh dear!" wailed the Queen. "THIS IS DREADFUL!"

"Tch! Tch! Tch!" said the Lord High Chancellor.

But the Chief Professor ran up the steps and stood by the King's throne.

"Who taught you these things, Majesty?" he demanded.

The King pointed with his sceptre to the Fool, who was throwing up his knuckle-bones.

"Him," said the King, ungrammatically.

The Chief Professor raised his bushy eyebrows. The Fool looked up at him and smiled. He tossed a knuckle-bone and the Professor, bending forward, caught it on the back of his hand.

"Ha!" he cried. "I know you! Even in that cap and bells, I know the Dirty Rascal!"

"Ha, ha!" laughed the Fool.

"What else did he teach you, Majesty?" The Chief Professor turned again to the King.

"To sing," answered the King.

And he stood up and sang —

"A black and white Cow
Sat up in a Tree
And if I were she
Then I shouldn't be me!"

"Very true," said the Chief Professor. "What else?"
The King sang again, in a pleasant, quavering voice —

"The Earth spins round
Without a tilt
So that the Sea
Shall not be spilt."

"So it does," remarked the Chief Professor. "Any
more?"

"Oh gracious, yes!" said the King, delighted at his suc-
cess. "There's this one"

"Oh, I could learn
Until I'm pink.
But then I'd have
No time to think!"

"Or perhaps, Professor, you'd prefer —

"We won't go round
The World for then

We'd only come
Back Home again!"

The Chief Professor clapped his hands.

"There's one more," said the King, "if you'd care to hear it."

"Please sing it, Sire!"

And the King cocked his head at the Fool and smiled wickedly and sang —

"Chief Professors
All should be
Drowned in early
Infancee!"

At the end of the song the Chief Professor gave a loud laugh and fell at the King's feet.

"Oh, King," he said, "live for ever! You have no need of me!"

And without another word he ran down the steps and took off his overcoat, coat and waistcoat. Then he flung himself down upon the grass and called for a plate of Strawberries-and-Cream and a large glass of Beer.

"Tch, tch, tch!" said the horrified Lord High Chancellor. For now all the courtiers were rushing down the steps and taking off their coats and rolling in the rainy grass.

"Strawberries and Beer! Strawberries and Beer!" they shouted thirstily.

"Give him the prize!" said the Chief Professor, sucking his beer through a straw, and nodding in the direction of the Fool.

"Pooh!" said the Fool. "I don't want it. What would I do with it?"

And he scrambled to his feet, put his knucklebones in his pocket and strolled off down the path.

"Hi, where are you going?" cried the King anxiously.

"Oh, anywhere, everywhere!" said the Fool airily, sauntering on down the path.

"Wait for me, wait for me!" called the King stumbling over his train as he hurried down the steps.

"Ethelbert! What *are* you doing? You forget yourself!" cried the Queen angrily.

"I do not, my dear!" The King called back. "On the contrary, I am remembering myself for the first time!"

He hurried down the path, caught up with the Fool, and embraced him.

"Ethelbert!" called the Queen again.

The King took no notice.

The rain had ceased but there was still a watery brightness in the air. And presently a rainbow streamed out of the sun and curved in a great arc down to the Castle path.

"I thought we might take this road," said the Fool, pointing.

"What? The rainbow? Is it solid enough? Will it hold us?"

"Try!"

The King looked at the rainbow and its shimmering stripes of violet, blue and green, and yellow and orange and red. Then he looked at the Fool.

"All right, I'm willing!" he said. "Come on!" He stepped up to the coloured path.

"It holds!" cried the King, delightedly. And he ran swiftly up the Rainbow, his train gathered in his hand.

"I'm the King of the Castle!" he sang triumphantly.

"And I'm the Dirty Rascal!" called the Fool, running after him.

"But — it's impossible!" said the Lord High Chancellor, gasping.

The Chief Professor laughed and swallowed another strawberry.

"How can anything that truly happens be impossible?" he enquired.

"But it is! It must be! It's against all the Laws!" The face
of the Lord High Chancellor was purple with anger.

A cry burst from the Queen.

"Oh, Ethelbert, come back!" she implored. "I don't
mind how foolish you are if you'll only come back!"

The King glanced down over his shoulder and shook
his head. The Fool laughed loudly. Up and up they went
together, steadily climbing the rainbow.

Something curved and shining fell at the Queen's feet.
It was the bent sceptre. A moment later it was followed by
the King's crown.

She stretched out her arms imploringly.

But the King's only answer was
a song, sung in his high, quavering
voice —

> "Say good-bye, Love,
>   Never cry, Love,
>   You are wise
>   And so am I, Love!"

The Fool, with a contemptuous flick of his hand,
tossed her down a knuckle-bone. Then he gave the King

a little push, and urged him onwards. The King picked up his train and ran, and the Fool pounded at his heels. On and on they went up the bright, coloured path until a cloud passed between them and the earth and the watching Queen saw them no longer.

> "You are wise,
>   And so am I, Love!"

The echo of the King's song came floating back. She heard the last thin thread of it after the King himself had disappeared.

"Tch, tch, TCH!" said the Lord High Chancellor. "Such things are simply NOT DONE!"

But the Queen sat down upon the empty throne and wept.

"Aie!" she cried softly, behind the screen of her hands. "My King is gone and I am very desolate and nothing will ever be the same again!"

Meanwhile, the King and the Fool had reached the top of the rainbow.

"What a climb!" said the King, sitting down and wrapping his cloak about him. "I think I shall sit here for a bit — perhaps for a long time. You go on!"

"You won't be lonely?" the Fool enquired.

"Oh, dear, no. Why should I be? It is very quiet and pleasant up here. And I can always think — or, better still, go to sleep." And as he said that he stretched himself out upon the rainbow with his cloak under his head.

The Fool bent down and kissed him.

"Good-bye, then, King," he said softly. "For you no longer have any need of me."

He left the King quietly sleeping and went whistling down the other side of the rainbow.

And from there he went wandering the world again, as he had done in the days before he met the King, singing and whistling and taking no thought for anything but the immediate moment.

Sometimes he took service with other Kings and high people, and sometimes he went among ordinary men living in small streets or lanes. Sometimes he would be wearing gorgeous livery and sometimes clothes as poor as any one ever stood up in. But no matter where he went he brought good fortune and great luck to the house that roofed him ——

Mary Poppins ceased speaking. For a moment her hands lay still in her lap and her eyes gazed out un-seeingly across the Lake.

Then she sighed and gave her shoulders a little shake and stood up.

"Now then!" she said briskly, "Best Feet Forward! And off home!"

She turned to find Jane's eyes fixed steadily upon her.

"You'll know me next time, I hope!" she remarked tartly. "And you, Michael, get down off that seat at once! Do
you want to break your neck and give me the trouble of
calling a Policeman?"

She strapped the Twins into the perambulator and
pushed it in front of her with a quick impatient movement.

Jane and Michael fell into step behind.

"I wonder where the King of the Castle went when the
rainbow disappeared?" said Michael thoughtfully.

"He went with it, I suppose, wherever it goes," said Jane.
"But what *I* wonder is — what happened to the Rascal?"

Mary Poppins had wheeled the perambulator into the
Elm Walk. And as the children turned the corner, Michael
caught Jane's hand.

"There he is!" he cried excitedly, pointing down the
Elm Walk to the Park Gates.

A tall slim figure, curiously dressed in red-and-yellow,
was swaggering towards the entrance. He stood for a moment, looking up and down Cherry-Tree Lane, and whistling. Then he slouched across to the opposite pavement
and swung himself lazily over one of the garden fences.

"It's ours!" said Jane, recognising it by the brick that
had always been missing. "He's gone into our garden.
Run, Michael, Let's catch up with him!"

They ran at a gallop after Mary Poppins and the perambulator.

"Now then, now then! No horse-play, please!" said Mary Poppins, grabbing Michael's arm firmly as he rushed by.

"But we want —— " he began, squirming.

"What did I say?" she demanded, glaring at him so fiercely that he dared not disobey. "Walk beside me, please, like a Christian. And Jane, you can help me push the pram!"

Unwillingly Jane fell into step beside her.

As a rule, Mary Poppins allowed nobody to push the perambulator except herself. But to-day it seemed to Jane that she was purposely preventing them from running ahead. For here was Mary Poppins, who usually walked so quickly that it was difficult to keep up with her, going at a snail's pace down the Elm Walk, pausing every few minutes to gaze about her, and standing for at least a minute in front of a basket of litter.

At last, after what seemed to them like hours, they came to the Park Gates. She kept them beside her until they reached the gate of Number Seventeen. Then they broke from her and went flying through the garden.

They darted behind the lilac tree. Not there! They searched among the rhododendrons and looked in the glasshouse, the tool-shed and the water-butt. They even peered into a circle of hose-piping. The Dirty Rascal was nowhere to be seen!

There was only one other person in the garden and that was Robertson Ay. He was sound asleep in the middle of the lawn with his cheek against the knives of the lawn-mower.

"We've missed him!" said Michael. "He must have taken a short-cut and gone out by the back way. Now we'll never see him again."

He turned back to the lawn-mower.

Jane was standing beside it, looking down affectionately at Robertson Ay. His old felt hat was pulled over his face, its crown crushed and dented into a curving peak.

"I wonder if he had a good Half-day!" said Michael, whispering so as not to disturb him.

But, small as the whisper was, Robertson Ay must have heard it. For he suddenly stirred in his sleep and settled himself more comfortably against the lawn-mower. And as he moved there was a faint, jingling sound as though, near at hand, small bells were softly ringing.

With a start, Jane lifted her head and glanced at Michael.

"Did you hear?" she whispered.

He nodded, staring.

Robertson Ay moved again and muttered in his sleep. They bent to listen.

"Black and white cow," he murmured indistinctly. "Sat up in a tree . . . mumble, mumble, mumble . . . it couldn't be me! Hum . . . !"

Across his sleeping body Jane and Michael gazed at each other with wondering eyes.

"Humph! Well to be him, I must say!"

Mary Poppins had come up behind them and she too was staring down at Robertson Ay. "The lazy, idle, Good-for-Nothing!" she said crossly.

But she couldn't really have been as cross as she sounded for she took her handkerchief out of her pocket and slipped it between Robertson Ay's cheek and the lawn-mower.

"He'll have a clean face, anyway, when he wakes up. *That'll* surprise him!" she said tartly.

But Jane and Michael noticed how careful she had been not to wake Robertson Ay and how soft her eyes were when she turned away.

They tip-toed after her, nodding wisely to one another. Each knew that the other understood.

Mary Poppins trundled the perambulator up the steps

and into the hall. The front door shut with a quiet little click.

Outside in the garden Robertson Ay slept on.

That night when Jane and Michael went to say goodnight to him, Mr. Banks was in a towering rage. He was dressing to go out to dinner and he couldn't find his best stud.

"Well, by all that's lively, here it is!" he cried suddenly. "In a tin of stove-blacking — of all things! on my dressing-table. That Robertson Ay's doing. I'll sack that fellow one of these days. He's nothing but a dirty rascal!"

And he could not understand why Jane and Michael, when he said that, burst into such peals of joyous laughter. . . .

CHAPTER SEVEN

THE EVENING OUT

What no pudding?" said Michael, as Mary Poppins, her arm full of plates, mugs and knives, began to lay the table for Nursery Tea.

She turned and looked at him fiercely.

"This," she snapped, "is my Evening Out. So you will eat bread and butter and strawberry-jam and be thankful. There's many a little boy would be glad to have it."

"*I'm* not," grumbled Michael. "I want rice-pudding with honey in it."

"You want! You want! You're always wanting. If it's not this it's that, and if it's not that it's the other. You'll ask for the Moon next."

He put his hands in his pockets and moved sulkily away to the window-seat. Jane was kneeling there, staring out at the bright, frosty sky. He climbed up beside her, still looking very cross.

"All right, then! I *do* ask for the Moon. So there!" He flung the words back at Mary Poppins. "But I know I shan't get it. Nobody ever gives me anything."

He turned hurriedly away from her angry glare.

"Jane," he said, "there's no pudding."

"Don't interrupt me, I'm counting!" said Jane, pressing her nose against the window-pane so that it was quite blunt and squashed at the tip.

"Counting what?" he asked, not very interested. His mind was full of rice-pudding and honey.

"Shooting stars. Look, there goes another. That's seven. And another! Eight. And one over the Park—that's nine!"

"O-o-h! And there's one going down Admiral Boom's chimney!" said Michael, sitting up suddenly and forgetting all about the pudding.

"And a little one—see!—streaking right across the Lane. Such frosty lights!" cried Jane. "Oh, *how* I wish we were out there! What makes stars shoot, Mary Poppins?"

"Do they come out of a gun?" enquired Michael.

Mary Poppins sniffed contemptuously.

"What do you think I am? An Encyclopaedia? Everything from A to Z?" she demanded crossly. "Come and eat your teas, please!" She pushed them towards their chairs and pulled down the blind. "And No Nonsense. I'm in a hurry!"

And she made them eat so quickly that they were both afraid they would choke.

"Mayn't I have just *one* more piece?" asked Michael, stretching out his hand to the plate of bread-and-butter.

"You may not. You have already eaten more than is good for you. Take a ginger biscuit and go to bed."

"But —— "

"But me no buts or you'll be sorry!" she flung at him sternly.

"I shall have indigestion, I know I shall," he said to Jane, but only in a whisper, for when Mary Poppins looked like that it was wiser not to make any remark at all. Jane took no notice. She was slowly eating her ginger biscuit and peering cautiously out at the frosty sky through a chink in the blind.

"Thirteen, Fourteen, Fifteen, Sixteen —— "

"Did I or did I not say BED?" enquired the familiar voice behind them.

"All right, I'm just going! I'm just going, Mary Poppins!" And they ran squealing to the Night-Nursery with Mary Poppins hurrying after them and looking Simply Awful.

Less than half-an-hour later Mary Poppins was tucking each one in tightly, pushing the sheets and blankets under the mattress with sharp furious little stabs.

"There!" she said, snapping the words between her lips. "That's all for tonight. And if I hear One Word —— " She did not finish the sentence but her look said all that was necessary.

"There'll be Trouble!" said Michael, finishing it for her. But he whispered it under his breath to his blanket for he knew what would happen if he said it aloud. She whisked out of the room, her starched apron rustling and crackling, and shut the door with an angry click. They heard her light feet hurrying away down the stairs — Tap-tap, Tap-tap — from landing to landing.

"She's forgotten to light the night-light," said Michael, peering around the corner of his pillow. "She *must* be in a hurry. I wonder where she's going!"

"And she's left the blind up!" said Jane, sitting up in bed. "Hooray, now we can watch the shooting stars!"

The pointed roofs of Cherry-Tree Lane were shiny with frost and the moonlight slid down the gleaming slopes and fell soundlessly into the dark gulfs between the houses. Everything glimmered and shone. The earth was as bright as the sky.

"Seventeen-Eighteen-Nineteen-Twenty — — "said Jane, steadily counting as the stars shot down. As fast as one disappeared another came to take its place until it seemed that the whole sky was alive and dancing with the dazzle of shooting stars.

"It's like fireworks," said Michael. "Oh, look at that one! Or the Circus. Do you think they have circuses in Heaven, Jane?"

"I'm not sure!" said Jane doubtfully. "There's the Great Bear and the Little Bear, of course, and Taurus-the-Bull and Leo-the-Lion. But I don't know about a Circus."

"Mary Poppins would know," said Michael, nodding wisely.

"Yes, but she wouldn't tell," said Jane, turning again to the window. "Where was I? Was it Twenty-one? Oh, Michael, *such* a beauty — do you see?" She bounced excitedly up and down in her bed, pointing to the window.

A very bright star, larger than any they had yet seen, was shooting through the sky towards Number Seventeen Cherry-Tree Lane. It was different from the others for, instead of leaping straight across the dark, it was turning over and over, curving through the air very curiously.

"Duck your head, Michael!" shouted Jane suddenly. "It's coming in here!"

They dived down into the blankets and burrowed their heads under the pillows.

"Do you think it's gone now?" came Michael's muffled voice presently. "I'm nearly smothercated."

"Of course I haven't gone!" A small clear voice answered him. "What do you take me for?"

Very surprised, Jane and Michael threw off the bedclothes and sat up. There, at the edge of the window-sill, perched on its shiny tail and gleaming brightly at them, was the shooting star.

"Come on, you two! Be quick!" it said, gleaming frostily across the room.

Michael stared at it.

"But — I don't understand —— " he began.

A bright, glittering, very small laugh sounded in the room.

"You never do, do you?" said the star.

"You mean — we're to come with you?" said Jane.

"Of course! And mind you wrap up. It's chilly!"

They sprang out of their beds and ran for overcoats.

"Got any money?" the star asked sharply.

"There's twopence in my coat pocket," said Jane doubt-fully.

"Coppers? They'll be no good! Here, catch!" And with a little sizzling sound, as though a firework squib was go-ing off, the star sent out a shower of sparks. Two of them shot right across the room and landed, one in Jane's hand and one in Michael's.

"Hurry, or we'll be late!"

The star streaked across the room, through the closed door and down the stairs, with Jane and Michael, tightly clasping their starry money, after it.

"Can I be dreaming I wonder?" said Jane to herself, as she hurried down Cherry-Tree Lane.

"Follow!" cried the star as, at the end of the Lane, where the frosty sky seemed to come down to meet the pavement, it leapt into the air and disappeared.

"Follow! Follow!" came the voice from somewhere in the sky. "Just as you are, step on a star!"

Jane seized Michael's hand and raised her foot uncer-tainly from the pavement. To her surprise she found that the lowest star in the sky was easily within her reach. She stepped up, balancing carefully. The star seemed quite steady and solid.

"Come on, Michael!"

They hurried up the frosty sky, leaping over the gulfs between the stars.

"Follow!" cried the voice, far ahead of them. Jane paused and, glancing down, caught her breath to see how high they were. Cherry-Tree Lane — indeed, the whole world — was as small and sparkly as a toy on a Christmas Tree.

"Are you giddy, Michael?" she said, springing on to a large flat star.

"N-o-o. Not if you hold my hand."

They paused. Behind them the great stairway of stars led down to earth, but before them there were no more to be seen, nothing but a thick blue patch of naked sky.

Michael's hand trembled in Jane's.

"W-w-what shall we do now?" he said, in a voice that tried not to sound frightened.

"Walk up! Walk up! Walk up and see the sights! Pay your money and take your choice! The two-Tailed Dragon or the Horse with Wings! Magical Marvels! Universal Wonders! Walk up! Walk up!"

A loud voice seemed to be shouting these words in their very ears. They stared about them. There was no sign of anybody.

"Step along everybody! Don't miss the Golden Bull and the Comical Clown! World-Famous Troupe of Performing Constellations! Once seen never forgotten! Push aside the curtain and walk in!"

Again the voice sounded close beside them. Jane put

out her hand. To her surprise she found that what had seemed a plain and starless patch of sky was really a thick dark curtain. She pressed against it and felt it yield; she gathered up a fold of it and, pulling Michael after her, pushed the curtain aside.

A bright flare of light dazzled them for a moment. When they could see again they found themselves standing at the edge of a ring of shining sand. The great blue curtain enfolded the ring on all sides and was drawn up to a point above as though it were a tent.

"Now then! Do you know you were almost too late? Got your tickets?"

They turned. Beside them, his bright feet gleaming in the sand, stood a strange and gigantic figure. He looked like a hunter, for a starry leopard-skin was slung across his shoulders, and from his belt, decorated with three large stars, hung down a shining sword.

"Tickets, please!" he held out his hand.

"I'm afraid we haven't got any. You see, we didn't know —— " began Jane.

"Dear, dear, how careless! Can't let you in without a ticket, you know. But what's that in your hand?"

Jane held out the golden spark.

"Well, if that isn't a ticket, I'd like to know what is!" He pressed the spark between his three large stars. "Another shiner for Orion's belt!" he remarked pleasantly.

"Is that who you are?" said Jane, staring at him.

"Of course — didn't you know? But — excuse me, I must attend to the door. Move along, please!"

The children, feeling rather shy, moved on hand in hand. Tier on tier of seats rose up at one side of them and at the other a golden cord separated them from the ring. And the ring itself was crowded with the strangest collection of animals, all shining bright as gold. A Horse with great gold Wings pranced by on glittering hooves. A golden Fish threshed up the dust of the ring with its fin. Three Little Kids were rushing wildly about on two legs instead of four. And it seemed to Jane and Michael, as they looked closer, that all these animals were made of stars. The wings of the Horse were of stars, not feathers, the Three Kids had stars on their noses and tails, and the Fish was covered with shining starry scales.

"Good-evening!" it remarked, bowing politely to Jane as it threshed by. "Fine night for the performance!"

But before Jane could reply it had hurried past.

"How very strange!" said she. "I've never seen animals like this before!"

"Why should it be strange?" said a voice behind them.

Two children, both boys and a little older than Jane, stood there smiling. They were dressed in shining tunics and their peaked caps had each a star for a pompon.

"I beg your pardon," said Jane, politely. "But, you see, we're used to — er — fur and feathers and these animals seem to be made of stars."

"But of course they are!" said the first boy, opening his eyes very wide. "What else could they be made of? They're the Constellations!"

"But even the sawdust is gold —— " began Michael.

The second boy laughed. "Star-dust, you mean! Haven't you been to a Circus before?"

"Not this kind."

"All circuses are alike," said the first boy. "Our animals are brighter, that's all."

"But who are you?" demanded Michael.

"The Twins. He's Pollux and I'm Castor. We're always together."

"Like the Siamese Twins?"

"Yes. But more so. The Siamese Twins are only joined in body but we have a single heart and a single mind between us. We can think each other's thoughts and dream each other's dreams. But we mustn't stay here talking. We've got to get ready — see you later!" And the Twins ran off and disappeared through a curtained exit.

"Hullo!" said a gloomy voice from inside the ring. "I suppose you don't happen to have a currant bun in your pocket?"

A Dragon with two large finny tails lumbered towards them, breathing steam from its nostrils.

"I'm sorry, we haven't," said Jane.

"Nor a biscuit or two?" said the Dragon eagerly.

They shook their heads.

"I thought not," said the Dragon, dropping a golden

tear. "It's always the way on Circus nights. I don't get fed till after the performance. On ordinary occasions I have a beautiful maiden for supper —— "

Jane drew back quickly, pulling Michael with her.

"Oh, don't be alarmed!" the Dragon went on, reassuringly. "You'd be *much* too small. Besides, you're human and therefore tasteless. They keep me hungry," he explained, "so that I shall do my tricks better. But after the show —— " A greedy light came into his eyes and he shuffled away, lolling out his tongue and saying "Yum-yum" in a soft, greedy, hissing voice.

"I'm glad we're only human," said Jane, turning to Michael. "It would be *dreadful* to be eaten by a Dragon!"

But Michael had hurried on ahead and was talking eagerly to the Three Little Kids.

"How does it go?" he was asking, as Jane caught up with him.

And the Eldest Kid, which apparently had offered to recite, cleared its throat, and began —

> "Horn and toe,
> Toe and horn —— — "

"Now, Kids!" Orion's voice interrupted loudly. "You can say your piece when the time comes. Get ready now, we're going to begin! Follow me, please!" he said to the children.

They trotted obediently after the gleaming figure, and

as they went the golden animals turned to stare at them. They heard snatches of whispered conversation as they passed.

"Who's that?" said a huge starry Bull, as it stopped pawing the star-dust to gaze at them. And a Lion turned and whispered something into the Bull's ear. They caught the words "Banks" and "Evening Out" but heard no more than that.

By now every seat on every tier was filled with a shining starry figure. Only three empty seats remained and to these Orion led the children.

"Here you are! We kept these for you. Just under the Royal Box. You'll see perfectly. Look! they're just beginning!"

And, turning, Jane and Michael saw that the ring was empty. The animals had hurried out while they had been climbing to their seats. They unbuttoned their overcoats and leaned forward excitedly.

From somewhere came a fanfare of trumpets. A blast of music echoed through the tent and above the sound could be heard a high, sweet neighing.

"The comets!" said Orion, sitting down beside Michael.

A wild nodding head appeared at the entrance and one by one nine comets galloped into the ring, their manes braided with gold, and silver plumes on their heads.

Suddenly the music rose to a great roar of sound and

with one movement the comets dropped upon their knees and bowed their heads. A warm gust of air came wafting across the ring.

"How hot it's getting!" cried Jane.

"Hush! He's coming!" said Orion.

"Who?" whispered Michael.

"The Ring-Master!"

Orion nodded to the far entrance. A light shone there, eclipsing the light of the constellations. It grew steadily brighter.

"Here he is!" Orion's voice had a curious softness in it.

And as he spoke there appeared between the curtains a towering golden figure with flaming curls upon his head and a wide, radiant face. And with him came a great swell of warmth that lapped the ring and spread out in ever-widening circles until it surrounded Jane and Michael and Orion. Half-consciously, made dreamy by that warmth, the children slipped off their overcoats.

Orion sprang to his feet holding his right hand above his head.

"Hail, Sun, hail!" he cried. And from the stars in the tiered seats the cry came echoing ——

"Hail!"

The Sun glanced round the wide dark-tented ring and, in answer to the greeting, swung his long gold whip three times about his head. As the lash turned in the air there was a quick, sharp crack. At once the comets sprang up and cantered out, their braided tails swinging wildly, their plumed heads high and erect.

"Here we are again, here we are again!" cried a loud, hoarse voice, and bouncing into the ring came a comical figure with silver-painted face, wide red mouth and huge silvery frills about his neck.

"Saturn — the Clown!" whispered Orion behind his hand to the children.

"When is a door not a door?" demanded the Clown of the audience, turning over and standing on one hand.

"When it's ajar!" answered Jane and Michael loudly.

A disappointed look came over the Clown's face.

"Oh, you know it!" he said, reproachfully. "That's not fair!"

The Sun cracked his whip.

"All right, all right!" said the Clown. "I've got another. Why does a hen cross the road?" he asked, sitting down with a bump on the star-dust.

"To get to the other side!" cried Jane and Michael.

The swinging whip caught the Clown round the knees.

"O-o-h! Don't do that! You'll hurt poor Joey. Look at them laughing up there! But I'll fix them! Listen!" He turned a double somersault in the air.

"What kind of jam did the chicken ask for when it came out of the egg. Tell me that!"

"Mar — me — lade!" yelled Michael and Jane.

"Be off with you!" cried the Sun, catching his whip

about the Clown's shoulders, and the Clown went bounding round the ring, head over heels, crying ——

"Poor old Joey! He's failed again! He's failed again!
They know all his best jokes, poor old fellow, poor
old — oh, beg pardon, Miss, beg pardon!"

He broke off for he had somersaulted against Pegasus,
the Winged Horse, as it entered carrying a bright spangly
figure on its back.

"Venus, the Evening Star," explained Orion.

Breathlessly, Jane and Michael watched the starry figure ride lightly through the ring. Round and round she
went, bowing to the Sun as she passed, and presently the
Sun, standing in her path, held up a great hoop covered
with thin gold paper.

She balanced on her toes for a moment. "Hup!" said the
Sun, and Venus, with the utmost grace, jumped through
the hoop and landed again on the back of Pegasus.

"Hurrah!" cried Jane and Michael, and the audience of
stars echoed back "Hurrah!"

"Let me try, let Poor Joey have a go, just a little one to
make a cat laugh!" cried the Clown. But Venus only tossed
her head and laughed and rode out of the ring.

She had hardly disappeared before the Three Kids
came prancing in, looking rather shy and bowing awkwardly to the Sun. Then they stood on their hind legs in
a row before him, and in high, thin voices recited the following song —

"Horn and hoof,
 Hoof and horn,
 Every night
 Three Kids are born,
Each with a Twinkly Nose,
Each with a Twinkly Tail.
 Blue and black,
 Black and blue
 Is the evening sky
 As the Kids come through,
Each with a Twinkly Nose,
Each with a Twinkly Tail.

Gay and bright
And white as May
The Three Kids drink
At the Milky Way,
Each with a Twinkly Nose,
Each with a Twinkly Tail.
All night long
From Dusk till Dawn
The Three Kids graze
On the starry lawn
Each with a Twinkly Nose.
Each with a Twink-ker-ly T-a-i-l!"

They drew out the last line with a long baa-ing sound and danced out.

"What's next?" asked Michael but there was no need for Orion to reply for the Dragon was already in the ring, his nostrils steaming and his two finny tails tossing up the star-dust. After him came Castor and Pollux carrying between them a large white shining globe faintly figured with a design of mountains and rivers.

"It looks like the Moon!" said Jane.

"Of course it's the Moon!" said Orion.

The Dragon was now on his hind legs and the Twins were balancing the Moon on his nose. It bobbed up and down uncertainly for a moment. Then it settled and the Dragon began to waltz about the ring to the tune of the starry music. Round he went, very carefully and steadily, once, twice, three times.

"That will do!" said the Sun cracking his whip. And the Dragon, with a sigh of relief, shook its head and sent the Moon flying across the ring. It landed, with a bumpy thud, right in Michael's lap.

"Good gracious!" said he, very startled. "What shall I do with this?"

"Whatever you like," said Orion. "I thought you asked for it."

And suddenly Michael remembered his conversation that evening with Mary Poppins. He had asked for the Moon then, and now he had got it. And he didn't know what to do with it. How very awkward!

But he had no time to worry about it for the Sun was cracking his whip again. Michael settled the Moon on his knee, folded his arms around it and turned back to the ring.

"What are two and three?" the Sun was asking the Dragon.

The two tails lashed five times on the star-dust.

"And six and four?" The Dragon thought for a minute. One, two, three, four, five, six, seven, eight, nine —— The tails stopped.

"Wrong!" said the Sun. "Quite wrong! No supper for you to-night!"

At that the Dragon burst into tears and hurried from the ring sobbing.

"Alas and alack,
    Boo-hoo, boo-hoo!"

he cried bitterly.

    "I wanted a Maiden
    Served in a stew,
    A succulent, seasoned, tasty Girl
    With star for her eye
    And comet for curl,
    And I wouldn't have minded if there'd
    been two,
    For I'm awfully hungry.
                    Boo-hoo!
                    Boo-hoo!"

    "Won't they give him even a small maiden?" said
Michael, feeling rather sorry for the Dragon.

"Hush!" said Orion, as a dazzling form sprang into the ring.

When the cloud of star-dust had cleared away, the children drew back, startled. It was the Lion and he was growling fiercely.

Michael moved a little closer to Jane.

The Lion, crouching, moved forward slowly till he reached the Sun. His long red tongue went out, lolling dangerously. But the Sun only laughed, and lifting his foot, he gently kicked the Lion's golden nose. With a roar, as though he had been burnt, the starry beast sprang up.

The Sun's whip cracked fiercely on the air. Slowly, unwillingly, growling all the time, the Lion rose on his hind legs. The Sun tossed him a skipping-rope and, holding it between his forepaws, the lion began to sing.

> "I am the Lion, Leo-the-Lion,
>   The beautiful, suitable, Dandy Lion,
>   Look for me up in the starry sky on
>   Clear cold nights at the foot of Orion,
>   Glimmering, glittering, gleaming there,
>   The Handsomest Sight in the atmos-
>   phere!"

And at the end of the song he swung the rope and skipped round the ring, rolling his eyes and growling.

"Hurry up, Leo, it's our turn!" A rumbling voice sounded from behind the curtain.

"Come on, you big cat!" a shrill voice added.

The Lion dropped his skipping-rope and with a roar sprang at the curtain, but the two creatures who entered next stepped carefully aside so that the Lion missed them.

"Great Bear and Little Bear," said Orion.

Slowly the two Bears lumbered in, holding paws and waltzing to slow music. Round the ring they went, looking very serious and solemn, and at the end of their dance they made a clumsy curtsey to the audience and remarked—

"We're the Gruffly Bear and the Squeaky
    Bear,
O Constellations, has any one here
A honeycomb square that they can spare
For the Squeaky Bear and the Gruffly Bear
To add to the store in their dark blue lair
Or to——
        or to——
            or to——"

The Great Bear and the Little Bear stammered and stumbled and looked at each other.

"Don't you remember what comes next?" rumbled the Gruffly Bear behind his paw.

"No, I don't!" The Squeaky Bear shook his head and stared anxiously down at the star-dust as though he thought the missing words might be there.

But at that moment the audience saved the situation. A shower of honeycombs came hurtling down, tumbling about the ears of the two Bears. The Gruffly Bear and the Squeaky Bear, looking very relieved, stooped and picked them up.

"Good!" rumbled the Great Bear, digging his nose into a comb.

"*Ex*-cellent!" squeaked the Little Bear, trying another. Then, with their noses streaming with honey, they bowed solemnly to the Sun and lumbered out.

The Sun waved his hand and the music grew louder and rang triumphantly through the tent.

"The signal for the Big Parade," said Orion, as Castor and Pollux came dancing in with all the Constellations at their heels.

The Bears came back, waltzing clumsily together, and Leo-the-Lion, still growling angrily, came sniffing at their heels. In swept a starry Swan, singing a high, clear chant.

"The Swan Song," said Orion.

And after the Swan came the Golden Fish, leading the Three Kids by a silver string, and the Dragon followed, still sobbing bitterly. A loud and terrible sound almost drowned the music. It was the bellowing of Taurus-the-Bull as he leapt into the ring, trying to toss Saturn the Clown from his back. One after another the creatures came rushing in to take their places. The ring was a swaying golden mass of horns and hooves and manes and tails.

"Is this the end?" Jane whispered.

"Almost," replied Orion. "They're finishing early to-night. She has to be in by half-past ten."

"Who has?" asked both the children together. But Orion did not hear. He was standing up in his seat waving his arm.

"Come along, be quick there, step along!" he called.

And in came Venus riding her Winged Horse followed by a starry Serpent that put its tail carefully in its mouth and bowled along like a hoop.

Last of all came the comets, prancing proudly through the curtains, swinging their braided tails. The music was louder now and wilder and a golden smoke rose up from the star-dust as the Constellations, shouting, singing, roaring, growling, formed themselves into a ring. And in the centre, as though they dared not go too near his presence, they left a clear, bare circle for the Sun.

There he stood, towering above them all, his whip folded in his arms. He nodded lightly to each animal as it passed him with bent head. And then Jane and Michael saw that bright gaze lift from the ring and wander round the great audience of watching stars until it turned in the direction of the Royal Box. They felt themselves growing warmer as his rays fell upon them and, with a start of surprise, they saw him raise his whip and nod his head towards them.

As the lash swung up every star and constellation

turned in its tracks. Then, with one movement, every one of them bowed.

"Are they — can they be bowing to *us?*" whispered Michael, clutching the Moon more tightly.

A familiar laugh sounded behind them. They turned quickly. There, sitting alone in the Royal Box, sat a well-known figure in a straw hat and blue coat and a gold locket round its neck.

"Hail, Mary Poppins, hail!" came the massed voices from the circus ring.

Jane and Michael looked at each other. So this was what Mary Poppins did on her Evening Out! They could hardly believe their eyes — and yet, there *was* Mary Poppins, as large as life and looking very superior.

"Hail!" came the cry again.

Mary Poppins raised her hand in greeting.

Then, stepping primly and importantly, she moved out of the box. She did not seem in the least surprised to see Jane and Michael but she sniffed as she went past.

"How often," she remarked to them across Orion's head, "have you been told that it is rude to stare?"

She passed on and down to the ring. The Great Bear lifted the golden rope. The Constellations drew apart and the Sun moved a pace forward. He spoke and his voice was warm and full of sweetness.

"Mary Poppins, my dear, you are welcome!"

Mary Poppins dropped to her knees in a deep curtsey.

There, all alone in the Royal Box, sat a well-known figure

"The Planets hail you and the Constellations give you greeting. Rise, my child!"

She stood up, bending her head respectfully before him.

"For you, Mary Poppins," the Sun went on, "the Stars have gathered in the dark blue tent, for you they have been withdrawn to-night from shining on the world. I trust, therefore, that you have enjoyed your Evening Out!"

"I never had a better one. Never!" said Mary Poppins, lifting her head and smiling.

"Dear child!" The Sun bowed. "But now the sands of night are running out, and you must be in by half-past ten. So, before you depart, let us all, for old sake's sake, dance the Dance of the Wheeling Sky!"

"Down you go!" said Orion, to the astonished children, giving them a little push. They stumbled down the stairs and almost fell into the star-dust ring.

"And where, may I ask, are your manners?" hissed the well-known voice in Jane's ear.

"What must I do?" stammered Jane.

Mary Poppins glared at her and made a little movement towards the Sun. And, suddenly, Jane realised. She grabbed Michael's arm, and, kneeling, pulled him down beside her. The warmth from the Sun lapped them about with fiery sweetness.

"Rise, children," he said kindly. "You are very welcome. I know you well — I have looked down upon you many a summer's day!"

Scrambling to her feet Jane moved towards him but his whip held her back. "Touch me not, child of earth!" he cried warningly, waving her further away. "Life is sweet and no man may come near the Sun — touch me not!"

"But are you truly the Sun?" demanded Michael, staring at him.

The Sun flung out his hand.

"O Stars and Constellations," he said, "tell me this. Who am I? This child would know?"

"Lord of the Stars, O Sun!" answered a thousand starry voices.

"He is King of the South and North," cried Orion, "and Ruler of the East and West. He walks the outer rim of the world and the Poles melt in his glory. He draws up the leaf from the seed and covers the land with sweetness. He is truly the Sun."

The Sun smiled across at Michael.

"Now do you believe?"

Michael nodded.

"Then, strike up! And you, Constellations, choose your Partners!"

The Sun waved his whip. The music began again, very swift and gay and dancey. Michael began to beat time with his feet as he hugged the Moon in his arms. But he squeezed it a little too tightly for suddenly there was a loud pop and the Moon began to dwindle.

"Oh! Oh! Look what's happening!" cried Michael, almost weeping.

Down, down, down, shrank the Moon, until it was as small as a soap-bubble, then it was only a wisp of shining light and then — his hands closed upon empty air.

"It couldn't have been a real Moon, could it?" he demanded.

Jane glanced questioningly at the Sun across the little stretch of star-dust.

He flung back his flaming head and smiled at her.

"What is real and what is not? Can you tell me or I you? Perhaps we shall never know more than this — that to think a thing is to make it true. And so, if Michael thought he had the Moon in his arms — why, then, he had indeed."

"Then," said Jane wonderingly, "is it true that we are here to-night or do we only think we are?"

The Sun smiled again, a little sadly.

"Child," he said, "seek no further! From the beginning of the world all men have asked that question. And I, who am Lord of the Sky — even I do not know the answer. I am certain only that this is the Evening Out, that the Constellations are shining in your eyes and that it is true if you think it is . . ."

"Come, dance with us, Jane and Michael!" cried the Twins.

And Jane forgot her question as the four of them swung out into the ring in time with the heavenly tune. But they were hardly half-way round the ring before, with a little start, she stumbled and stood still.

"Look! Look! She is dancing with him!"

Michael followed her gaze and stood still on his short
fat legs, staring.

Mary Poppins and the Sun were dancing together. But
not as Jane and he were dancing with the Twins, breast to
breast and foot to foot. Mary Poppins and the Sun never

once touched, but waltzed with arms outstretched, opposite each other, keeping perfect time together in spite of the space between them.

About them wheeled the dancing constellations: Venus with her arms round the neck of Pegasus, the Bull and the Lion arm in arm and the Three Kids prancing in a row. Their moving brightness dazzled the children's eyes as they stood in the star-dust gazing.

Then suddenly the dance slackened and the music died away. The Sun and Mary Poppins, together yet apart, stood still. And at the same time every animal paused in the dance and stood quietly in its tracks. The whole ring was silent.

The Sun spoke.

"Now," he said quietly, "the time has come. Back to your places in the sky, my stars and constellations. Home and to sleep, my three dear mortal guests. Mary Poppins, good-night! I do not say good-bye for we shall meet again. But — for a little time — farewell, farewell!"

Then, with a large and gracious movement of his head, the Sun leaned across the space that separated him from Mary Poppins and, with great ceremony, carefully, lightly, swiftly, he brushed her cheek with his lips.

"Ah!" cried the Constellations, enviously, "The Kiss! The Kiss!"

But as she received it, Mary Poppins' hand flew to her cheek protectingly, as though the kiss had burnt it. A look of pain crossed her face for a moment. Then, with a smile, she lifted her head to the Sun.

"Farewell!" she said softly, in a voice Jane and Michael had never heard her use.

"Away!" cried the Sun, stretching out his whip. And obediently the Constellations began to rush from the ring. Castor and Pollux joined arms protectingly about the children, that the Great Bear might not brush them as he lumbered by, nor the Bull's horns graze them, nor the Lion do them harm. But in Jane's ears and Michael's the sounds of the ring were growing fainter. Their heads fell sideways, dropping heavily upon their shoulders. Other arms came round them and, as in a dream, they heard the voice of Venus saying — "Give them to me! I am the Homeward Star. I bring the lamb to the fold and the child to its Mother."

They gave themselves up to her rocking arms, swinging lightly with her as a boat swings with the tide.

To-and-fro, to-and-fro.

A light flickered across their eyes. Was that the Dragon
going brightly by or the nursery candle held guttering
above them?

To-and-fro, to-and-fro.

They nestled down into soft, sweet warmth. Was it the
lapping heat of the Sun? Or the eiderdown on a nursery
bed?

"I think it is the Sun," thought Jane, dreamily.

"I think it is my eiderdown," thought Michael.

And a far-away voice, like a dream, like a breath,
cried faintly, faintly — "It is whatever you think it is.
Farewell . . . Farewell . . ."

Michael woke with a shout. He had suddenly remembered something.

"My overcoat! My overcoat! I left it under the Royal
Box!"

He opened his eyes. He saw the painted duck at the end
of his bed. He saw the mantelpiece with the clock and the
Royal Doulton Bowl and the jam-jar full of green leaves.
And he saw, hanging on its usual hook, his overcoat with
his hat just above it.

"But where are the stars?" he called, sitting up in bed
and staring. "I want the stars and Constellations!"

"Oh? Indeed?" said Mary Poppins, coming into the

room and looking very stiff and starched in her clean apron. "Is that all? I wonder you don't ask for the Moon, too!"

"But I did!" he reminded her reproachfully. "And I got it, too! But I squeezed it too tight and it bust!"

"Burst!"

"Well, burst, then!"

"Stuff!" said Mary Poppins, tossing him his dressing-gown.

"Is it morning already?" said Jane, opening her eyes and gazing round the room very surprised to find herself in her own bed. "But how did we get back? I was dancing with the Twin stars, Castor and Pollux."

"You two and your stars," said Mary Poppins crossly, pulling back the blankets. "I'll star you. Spit-spot out of bed, please. I'm late already."

"I suppose you danced too long last night," said Michael, bundling unwillingly out on to the floor.

"Danced? Humph, a lot of dancing I get a chance for, don't I—looking after the five worst children in the world!"

Mary Poppins sniffed and looked very sorry for herself and as if she had not had enough sleep.

"But weren't you dancing—on your Evening Out?" said Jane. For she was remembering how Mary Poppins and the Sun had waltzed together in the centre of the star-dust ring.

Mary Poppins opened her eyes wide.

"I hope," she remarked, drawing herself up haughtily, "I have something better to do with my Evening Out than to go round and round like a Careering Whirligig."

"But I saw you!" said Jane. "Up in the sky. You jumped down from the Royal Box and went to dance in the ring."

Holding their breaths, she and Michael gazed at Mary Poppins as her face slowly flushed red with fury.

"You," she said shortly, "have been having a nice sort of a nightmare, I must say. Who ever heard of me, a person in my position, jumping down from —— "

"But I had the nightmare, too," interrupted Michael, "and it was lovely. I was in the sky with Jane and I *saw* you!"

"What, jumping?"

"Er — yes — and dancing."

"In the sky?" He trembled as she came towards him. Her face was dark and terrible.

"One more insult —— " she said threateningly, "Just *one more* and you'll find yourself dancing in the corner. So I warn you!"

He hurriedly looked the other way, tying the cord of his dressing-gown, and Mary Poppins, her very apron crackling with anger, flounced across the room to wake up the Twins.

Jane sat on her bed staring at Mary Poppins as she bent over the cots.

Michael slowly put on his slippers and sighed.

"We *must* have dreamt it after all," he said sadly. "I wish it had been true."

"It *was* true," said Jane in a cautious whisper, her eyes still fixed on Mary Poppins.

"How do you know? Are you sure?"

"Quite sure. Look!"

Mary Poppins' head was bent over Barbara's cot. Jane nodded towards it. "Look at her face," she whispered in his ear.

Michael regarded Mary Poppins' face steadily. There was the black hair looped back behind the ears, there the familiar blue eyes so like a Dutch doll's, and there were the turned-up nose and the bright red shiny cheeks.

"I can't see anything——" he began and broke off suddenly. For now, as Mary Poppins turned her head, he saw what Jane had seen.

Burning bright, in the very centre of her cheek, was a small fiery mark. And, looking closer, Michael saw that it was curiously shaped. It was round, with curly, flame-shaped edges and like a very small sun.

"You see?" said Jane softly. "That's where he kissed her."

Michael nodded — once, twice, three times.

"Yes," he said, standing very still and staring at Mary Poppins. "I do see. I do . . ."

CHAPTER EIGHT

BALLOONS *AND* BALLOONS

I wonder, Mary Poppins," said Mrs. Banks, hurrying into the Nursery one morning, "if you will have time to do some shopping for me?"

And she gave Mary Poppins a sweet, nervous smile as though she were uncertain what the answer would be.

Mary Poppins turned from the fire where she was airing Annabel's clothes.

"I might," she remarked, not very encouragingly.

"Oh, I see —— " said Mrs. Banks, and she looked more nervous than ever.

"Or again — I might not," continued Mary Poppins, busily shaking out a woollen jacket and hanging it over the fire-guard.

"Well — in case you *did* have time, here is the List and here is a Pound Note. And if there is any change left over you may spend it!"

Mrs. Banks put the money on the chest of drawers.

Mary Poppins said nothing. She just sniffed.

"Oh!" said Mrs. Banks, suddenly remembering something. "And the Twins must walk to-day, Mary Poppins. Robertson Ay sat down on the perambulator this morning. He mistook it for an arm-chair. So it will have to be mended. Can you manage without it — and carry Annabel?"

Mary Poppins opened her mouth and closed it again with a snap.

"I," she remarked tartly, "can manage anything — and more, if I choose."

"I — I know!" said Mrs. Banks, edging towards the door. "You are a Treasure — a perfect Treasure — an absolutely wonderful and altogether suitable Treas——" Her voice died away as she hurried down the stairs.

"And yet — and yet — I sometimes wish she wasn't!" Mrs. Banks remarked to her great-grandmother's portrait as she dusted the Drawing-room. "She makes me feel small and silly, as though I were a little girl again. And I'm not!" Mrs. Banks tossed her head and flicked a speck of dust from the spotted cow on the mantelpiece. "I'm a very important person and the Mother of five children. She forgets that!" And she went on with her work thinking out all the things she would like to say to Mary Poppins but knowing all the time that she would never dare.

Mary Poppins put the list and the Pound Note into her bag and in no time she had pinned on her hat and was hurrying out of the house with Annabel in her arms and Jane and Michael, each holding the hand of a Twin, following as quickly as they could.

"Best foot forward, please!" she remarked, turning sternly upon them.

They quickened their pace, dragging the poor Twins with a shuffling sound along the pavement. They forgot that John's arm and Barbara's were being pulled nearly out of their sockets. Their only thought was to keep up with Mary Poppins and see what she did with the change from the Pound Note.

"Two packets of candles, four pounds of rice, three of brown sugar and six of castor; two tins of tomato soup and a hearth-brush, a pair of housemaid's gloves, half-a-stick of sealing-wax, one bag of flour, one firelighter, two boxes of matches, two cauliflowers and a bundle of rhubarb!"

Mary Poppins, hurrying into the first shop beyond the Park, read out the list.

The Grocer, who was fat and bald and rather short of breath, took down the order as quickly as he could.

"One bag of housemaid's gloves —— " he wrote, nervously licking the wrong end of his blunt little pencil.

"Flour, I said!" Mary Poppins reminded him tartly.

The Grocer blushed as red as a mulberry.

"Oh, I'm sorry. No offense meant, I'm sure. Lovely day, isn't it? Yes. My mistake. One bag of house — er — flour."

He hurriedly scribbled it down and added ——

"Two boxes of hearth-brushes —— "

"Matches!" snapped Mary Poppins.

The Grocer's hands trembled on his pad.

"Oh, of course. It must be the pencil — it seems to write all the wrong things. I must get a new one. Matches, of course! And then you said —— ?" He looked up nervously and then down again at his little stub of pencil.

Mary Poppins, unfolded the list, read it out again in an angry, impatient voice.

"Sorry," said the Grocer, as she came to the end. "But rhubarb's off. Would damsons do?"

"Certainly not. A packet of tapioca."

"Oh, no, Mary Poppins — not Tapioca. We had that last week," Michael reminded her.

She glanced at him and then at the Grocer, and by the look in her eye they both knew that there was no hope. Tapioca it would be. The Grocer, blushing redder than ever, went away to get it.

"There won't be any change left if she goes on like this," said Jane, watching the pile of groceries being heaped upon the counter.

"She might have enough left over for a bag of acid-drops — but that's all," Michael said mournfully, as Mary Poppins took the Pound Note out of her bag.

"Thank you," she said, as the Grocer handed her the change.

"Thank *you!*" he remarked politely, leaning his arms on the counter. He smiled at her in a manner that was meant to be pleasant and continued, "Keeps nice and fine, doesn't it?" He spoke proudly as though he, himself, had complete charge of the weather and had made it fine for her on purpose.

"We want rain!" said Mary Poppins, snapping her mouth and her hand-bag at the same time.

"That's right," said the Grocer hurriedly, trying not to offend her. "Rain's always pleasant."

"Never!" retorted Mary Poppins, tossing Annabel into a more comfortable position on her arm.

The Grocer's face fell. *Nothing* he said was right.

"I hope," he remarked, opening the door courteously for Mary Poppins, "that we shall be favoured with your further custom, Madam."

"Good-day!" Mary Poppins swept out.

The Grocer sighed.

"Here," he said, scrabbling hurriedly in a box near the door. "Take these. I meant no harm, truly I didn't. I only wanted to oblige."

Jane and Michael held out their hands. The Grocer slipped three chocolate drops into Michael's and two into Jane's.

"One for each of you, one for the two little ones and one for —— " he nodded towards Mary Poppins' retreating figure — "her!"

They thanked the Grocer and hurried after Mary Poppins, munching their chocolate drops.

"What's that you're eating?" she demanded, looking at the dark rim round Michael's mouth.

"Chocolates. The Grocer gave us one each. And one for you." He held out the last drop. It was very sticky.

"Like his impudence!" said Mary Poppins, but she took the chocolate drop and ate it in two bites as though she thoroughly enjoyed it.

"Is there much change left?" enquired Michael anxiously.

"That's as may be."

She swept into the Chemist's and came out with a cake of soap, a mustard plaster and a tube of toothpaste.

Jane and Michael, waiting with the Twins at the door, sighed heavily.

The Pound Note, they knew, was disappearing fast.

"She'll hardly have enough left over for a stamp and, even if she has, *that* won't be very interesting," said Jane.

"Now to Mr. Tip's!" snapped Mary Poppins, swinging the Chemist's packages and her bag from one hand and holding Annabel tightly with the other.

"But what can we buy *there*?" said Michael in despair. For there was not much jingle in Mary Poppins' purse.

"Coal — two tons and a half," she said, hurrying ahead.

"How much is coal?"

"Two pounds a ton."

"But — Mary Poppins! We can't buy *that*!" Michael stared at her, appalled.

"It will go on the bill."

This was such a relief to Jane and Michael that they

bounded beside her, dragging John and Barbara behind them at a trot.

"Well, is that all?" Michael asked, when Mr. Tip and his coals had been left safely behind.

"Cake shop!" said Mary Poppins, examining her list and darting in at a dark door. Through the window they could see her pointing to a pile of macaroons. The assistant handed her a large bag.

"She's bought a dozen at least," said Jane sadly. Usually the sight of anybody buying a macaroon filled them with delight, but to-day they wished and wished that there wasn't a macaroon in the world.

"*Now* where?" demanded Michael, hopping from one leg to the other in his anxiety to know if there was any of the Pound Note left. He felt sure there couldn't be and yet — he hoped.

"Home," said Mary Poppins.

Their faces fell. There was no change, after all, not even a penny or Mary Poppins would surely have spent it. But Mary Poppins, as she dumped the bag of macaroons up on Annabel's chest and strode ahead, had such a look on her face that they did not dare to make any remark. They only knew that, for once, she had disappointed them and they felt they could not forgive her.

"But — this isn't the way home," complained Michael, dragging his feet so that his toes scraped along the pavement.

"Isn't the Park on the way home, I'd like to know?" she demanded, turning fiercely upon him.

"Yes — but —— "

"There are more ways than one of going through a Park," she remarked and led them round to a side of it they had never seen before.

The sun shone warmly down. The tall trees bowed over the railings and rustled their leaves. Up in the branches two sparrows were fighting over a piece of straw. A squirrel hopped along the stone balustrade and sat up on his hindquarters, asking for nuts.

But to-day these things did not matter. Jane and Michael were not interested. All they could think of was the fact that Mary Poppins had spent the whole Pound Note on unimportant things and had kept nothing over.

Tired and disappointed, they trailed after her towards the Gates.

Over the entrance, a new one they had never seen before, spread a tall stone arch, splendidly carved with a Lion and a Unicorn. And beneath the arch sat an old, old woman, her face as grey as the stone itself and as withered and wrinkled as a walnut. On her little old knees she held a tray piled up with what looked like small coloured strips of rubber and above her head, tied firmly to the Park railings, a cluster of bright balloons bobbed and bounced and bounded.

"Balloons! Balloons!" shouted Jane. And, loosening

her hand from John's sticky fingers, she ran towards the old woman. Michael bounded after her, leaving Barbara alone and lost in the middle of the pavement.

"Well, my deary-ducks!" said the Balloon Woman in an old cracked voice. "Which will you have? Take your choice! And take your time!" She leant forward and shook her tray in front of them.

"We only came to look," Jane explained. "We've got no money."

"Tch, tch, tch! What's the good of *looking* at a balloon? You've got to feel a balloon, you've got to hold a balloon, you've got to *know* a balloon! Coming to look! What good will that do you?"

The old woman's voice crackled like a little flame. She rocked herself on her stool.

Jane and Michael stared at her helplessly. They knew she was speaking the truth. But what could they do?

"When I was a girl," the old woman went on, "people really *understood* balloons. They didn't just come and look! They took — yes, they *took!* There wasn't a child that went through these gates without one. They wouldn't have insulted the Balloon Woman in those days by just looking and passing by!"

She bent her head back and gazed up at the bouncing balloons above her.

"Ah, my loves and doves!" she cried. "They don't understand you any more — nobody but the old woman understands. You're old-fashioned now. Nobody wants you!"

"We *do* want one," said Michael stoutly. "But we haven't any money. *She* spent the whole Pound Note on ——"

"And who is 'she'?" enquired a voice close behind him.

He turned and his face went pink.

"I meant — er — that you — er ——" he began nervously.

"Speak politely of your betters!" remarked Mary Poppins and, stretching her arm over his shoulder, she put half-a-crown on the Balloon Woman's tray.

Michael stared at it, shining there among the limp unblown balloons.

"Then there was some change over!" said Jane, wishing she had not thought so crossly of Mary Poppins.

The Balloon Woman her old eyes sparkling, picked up the coin, and gazed at it for a long moment.

"Shiny, shiny, King-and-Crown!" she cried. "I haven't seen one of these since I was a girl." She cocked her head at Mary Poppins. "Do you want a balloon, my lass?"

"*If* you please!" said Mary Poppins with haughty politeness.

"How many, my deary-duck, how many?"

"Four!"

Jane and Michael, almost jumping out of their skins, turned and flung their arms round her.

"Oh, Mary Poppins, do you mean it? One each? Really-really?"

"I hope I always say what I mean," she said primly, looking very conceited.

They sprang towards the tray and began to turn over the coloured balloon-cases.

The Balloon Woman slipped the silver coin into a pocket in her skirt. "There, my shiny!" she said, giving the pocket a loving pat. Then, with excited trembling hands, she helped the children turn over the cases.

"Go carefully, my deary-ducks!" she warned them. "Remember, there's balloons *and* balloons, and one for everybody! Take your choice and take your time. There's many a child got the wrong balloon and his life was never the same after."

"I'll have this one!" said Michael, choosing a yellow one with red markings.

"Well, let me blow it up and you can see if it's the right one!" said the Balloon Woman.

She took it from him and with one gigantic puff blew it up. Zip! There it was! You would hardly think such a tiny person could have so much breath in her body. The yellow balloon, neatly marked with red, bobbed at the end of its string.

"But, I say!" said Michael staring. "It's got my name on it!"

And, sure enough, the red markings on the balloon were letters spelling out the two words — "MICHAEL BANKS."

"Aha!" cackled the Balloon Woman. "What did I tell you? You took your time and the choice was right!"

"See if mine is!" said Jane, handing the Balloon Woman a limp blue balloon.

She puffed and blew it up and there appeared across the fat blue globe the words "JANE CAROLINE BANKS" in large white letters.

"Is that your name, my deary-duck?" said the Balloon Woman.

Jane nodded.

The Balloon Woman laughed to herself, a thin, old cackling laugh, as Jane took the balloon from her and bounced it on the air.

"Me! Me!" cried John and Barbara, plunging fat hands

among the balloon-cases. John drew out a pink one and, as she blew it up, the Balloon Woman smiled. There, round the balloon, the words could clearly be seen. "JOHN AND BARBARA BANKS — ONE BETWEEN THEM BECAUSE THEY ARE TWINS."

"But," said Jane, "I don't understand. How did you know? You never saw us before."

"Ah, my deary-duck, didn't I tell you there were balloons *and* balloons and that these were extra-special?"

"But did you put the names on them?" said Michael.

"I?" the old woman chuckled. "Nary I!"

"Then who did?"

"Ask me another, my deary-duck! All I know is that the names *are* there! And there's a balloon for everybody in the world if only they choose properly."

"One for Mary Poppins, too?"

The Balloon Woman cocked her head and looked at Mary Poppins with a curious smile.

"Let her try!" She rocked herself on her little stool. "Take your choice and take your time! Choose and see!"

Mary Poppins sniffed importantly. Her hand hovered for a moment over the empty balloons and then pounced on a red one. She held it out at arm's length and, to their astonishment, the children saw it slowly filling with air of its own accord. Larger and larger it grew till it became the size of Michael's. But still it swelled until it was three times as large as any other balloon. And across it appeared in letters of gold the two words "MARY POPPINS."

The red balloon bounced through the air and the old woman tied a string to it and with a little cackling laugh, handed it back to Mary Poppins.

Up into the dancing air danced the four balloons. They tugged at their strings as though they wanted to be free of their moorings. The wind caught them and flung them backwards and forwards, to the North, to the South, to the East, to the West.

"Balloons *and* balloons, my deary-ducks! One for everybody if only they knew it!" cried the Balloon Woman, happily.

At that moment an elderly gentleman in a top hat, turning in at the Park Gates, looked across and saw the balloons. The children saw him give a little start. Then he hurried up to the Balloon Woman.

"How much?" he said, jingling his money in his pocket.

"Sevenpence halfpenny. Take your choice and take your time!"

He took a brown one and the Balloon Woman blew it up. The words "The Honourable WILLIAM WETHERILL WILKINS" appeared on it in green letters.

"Good Gracious!" said the elderly gentleman. "Good gracious, that's *my* name!"

"You choose well, my deary-duck. Balloons *and* balloons!" said the old woman.

The elderly gentleman stared at his balloon as it tugged at its string.

"Extraordinary!" he said, and blew his nose with a

trumpeting sound. "Forty years ago, when I was a boy, I tried to buy a balloon here. But they wouldn't let me. Said they couldn't afford it. Forty years — and it's been waiting for me all this time. Most extraordinary!"

And he hurried away, bumping into the arch because his eyes were fixed on the balloon. The children saw him giving little excited leaps in the air as he went.

"Look at him!" cried Michael as the Elderly Gentleman bobbed higher and higher. But at that moment his own balloon began pulling at the string and he felt himself lifted off his feet.

"Hello, hello! How funny! Mine's doing it, too!"

"Balloons *and* balloons, my deary-duck!" said the Balloon Woman and broke into her cackling laugh, as the Twins, both holding their balloon by its single string, bounced off the ground.

"I'm going, I'm going!" shrieked Jane as she, too, was borne upwards.

"Home, please!" said Mary Poppins.

Immediately, the red balloon soared up, dragging Mary Poppins after it. Up and down she bounced, with Annabel and the parcels in her arms. Through the Gates and above the path the red balloon bore Mary Poppins, her hat very straight, her hair very tidy and her feet as trimly walking the air as they usually walked the earth. Jane and Michael and the Twins, tugged jerkily up and down by their balloons, followed her.

"Oh, oh, oh!" cried Jane as she was whirled past the branch of an elm tree, "What a *delicious* feeling!"

"I feel as if I were made of air!" said Michael, knocking into a Park seat and bouncing off it again. "What a lovely way to go home!"

"O-o-h! E-e-eh!" squeaked the Twins, tossing and bobbing together.

"Best foot forward, please, and don't dawdle!" said Mary Poppins, looking fiercely over her shoulder, for all the world as if they were walking sedately on the ground instead of being tugged through the air.

Past the Park Keeper's house they went and down the Lime Walk. The Elderly Gentleman was there bouncing along ahead of them.

Michael turned for a moment and looked behind him.

"Look, Jane, look! Everybody's got one!"

She turned. In the distance a group of people, all carrying balloons, were being jerked up and down in the air.

"The Ice Cream Man has bought one!" she cried, staring and just missing a statue.

"Yes, and the Sweep! And there — do you see? — is Miss Lark!"

Across the lawn a familiar figure came bouncing, hatted and gloved, and holding a balloon bearing the name "LUCINDA EMILY LARK." She bobbed across the Elm Walk, looking very pleased and dignified, and disappeared round the edge of a fountain.

By this time the Park was filling with people and every one of them had a balloon with a name on it and every one was bouncing in the air.

"Heave ho, there! Room for the Admiral! Where's my port? Heave ho!" shouted a huge, nautical voice as Admiral and Mrs. Boom went rolling through the air. They held the string of a large white balloon with their names on it in blue letters.

"Masts and mizzens! Cockles and shrimps! Haul away,

my hearties!" roared Admiral Boom, carefully avoiding a large oak tree.

The crowd of balloons and people grew thicker. There was hardly a patch of air in the Park that was not rainbowy with balloons. Jane and Michael could see Mary Poppins threading her way primly among them and they, too, hurried through the throng, with John and Barbara bobbing at their heels.

"Oh, dear! Oh, dear! My balloon won't bounce me. I must have chosen the wrong one!" said a voice at Jane's elbow.

An old-fashioned lady with a quill in her hat and a feather boa round her neck was standing on the path just below Jane. At her feet lay a purple balloon across which was written in letters of gold, "THE PRIME MINISTER."

"What shall I do?" she cried. "The old woman at the Gates said 'Take your choice and take your time, my deary-duck!' And I did. But I've got the wrong one. *I'm* not the Prime Minister!"

"Excuse me, but I am!" said a voice at her side, as a tall man, very elegantly dressed and carrying a rolled umbrella, stepped up to her.

The lady turned. "Oh, then this is your balloon! Let me see if you've got mine!"

The Prime Minister, whose balloon was not bouncing him at all, showed it to her. Its name was "LADY MURIEL BRIGHTON-JONES."

"Yes, you have! We've got mixed!" she cried, and handing the Prime Minister his balloon, she seized her own. Presently they were off the ground and flying among the trees, talking as they went.

"Are you married?" Jane and Michael heard Lady Muriel ask.

And the Prime Minister answered, "No. I can't find the right sort of middle-aged lady — not too young and not too old and rather jolly because I'm so serious myself."

"Would I do?" said Lady Muriel Brighton-Jones. "I enjoy myself quite a lot."

"Yes, I think you'd do very nicely," said the Prime Minister and, hand in hand, they joined the tossing throng.

By this time the Park was really rather crowded. Jane and Michael, bobbing across the lawns after Mary Poppins, constantly bumped into other bouncing figures who had bought balloons from the Balloon Woman. A tall man, wearing a long moustache, a blue suit, and a helmet, was being tugged through the air by a balloon marked "POLICE INSPECTOR"; and another, bearing the words "LORD MAYOR," dragged along a round, fat person in a three-cornered hat, a red overall and a large brass necklace.

"Move on, please! Don't crowd the Park. Observe the Regulations! All litter to be Deposited in the Rubbish Baskets!"

The Park Keeper, roaring and ranting, and holding a small cherry-coloured balloon marked "F. SMITH," threaded his way through the crowd. With a wave of his hand he moved on two dogs — a bulldog with the word "CU" written on his balloon and a fox-terrier whose name appeared to be "ALBERTINE."

"Leave my dogs alone! Or I shall take your number and report you!" cried a lady whose balloon said she was "THE DUCHESS OF MAYFIELD."

But the Park Keeper took no notice and went bobbing by, crying "All Dogs on a Lead! Don't crowd the Park! No Smoking! Observe the Regulations!" till his voice was hoarse.

"Where's Mary Poppins?" said Michael, whisking up to Jane.

"There! Just ahead of us!" she replied and pointed to the prim, tidy figure that bounced at the end of the largest balloon in the Park. They followed it homewards.

"Balloons *and* Balloons, my deary-ducks!" cried a cackling voice behind them.

And, turning, they saw the Balloon Woman. Her tray was empty and there was not a balloon anywhere near her, but in spite of that she was flying through the air as though a hundred invisible balloons were drawing her onwards.

"Every one sold!" she screamed as she sped by. "There's a balloon for every one if only they knew it. They took their choice and they took their time! And I've sold the lot! Balloons *and* Balloons."

Her pockets jingled richly as she flew by, and standing still in the air, Jane and Michael watched the small, withered figure shooting past the bobbing balloons, past the Prime Minister and the Lord Mayor, past Mary Poppins and Annabel, until the tiny shape grew tinier still and the Balloon Woman disappeared into the distance.

By this time the Park was really rather crowded

"Balloons and Balloons, my deary-ducks!" The faint echo came drifting back to them.

"Step along, please!" said Mary Poppins. They flocked round her, all four of them. Annabel, rocked by the movement of Mary Poppins' balloon, nestled closer to her and went to sleep.

The gate of Number Seventeen stood open, the front door was ajar. Mary Poppins, leaping neatly and bouncing primly, passed through and up the stairs. The children followed, jumping and bobbing. And when they reached the nursery door, their four pairs of feet clattered noisily to the ground. Mary Poppins floated down and landed without a sound.

"Oh, what a *lovely* afternoon!" said Jane, rushing to fling her arms round Mary Poppins.

"Well, that's more than *you* are, at this moment. Brush your hair, please. I don't care for scarecrows," Mary Poppins said tartly.

"I feel like a balloon myself," said Michael joyfully, "All airy-fairy-free!"

"I'd be sorry for the fairy that looked like you!" said Mary Poppins. "Go and wash your hands. You're no better than a sweep!"

When they came back, clean and tidy, the four balloons were resting against the ceiling, their strings firmly moored behind the picture over the mantelpiece.

Michael gazed up at them — his own yellow one,

Jane's blue, the Twins' pink and Mary Poppins' red. They were very still. No breath of wind moved them. Light and bright, steady and still, they leaned against the ceiling.

"I wonder!" said Michael softly, half to himself.

"You wonder what?" said Mary Poppins, sorting out her parcels.

"I wonder if it would all have happened if you hadn't been with us."

Mary Poppins sniffed.

"I shouldn't wonder if you didn't wonder much too much!" she replied.

And with that Michael had to be content.

CHAPTER NINE

NELLIE-RUBINA

I don't believe it will ever stop — ever!"

Jane put down her copy of *Robinson Crusoe* and gazed gloomily out of the window.

The snow fell steadily, drifting down in large soft flakes, covering the Park and the pavements and the houses in Cherry-Tree Lane with its thick white mantle. It had not stopped snowing for a week and in all that time the children had not once been able to go out.

"I don't mind — not very much," said Michael from the floor where he was busy arranging the animals of his Noah's Ark. "We can be Esquimos and eat whales."

"Silly — how could we get whales when it's too snowy even to go and buy cough drops!"

"They might come here. Whales do, sometimes," he retorted.

"How do you know?"

"Well, I don't *know*, exactly. But they might. Jane, where's the second giraffe? Oh, here he is — under the tiger!"

He put the two giraffes into the Ark together.

> "The Animals went in Two-by-Two,
> The Elephant and the Kangaroo,"

sang Michael. And, because he hadn't got a kangaroo, he sent an antelope in with the elephant and Mr. and Mrs. Noah behind them to keep order.

"I wonder why they never have any relatives!" he remarked presently.

"*Who* don't?" said Jane crossly, for she didn't want to be disturbed.

"The Noahs. I've never seen them with a daughter or a son or an uncle or an aunt. Why?"

"Because they don't have them," said Jane. "Do be quiet."

"Well, I was only remarking. Can't I remark if I want to?"

He was beginning to feel cross now, and very tired of being cooped up in the Nursery. He scrambled to his feet and swaggered over to Jane.

"I only said ——" he began annoyingly, jogging the hand that held the book.

But at that, Jane's patience gave way and she hurled *Robinson Crusoe* across the room.

"How dare you disturb me!" she shouted, turning on Michael.

"How dare you not let me make a remark!"

"I didn't!"

"You did!"

And in another moment Jane was shaking Michael furiously by the shoulders and he had gripped a great handful of her hair.

"WHAT IS ALL THIS?"

Mary Poppins stood in the doorway, glowering down at them.

They fell apart.

"She sh-sh-shook me!" wailed Michael, but he looked guiltily at Mary Poppins.

"He p-p-pulled my hair!" sobbed Jane, hiding her head in her arms, for she dared not face that stern gaze.

Mary Poppins stalked into the room. She had a pile of coats, caps and mufflers on her arm, and the Twins, round-eyed and interested, were at her heels.

"I would rather," she remarked with a sniff, "have a family of Cannibals to look after. They'd be more human!"

"But she did sh-sh-shake me ——" Michael began again.

"Tell-Tale-Tit, Your tongue shall be slit!" jeered Mary Poppins. Then, as he seemed to be going to protest, "Don't dare answer back!" she said warningly and tossed him his overcoat. "Get your things on, please! We're going out!"

"Out?"

They could hardly believe their ears! But at the sound

of that word all their crossness melted away. Michael, buttoning up his leggings, felt sorry he had annoyed Jane and looked across to find her putting on her woolen cap and smiling at him.

"Hooray, hooray, hooray!" They shouted, stamping and clapping their woolen-gloved hands.

"Cannibals!" she said fiercely and pushed them in front of her down the stairs. . . .

The snow was no longer falling but was piled in heavy drifts all over the garden, and beyond, in the Park, it lay over everything like a thick white quilt. The naked branches of the cherry-trees were covered with a glistening rind of snow, and the Park railings, that had once been green and slender, were now white and rather woolly.

Down the garden path Robertson Ay was languidly trailing his shovel, pausing every few inches to take a long rest. He was wearing an old overcoat of Mr. Banks' that was much too big for him. As soon as he had shovelled the snow from one piece of path, the coat, drifting behind him, swept a new drift of snow over the cleared patch.

But the children raced past him and down to the gate, crying and shouting and waving their arms.

Outside in the Lane everybody who lived in it seemed to be taking the air.

"Ahoy there, shipmates!" cried a roaring, soaring voice as Admiral Boom came up and shook them all by the hand. He was wrapped from head to foot in a large

Inverness cape and his nose was redder than they had ever seen it.

"Good-day!" said Jane and Michael politely.

"Port and starboard!" cried the Admiral. "I don't call *this* a good day. Hur-rrrrrumph! A hideous, hoary, land lubberly sort of a day, I call it. Why doesn't the Spring come? Tell me that!"

"Now, Andrew! Now, Willoughby! Keep close to Mother!"

Miss Lark, muffled up in a long fur coat and wearing a fur hat like a tea-cosy, was taking a walk with her two dogs.

"Good-morning, everybody!" She greeted them fussily. "*What* weather! *Where* has the sun gone? And *why* doesn't the Spring come?"

"Don't ask me, Ma'am!" shouted Admiral Boom. "No affair of mine. You should go to sea. Always good weather there! Go to sea!"

"Oh, Admiral Boom, I couldn't do that! I haven't the time. I am just off to buy Andrew and Willoughby a fur coat each."

A look of shame and horror passed between the two dogs.

"Fur coats!" roared the Admiral. "Blast my binnacle! Fur coats for a couple of mongrels? Heave her over! Port, I say! Up with the Anchor! Fur coats!"

"Admiral! Admiral!" cried Miss Lark, stopping her ears

with her hands. "Such *language!* Please, please remember I am not used to it. And my dogs are *not* mongrels. Not at all! One has a long pedigree and the other has at least a Kind Heart. Mongrels, indeed!"

And she hurried away, talking to herself in a high, angry voice, with Andrew and Willoughby sidling behind her, swinging their tails and looking very uncomfortable and ashamed.

The Ice Cream Man trundled past on his cycle, going at a terrific rate and ringing his bell madly.

"DON'T STOP ME OR I SHALL CATCH COLD" said the notice in front of his cart.

"Whenever's that there Spring coming?" shouted the Ice Cream Man to the Sweep, who at that moment came trudging round the corner. To keep out the cold he had completely covered himself with brushes so that he looked more like a porcupine than a man.

"Bur-rum, bur-rum, bumble!" came the voice of the Sweep through the brushes.

"What's that?" said the Ice Cream Man.

"Bumble!"

The Sweep remarked, disappearing in at Miss Lark's Tradesman's Entrance.

In the gateway to the Park stood the Keeper, waving his arms and stamping his feet and blowing on his hands.

"Need a bit of Spring, don't we?" he said cheerfully to Mary Poppins as she and the children passed through.

"*I'm* quite satisfied!" replied Mary Poppins primly, tossing her head.

"*Self*-satisfied, I'd call it," muttered the Keeper. But as he said it behind his hand, only Jane and Michael heard him.

Michael dawdled behind. He stooped and gathered up a handful of snow and rolled it between his palms.

"Jane, dear!" he called in a wheedling voice. "I've got something for you!"

She turned, and the snowball, whizzing through the air, caught her on the shoulder. With a squeal she began to burrow in the snow and presently there were snowballs flying through the air in every direction. And in and out, among the tossing, glistening balls, walked Mary Poppins, very prim and neat, and thinking to herself how handsome she looked in her large woolen gloves and her rabbit-skin coat.

And just as she was thinking that, a large snowball grazed past the brim of her hat and landed right on her nose.

"Oh!" screamed Michael, putting up both hands to his mouth. "I didn't mean to, Mary Poppins! I didn't, really. It was for Jane."

Mary Poppins turned and her face, as it appeared through the fringe of broken snowball, was terrible.

"Mary Poppins," he said earnestly. "I'm sorry. It was a Naccident!"

"A Naccident or not!" she retorted. "That's the end of

your snowballing. Naccident, indeed! A *Zulu* would have better manners!"

She plucked the remains of the snowball from her neck and rolled them into a small ball between her woolen palms. Then she flung the ball right across the snowy lawn and went stamping haughtily after it.

"Now you've done it," whispered Jane.

"I didn't mean to," Michael whispered back.

"I know. But you know what she is!"

Mary Poppins, arriving at the place where the snowball had fallen, picked it up and threw it again, a long powerful throw.

"Where is she going?" said Michael suddenly. For the snowball was bowling away under the trees and, instead of keeping to the path, Mary Poppins was hurrying after it. Every now and then she dodged a little fall of snow as it tumbled softly from a branch.

"I can hardly keep up!" said Michael, stumbling over his own feet.

Mary Poppins quickened her steps. The children panted behind her. And when at last they caught up with the snowball, they found it lying beside the strangest building they had ever seen.

"I don't remember seeing this house before!" exclaimed Jane, her eyes wide with surprise.

"It's more like an Ark than a house," said Michael, staring.

The house stood solidly in the snow, moored by a thick

rope to the trunk of a tree. Round it, like a verandah, ran a long narrow deck and its high peaked roof was painted bright scarlet. But the most curious thing about it was that though it had several windows there was not a single door.

"Where *are* we?" said Jane, full of curiosity and excitement.

Mary Poppins made no reply. She led the way along the deck and stopped in front of a notice that said,

"KNOCK THREE AND A HALF TIMES"

"What is half a knock?" whispered Michael to Jane.

"Sh!" she said, nodding towards Mary Poppins. And her nod said as clearly as if she had spoken — "We're on the brink of an Adventure. Don't spoil it by asking questions!"

Mary Poppins, seizing the knocker that hung above the notice, swung it upwards and knocked three times against the wall. Then, taking it daintily between the finger and thumb of her woolen glove, she gave the merest, tiniest, smallest, gentlest tap.

Like this.

RAP! RAP! RAP! . . . tap.

Immediately, as though it had been listening and waiting for that signal, the roof of the building flew back on its hinges.

"Goodness Graciousness!" Michael could not restrain the exclamation, for the wind of the roof, as it swung open, nearly lifted his hat off.

Mary Poppins walked to the end of the narrow deck and began to climb a small, steep ladder. At the top she turned, and looking very solemn and important, beckoned with a woolly finger.

"Step up, please!"

The four children hurried after her.

"Jump!" cried Mary Poppins, leaping down from the top of the ladder into the house. She turned and caught the Twins as they came tumbling over the edge with Jane and Michael after them. And as soon as they were all safely inside, the roof closed over again and shut with a little click.

They gazed round them. Four pairs of eyes popped with surprise.

"*What* a funny room!" exclaimed Jane.

But it was really more than funny. It was extraordinary. The only piece of furniture in it was a large counter that ran along one end of the room. The walls were whitewashed, and leaning against them were piles of wood cut into the shape of trees and branches and all painted green. Small wooden sprays of leaves, newly painted and polished, were scattered about the floor. And several notices hung from the walls saying:

"MIND THE PAINT!"

or

"DON'T TOUCH!"

or

"KEEP OFF THE GRASS!"

But this was not all.

In one corner stood a flock of wooden sheep with the dye still wet on their fleeces. Crowded in another were small stiff groups of flowers — yellow aconites, green-and-white snow-drops and bright blue scyllas. All of them looked very shiny and sticky as though they had been newly varnished. So did the wooden birds and butterflies that were neatly piled in a third corner. So did the flat white wooden clouds that leant against the counter.

But the enormous jar that stood on a shelf at the end of the room was not painted. It was made of green glass and filled to the brim with hundreds of small flat shapes of every kind and colour.

"You're quite right, Jane," said Michael staring. "It is a funny room!"

"Funny!" said Mary Poppins, looking as though he had said something insulting.

"Well — peculiar."

"PECULIAR?"

Michael hesitated. He could not find the right word.

"What I meant was —— "

"I think it's a lovely room, Mary Poppins —— " said Jane, hastily coming to the rescue.

"Yes it is," said Michael, very relieved. "And — " he added cleverly, "I think you look very nice in that hat."

He watched her carefully. Yes, her face was a little softer — there were even faint beginnings of a conceited smile around her mouth.

"Humph!" she remarked and turned towards the end of the room.

"Nellie-Rubina!" she called. "Where are you? We've arrived!"

"Coming! Coming!"

The highest, thinnest voice they had ever heard seemed to rise up from beneath the counter. And, presently, from the same direction as the voice, a head, topped with a small flat hat, popped up. It was followed by a round, rather solid body that held in one hand a pot of red paint and in the other a plain wooden tulip.

Surely, surely, thought Jane and Michael, this was the strangest person they had ever seen.

From her face and size she seemed to be quite young but somehow she looked as though she were made, not of flesh, but of wood. Her stiff, shiny black hair seemed to have been carved on her head and then painted. Her eyes were like small black holes drilled in her face, and surely that bright pink patch on her shiny cheek was paint!

"Well, Miss Poppins!" said this curious person, her red lips glistening as she smiled. "This *is* nice of you, I must say!" And putting down the paint and the tulip, she came round the counter and shook hands with Mary Poppins.

Then it was that the children noticed she had no legs at all! She was quite solid from the waist downwards and moved with a rolling motion by means of a round flat disc that was where her feet should have been.

"Not at all, Nellie-Rubina," said Mary Poppins, with unusual politeness. "It is a Pleasure and a Treat!"

"We've been expecting you, of course," Nellie-Rubina went on, "because we wanted you to help with the —— " She broke off, for not only had Mary Poppins flashed her a warning look, but she had caught sight of the children.

"Oh," she cried in her high friendly voice. "You've brought Jane and Michael! And the Twins, too. What a surprise!" She bowled across and shook hands jerkily with them all.

"Do you know us, then?" said Michael, staring at her amazed.

"Oh, dear me, yes!" she trilled gaily. "I've often heard my Father and Mother speak of you. Pleased to make your acquaintance." She laughed, and insisted on shaking hands all round again.

"I thought, Nellie-Rubina," said Mary Poppins, "that maybe you could spare an ounce of Conversations."

"Most certainly!" said Nellie-Rubina, smiling and rolling towards the counter. "To do anything for *you*, Miss Poppins, is an Honour and a Joy!"

"But can you have conversation by the ounce?" said Jane.

"Yes, indeed. By the pound, too. Or the ton, if you like." Nellie-Rubina broke off. She lifted her arms to the large jar on the shelf. They were just too short to reach it. "Tch, tch, tch! Not long enough. I must have a bit added. In the meantime, I'll get my Uncle to lift them down. Uncle Dodger! Uncle Dod-GER!"

She screamed the last words through a door behind the counter and immediately an odd-looking person appeared.

He was as round as Nellie-Rubina, but much older and with a sadder sort of face. He, too, had a little flat hat on his head and his coat was tightly buttoned across a chest as woodeny as Nellie-Rubina's. And Jane and Michael could see, as his apron swung aside for a moment, that, like his niece, he was solid from the waist downwards. In his hand he carried a wooden cuckoo half-covered with grey paint and there were splashes of the same paint on his own nose.

"You called, my dear?" he asked, in a mild, respectful voice.

Then, he saw Mary Poppins.

"Ah, here you are at last, Miss Poppins! Nellie-Rubina *will* be pleased. She's been expecting you to help us with —— "

He caught sight of the children and broke off suddenly.

"Oh, I beg pardon. I didn't know there was Company, my dear! I'll just go and finish this bird —— "

"You will not, Uncle Dodger!" said Nellie-Rubina, sharply. "I want the Conversations lifted down. Will you be so good?"

Although she had such a jolly, cheerful face, the children noticed that when she spoke to her Uncle she gave orders rather than asked favours.

Uncle Dodger sprang forward as swiftly as anybody could who had no legs.

"Certainly, my dear, certainly!" He lifted his arms jerkily and set the jar on the counter.

"In front of me, please!" ordered Nellie-Rubina haughtily.

Fussily Uncle Dodger edged the Jar along.

"There you are, my dear, begging your pardon!"

"Are *those* the Conversations?" asked Jane, pointing to the Jar. "They look more like sweets."

"So they are, Miss! They're Conversation Sweets," said Uncle Dodger, dusting the jar with his apron.

"Does one eat them?" inquired Michael.

Uncle Dodger, glancing cautiously at Nellie-Rubina, leaned across the counter.

"*One* does," he whispered behind his hand. "But I don't, being only an Uncle-by-Marriage. But she —— " he nodded respectfully towards his niece, "she's the Eldest Daughter and a Direct Descendant!"

Neither Jane nor Michael knew in the least what he meant but they nodded politely.

"Now," cried Nellie-Rubina gaily as she unscrewed the lid of the Jar. "Who'll choose first?"

Jane thrust in her hand and brought out a flat star-shaped sweet rather like a peppermint.

"There's writing on it!" she exclaimed.

Nellie-Rubina shrieked with laughter. "Of course there is! It's a Conversation! Read it."

"You're My Fancy," read Jane aloud.

"How *very* nice!" tinkled Nellie-Rubina, pushing the jar towards Michael. He drew out a pink sweet shaped like a shell.

"I Love You. Do You Love Me?" He spelled out.

"Ha, ha! That's a good one! Yes, I do!" Nellie-Rubina laughed loudly, and gave him a quick kiss that left a sticky patch of paint on his cheek.

John's yellow Conversation read "Deedle, deedle, dumpling!" and on Barbara's was written in large letters, "Shining-bright and airy."

"And so you are!" cried Nellie-Rubina, smiling at her over the counter.

"Now you, Miss Poppins!" And as Nellie-Rubina tipped the Jar towards Mary Poppins, Jane and Michael noticed a curious, understanding look pass between them.

Off came the large woolen glove and Mary Poppins, shutting her eyes, put in her hand and scrabbled for a moment among the Conversations. Then her fingers closed on a white one shaped like a half-moon and she held it out in front of her.

"Ten o'clock to-night," said Jane, reading the inscription aloud.

Uncle Dodger rubbed his hands together.

"That's right. That's the time when we —— "

"Uncle Dod-GER!" cried Nellie-Rubina in a warning voice.

The smile died away from his face and left it sadder than before.

"Begging your pardon, my dear!" He said humbly. "I'm an old man, I'm afraid, and I sometimes say the wrong thing — beg pardon." He looked very ashamed of himself but Jane and Michael could not see that he had done anything very wrong.

"Well," said Mary Poppins, slipping her Conversation carefully into her hand-bag. "If you'll excuse us, Nellie-Rubina, I think we'd better be going!"

"Oh, must you?" Nellie-Rubina rolled a little on her disc. "It has been Such a Satisfaction! Still," she glanced out of a window, "it might snow again and keep you imprisoned here. And you wouldn't like that, would you?" she trilled, turning to the children.

"I would," said Michael, stoutly. "I would love it. And then, perhaps, I'd find out what these are for." He pointed to the painted branches, the sheep and birds and flowers.

"Those? Oh, those are just decorations," said Nellie-Rubina, airily dismissing them with a jerky wave of her hand.

"But what do you do with them?"

Uncle Dodger leaned eagerly across the counter.

"Well, you see, we take them out and —— "

"Uncle Dod-GER!" Nellie-Rubina's dark eyes were snapping dangerously.

"Oh — dear! There I go again. Always speaking out of my turn. I'm too old, that's what it is," said Uncle Dodger mournfully.

Nellie-Rubina gave him an angry look. Then she turned smiling to the children.

"Good-bye," she said, jerkily shaking hands. "I'll remember our Conversations. You're my Fancy, I love You, Deedle-deedle and Shining-bright!"

"You've forgotten Mary Poppins' Conversation. It's 'Ten o'clock to-night,'" Michael reminded her.

"Ah, but *she* won't!" said Uncle Dodger, smiling happily.

"Uncle Dod-GER!"

"Oh, begging your pardon, begging your pardon!"

"Good-bye!" said Mary Poppins. She patted her handbag importantly and another strange look passed between her and Nellie-Rubina.

"Good-bye, good-bye!"

When Jane and Michael thought about it afterwards, they could not remember how they had got out of that curious room. One moment they were inside it saying good-bye to Nellie-Rubina and the next they were out in the snow again, licking their Conversations and hurrying after Mary Poppins.

"Do you know, Michael," said Jane, "I believe that sweet was a message."

"Which one? Mine?"

"No. The one Mary Poppins chose."

"You mean —— ?"

"I think something is going to happen at ten o'clock to-night and I'm going to stay awake and see."

"Then so will I," said Michael.

"Come along, please! Keep up!" said Mary Poppins. "I haven't *all* day to waste . . ."

Jane was dreaming deeply. And in her dream somebody was calling her name in a small urgent voice. She sat up with a start to find Michael standing beside her in his pyjamas.

"You said you'd stay awake!" he whispered accusingly.

"What? Where? Why? Oh, it's you, Michael! Well, you said you would, too."

"Listen!" he said.

There was a sound of somebody tip-toeing in the next room.

Jane drew in her breath sharply. "Quick! Get back into bed. Pretend to be asleep. Hurry!"

With a bound Michael was under the blankets. In the darkness he and Jane held their breath, listening.

From the other Nursery, the door opened stealthily. The thin gap of light widened and grew larger. A head came round the edge and peered into the room. Then somebody slipped through and silently shut the door behind her.

Mary Poppins, wrapped in her fur coat and holding her shoes in her hands, tip-toed through their room.

They lay still, listening to her steps hurrying down the stairs. Far away the key of the front door scraped in its lock. There was a scurry of steps on the garden path and the front gate clicked.

And at that moment the clock struck ten!

Out of bed they sprang and rushed into the other Nursery, where the windows opened on the Park.

The night was black and splendid, lit with high swinging stars. But to-night it was not stars they were looking for. If Mary Poppins' Conversation had really been a message, there was something more interesting to be seen.

"Look!" Jane gave a little gulp of excitement and pointed.

Over in the Park, just by the entrance gate, stood the curious ark-shaped building, loosely moored to a tree-trunk.

"But how did it get *there?*" said Michael staring. "It was at the other side of the Park this morning."

Jane did not reply. She was too busy watching.

The roof of the Ark was open and on the top of the ladder stood Nellie-Rubina, balancing on her round disc. From inside Uncle Dodger was handing up to her bundle after bundle of painted wooden branches.

"Ready, Miss Poppins?" tinkled Nellie-Rubina, passing an armful down to Mary Poppins who was standing on the deck waiting to receive them.

The air was so clear and still that Jane and Michael, crouched in the window-seat, could hear every word.

Suddenly there was a loud noise inside the Ark as a wooden shape clattered to the floor.

"Uncle Dod-GER! Be careful, please! They're fragile!" said Nellie-Rubina sternly. And Uncle Dodger, as he lifted out a pile of painted clouds, replied apologetically, "Begging your pardon, my dear!"

The flock of wooden sheep came next, all very stiff and solid. And last of all, the birds, butterflies and flowers.

"That's the lot!" said Uncle Dodger, heaving himself up through the open roof. Under his arm he carried the wooden cuckoo, now entirely covered with grey paint. And in his hand swung a large green paint-pot.

"Very well," said Nellie-Rubina. "Now, if you're ready, Miss Poppins, we'll begin!"

And then began one of the strangest pieces of work Jane and Michael had ever seen. Never, never, they thought, would they forget it, even if they lived to be ninety.

From the pile of painted wood Nellie-Rubina and Mary Poppins each took a long spray of leaves and, leaping into the air, attached them swiftly to the naked frosty branches of the trees. The sprays seemed to clip on easily for it did not take more than a minute to attach them. And as each was slipped into place, Uncle Dodger would spring up and neatly dab a spot of green paint at the point where the spray joined the tree.

"My Goodness *Goodness!*" exclaimed Jane, as Nellie-

Rubina sailed lightly up to the top of a tall poplar and fixed a large branch there. But Michael was too astonished to say anything.

All over the Park went the three, jumping up to the tallest branch as if they were on springs. And in no time every tree in the Park was decked out with wooden sprays of leaves and neatly finished off with dabs of paint from Uncle Dodger's brush.

Every now and then Jane and Michael heard Nellie-Rubina's shrill voice crying,

"Uncle Dod-GER! Be CAREFUL!" and Uncle Dodger's voice begging her pardon.

And now Nellie-Rubina and Mary Poppins took up in their arms the flat white wooden clouds. With these they soared higher than ever before, shooting right above the trees and pressing the clouds carefully against the sky.

"They're sticking, they're sticking!" cried Michael excitedly, dancing on the window-seat. And, sure enough,

against the sparkling, darkling sky the flat white clouds stuck fast.

"Who-o-o-op!" cried Nellie-Rubina as she swooped down. "Now for the sheep!"

Very carefully, on a snowy strip of lawn, they set up the wooden flock, huddling the larger sheep together with the stiff white lambs among them.

"We're getting on!" Jane and Michael heard Mary Poppins say, as she put the last lamb on its legs.

"I don't know what we'd have done without you, Miss Poppins, indeed I don't!" said Nellie-Rubina, pleasantly. Then, in quite a different voice,

"Flowers, please, Uncle Dodger! And look sharp!"

"Here, my dear!" He rolled hurriedly up to her, his apron bulging with snow-drops, scyllas and aconites.

"Oh, look! Look!" Jane cried, hugging herself delightedly. For Nellie-Rubina was sticking the wooden shapes round the edge of an empty flower-bed. Round and round she rolled, planting her wooden border and reaching up her hand again and again for a fresh flower from Uncle Dodger's apron.

"That's neat!" said Mary Poppins admiringly, and Jane and Michael were astonished at the pleasant friendly tone of her voice.

"Yes, isn't it?" trilled Nellie-Rubina, brushing the snow from her hands, "Quite a Sight! What's left, Uncle Dodger?"

Against the sparkling, darkling sky the flat white clouds stuck fast

"The birds, my dear, and the butterflies!" He held out his apron. Nellie-Rubina and Mary Poppins seized the remaining wooden shapes and ran swiftly about the Park, setting the birds on branches or in nests and tossing the butterflies into the air. And the curious thing was that they *stayed* there, poised above the earth, their bright patches of paint showing clearly in the starlight.

"There! I think that's all!" said Nellie-Rubina, standing still on her disc, with her hands on her hips, as she gazed round at her handiwork.

"One thing more, my dear!" said Uncle Dodger.

And, rather unevenly, as though the evening's work had made him feel old and tired, he bowled towards the ash tree near the Park Gates. He took the cuckoo from under his arm and set it on a branch among the wooden leaves.

"There, my bonny! There, my dove!" he said, nodding his head at the bird.

"Uncle Dod-GER! When *will* you learn? It's *not* a dove. It's a cuckoo!"

He bent his head humbly.

"A dove of a cuckoo — that's what I meant. Begging your pardon, my dear!"

"Well, now, Miss Poppins, I'm afraid we must really be going!" said Nellie-Rubina and, rolling towards Mary Poppins, she took the pink face between her two woodeny hands and kissed it.

"See you soon, Tra-la!" she cried airily, bowling along the deck of the Ark and up the little ladder. At the top she turned and waved her hand jerkily to Mary Poppins. Then, with a woodeny clatter, she leapt down and disappeared inside.

"Uncle Dod-GER! Come along! Don't keep me waiting!" her thin voice floated back.

"Coming, my dear, coming! Begging your pardon!" Uncle Dodger rolled toward the deck, shaking hands with Mary Poppins on the way. The wooden cuckoo stared out from its leafy branch. He flung it a sad, affectionate glance. Then his flat disc rose in the air and echoed woodenly as he landed inside. The roof flew down and shut with a click.

"Let her go!" came Nellie-Rubina's shrill command from within. Mary Poppins stepped forward and unwound the mooring-rope from the tree. It was immediately drawn in through one of the windows.

"Make way, there, please! Make way!" shouted Nellie-Rubina. Mary Poppins stepped back hurriedly.

Michael clutched Jane's arm excitedly.

"They're off!" he cried, as the Ark rose from the ground and moved top-heavily above the snow. Up it went, rocking drunkenly between the trees. Then it steadied itself and passed lightly up and over the topmost boughs.

A jerky arm waved downwards from one of the windows but before Jane and Michael could be certain whether it was Nellie-Rubina's or Uncle Dodger's, the Ark swept into the star-lit air and a corner of the house hid it from view.

Mary Poppins stood for a moment by the Park Gates waving her woolen gloves.

Then she came hurrying across the Lane and up the garden path. The front door key scraped in the lock. A cautious footstep creaked on the stairs!

"Back to bed, quick!" said Jane. "She mustn't find us here!"

Down from the window-seat and through the door they fled and with two quick jumps landed in their beds. They had just time to put the bedclothes over their heads before Mary Poppins opened the door quietly and tip-toed through.

Zup! That was her coat being hung on its hook. Crackle! That was her hat rustling down into its paper-bag. But they heard no more. For by the time she had undressed and climbed into her camp-bed, Jane and Michael had huggled down under the blankets and were fast asleep. . . .

"Cuckoo! Cuckoo! Cuckoo!"

Across the Lane the soft bird note came floating.

"Jumping giraffes!" cried Mr. Banks, as he lathered his face, "The Spring is here!"

And he flung down his shaving-brush and rushed out

into the garden. He gave one look at it and then, flinging back his head, he made a trumpet with his hands.

"Jane! Michael! John! Barbara!" he called up to the Nursery windows. "Come down! The snow's gone and Spring has come!"

They came tumbling down the stairs and out of the front door to find the whole Lane alive with people.

"Ship ahoy!" roared Admiral Boom waving his muffler. "Rope and Rigging! Cockles and Shrimps! Here's the Spring!"

"Well!" said Miss Lark, hurrying out through her gate. "A fine day at last! I was thinking of getting Andrew and Willoughby two pairs of leather boots each, but now the snow's gone I shan't have to!"

At that Andrew and Willoughby looked very relieved and licked her hand to show they were glad she had not disgraced them.

The Ice Cream Man wheeled slowly up and down, keeping an eye open for customers. And today his notice board read —

"SPRING HAS COME,

RUM-TI-TUM,

STOP AND BUY ONE,

SPRING HAS COME!"

And the Sweep, carrying only one brush, walked along

the Lane, looking from right to left with a satisfied air, as though he himself had arranged the lovely day.

And in the middle of all the excitement Jane and Michael stood still, staring about them.

Everything shone and glistened in the sunlight. There was not a single flake of snow to be seen.

From every branch of every tree, the tender pale-green buds were bursting. Round the edge of the flower-bed just inside the Park fragile green shoots of aconites, snow-drops and scyllas were breaking into a border of yellow, white and blue. Presently the Park Keeper came along and picked a tiny bunch and put them carefully in his button hole.

From flower to flower brightly coloured butter-flies were darting on downy wings, and in the branches thrushes and tits and swallows and finches were singing and building nests.

A flock of sheep with soft young lambs at their heels went by, baa-ing loudly.

And from the bough of the ash tree by the Park Gates came the clear double-noted call —

"Cuckoo! Cuckoo!"

Michael turned to Jane. His eyes were shining.

"So that's what they were doing — Nellie-Rubina and Uncle Dodger and Mary Poppins!"

Jane nodded, gazing wonderingly about her.

Among the faint green smoke of buds a grey body rocked backwards and forwards on the ash-bough.

"Cuckoo! Cuckoo!"

"But — I thought they were all made of painted wood!" said Michael. "Did they come alive in the night, do you think?"

"Perhaps," said Jane.

"Cuckoo! Cuckoo!"

Jane seized Michael's hand and, as though he guessed the thought in her mind, he ran with her through the garden, across the Lane and into the Park.

"Hi! Where are you going, you two?" called Mr. Banks.

"Ahoy, there, messmates!" roared Admiral Boom.

"You'll get lost!" warned Miss Lark shrilly.

The Ice Cream Man tingled his bell wildly and the Sweep stood staring after them.

But Jane and Michael took no notice. They ran on, right through the Park under the trees to the place where they had first seen the Ark.

They drew up panting. It was cold and shadowy here under the dark branches and the snow had not yet melted. They peered about, seeking, seeking. But there was only a heavy drift of snow-flakes spread under the dark green boughs.

"It's really gone, then!" said Michael, gazing round.

"Do you think we only imagined it, Jane?" he asked

doubtfully. She bent down suddenly and picked up something from the snow.

"No," she said slowly, "I'm sure we didn't." She held
out her hand. In her palm lay a round pink Conversation
Sweet. She read out the words.

> "Good-bye till Next Year,
> Nellie-Rubina Noah."

Michael drew a deep breath.

"So that's who she was! Uncle Dodger said she was the
Eldest Daughter. But I never guessed."

"She brought the Spring!" said Jane dreamily, gazing at
the Conversation.

"I'll thank you," said a voice behind them "to come home at once and eat your breakfast," said Mary Poppins.

They turned guiltily.

"We were just — " Michael began to explain.

"Then don't," snapped Mary Poppins. She leant over Jane's shoulder and took the Conversation.

"That, I believe, is mine!" she remarked and, putting it in her apron pocket, she led the way home through the Park.

Michael broke off a spray of green buds as he went. He examined them carefully.

"They seem quite real now," he said.

"Perhaps they always were," said Jane.

And a mocking voice came fluting from the ash tree,

"Cuckoo! Cuckoo! Cuckoo!"

CHAPTER TEN

MERRY-GO-ROUND

I t had been a quiet morning.

More than one person, passing along Cherry-Tree Lane, had looked over the fence of Number Seventeen and said — "How very extraordinary! Not a sound!"

Even the house, which usually took no notice of anything, began to feel alarmed.

"Dear me! Dear me!" it said to itself, listening to the silence. "I hope nothing's wrong!"

Downstairs in the Kitchen, Mrs. Brill, with her spectacles on the tip of her nose, was nodding over the newspaper.

On the first-floor landing, Mrs. Banks and Ellen were tidying the Linen-cupboard and counting the sheets.

Upstairs in the Nursery Mary Poppins was quietly clearing away the luncheon things.

"I feel very good and sweet to-day," Jane was saying drowsily, as she lay stretched on the floor in a patch of sunlight.

"That must be a change!" remarked Mary Poppins with a sniff.

Michael took the last chocolate out of the box Aunt Flossie had given him for his sixth birthday last week.

Should he offer it to Jane? He wondered. Or to the Twins? Or Mary Poppins?

No. After all, it had been *his* birthday.

"Last, lucky last!" he said quickly and popped it into his own mouth. "And I wish there were more!" he added regretfully, gazing into the empty box.

"All good things come to an end, sometime," said Mary Poppins primly.

He cocked his head on one side and looked up at her.

"*You* don't!" he said daringly. "And you're a good thing."

The beginnings of a satisfied smile glimmered at the corners of her mouth but it disappeared as quickly as it had come.

"That's as may be," she retorted. "Nothing lasts for ever."

Jane looked round, startled.

If nothing lasted for ever it meant that Mary Poppins ——

"Nothing?" she said uneasily.

"Nothing at all," snapped Mary Poppins.

And as if she had guessed what was in Jane's mind she went to the mantelpiece and took down her large Thermometer. Then she pulled her carpet bag from under the camp-bed and popped the Thermometer into it.

Jane sat up quickly.

"Mary Poppins, why are you doing that?"

Mary Poppins gave her a curious look.

"Because," she said priggishly. "I was always taught to be tidy." And she pushed the carpet bag under the bed again.

Jane sighed. Her heart felt tight and heavy in her chest.

"I feel rather sad and anxious," she whispered to Michael.

"I expect you had too much steam pudding!" he retorted.

"No, it's not that kind of a feeling —— " she began, and broke off suddenly for a knock had sounded at the door.

Tap! Tap!

"Come in!" called Mary Poppins.

Robertson Ay stood there yawning.

"Do you know what?" he said sleepily.

"No, what?"

"There's a Merry-go-round in the Park!"

"That's no news to me!" snapped Mary Poppins.

"A Fair?" cried Michael excitedly. "With swinging-boats and a Hoop-la?"

"No," said Robertson Ay, solemnly shaking his head. "A Merry-go-round, all by itself. Came last night. Thought you would like to know."

He shuffled languidly to the door and closed it after him.

Jane sprang up, her anxiety forgotten.

"Oh, Mary Poppins, may we go?"

"Say Yes, Mary Poppins, say Yes!" cried Michael dancing round her.

She turned, balancing a tray of plates and cups on her arm.

"*I* am going," she remarked, calmly. "Because I have the fare. I don't know about you."

"There's sixpence in my money-box!" said Jane eagerly.

"Oh, Jane, lend me twopence!" pleaded Michael. He had spent all his money the day before on a stick of Liquorice.

They gazed anxiously at Mary Poppins, waiting for her to make up her mind.

"No borrowing or lending in this Nursery, please," she said tartly. "I will pay for one ride each. And one is all you will have." She swept from the room carrying the tray.

They stared at each other.

"What can be the matter?" said Michael. It was now his turn to be anxious. "She's never paid for anything before!"

"Aren't you well, Mary Poppins?" he asked uneasily, as she came hurrying back.

"Never better in my life!" she replied, tossing her head. "And I'll thank you, if you please, not to stand there, peeking and prying at me as if I were a Waxwork! Go and get ready!"

Her look was so stern, and her eyes so fiercely blue,

and she spoke so like her usual self that their anxiety vanished away and they ran, shouting, to get their hats.

Presently the quietness of the house was broken by the noise of slamming doors, screaming voices and stamping feet.

"Dear me! Dear me! What a relief! I was getting quite anxious!" said the house to itself, listening to Jane and Michael and the Twins plunging and tumbling downstairs.

Mary Poppins paused for a moment to glance at her reflection in the hall mirror.

"Oh, do come on, Mary Poppins! You look all right," said Michael impatiently.

She wheeled about. Her expression was angry, outraged and astonished all at once.

All right, indeed! That was hardly the word. All right, in her blue jacket with the silver buttons! All right with her gold locket round her neck! All right with the parrot-headed umbrella under her arm!

Mary Poppins sniffed.

"That will be enough from you — and more!" she said shortly. Though what she meant was that it wasn't nearly sufficient.

But Michael was too excited to care.

"Come on, Jane!" he cried, dancing wildly. "I simply can't wait! Come on!"

They ran on ahead while Mary Poppins strapped the

Twins into the perambulator. And presently the garden-gate clicked behind them and they were on the way to the Merry-go-round.

Faint sounds of music came floating across from the Park, humming and drumming like a humming-top.

"Good-afternoon! And how are *we* to-day?" Miss Lark's high voice greeted them as she hurried down the Lane with her dogs.

But before they had time to reply she went on, "Off to the Merry-go-round, I suppose! Andrew and Willoughby and I have just been. A *very* superior Entertainment. *So* nice and clean. And *such* a polite Attendant!" She fluttered past with the two dogs prancing beside her. "Good-bye! Good-bye!" she called back over her shoulder as she disappeared round the corner.

"All hands to the pump! Heave ho, my hearties!"

A well-known voice came roaring from the direction of the Park. And through the gates came Admiral Boom, looking very red in the face and dancing a Sailor's Hornpipe.

"Yo, ho, ho! And a bottle of Rum! The Admiral's been on the Merry-go-round. Bail her out! Cockles and Shrimps! It's as good as a long sea-voyage!" he roared, as he greeted the children.

"We're going, too!" said Michael excitedly.

"What? You're going?" The Admiral seemed quite astonished.

"Yes, of course!" said Jane.

"But — not all the way, surely?" The Admiral looked curiously at Mary Poppins.

"They're having one ride each, Sir!" she explained primly.

"Ah, well! Farewell!" he said in a voice that for him was almost gentle.

Then to the children's astonishment, he drew himself up, put his hand to his forehead, and smartly saluted Mary Poppins.

"Ur-rrrrrumph!" he trumpeted into his handkerchief. "Hoist your sail! And up with your Anchor! And away, Love, away!"

And he waved his hand and went off rolling from side to side of the pavement and singing,

"Every nice Girl loves a Sailor!"

in a loud, rumbling voice.

"Why did he say Farewell and call you Love?" said Michael, staring after the Admiral as he walked on beside Mary Poppins.

"Because he thinks I'm a Thoroughly Respectable Person!" she snapped. But there was a soft dreamy look in her eyes.

Again Jane felt the strange sad feeling and her heart tightened inside her.

"What *can* be going to happen?" she asked herself anxiously. She put her hand on Mary Poppins' hand as it lay on the handle of the perambulator. It felt warm and safe and comforting.

"How silly I am!" she said softly. "There *can't* be anything wrong!"

And she hurried beside the perambulator as it trundled towards the Park.

"Just a moment! Just a moment!" A panting voice sounded behind them.

"Why," said Michael, turning. "It's Miss Tartlet!"

"Indeed, it is not," said Miss Tartlet breathlessly. "It's Mrs. Turvy!"

She turned, blushing to Mr. Turvy. He stood beside her smiling a little sheepishly.

"Is this one of your Second Mondays?" Jane enquired. He was right-side up, so she did not think it could be.

"Oh, no! Thank goodness, no!" he said hastily. "We — er — were just coming to say — oh, Good-Afternoon, Mary!"

"Well, Cousin Arthur?" They all shook hands.

"I wondered if you were going on the Merry-go-round?" he enquired.

"Yes I am. We all are!"

"All!" Mr. Turvy's eyebrows shot up to the top of his head. He seemed very surprised.

"They're going for one ride each!" said Mary Poppins, nodding at the children. "Sit still, please!"

she snapped at the Twins, who had bobbed up excitedly. "You're not Performing Mice!"

"Oh, I see. And then — they're getting off? Well — Good-bye, Mary, and Bon Voyage!" Mr. Turvy raised his hat high above his head, very ceremoniously.

"Good-bye — and thank you for coming!" said Mary Poppins, bowing graciously to Mr. and Mrs. Turvy.

"What does Bon Voyage mean?" said Michael, looking over his shoulder at their retreating figures — Mrs. Turvy very fat and curly, Mr. Turvy very straight, and thin.

"Good journey! Which is something *you* won't have unless you walk up!" snapped Mary Poppins. He hurried after her.

The music was louder now, beating and drumming on the air, drawing them all towards it.

Mary Poppins, almost running, turned the perambulator in at the Park Gates. But there a row of pavement pictures caught her eye and she pulled up suddenly.

"What is she stopping for now?" said Michael in an angry whisper to Jane. "We'll never get there at this rate!"

The Pavement Artist had just completed a set of fruit in coloured chalks — an Apple, a Pear, a Plum, and a Banana. Underneath them he was busy chalking the words —

TAKE ONE

"Ahem!" said Mary Poppins, with a lady-like cough.

The Pavement Artist leapt to his feet, and Jane and Michael saw that it was Mary Poppins' great friend, the Match Man.

"Mary! At last! I've been waiting all day!"

The Match Man seized her by both hands and gazed admiringly into her eyes.

Mary Poppins looked very shy and rather pleased.

"Well, Bert, we're off to the Merry-go-round," she said, blushing.

He nodded. "I thought you would be. They going with you?" he added, jerking his thumb at the children.

Mary Poppins shook her head mysteriously.

"Just for a ride," she said quickly.

"Oh —— " He pursed up his mouth. "I see."

Michael stared. What else could they do on a Merry-go-round *except* go for a ride? He wondered.

"A nice set of pictures you've got!" Mary Poppins was saying admiringly, gazing down at the fruit.

"Help yourself!" said the Match Man airily.

And with that Mary Poppins, before their astonished eyes, bent down and picked the painted Plum from the pavement and took a bite out of it.

"Won't you take one?" said the Match Man, turning to Jane.

She stared at him. "But *can* I?" It seemed so impossible. "Try!"

She bent towards the Apple and it leapt into her hand. She bit into the red side. It tasted very sweet.

"But how do you do it?" said Michael, staring.

"I don't," said the Match Man. "It's Her!" He nodded at Mary Poppins as she stood primly beside the perambulator. "It only happens when She's around, I assure you!"

Then he bent down and picked the pear clean out of the pavement and offered it to Michael.

"But what about you?" said Michael, for though he wanted the Pear, he also wanted to be polite.

"That's all right!" said the Match Man. "I can always paint more!" And with that he plucked the Banana, peeled it, and gave half each to the Twins.

A clear sweet strain of music came floating urgently to their ears.

"Now, Bert, we must really be going!" said Mary Poppins hurriedly, as she neatly hid her Plum-stone between two Park railings.

"Must you, Mary?" said the Match Man, very sadly. "Well, Good-bye, my Dear! And Good Luck!"

"But you'll see him again, won't you?" said Michael, as he followed Mary Poppins through the Gates.

"Maybe and maybe not!" she said shortly. "And it's no affair of yours!"

Jane turned and looked back. The Match Man was standing by his box of chalks, gazing with all his eyes after Mary Poppins.

"This *is* a curious day!" she said, frowning.

Mary Poppins glared at her.

"What's wrong with it, pray?"

"Well — everyone's saying Good-bye, and looking at you so strangely."

"Speech costs nothing!" snapped Mary Poppins. "And a Cat can look at a King, I suppose?"

Jane was silent. She knew it was no good saying anything to Mary Poppins because Mary Poppins never explained.

She sighed. And because she was not quite sure why she sighed, she began to run, streaking past Michael and Mary Poppins and the perambulator towards the thundering music.

"Wait for me! Wait for me!" screamed Michael, dashing after her. And behind him came the rumbling trundle of the perambulator as Mary Poppins hurried after them both.

There stood the Merry-go-round on a clear patch of lawn between the lime trees. It was a new one, very bright and shiny, with prancing horses going up and down on their brass poles. A striped flag fluttered from the top, and everywhere it was gorgeously decorated with golden scrolls and silver leaves and coloured birds and stars. It was, in fact, everything Miss Lark had said, and more.

The Merry-go-round slowed up and drew to a standstill as they arrived. The Park Keeper ran up officiously and held on to one of the brass poles.

"Come along, come along! Threepence a ride!" he called importantly.

"I know which horse I'll have!" said Michael, dashing up to one painted blue-and-scarlet with the name "Merry-Legs" on its gold collar. He clambered on to its back and seized the pole.

"No Litter Allowed and Observe the Bye-Laws," called the Keeper fussily as Jane sped past him.

"I'll have Twinkle!" she cried, climbing upon the back of a fiery white horse with its name on a red collar.

Then Mary Poppins lifted the Twins from the perambulator and put Barbara in front of Michael and John behind Jane.

"Penny, Tuppeny, Threepenny, Fourpenny or Fivepenny rides?" said the Merry-go-round Attendant, as he came to collect the money.

"Sixpenny," said Mary Poppins, handing him four sixpenny bits.

The children stared, amazed. They had never before had a sixpenny ride on a Merry-go-round.

"No Litter Allowed!" called the Keeper, his eye on the tickets in Mary Poppins' hands.

"But aren't you coming?" Michael called down to her.

"Hold tight, please! Hold tight! I'll take the next turn!" she replied snappily.

There was a hoot from the Merry-go-round's chimney. The music broke out again. And slowly, slowly the horses began to move.

"Hold on, please!" called Mary Poppins sternly.

They held on.

The trees were moving past them. The brass poles slipped up and down through the horses' backs. A dazzle of light fell on them from the rays of the setting sun.

"Sit tight!" came Mary Poppins' voice again.

They sat tight.

Now the trees were moving more swiftly, spinning about them as the Merry-go-round gathered speed. Michael tightened his arm about Barbara's body. Jane flung back her hand and held John firmly. On they rode, turning ever more quickly, with their hair blowing out behind them and the wind sharp on their faces. Round and round went Merry-Legs and Twinkle, with the children on their backs and the Park tipping and rocking, whirling and wheeling about them.

It seemed as if they would never stop, as if there were no such thing as Time, as if the world was nothing but a circle of light and a group of painted horses.

The sun died in the West and the dusk came fluttering down. But still they rode, faster and faster, till at last they could not distinguish tree from sky. The whole broad earth was spinning now about them with a deep, drumming sound like a humming top.

Never again would Jane and Michael and John and Barbara be so close to the centre of the world as they were on that whirling ride. And somehow, it seemed, they knew it.

"For —— Never again! Never again!" was the thought in their hearts as the earth whirled about them and they rode through the dropping dusk.

Presently the trees ceased to be a circular green blur and their trunks again became visible. The sky moved away from the earth and the Park stopped spinning. Slower and slower went the horses. And at last the Merry-go-round stood still.

"Come along, come along! Threepence a ride!" the Park Keeper was calling in the distance.

Stiff from their long ride, the four children clambered down. But their eyes were shining and their voices trembled with excitement.

"Oh, lovely, lovely, lovely!" cried Jane, gazing at Mary Poppins with sparkling eyes, as she put John into the perambulator.

"If only we could have gone on for ever!" exclaimed Michael, lifting Barbara in beside him.

Mary Poppins gazed down at them. Her eyes were strangely soft and gentle in the gathering dusk.

"All good things come to an end," she said, for the second time that day.

Then she flung up her head and glanced at the Merry-go-round.

"*My* turn!" she cried joyfully, as she stooped and took something from the perambulator.

Then she straightened and stood looking at them for a moment — that strange look that seemed to plunge right down inside them and *see* what they were thinking.

"Michael!" she said, lightly touching his cheek with her hand. "Be good!"

He stared up at her uneasily. Why had she done that? What could be the matter?

"Jane! Take care of Michael and the Twins!" said Mary Poppins. And she lifted Jane's hand and put it gently on the handle of the perambulator.

"All aboard! All aboard!" cried the Ticket Collector.

The lights of the Merry-go-round blazed up.

Mary Poppins turned.

"Coming!" she called, waving her parrot-headed umbrella.

She darted across the little gulf of darkness that lay between the children and the Merry-go-round.

"Mary Poppins!" cried Jane, with a tremble in her voice. For suddenly — she did not know why — she felt afraid.

"Mary Poppins!" shouted Michael, catching Jane's fear.

But Mary Poppins took no notice. She leapt gracefully upon the platform, and, climbing upon the back of a dappled horse called Caramel, she sat down neatly and primly.

"Single or Return?" said the Ticket Collector.

For a moment she appeared to consider the question. She glanced across at the children and back at the Collector.

"You never know," she said, thoughtfully. "It might come in useful. I'll take a Return."

The Ticket Collector snapped a hole in a green ticket and handed it to Mary Poppins. Jane and Michael noticed that she did not pay for it.

The music broke out again, softly at first, then loudly, wildly, triumphantly. Slowly the painted horses began to move.

Mary Poppins, looking straight ahead of her, was borne past the children. The parrot's head of her umbrella nestled under her arm. Her neatly gloved hands were closed on the brass pole. And in front of her, on the horse's neck——

"Michael!" cried Jane, clutching his arm. "Do you see? She must have hidden it under the rug! Her Carpet bag!"

Michael stared.

"Do you think——?" he began in a whisper.

Jane nodded.

"But — she's wearing the locket! The chain hasn't broken! I distinctly saw it!"

Behind them the Twins began to whimper but Jane and Michael took no notice. They were gazing anxiously at the shining circle of horses.

The Merry-go-round was moving swiftly now, and soon the children could no longer tell which horse was which, nor distinguish Merry-Legs from Twinkle. Everything before them was a blaze of spinning light, except for the dark figure, neat and steady, that ever and again approached them and sped past and disappeared.

Wilder and wilder grew the drumming music. Faster and faster whirled the Merry-go-round. Again the dark shape rode towards them upon the dappled horse. And this time, as she came by, something bright and gleaming broke from her neck and came flying through the air to their feet.

Jane bent and picked it up. It was the gold locket, hanging loosely from its broken golden chain.

"It's true, then, it's true!" came Michael's bursting cry. "Oh, open it, Jane!"

With trembling fingers she pressed the catch and the locket flew open. The flickering light fell across the glass and they saw before them their own pictured faces, clustered about a figure with straight black hair, stern blue

eyes, bright pink cheeks, and a nose turning upwards like
the nose of a Dutch doll.

> "Jane, Michael, John, Barbara and Annabel Banks,
> and
> Mary Poppins."

read Jane from the little scroll beneath the picture.

"So that's what was in it!" said Michael, miserably, as
Jane shut the locket and put it in her pocket. He knew
there was no hope now.

They turned again to the Merry-go-round, dazzled
and giddy in the spinning light. For by now the horses
were flying more swiftly than ever and the pealing music
was louder than before.

And then a strange thing happened. With a great blast
of trumpets, the whole Merry-go-round rose, spinning,
from the ground. Round and round, rising ever higher,
the coloured horses wheeled and raced with Caramel and
Mary Poppins at their head. And the swinging circle of
light went lifting among the trees, turning the leaves to
gold as the light fell upon them.

"She's going!" said Michael.

"Oh, Mary Poppins, Mary Poppins! Come back, come
back!" they cried, lifting their arms towards her.

But her face was turned away, she looked out serenely above her horse's head and gave no sign that she had
heard.

"Mary Poppins!" It was a last despairing cry.

No answer now came from the air.

By now the Merry-go-round had cleared the trees and was whirling up towards the stars. Away it went and away, growing smaller and smaller, until the figure of Mary Poppins was but a dark speck in a wheel of light.

On and on, pricking through the sky, went the Merry-go-round, carrying Mary Poppins with it. And at last it was just a tiny twinkling shape, a little larger but not otherwise different from a star.

Michael sniffed and fumbled for his handkerchief.

"I've got a crick in my neck," he said to explain the sniff. But when she was not looking he hurriedly wiped his eyes.

Jane, still watching the bright spinning shape, gave a little sigh. Then she turned away.

"We must go home," she said flatly, remembering that Mary Poppins had told her to take care of Michael and the Twins.

"Come along, come along! Threepence a ride!" The Park Keeper, who had been putting litter in the baskets returned to the scene. He glanced at the place where the Merry-go-round had been and started violently. He looked around him and his mouth fell open. He looked up and his eyes nearly burst out of his head.

"See here!" he shouted. "This won't do! Here one minute and gone the next! It's against the regulations! I'll have the law on you." He shook his fist wildly at the empty

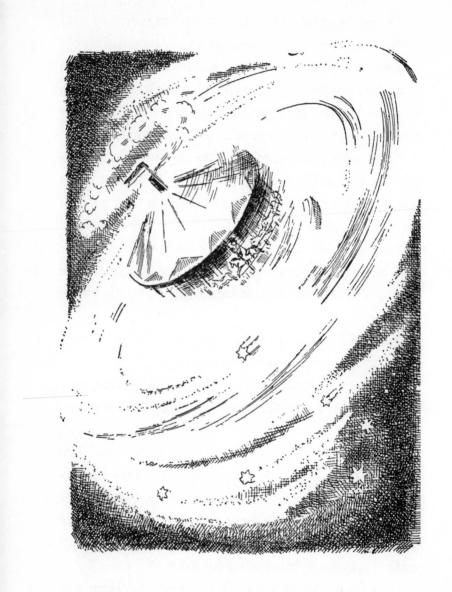

Away it went and away, growing smaller and smaller

air. "I never saw such a thing! Not even when I was a boy! I must make a report! I shall tell the Lord Mayor!"

Silently the children turned away. The Merry-go-round had left no trace in the grass, not a dent in the clover. Except for the Park Keeper, who stood there shouting and waving his arms, the green lawn was quite empty.

"She took a Return," said Michael, walking slowly beside the perambulator. "Do you think that means she'll come back?"

Jane thought for a moment. "Perhaps. If we want her enough," she said slowly.

"Yes, perhaps . . . !" he repeated, sighing a little, and said no more till they were back in the Nursery. . . .

"I say! I say! I say!"

Mr. Banks came running up the path and burst in at the front door.

"Hi! Where's everybody?" he shouted, running up the stairs three at a time.

"Whatever is the matter?" said Mrs. Banks, hurrying out to meet him.

"The most wonderful thing!" he cried, flinging open the Nursery door. "A new star has appeared. I heard about it on the way home. The Largest Ever. I've borrowed Admiral Boom's telescope to look at it. Come and see!"

He ran to the window and clapped the telescope to his eye.

"Yes! Yes!" he said, hopping excitedly. "There it is! A Wonder! A Beauty! A Marvel! A Gem! See for yourself!"

He handed Mrs. Banks the telescope.

"Children!" he shouted. "There's a new star!"

"I know——" began Michael. "But it's not really a star. It's——"

"You know? And it isn't? What on earth do you mean?"

"Take no notice. He is just being silly!" said Mrs. Banks. "Now, where is this star? Oh, I see! *Very* pretty! Quite the brightest in the sky! I wonder where it came from! Now, children!"

She gave the telescope in turn to Jane and Michael, and as they looked through the glass they could clearly see the circle of painted horses, the brass poles and the dark blur that ever and again whirled across their sight for a moment and was gone.

They turned to each other and nodded. They knew what the dark blur was — a neat, trim figure in a blue coat with silver buttons, a stiff straw hat on its head, and a parrot-headed umbrella under its arm. Out of the sky she had come, back to the sky she had gone. And Jane and Michael would not explain to anyone for they knew there were things about Mary Poppins that could never be explained.

A knock sounded at the door.

"Excuse me, Ma'am," said Mrs. Brill, hurrying in, very red in the face. "But I think you ought to know that that there Mary Poppins has gone again!"

"Gone!" said Mrs. Banks unbelievingly.

"Lock, stock and barrer — gone!" said Mrs. Brill, triumphantly. "Without a word or By Your Leave. Just like last time. Even her Camp-bed and her Carpet bag — clean gone! Not even her Postcard album as a Memento. So there!"

"Dear, dear!" said Mrs. Banks. "How very tiresome! How thoughtless, how and — George!" she turned to Mr. Banks. "George, Mary Poppins has gone again!"

"Who? What? Mary Poppins? Well, never mind that! We've got a new star!"

"A new star won't wash and dress the children!" said Mrs. Banks crossly.

"It will look through their window at night!" cried Mr. Banks, happily. "That's better than washing and dressing."

He turned back to the telescope.

"Won't you, my Wonder? My Marvel? My Beauty!" he said, looking up at the star.

Jane and Michael drew close and leant against him, gazing across the window-sill into the evening air.

And high above them the great shape circled and wheeled through the darkening sky, shining and keeping its secret for ever and ever and ever. . . .

A day in the Park

MARY
POPPINS
OPENS THE
DOOR

TO
KATHARINE CORNELL

CONTENTS

ILLUSTRATIONS

Also insets and tailpieces

NOTE

The Fifth of November is Guy Fawkes' Day in England. In peace-time it is celebrated with bonfires on the greens, fireworks in the parks and the carrying of "guys" through the streets. "Guys" are stuffed, straw figures of unpopular persons; and after they have been shown to everybody they are burnt in the bonfires amid great acclamation. The children black their faces and put on comical clothes, and go about begging for a Penny for the Guy. Only the very meanest people refuse to give pennies and these are always visited by Extreme Bad Luck.

The Original Guy Fawkes was one of the men who took part in the Gunpowder Plot. This was a conspiracy for blowing up King James I and the Houses of Parliament on November 5th, 1605. The plot was discovered, however, before any damage was done. The only result was that King James and his Parliament went on living but Guy Fawkes, poor man, did not. He was executed with the other conspirators. Nevertheless, it is Guy Fawkes who is remembered to-day and King James who is forgotten. For since that time, the Fifth of November in England, like the Fourth of July in America, has been devoted to Fireworks. From 1605 till 1939 every village green in the shires had a bonfire on Guy Fawkes' Day. In the village where I live, in Sussex, we made our bonfire in the Vicarage paddock and every year, as soon as it was lit, the Vicar's cow would begin to dance. She danced while the flames roared up to the sky, she danced till the ashes were black and cold. And the next morning — it was always the same — the Vicar would have no milk for his breakfast. It is strange to think of a simple cow rejoicing so heartily at the saving of Parliament so many years ago.

Since 1939, however, there have been no bonfires on the village greens. No fireworks gleam in the blackened parks and the streets are dark and silent. But this darkness will not last forever. There will some day come a Fifth of November — or another date, it doesn't matter — when fires will burn in a chain of brightness from Land's End to John O'Groats. The children will dance and leap about them as they did in the times before. They will take each other by the hand and watch the rockets breaking, and afterwards they will go home singing to the houses full of light. . . .

P. L. T. (1943)

CHAPTER
ONE

THE FIFTH OF NOVEMBER*

t was one of those bleak and chilly mornings that remind you winter is coming. Cherry-Tree Lane was quiet and still. The mist hung over the Park like a shadow. All the houses looked exactly alike as the grey fog wrapped them round. Admiral Boom's flagstaff, with the telescope at the top of it, had entirely disappeared.

The Milkman, as he turned into the Lane, could hardly see his way.

"Milk Be-l-o-o-ow!" he called, outside the Admiral's door. And his voice sounded so queer and hollow that it gave him quite a fright.

"I'll go 'ome till the fog lifts," he said to himself. " 'Ere! Look where you're goin'!" he went on, as a shape loomed suddenly out of the mist and bumped against his shoulder.

"Bumble, bumble, bum-bur-um-bumble," said a gentle, muffled voice.

---

* *See note, page 507.*

"Oh, it's you!" said the Milkman, with a sigh of relief.

"Bumble," remarked the Sweep again. He was holding his brushes in front of his face to keep his moustache dry.

"Out early, aren't you?" the Milkman said.

The Sweep gave a jerk of his black thumb towards Miss Lark's house.

"Had to do the chimbley before the dogs had breakfast. In case the soot gave them a cough," he explained.

The Milkman laughed rudely. For that was what everybody did when Miss Lark's two dogs were mentioned.

The mist went wreathing through the air. There was not a sound in the Lane.

"Ugh!" said the Milkman, shivering. "This quiet gives me the 'Orrors!"

And as he said that, the Lane woke up. A sudden roar came from one of the houses and the sound of stamping feet.

"That's Number Seventeen!" said the Sweep. "Excuse me, old chap. I think I'm needed." He cautiously felt his way to the gate and went up the garden path. . . .

Inside the house, Mr. Banks was marching up and down, kicking the hall furniture.

"I've had about all I can stand!" he shouted, waving his arms wildly.

"You keep on saying that," Mrs. Banks cried. "But you won't tell me what's the matter." She looked at Mr. Banks anxiously.

"Everything's the matter!" he roared. "Look at this!" He waggled his right foot at her. "And this!" he went on, as he waggled his left.

Mrs. Banks peered closely at the feet. She was rather short-sighted and the hall was misty.

"I — er — don't see anything wrong," she began timidly.

"Of course you don't!" he said, sarcastically. "It's only imagination, of course, that makes me think Robertson Ay has given me one black shoe and one brown!" And again he waggled his feet.

"Oh!" said Mrs. Banks hurriedly. For now she saw clearly what the trouble was.

"You may well say 'Oh!' So will Robertson Ay when I give him the sack tonight."

"It's not his fault, Daddy!" cried Jane, from the stairs. "He couldn't see — because of the fog. Besides, he's not strong."

"He's strong enough to make my life a misery!" said Mr. Banks angrily.

"He needs rest, Daddy!" Michael reminded him, hurrying down after Jane.

"He'll get it!" promised Mr. Banks, as he snatched up his bag. "When I think of the things I could have done if I hadn't gone and got married! Lived alone in a Cave, perhaps. Or I might have gone Round the World."

"And what would *we* have done, then?" asked Michael.

"You would have had to fend for yourselves. And serve you right! Where's my overcoat?"

"You have it on, George," said Mrs. Banks, meekly.

"Yes!" he retorted. "And only one button! But anything's good enough for *me!* *I'm* only the man who Pays the Bills. I shall not be home for dinner."

A wail of protest went up from the children.

"But it's Guy Fawkes' Day," wheedled Mrs. Banks. "And you so good at letting off rockets."

"No rockets for me!" cried Mr. Banks. "Nothing but trouble from morning till night!" He shook Mrs. Banks' hand from his arm and dashed out of the house.

"Shake, sir!" said the Sweep in a friendly voice as Mr. Banks knocked into him, "It's lucky, you know, to shake hands with a Sweep."

"Away, away!" said Mr. Banks wildly. "This is not my lucky day!"

The Sweep looked after him for a moment. Then he smiled to himself and rang the door-bell. . . .

"He doesn't mean it, does he, Mother? He *will* come home for the fireworks!" Jane and Michael rushed at Mrs. Banks and tugged at her skirt.

"Oh, I can't promise anything, children!" she sighed, as she looked at her face in the front hall mirror.

And she thought to herself — Yes, I'm getting thinner. One of my dimples has gone already and soon I shall lose

the second. No one will look at me any more. And it's all *her* fault!

By her, Mrs. Banks meant Mary Poppins, who had been the children's nurse. As long as Mary Poppins was in the house, everything had gone smoothly. But since that day when she had left them — so suddenly and without a Word of Warning — the family had gone from Bad to Worse.

Here am I, thought Mrs. Banks miserably, with five wild children and no one to help me. I've advertised. I've asked my friends. But nothing seems to happen. And George is getting crosser and crosser; and Annabel's teething; and Jane and Michael and the Twins are so naughty, not to mention that awful Income Tax——

She watched a tear run over the spot where the dimple had once been.

"It's no good," she said, with sudden decision. "I shall have to send for Miss Andrew."

A cry went up from all four children. Away in the Nursery, Annabel screamed. For Miss Andrew had once been their Father's governess and they knew how frightful she was.

"I won't speak to her!" shouted Jane, in a rage.

"I'll spit on her shoes if she comes!" threatened Michael.

"No, no!" wailed John and Barbara miserably.

Mrs. Banks clapped her hands to her ears. "Children, have mercy!" she cried in despair.

"Beg pardon, ma'am," said Ellen the housemaid, as she tapped Mrs. Banks on the shoulder. "The Sweep is 'ere for the Drawing-room Chimbley. But I warn you, ma'am, it's my Day Out! And I can't clean up after 'im. So there!" She blew her nose with a trumpeting sound.

"Excuse me!" said the Sweep cheerfully, as he dragged in his bags and brushes.

" 'Oo's that?" came the voice of Mrs. Brill as she hurried up from the kitchen. "The Sweep? On Baking Day? No, you don't! I'm sorry to give you notice, ma'am. But if that Hottentot goes into the chimney, I shall go out of the door."

Mrs. Banks glanced round desperately.

"I didn't ask him to come!" she declared. "I don't even know if the chimney wants sweeping!"

"A chimbley's always glad of a brush." The Sweep stepped calmly into the Drawing-room and began to spread out his sheet.

Mrs. Banks looked nervously at Mrs. Brill. "Perhaps Robertson Ay could help — " she began.

"Robertson is asleep in the pantry, wrapped in your best lace shawl. And nothing will wake him," said Mrs. Brill, "but the sound of the Last Trombone. So, if you please, I'll be packing my bag. 'Ow! Let me go, you Hindoo!"

For the Sweep had seized Mrs. Brill's hand and was shaking it vigorously. A reluctant smile spread over her face.

"Well — just this once!" she remarked cheerfully. And she went down the kitchen stairs.

The Sweep turned to Ellen with a grin.

"Don't touch me, you black heathen!" she screamed in a terrified voice. But he took her hand in a firm grip and she, too, began to smile. "Well, no messing up the carpet!" she warned him, and hurried off to her work.

"Shake!" said the Sweep, as he turned to the children. "It's sure to bring you luck!" He left a black mark on each of their palms and they all felt suddenly better.

Then he put out his hand to Mrs. Banks. And as she took his warm black fingers her courage came flowing back.

"We must make the best of things, darlings," she said. "I shall advertise for another nurse. And perhaps something good will happen."

Jane and Michael sighed with relief. At least she was not going to send for Miss Andrew.

"What do you do when *you* need luck?" asked Jane, as she followed the Sweep to the Drawing-room.

"Oh, I just shake 'ands with meself," he said, cheerfully, pushing his brush up the chimney.

All day long the children watched him and argued over who should hand him the brushes. Now and again Mrs. Banks came in, to complain of the noise and hurry the Sweep.

And all day long, beyond the windows, the mist crept through the Lane. Every sound was muffled. The birds were gone. Except for an old and moulting Starling who kept on peering through the cracks in the blinds as if he were looking for someone.

At last the Sweep crept out of the chimney and smiled at his handiwork.

"So kind of you!" said Mrs. Banks hurriedly. "Now, I'm sure you must want to pack up and go home —— "

"*I'm* in no 'Urry," remarked the Sweep. "Me Tea isn't ready till six o'clock and I've got an hour to fill in —— "

"Well, you can't fill it in here!" Mrs. Banks shrieked. "I have to tidy up this room before my husband comes home!"

"I tell you what — " the Sweep said calmly. "If you've got a rocket or two about you, I could take them children into the Park and show 'em a few fireworks. It'd give you a rest and meself a Treat. I've always been very partial to rockets, ever since a boy — and before!"

A yell of delight went up from the children. Michael ran to a window and lifted the blind.

"Oh, look what's happened!" he cried in triumph.

For a change had come to Cherry-Tree Lane. The chill grey mist had cleared away. The houses were lit with warm soft lights. And away in the West shone a glimmer of sunset, rosy and clear and bright.

"Remember your coats!" cried Mrs. Banks, as the children darted away. Then she ran to the cupboard under the staircase and brought out a nobbly parcel.

"Here you are!" she said breathlessly to the Sweep. "And, mind, be careful of sparks!"

"Sparks?" said the Sweep. "Why, sparks is my 'Obby. Them and the soot wot comes after!"

The children leapt like puppies about him as he went down the garden path. Mrs. Banks sat down for two minutes' rest on one of the sheet-covered chairs. The Starling looked in at her for a moment. Then he shook his head disappointedly and flew away again. . . .

Daylight was fading as they crossed the road. By the Park railings Bert, the Matchman, was spreading out his tray. He lit a candle with one of his matches and began to draw pictures on the pavement. He nodded gaily to the children as they hurried through the Gates.

"Now, all we need," the Sweep said fussily, "is a clear patch of grass —— "

"Which you won't get!" said a voice behind them. "The Park is closed at 5:30."

Out from the shadows came the Park Keeper, looking very belligerent.

"But it's Guy Fawkes' Day — the Fifth of November!" the children answered quickly.

"Orders is orders!" he retorted, "and all days are alike to me."

"Well, where can we let off the fireworks?" Michael demanded impatiently.

A greedy look leapt to the Keeper's eyes.

"You got some fireworks?" he said hungrily. "Well, why not say so before!" And he snatched the parcel from the Sweep and began to untie the string. "Matches — that's what we need!" he went on, panting with excitement.

"Here," said the Matchman's quiet voice. He had followed the children into the Park and was standing behind them with his lighted candle.

The Park Keeper opened a bundle of Squibs.

"They're *ours*, you know!" Michael reminded him.

"Ah, let me help you — do!" said the Keeper. "I've never 'ad fun on Guy Fawkes' Day — never since I was a boy!"

And without waiting for permission, he lit the Squibs at the Matchman's candle. The hissing streams of fire poured out, and pop, pop, pop, went the crackers. The Park Keeper seized a Catherine Wheel and stuck it on a branch. The rings of light began to turn and sparkled on the air. And after that he was so excited that nothing could stop him. He went on lighting fuse after fuse as though he had gone mad.

Flower Pots streamed from the dewy grass and Golden Rain flowed down through the darkness. Top Hats burned for a bright short moment; Balloons went floating up to the branches; and Firesnakes writhed in the shadows. The children jumped and squeaked and shouted. The Park Keeper ran about among them like a large frenzied dog. And amid the noise and the sparkling lights the Matchman waited quietly. The flame of his candle never wavered as they lit their fuses from it.

"Now!" cried the Keeper, who was hoarse with shouting. "Now we come to the rockets!"

All the other fireworks had gone. Nothing remained in the nobbly parcel except three long black sticks.

"No you don't!" said the Sweep, as the Keeper snatched them. "Share and share. That's fair!" He gave the Keeper one rocket and kept the others for himself and the children.

"Make way, make way!" said the Keeper importantly,

as he lit the fuse at the candle flame and stuck the stick in the ground.

Hissing and guttering, the spark ran down like a little golden thread. Then — whoop! went the stick as it shot away. Up in the sky the children heard a small faraway bang. And a swirl of red-and-blue stars broke out and rained upon the Park.

"Oh!" cried the children. And "Oh!" cried the Sweep. For that is the only word anyone can say when a rocket's stars break out.

Then it was the Sweep's turn. The candle-light gleamed on his black face as he lit the fuse of his rocket. Then came a whoop and another bang and white-and-green stars spread over the sky like the ribs of a bright umbrella. And again the watchers all cried "Oh!" and sighed for sheer joy.

"It's our turn now!" cried Jane and Michael. And their fingers trembled as they lit the fuse. They pressed the stick down into the earth and stepped back to watch. The thread of golden fire ran down. Whe-e-e-ew! Up went the stick with a singing sound, up to the very top of the sky. And Jane and Michael held their breath as they waited for it to burst.

At last, far away and very faint, they heard the little bang.

Now for the stars, they thought to themselves.

But — alas! — nothing happened.

"Oh!" said everyone again — not for joy this time, but for disappointment. For no stars broke from the third rocket. There was nothing but darkness and the empty sky.

"Tricksy — that's what they are!" said the Sweep. "There are some as just doesn't go off! Well, come on home, all. There's no good staring. Nothing will come down now!"

"Closing Time! Everyone out of the Park!" cried the Park Keeper importantly.

But Jane and Michael took no notice. They stood there watching, hand in hand. For their hopeful eyes had no-

ticed something that nobody else had seen. Up in the sky
a tiny spark hovered and swayed in the darkness. What
could it be? Not the stick of the rocket, for that must have
fallen long ago. And certainly not a star, they thought, for
the little spark was moving.

"Perhaps it's a special kind of rocket that has only one
spark," said Michael.

"Perhaps," Jane answered quietly, as she watched the
tiny light.

They stood together, gazing upwards. Even if there
was only one spark they would watch till it went out. But,
strangely enough, it did not go out. In fact, it was growing
larger.

"Let's get a move on!" urged the Sweep. And again the
Park Keeper cried:

"Closing Time!"

But still they waited. And still the spark grew ever larger and brighter. Then suddenly Jane caught her breath.
And Michael gave a gasp. Oh, was it possible — ? Could it
be — ? they silently asked each other.

Down came the spark, growing longer and wider. And
as it came, it took on a shape that was strange and also
familiar. Out of the glowing core of light emerged a curious figure — a figure in a black straw hat and a blue coat
trimmed with silver buttons — a figure that carried in
one hand something that looked like a carpet bag, and in
the other — oh, could it be true? — a parrot-headed umbrella.

Behind them the Matchman gave a cry and ran through the Park Gates.

The curious figure was drifting now to the tops of the naked trees. Its feet touched the highest bough of an oak and stepped down daintily through the branches. It stood for a moment on the lowest bough and balanced itself neatly.

Jane and Michael began to run and their breath broke from them in a happy shout.

"Mary Poppins! Mary Poppins! Mary Poppins!" Half-laughing, half-weeping, they flung themselves upon her.

"You've c-come b-back, at l-last!" stammered Michael excitedly, as he clutched her neatly shod foot. It was warm and bony and quite real and it smelt of Black Boot-polish.

"We knew you'd come back. We trusted you!" Jane seized Mary Poppins' other foot and dragged at her cotton stocking.

Mary Poppins' mouth crinkled with the ghost of a smile. Then she looked at the children fiercely.

"I'll thank you to let go my shoes!" she snapped. "I am not an object in a Bargain Basement!"

She shook them off and stepped down from the tree, as John and Barbara, mewing like kittens, rushed over the grass towards her.

"Hyenas!" she said with an angry glare, as she loosened their clutching fingers. "And what, may I ask, are you all doing — running about in the Park at night and looking like Blackamoors?"

Quickly they pulled out handkerchiefs and began to
rub their cheeks.

"My fault, Miss Poppins," the Sweep apologised. "I
been sweeping the Drawing-room chimbley."

"Somebody will be sweeping *you,* if you don't look
out!" she retorted.

"But-but!   Glog-glog!   Er-rumph!   Glug-glug!"
Speechless with astonishment, the Park Keeper blocked
their path.

"Out of my way, please!" said Mary Poppins, haughtily
brushing him aside as she pushed the children in front of
her.

"This is the Second Time!" he gasped, suddenly finding his voice. "First it's a Kite and now it's a — You can't

Out of the glowing core of light emerged a curious figure

do things like this, I tell you! It's against the Law. And, furthermore, it's all against Nature."

He flung out his hand in a wild gesture and Mary Poppins popped into it a small piece of cardboard.

"Wot's this?" he demanded, turning it over.

"My Return Ticket," she calmly replied.

And Jane and Michael looked at each other and nodded wisely together.

"Ticket — wot ticket? Buses have tickets and so do trains. But you came down on I-don't-know-what! Where did you come from? 'Ow did you get 'ere? That's what I want to know!"

"Curiosity Killed a Cat!" said Mary Poppins primly. She pushed the Park Keeper to one side and left him staring at the little green ticket as though it were a ghost.

The children danced and leapt about her as they came to the Park Gates.

"Walk quietly, please," she told them crossly. "You are not a School of Porpoises! And which of you, I'd like to know, has been playing with lighted candles?"

The Matchman scrambled up from his knees.

"I lit it, Mary," he said eagerly. "I wanted to write you a ——" He waved his hands. And there on the pavement, not quite finished, was the one word

WELCOM

Mary Poppins smiled at the coloured letters. "That's a lovely greeting, Bert," she said softly.

The Matchman seized her black-gloved hand, and looked at her eagerly. "Shall I see you on Thursday, Mary?" he asked.

She nodded. "Thursday, Bert," she said. Then she flung a withering look at the children. "No dawdling, if you please!" she commanded, as she hurried them across the Lane to Number Seventeen.

Up in the Nursery Annabel was screaming her head off. Mrs. Banks was running along the hall, calling out soothing phrases. As the children opened the Front Door, she gave one look at Mary Poppins, and collapsed upon the stairs.

"Can it be you, Mary Poppins?" she gasped.

"It can, ma'am," Mary Poppins said calmly.

"But — where did you spring from?" Mrs. Banks cried.

"She sprang right out of a——" Michael was just about to explain when he felt Mary Poppins' eyes upon him. He knew very well what that look meant. He stammered and was silent.

"I came from the Park, ma'am," said Mary Poppins, with the patient air of a martyr.

"Thank goodness!" breathed Mrs. Banks from her

heart. Then she remembered all that had happened since Mary Poppins had left them. I mustn't seem *too* pleased, she thought. Or she'll be more uppish than ever!

"You left me Without a Word, Mary Poppins," she said with an air of dignity. "I think you might tell me when you're coming and going. I never know where I am."

"Nobody does, ma'am," said Mary Poppins, as she calmly unbuttoned her gloves.

"Don't *you*, Mary Poppins?" asked Mrs. Banks, in a very wistful voice.

"Oh, *she* knows," Michael answered daringly. Mary Poppins gave him an angry glare.

"Well, you're here now, anyway!" Mrs. Banks cried. She felt extremely relieved. For now she need neither advertise nor send for Miss Andrew.

"Yes, ma'am. Excuse me," said Mary Poppins.

And she neatly stepped past Mrs. Banks and put her carpet bag on the bannisters. It slid up swiftly with a whistling sound and bounced into the Nursery. Then she gave the umbrella a little toss. It spread its black silk wings like a bird and flew up after the carpet bag with a parrot-like squawk.

The children gave an astonished gasp and turned to see if their Mother had noticed.

But Mrs. Banks had no thought for anything but to get to the telephone.

"The Drawing-room chimney has been cleaned. We are having Lamb Chops and peas for dinner. And Mary Poppins is back!" she cried, breathlessly.

"I don't believe it!" crackled Mr. Banks' voice. "I shall come and see for myself!"

Mrs. Banks smiled happily as she hung up the receiver. . . .

Mary Poppins went primly up the stairs and the children tore past her into the Nursery. There on the hearth lay the carpet bag. And standing in its usual corner was the parrot-headed umbrella. They had a settled, satisfied air as though they had been there for years. In the cradle, Annabel, blue in the face, was tying herself into knots. She stared in surprise at Mary Poppins, and smiled a toothless smile. Then she put on her Innocent Angel look and began to play tunes on her toes.

"Humph!" said Mary Poppins grimly, as she put her straw hat in its paper bag. She took off her coat and hung it up on the hook behind the door. Then she glanced at herself in the Nursery mirror and stooped to unlock the carpet bag.

It was quite empty except for a curled-up Tape Measure.

"What's that for, Mary Poppins?" asked Jane.

"To measure you," she replied quickly. "To see how you've grown."

"You needn't bother," Michael informed her. "We've all grown two inches. Daddy measured us."

"Stand straight, please!" Mary Poppins said calmly, ignoring the remark. She measured him from his head to his feet and gave a loud sniff.

"I might have known it!" she said, snorting. "You've grown Worse and Worse."

Michael stared. "Tape Measures don't tell words, they tell inches," he said, protestingly.

"Since when?" she demanded haughtily, as she thrust it under his nose. There on the Tape were the tell-tale words in big blue letters:

W-O-R-S-E A-N-D W-O-R-S-E

"Oh!" he said, in a horrified whisper.

"Head up, please!" said Mary Poppins, stretching the Tape against Jane.

"Jane has grown into a Wilful, Lazy, Selfish child," she read out in triumph.

The tears came pricking into Jane's eyes. "Oh, I haven't, Mary Poppins!" she cried. For, funnily enough, she only remembered the times when she had been good.

Mary Poppins slipped the Tape round the Twins. "Quarrelsome" was their measurement. "Fretful and Spoilt," was Annabel's.

"I thought so!" Mary Poppins said, sniffing. "I've only got to turn my back for you to become a Menagerie!"

She drew the Tape round her own waist; and a satisfied smile spread over her face.

"Better Than Ever. Practically Perfect," her own measurement read.

"No more than I expected," she preened. And added, with a furious glare, "Now, spit-spot into the Bathroom!"

They hurried eagerly to obey her. For now that Mary Poppins was back, everything went with a swing. They undressed and bathed in the wink of an eye. Nobody dawdled over Supper, nobody left a crumb or a drop. They pushed in their chairs, folded their napkins and scrambled into bed.

Up and down the Nursery went Mary Poppins, tucking them all in. They could smell her old familiar smell, a mixture of toast and starchy aprons. They could feel her old familiar shape, solid and real beneath her clothes. They watched her in adoring silence, drinking her in.

Michael, as she passed his bed, peered over the edge and under it. There was nothing there except dust and slippers. Then he peeped under Jane's bed. Nothing there, either.

"But where are you going to sleep, Mary Poppins?" he enquired curiously.

As he spoke, she touched the door of the clothes cupboard. It burst open noisily and out of it, with a graceful sweep, came the old camp bed. It was made up, ready to be slept in. And upon it, in a neat pile, were Mary Poppins' possessions. There were the Sun-light Soap and the hairpins, the bottle of scent, the folding armchair, the toothbrush and the lozenges. The nightgowns, cotton, and flannel as well, were tidily laid on the pillow. And beside them were the boots and the dominoes, and the bathing-caps and the postcard album.

The children sat up in a gaping row.

"But how did it get in there?" demanded Michael. "There wasn't a sign of it today. I know, 'cos I hid there from Ellen!"

He dared not go on with his questions, however, for Mary Poppins looked so haughty that the words froze on his lips. With a sniff, she turned away from him and un-folded a flannel nightgown.

Jane and Michael looked at each other. And their eyes said all that their tongues could not: It's no good expect-ing her to explain, they told each other silently.

They watched her comical scarecrow movements as she undressed beneath the nightgown. Clip, clip — the buttons flew apart. Off went her petticoat — swish, swish, swish! A peaceful feeling stole into the children. And they knew that it came from Mary Poppins. Dreamily watch-ing the wriggling nightgown, they thought of all that had happened. How she had first arrived at the house, blown by the West Wind. How her umbrella had carried her off when the wind went round to the East. They thought how she had come back to them on the day when they flew the Kite; and how she had ridden away once more and left them lonely for her comforting presence.

Well, now — they sighed happily — she was back again, and just the same as ever. Here she was, settling down in the Nursery, as calmly as though she had never left it. The thoughts he was thinking rose up in Michael like bubbles in soda water. And before he could stop them, they burst right out.

"Oh, Mary Poppins," he cried, eagerly, "it's been just awful without you!"

Her lip quivered. It seemed as though a smile might break out. But it changed its mind and didn't.

"*You've* been awful — that's more like it! This house is nothing but a Bear Garden. I wonder anyone stays in it!"

"But *you* will, won't you?" he said wheedlingly.

"We'll be good as gold, if only you'll stay!" Jane promised solemnly.

She looked from one to the other calmly, seeing right down inside their hearts and understanding everything.

"I'll stay —— " she said, after a little pause. "I'll stay till the door opens." And as she spoke she gazed thoughtfully at the door of the Nursery.

Jane gave a little anxious cry. "Oh, don't say that, Mary Poppins!" she wailed. "That door is always opening!"

Mary Poppins glared.

"I meant the Other Door," she said, as she buttoned up her nightgown.

"What can she mean?" Jane whispered to Michael.

"I know what she means," he answered cleverly. "There

isn't any other door. And a door that isn't there, *can't* open. So she's going to stay forever." He hugged himself happily at the thought.

Jane, however, was not so sure. I wonder, she thought to herself.

But Michael went on cheerfully babbling.

"I'm glad I shook hands with the Sweep," he said. "It brought us wonderful luck. Perhaps he'll do the Nursery next and shake hands with *you*, Mary Poppins!"

"Pooh!" she replied, with a toss of her head. "I don't need any luck, thank you!"

"No," he said thoughtfully, "I suppose you don't. Anyone who can come out of a rocket — as you did to-night — must be born lucky. I mean — er — oh, don't *look* at me!"

He gave a little beseeching cry, for Mary Poppins was glaring at him in a way that made him shudder. Standing there in her flannel nightgown, she seemed to freeze him in his cosy bed.

"I wonder if I heard you correctly?" she enquired in an icy voice. "Did I understand you to mention *Me* — in connection with a Rocket?" She said the word "Rocket" in such a way as to make it seem quite shocking.

In terror, Michael glanced about him. But no help came from the other children. And he knew he would have to go through with it.

"But you did, Mary Poppins!" he protested bravely.

"The rocket went pop! and there you were, coming out of it down the sky!"

She seemed to grow larger as she came towards him.

"Pop?" she repeated, furiously. "I popped — and came out of a rocket?"

He shrank back feebly against the pillow. "Well — that's what it looked like — didn't it, Jane?"

"Hush!" whispered Jane, with a shake of her head. She knew it was no good arguing.

"I have to say it, Mary Poppins! We saw you!" Michael wailed. "And if *you* didn't come out of the rocket, what did! There weren't any stars!"

"Pop!" said Mary Poppins again. "Out of a rocket with a pop! You have often insulted me, Michael Banks, but this is the Very Worst. If I hear any more about Pops — or Rockets — — " She did not tell him what she would do but he knew it would be dreadful.

"Wee-twee! Wee-twee!"

A small voice sounded from the window-sill. An old Starling peered into the Nursery and flapped his wings excitedly.

Mary Poppins bounded to the window.

"Be off, you sparrer!" she said fiercely. And as the Starling darted away she switched out the light and pounced into bed. They heard her angrily muttering "Pop!" as she pulled the blankets up.

Then silence settled over them like a soft comforting

cloud. It had almost folded them to sleep when the faintest murmur came from Jane's bed.

"Michael!" she said, in a careful whisper.

He sat up cautiously and looked in the direction of her
pointing finger.

From the corner by the fireplace came a little glow of
light. And they saw that the folds of the parrot umbrella
were full of coloured stars — the kind of stars you expect
to see when a rocket breaks in the sky. Their eyes grew
wide with astonishment as the parrot's head bent down.
Then, one by one, its beak plucked the stars from the silk-
en folds and threw them on the floor. They gleamed for a
moment, gold and silver, then faded and went out. Then
the parrot head straightened upon the handle, and Mary
Poppins' black umbrella stood stiff and still in its corner.

The children looked at each other and smiled. But they
said nothing. They could only wonder and be silent. They

knew there were not enough words in the Dictionary for the things that happened to Mary Poppins.

"Tick-tock!" said the clock on the mantelpiece. "Go to sleep, children! Tick, tock, tick!"

Then they closed their eyes on the happy day and the clock kept time with their quiet breathing.

Mr. Banks sat and snored in his study with a newspaper over his face.

Mrs. Banks was sewing new black buttons on his old overcoat.

"Are you still thinking what you might have done if you hadn't got married?" she asked.

"Eh, what?" said Mr. Banks, waking up. "Well, no. It's much too much trouble. And now that Mary Poppins is back, I shan't have to think about anything."

"Good," said Mrs. Banks, sewing briskly. "And I'll try and teach Robertson Ay."

"Teach him what?" Mr. Banks said, sleepily.

"Not to give you one black and one brown, of course!"

"You'll do nothing of the kind," Mr. Banks insisted. "The mixture was much admired at the Office. I shall always wear them that way in future."

"Indeed?" said Mrs. Banks, smiling happily. On the whole, she felt glad Mr. Banks had married. And now that Mary Poppins was back, she would tell him so more often. . . .

Downstairs in the kitchen sat Mrs. Brill. The Policeman had just brought Ellen home and was staying for a Cup of Tea.

"That Mary Poppins!" he said, sipping. "She's 'ere today and gone tomorrer, just like them Willy-the-Wisps!"

"Ow! Don't say that!" said Ellen, sniffling. "I thought she was come to stay."

The Policeman gave her his handkerchief.

"Maybe she will!" he told her fondly. "You never can tell, you know."

"Well, I'm sure I hope so," sighed Mrs. Brill. "This 'ouse is a Model Residence whenever she's in it."

"I hope so, too. I need a rest," said Robertson Ay to the brooms. And he snuggled down under Mrs. Banks' shawl and went to sleep again.

But what Mary Poppins hoped, none of them knew. For Mary Poppins, as everyone knows, never told anyone anything....

CHAPTER TWO

MR. TWIGLEY'S WISHES

h, do come on, Mary Poppins!" said Michael impatiently, as he danced up and down on the pavement.

Mary Poppins took no notice. She was standing in the Lane admiring her reflection in the brass plate on Dr. Simpson's gate.

"You look quite tidy!" Jane assured her.

"Tidy!" Mary Poppins snorted. Tidy in her new black hat with the blue bow? Tidy indeed! Handsome, she thought, would be nearer the mark. Tossing her head, she strode on quickly and they had to run to keep up with her.

The three of them were walking through the fine May afternoon to find Mr. Twigley. For the Drawing-room piano was out of tune and Mrs. Banks had asked Mary Poppins to find a piano-tuner.

"There's my cousin, Ma'am, Mr. Twigley. Just three blocks from here." Mary Poppins had announced. And when Mrs. Banks said she had never heard of him, Mary Poppins, with her usual sniff, had reminded Mrs. Banks that *her* relatives were composed of the Very Best People.

And now Jane and Michael, who had already met two members of Mary Poppins' family, were wondering what Mr. Twigley would be like.

"I think he will be tall and thin, like Mr. Turvy," said Michael.

"I think he will be round and fat, like Mr. Wigg," said Jane.

"I never knew such a pair for thinking!" said Mary Poppins. "You'll wear your brains out. Turn here, please!"

They hurried along and turned a corner and found themselves standing in a narrow street lined with small, old-fashioned houses.

"Why, what street is this? I never saw it before! And I've been here lots of times!" cried Jane.

"Well, don't blame *me!*" Mary Poppins snapped. "You don't suppose I put it there!"

"I shouldn't wonder if you did!" said Michael, as he gazed at the strange little houses. Then he added, with a flattering smile, "You're so very clever, you know!"

"Humph!" she said tartly, though her mouth took on a conceited look. "Clever is as clever does. And it's more than you are, anyway!" And, sniffing, she led them down the street and rang the bell of one of the houses.

"Pang!" said the bell loudly. And at the same moment an upstairs window swung open. A large head, with a knob of hair at the back, popped out like a Jack-in-the-Box.

"Well, what's the matter now?" a harsh voice cried. Then the woman looked down and spied Mary Poppins. "Oh, it's you, is it?" she said angrily. "Well, you can just turn round and go back to wherever you came from. He isn't in!" The window swung to and the head disappeared.

The children felt very disappointed.

"Perhaps we can come again tomorrow," said Jane anxiously.

"Today — or Never. That's my motto!" snapped Mary Poppins. And she rang the bell again.

This time it was the front door that burst open. The owner of the head stood before them glowering. She wore large black boots, a blue-and-white checked apron and a black shawl round her shoulders. Jane and Michael thought she was the ugliest person they had ever seen. And they felt very sorry for Mr. Twigley.

"What — you again!" the huge woman shouted. "I told you he wasn't in. And in he is not, or my name's not Sarah Clump!"

"Then you aren't Mrs. Twigley!" exclaimed Michael, with relief.

"Not *yet*," she remarked, with an ominous smile. "Here! Down you come, all of you!" she added. For Mary Poppins, with the speed of a serpent, had slipped through the doorway and was dragging the children up the stairs. "Do you hear me? I'll have the Law on you, bursting into a decent woman's house like a set of Vampires!"

"Decent!" said Mary Poppins, snorting. "If you're decent I'm a Dromedary!" And she rapped three times on a door at her right.

"Who's there?" called an anxious voice from within. Jane and Michael trembled with excitement. Perhaps Mr. Twigley was at home, after all!

"It's me, Cousin Fred. Unlock the door, please!"

There was a moment's silence. Then the sound of a key being turned in the lock. The door opened and Mary Poppins, pulling the children after her, shut it and locked it again.

"Let me in — you Pirate!" roared Mrs. Clump, angrily rattling the handle.

Mary Poppins laughed quietly. The children glanced

about them. They were in a large attic littered with scraps
of wood, tins of paint and bottles of glue. Every available
space in the room was filled with musical instruments.
A harp stood in one corner and in another was a pile of
drums. Trumpets and violins hung from the rafters; flutes
and tin-whistles were stacked on the shelves. A dusty table by the window was littered with carpenter's tools. And
on the edge of the bench was a small polished box with a
tiny screw-driver tossed beside it.

In the middle of the floor stood five half-finished musi-

cal boxes. Brightly they shone in their fresh new colours
and round them, chalked on the boards in large white letters, were the words

WET PAINT

The whole attic smelt deliciously of wood-shavings,
paint and glue. There was only one thing missing from it.
And that was Mr. Twigley.

"Will you let me in or shall I go for the Police?" shouted
Mrs. Clump, banging again. Mary Poppins took no notice. And presently they heard her thumping downstairs,
muttering furiously as she went.

"Has she gone?" a thin voice cackled anxiously.

"She's gone downstairs and I've locked the door! Now,
what have you done with yourself, please, Fred?" Mary
Poppins gave an impatient sniff.

"I've wished, Mary!" chirped the voice again.

Jane and Michael stared round the dusty attic. Where
could Mr. Twigley be?

"Oh, Fred! Don't tell me it's the ——! Well, wish
again, please, wherever you are! I haven't all day to waste."

"All right! I'm coming! No need for excitement!"

The violins played a stave of music. Then, out of the
air — as it seemed to the children — came two short legs
clad in baggy trousers. They were followed by a body in
an old frock-coat. And last of all came a long white beard,

a wrinkled face with glasses on its nose and a bald head in a smoking cap.

"Really, Cousin Fred!" said Mary Poppins crossly. "You're old enough to know better!"

"Nonsense, Mary!" said Mr. Twigley, beaming. "Nobody's ever old enough to know better! I'm sure you agree with me, young man!" He looked at Michael with his twinkly eyes. And Michael couldn't help twinkling back.

"But where were you hiding?" he demanded. "You couldn't have just come out of the air."

"Oh, yes, I could!" said Mr. Twigley. "If I wished," he added, as he skipped round the room.

"You mean, you just wished — and you disappeared?"

With a glance at the door, Mr. Twigley nodded.

"I had to — to get away from *her!*"

"Why? What would she do to you?" asked Jane.

"Why? Because she wants to marry me! She wants to get my wishes."

"Do you get everything you wish for?" asked Michael enviously.

"Oh, everything. That is, if I wish on the first New Moon, after the Second Wet Sunday, after the Third of May. And she —— " Mr. Twigley waved at the door. "*She* wants me to wish for a Golden Palace and Peacock Pie every day for dinner. What would *I* do with a golden palace? All that I want is —— "

"Be careful, Fred!" warned Mary Poppins.

Mr. Twigley clapped his hand to his mouth. "Tut, tut! I really must remember! I've used up two wishes already!"

"How many do you get?" asked Jane.

"Seven," said Mr. Twigley, sighing. "My Godmother thought that a suitable number. I know the old lady meant it kindly. But I'd rather have had a Silver Mug. More useful. And much less trouble."

"I'd rather have wishes," said Michael, stoutly.

"Oh, no, you wouldn't!" cried Mr. Twigley. "They're tricky. And hard to handle. You think out the loveliest things to ask for — then Supper Time comes and you're feeling hungry and you find yourself wishing for Sausage and Mashed!"

"What about the two you've already had? Were they any good?" demanded Michael.

"Well, not so bad, now I come to think of it. I was working on my Birdie there —— " Mr. Twigley nodded towards his bench —— " when I heard *her* coming up the stairs. 'Oh, Goodness!' I thought, 'I wish I could vanish!' And — when I looked round, I wasn't there! It gave me quite a turn for a moment. No wonder she told you I was out!"

Mr. Twigley gave a happy cackle as he beamed at the children and swung his coat-tails. They had never seen such a twinkly person. He seemed to them more like a star than a man.

"Then, of course," Mr. Twigley went on blandly, "I had

to wish myself back again in order to see Mary Poppins! Now, Mary, what can I do for you?"

"Mrs. Banks would like her piano tuned, please, Fred. Number Seventeen, Cherry-Tree Lane, Opposite the Park," Mary Poppins said primly.

"Ah! Mrs. Banks. Then these must be——?" Mr. Twigley waved his hand at the children.

"They're Jane and Michael Banks," she explained, glancing at them with a look of disgust.

"Delighted. I call this a very great honour!" Mr. Twigley bowed and flung out his hands. "I wish I could offer you something to eat but I'm all at sixes and sevens today."

A flute rang gaily through the attic.

"What's this?" Mr. Twigley staggered back. In each of his upturned, outstretched hands lay a dish of Peaches-and-Cream.

Mr. Twigley stared. Then he sniffed at the peaches.

"There goes my third wish!" he said ruefully, as he handed the dishes to the children. "Well, it can't be helped. I've still got four more. And now I shall have to be really careful!"

"If you must waste wishes, Cousin Fred, I wish you would waste them on Bread and Butter. You'll spoil their Supper!" snapped Mary Poppins.

Jane and Michael spooned up their peaches hurriedly. They were not going to give Mr. Twigley the chance of wishing them away again.

"And now," said Mary Poppins, as the last mouthful

disappeared. "Say Thank You to Mr. Twigley and we'll get along home."

"Oh, *no*, Mary! Why, you've only just come!" Mr. Twigley was so shocked that for once he stood quite still.

"Oh, do stay a little longer, Mary Poppins!" Jane and Michael begged. The thought of leaving Mr. Twigley all alone with his wishes was too much for them.

Mr. Twigley took Mary Poppins' hand.

"I feel so much safer when you're here, Mary! And it's ages since we've seen each other! Why not stay for a while — I wish you would!"

Jug, jug, jug, jug!

A shower of bird notes broke on the air. At the same moment the determined look on Mary Poppins' face changed to a polite smile. She took off her hat and laid it on the bench beside the glue-pot.

"Oh, my!" Mr. Twigley gasped in horror. "I've been and gone and done it again!"

"That's four!" cried Jane and Michael gaily, shouting with laughter at his look of surprise.

Four, four, four, four! The bird notes echoed.

"Dear me! How careless! I'm ashamed of myself!" For a moment Mr. Twigley looked almost sad. Then his face and his feet began to twinkle. "Well, it's no good crying over spilt wishes. We must just take care of the ones that are left. I'm coming, my Duckling! I'm coming, my Chick!" he called in the direction of the bird notes.

And, tripping to the dusty table, he took up the little polished box. His fingers touched a hidden spring. The lid flew open and the smallest, brightest bird the children had ever seen leapt up from a nest of gold. Clear jets of music poured from its beak. Its small throat throbbed with the stream of notes.

Jug, jug, jug, jug — tereu! it sang. And when the burning song was ended the bird dropped back to its golden nest.

"Oh, Mr. Twigley, what bird is that?" Jane looked at the box with shining eyes.

"A Nightingale," Mr. Twigley told her. "I was working on him when you came in. He has to be finished tonight, you see. Such lovely weather for nightingales."

"Why don't you just wish?" suggested Michael. "Then you needn't do any work."

"What! Wish on my Birdie? Certainly not! You see what happens when *I* start wishing. Why — he might turn into a Bald-headed Eagle!"

"Will you keep him to sing to you always?" Jane asked enviously. She wished she could have a bird like that.

"Keep him? Oh, dear, no! I'll set him free! Can't litter the place up with finished work. I've more things to do than take care of a bird. I have to put figures on those —— " he nodded at the half-finished musical boxes. "And I've got a rush order that *must* be finished — a music box playing 'A Day in the Park.' "

"A Day in the Park?" The children stared.

"The Band, you know!" Mr. Twigley explained. "And the sound of the fountains. And gossiping ladies. Rooks caw-cawing, and children laughing, and the slow, soft murmur of trees as they grow."

Mr. Twigley's eyes glowed behind his spectacles as he thought of all the lovely things he would put in the musical box.

"But you can't hear trees growing," protested Michael. "There's no music for that!"

"Tut!" said Mr. Twigley impatiently. "Of course there is! There's a music for everything. Didn't you ever hear the earth spinning? It makes a sound like a humming-top. Buckingham Palace plays 'Rule Britannia'; the River Thames is a drowsy flute. Dear me, yes! Everything in the world — trees, rocks and stars and human beings — they all have their own true music."

As he spoke Mr. Twigley tripped across the floor and wound up a musical box. Immediately the little platform at the top began to turn. And from within came a clear high piping like the sound of a penny whistle.

"That's mine!" said Mr. Twigley proudly, as he cocked his head to listen. He wound up another musical box and a new tune fell on the air.

"That's 'London Bridge Is Falling Down'! It's my favourite song!" cried Michael.

"What did I tell you?" smiled Mr. Twigley, as he turned another handle. The tune broke gaily from the box.

"That's mine!" said Jane, with a crow of delight. "It's 'Oranges and Lemons.'"

"Of course it is!" twinkled Mr. Twigley.

And gaily seizing the children's hands he swept them away across the attic. The three little platforms turned and spun and the three tunes mingled in the air.

> "London Bridge is Falling Down,
>   Dance over, my Lady Leigh!"

sang Michael.

> "Oranges and Lemons,
>   Said the Bells of St. Clements."

sang Jane.

And Mr. Twigley whistled like a happy blackbird.

The feet of the children were light as wings as they danced to their own true music. Never before, they told themselves, had they felt so light and merry.

Bang! The front door slammed and shook the house. Mr. Twigley paused on one toe and listened. Thump! Thump! came the footsteps on the stairs. A loud voice rumbled across the landing.

Mr. Twigley gave a gasp of horror, and swung his coat-tails over his ears.

"She's coming!" he shrieked. "Oh, dear! Oh, my! I wish I were in a nice safe place!"

A blast of music came from the trumpets. And then a strange thing happened.

Mr. Twigley, as though by an unseen hand, was snatched from the floor of the attic. Off he went, hurtling past the children, like a seed of thistledown tossed by the wind. Then choking and gasping, shaking and panting, he landed upon his musical box. He did not seem to have grown smaller nor the box larger. Yet, somehow, they fitted perfectly together.

Round and round Mr. Twigley spun and upon his face spread a smile of triumph.

"I'm safe!" he yelled, as he waved to the children, "She'll never catch me now!"

"Hooray!" they were just about to shout but the word was caught in their throats, like a hiccup. For something had seized them by the hair and was flinging them both across the attic. Their arms and legs went sprawling wildly as they landed upon their musical boxes. They wobbled a little for a moment, but soon they were steadily whirling round.

"Oh!" panted Jane. "What a lovely surprise!"

"I feel like a spinning top!" shouted Michael.

Mr. Twigley gave a little start and stared at them in astonishment.

"Did *I* do that? Good Gracious me! I'm getting quite clever at wishing."

"Clever!" said Mary Poppins sniffing. "Ridiculous — that's what *I* call it!"

"Well, at least it's safe," said Mr. Twigley. "And rather pleasant. Why don't you try it?"

"Wish!" urged Michael, with a wave of his hand.

"Ah! *She* doesn't need to," said Mr. Twigley, with a curious glance at Mary Poppins.

"Well, if you insist . . ." she said with a sniff. And placing her two feet neatly together she rose from the floor and swept past the rafters. Then, without a smile, not even a wobble, she alighted upon a musical box. Immediately, though no one had wound it, the tune broke gaily out.

> "Round and round the Cobbler's bench,
>   The Monkey chased the Weasel,
>   The Monkey said it was all in fun —
>   Pop goes the Weasel!"

it sang.

And round and round went Mary Poppins, as calmly as though she had turned and spun from the very day she was born.

"Now we're all together!" Jane cried happily. She glanced at the window and waved her hand to draw Michael's attention.

Outside in the street the little houses were revolving on their foundations. Above in the sky spun two white clouds. And the attic itself, like the musical boxes, was turning round and round.

But loudly though the four tunes rang, another sound

could be heard above them. Thump! Thump! The heavy steps came nearer.

And the next moment somebody banged on the door.

"Open, I say, in the name of the Law!" cried a voice that was somehow familiar.

A strong hand twisted the rickety lock. And then, with a crash, the door burst open. On the threshold stood Mrs. Clump and the Policeman. They stared. Their eyes popped. Their mouths fell open with astonishment.

"Well, of all the shameful sights!" cried Mrs. Clump. "I never thought to see this house turned into an Amusement Park!" She shook her fist at Mary Poppins. "You're going to get your reward, my girl. The Policeman here will deal with you! And as for you, Mr. Twigley, down you get from that silly razzle-dazzle and comb your hair and put on your hat. We're going off to be married!"

Mr. Twigley shuddered. But he swung his coattails jauntily.

> "Don't shout and thump
> Please, Mrs. Clump,
> It makes me jump!"

he sang, as he sped round. The Policeman took out notebook and pencil.

"Come on! Stop spinning, all of you. I'm as giddy as a Garden Goat. And I want an Explanation!"

She alighted upon a musical box

Mr. Twigley gave a gleeful cackle.

"You've come to the wrong place, Officer dear! I've never yet made an Explanation. And what's more, as I used to say to my boy, Methuselah, I don't believe in 'em!"

"Now, now, joking'll only make things worse. You can't tell *me* you're Methuselah's father!" The Policeman smiled a knowing smile.

"Grandfather!" Mr. Twigley retorted, as he sailed gracefully round.

"Now, that's enough. You just come down! This spinning and twirling is bad for the 'Ealth. And not permitted in Private Dwellings. 'Ere! 'Oo's that pulling me! Let me go!" The Policeman gave a frightened shriek as he shot off his feet and through the air. A music box broke into noisy song as he dropped like a stone upon it.

"Daisy, Daisy, give me your answer, do!
     I've gone crazy, all for the love of you!"

it shouted.

" 'Elp! 'Elp! It's me — P.C. 32 calling!" The Policeman wildly snatched at his whistle and blew a resounding blast.

"Officer!" shouted Mrs. Clump. "You do your duty or I'll have the Law on you, too. Get down and arrest that woman!" She thrust a huge finger at Mary Poppins. "I'll have you put behind bars, my girl. I'll have you —— Here! Stop spinning me round!" Her eyes grew wide with angry amazement. For a curious thing was happening.

Slowly, on the spot where she stood, Mrs. Clump began to revolve. She had no musical box, no platform, she simply went round and round on the floor. The boards gave a loud protesting creak as the huge shape turned upon them.

"Well, that's fixed *you!*" cried Mr. Twigley.

> "Try and jump
> Dear Mrs. Clump!"

he advised her, with a gleeful shriek.

A shudder of horror shook Mrs. Clump as she tried to move her large black boots. She struggled. She writhed. She wriggled her body. But her feet were firmly glued to the floor.

"Clever girl, Mary! I'd never have thought of it!" Mr. Twigley smiled at Mary Poppins with pride and admiration.

"This is your doing — you wilful, wicked, cold-hearted Varmint!" Mrs. Clump gave an angry shout as she tried to clutch at Mary Poppins. "But I'll get even with you yet — or my name's not Sarah Clump!"

"It'll never be Twigley, anyway!" shrieked Mr. Twigley joyously.

"I want to go home! I want the Police Station!" wailed the Policeman, spinning madly.

"Well, nobody's keeping *you*, I'm sure!" said Mary Poppins, sniffing. As she spoke the Policeman's box came to a standstill and he stumbled off it, panting.

"Scotland Yard!" he cried, staggering to the door. "I must see the Chief! I must make a Report." And, blowing a frantic peal on his whistle, he fled downstairs and out of the house.

"Come back, you Villain!" screamed Mrs. Clump. "He's gone!" she went on, as the front door banged. "Oh, what shall I do? Help! Murder! Fire!"

Her face grew red as she tried to free herself. But it was no good. Her feet were firmly fixed to the floor, and she flung out her arms with a cry of anguish.

"Mr. Twigley!" she begged. "Please help me, Sir! I've always cooked you tasty meals. I've always kept you clean and tidy. You won't have to marry me, I promise. If you'll only wish something to set me free!"

"Be careful, Fred!" warned Mary Poppins, as she twirled in a dignified manner.

"A Wish in Time saves Nine! Now, let me think!" murmured Mr. Twigley.

He pressed his fingers to his eyes. Jane and Michael could see he was making an effort to wish Something Really Useful. For a moment he spun round, deep in thought. Then he looked up, smiling, and clapped his hands.

"Mrs. Clump," he cried gaily. "You *shall* be free! I wish for you a Golden Palace and Peacock Pie every day for dinner. But —— " he winked across at Mary Poppins, "my kind of palace, Mrs. Clump! And *my* kind of pie!"

A roll of drums boomed through the attic.

Mrs. Clump looked at Mary Poppins and smiled a smile of triumph.

"Aha!" she said smugly. "What did I tell you?"

But even as she spoke the proud smile faded. It changed to a look of purest terror.

For Mrs. Clump was no longer a large fat woman. Her buxom body was rapidly shrinking. Her feet as they spun on the creaking floor grew smaller with every turn.

"What's this?" she panted. "Oh, what can it be?" Her arms and her legs grew short and skinny as her figure dwindled to half its size.

"Police! Fire! Murder! S.O.S." Her voice grew thinner as she shrank.

"Oh, Mr. Twigley! What have you done? Police! Police!" squeaked the tiny voice.

As she spoke the floor gave an angry heave and flung her, spinning, into the air. She bounced back with a frantic shriek and stumbled away across the room. And as she ran she grew smaller than ever and her movements more and more jerky. One moment she was the size of a kitten and the next no bigger than a small-sized mouse. Away she went, stumbling and bouncing and tripping, till at the end of the attic she dashed into a tiny golden palace that had suddenly appeared.

"Oh, why did I speak to him? What has he done?" Mrs. Clump cried out in a tinny voice.

And looking through one of the golden windows, the children saw her collapse on a chair before a small tin pie. She began to cut it with jerky movements as the palace door closed with a bang.

At that moment the boxes ceased to spin. The music stopped and the attic was silent.

Down from his box sprang Mr. Twigley and ran to the golden palace. With a cry of delight he picked it up and gazed at the scene within.

"Very clever! I really must congratulate myself. All it needs now is a penny-in-the-slot and then it will do for Brighton Pier. One Penny, Only One Penny, folks! To see the Fat Woman Eating the Pie! Roll up! Roll up! Only one Penny!"

Waving the palace, Mr. Twigley went gaily capering round the room. Jane and Michael, leaping down from their boxes, ran after him and caught his coattails. They peered through the windows at Mrs. Clump. There was a look of horror on her mechanical face as she cut her mechanical pie.

"That was your sixth wish!" Michael reminded him.

"It was indeed!" Mr. Twigley agreed. "A Really useful idea, for once! Where there's a wish, there's a way, you see! Especially if *she's* around!" He nodded at Mary Poppins, who was stepping off her musical box in the most majestic manner.

"Get your hats, please!" she commanded sharply.

"I want to get home for a Cup of Tea. I am not a Desert Camel."

"Oh, just one moment, please, Mary Poppins! Mr. Twigley's got one more wish!"

Jane and Michael, both talking at once, were tugging at her hands.

"Why, so I have! I'd quite forgotten. Now, what shall I——?"

"Cherry-Tree Lane, remember, Fred!" Mary Poppins' voice had a warning note.

"Oh, I'm glad you reminded me. Just a second!" Mr. Twigley put his hand to his brow and a scale of music sounded.

"What did you wish?" asked Jane and Michael.

But Mr. Twigley seemed suddenly to have become deaf, for he took no notice of the question. He shook hands hurriedly as though, having wished all his wishes, he was now anxious to be alone.

"You have to be going, you said? How sad! Is this your hat? Well, delighted you came! I hope — are these your gloves, dear Mary? — I hope you'll pay me another visit when my wishes come round again!"

"When will that be?" demanded Michael.

"Oh, in about ninety years or so." Mr. Twigley answered airily.

"But we'll be quite old by then!" said Jane.

"Maybe," he replied, with a little shrug. "But at least not as old as I am!"

And with that he kissed Mary Poppins on both cheeks and hustled them out of the room.

The last thing they saw was his jubilant smile as he began to fix a Penny-in-the-Slot to Mrs. Clump's palace. . . .

Later, when they came to think about it, Jane and Michael could never remember how they got out of Mr. Twigley's house and into Cherry-Tree Lane. It seemed as though at one moment they were on the dusty stairs and the next were following Mary Poppins through the pearly evening light.

Jane glanced back for one last look at the little house.

"Michael!" she said in a startled whisper. "It's gone. Everything's gone!"

He looked round. Yes! Jane was right. The little street and the old-fashioned houses were nowhere to be seen. There was only the shadowy Park before them and the well-known curve of Cherry-Tree Lane.

"Well, where have we been all the afternoon?" said Michael, staring about him.

But it needed someone wiser than Jane to answer that question truly.

"We must have been somewhere," she said sensibly.

But that was not enough for Michael. He rushed away to Mary Poppins and pulled at her best blue skirt.

"Mary Poppins, where have we been today? What's happened to Mr. Twigley?"

"How should I know?" snapped Mary Poppins. "I'm not an Encyclopaedia."

"But he's gone! And the street's gone! And I suppose the musical box has gone, too — the one he went round on this afternoon!"

Mary Poppins stood still on the kerb, and stared.

"A cousin of mine on a musical box? What nonsense you do talk, Michael Banks!"

"But he did!" cried Jane and Michael together. "We *all* went round on musical boxes. Each of us to our own true music. And yours was 'Pop Goes the Weasel.'"

Her eyes blazed sternly through the darkness. She seemed to grow larger as she glared.

"Each to our — weasel? Round and round?" Really, she was so angry she could hardly get the words out.

"On top of a musical box, did you say? So, *this* is what I get for my pains! You spend the afternoon with a well-brought up, self-respecting pair like my cousin and myself. And all you can do afterwards is to make a mock of us. Round and round with a weasel, indeed! For Two Pins I'd leave you — here, on this spot — and never come back! I warn you!"

"On top of a musical weasel!" she fumed, as she stalked through the gathering dusk.

Snap, snap, went her heels along the pavement. Even her back had an angry look.

Jane and Michael hurried after her. It was no good arguing with Mary Poppins, especially when she looked like that. The best thing to do was to say nothing. And be glad there was nobody in the Lane to offer her Two Pins. In silence they walked along beside her, and thought of the afternoon's adventure and looked at each other and wondered. . . .

"Oh, Mary Poppins!" said Mrs. Banks brightly, as she opened the front door. "I'm sorry, but I don't need your cousin, after all. I tried the piano again just now. And it's quite in tune. In fact, better than ever."

"I'm glad of that, ma'am," said Mary Poppins, stealing

a glance at herself in the mirror. "My cousin will make no charge."

"Well, I should think not!" cried Mrs. Banks indignantly. "Why, he hasn't even been here."

"Exactly, ma'am," said Mary Poppins. She sniffed as she turned towards the stairs.

Jane and Michael exchanged a secret look.

"That must have been the seventh wish!" Michael whispered. And Jane gave an answering nod.

Jug, jug, jug, jug — tereu!

From the Park came a shower of wild sweet music. It had a familiar sound.

"What can that be?" cried Mrs. Banks as she ran to the door to listen. "Good gracious! It's a Nightingale!"

Down from the branches fell the song, note by note, like plums from a tree. It burnt upon the evening air. It throbbed through the listening dusk.

"How very strange!" said Mrs. Banks. "They never sing in the city!"

Behind her back the children nodded and looked at each other wisely.

"It's Mr. Twigley's," murmured Jane.

"He's set it free!" answered Michael softly.

And they knew, as they listened to the burning song, that somewhere, somehow, Mr. Twigley was true — as true as his little golden bird that was singing now in the Park.

The Nightingale sang once more and was silent.

Mrs. Banks sighed and shut the door. "I wish I knew where he came from!" she said dreamily.

But Jane and Michael, who could have told her, were already half-way up the stairs. So they said nothing. There were things that could be explained, they knew, and things that could not be explained.

Besides, there were Currant Buns for Tea and they knew what Mary Poppins would say if they dared to keep her waiting. . . .

CHAPTER THREE

THE CAT THAT LOOKED AT A KING

ichael had toothache. He lay in bed groaning and looking at Mary Poppins out of the corner of his eye.

There she sat, in the old arm chair, busily winding wool. Jane knelt before her, holding the skein. Up from the garden came the cries of the Twins as they played on the lawn with Ellen and Annabel. It was quiet and peaceful in the Nursery. The clock made a clucking, satisfied sound like a hen that has laid an egg.

"Why should *I* have toothache and not Jane?" complained Michael. He pulled the scarf Mary Poppins had lent him more tightly round his cheek.

"Because you ate too many sweets yesterday," Mary Poppins replied tartly.

"But it was my Birthday!" he protested.

"A Birthday's no reason for turning yourself into a Dustbin! *I* don't have toothache after mine."

Michael glared at her. Sometimes he wished Mary

Poppins was not quite so Perfectly Perfect. But he never dared to say so.

"If I die," he warned her, "you'll be sorry. You'll wish you'd been a bit nicer!"

She sniffed contemptuously and went on winding.

Holding his cheek in his two hands he gazed round the Nursery. Everything there had the familiar look of an old friend. The wall paper, the rocking-horse, the worn red carpet. His eyes wandered to the mantelpiece.

There lay the Compass and the Doulton Bowl, the jam-jar full of daisies, the stick of his old Kite and Mary Poppins' Tape Measure. And there, too, was the present Aunt Flossie had given him yesterday — the little Cat of white china patterned with blue-and-green flowers. It sat there with its paws together and its tail neatly curled about them. The sunlight shone on its china back; its green eyes gazed gravely across the room. Michael gave it a friendly smile. He was fond of Aunt Flossie and he liked the present she had brought him.

Then his tooth gave another dreadful stab.

"Ow!" he shrieked, "It's digging a hole right into my gum!" He glanced pathetically at Mary Poppins. "And nobody cares!" he added bitterly.

Mary Poppins tossed him a mocking smile.

"Don't look at me like that!" he complained.

"Why not? A Cat can look at a King, I suppose!"

"But I'm not a king——" he grumbled crossly, "and

you're not a cat, Mary Poppins!" He hoped she would argue with him about it and take his mind off his tooth.

"Do you mean *any* cat can look at the King? Could Michael's cat?" demanded Jane.

Mary Poppins glanced up. Her blue eyes gazed at the Cat's green eyes and the Cat returned her look.

There was a pause.

"Any cat," said Mary Poppins at last. "But that cat more than most."

Smiling to herself, she took up the ball of wool again and something stirred on the mantelpiece. The china cat twitched its china whisker and lifted its head and yawned. The children could see its glistening teeth and a long pink cat's tongue. The Cat then arched its flowery back and stretched itself lazily. And after that, with a wave of its tail, it leapt from the mantelpiece.

Plop! went the four paws on the carpet. Purr! said the Cat as it crossed the hearth-rug. It paused for a moment by Mary Poppins and gave her a little nod. Then it sprang upon the window-sill, dived out into the shining sunlight and disappeared.

Michael forgot his toothache and gaped.

Jane dropped her skein and stared.

"But —— " they both stammered. "How? Why? Where?"

"To see the Queen," Mary Poppins answered. "She's At Home every Second Friday. Don't stare like that,

Jane — the wind might change! Close your mouth, Michael! Your tooth will get cold."

"But I want to know what happened!" he cried. "He's made of china. He isn't real. And yet — he jumped! I saw him."

"Why did he want to see the Queen?" asked Jane.

"Mice," replied Mary Poppins calmly. "And partly for Old Sake's Sake."

A faraway look came into her eyes and the hands on the ball of wool fell idle. Jane flung a warning glance at Michael. He wriggled cautiously out of bed and crept across the room. Mary Poppins took no notice. She was gazing thoughtfully out of the window with distant dreamy eyes.

"Once upon a time," she began slowly, as though she were reading from the sheet of sunlight. . . .

Once upon a time, there lived a King who thought he knew practically everything. I couldn't even begin to tell you the things he thought he knew. His head was as full of facts and figures as a pomegranate of pips. And this had the effect of making the King extremely absent-minded. You will hardly believe me when I say that he even forgot his own name, which was Cole. The Prime Minister, however, had an excellent memory, and reminded him of it from time to time.

Now, this King's favourite pursuit was thinking. He thought all night and he thought in the morning. He thought at mealtimes, he thought in his bath. He never noticed what was happening in front of his nose because, of course, he was always thinking about something else.

And the things he thought about were not, as you might imagine, the welfare of his people and how to make them happy. Not at all. His mind was busy with other questions. The number of baboons in India, for instance; and whether the North Pole was as long as the South; and if pigs could be taught to sing.

He not only worried about these things himself. He

forced everybody else to worry about them, too. All except the Prime Minister, who was not at all a thinking kind of person but an old man who liked to sit in the sun and do absolutely nothing. But he was careful not to let this be known for fear the King would cut off his head.

The King lived in a palace made entirely of crystal. In the early days of his reign it had shone so brightly that passers-by would hide their eyes, for fear of being dazzled. But gradually the crystal grew duller and the dust of the seasons covered its brightness. Nobody could be spared to polish it for everyone was far too busy helping the King think his thoughts. At any moment they might be ordered to leave their work and hurry away on the King's business. To China, perhaps, to count the silkworms. Or to find out if the Solomon Islands were ruled by the Queen of Sheba. When they came back with their lists of facts, the King and the courtiers would write them down in large books bound in leather. And if anyone returned without an answer, his head was at once cut off.

The only person in the palace who had nothing to do was the Queen. All day long she sat on her golden throne, twisting the necklace of blue-and-green flowers that was clasped about her throat. Sometimes she would start up with a cry and pull her ermine robes about her. For the palace, as it grew more and more dirty, became infested with mice. And mice, as anyone will tell you, are the things no Queen can stand.

"O-o-o-h!" she would say, with a little gasp, as she leapt on the seat of the throne.

And each time she cried out the King would frown.

"Silence please!" he would say, in a fractious voice, for the least little noise disturbed his thinking. Then the mice would scatter for a little while and no sound would be heard in the room. Except for the scratching of goose-quill pens as the King and the courtiers added new facts to the ones in the leather books.

The Queen never gave orders, not even to her Ladies-of-the-Bedchamber. For as likely as not the King would countermand them.

"Mend the Queen's petticoat?" he would say crossly. "What petticoat? Why waste time talking about petticoats? Take a pen and write out these facts about the Phoenix!"

What a dreadful state of affairs, you will say! And, indeed, I wouldn't blame you. But you must not think it was always like that. The Queen, sitting lonely upon her throne, would often remind herself of the days when she first had married the King. How tall and handsome he had been, with his strong white neck and ruddy cheeks, and locks of hair folded round his head like the leaves of camellia flowers.

"Ah!" she would sigh, remembering back. How he had fed her with honey-cakes and fingers of buttered bread from his plate. How his face had been so full of love that her heart would turn over in her breast and force her to look away, for sheer joy.

But at last there came a fateful evening.

"Your eyes are brighter than stars," he said, as he glanced from her face to the shining sky. But instead of turning to her again as usual, he continued to gaze upwards.

"I wonder," he said dreamily, "just how many stars there are! I think I shall count them. One, two, three, four, five, six, seven —— " And he went on counting till the Queen fell asleep beside him.

"One thousand, two hundred and forty-nine —— " he was saying as she woke up.

And after that he would not be satisfied till he got the courtiers out of their beds and set them to counting stars. And as no two answers came out alike the King was very angry.

That was how it all began.

The next day, the King exclaimed, "Your cheeks, my Darling, are like two roses!"

And the Queen was very happy till he added, "But why roses? Why not cabbages? Why are cheeks pink and cabbages green? And vice versa? This is a very serious question."

The third day he told her that her teeth were like pearls. But before she even had time to smile, he went on ——

"And what if they are? Everybody has, after all, a certain number of teeth, and most of them are pearly. Pearls themselves, however, are very rare. It is more important to think about them."

So he summoned the best divers in the kingdom and sent them down under the sea.

And from that day onwards he was always thinking. He was only concerned with gaining knowledge and he never even looked at the Queen. Indeed, if he had glanced in her direction, he would probably not have seen her, for he worked so hard at his books and papers that he soon became very short-sighted. His round red face grew thin and wrinkled, and his hair turned grey at an early age. He ate practically nothing—except for a cheese-and-onion sandwich whenever the old Prime Minister told him that dinner was on the table.

Well! You can imagine how lonely the Queen was. Sometimes the Prime Minister would shuffle cautiously to the throne and pat her hand kindly. Sometimes the little page who filled the inkwells would raise his eyes and smile at her from behind the King's back. But neither the old man nor the boy could spare much time to amuse the Queen, for fear of losing their heads.

You must not think the King meant to be unkind. Indeed, it seemed to him that his subjects were luckier than most, for hadn't they a King who knew practically everything? But while he was busy gathering knowledge his people grew poorer and poorer. Houses fell into ruin and fields went untilled, because the King needed all the men to help him in his thinking.

At last there came a day when the King and the courtiers were busy, as usual, at their desks in the Council Chamber. The Queen sat listening to the scratching of pens and the squeaking of mice in the wainscot. And presently, as she sat so still, a bold mouse streaked across the floor and began to wash its whiskers right under the throne. The Queen gave a little frightened gasp. But she quickly clapped her hand to her mouth for fear of disturbing the King. Then she pulled her ermine train about her and sat trembling within it. And at that moment, over the edge of her hand, her startled eyes glanced across the room and saw on the threshold — a cat.

A small cat it was, as fluffy as a dandelion, and white as sugar from tail to whisker. It walked with a lazy swinging step as though it had nothing at all to do and all time to do it in. A pair of green eyes glowed in its head as it sauntered through the door.

For a moment it paused at the carpet's edge, glancing curiously at the King and the courtiers as they bent above their books. Then the green eyes turned towards the Queen. The Cat gave a start and its body stiffened. Up went its back like the hump of a camel. Its whiskers stretched into threads of steel. Then it leapt across the Council Chamber and dived beneath the throne. There was a hoarse cat-cry. And a smothered squeak. And the mouse was there no longer.

"Silence, please! Don't make such extraordinary noises, my dear! They interrupt my thoughts!" said the King fractiously.

"It wasn't me," said the Queen timidly. "It was a Cat."

"Cats?" said the King absent-mindedly, without even lifting his head. "Cats are four-footed creatures covered with fur. They eat mice, fish, liver and birds and communicate either in a purr or a caterwaul. They keep themselves to themselves and are popularly supposed to possess nine lives. For further information on Cats, see Page Two, Volume Seven, Shelf D in Library Number Five to the left as you go in the door. Here! Hi! What's all this —— ?"

With a start the King looked up from his page. For the Cat was sitting on the desk before him.

"Kindly be careful!" the King said crossly. "You're right on my latest facts. They deal with a very important question. Do turkeys really come from Turkey and if not, why? Well, what do you want? Speak up! Don't mumble."

"I want to have a look at you," the Cat said calmly.

"Oho! You do, do you? Well, a Cat may look at a King, they say! And I've no objection. Go ahead!"

The King leaned backwards in his chair and turned his face from left to right so the Cat could see both sides.

The Cat gazed thoughtfully at the King.

There was a long pause.

"Well?" said the King, with a tolerant smile. "And what do you think of me, may I ask?"

The Cat was sitting on the desk before him

"Not much," said the Cat casually, licking its right front paw.

"What?" cried the King. "Not much, indeed! My poor ignorant animal, you are evidently not aware *which* King you are looking at!"

"All kings are pretty much alike," said the Cat.

"Nothing of the kind," the King said angrily. "I defy you to name a single king that knows as much as I do. Why, professors come from the ends of the earth to consult with me for half an hour. My court is composed of the Very Best People. Jack-the-Giant-Killer digs my garden. My flocks are tended by no less a person than Bo-Peep. And all my pies contain Four-and-Twenty Blackbirds. Not much to look at, forsooth! And who are you, I'd like to know, to speak to a King like that!"

"Oh, just a cat," the Cat replied. "Four legs and a tail and a couple of whiskers."

"I can see that for myself!" snapped the King. "It doesn't matter to me what you *look* like. What *I* care about is, how much do you know?"

"Oh, everything," the Cat said calmly, as it licked the tip of its tail.

"What!" The King burst out with an angry splutter. "Well, of all the vain, conceited creatures! I've a jolly good mind to chop off your head."

"So you shall," said the Cat. "But all in good time."

"Everything! Why, you preposterous animal! There's

no one alive — not even myself — who could be as wise as that!"

"With the single exception of cats," said the Cat. "All cats, I assure you, know everything!"

"Very well," growled the King. "But you've got to prove it. If you're so clever I shall ask you three questions. And then we shall see what we'll see."

He smiled a supercilious smile. If the wretched Cat insisted on boasting, it would have to take the consequences!

"Now," he said, leaning back in his chair and putting his fingers together. "My first question is — — "

"One moment, please!" the Cat said calmly. "I cannot undertake to answer your questions until we have settled the terms. No cat would do anything so foolish. I am prepared to make a bargain with you. And these are my conditions. It is agreed between us that you shall ask me three questions. After that, it is only fair that I should question you. And whichever one of us wins the contest shall have command of your kingdom."

The courtiers dropped their pens in surprise. The King's eyes goggled with astonishment.

But he swallowed the words that sprang to his mouth and gave a disdainful laugh.

"Very well," he said haughtily. "It's a great waste of time and you, not I, will be the one to regret it. But I accept your bargain."

"Then take off your crown," commanded the Cat, "and lay it on the table between us."

The King tore the crown from his tattered head and the jewels flashed in the sunlight.

"Let's get this nonsense over and done with! I have to go on with my work," he said crossly. "Are you ready? Well, here is my first question. If you laid them carefully, end to end, how many six-foot men would it take to go right round the Equator?"

"That's easy," the Cat replied, with a smile. "You simply divide the length by six."

"Aha!" cried the King with a crafty look. "That's all very well — but what *is* the length?"

"Any length you like," the Cat said airily. "It doesn't really exist, you know. The Equator is purely an imaginary line."

The King's face darkened with disapproval.

"Well," he said sulkily, "tell me this. What is the difference between an Elephant and a Railway Porter?"

"No difference at all," said the Cat at once. "Because they both carry trunks."

"But — but — but — but —— " the King protested. "These are not the answers I expected. You really must try to be more serious."

"I can't help what you expected," said the Cat. "These are the proper replies to your questions, as any cat will tell you."

The King made an angry click with his tongue.

"This nonsense is getting beyond a joke! It's a farce! It's nothing but twiddle-twaddle. Well, here is my third question — *if* you can answer it."

You could see by the smile on the King's face that *this* time he thought he had the Cat exactly where he wanted it.

He held up a pompous hand and began.

"If a dozen men, working eight hours a day, had to dig a hole ten-and-a-half miles deep — how long would it be, including Sundays, before they put down their spades?"

The King's eyes shone with a cunning sparkle. He gazed at the Cat with a look of triumph. But the Cat had its answer ready.

"Two seconds," it said quickly, with a little flick of its tail.

"Two seconds! Are you mad? The answer's in years!" The King rubbed his hands together with glee at the thought of the Cat's mistake.

"I repeat," said the Cat. "It would take them two seconds. To dig such a hole would be utterly foolish. 'Ten miles deep?' they would say. 'Why, what on earth for?' "

"That isn't the point," the King said angrily.

"But every question must have a point. A point is exactly what questions are for. And now," said the Cat, "it's my turn, I believe!"

The King gave an angry shrug of his shoulders.

"Well, be quick. You've wasted enough of my time!"

"My questions are short and very simple," the Cat assured him. "A cat could solve them in a flick of the whisker. Let us hope that a King will be equally clever. Now, here is my first. How high is the sky?"

The King gave a grunt of satisfaction. This was exactly the kind of question he liked, and he smiled a knowing smile.

"Well, of course," he began, "it all depends. If you measured it from a level plain it would be one height. From the top of a mountain another. And after taking this into account, we should have to determine the latitude and longitude, the amplitude, magnitude and multitude, not forgetting the atmospherics, mathematics, acrobatics and hysterics; and the general depressions, expressions, impressions and confessions, together with —— "

"Excuse me," interrupted the Cat. "But that is not the answer. Try again, please. How high is the sky?"

The King's eyes popped with angry astonishment. Nobody had ever dared to interrupt him before.

"The sky," he bellowed, "is — er — it's ——. Well, of course I can't tell you in so many yards. Neither could anyone else, I assure you. It is probably —— "

"I want an exact reply," said the Cat. He glanced from the King to the gaping courtiers. "Has anyone here, in this hall of learning, the answer to my question?"

Nervously glancing at the King, the Prime Minister raised a trembling hand.

"I have always supposed," he murmured shyly, "that the sky was just a little higher than the Eagle flies. I'm an old man, of course, and I'm probably wrong —— "

The Cat clapped its sugar-white paws together.

"No! No! You are right," it protested gently.

The King gave a sullen snort of rage.

"Tomfoolery! Nonsensical bosh!"

The Cat held up its paw for silence. "Will you answer my second question, please! Where is the sweetest milk to be found?"

Immediately the King's face cleared, and took on a confident smirk.

"As simple as A.B.C.," he said loftily. "The answer, of course, is Sardinia. For there the cows live on honey and roses and their milk is as sweet as Golden Syrup. Or perhaps I should say the Elegant Islands, where they feed upon nothing but sugar cane. Or Greece, where they browse in the Candytuft. Now, taking into consideration —— "

"I can take nothing into consideration," said the Cat, "except the fact that you have not answered my question. Where is the sweetest milk, O King?"

"I know!" cried the little Page, pausing for a moment above a half-filled inkwell. "In a saucer by the fire."

The Cat gave the child an approving nod and yawned in the face of the King.

"I thought you were so clever!" it said slyly. "You may

indeed be the wisest of Kings — but somebody else has answered my question. Do not frown, however — " for the King was glowering at the Page — "you still have one more chance to win. Here is my third question. What is the strongest thing in the world?"

The King's eyes glittered. This time he was certain he had the right answer.

"The Tiger," he said thoughtfully, "is a very strong thing. So also are the Horse and the Lion. Then, of course, there are the tides of the sea. And the granite veins of the mountains. Volcanoes, too, have a mighty strength and the snowy caps of ice at the Poles. Or, again, it might be the Wall of China ——"

"Or again it might not!" the Cat broke in. "Can anyone tell me the strongest thing?"

It glanced once more round the Council Chamber. And this time it was the Queen who spoke.

"I think," she said gently, "it must be Patience. For, in the long run, it is Patience that overcomes all things."

The green eyes dwelt gravely upon her for a moment.

"It is indeed," the Cat agreed quietly. And turning, it laid a paw on the crown.

"Oh, wisest of monarchs!" cried the Cat. "You are, without doubt, a mighty scholar and I am a common-or-garden cat. But I have answered all three of your questions and you have not answered one of mine. The result of the contest is clear, I think. The crown belongs to me."

The King gave a short contemptuous laugh.

"Don't be so silly! What would you do with it? You can't make laws and rule the people. You don't even know how to read or write. Turn over my kingdom to a Cat? I'm hanged if I will!"

The Cat smiled broadly.

"I see that your wisdom does not include a knowledge of fairy-tales. If it did, you would know that it is only necessary to cut off a cat's head to discover a Prince in disguise."

"Fairy-tales? Pooh! They're nothing to me. I'm thinking about my kingdom."

"Your kingdom," said the Cat, "if you'll forgive me mentioning it, is no longer your affair. All that need concern you now is quickly to cut off my head. The rest you may leave to me. Furthermore, since you apparently have no use for them, I shall take into my service this wise man, your Prime Minister, this understanding woman, your wife, and this sensible child, your page. Let them get their hats and come with me and together we four shall rule the kingdom."

"But what's going to happen to *me?*" cried the King. "Where shall I go? How shall I live?"

The Cat's eyes narrowed sternly.

"You should have thought of that before. Most people think twice before making a bargain with a Cat. Well, out with your sword now, learned man! And I trust the blade is sharp."

"Stop!" cried the Prime Minister, as he laid his hand on the hilt of the King's sword. Then he turned to the Cat and bowed respectfully.

"Sir," he said quietly, "listen to me! It is true that you have won the crown, in fair and equal contest. And it may be you are indeed a Prince. But I must decline your offer. I have served the King faithfully since the days when I was a page in his father's court. And whether he be crowned or uncrowned, head of a kingdom or a tramp on the lonely roads, I love him and he needs me. I will not go with you."

"Nor I," said the Queen, as she rose from her golden throne. "I have stood at the King's side since he was young and comely. I have waited for him in silence through long, lonely years. Whether he be wise or foolish, rich or without bread, I love him and I need him. I will not go with you."

"Nor I," said the little Page, as he corked up his bottle of ink. "This is the only home I have ever known. And the King is my king and I am sorry for him. Besides, I like filling up the inkwells. I will not go with you."

At that the Cat smiled a curious smile and its green eyes shone on the three who had refused him.

"What have you to say to this, O King?" said the Cat as it turned to the desk.

But no words came to answer the question. For the King was weeping.

"O wise man, why do you weep?" asked the Cat.

"Because I am ashamed," sobbed the King. "I

boasted about how clever *I* was. I thought I knew every-thing — pretty nearly. And now I find that an old man and a woman and a little lad are all far wiser than I am. Do not try to comfort me!" he wept, as the Queen and the Prime Minister touched his hands. "I am not worth it. I know nothing at all. Not even who I am!"

He hid his face in the crook of his arm. "Oh, I know that I'm a King!" he cried. "I know my name and address, of course! But I do not know, after all these years, who I really, truly am!"

"Look at me and you will find out," said the Cat quietly.

"But I h-h-have looked at you!" sobbed the King into his handkerchief.

"Not really," the Cat insisted gently. "You have only glanced at me, now and again. A Cat may look at a King you say. But a King may also look at a Cat. If you did that, you would know who you are. Look in my eyes — and see!"

The King took his face out of the handkerchief and peered at the Cat through his tears. His eyes wandered over the calm white face and came at last to the Cat's green eyes. Within that shining, piercing gaze he saw his own reflection.

"Closer. Closer," the Cat commanded.

Obediently the King bent nearer.

And as he gazed at those fathomless eyes, a change came over the man within them. Slowly, his thin, pinched face grew fatter. The pale cheeks plumped into round red pouches and the wrinkles smoothed themselves out of his brow. Bright locks of brown curled upon his head; a brown beard sprang from his greying chin. The King gave a start of surprise and smiled. And a big broad rosy man smiled back from the mirroring eyes of the Cat.

"My Glorious Ghosts! That's *me!*" he cried. "I know who I really am at last! Why, *I'm* not the cleverest man in the world!" He flung up his head with a gusty laugh. "Ho-ho! Ha-ha! I see it all now! I'm not a thinking person at all. I'm nothing but a Merry Old Soul!"

He waved his arms at the gaping courtiers. "Here, you! Take away those pens and papers. Tear up the notebooks! Bury the desks! And if anyone mentions a fact to me I shall cut off his head myself!"

He gave another uproarious laugh and embraced the Prime Minister so tightly that he nearly killed the old man.

"Forgive me, my faithful friend!" he cried. "And bring me my Pipe and a Bowl of Punch and call in my Fiddlers Three!"

"And you, my Joy, my Treasure, my Dove —— " he turned to the Queen with outstretched arms. "Oh, give me your hand again, dear heart, and I'll never let it go!"

Happy tears crept down the cheeks of the Queen, and the King touched them gently away. "I don't need stars in the sky," he whispered, "I have them here, in your eyes."

"Forgive me if I interrupt. But what about me?" exclaimed the Cat.

"Well, you've got the kingdom. You've got the crown! What more do you want?" the King demanded.

"Pooh!" said the Cat. "They're no use to me! Accept them, I pray, as a friendly gift. But as no cat ever gives something for nothing, I demand in return two small requests —— "

"Oh, anything. Anything at all," said the King with a lordly gesture.

"I should like, every now and then," said the Cat, "to come to the Palace and see —— "

"Me? Why, of course! You're always welcome!" The King broke in with a satisfied smile.

"To see the Queen," the Cat continued, ignoring the King's remark.

"Oh — the Queen! All right. Whenever you like. You can help us to keep down the mice."

"My second request," the Cat went on, "is the little chain of blue-and-green flowers that the Queen wears round her neck."

"Take it — and welcome!" the King said airily. "It was only a cheap one, anyway."

Slowly the Queen put up her hands and unfastened the clasp at her throat. She twined the necklace about the Cat, looping it round the furry body and over and under the tail. Then for a long moment she looked deep into the

Cat's green eyes and the Cat looked into hers. And in that look lay all the secrets that Queens and cats carry in their hearts and never tell to anyone.

"My At Home days are every Second Friday," said the Queen, as she smiled at the Cat.

"I shall come," the Cat said nodding.

And having said that, he turned away and, without a glance at anyone else, sailed out of the Council Chamber. The blue-and-green necklace shone in his fur and his tail waved to and fro like a banner.

"By the way!" called the King, as the Cat departed.

"Are you sure you're really a prince in disguise? Could I have safely cut off your head?"

The Cat turned about and regarded him gravely. Then it smiled its mocking smile.

"Nothing is certain in this world. Good-bye!" said the green-eyed Cat.

It sprang across the sunny threshold and down the Castle steps.

On the Palace lawn a red cow was admiring her reflection in an ornamental pond.

"Who are you?" she enquired, as the Cat passed by.

"I'm the Cat that Looked at a King," he replied.

"And I," she remarked with a toss of her head, "am the Cow that Jumped Over the Moon."

"Is that so?" said the Cat. "Whatever for?"

The Cow stared. She had never before been asked that question. And suddenly it occurred to her that there might be something else to do than jumping over moons.

"Now that you mention it," she said shyly, "I don't think I really know." And she trotted away across the lawn to think the matter over.

On the garden path a large grey bird was noisily flapping its wings.

"I'm the Goose that Lays the Golden Eggs!" it quacked haughtily.

"Indeed?" said the Cat, "and where are your goslings?"

"Goslings?" The Goose turned a trifle pale. "Well, now

that you mention it, I have none. I always felt there was something missing." And she hurried off to make a nest and lay a common egg.

Plop! A green shape dropped in front of the Cat.

"I'm the Frog that Would a-Wooing Go," it said proudly.

"Do you tell me that, now?" the Cat said gravely. "Well, I trust you are happily married."

"Er —— now that you mention it — not exactly. In fact — er — no!" confessed the Frog.

"Ah," said the Cat, with a shake of his head. "You should have obeyed your Mother!"

And before the Frog could do more than blink, the Cat had passed on. Away he went down the garden path, his whiskers twitching in the morning air, his blue-and-green necklace shining in the sun and his white tail waving like a banner behind him.

And as he disappeared through the Palace gates, all those who had seen him felt rich and happy.

The Cow and the Goose and the Frog were happy for now they could stop doing foolish things that had no rhyme or reason. The courtiers all were happy men, dancing by day to the Fiddlers' tunes and drinking at night from the flowing Bowl. The King himself was extremely happy because he no longer thought about anything. And the Queen was happy for a very good reason — because the King was happy. The little Page was happy, too. For now he could fill the inkwells with ink, and empty them back in the bottle again with no one to say him nay. But the happiest person in all the world was the old Prime Minister.

Do you know what he did?

He issued a proclamation.

The King commanded his subjects (it said) to put up Maypoles and dance around them; to get out Merry-go-rounds and ride them; to dance and feast and sing and grow fat and love one another dearly. And, furthermore, (it was clearly printed) if anyone disobeyed these laws, the King would immediately cut off his head.

And, having done that, the Prime Minister felt he had done enough. He spent the rest of his days doing nothing — just sitting in the sun in a rocking-chair, making himself a gentle breeze with a fan of cocoanut palm.

As for the Cat, he went his way through the ways of the world, decked in the Queen's bright necklace; and gazing at everything he saw with his green and piercing eyes.

He is still wandering, some folks say, for Near and Far are alike to him. And always as he goes, he watches out for one or another who will return his gaze. A king, it may be, or perhaps a shepherd, or a man going by through the city streets. If he comes upon anyone like that, he will stay with them for a little while. Not very long, but long enough. It takes no more than the tick of a second to look down deep in his deep green eyes and discover who they are. . . .

The dreamy voice was hushed and silent. The sunlight crept away from the window and dusk came slowly in. Not a sound could be heard in the Nursery but the ticking of the clock.

Then, with a start, as though she were coming back from a great distance, Mary Poppins turned to the children. Her eyes snapped angrily.

"May I ask what you're doing out of bed? I thought you were dying of toothache, Michael! What are you gaping at me for, Jane? I am not a Performing Bear!"

And, snatching up her wool, she became her usual whirlwind self.

With a squeak, Michael hurled himself into bed. But Jane did not move.

"I wonder who I am!" she said softly, half to herself and half to Michael.

"I *know* who I am," said Michael stoutly. "I'm Michael George Banks, of Cherry-Tree Lane. And I don't need a Cat to tell me."

"He doesn't need anyone to tell him anything. Clever Mr. Smarty!" Mary Poppins tossed him a scornful smile.

"When he comes back," Jane murmured slowly, "I shall look right into his deep green eyes!"

"You and your deep green eyes, indeed! Better look into your own black face and see that it's clean for Supper!" Mary Poppins sniffed her usual sniff.

"Perhaps he won't come back!" said Michael. A Cat

that could look at a King, he thought, would hardly want to spend its days on the top of a mantelpiece.

"Oh, yes, he will — won't he, Mary Poppins?" Jane's voice was full of anxiety.

"How should I know?" snapped Mary Poppins. "I'm not a Public Library!"

"But it's Michael's cat ——" Jane began to argue, when Mrs. Banks' voice interrupted her.

"Mary Poppins!" it called from the foot of the stairs. "Could you possibly spare me a moment?"

The children looked at each other questioningly. Their Mother's voice was shrill with alarm. Mary Poppins hurried out of the room. Michael pushed the blankets away once more and crept with Jane to the top of the stairs.

Down in the front hall Mr. Banks sat huddled upon a chair. Mrs. Banks was anxiously stroking his head and giving him sips of water.

"He seems to have had some kind of shock," she explained to Mary Poppins. "Can't you tell us, George, exactly what happened? Whatever can be the matter?"

Mr. Banks raised a ghostly face. "A Nervous Breakdown — that's what's the matter. I'm overworking. I'm seeing things."

"What things?" demanded Mrs. Banks.

Mr. Banks took a sip of water.

"I was turning in at the end of the Lane when ——" he gave a shudder and closed his eyes. "I saw it standing right by our gate."

"You saw what standing?" cried Mrs. Banks frantically.

"A white thing. Sort of leopard it was. And forget-me-nots growing all over its fur. When I got to the gate it — looked at me. A wild green look — right into my eyes. Then it nodded and said 'Good-evening, Banks!' and hurried up the path."

"But —— " Mrs. Banks began to argue.

Mr. Banks raised a protesting hand.

"I know what you're going to say. Well, don't. The leopards are all locked up in the Zoo. And they don't have forget-me-nots on them, anyway. I'm perfectly well aware of that. But it just goes to show that I'm very ill. You'd better send for Dr. Simpson."

Mrs. Banks ran to the telephone. And a stifled hiccup came from the landing.

"What's the matter with you up there?" asked Mr. Banks faintly.

But Jane and Michael could not answer. They were overcome by a storm of giggles. They writhed and rolled and rocked on the floor and gulped and gurgled with laughter.

For while Mr. Banks was describing his shock, a white shape had appeared at the Nursery window. Lightly it leapt from the sill to the floor and up to its place on the mantelpiece. It sat there now with its tail curled round it and its whiskers folded against its cheeks. Dappled with small, blue, shining flowers, its green eyes gazing across the room, silent and still on the mantelpiece, sat Michael's China Cat.

"Well, of all the hard-hearted, unfeeling children!" Mr. Banks stared up at them, shocked and hurt.

But that only made them laugh more loudly. They giggled and coughed and choked and exploded till Mary Poppins bent back her head and fixed them with one of her fiercest glares.

Then there was silence. Not even a hiccup. For that look, as Jane and Michael knew, was enough to stop anyone laughing. . . .

CHAPTER FOUR

THE MARBLE BOY

ND DON'T forget to buy me an evening paper!" said Mrs. Banks, as she handed Jane two pennies and kissed her good-bye.

Michael looked at his Mother reproachfully.

"Is that all you're going to give us?" he asked. "What'll happen if we meet the Ice Cream Man?"

"Well," said Mrs. Banks reluctantly. "Here's another sixpence. But I do think you children get too many treats. *I* didn't have Ices every day when *I* was a little girl."

Michael looked at her curiously. He could not believe she had ever been a little girl. Mrs. George Banks in short skirts and her hair tied up with ribbons? Impossible!

"I suppose," he said smugly, "you didn't deserve them!"

And he tucked the sixpence carefully into the pocket of his sailor suit.

"That's Fourpence for the Ice Creams," said Jane. "And we'll buy a *Lot-o'-Fun*, with the rest."

"Out of my way, Miss, if you please!" said a haughty voice behind her.

As neat and trim as a fashion-plate, Mary Poppins came down the steps with Annabel. She dumped her into the perambulator and pushed it past the children.

"Now, Quick March into the Park!" she snapped. "And no meandering!"

Down the path straggled Jane and Michael, with John and Barbara at their heels. The sun spread over Cherry-Tree Lane like a bright enormous umbrella. Thrushes and blackbirds sang in the trees. Down at the corner Admiral Boom was busily mowing his lawn.

From the distance came sounds of martial music. The Band was playing at the end of the Park. Along the walks went the flowery sunshades and beneath them sauntered gossiping ladies, exchanging the latest news.

The Park Keeper, in his summer suit — blue with a red stripe on the sleeve — was keeping an eye on everyone as he tramped across the lawns.

"Observe the Rules! Keep Off the Grass! All Litter to be Placed in the Baskets!" he shouted.

Jane gazed at the sunny, dreamy scene. "It's just like Mr. Twigley's box," she said with a happy sigh.

Michael put his ear to the trunk of an oak.

"I believe I can hear it growing!" he cried. "It makes a small, soft, creeping sound —— "

"You'll be creeping in a minute! Right back home, unless you hurry!" Mary Poppins warned him.

"No Rubbish Allowed in the Park!" shouted the Keeper, as she swept along the Lime Walk.

"Rubbish yourself!" she retorted briskly, with a haughty toss of her head.

He took off his hat and fanned his face as he stared at her retreating back. And you knew from the way Mary Poppins smiled that she knew quite well he was staring. How could he help it, she thought to herself. Wasn't she wearing her new white jacket, with the pink collar and the pink belt and the four pink buttons down the front?

"Which way are we going today?" asked Michael.

"That remains to be seen!" she answered him priggishly.

"I was only enquiring —— " Michael argued.

"Don't, then!" she advised, with a warning sniff.

"She never lets me say anything!" he grumbled under his hat to Jane. "I'll go dumb some day and then she'll be sorry!"

Mary Poppins thrust the perambulator in front of her as though she were running an obstacle race.

"This way, please!" she commanded presently, as she swung the pram to the right.

And they knew, then, where they were going. For the little path that turned out of the Lime Walk led away towards the Lake.

There, beyond the tunnels of shade, lay the shining patch of water. It sparkled and danced in its net of sunlight and the children felt their hearts beat faster as they ran through the shadows towards it.

"I'll make a boat, and sail it to Africa!" shouted Michael, forgetting his crossness.

"I'll go fishing!" cried Jane, as she galloped past him.

Laughing and whooping and waving their hats, they came to the shining water. All round the Lake stood the dusty green benches, and the ducks went quacking along the edge, greedily looking for crusts.

At the far end of the water stood the battered marble statue of the Boy and the Dolphin. Dazzling white and bright it shone, between the Lake and the sky. There was a small chip off the Boy's nose and a line like a black thread round his ankle. One of the fingers of his left hand was broken off at the joint. And all his toes were cracked.

There he stood, on his high pedestal, with his arm

flung lightly round the neck of the Dolphin. His head, with its ruffle of marble curls, was bent towards the water. He gazed down at it thoughtfully with wide marble eyes. The name NELEUS was carved in faded gilt letters at the base of the pedestal.

"How bright he is today!" breathed Jane, blinking her eyes at the shining marble.

And it was at that moment that she saw the Elderly Gentleman.

He was sitting at the foot of the statue, reading a book with the aid of a magnifying glass. His bald head was sheltered from the sun by a knotted silk handkerchief, and lying on the bench beside him was a black top-hat.

The children stared at the curious figure with fascinated eyes.

"That's Mary Poppins' favourite seat! She *will* be cross!" exclaimed Michael.

"Indeed? And when was I ever cross?" her voice enquired behind him.

The remark quite shocked him. "Why, you're *often* cross, Mary Poppins!" he said. "At least fifty times a day!"

"Never!" she said with an angry snap. "I have the patience of a Boa Constrictor! I merely Speak My Mind!"

She flounced away and sat down on a bench exactly opposite the Statue. Then she glared across the Lake at the Elderly Gentleman. It was a look that might have killed anybody else. But the Elderly Gentleman was quite unaffected. He went on poring over his book and took no notice of anyone. Mary Poppins, with an infuriated sniff, took her mending-bag from the perambulator and began to darn the socks.

The children scattered round the sparkling water.

"Here's my boat!" shrieked Michael, snatching a piece of coloured paper from a litter basket.

"I'm fishing," said Jane, as she lay on her stomach and stretched her hand over the water. She imagined a fishing-rod in her fingers and a line running down, with a hook and a worm. After a little while, she knew, a fish would swim lazily up to the hook and give the worm a tweak. Then, with a jerk, she would land him neatly and take him home in her hat. "Well, I never!" Mrs. Brill would say. "It's just what we needed for supper!"

Beside her the Twins were happily paddling. Michael steered his ship through a terrible storm. Mary Poppins sat primly on her bench and rocked the perambulator with one foot. Her silver needle flashed in the sunlight. The Park was quiet and dreamy and still.

Bang!

The Elderly Gentleman closed his book and the sound shattered the silence.

"Oh, I say!" protested a shrill sweet voice. "You might have let me finish!"

Jane and Michael looked up in surprise. They stared. They blinked. And they stared again. For there, on the grass before them, stood the little marble statue. The marble Dolphin was clasped in his arms and the pedestal was quite empty.

The Elderly Gentleman opened his mouth. Then he shut it and opened it again.

"Er — did you say something?" he said at last, and his eyebrows went up to the top of his head.

"Yes, of course I did!" the Boy replied. "I was reading over your shoulder there ——" he pointed towards the empty pedestal, "and you closed the book too quickly. I wanted to finish the Elephant story and see how he got his Trunk."

"Oh, I *beg* your pardon," said the Elderly Gentleman. "I

had no idea — er — of such a thing. I always stop reading at four, you see. I have to get home to my Tea."

He rose and folded the handkerchief and picked up the black top hat.

"Well, now that you've finished," the Boy said calmly, "you can give the book to me!"

The Elderly Gentleman drew back, clutching the book to his breast.

"Oh, I couldn't do that, I'm afraid," he said. "You see, I've only just bought it. I wanted to read it when I was young, but the grown-ups always got it first. And now that I've got a copy of my own, I really feel I must keep it."

He eyed the statue uneasily as though he feared that at any moment it might snatch the book away.

"*I* could tell you about the Elephant's Child — — " Jane murmured shyly to the Boy.

He wheeled around with the fish in his arms.

"Oh, Jane — would you really?" he cried in surprise. His marble face gleamed with pleasure.

"And I'll tell you *Yellow Dog Dingo*," said Michael, "and *The Butterfly That Stamped*."

"No!" said the Elderly Gentleman suddenly. "Here am I with a suit of clothes and a hat. And he's quite naked. I'll *give* him the book! I suppose," he added, with a gloomy sigh, "I was never meant to have it."

He gave the book a last long look, and, thrusting it at the Marble Boy, he turned away quickly. But the Dolphin wriggled and caught his eye and he turned to the Boy again.

"By the way," he said, curiously, "I wonder how you caught that Porpoise? What did you use — a line or a net?"

"Neither," replied the Boy, with a smile. "He was given to me when I was born."

"Oh — I see." The Elderly Gentleman nodded, though he still looked rather puzzled. "Well — I must be getting along. Good-day!" He lifted the black top-hat politely and hurried off down the path.

"Thank you!" the Marble Boy shouted after him, as he eagerly opened the book. On the fly-leaf was written, in spidery writing, *"William Weatherall Wilkins."*

"I'll cross out his name and put mine instead." The Boy smiled gaily at Jane and Michael.

"But what is your name? And how can you read?" cried Michael, very astonished.

"My name is Neleus," the Boy said laughing. "And I read with my eyes, of course!"

"But you're only a statue!" Jane protested. "And statues don't usually walk and talk. However did you get down?"

"I jumped," replied Neleus, smiling again, as he tossed his marble curls. "I was so disappointed not to finish that story, that something happened to my feet. First they twitched, and then they jumped and the next thing I knew I was down on the grass!" He curled his little marble

toes and stamped on the earth with his marble feet. "Oh, lucky, lucky human beings to be able to do this every day! I've watched you so often, Jane and Michael, and wished I could come and play with you. And now at last my wish has come true. Oh, tell me you're glad to see me!"

He touched their cheeks with his marble fingers and crowed with joy as he danced around them. Then before they could utter a word of welcome he sped like a hare to the edge of the Lake and dabbled his hand in the water.

"So — this is what water feels like!" he cried. "So deep and so blue — and as light as air!" He leaned out over the sparkling Lake and the Dolphin gave a flick of its tail and slipped from his arms with a splash.

"Catch him! He'll sink!" cried Michael quickly.

But the Dolphin did nothing of the kind. It swam round the Lake and threshed the water; it dived and caught its tail in its mouth and leapt in the air and dived again. The performance was just like a turn in the circus. And as it sprang, dripping, to the arms of its master, the children could not help clapping.

"Was it good?" asked Neleus enviously. And the Dolphin grinned and nodded.

"Good!" cried a well-known voice behind them. "I call it extremely naughty!"

Mary Poppins was standing at the edge of the Lake and her eyes were as bright as her darning needle. Neleus sprang to his feet with a little cry and hung his head before her. He looked very young and small and shy as he waited for her to speak.

"Who said you might get down, may I ask?" Her face had its usual look of fury.

He shook his head guiltily.

"No one," he mumbled. "My feet jumped down by themselves, Mary Poppins."

"Then they'd better jump up again, spit-spot. You've no right to be off your pedestal."

He tilted back his marble head and the sunlight glanced off his small chipped nose.

"Oh, can't I stay down, Mary Poppins?" he pleaded. "Do let me stay for a little while and play with Jane and

Michael! You don't know how lonely it is up there, with only the birds to talk to!" The earnest marble eyes entreated her. "Please, Mary Poppins!" he whispered softly, as he clasped his marble hands.

She gazed down thoughtfully for a moment, as though she were making up her mind. Then her eyes softened. A little smile skipped over her mouth and crinkled the edge of her cheek.

"Well, just for this afternoon!" she said. "This one time, Neleus! Never again!"

"Never — I promise, Mary Poppins!" He gave her an impish grin.

"Do you know Mary Poppins?" demanded Michael. "Where did you meet her?" he wanted to know. He was feeling a little jealous.

"Of course I do!" exclaimed Neleus laughing. "She's a very old friend of my Father's."

"What is your Father's name? Where is he?" Jane was almost bursting with curiosity.

"Far away. In the Isles of Greece. He is called the King of the Sea." As he spoke, the marble eyes of Neleus brimmed slowly up with sadness.

"What does he do?" demanded Michael. "Does he go to the City — like Daddy?"

"Oh, no! He never goes anywhere. He stands on a cliff above the sea, holding his trident and blowing his horn. Beside him my Mother sits, combing her hair. And Pelias, that's my younger brother, plays at their feet with a marble shell. And all day long the gulls fly past them, making black shadows on their marble bodies, and telling them news of the harbour. By day they watch the red-sailed ships going in and out of the bay. And at night they listen to the wine-dark waters that break on the shore below."

"How lovely!" cried Jane. "But why did you leave them?"

She was thinking that she would never have left Mr. and Mrs. Banks and Michael alone on the cliffs of Greece.

"I didn't want to," said the Marble Boy. "But what can a statue do against men? They were always coming to stare at us — peeking and prying and pinching our arms. They said we were made a long time ago by a very famous artist. And one day somebody said — 'I'll take *him!*' — and he pointed at me. So — I had to go."

He hid his eyes for a moment behind the Dolphin's fin.

"What happened then?" demanded Jane. "How did you get to our Park?"

"In a packing-case," said Neleus calmly, and laughed at their look of astonishment. "Oh, we always travel that way, you know. My family is very much in demand. People want us for Parks or Museums or Gardens. So they buy us and send us by Parcel Post. It never seems to occur to them that some of us might be — lonely." He choked a little on the word. Then he flung up his head with a lordly gesture. "But don't let's think about that!" he cried. "It's been much better since you two came. Oh, Jane and Michael, I know you so well — as if you were part of my family. I know about Michael's Kite and his Compass; and the Doulton Bowl, and Robertson Ay, and the things you have for supper. Didn't you ever notice me listening? And reading the fairy-tales over your shoulders?"

Jane and Michael shook their heads.

"I know *Alice in Wonderland* by heart," he went on. "And most of *Robinson Crusoe.* And *Everything a Lady Should Know,* which is Mary Poppins' favourite. But best of all are the coloured comics, especially the one called *Lot-o'-Fun.* What happened to Tiger Tim this week? Did he get away safely from Uncle Moppsy?"

"The new one comes out today," said Jane. "We'll all read it together!"

"Oh, dear! How happy I am!" cried Neleus. "The Elephant's Child, and a new *Lot-o'-Fun,* and my legs like the wings of a bird. I don't know when my Birthday is, but I think it must be today!" He hugged the Dolphin and the book in his arms and capered across the grass.

"Hi! Ting-aling-aling! Look where you're going!" the Ice Cream Man gave a warning cry. He was wheeling his barrow along by the Lake. The printed notice in front of it said:

STOP ME AND BUY ONE

WHAT WONDERFUL WEATHER!

"Stop! Stop! Stop! Stop!" cried the children wildly, as they ran towards the barrow.

"Chocolate!" said Michael.

"Lemon!" cried Jane.

And the fat little Twins put out their hands and gladly took what was given them.

"And wot about you!" said the Ice Cream Man, as Neleus came and stood shyly beside him.

"I don't know what to choose," said Neleus. "I never had one before."

"Wot! Never 'ad a Nice? Wot's the matter — weak stummick? A boy your size should know all about Ices! 'Ere!" The Ice Cream Man fished inside his barrow and brought out a Raspberry Bar. "Take this and see 'ow you like it!"

Neleus broke the bar with his marble fingers. He popped one half in the Dolphin's mouth and began to lick the other.

"Delicious," he said, "much better than seaweed."

"Seaweed? I should think so! Wot's seaweed got to do with it? But — talking of seaweed, that's a nice big Cod!"

The Ice Cream Man waved his hand at the Dolphin. "If you took it along to the Fishmonger 'e'd give you a fancy price."

The Dolphin gave its tail a flick and its face looked very indignant.

"Oh, I don't want to sell him," said Neleus quickly. "He isn't just a fish — he's a friend!"

"A fishy kind of friend!" said the man. "Why doesn't 'e tell you to put on your clothes? You'll catch your death running round stark naked. Well, no offence meant! Ting-aling! Ting-aling!" He rode away whistling and ringing his bell.

Neleus glanced at the children out of the corner of his eye and the three burst out into peals of laughter.

"Oh, dear!" cried Neleus, gasping for breath. "I believe he thinks I'm human! Shall I run and tell him he's made a mistake? That I haven't worn clothes for two thousand years and never caught even a sniffle?"

He was just about to dart after the barrow when Michael gave a shout.

"Look out! Here's Willoughby!" he cried, and swallowed the rest of his Ice in one gulp.

For Willoughby, who belonged to Miss Lark, had a habit of jumping up at the children and snatching the food from their hands. He had rough, bouncy, vulgar manners and no respect for anyone. But what else could you expect of a dog who was half an Airedale and half a Retriever and the worst half of both?

There he came, lolloping over the grass, sticking out his tongue. Andrew, who was as well-bred as Willoughby was common, tripped gracefully after him. And Miss Lark herself followed breathlessly.

"Just out for a spin before Tea!" she trilled. "Such a beautiful day and the dogs insisted—Good gracious, what is that I see?"

She broke off, panting, and stared at Neleus. Her face, already red, grew redder, and she looked extremely indignant.

"You naughty, wicked boy!" she cried. "What are you doing to that poor fish? Don't you know it will die if it stays out of water?"

Neleus raised a marble eyebrow. The Dolphin swung its tail over its mouth to hide a marble smile.

"You see?" said Miss Lark. "It's writhing in agony! You must put it back into water this minute!"

"Oh, I couldn't do that," said Neleus quickly. "I'm afraid he'd be lonely without me." He was trying to be polite to Miss Lark. But the Dolphin was not. He flapped his tail and wriggled and grinned in a very discourteous manner.

"Don't answer me back! Fish are never lonely! You are just making silly excuses."

Miss Lark made an angry gesture towards the green bench.

"I do think, Mary Poppins," she said, "you might keep an eye on the children! This naughty boy, whoever he is, must put that fish back where he got it!"

Mary Poppins favoured Miss Lark with a stare. "I'm afraid that's quite impossible, ma'am. He'd have to go too far."

"Far or near — it doesn't matter. He must put it back this instant. It's cruelty to animals and it shouldn't be allowed. Andrew and Willoughby — come with me! I shall go at once and tell the Lord Mayor!"

Away she bustled, with the dogs at her heels. Willoughby, as he trotted by, winked rudely at the Dolphin.

"And tell him to put his clothes on! He'll get sunburnt, running about like that!" shrieked Miss Lark, as she hurried off.

Neleus gave a little spurt of laughter and flung himself down on the grass.

"Sunburnt!" he choked. "Oh, Mary Poppins, does nobody guess I'm made of marble?"

"Humph!" replied Mary Poppins, snorting. And Neleus tossed her a mischievous smile.

"That's what the Sea Lions say!" he said, "They sit on the rocks and say 'Humph!' to the sunset!"

"Indeed?" she said tartly. And Jane and Michael waited, trembling, for what was surely coming. But nothing happened. Her face had an answering look of mischief and the blue eyes and the marble eyes smiled gently at each other.

"Neleus," she said quietly, "you have ten minutes more. You can come with us to the Bookstall and back."

"And then —— ?" he said, with a questioning look, as he tightened his arms round the Dolphin.

She did not answer. She looked across the sparkling Lake and nodded towards the pedestal.

"Oh, can't he stay longer, Mary Poppins —— ?" the children began to protest. But the eager question froze on their lips, for Mary Poppins was glaring.

"I said ten minutes," she remarked. "And ten minutes is what I meant. You needn't look at me like that, either. I am not a Grisly Gorilla."

"Oh, don't start arguing!" cried Neleus. "We mustn't waste a second!" He sprang to his feet and seized Jane's hand. "Show me the way to the Bookstall!" he said. And drew her away through the spreading sunlight and over the grassy lawns.

Behind them Mary Poppins lifted the Twins into the perambulator and hurried along with Michael.

Lightly across the summer grasses ran Jane and the Marble Boy. His curls flew out on the wind with hers and her hot breath blew on his marble cheeks. Within her soft and living fingers the marble hand grew warmer.

"This way!" she cried, as she tugged at his arm and drew him into the Lime Walk.

At the end of it, by the Far Gate, stood the gaily painted bookstall. A bright sign nailed above it said:

MR. FOLLY

BOOKS PAPERS AND MAGAZINES

YOU WANT THEM

I'VE GOT THEM

A frill of coloured magazines hung round the Bookstall; and as the children raced up, Mr. Folly popped his head through a gap in the frill. He had a round, quiet, lazy face that looked as though nothing in the world could disturb it.

"Well, if it isn't Jane Banks and Friend!" he remarked mildly. "I think I can guess what you've come for!"

"*The Evening News* and *Lot-o'-Fun*," panted Jane, as she put down the pennies.

Neleus seized the coloured comic and skimmed the pages quickly.

"Does Tiger Tim get away?" cried Michael, as he dashed up, breathless, behind them.

"Yes, he does!" cried Neleus, with a shout of joy. "Listen! Tiger Tim Escapes Clutches of Uncle Moppsy. His New Adventure with Old Man Dogface. Watch Out For Another Tiger Tim Story Next Week!"

"Hooray!" shouted Michael, peering round the Dolphin's shoulder to get a look at the pictures.

Mr. Folly was eyeing Neleus with interest. "That's a fine young whale you got there, sonny! Seems almost 'uman. Where did you catch him?"

"I didn't," said Neleus, glancing up. "He was given to me as a present."

"Fancy that! Well, he makes a nice pet! And where do *you* come from? Where's yer Ma?"

"She's a long way from here," replied Neleus gravely.

"Too bad!" Mr. Folly wagged his head. "Dad away, too?" Neleus smiled and nodded.

"You don't say! Goodness, you must be lonely!" Mr. Folly glanced at the marble body. "And cold as well, I shouldn't wonder, with not a stitch on your bones!" He made a jingling noise in his pocket and thrust out his hand to Neleus.

"There! Get yourself something to wear with that. Can't go around with nothing on. Pneumonia, you know! And chilblains!"

Neleus stared at the silver thing in his hand.

"What is it?" he asked curiously.

"That's a 'Arf-crown," said Mr. Folly. "Don't tell me you never saw one!"

"No, I never did," said Neleus, smiling. And the Dolphin gazed at the coin with interest.

"Well, I declare! You poor little chap! Stark naked and never seen a 'Arf-crown! Someone ought to be taking care of you!" Mr. Folly glanced reproachfully at Mary Poppins. And she gave him an outraged glare.

"Someone *is* taking care of him, thank you!" she said. As she spoke she unbuttoned her new white jacket and slipped it round Neleus' shoulders.

"There!" she said gruffly. "You won't be cold now. And no thanks to *you*, Mr. Folly!"

Neleus looked from the coat to Mary Poppins and his marble eyes grew wider. "You mean — I can keep it always?" he asked.

She nodded, and looked away.

"Oh, dear sweet Sea Lion — thank you!" he cried, and he hugged her waist in his marble arms. "Look at me, Jane, in my new white coat! Look at me, Michael, in my beautiful buttons." He ran excitedly from one to the other to show off his new possession.

"That's right," said Mr. Folly, beaming. "Much better be sure than sorry! And the 'Arf-crown will buy you a nice pair of trousers ——"

"Not tonight," interrupted Mary Poppins. "We're late

as it is. Now Best Foot Forward and home we go, and I'll thank you all not to dawdle."

The sun was swiftly moving westwards as she trundled the pram down the Lime Walk. The Band at the end of the Park was silent. The flowery sunshades had all gone home. The trees stood still and straight in the shadows. The Park Keeper was nowhere to be seen.

Jane and Michael walked on either side of Neleus and linked their hands through his marble arms. A silence was over the human children and over the marble child between them.

"I love you, Neleus," Jane said softly. "I wish you could stay with us always."

"I love you, too," he answered, smiling. "But I must go back. I promised."

"I suppose you couldn't leave the Dolphin?" said Michael, stroking the marble fin.

Jane looked at him angrily.

"Oh, Michael — how can you be so selfish! How would you like to spend your life, all alone up there on a pedestal?"

"I'd like it — if I could have the Dolphin, and call Mary Poppins a Sea Lion!"

"I tell you what, Michael!" said Neleus quickly. "You can't have the Dolphin — he's part of me. But the Half-crown isn't. I'll give you that." He pushed the money into Michael's hand. "And Jane must have the book," he went on. "But promise, Jane, and cross your heart, that you'll let me read it over your shoulder. And every week you must come to the bench and read me the new *Lot-o'-Fun*."

He gave the book a last long look and tucked it under her arm.

"Oh, I promise, Neleus!" she said faithfully, and crossed her heart with her hand.

"I'll be waiting for you," said Neleus softly. "I'll never, never forget."

"Walk up and don't chatter!" hissed Mary Poppins, as she turned towards the Lake.

The perambulator creaked and groaned as it trundled on its way. But high above the creak of the wheels they could hear a well-known voice. They tiptoed up behind Mary Poppins as she walked to the shadowy water.

"I never done it!" the voice protested. "And wouldn't — not if you paid me!"

At the edge of the Lake, by the empty pedestal, stood the Lord Mayor with two Aldermen. And before them, waving his arms and shouting, and generally behaving in a peculiar manner, was the Park Keeper.

"It's none of my doing, Your Honour!" he pleaded. "I can look you straight in the eye!"

"Nonsense, Smith!" said the Lord Mayor sternly. "You are the person responsible for the Park statues. And only you could have done it!"

"You might as well confess!" advised the First Alderman.

"It won't save you, of course," the Second added, "but you'll *feel* so much better!"

"But I didn't *do* it, I'm telling you!" The Park Keeper clasped his hands in a frenzy.

"Stop quibbling, Smith. You're wasting my time!" The Lord Mayor shook his head impatiently. "First, I have to go looking for a naked boy who I hear is maltreating some wretched fish. A salmon, Miss Lark said — or was it a halibut? And now, as if this wasn't enough, I find the most valuable of our statues is missing from its pedestal. I am shocked and disgusted. I trusted you, Smith. And look how you repay me!"

"I *am* looking. I mean, I don't *have* to look! Oh, I don't know what I'm saying, Your Grace! But I *do* know I never touched that statchew!"

The Keeper glanced round wildly for help and his eye fell on Mary Poppins. He gave a cry of horrified triumph and flung out his hand accusingly.

"Your Worship, *there's* the guilty party! She done it or I'll eat me 'At!"

The Lord Mayor glanced at Mary Poppins and back to the Park Keeper.

"I'm ashamed of you, Smith!" he shook his head sorrowfully. "Putting the blame on a perfectly respectable, innocent young woman taking her charges for an afternoon airing! How could you?"

He bowed courteously to Mary Poppins, who returned the bow with a lady-like smile.

"Innocent! *'Er!*" the Park Keeper screamed. "You don't know what you're sayin', my Lord! As soon as that girl comes into the Park, the place begins to go crosswise. Merry-go-rounds jumpin' up in the sky, people coming down on kites and rockets, the Prime Minister bobbing round on balloons — and it's all *your* doing — you Caliban!" He shook his fist wildly at Mary Poppins.

"Poor fellow! Poor fellow! His mind is unhinged!" said the First Alderman sadly.

"Perhaps we'd better get some handcuffs," the Second whispered nervously.

"Do what you like with me! 'Ang me, why don't yer? But it wasn't me wot done it!" Overcome with misery, the Park Keeper flung himself against the pedestal and sobbed bitterly.

Mary Poppins turned and beckoned to Neleus. He ran to her side on marble feet and leaned his head gently against her.

"Is it time?" he whispered, glancing up.

She nodded quickly. Then bending she took him in her arms and kissed his marble brow. For a moment Neleus clung to her as though he could never let her go. Then he broke away, smothering a sob.

"Good-bye, Jane and Michael. Don't forget me!" He pressed his chilly cheek to theirs. And before they could even say a word he had darted away among the shadows and was running towards his pedestal.

The Park Keeper flung himself against the pedestal

"I never 'ad no luck!" wailed the Keeper. "Never since I was a boy!"

"And you won't have any now, my man, unless you put back that statue." The Lord Mayor fixed him with an angry eye.

But Jane and Michael were looking neither at the Park Keeper nor the Lord Mayor. They were watching a curly head appear at the far side of the pedestal.

Up scrambled Neleus, over the ledge, dragging the Dolphin after him. His marble body blazed white and bright in a fading shaft of sunlight. Then with a gesture, half-gay, half-sad, he put up a little marble hand and waved them all farewell. As they waved back he seemed to tremble, but that may have been the tears in their eyes. They watched him draw the Dolphin to him, so close that its marble melted to his. Then he smoothed his curls with a marble hand and bent his head and was still. Even Mary Poppins' pink-and-white jacket seemed turned to lifeless marble.

"I can't put it back if I never took it!" the Park Keeper went on sobbing and shouting.

"Now, see here, Smith ——" the Lord Mayor began. Then he gave a gasp and staggered sideways with his hand clasped to his brow. "My Jumping Giraffes! It's come back ——" he cried. "And there's something different about it!"

He peered more closely at the statue and burst into

roars of delighted laughter. He took off his hat and waved it wildly and slapped the Park Keeper on the back.

"Smith — you rogue! So *that* was your secret! Why didn't you tell us at first, my man? It certainly is a splendid surprise! Well, you needn't go on pretending now —— "

For the Park Keeper, speechless with amazement, was goggling up at Neleus.

"Gentlemen!" The Lord Mayor turned to the Aldermen. "We have sadly misjudged this poor fellow. He has proved himself not only an excellent servant of the community — but an artist as well. Do you see what he has done to the statue? He has added a little marble coat with collar and cuffs of pink. A *great* improvement, to my mind, Smith! I *never* approved of naked statues."

"Nor I!" the First Alderman shook his head.

"Certainly not!" said the Second.

"Never fear, my dear Smith. You shall have your reward. From today your wages will be raised one shilling and an extra stripe will be sewn on your sleeve. Furthermore, I shall speak of you to His Majesty when I make my next report."

And the Lord Mayor, with another ceremonious bow to Mary Poppins, swept majestically away, humbly followed by the two Aldermen.

The Park Keeper, looking as though he were not sure if he were on his head or his heels, stared after them. Then he turned his popping eyes to the statue and stared again at that. The Marble Boy and his marble fish gazed thoughtfully down at the Lake. They were as still and quiet and silent as they had always been.

"Now home again, home again, jiggety-jog!" Mary Poppins raised a beckoning finger and the children followed without a word. The Half-crown lay in Michael's palm, burning and bright and solid. And cold as the marble hand of Neleus was the book beneath Jane's arm.

Along the Walk they marched in silence thinking their secret thoughts. And presently, on the grass behind them, there came the thud of feet. They turned to find the Park Keeper running heavily towards them. He had taken off his coat and was waving it, like a blue-and-red flag, at the end of his walking stick. He pulled up, panting, beside the perambulator and held out the coat to Mary Poppins.

"Take it!" he said breathlessly. "I just been looking at that Boy back there. He's wearin' yours — with the four pink buttons. And you'll need one when it gets chilly."

Mary Poppins calmly took the coat and slipped it over her shoulders. Her own reflection smiled conceitedly at her from the polished brass buttons.

"Thank you," she said primly, to the Park Keeper.

He stood before her in his shirt-sleeves, shaking his head like a puzzled dog.

"I suppose *you* understand what it all means?" he said wistfully.

"I suppose I do," she replied smugly.

And without another word, she gave the perambulator a little push and sent it bowling past him. He was still staring after her, scratching his head, as she passed through the gate of the Park.

Mr. Banks, on his way home from the Office, whistled to them as they crossed the Lane.

"Well, Mary Poppins!" he greeted her. "You're very smart in your blue-and-red jacket! Have you joined the Salvation Army?"

"No, sir," she replied, primly. And the look she gave him made it quite clear she had no intention of explaining.

"It's the Park Keeper's coat," Jane told him hurriedly.

"He gave it to her just now," added Michael.

"What — Smith? He gave her the jacket of his uniform? Whatever for?" exclaimed Mr. Banks.

But Jane and Michael were suddenly silent. They could feel Mary Poppins' gimlet eyes making holes in the backs of their heads. They dared not go on with the story.

"Well, never mind!" said Mr. Banks calmly. "I suppose she did something to deserve it!"

They nodded. But they knew he would never know what she had done, not even if he lived to be fifty. They walked up the garden path beside him, clasping the coin and the book.

And as they went they thought of the child who had
given them those gifts, the Marble Boy who for one short
hour had danced and played in the Park. They thought
of him standing alone on his pedestal, with his arm flung
lovingly round his Dolphin — forever silent, forever still
and the sweet light gone from his face. Darkness would
come down upon him and the stars and the night would
wrap him round. Proud and lonely he would stand there,
looking down upon the waters of the little Lake, dreaming of the great sea and his home so far away. . . .

CHAPTER FIVE

PEPPERMINT HORSES

i!" shouted Mr. Banks, angrily, as he rattled the umbrellas in the Elephant's Leg that stood in the front hall.

"What is it now, George?" called Mrs. Banks, from the foot of the kitchen stairs.

"Somebody's taken my walking sticks!" Mr. Banks sounded like a wounded tiger.

"Here they are, Sir!" said Mary Poppins, as she tripped down from the Nursery. In one hand she carried a silver-headed ebony cane. From the other swung a grey ash stick with a curved nobbly handle. Without another word, and looking very superior, she handed the sticks to Mr. Banks.

"Oh!" he said, rather taken aback. "Why did you want them, Mary Poppins? I hope you haven't got a bad leg!"

"No, thank you, Sir!" she said with a sniff. And you knew by the haughty tone of her voice that Mr. Banks had insulted her. A bad leg, indeed! As if her legs, as well as every other part of her, were not in perfect condition!

"It was us!" said Jane and Michael together, peering out at their Father from behind Mary Poppins.

"You! What's the matter with *your* fat legs? Are they lame, or crippled or what?"

"Nothing's the matter," said Michael plaintively. "We wanted the sticks for horses."

"What! My Great-uncle Herbert's ebony cane and the stick I won in the Church Bazaar!" Mr. Banks could hardly believe his ears.

"Well, we've nothing to ride on!" grumbled Jane.

"Why not the rocking-horse — dear old Dobbin?" called Mrs. Banks from the kitchen.

"I hate old Dobbin. He creaks!" said Michael, and he stamped his foot at his Mother.

"But Dobbin doesn't *go* anywhere. We want real horses!" protested Jane.

"And I'm to provide them, I suppose!" Mr. Banks strode, fuming, down the hall. "Three meals a day are not enough! Warm clothes and shoes are merely trifles! Now you want horses! Horses, indeed! Are you sure you wouldn't prefer a camel?"

Michael looked at his Father with a pained expression. Really, he thought, what shocking behaviour! But aloud he said patiently — —

"No, thank you. Just horses!"

"Well, you'll get them when the moon turns blue! That's all I can say!" snapped Mr. Banks.

"How often does that happen?" Jane enquired.

Mr. Banks looked at her angrily. What stupid children I've got, he thought. Can't understand a figure of speech!

"Oh — every thousand years or so. Once in a life-time — if you're lucky!" he said crossly. And, stuffing the cane into the Elephant's Leg, he hooked the ash stick over his arm and started for the City.

Mary Poppins smiled as she watched him go. A curious, secret smile it was, and the children wondered what it meant.

Mrs. Banks came bustling up the kitchen stairs. "Oh dear! Mary Poppins, what do you think! Miss Lark's dog Willoughby has just been in and eaten a tyre off the perambulator!"

"Yes, ma'am," replied Mary Poppins calmly, as though nothing that Willoughby ever did could possibly surprise her.

"But what shall we do about the shopping?" Mrs. Banks was almost in tears.

"I really couldn't say, I'm sure." Mary Poppins gave her head a toss, as though neither dogs nor perambulators were any concern of hers.

"Oh, must we go shopping?" grumbled Jane.

"I'm sick of walking," said Michael crossly. "I'm sure it's bad for my health."

Mrs. Banks took no notice of them. "Perhaps, Mary Poppins," she suggested nervously, "you could leave Annabel at home today and take Robertson Ay to carry the parcels."

"He's asleep in the wheelbarrow," Jane informed them.

She had looked through the window, just after breakfast, and seen him taking his morning rest.

"Well, he won't be there long," said Mary Poppins. And she stalked out into the garden.

She was quite right. He wasn't there long. She must have said something Really Awful, for as they trailed after her down the path Robertson Ay was waiting at the garden gate.

"Keep up and don't straggle, if you please! This is not a Tortoise Parade." Mary Poppins took a Twin by each hand and hurried them along beside her.

"Day in and day out, it's always the same. I never get a moment's peace." Robertson Ay gave a stifled yawn as he handed Jane his hat to carry and stumbled along beside her.

Down the High Street marched Mary Poppins, glancing at the windows now and again to admire her own reflection.

Her first stop was at Mr. Trimlet's — Ironmonger, Hardware and Garden Tools.

"One mouse-trap!" she said haughtily, as she darted in at the door of the shop and read from Mrs. Banks' list.

Mr. Trimlet was a bony man with a large purplish face. He was sitting behind the counter with his hat on the back of his head. And the morning paper was propped around him like an old Chinese screen.

"Only one?" he asked rudely, peering round the edge of

the screen to look at Mary Poppins. "Sorry, Miss!" he said with a leer. "But one trap wouldn't be worth me while!" He shook his head and was about to turn away when he caught the look on her face. His purple cheeks turned the colour of lilac.

"Just my joke," he said hurriedly. "No offence meant! Why, I'd sell 'alf a mouse-trap if I thought *you* wanted it. Not to mention a nice bit o' cheese to go with it."

"One mincing machine," said Mary Poppins, as she fixed him with a stare.

"And I'll throw in a pound of steak for luck," said Mr. Trimlet eagerly.

Mary Poppins took no notice.

"Half-a-dozen pot cleaners, one tin of bees' wax, one floor mop," she read out quickly.

"Setting up 'ouse?" enquired Mr. Trimlet, smiling nervously as he tied up the parcels.

"A packet of nails and a garden rake," she went on. She looked right through his purple face as though it were made of glass.

"And wot about the sawdust?" he enquired. "All that wot them children has spilt?"

Mary Poppins spun round. Jane and Michael and the Twins were sitting comfortably on a fat brown sack, and their weight had squeezed a stream of sawdust out on to the floor. Her eyes blazed.

"If you don't get up this minute —— " she began. And

her voice was so frightful that they sprang to their feet without waiting to hear the rest of the sentence. Robertson Ay, who had been asleep on a garden-roller, woke up with a start and began to collect the parcels.

"We were only resting our legs —— " Michael began.

"One More Word and you'll find yourself resting in Bed! I warn you!" she told him fiercely.

"I'll make no charge," declared Mr. Trimlet, as he hurriedly swept up the sawdust. "Seein' it's you!" he added eagerly, still trying to be friendly.

Mary Poppins gave him a contemptuous stare.

"There's paint on your nose," she announced calmly, and stalked out of the shop.

Then off she went, like a human whirlwind, speeding up the High Street. And off went the children and Robertson Ay, wheeling behind her like the tail of a comet.

At the Baker's she bought a loaf of bread, two boxes of tarts and some ginger biscuits.

"Don't mind me," sighed Robertson Ay as she piled them into his arms.

"I won't!" she retorted cheerfully, as she hurried on to the Greengrocer's for peas, beans and cherries.

"The Last Straw breaks the Camel's back," said Robertson Ay, as she thrust them at him.

"So they say!" she remarked with a chilly smile and consulted her list again.

The next place was the Stationer's, where she bought a bottle of ink; and then she went to the Chemist for a packet of mustard plasters.

By now they had come to the end of the High Street. But still Mary Poppins did not stop. The children looked at each other and sighed. There were no more shops. Where could she be going?

"Oh, dear, Mary Poppins, my legs are breaking!" said Michael, limping pathetically.

"Can't we go home now, Mary Poppins? My shoes are worn out!" complained Jane.

And the Twins began to whimper and whine like a couple of fretful puppies.

Mary Poppins regarded them all with disgust.

"A set of Jellyfish — that's what you are! You haven't a backbone between you!"

And popping the shopping-list into her bag, she gave a quick contemptuous sniff and hurried round the corner.

"A Jellyfish swims," said Michael angrily. "And it doesn't have to go shopping!" He was so tired that he almost didn't care whether Mary Poppins heard him or not.

The breeze blew gently from the Park, full of the scents of the morning. It smelt of laurel leaves and moss, and something else that was vaguely familiar. What could it be? Jane sniffed the air.

"Michael!" she whispered. "I smell Peppermint!"

Michael sniffed like a sulky little dog.

"Um-hum," he admitted, "I do, too!"

And then it was that they both noticed the red-and-green umbrella. It stood beside the iron railings on the Town side of the Park. Against it leaned a large white signboard.

MISS CALICO

CONFECTIONER

HORSES FOR HIRE

said the words in big black letters.

The children stared.

For beneath the red-and-green umbrella sat one of the strangest little figures they had ever seen. At first they could not make out what it was, for it sparkled and glittered like a diamond. Then they saw that it was a small elderly lady with a skinny, leathery, yellow face and a mane of short white hair. The glitter and sparkle came from her dress, which was covered from collar to hem with pins. They stuck out all over her, like the quills of a hedgehog, and whenever she moved they flashed in the sunlight. In her hand she held a riding-whip. And every now and again she cracked it at one of the passers-by.

"Peppermint Candy! Bargain Prices! All of it made of Finest Sugar!" she cried in a little whinnying voice as the whip swished through the air.

"Come on, Michael!" said Jane excitedly, forgetting how tired she was.

He took her hand and let her drag him towards the striped umbrella. And as they drew nearer the sparkling figure, they saw a sight that filled them with hunger. For beside her stood a pottery jar that was filled with peppermint walking-sticks.

> "Sugar and Spice
> And all that's nice
> At a Very Special
> Bargain Price!"

sang the little old lady, cracking her whip.

And just at that moment she turned her head and spied the straggling group. Her dark eyes glittered like little black currants as she thrust out a bird-like hand.

"Well, I never! If it isn't Mary Poppins! I haven't seen you in a month of Tuesdays!"

"The same to you, so to speak, Miss Calico!" Mary Poppins replied politely.

"Well, it all just goes to show!" said Miss Calico. "If you know what I mean!" she added, grinning. Then her bright black gaze fell upon the children.

"Why, Mercy Me and a Jumping Bean! What a quartet of sulky faces! Cross-patch, draw the latch! You all look as if you'd lost something!"

"Their tempers," said Mary Poppins grimly.

Miss Calico's eyebrows went up with a rush, and her pins began to flash.

"Thundering Tadpoles! Think of that! Well, what's lost must be found — that's the law! Now — where did you lose 'em?"

The little black eyes went from one to another and somehow they all felt guilty.

"I think it must have been in the High Street," said Jane in a stifled whisper.

"Tut! Tut! All that way back? And *why* did you lose 'em, might one ask?"

Michael shuffled his feet and his face grew red. "We

didn't want to go on walking——" he began shamefac-
edly. But the sentence was never finished. Miss Calico interrupted him with a loud shrill cackle.

"Who does? Who does? I'd like to know? Nobody
wants to go on walking. I wouldn't do it myself if you paid
me. Not for a sackful of rubies!"

Michael stared. Could it really be true? Had he found
at last a grown-up person who felt as he did about walking?

"Why, I haven't walked for centuries," said Miss Calico.
"And what's more, none of my family does. What — stump
on the ground on two flat feet? They'd think that quite
beneath them!" She cracked her whip and her pins flashed
brightly as she shook her finger at the children.

"Take my advice and always ride. Walking will only
make you grow. And where does it get you? Pretty near
nowhere! Ride, I say! Ride — and see the world!"

"But we've nothing to ride on!" Jane protested, looking round to see what Miss Calico rode. For, in spite of
the notice "Horses for Hire" there wasn't even a donkey
in sight.

"Nothing to ride on? Snakes alive! That's a very unfortunate state of affairs!"

Miss Calico's voice had a mournful sound but her black
eyes twinkled impishly as she glanced at Mary Poppins.
She gave a little questioning nod and Mary Poppins nodded back.

"Well, it might have been worse!" cried Miss Calico, as she whipped up a handful of sticks. "If you can't have horses — what about these? *At* least they'll help you along a bit. I can let you have 'em for a pin apiece."

The scent of peppermint filled the air, The four lost tempers came creeping back as they searched their clothes for pins. They wriggled and giggled, and peeked and pried, but never a pin could they find.

"Oh, what shall we do, Mary Poppins?" cried Jane. "We haven't a pin between us!"

"I should hope not!" she replied, with a snort. "The children *I* care for are properly mended."

She gave a little disgusted sniff. Then turning back the lapel of her coat, she handed a pin to each of the children. Robertson Ay, who was dozing against the railings, woke up with a start as she handed him another.

"Stick 'em in!" shrieked Miss Calico, leaning towards them. "Don't mind if they prick. I'm too tough to feel 'em!"

They pushed their pins in among the others and her dress seemed to shine more brightly than ever as she handed out the sticks.

Laughing and shouting, they seized and waved them and the scent of peppermint grew stronger.

"I shan't mind walking now!" cried Michael, as he nibbled the end of his stick. A shrill little cry broke on the air, like a faint protesting neigh. But Michael was sampling the Peppermint Candy and was far too absorbed to hear it.

"I'm not going to eat mine," Jane said quickly. "I'm going to keep it always."

Miss Calico glanced at Mary Poppins and a curious look was exchanged between them.

"If you can!" said Miss Calico, cackling loudly. "You may keep 'em *all*, if you can — and welcome! Stick 'em in firmly, don't mind me!" She handed a stick to Robertson Ay as he stuck his pin in her sleeve.

"And now," said Mary Poppins politely, "if you'll excuse us, Miss Calico, we'll get along home to dinner!"

"Oh, wait, Mary Poppins!" protested Michael. "We haven't bought a stick for you!" An awful thought had come to him. What if she hadn't another pin? Would he have to share his stick with her?

"Humph!" she said, with a toss of her head. "*I'm* not afraid of breaking my legs, like some people I could mention!"

"Tee-hee! Ha-ha! Excuse me laughing! As if *she* needed a walking stick!"

Miss Calico gave a bird-like chirp, as though Michael had said something funny.

"Well, pleased to have met you!" said Mary Poppins, as she shook Miss Calico's hand.

"The Pleasure is mine, I assure you, Miss Poppins! Now, remember my warning! Always ride! Good-bye,

good-bye!" Miss Calico trilled. She seemed to have quite
forgotten the fact that none of them had any horses.

"Peppermint Candy! Bargain Prices! All of it made of
the Finest Sugar!" they heard her shouting as they turned
away.

"Got a Pin?" she enquired of a passer-by, a well-dressed
gentleman wearing an eye-glass. He carried a brief-case
under his arm. It was marked in gold letters

LORD CHANCELLOR
DISPATCHES

"Pin?" said the gentleman. "Certainly not! Where
would *I* get such a thing as a Pin?"

"Nothing for nothing, that's the law! You can't get a
stick if you've got no pin!"

"Take one o' mine, duck! I got plenty!" said a large
fat woman who was tramping past. She hitched a basket
under her arm and, plucking a handful of pins from her
shawl, she offered them to the Lord Chancellor.

"One Pin Only! Bargain Prices! Never Pay Two when
you're asked for One!" Miss Calico cried in her hen-
like cackle. She gave the Lord Chancellor a stick and he
hooked it over his arm and went on.

"You and your laws!" said the fat woman laughing,
as she stuck a pin in Miss Calico's skirt. "Well, gimme
a strong one, ducky, do! I'm hardly a Fairy Fay!" Miss

Calico gave her a long, thick stick and she grasped the
handle in her hand and leaned her weight against it.

"Feed the birds! Tuppence a bag! Thank you, my dear!"
cried the fat woman gaily.

"Michael!" cried Jane, with a gasp of surprise, "I do believe it's the Bird Woman!"

But before he had a chance to reply, a very strange
thing happened. As the fat woman leaned her weight on
the stick it gave a little upward swing. Then, swooping under her spreading skirts, it heaved her into the air.

"Ups a daisy! 'Ere I go!" The Bird Woman seized the
peppermint handle and wildly clutched her basket.

Off swept the walking stick over the pavement and up

across the railings. A long, loud neighing filled the air and the children stared in amazement.

"Hold tightly!" Michael shouted anxiously.

"'Old tight yourself!" the Bird Woman answered, for his stick was already leaping beneath him.

"Hi, Jane! Mine's doing it, too!" he shrieked, as the stick bore him swiftly away.

"Be careful, Michael!" Jane called after him. But just at that moment her own stick wobbled and made a long plunge upwards. Away it swooped on the trail of Michael's, with Jane astride its pink-and-white back. Over the laurel hedge she rode and as she cleared the lilac bushes a crackling shape sped past her. It was Robertson Ay with his arms full of parcels. He was lying lengthways along his stick and dozing as he rode.

"I'll race you to the oak tree, Jane!" cried Michael, as she trotted up.

"Quietly, please! No horseplay, Michael! Put your hats straight and follow me!"

Mary Poppins, on her parrot umbrella, rode past them at a canter. Neatly and primly, as though she were in a rocking chair, she sat on the black silk folds. In her hand she held two leading strings attached to the Twins' pink sticks.

"All of 'em made of the Finest Sugar!" Miss Calico's voice came floating up as the earth fell away beneath them.

"She's selling hundreds of sticks!" cried Michael. For the sky was quickly filling with riders.

"There goes Aunt Flossie — over the dahlias!" cried Jane, as she pointed downwards. Below them rode a middle-aged lady. Her feather boa streamed out on the wind and her hat was blowing sideways.

"So it is!" said Michael, staring with interest. "And there's Miss Lark — with the dogs!"

Above the weeping-willow trees a neat little peppermint stick came trotting. On its back sat Miss Lark, looking rather nervous, and behind her rode the dogs. Willoughby, looking none the worse for the perambulator tyre, smiled rudely at the children. But Andrew kept his eyes tight shut as heights always made him giddy.

Ka-lop! Ka-lop! Ka-lop! Ka-lop! came the sound of galloping hooves.

"Help! Help! Murder! Earthquakes!" cried a hoarse, distracted voice.

The children turned to see Mr. Trimlet riding madly up behind them. His hands clung tightly to the Peppermint Candy and his face had turned quite white.

"I tried to eat my stick," he wailed, "and look what it did to me!"

"Bargain Prices! Only one Pin! You get what you give!" came Miss Calico's voice.

By this time the sky was like a race-course. The riders came from all directions; and it seemed to the children that everyone they knew had bought a peppermint horse. A man in a feathered hat rode by and they recognised him as one of the Aldermen. In the distance they caught a glimpse of the Matchman, as he trotted along on a bright pink stick. The Sweep raced past with his sooty brushes and the Ice Cream Man cantered up beside him, licking a Strawberry Bar.

"Out of the way! Make room! Make room!" cried a loud, important voice.

And they saw the Lord Chancellor dashing along at break-neck speed. He leaned low over the neck of his stick as though he were riding a Derby Winner. His eye-glass was firmly stuck in his eye and his briefcase bounced up and down as he rode.

"Important Dispatches!" they heard him shout. "I must get to the Palace in time for Lunch! Make room! Make room!" And away he galloped and soon was out of sight.

What a commotion there was in the Park! Everyone jostled everyone else. "Get up!" and "Whoa there!" the riders yelled. And the walking sticks snorted like angry horses.

"Keep to the Left! No overtaking!" the Park Keeper cried, as he cantered among them.

"No Parking!" he bawled. "Pedestrians Crossing! Speed Limit Twenty Miles an Hour!"

"Feed the Birds! Tuppence a Bag!" The Bird Woman trotted among the crowd. She moved through a tossing

"Out of the way! Make room! Make room!"

surge of wings — pigeons and starlings, blackbirds and sparrows. "Feed the Birds! Tuppence a Bag!" she cried as she tossed her nuts in the air.

The Park Keeper pulled up his stick and shouted.

"Why, Mother, wot are *you* doin' 'ere? You ought to be down at St. Paul's!"

" 'Ullo, Fred, my boy! I'm feedin' the Birds! See you at Tea-time! Tuppence a Bag!"

The Park Keeper stared as she rode away.

"I never saw 'er do that before, not even when I was a boy! 'Ere! Whoa, there! Look where you're goin'!" he cried, as a bright pink walking stick streaked by.

On it rode Ellen and the Policeman who were off for their Afternoon Out.

"Oh! Oh!" shrieked Ellen. "I daren't look down! It makes me feel quite giddy!"

"Well, don't, then. Look at me instead!" said the Policeman, holding her round the waist as their stick galloped swiftly away.

On and on went the peppermint walking sticks and their pinkness shone in the morning sun. Over the trees they bore their riders, over the houses, over the clouds.

Down below them Miss Calico's voice grew fainter every moment.

"Peppermint Candy! Bargain Prices! All of them made of the Finest Sugar!"

And at last it seemed to Jane and Michael that the voice

was no longer Miss Calico's, but the faint shrill neigh of a little horse in a very distant meadow.

They threaded their way through the crowding riders, bouncing upon their peppermint sticks. The wind ran swiftly by their faces and the echo of hooves was in their ears. Oh, where were they riding? Home to dinner? Or out to the uttermost ends of the earth?

And ever before them, showing the way, went the figure of Mary Poppins. She sat her umbrella with elegant ease, her hands well down on its parrot head. The pigeon's wing flew at a perfect angle, not a fold of her dress was out of place. What she was thinking, they could not tell. But her mouth had a small self-satisfied smile as though she were thoroughly pleased with herself.

Cherry-Tree Lane grew nearer and nearer. The Admiral's telescope shone in the sun.

"Oh, I wish we need never go down!" cried Michael.

"I wish we could ride all day!" cried Jane.

"I wish to be home by One O'clock. Keep up with me, please!" said Mary Poppins. She pointed the beak of her parrot umbrella towards Number Seventeen.

They sighed, though they knew it was no good sighing. They patted the necks of their walking sticks and followed her downwards through the sky.

The garden lawn, like a bright green paddock, rose slowly up to meet them. Down to it raced the peppermint sticks, rearing and prancing like polo ponies. Robertson

Ay was the first to land. His stick pulled up in the pan-sy bed and Robertson opened his eyes and blinked. He yawned and gathered his parcels together and staggered into the house.

Down past the Cherry-Trees trotted the children. Down, down, till the grasses grazed their feet, and the sticks stood still on the lawn.

At the same moment, the parrot-headed umbrella, its black silk folds like a pair of wings, swooped down among the flowers. Mary Poppins alighted with a ladylike jump. Then she gave the umbrella a little shake and tucked it under her arm. To look at that neat, respectable pair, you would never have guessed they had crossed the Park in such a curious fashion.

"Oh, what a glorious ride!" cried Michael. "How lucky you had those pins, Mary Poppins!" He rushed to her across the lawn and hugged her round the waist.

"Is this a garden or a Jumble Sale? I'll thank you to let me go!" she snapped.

"I'll never lose my temper again! I feel so sweet and good!" said Jane.

Mary Poppins smiled disbelievingly. "How very unu-sual!" she remarked, as she stooped to pick up the sticks.

"I'll take mine, Mary Poppins!" said Michael, as he made a grab at a sugary handle.

But she swung the walking sticks over her head and stalked away into the house.

"I won't eat it, Mary Poppins!" he pleaded. "I shan't even nibble the handle!"

Mary Poppins took not the slightest notice. Without a word she sailed upstairs with the walking sticks under her arm.

"But they're ours!" complained Michael, turning to Jane. "Miss Calico told us to keep them!"

"No, she didn't," said Jane, with a shake of her head. "She said we might keep them if we could."

"Well, of course we can!" said Michael stoutly. "We'll keep them to ride on always!"

And indeed, the sight of the walking sticks, as they stood in a corner by Mary Poppins' bed, was very reassuring. For who, the children fondly thought, would want to steal four sticky poles of sugar? Already the pink-and-white-striped sticks seemed part of the nursery furniture.

They leaned together with handles locked, like four faithful friends. Not a movement came from any of them. They were just like any other sticks, quietly waiting in a dusty corner to go for a walk with their owners. . . .

The afternoon passed and bed-time came and the scent of peppermint filled the Nursery. Michael sniffed as he hurried in from his bath.

"They're all right!" he whispered, as Jane came in. "But I think we should stay awake tonight and see that nothing happens."

Jane nodded. She had seen those sticks do curious things and she felt that Michael was right.

So, long after Mary Poppins had gone, they lay awake and stared at the corner. The four dim shapes stood still and silent beside the neat camp bed.

"Where shall we go tomorrow?" asked Michael. "I think I'll ride over to see Aunt Flossie and ask her how she liked it." He gave a yawn and shut his right eye. He could see just as well with one, he thought. And the other could take a rest.

"I'd like to see Timbuctoo," said Jane. "It has such a beautiful sound."

There was a long pause.

"Don't you think that's a good idea, Michael?"

But Michael did not answer. He had closed the other eye — just for a moment. And in that moment he had fallen asleep.

Jane sat up, faithfully watching the sticks. She watched and watched and watched and watched, till her head fell sideways upon the pillow.

"Timbuctoo," she murmured drowsily, with her eyes on the slender shapes in the corner. And after that she said nothing more because she was much too sleepy. . . .

Downstairs the Grandfather Clock struck ten. But Jane did not hear it. She did not hear Mary Poppins creep in and undress beneath her cotton nightgown. She did not

hear Mr. Banks locking the doors, nor the house as it settled down for the night. She was dreaming a beautiful
dream of horses and through it came Michael calling her
name.

"Jane! Jane! Jane!" came the urgent whisper.

She sprang up and tossed the hair from her eyes.
Beyond Mary Poppins' sleeping shape she could see
Michael sitting on the edge of his bed with his finger to
his lips.

"I heard a funny noise!" he hissed.

Jane listened. Yes! She heard it, too. She held her breath
as she caught the sound of a high, shrill, faraway whistle.

"Whew — ee! Whew — ee!"

It came nearer and nearer. Then, suddenly, from the
night outside, they heard a shrill voice calling.

"Come, Sugar! Come, Lightfoot! Come, Candy!
Come, Mint! Don't wait or you'll be late. That's the law!"

And at the same moment there was a quick scuffle in
the corner by Mary Poppins' bed.

Rattle! Clash! Bang! Swoop!

And the four walking sticks, one after another, rose up
and leapt out of the window.

In a flash the children were out of bed and leaning
across the sill. All was darkness. The night had not a single star. But over the Cherry-Trees something shone with
a queer unearthly brilliance.

It was Miss Calico. She flashed like a little silver hedgehog, as she rode through the sky on a peppermint stick. Her whip made little cracks in the air and her whistle pierced the still, dark night.

"Come up, you slow-coaches!" she screamed, as the four sticks followed her, neighing wildly.

"Dancer, you donkey, come up!" she called. And from somewhere, down by the kitchen steps, another stick came trotting.

"That must be Robertson Ay's!" said Jane.

"Where are you, Trixie? Come up, my girl!" Miss Calico cracked her whip again. And out from Miss Lark's best bedroom window another stick leapt to join the throng.

"Come, Stripe! Come Lollipop! Dapple and Trot!" From every direction the sticks came racing.

"Shake a leg, Blossom! Look sharp, there, Honey! Those who roam, must come home. That's the law!" She whistled them up and cracked her whip and laughed as they leapt through the air towards her.

The whole sky now was studded with sticks. It rang with the thunder of galloping hooves and the trumpeting neighs of peppermint horses. At first they looked like small black shadows with the colour gone from their shining backs. But a glow of moonrise came from the Park and soon they appeared in all their brightness. They shone and shimmered as they galloped; their pink legs flashed in the rising light.

"Come up, my fillies! Come up, my nags! All of you made of the Finest Sugar!"

High and sweet came Miss Calico's voice, as she called her horses home. Crack! went her whip as they trotted behind her, snorting and tossing their peppermint heads.

Then the moon rose, full and round and clear, above the trees of the Park. And Jane, as she saw it, gave a gasp and clutched her brother's hand.

"Oh, Michael! Look! It's blue!" she cried.

And blue indeed it was.

Out from the other side of earth the great blue moon came marching. Over the Park and over the Lane it spread its bright blue rays. It hung from the topmost peak of the sky, and shone like a lamp on the sleeping world.

And across its light, like a flock of bats, rode Miss Calico and her string of horses. Their shapes sped past the big blue moon and flashed for a moment in its brightness. Then away went the racing peppermint sticks, through the distant shining sky. The crack of the whip grew smaller and smaller. Miss Calico's voice grew far and faint. Till at last it seemed as though she and her horses had faded into the moonlight.

"All of them made of the Finest Sugar!"

A last small echo came floating back.

The children leaned on the window-sill and were silent for a moment.

Then Michael spoke.

"We couldn't keep them, after all," he said in a mournful whisper.

"She never meant us to," said Jane, as she gazed at the empty sky.

They turned together from the window, and the moon's blue light streamed into the room. It lay like water upon the floor. It crept across the children's cots till it reached the bed in the corner. Then, full and clear and bold and blue, it shone upon Mary Poppins. She did not wake. But she smiled a secret, satisfied smile as though, even in her deepest dreams, she was thoroughly pleased with herself.

They stood beside her, hardly breathing, as they watched that curious smile. Then they looked at each other and nodded wisely.

"She knows," said Michael, in a whisper. And Jane breathed an answering "Yes."

For a moment they smiled at her sleeping figure. Then they tip-toed back to their beds.

The blue moonlight lay over their pillows. It lapped them round as they closed their eyes. It gleamed upon Mary Poppins' nose as she lay in her old camp bed. And presently, as though blue moons were nothing to her, she turned her face away. She pulled the sheet up over her head and huddled down deeper under the blankets. And soon the only sound in the Nursery was Mary Poppins' snoring.

CHAPTER SIX

HIGH TIDE

nd be sure you don't drop it!" said Mary Poppins, as she handed Michael a large black bottle.

He met the warning glint in her eye and shook his head earnestly.

"I'll be extra specially careful," he promised. He could not have gone more cautiously if he had been a Burglar.

He and Jane and Mary Poppins had been on a visit to Admiral Boom to borrow a Bottle of Port for Mr. Banks. Now it was lying in Michael's arms and he was walking gingerly — pit-pat, pit-pat — like a cat on hot bricks. And dawdling along behind came Jane, holding the Spotted Cowrie Shell that Mrs. Boom had given her.

They had had a wonderful afternoon. The Admiral had sung "I Saw Three Ships a-Sailing" and shown them his full-rigged Ship in a Bottle. Mrs. Boom had provided Ginger Pop and a plate of macaroons. And Binnacle, the retired Pirate who did the Admiral's cooking and mending, had allowed them to look at the Skull and Crossbones tattooed upon his chest.

Yes, thought Michael, looking down at the bottle, it had really been a lovely day.

Then, aloud, he said wistfully, "I wish *I* could have a Glass of Port. I'm sure it must be delicious!"

"Step up, please!" Mary Poppins commanded. "And don't keep scratching at that label, Michael! You are not a Tufted Woodpecker!"

"I can't step up any quicker!" he grumbled. "And why must we hurry, Mary Poppins?" He was thinking that when the bottle was empty he would make a ship to put in it.

"We are hurrying," said Mary Poppins, with awful distinctness, "because this is the Second Thursday and I am going out."

"Oh!" groaned Michael, who had quite forgotten. "That means an evening with Ellen!"

He looked at Jane for sympathy but Jane took no notice. She was holding her Cowrie Shell to her ear and listening to the sound of the sea.

"I can't bear Ellen!" Michael grumbled. "She's always got a cold and her feet are too big."

"I wish I could *see* the Sea!" Jane murmured, as she peered inside the shell.

Mary Poppins gave an impatient snort. "There you go! Wish, wish, wishing — all day long! If it isn't a Glass of Port, it's the Sea! I never knew such a pair for wishing!"

"Well, you never *need* to wish!" said Michael. "You're perfect, just as you are!"

She'll be pleased with that, he thought to himself, as he gave her a flattering smile.

"Humph!" said her disbelieving look. But a dimple danced suddenly into her cheek.

"Get along with you, Michael Banks!" she cried, and hustled them through the gate....

It turned out later, to Michael's surprise, that Ellen had no cold. She had another ailment, however, which went by the name of 'Ay Fever. She sneezed and sneezed till her face grew red. And it seemed to Michael that her feet grew bigger.

"I'm afraid I'll sneeze me 'ead right off!" she said lugubriously. And Michael almost wished she would.

"If there weren't any Thursdays," he said to Jane, "Mary Poppins would *never* go out!"

But, unfortunately, every week had a Thursday and once Mary Poppins was out of the house, it was no good calling her back.

There she went now, tripping down the Lane. She wore her black straw hat with the daisies and her best blue coat with the silver buttons. The children leaned from the nursery window and watched her retreating back. The parrot-head of her umbrella had a perky look, and she walked with a jaunty, expectant air as though she knew that a pleasant surprise awaited her round the corner.

"I wonder where she's going!" said Jane.

"I wish I were going, too!" groaned Michael. "Oh, Ellen, can't you stop sneezing!"

"Colder-hearted than a Toad, that boy is!" observed Ellen to her handkerchief. "As if I did it for choice! A-tishoo!"

She sneezed till the nursery furniture trembled. She sneezed the afternoon away and she sneezed all through supper. She sneezed the five of them through their baths and put them into bed, still sneezing. Then she sneezed on the night-light, sneezed the door shut and sneezed herself down the stairs.

"Thank goodness!" said Michael. "Now, let's do something!"

If Mary Poppins had been on duty they would never have dared to do anything. But nobody took any notice of Ellen.

Jane pattered over to the mantelpiece and took down the Cowrie Shell.

"It's still going on!" she said with delight. "Singing and gently roaring!"

"Good Gracious!" cried Michael, as he, too, listened. "I can even hear the fish swimming!"

"Don't be so silly! What nonsense you talk! Nobody ever heard a fish swim!"

Jane and Michael glanced round hurriedly. Whose voice was that? And where did it come from?

"Well, don't stand goggling at each other! Come on

in!" the strange voice cried. And this time it seemed to come from the Shell.

"It's perfectly simple! Just shut your eyes and hold your breath — and dive!"

"Dive where?" said Michael disbelievingly. "We don't want to hit our heads on the hearth-rug!"

"Hearth-rug? Don't be so silly! Dive!" the voice commanded again.

"Come on, Michael! Stand beside me! At least we can try!" said Jane.

So, holding the Cowrie Shell between them, they shut their eyes and drew in their breath and dived as the voice had told them. To their surprise, their heads hit nothing. But the roaring sound from the Shell grew louder and a wind ran swiftly by their cheeks. Down they went, swooping like a pair of swallows, till suddenly water splashed around them and a wave went over their heads.

Michael opened his mouth and gave a splutter. "Oh, oh!" he cried loudly, "it tastes of salt!"

"Well, what did you think it would taste of? Sugar?" said the same little voice beside them.

"Are you all right, Michael?" Jane called anxiously.

"Ye-yes," he said bravely. "As long as you're there!"

She seized his hand and they dived together through rising walls of water.

"Shan't be long now," the voice assured them. "I can see the lights already."

Lights in the water — how strange! thought Jane. And she opened her eyes for a peep.

Below shone a ripple of coloured flares — blue, rose and silver, scarlet and green.

"Pretty, aren't they?" said the voice in her ear. And, turning, she saw, looking gleefully at her, the round, bright eye of a Sea-Trout. He was perched like a bird on the bough of a tree, whose branches were all of crimson.

"That's coral!" she cried in astonishment. "We must be down in the deeps of the sea!"

"Well, wasn't that what you wanted?" said the Trout. "I thought you wished you could see the sea!"

"I did," said Jane, looking very surprised. "But I never expected the wish to come true."

"Great Oceans! Why bother to wish it, then? I call that simply a waste of time. But come on! We mustn't be late for the Party!"

And before they had time to wonder where the Party was, he swept away through forests of coral and they dived behind him with the greatest of ease.

"Jumping Jellyfish!" cried a frightened voice. "What a start you gave me! It looked like a net!" A large fish darted through a curl of Jane's hair and hurtled away, looking very upset.

"That's the Haddock. He's nervous," the Trout explained. "He's lost so many old friends up there——" he pointed his fin up through the water, "and he's always afraid it's his turn next."

Jane thought how often she had eaten haddock for breakfast and felt a little guilty.

"I'm sorry —— " she began to say, when a loud rough voice interrupted her.

"Move along, please! Don't block up the sea-lanes! Why can't you keep your fins to yourself!" A huge Cod shouldered his way between them.

"Cluttering up the Ocean like this! It's disgraceful! I'll be late for the Party!" He flung an angry glance at the children. "And who are you, anyway?" he demanded.

They were just about to tell him their names when the Trout swam up beside the Cod and whispered in his ear.

"Oh, I see! Well, I hope they've got money to pay for their tickets!"

"Well — no —— " Jane fumbled in her pocket.

"Tch, tch, tch! It's always the way. No method in anyone's madness. Here!" The Cod whisked a couple of flat white discs from a pocket under his tail. "Sand dollars," he explained importantly. "I always keep a few about me. Never know when I may need 'em." He tossed the dollars at the children and floundered away through the coral.

"Silly Old Codger!" remarked the Trout. "You needn't worry about your tickets. You're Guests of Honour. You'll get in free."

Jane and Michael looked at each other in surprise. They had never before been guests of honour and they felt very proud and superior.

"*Who'll* get in free, I'd like to know? Nobody's going

to get in free while I'm around in the Ocean. Nor out, either, if it comes to that!" a grating, sawlike voice informed them.

Jane and Michael spun round. A pair of staring eyes met theirs, and a set of hairy, hungry feelers reached out in every direction. It was an Octopus.

"Yum, yu-u-um!" said the Octopus, leering at Michael. "Bobby Shafto's fat and fair — and just what I need for my Supper!" He reached out one of the dreadful feelers and Michael gave a squeak of terror.

"Oh, no, you don't!" the Trout said quickly. And he whispered a word to the Octopus as Jane whisked Michael away.

"What? Speak up, can't you? I'm hard of hearing! Oh, I see. They belong to — all right, all right!"

The Octopus drew in his feeler regretfully. "We are always delighted," he went on loudly, "to have among us at High Tide anybody belonging to —— "

"What in the Sea is all that chatter? I never get a moment's peace!" a querulous voice broke in.

The children turned in its direction. But all they saw was one small claw waving from inside a shell.

"That's the Hermit Crab!" the Trout explained. "Lives by himself and does nothing but grumble. Shuts up like a clam if anyone speaks to him. But, come! We must hurry. The music's starting."

Soft sounds of music came to their ears as they fol-

lowed him through a tunnel of rock. A faint glow shone
at the end of the tunnel and the music grew louder as they
swam towards it. Then suddenly their eyes were dazzled as a flood of brilliance broke upon them. They had
reached the end of the shadowy tunnel and before them
was the loveliest sight the children had ever seen.

There lay the stretching floor of the sea, sown with soft
lawns of greenest seaweed. It was threaded with paths
of golden sand and dappled with flowers of every colour.
Up from the sand stretched trees of coral, and plumes of
sea-fern lolled on the water. The dark rocks glittered with
shining shells and one of them, the largest of all, was covered with mother-of-pearl. Behind this rock lay a deep
dark cavern, as black as the sky on a moonless night. And
far within it faint lights twinkled as though stars shone in
the depths of the sea.

Jane and Michael, at the tunnel's edge, looked out and
gasped with delight.

Nothing in that bright scene was still. The rocks themselves seemed to bow and swing in the endless ripple of
water. The small fish fluttered like butterflies between the
swaying flowers. And festoons of seaweed, slung from the
coral, were hung with a thousand swinging lights.

Chinese lanterns! thought Jane to herself. But, looking
closer, she saw that the lights were really luminous fish.
They hung by their mouths from the strings of seaweed
and lit up the lawns with their brightness.

The music was playing more loudly now. It came from a little terrace of coral where several Crabs were playing on fiddles. A Flounder was puffing out its cheeks and blowing down a conch shell; while Cornet fish played on silver cornets and a Bass beat time on a big bass drum. About the players swam the bright sea-creatures, darting between the rock and the coral and leaping and plunging in time with the music. Mermaids in necklaces of pearl swam daintily round among the fish. And the silver sheen of tail and fin went sparkling everywhere.

"Oh!" cried Jane and Michael together, for it seemed the only thing to say.

"Well, here you are at last!" said a booming voice, as a big Bronze Seal came flapping towards them. "You're just in time for the Garden Party." He offered a flipper to each of the children and waddled along between them.

"Do you often give Garden Parties?" asked Michael. He was wishing he, too, could live in the sea.

"Oh, dear me, no!" the Seal replied. "Only when High Tide falls on — I say! I say! Were you invited?" He broke off to speak to a large grey shape. "I was told no whales were to be admitted!"

"Get out! Get out! No whales allowed!" came a chorus of fishy voices.

The Whale gave a flick of his monstrous tail and darted between two rocks. He had a large pathetic face and great sad eyes which he turned on the children.

"It's the same each time," he said, shaking his head.

"They say I'm too big, and I eat too much. Can't *you* persuade them to make an Exception? I do want to see the Distant Relative!"

"Whose distant relative?" Jane began, when the Seal interrupted loudly.

"Now, don't be pathetic, Whale. Get moving! Remember the last Unfortunate Incident. He ate up all the Sardine Sandwiches," the Seal said to Jane behind his flipper.

"No Admission Except on Business. All Riff-Raff keep outside the gates. Off with you, now. Swim along! No nonsense!" A fish with a sharp sword on his nose came bustling across the lawns.

"I never have any fun!" blubbered the Whale, as the Seal and the Swordfish chased him away.

Jane felt very sorry for him. "But, after all," she said, turning to Michael, "he does take up a lot of space!"

But Michael was no longer beside her. He had swum away with one of the mermaids who was dabbing at her face with a little pink sponge.

"Well, skirts, I suppose. And blouses and boots," Jane heard him saying as she swam towards them.

The Mermaid turned to Jane and smiled. "I was asking him about fashions up there ——" she nodded upwards through the sea, "and he says they are wearing blouses and boots." She spoke the words with a little laugh as though they could not be true.

"And coats," Jane added. "And galoshes, of course!"

"Galoshes?" The Mermaid raised her eyebrows.

"To keep our feet dry," Jane explained.

The Mermaid gave a trill of laughter. "How very extraordinary!" she said. "Down here, we prefer to keep everything wet!" She turned on her tail to swim away when a clear voice suddenly hailed her.

"Hullo, Anemone!" it cried. And out from behind a bed of lilies a silver shape came leaping. At the sight of the children it stopped in mid-water and stared at them with its great bright eyes. "Why, Bless my Sole!" it cried in surprise. "Whoever caught those creatures?"

"Nobody," tinkled the Mermaid gaily, as she whispered behind her hand.

"Oh, really? How very delightful!" said the fish, with a supercilious smile.

"I suppose I should introduce myself. I'm the Deep-Sea Salmon," he explained, preening his silver fins. "King of the Fish, you know, and all that. I dare say you've heard of me now and again!" Indeed, by the way he swaggered and preened, you would have thought there was nothing else worth hearing about!

"Refreshments! Refreshments!" said a gloomy voice, as a Pike, with the air of an elderly butler, came hovering past with a tray.

"Help yourself!" said the Salmon, bowing to Jane, "A Sardine Sandwich or a Salted Shrimp? Or Jelly — the fishy kind, of course! And what about you —— ?" he turned to

Michael. "Some Sea-Cow milk or Barnacle Beer? Or perhaps you'd prefer just Plain Sea Water!"

"I was given to h'understand, your 'Ighness, that the h'young gentleman h'wished for Port!" The Pike stared before him gloomily as he held out the tray towards them.

"Then Port he shall have!" said the Salmon imperiously, as he whisked a dark red drink from the tray.

With a start of surprise, Michael remembered his wish. He took the glass and sipped it eagerly. "It's igzactly like Raspberry Fizz!" he cried.

"Good!" said the Salmon conceitedly, as though he had made the Port himself. "Now, how would you like to look at the Catch? They're probably reeling the last ones in and we'll just have time if we hurry!"

"I wonder what has been caught!" thought Jane, as they darted along beside the Salmon. The sea-lanes by now were crowded with fish who were leaping towards the lawn.

"Now! Now! Remember whom you're pushing!" said the Salmon in a haughty voice as he scattered them right and left. "My Fins and Flippers! Look at those children!" He pointed to a group of Sea-Urchins who were tumbling noisily by. "Schoolmaster! Keep an eye on your pupils! This Ocean's becoming an absolute Bear Garden!"

"Eh what?" said an absent-minded fish who was floating along with his nose in a book. "Here, Winkle and

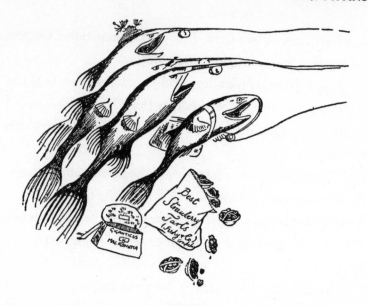

Twinkle! And you, too, Spiky! Behave — or I shan't let you go to the Party!"

The urchins looked at each other and grinned. Then they solemnly swam along with the Schoolmaster, looking as though butter wouldn't melt in their mouths.

"Ah, here we are!" cried the Salmon gaily, as he led the children round a cluster of coral.

On a large flat rock sat a row of fish, all solemnly staring upward. Each fish held a fishing-rod in his fin and watched his line with an earnest gaze as it ran up through the water.

"The Angler-fish," the Salmon explained. "Talk softly! They don't like to be disturbed."

"But —— " whispered Jane, looking very surprised, "the lines are going upwards!"

The Salmon stared. "Where else would they go?" he wanted to know. "You could hardly expect them to go downwards, could you? Bait!" he added, pointing to several water-proof bags that were filled with pastry tarts.

"But — what do they catch?" whispered Michael hoarsely.

"Oh, humans, mostly," the Salmon replied. "You can get almost anyone with a Strawberry Tart. They've taken a pretty good catch already. Look at them squirming and twitching!"

He flicked his tail at a nearby cave and the children gasped with astonishment. For there, looking very cross and disgruntled, stood a cluster of human beings. Men in dark goggles and summer hats were shaking their fists and stamping. Three elderly ladies were waving umbrellas and a younger one in rubber boots was wringing her hands in despair. Beside her holding a shrimping net, stood two disconsolate children.

"Well, how do *you* like it?" jeered the Salmon. "I must say you look extremely funny! Exactly like fish out of water!"

The humans all gave a furious snort and turned their backs on the Salmon. And at the same moment, from somewhere above, a wild cry rent the sea.

"Let me go, I say! Take this hook out at once! How dare you do such a thing to me!"

One of the Angler-fish, smiling quietly, began to reel in his line.

"Take it out, I tell you!" came the voice again.

And down through the sea, with a rush of bubbles, came a most extraordinary figure. Its body was clothed in a thick tweed coat; a grey veil floated from the hat on its head; and upon its feet were thick wool stockings and large-size button boots.

Michael opened his mouth and stared and made a gargling noise.

"Jane! Do you see? I believe it's —— "

"Miss Andrew!" said Jane, who was gargling, too.

And Miss Andrew indeed it was. Down she came, coughing and choking and shouting. The Angler-fish jerked the hook from her mouth and pushed her towards the cave.

"Outrageous! Preposterous!" she spluttered. "How was *I* to know that Tart had a hook on it! You villains!" She shook her fist at the Anglers. "I shall write to *The Times*! I shall have you fried!"

"Look at her writhing!" crowed the Salmon. "She's a whopper! She'll wriggle for hours and hours."

Jane felt that Miss Andrew deserved all she got, but she looked at the children anxiously. How terrible, she thought to herself, if *she* had been caught — or Michael!

"What will the Anglers do with them?" she asked the Salmon earnestly.

"Oh, throw them back again, of course! We only catch them for sport, you know. They're far too tough for eating."

"Hey! Come along, Salmon!" called the Seal from the distance. "We can't let the children miss the Greeting. And she's due to arrive any minute."

Jane looked at Michael in silent question. Who could *she* be? An important Mermaid? Or perhaps the Queen of the Sea!

"Kippers and Catfish! I'd forgotten! Come on, you two!" cried the Salmon.

He went before them, leaping and curving. Beside them a sea-horse trotted swiftly. And fish swam in and out among them as they hurried towards the lawns.

"Hullo, Jane and Michael!" piped a friendly voice. "Remember me — in your goldfish bowl? I'm back at home now. Give my love to your Mother!" The Goldfish smiled and darted away before they had time to answer.

"What a crush! One might as well be tinned!" said the Salmon, threshing his tail.

"Refreshments! Refreshments!" the Pike cried hoarse-ly.

"Yo, ho, ho! And a bottle of rum!" a familiar voice answered. And Admiral Boom came plunging past and seized a glass from the tray. Beside him swam Mrs. Boom's dove-like figure. And, floundering in their wake, came Binnacle.

"Shiver my timbers! Ahoy there, messmates! For I'm bound for the Rio Grande!" bawled the Admiral.

The Pike stared after him, shaking his head. " 'Ooligans — that's what they are!" he said gloomily. "I h'really don't know h'what the h'Ocean's coming to!"

"Ah, there you are, children!" the Bronze Seal cried, as he shouldered his way through the throng. "Hang on to my tail and I'll pull you through. Excuse me! Let me pass, please, fish! These are Jane and Michael, the Guests of Honour!"

The fish drew back and stared at them. Polite murmurs of welcome sounded amid the noise. The Seal pushed the crowd aside with his flippers and dragged the children after him to the rock of shining pearl.

"We're just in time for the Greeting!" he panted. They could hardly hear his booming voice because of the shouting and laughter.

"What greeting?" Jane was about to ask, when, all of a sudden, the shouting ceased. The music and laughter died away and a deep hush fell on the sea. Each fish in the crowd was as still as stone. The swaying flowers stood quiet in the water. And the tide itself was still.

"He's coming!" said the Seal in a whisper, as he nodded towards the cave.

"He's coming!" the watching creatures echoed.

Then, out from the black mysterious cave, a withered head emerged. A pair of ancient sleepy eyes blinked at the dazzle of lights. Two wrinkled flippers stretched from the darkness and a domed black shell heaved up behind them.

The children clutched the Bronze Seal's flippers.

"Who is it?" whispered Jane in his ear. She thought it might be a tortoise, perhaps, or a strange kind of turtle.

"The Terrapin," the Seal replied gruffly. "The oldest and wisest thing in the world."

Inch by inch on trembling flippers the Terrapin crept to the pearly rock. His eyes beneath the half-closed lids were like two small black stars. He gazed at the assembled creatures for a moment. Then lifting his withered, ancient head the Terrapin smiled, and spoke.

"My friends," he began majestically, in a voice like an old, cracked bell, "I greet you, creatures of the Sea! And I wish you a happy High-Tide Party!"

He bowed his withered head to the rock and the fish bowed humbly in the water.

"This is a great occasion for us all," the Terrapin went on quietly. "I am glad indeed to see tonight so many old acquaintances." His black-star gaze swept the crowded

lawns, as though in one glance he recognized every creature in the sea. "But surely," the wrinkled brows went up,
"there is one of us missing!"

The Seal glanced round towards the tunnel and his
voice boomed out with a cry of triumph.

"She is here, my lord! She has just arrived!"

As he spoke a clamour of voices rose and the creatures
clapped and cheered. At the same moment, to the children's amazement, a figure that was strangely familiar appeared at the edge of the tunnel. There it stood, dressed
in its best blue coat and the straw hat trimmed with daisies. Then, dainty and graceful, neat and prim, it swooped
across the shining gardens. The cheering rose to a roar of
joy as it landed upon the Terrapin's rock.

"Welcome, Mary Poppins!" cried a thousand happy
voices.

She waved her parrot umbrella in greeting, then she
turned and curtsied to the Terrapin.

For a long moment he gazed at her, as though his ancient glittering eyes were looking into her heart. Then he
waved his little naked head and gave her a friendly smile.

"My dear young relative!" he said, graciously. "This is
indeed a pleasure. It is long since I had a visitor from the
world above the water. And long, too, since your Second
Thursday fell upon our High Tide. Therefore, in the
name of the creatures of the deep, I bid you welcome,
Mary!" And, blinking, he offered her a small withered
flipper.

Mary Poppins took it and bowed respectfully. Then the china blue eyes looked into the black ones and a strange smile passed between them. It was as though neither of them had any secrets from the other.

"And now, dear Mary," the Terrapin continued, "since nobody comes down to the depths of the sea without taking something away with them, let me give you a little present."

He reached his flipper back into the cave and brought out a small bright object. "Take this to remind you of your visit. It will make a nice brooch, or perhaps a hatpin." And, leaning forward, he pressed a starfish on Mary

Poppins' coat. It shone and twinkled upon the blue like a little cluster of diamonds.

"Oh, thank you!" she said, with a cry of delight. "It's exactly what I wanted!"

She smiled at the Terrapin and then at the star and her glance slid away to the children. The smile faded instantly. She gave a disgusted sniff.

"If I've told you once, Jane, not to gape, I've told you a thousand times! Close your mouth, Michael! You are not a Codfish!"

"I should think not!" muttered the Cod indignantly, from his place behind the children.

"So — these are Jane and Michael!" said the Terrapin, as he turned his sleepy eyes upon them. "I am very glad to meet you at last. Welcome, my children, to our High-Tide Party!"

He bowed gravely and, urged by Mary Poppins' glare, they bowed in return. "You see," he went on in his old, cracked voice, "I know who Jane and Michael are. But I wonder — yes, I wonder indeed, if *they* know who *I* am!"

They shook their heads and gazed at him speechlessly.

He moved his carapace a little and thoughtfully blinked for a moment. Then he spoke.

"I am the Terrapin. I dwell at the roots of the world. Under the cities, under the hills, under the very sea itself, I make my home. Up from my dark root, through the waters, the earth rose with its flowers and forests. The man and the mountain sprang from it. The great beasts, too, and the birds of the air."

He ceased for a moment and the creatures in the sea about him were quiet as they watched him. Then he went on. "I am older than all things that are. Silent and dark and wise am I, and quiet and very patient. Here in my cave all things have their beginning. And all things return to me in the end. I can wait. I can wait . . ."

He folded his lids upon his eyes and nodded his naked wrinkled head as though he were talking to himself. "I have no more to say," he said, blinking. "So —— " he held up a little lordly flipper. "Bid the music play!" he commanded the Seal. "And let the sea-people choose their dance. What shall it be this time, my children?"

"Tiddy-um-pom-pom, tiddy-um-pom-pom!" hummed a voice like a bee in a bottle.

"Ah, yes, my dear Admiral!" the Terrapin nodded. "A very suitable suggestion. Strike up the Sailor's Hornpipe!"

At once a wild commotion rose. The band broke into swift gay music and the still fish flickered their tails again. Voices and laughter filled the sea and the tide began to move.

Tiddy-um-pom-pom! Away they went — fishes and mermaids, urchins, seals.

Tiddy-um-pom-pom! cried Admiral Boom, as he pulled on invisible tarry ropes. Tiddy-um-pom-pom! sang Mrs. Boom, clasping her hands and rocking her feet. Tiddy-um-pom-pom! sang Binnacle loudly, as he thought

"Tiddy-um-pom-pom!"

of his happy pirate days. And the fish danced in and out among them and waved their shining fins.

The Bronze Seal flapped up and down on his tail and the Salmon swooped over the lawns like a bird. The Angler-fish pranced by with their rods and the Swordfish and School-master danced together. And ever among the scaly throng, a dark shape moved like a graceful shadow. Heel and toe, went Mary Poppins as she danced the Hornpipe on the floor of the sea.

The children stood by the pearly rock and stared at the curious scene.

"You find it strange, do you not?" said the Terrapin. "I can see you are feeling all at sea!" He cackled gently at his own little joke.

Jane nodded. "I thought the sea would be so different, but really, it's very like the land!"

"And why not?" said the Terrapin, blinking. "The land came out of the sea, remember. Each thing on the earth has a brother here — the lion, the dog, the hare, the elephant. The precious gems have their kind in the sea, so have the starry constellations. The rose remembers the salty waters and the moon the ebb and flow of the tide. You, too, must remember it, Jane and Michael! There are more things in the sea, my children, than ever came out of it. And I don't mean fish!" the Terrapin smiled. "But I see that your twenty toes are twitching! Be off with you, now, and join the dance."

Jane seized Michael by the hand. Then, because she remembered he was very old, she curtsied to the Terrapin before they darted away.

They plunged together among the fish in time to the beat of the music. Oh, how their bare feet twinkled and pranced! Oh, how their arms waved through the water! And their bodies swayed like strands of seaweed as they went through the steps of the Sailor's Hornpipe.

Tiddy-um-pom-pom! cried the merry music, as Mary Poppins came swimming towards them. She took their hands and they danced together, pulling and rocking through the boughs of coral. Round they went, faster and ever faster, spinning like tops in the spinning water. Till, dazed with the dance and dazzled with lights, they closed their eyes and leaned against her. And her arms went round them, firmly, strongly, as she lifted them through the moving tide.

Tiddy-um-pom-pom! They swung together and the music grew fainter as they swung. Tiddy-um-pom-pom! Oh, the circling sea, that rocks us all in its mighty cradle! Tiddy-um-pom-pom! Oh, Mary Poppins, swing me round like a bubble in the falling tide. Swing me round — tiddy-um . . . Swing me round — pom-pom . . . Swing me . . . Swing me . . . Swing. . . .

"Hold me tight, Mary Poppins!" murmured Michael drowsily, as he felt for her comforting arm.

There was no answer.

"Are you there, Mary Poppins?" he said with a yawn, as he leaned on the rocking sea.

Still no answer.

So, keeping his eyes closed, he called again and the sea seemed to echo his voice. "Mary Poppins, I want you! Mary Poppins, where are you?"

"Where I always am at this hour of the morning!" she replied with an angry snap.

"Oh, what a beautiful dance!" he said sleepily. And he put out his hand to draw her to him.

It touched nothing. All that his searching fingers found was a warm, soft bulkiness suspiciously like a pillow.

"I'll thank you to dance yourself out of bed! It is nearly time for breakfast!"

Her voice had the rumble of distant thunder. And Michael opened his eyes with a start.

Good gracious! Where was he? Surely it could not be the Nursery! Yet there was Old Dobbin standing still in the corner; and Mary Poppins' neat camp bed and the toys and the books and his slippers. All the old familiar things were there but the last thing Michael wanted just now was an old familiar thing.

"But where's the sea gone?" he said crossly. "I want to be back in the sea!"

Her face popped round the bathroom door and he knew at once she was furious.

"The sea is at Brighton where it always is!" she said,

with fierce distinctness. "Now, spit-spot and up you get. And Not Another Word!"

"But I was in it a moment ago! And so were you, Mary Poppins. We were dancing around among the fish and doing the Sailor's Hornpipe!"

"Humph!" she said, giving the bath-mat a shake. "I hope I have something better to do than to go out dancing with sailors!"

"Well, what about all the fish?" he demanded. "And the Seal and the Salmon and that funny old Turtle? We were down there with them, Mary Poppins, right on the floor of the sea!"

"Down in the sea? With a funny old Salmon? Well, you certainly have the fishiest dreams! I suppose you had too many buns for Supper! Sailors and Turtles, indeed! What next?" Her apron gave an angry crackle as she flounced away, muttering.

He gazed at her retreating back and frowned and shook his head. He dared not say any more, he knew, but she couldn't stop him wondering.

So he wondered and wondered as he got out of bed and poked his toes into his slippers. And as he wondered his eyes met Jane's as she peeped from under the blankets. She had heard every word of the argument and while she had listened, she had thought her own thoughts and her eyes had noticed something. Now she smiled a secret smile at Michael and nodded her head wisely.

"It was fishy," she said. "But it wasn't a dream." And she pointed to the mantelpiece.

He looked up. He gave a start of surprise. Then a smile of triumph spread over his face.

For there, beside the Cowrie Shell, were the two Sand Dollars and a little pink Starfish.

"You remember what the Terrapin said? Everyone who goes down to the sea brings something back," Jane reminded him.

Michael nodded as he gazed at the Sand Dollars. And at that moment the door burst open and Mary Poppins bounced back. She plucked the Starfish from the mantelpiece and pinned it to her collar. It twinkled brightly as she prinked and pranked in front of the Nursery mirror.

Michael turned to Jane with a smothered giggle.

"Tiddy-um-pom-pom!" he hummed under his breath.

"Tiddy-um-pom-pom!" Jane said in a whisper.

And, daringly, behind Mary Poppins' stiff straight back, they danced a few steps of the Hornpipe.

They never noticed that her bright blue eyes were watching them in the mirror and calmly exchanging with her own reflection a very superior smile. . . .

CHAPTER SEVEN

HAPPY EVER AFTER

I t was the last day of the Old Year.

Upstairs in the Nursery, Jane and Michael and the Twins were going through that magical performance known as Undressing. When Mary Poppins set to work, it was almost as good as watching a Conjuror!

She moved along the row of children and their clothes seemed to fall away at her touch. Over John's head she pulled the sweater as quickly as though she were skinning a rabbit. Jane's frock dropped off at a single touch; Barbara's socks literally ran off her toes. As for Michael, he always felt that Mary Poppins undressed him simply by giving him one of her looks.

"Now, spit-spot into bed!" she ordered.

And with the words went such a glare that they fled squealing in all directions and darted under the bedclothes.

She moved about the Nursery, folding up the scattered clothes and tidying the toys. The children lay cosily in their beds, watching the crackling wing of her apron as it whisked about the room. Her eyes were blue and her cheeks were pink and her nose turned up with a perky air like the nose of a Dutch Doll. To look at her, they thought to themselves, you would never imagine she was anything but a perfectly ordinary person. But, as you know and I know, they had every reason to believe that Appearances are Deceptive.

Suddenly Michael had an idea that seemed to him very important.

"I say!" he said, sitting up in bed. "When igzackly does the Old Year end?"

"Tonight," said Mary Poppins shortly. "At the first stroke of twelve."

"And when does it begin?" he went on.

"When does what begin?" she snapped.

"The New Year," answered Michael patiently.

"On the last stroke of twelve," she replied, giving a short sharp sniff.

"Oh? Then what happens in between?" he demanded.

"Between what? Can't you speak properly, Michael? Do you think I'm a Mind Reader?"

He wanted to say Yes, for that was exactly what he did think. But he knew he would never dare.

"Between the first and the last stroke," he explained hurriedly.

Mary Poppins turned and glared at him.

"Never trouble Trouble till Trouble troubles you!" she advised priggishly.

"But I'm not troubling Trouble, Mary Poppins. I was only wanting to know——" he broke off quickly, for Mary Poppins' face had a Very Ominous look.

"Then Want must be your Master. Now! If I have One More Word from you——" At the sound of that phrase he dived under the blankets. For he knew very well what it meant.

Mary Poppins gave another sniff and moved along the row of beds, tucking them all in.

"I'll take that, thank you!" she remarked, as she plucked the Blue Duck from John's arms.

"Oh, *no!*" cried John. "Please give him to me!"

"I want my Monkey!" Barbara wailed, as Mary Poppins uncurled her fingers from the moth-eaten body of Pinnie. Pinnie was an old rag Monkey who had belonged first to Mrs. Banks when she was a little girl, and then to each of the children in turn.

But Mary Poppins took no notice. She hurried on to Jane's bed and Alfred, the grey-flannel Elephant, was plucked from under the blankets. Jane sat up quickly.

"But why are you taking the toys?" she demanded. "Can't we sleep with them as we always do?"

Mary Poppins' only answer was an icy glare flung over her shoulder as she stooped to Michael's bed.

"The Pig, please!" she commanded, sternly. She put

out her hand for the small, gilt cardboard Pig that Aunt Flossie had given him for Christmas.

At first the Pig had been filled with chocolates but now he was quite empty. A large hole yawned in the back of his body at the place where the tail should have been. On Christmas Day Michael had wrenched it off to see how it was stuck on. Since then it had lain on the mantelpiece and the Pig had gone without it.

Michael clutched the Golden Pig in his arms.

"No, Mary Poppins!" he said bravely. "He's *my* Pig! And I want him!"

"What did I say?" asked Mary Poppins. And her look was so awful that Michael loosened his hold at once and let her take it from him.

"But what are you going to do with them?" he asked curiously.

For Mary Poppins was arranging the animals in a row on top of the toy-cupboard.

"Ask no Questions and you'll be Told no Lies," she retorted priggishly. Her apron gave another crackle as she crossed the room to the book-case.

They watched her take down three well-known books: *Robinson Crusoe, The Green Fairy Book* and *Mother Goose Nursery Rhymes.* Then she opened them and laid them down in front of the four animals.

Does she mean the animals to read the books? Jane wondered to herself.

"And now," said Mary Poppins, primly, as she moved towards the door, "turn over, all of you — if you please — and go to sleep at once!"

Michael sat bolt upright.

"But I want to stay awake, Mary Poppins, and watch for the New Year!"

"A Watched Pot Never Boils!" she reminded him. "Lie down, please, Michael, in that bed — and don't say Another Word!"

Then, sniffing loudly, she snapped out the light, and shut the Nursery door behind her with an angry little click.

"I will watch all the same," said Michael, as soon as she had gone.

"So will I," agreed Jane quickly, with a very determined air.

The Twins said nothing. They were fast asleep. But it was at least ten minutes before Michael's head fell sideways on his pillow. And quite fifteen before Jane's eyelashes fluttered down on her cheeks.

The four eiderdowns rose and fell with the children's steady breathing.

For a long time nothing stirred the silence of the Nursery.

Ding-dong! Ding-dong! Ding-dong! Ding-dong!

Suddenly, through the silent night, a peal of bells rang out.

Ding-dong! Ring-ting! Ding-dong!

From every tower and steeple the swinging chimes went forth. The bells of the city echoed and tossed and floated across the Park to the Lane. From North and South and East and West they pealed and clanged and chimed. People leaned over their window-sills and rattled their dinner bells. And those who hadn't a dinner bell played tunes on their Front Door knockers.

Along the Lane came the Ice Cream Man, twanging his bicycle bell with gusto. In the garden of Admiral Boom, at the corner, a ship's bell clanged through the frosty air. And Miss Lark, in the Next Door drawing-room, tinkled her little breakfast bell, while the two dogs barked and howled.

Clang-clang! Tinkle-tinkle! Ding-dong! Bow-wow!

Everybody in the world was ringing a bell. The echoes clashed and chimed and rhymed in the chilly midnight dark.

Then all of a sudden, there was silence. And out of the stillness, solemn and deep, the sound of a great clock striking.

"Boom!" said Big Ben.

It was the first stroke of Midnight.

At that moment something stirred in the Nursery. Then came the sound of clattering hooves.

Jane and Michael were wide awake in an instant. They both sat up with a start.

"Goodness!" said Michael.

"Gracious!" said Jane.

For before them lay an astounding sight. There on the floor, stood the Golden Pig, prancing about on his gold hind trotters and looking very important.

Plump! With a heavy muffled thud, Alfred the Elephant landed beside him. And, leaping lightly from the top of the cupboard, came Pinnie the Monkey and the old Blue Duck.

Then, to the children's astonishment, the Golden Pig spoke.

"Will somebody kindly put on my tail?" he enquired in a high, shrill voice.

Michael flung himself out of bed and rushed to the mantelpiece.

"That's better," remarked the Pig, with a smile. "I've been most uncomfortable ever since Christmas. A Pig without a tail, you know, is almost as bad as a tail without a Pig. And now," he went on, as he glanced round the room, "are we all ready? Then, hurry, please!"

As he spoke he pranced daintily to the door, followed by Alfred, Pinnie and the Duck.

"Where are you going?" Jane cried, staring.

"You'll soon see," answered the Pig. "Come on!"

In a flash they had flung on gowns and slippers and were following the four toys down the stairs and out through their own Front Door.

"This way!" said the Pig, as he pranced across Cherry-Tree Lane and through the Gates of the Park.

Pinnie and the Blue Duck danced beside him, wildly squealing and quacking. And after them lumbered Alfred the Elephant with Jane and Michael at his grey-flannel heels.

Above the trees hung a round white moon. Its gleaming silver rays poured down on the wide lawns of the Park. And there on the grass was a throng of figures, moving backwards and forwards in the shimmering light.

Alfred flung up his flannel trunk and eagerly sniffed the air.

"Ha!" he remarked delightedly. "We're safely inside, Pig, don't you think?"

"Inside what?" asked Michael curiously.

"The Crack," said Alfred, flapping his ears.

The children stared at each other. What on earth could Alfred mean?

But the Pig was beckoning them towards him with a wave of his golden trotter; and bright forms flickered behind and around them as they hurried to the lawn.

"Excuse us, please!" said three small shapes as they brushed against the children.

"The Three Blind Mice," explained Alfred, smiling. "They're always under everyone's feet!"

"Are they running away from the Farmer's Wife?" cried Michael, very surprised and excited.

"Oh, dear no! Not tonight," said Alfred. "They're hurrying to meet her. The Three Blind Mice and the Farmer's Wife are all inside the Crack!"

"Hullo, Alfred — you got in safely!"

"Why, it's dear old Pinnie!"

"What, the Blue Duck, too?"

"Hooray, hooray! Here's the Golden Pig!"

There were cries of welcome and shouts of joy as everyone greeted everyone else. A Tin Soldier who was marching past, saluted the Pig and he waved his trotter. Pinnie shook hands with a pair of birds whom he hailed as Cock Robin and Jenny Wren. And the Blue Duck quacked at an Easter Chicken half-in and half-out of its egg. As for Alfred, he flung up his trunk in all directions and loudly trumpeted greetings.

"Aren't you cold, my dear? It's chilly tonight!" A gruff voice spoke behind Jane's shoulder.

She turned to find a bearded man dressed in the strangest garments. He had goatskin trousers, a beaver cap and a large umbrella of rabbit-tails. Behind him, with an armful of furs, stood a black, half-naked figure.

"Friday," said the bearded man. "Oblige me by giving this lady a coat."

"Suttinly, Massa! Ah aims to please!" And the great black creature, with a graceful movement, flung a sealskin cloak about Jane's shoulders.

She stared.

"So you're —— " she began, and smiled at him shyly.

"Of course I am," said the tall man, bowing. "Please call me Robinson! All my friends do. Mr. Crusoe sounds so formal."

"But I thought you were in a book!" said Jane.

"I am," said Robinson Crusoe, smiling. "But tonight someone kindly left it open. And so I escaped, you see!"

Jane thought of the books on top of the toy-cupboard. She remembered how Mary Poppins had opened them before she put out the light.

"Does it often happen?" she questioned eagerly.

"Alas, no! Only at the end of the year. The Crack's

our one and only chance. But, excuse me! I must speak to——"

Robinson Crusoe turned to greet a curious egg-shaped little man who was hurrying past on spindly legs. His pointed head was as bald as an egg and his neck was muffled in a woolen scarf. He stared inquisitively at the children, as he greeted Robinson Crusoe.

"Good Gracious!" cried Michael in surprise. "You're igzackly like Humpty-Dumpty!"

"Like?" shrilled the little man, haughtily. "How can any-one be like himself, I'd like to know? I've heard of people being *un*like themselves — when they've been naughty or eaten too much — but never like. Don't be so silly!"

"But — you're quite whole!" said Michael, staring. "I thought Humpty-Dumpty couldn't be mended."

"Who said I couldn't?" cried the little man, angrily.

"Well, I just thought — er — that all the King's horses and — er — all the King's men——" Michael began to stammer.

"Pooh — horses! What do they know about it? And as for the King's men — stupid creatures! — they only know about horses! And because *they* couldn't put me together, it doesn't say no one else could, does it?"

Not wishing to contradict him, Jane and Michael shook their heads.

"As a matter of fact," Humpty-Dumpty went on, "the King himself mended me — didn't you — heh?"

He shrieked the last words at a round fat man who was holding a crown on his head with one hand and carrying a pie-dish in the other.

"He's just like the King in Mary Poppins' story! He must be Old King Cole!" said Jane.

"Didn't I what?" the King enquired, carefully balancing his pie and his crown.

"Stick me together!" shrieked Humpty-Dumpty.

"Of course I did. Just for tonight, you know. With honey. In the Queen's parlour. But you really mustn't bother me now. My Four-and-Twenty Blackbirds are going to sing and I have to open the Pie."

"There, what did I tell you?" screamed Humpty-Dumpty. "How dare you suggest I'm a Broken Egg!" He turned his back upon them rudely and his big cracked head shone white in the moonlight.

"Don't argue with him! It's no good," said Alfred. "He's

always so touchy about that fall. Here! Step on your own toes! Look who you're pushing!" He turned and made a sweep with his trunk and a crowned Lion lightly leapt aside.

"Sorry!" exclaimed the Lion, politely. "It's such a frightful crush tonight. Have you seen the Unicorn, by the way? Ah, there he is! Hi! Wait a minute!" And, growling softly in his throat, he pounced upon a silvery figure that was daintily trotting by.

"Oh, stop him! Stop him!" Jane cried anxiously. "He's going to beat the Unicorn all round the Town!"

"Not tonight," said Alfred, reassuringly. "You just watch!"

Jane and Michael stared with astonishment as they saw the Lion bowing. Then he took the golden crown from his head and offered it to the Unicorn.

"It's your turn to wear it," the Lion said courteously. Then the two exchanged a tender embrace and danced off into the crowd.

"Children behaving nicely tonight?" they heard the Unicorn enquire of a withered old woman who was dancing past. She was pulling along an enormous Shoe, full of laughing boys and girls.

"Oh, *so* nicely!" cried the Old Woman gaily. "I haven't used my whip once! George Porgie is *such* a help with the girls. They *insist* on being kissed tonight. And as for the boys, they're just *sugar* and spice. *Look* at Red Riding Hood hugging that Wolf! She's trying to teach him to *beg* for supper. Sit down, please, Muffet. And hold on *tight!*"

The Old Woman waved at a fair little girl who sat at the back of the Shoe. She was deep in conversation with

a large black Spider; and as the Shoe went rumbling past, she reached out her hand and patted him gently.

"She's not even running away!" cried Michael. "Why isn't she frightened?" he wanted to know.

"Because of the Crack," said Alfred again, as he hurried them before him.

Jane and Michael couldn't help staring at Red Riding Hood and Miss Muffett. Fancy not being afraid of the Wolf and that black enormous Spider!

Then a filmy whiteness brushed them lightly and they turned to find a shining shape yawning behind its hand.

"Still sleepy, Beauty?" trumpeted Alfred, as he slipped his trunk round her waist.

She patted the trunk and leaned against him.

"I was deep in a dream," she murmured softly. "But the First Stroke, luckily, woke me up!"

As she said that, Michael's curiosity could contain itself no longer.

"But I don't understand!" he burst out loudly. "Everything's upside down tonight! Why doesn't the

Spider frighten Miss Muffett? And the Lion beat the
Unicorn?"

"Alfred has told you," said Sleeping Beauty. "Because
we are all in the Crack."

"*What* crack?" demanded Michael.

"The Crack between the Old Year and the New. The
Old Year dies on the First Stroke of Midnight and the New
Year is born on the Last Stroke. And in between — while
the other ten strokes are sounding — there lies the secret
Crack."

"Yes?" said Jane, breathlessly, for she wanted to know
more.

The Sleeping Beauty gave a charming yawn and smiled
upon the children.

"And inside the Crack all things are as one. The eternal opposites meet and kiss. The wolf and the lamb lie
down together, the dove and the serpent share one nest.
The stars bend down and touch the earth and the young
and the old forgive each other. Night and day meet here,
so do the poles. The East leans over towards the West and
the circle is complete. This is the time and place, my darlings — the *only* time and the *only* place — where everybody lives happily ever after. Look!"

The Sleeping Beauty waved her hand.

Jane and Michael, glancing past it, saw three Bears
hopping clumsily round a little bright-haired girl.

"Goldilocks," explained the Sleeping Beauty. "As safe

and sound as you are. Oh, good-evening, Punch! How's
the baby, Judy?"

She waved to a pair of long-nosed puppets who were
strolling arm in arm. "They're a loving couple tonight,
you see, because they're inside the Crack. Oh, look!"

This time she pointed to a towering figure. His great
feet stamped upon the lawn and his head was as high as
the tallest tree. A huge club was balanced on one shoulder; and perched on the other sat a laughing boy who was
tweaking the big man's ear.

"That's Jack-the-Giant-Killer with his Giant. The two
are bosom friends tonight." The Sleeping Beauty glanced
up, smiling. "And here, at last, come the Witches!"

There was a whirr above the children's heads as a
group of beady-eyed old women swooped through the air
on broomsticks. A cry of welcome rose to greet them as
they plunged into the crowd. Everyone rushed to shake
their hands and the old women cackled with witch-like
laughter.

"Nobody's frightened of them tonight. They're happy
ever after!" The Sleeping Beauty's drowsy voice was like a
lullaby. She stretched her arms about the children and the
three stood watching the thronging figures. A Hare and
a Tortoise danced by together, the Queen and the Knave
of Hearts embraced, and Beauty gave her hand to the
Beast. The lawns bent under the tripping feet and the air
was dizzy with nodding heads as Kings and Princesses,

Jack-the-Giant-Killer with his Giant

Heroes and Witches saluted each other in the Crack between the years.

"Gangway! Gangway! Let me pass!" cried a high, clear
voice.

And far away at the end of the lawn they saw the
Golden Pig. He plunged through the crowd on his stiff
hind legs, dividing it to left and right with a wave of his
golden trotter.

"Make way! Make way!" he shouted importantly. And
the crowd parted and drew aside so that it formed a double row of bowing, curtsying creatures.

For now there appeared, at the heels of the Pig, a figure
that was curiously familiar. A hat with a bow was upon its
head and its coat shone brightly with silver buttons. Its
eyes were as blue as Willow-Pattern and its nose turned
up in an airy way like the nose of a Dutch Doll.

Lightly she tripped along the path, with the Golden Pig
prancing neatly before her. And as she came a cry of greeting rose up from every throat. Hats and caps and crowns
and coronets were tossed into the air. And the moon itself
seemed to shine more brightly as she walked beneath its
rays.

"But why is *she* here?" demanded Jane, as she watched
that shape come down the clearing. "Mary Poppins is not
a fairy-tale."

"She's even better!" said Alfred loyally. "She's a fairy-
tale come true. Besides," he rumbled, "she's the Guest of
the Evening! It was she who left the books open."

Amid the happy shouts of welcome, Mary Poppins bowed to right and left. Then she marched to the centre of the lawn and, opening her black hand-bag, she took out a concertina.

"Choose your partners!" cried the Golden Pig, as he drew a flute from a pocket in his skin and put it to his mouth.

At that command, every creature there turned swiftly to his neighbour. Then the flute broke into a swinging tune; the concertina and the Four-and-Twenty Blackbirds took up the gay refrain; and a white Cat played the chorus sweetly on a hey-diddle Fiddle.

"Can it be *my* cat?" Michael wondered, as he looked for the pattern of flowers and leaves. He had no time to decide, however, for his attention was attracted by Alfred.

The grey-flannel Elephant lumbered past, uttering happy jungle cries and using his trunk as a trumpet.

"May I have the Pleasure, my dear young Lady?" He bowed to the Sleeping Beauty. She gave him her hand and they danced away, Alfred taking care not to tread on her toes and the Sleeping Beauty yawning daintily and looking very dreamy.

Everyone seemed to be choosing a partner or finding a friend in the throng.

"Kiss *me!* Kiss *me!*" cried a group of girls, as they twined their arms round a large fat schoolboy.

"Out of my way, young Georgie Porgie!" cried the Farmer's Wife, dancing with Three Blind Mice.

"Choose your partners!" cried the Golden Pig

And the fat boy plunged off into the crowd with the girls all laughing about him.

"One and two and hop and turn — that's the way it goes." Red Riding Hood, holding the Wolf by the paw, was teaching him how to dance. The Wolf, looking very humble and shy, was watching his feet as she counted.

Jane and Michael could hardly believe their eyes. But before they had time to think about it, a friendly voice hailed them.

"Do you dance?" said Robinson Crusoe gaily, as he took Jane's hand and whirled her away. She swung around, pressed to his goatskin coat, as Michael pranced off in the arms of Man Friday.

"Who is that?" asked Jane as they danced along. For there was the Blue Duck waddling past, clasped to the bosom of a large grey bird.

"That's Goosey Gander!" said Robinson Crusoe. "And there is Pinnie — with Cinderella."

She glanced round quickly. And there, sure enough, was old rag Pinnie, looking very important and proud of himself as he danced with a beautiful Lady.

Everybody had a partner. No one was lonely or left out. All the fairy-tales ever told were gathered together on that square of grass, embracing each other with joy.

"Are you happy, Jane?" Michael called to her, as he and Friday went galloping past.

"For ever and ever!" she answered smiling, and for that moment knew it was true.

The music was swifter now and wilder. It tossed among the tossing trees, it echoed above the strokes of the clock. Mary Poppins, the Pig and the Fiddling Cat were bending and swaying as they played. Again and again the Blackbirds sang and never seemed to grow weary. The fairy-tale figures swung about the children; and in their ears the fairy-tale voices were sweetly singing and laughing.

"Happy ever after!" came the echoing cry, from everyone in the Park.

"What was that?" cried Jane to her partner. For behind the shouting and the music, she had heard the boom of the clock.

"Time's nearly up!" said Robinson Crusoe. "That must have been the Sixth Stroke!"

They paused for a moment in their dance and listened to the clock.

Seven! Above the sound rose the fairy-tale music, rocking them all in its golden net.

Eight! said the steady, distant boom. And the dancing feet seemed to move more swiftly.

Nine! The trees themselves were dancing now, bending their boughs to the fairy tune.

Ten! O Lion and Unicorn, Wolf and Lamb! Friend and Enemy! Dark and Light!

Eleven! O fleeting moment! O time on the wing! How short is the space between the years! Let us be happy — happy ever after!

Twelve!

Solemn and deep the last stroke struck.

"Twelve!" The cry went up from every throat and the ring immediately broke and scattered. Bright shapes brushed swiftly past the children, Jack and his Giant, Punch and Judy. Away sped the Spider with Miss Muffett; and Humpty-Dumpty on his spindly legs. The Lion, the

Unicorn, Goldilocks, Red Riding Hood and Three Blind Mice — they streamed away across the grass and seemed to melt in the moonshine.

Cinderella and the Witches vanished. The Sleeping Beauty and the Cat with the Fiddle fled, and were lost in light. And Jane and Michael, looking round for their partners, found that Robinson Crusoe and his Man Friday had dissolved into the air.

The fairy-tale music died away, it was lost in the lordly peal of bells. For now from every tower and steeple the chimes rang out, triumphant. Big Ben, St. Paul's, St. Bride's, Old Bailey, Southwark, St. Martin's, Westminster, Bow.

But one bell sounded above the others, merry and clear and insistent.

Ting-aling-aling-aling! It was different, somehow, from the New Year bells, familiar and friendly and nearer home.

Ting-aling-aling! it cried. And mixed with its echoes was a well-known voice.

"Who wants crumpets?" the voice said loudly, demanding immediate answer.

Jane and Michael opened their eyes. They sat up and stared about them. They were in their beds, under the eiderdowns, and John and Barbara were asleep beside them. The fire glowed gaily in the grate. The morning light streamed through the Nursery window. Ting-aling!

From somewhere down below in the Lane came the sound of the tinkling bell.

"I said 'Who wants crumpets?' Didn't you hear me? The Crumpet Man's down in the Lane."

There was no mistaking it. The voice was the voice of Mary Poppins, and it sounded very impatient.

"I do!" said Michael, hurriedly.

"I do!" echoed Jane.

Mary Poppins sniffed. "Then why not say so at once!" she said snappily. She crossed to the window and waved her hand to summon the Crumpet Man.

Downstairs the front gate opened quickly with its usual noisy squeak. The Crumpet Man ran up the path and knocked at the Back Door. He was sure of an order from Number Seventeen for all the Banks family were partial to crumpets.

Mary Poppins turned away from the window and put a log on the fire.

Michael gazed at her sleepily for a moment. Then he rubbed his eyes and, with a start, he woke up completely.

"I say!" he shouted. "I want my Pig! Where is it, Mary Poppins?"

"Yes!" joined in Jane. "And I want Alfred! And where are the Blue Duck and Pinnie?"

"On the top of the cupboard. Where else would they be?" said Mary Poppins crossly.

They glanced up. There were the four toys standing in a row, exactly as she had left them. And in front of them lay *Robinson Crusoe, The Green Fairy Book* and *Mother Goose Nursery Rhymes*. But the books were no longer open as they had been last night. They were piled upon one another neatly and all were firmly closed.

"But — how did they get back from the Park?" said Michael, very surprised.

"And where is the Pig's flute?" Jane exclaimed. "And your concertina!"

It was now Mary Poppins' turn to stare.

"My — what?" she enquired, with an ominous look.

"Your concertina, Mary Poppins! You played it last night in the Park!"

Mary Poppins turned from the fire and came towards Jane, glaring.

"I'd like you to repeat that, please!" Her voice was quiet but dreadful. "Did I understand you to say, Jane Banks, that I was in the Park last night, playing a musical instrument? Me?"

"But you were!" protested Michael bravely. "We were all there. You and the Toys and Jane and I. We were dancing with the Fairy-tales inside the Crack!"

Mary Poppins stared at them as though her ears had betrayed her. The look on her face was Simply Frightful.

"Fairy-tales inside the Crack? Humph! *You'll* have Fairy-tales inside the Bath-room, if I hear One More Word. *And* the door locked, I promise you! Crack, indeed! Cracked, more likely!"

And turning away disgustedly, she opened the door with an angry fling and hurried down the stairs.

Michael was silent for a minute, thinking and remembering.

"It's funny," he said presently. "I thought it was true. But I must have dreamed it."

Jane did not answer.

She had suddenly darted out of bed and was putting a chair against the toy-cupboard. She climbed up quickly and seized the animals and ran across to Michael.

"Feel their feet!" she whispered excitedly.

He ran his hand over the Pig's trotters; he felt the grey-flannel hooves of Alfred, the Duck's webbed feet and Pinnie's paws.

"They're wet!" he said, with astonishment.

Jane nodded.

"And look!" she cried, snatching their slippers from under the beds and Mary Poppins' shoes from the boot-box.

The slippers were drenched and stained with dew; and on the soles of Mary Poppins' shoes were wet little broken blades of grass, the sort of thing you would expect to find on shoes that have danced at night in the Park.

Michael looked up at Jane and laughed.

"It wasn't a dream, then!" he said happily.

Jane shook her head, smiling.

They sat together on Michael's bed, nodding knowingly at each other, saying in silence the secret things that could not be put into words.

Presently Mary Poppins came in with the crumpets in her hand.

They looked at her over the shoes and slippers.

She looked at them over the plate of crumpets.

A long, long look of understanding passed between the three of them. They knew that she knew that they knew.

"Is today the New Year, Mary Poppins?" asked Michael.

"Yes," she said calmly, as she put the plate down on the table.

Michael looked at her solemnly. He was thinking about the Crack.

"Shall we, too, Mary Poppins?" he asked, blurting out the question.

"Shall you, too, what?" she enquired with a sniff.

"Live happily ever afterwards?" he said eagerly.

A smile, half sad, half tender, played faintly round her mouth.

"Perhaps," she said, thoughtfully. "It all depends."

"What on, Mary Poppins?"

"On you," she said, quietly, as she carried the crumpets to the fire. . . .

CHAPTER EIGHT

THE OTHER DOOR

I t was a Round-the-Mulberry-Bush sort of morning, cold and rather frosty. The pale grey daylight crept through the Cherry-Trees and lapped like water over the houses. A little wind moaned through the gardens. It darted across the Park with a whistle and whined along the Lane.

"Brrrrrr!" said Number Seventeen. "What can that wretched wind be doing — howling and fretting around like a ghost! Hi! Stop that, can't you? You're making me shiver!"

"Whe-ew! Whe — ew! What shall I do?" cried the wind, taking no notice.

A raking noise came from inside the house. Robertson Ay was removing the ashes and laying fresh wood in the fireplaces.

"Ah, *that's* what I need!" said Number Seventeen, as Mary Poppins lit a fire in the Nursery. "Something to warm my chilly old bones. There goes that mournful wind again! I wish it would howl somewhere else!"

"Whe — ee! Whe — ee! When will it be?" sobbed the wind among the Cherry-Trees.

The Nursery fire sprang up with a crackle. Behind their bars the bright flames danced and shone on the window-pane. Robertson Ay slouched down to the broom cupboard to take a rest from his morning labours. Mary Poppins bustled about, as usual, airing the clothes and preparing the breakfast.

Jane had wakened before anyone else, for the howl of the wind had disturbed her. And now she sat on the window-seat, sniffing the delicious scent of toast and watching her reflection in the window. Half of the Nursery shone in the garden, a room made entirely of light. The flames of the fire were warm on her back but another fire leapt and glowed before her. It danced in the air between the houses beneath the reflection of the mantelpiece. Out there another rocking-horse was tossing his dappled head; and from the other side of the window another Jane watched and nodded and smiled. When Jane breathed on the window-pane and drew a face in the misty circle, her reflection did the very same thing. And all the time she was breathing and drawing, she could see right through herself. Behind the face that smiled at her were the bare black boughs of the Cherry-Trees, and right through the middle of her body was the wall of Miss Lark's house.

Presently the front door banged and Mr. Banks went away to the City. Mrs. Banks hurried into the drawing-

room to answer the morning's letters. Down in the kitch-
en Mrs. Brill was having a kipper for breakfast. Ellen had
caught another cold and was busily blowing her nose. And
up in the Nursery the fire went pop! and Mary Poppins'
apron went crackle! Altogether, except for the wind outside, it was a peaceful morning.

Not for very long, however. For Michael burst in with
a sudden rush and stood in the doorway in his pajamas.
His eyes had a silver, sleepy look as he stood there staring
at Mary Poppins. He stared at her face and he stared at
her feet with an earnest, measuring, searching gaze that
missed out no part of her. Then he said "Oh!" in a disappointed voice and rubbed the sleep from his eyes.

"Well? What's the matter with *you?*" she enquired.
"Lost sixpence and found a penny?"

He shook his head dejectedly. "I dreamed you had
turned into a beautiful princess. And here you are just the
same as ever!"

She bridled and gave her head a toss. "Handsome is as
Handsome does!" she said with a haughty sniff. "I'm perfectly well as I am, thank you! *I'm* satisfied, if you're not."

He flew to her side and tried to appease her.

"Oh, I *am* satisfied, Mary Poppins!" he said eagerly.
"I just thought that if the dream had come true it would
be — er — a sort of a change."

"Change!" she exclaimed with another sniff. "You'll
get all the changes you want soon enough — I promise
you, Michael Banks!"

He looked at her uneasily. What did she mean by that, he wondered.

"I was only joking, Mary Poppins. I don't want any changes, really! I only want you — for always!"

And suddenly it seemed to him that princesses were very silly creatures with nothing to be said in their favour.

"Humph!" said Mary Poppins crossly, as she planked the toast on the table. "You can't have *anything* for always — and don't you think it, sir!"

"Except you!" he retorted confidently, smiling his mischievous smile.

A strange expression came over her face. But Michael did not notice it. Out of the corner of his eye he had seen what Jane was doing. And now he was climbing up beside her to breathe on another patch of window.

"Look!" he said proudly. "I'm drawing a ship. And there's another Michael outside drawing one igzactly like it!"

"Um-hum!" said Jane, without looking up, as she gazed at her own reflection. Then suddenly she turned away and called to Mary Poppins.

"Which is the real me, Mary Poppins? The one in here or the one out there?"

With a bowl of porridge in her hand, Mary Poppins came and stood between them. Each time she breathed, her apron crackled, and the steam from the bowl went up with a puff. In silence she looked at her own reflection and smiled a satisfied smile.

Then: "—— Is this a riddle?" she demanded, sniffing.

"No, Mary Poppins," Jane said eagerly. "It's something I want to know."

For a moment they thought, as they looked at her, that she might be going to tell them. Then, apparently, she thought better of it, for she gave her head a scornful toss and turned away to the table.

"I don't know about *you*," she said, conceitedly, "but I'm glad to say that *I'm* real *wherever* I happen to be! Dress yourself, Michael, if you please! And Jane, you come to breakfast!"

Under the gleam of those steely eyes they hurried to obey her. And by the time breakfast was over and they were sitting on the floor building a Castle out of rubber bricks, they had quite forgotten their reflections. Indeed, had they looked, they would not have found them, for the fire had settled to a rosy glow and the bright flames had gone.

"That's better!" said Number Seventeen, snuggling closer into the earth.

The warmth from the fire crept through its bones and the house came alive as Mary Poppins went scuttling about it.

Today she seemed even busier than usual. She sorted the clothes and tidied the drawers, sewed on odd buttons and mended socks. She put fresh papers on the shelves; let down the hems of Jane's and Barbara's frocks; and stitched new elastics into John's hat and Michael's. She collected Annabel's old clothes and made them into a bundle for Mrs. Brill's niece's baby. She cleaned out cupboards, sorted the toys and put the books straight in the bookcases.

"How busy she is! It makes me quite giddy!" said Michael in a whisper.

But Jane said nothing. She gazed at the crackly, bustling figure. And a thought that she could not quite get hold of was wandering round in her mind. Something — was it a memory? — whispered a word that she couldn't quite catch.

And all through the morning, the Starling sat on the Next Door chimney and screeched his endless song. Every now and then he would dart across the garden and peer through the window at Mary Poppins with bright anxious eyes. And the wind went round and round the house, sighing and crying.

The hours went by and lunch time came. And still Mary Poppins went on bustling like a very tidy tornado. She put fresh daffodils in the jam-jar; she straightened the furniture and shook out the curtains. The children felt the Nursery tremble beneath her ministering hand.

"Will she *never* stop!" Michael complained to Jane, as he added a room to the Castle.

And at that moment, as though Mary Poppins had heard what he said, she suddenly stood still.

"There!" she exclaimed, as she looked at her handi-work. "It's as Neat as a Pin. And I hope it remains so!"

Then she took down her best blue coat and brushed it. She breathed on the buttons to make them shine and pinned the starfish brooch on her collar. She tweaked and pulled at her black straw hat till the daisies stood up as stiff as soldiers. Then she took off her white crackling apron and buckled the snake-skin belt round her waist. The message written on it was clearly visible: "A Present from the Zoo."

"You haven't worn that for a long, long time," said Michael, watching with interest.

"I keep it for Best," she replied calmly, as she twitched the belt into place.

Then she took her umbrella from the corner and pol-ished the parrot-head with bees' wax. And after that, with a quiet smile, she plucked the Tape Measure from the mantelpiece and popped it into the pocket of her coat.

Jane lifted her head quickly. Somehow, the sight of that bulging pocket made her feel strangely anxious.

"Why don't you leave the Tape Measure there? It's per-fectly safe, Mary Poppins."

There was a pause. Mary Poppins appeared to be con-sidering the question.

"I have my reasons," she said at last, as she gave a supe-rior sniff.

"But it's always been on the mantelpiece, ever since you came back!"

"That doesn't mean that it always will be. What's good for Monday won't do for Friday," she replied with her priggish smile.

Jane turned away. What was the matter with her heart? It suddenly felt too big for her chest.

"I'm lonely," she said in a whisper to Michael, taking care not to look at him.

"You can't be lonely as long as I'm here!" he put his last brick on the roof of the Castle.

"It's not that kind of loneliness. I feel I'm going to lose something."

"Perhaps it's your tooth," he said, with interest. "Try it and see if it wobbles."

Jane shook her head quickly. Whatever it was she was going to lose, she knew it was not a tooth.

"Oh, for just one more brick!" sighed Michael. "Everything's done but the chimney!"

Mary Poppins came swiftly across the room.

"There you are! That's what it needs!" she said. And she stooped and put one of her own dominoes in the place where the chimney should be.

"Hooray! It's completely finished!" he cried, glancing up at her with delight. Then he saw that she had placed the box of dominoes beside him. The sight of them made him queerly uneasy.

"You mean——" he said, swallowing. "You mean — we may keep them?"

He had always wanted those dominoes. But never be-

fore had Mary Poppins allowed him to touch her possessions. What did it mean? It was so unlike her. And suddenly, as she nodded at him, he, too, felt a pang of loneliness.

"Oh!" he broke out, with an anxious wail. "What's
wrong, Mary Poppins? What can be the matter?"

"Wrong!" Her eyes snapped angrily. "I give you a nice
respectable present and that's all the thanks I get! What's
wrong indeed! I'll know better next time."

He rushed at her wildly and clutched her hand. "Oh,
I didn't mean that, Mary Poppins! I — thank you. It was
just a sudden idea I had —— "

"Those ideas are going to get you into trouble one of
these fine bright days. You mark my words!" she snorted.
"Now, get your hats, please, all of you! We'll go for a walk
to the Swings."

At the sight of that familiar glare their anxiety melted
away. They flew to get ready, shouting and laughing, and
knocking the Castle down as they ran.

The thin Spring sun shone over the Park as they hurried across the Lane. Green smoke hung around the
Cherry-Trees where the small new leaves were sprouting.
The scent of primroses was in the air and the birds were
rehearsing their songs for summer.

"I'll race you to the Swings!" shouted Michael.

"We'll have them all to ourselves!" cried Jane. For nobody else was in the clearing where the five swings stood
and waited.

In no time they had scrambled for places and Jane and
Michael, John and Barbara were each on a swing of their
own. Annabel, looking like a white woollen egg, shared
hers with Mary Poppins.

"Now — one, two, THREE!" cried Michael loudly,
and the swings swayed from the cross-beam. Higher and
higher the children swung, swooping like birds through
the delicate sunlight. Up they went with their heads to
the sky and down they came with their feet to the earth.
The trees seemed to spread their branches below them;
the roofs of the houses nodded and bowed.

"It's like flying!" Jane cried happily, as the earth turned
a somersault under her feet. She glanced across at Michael.
His hair was tossing in all directions as he rode through
the air. The Twins were squeaking like excited mice. And
beyond them, with a dignified air, Mary Poppins swung
backwards and forwards. One hand held Annabel on her
knee and the other grasped her umbrella. Her eyes, as she
rode her flying swing, shone with a strange, bright gleam.
They were bluer than Jane had ever seen them, blue with
the blueness of faraway. They seemed to look past the
trees and houses, and out beyond all the seas and mountains, and over the rim of the world.

The afternoon faded and the Park grew grey as it tilted
beneath their feet. But Jane and Michael took no notice.
They were wrapped in a dream with Mary Poppins, a
dream that swung them up and down between the earth

and the sky, a rocking, riding, lulling dream that would
never come to an end.

But come to an end it did, at last. The sun went over
and the dream went with it. As the last rays spread across
the Park, Mary Poppins put her foot to the ground and
her swing stopped with a jerk.

"It is time to go," she said, quietly. And because her
voice had, for once, no sternness, they stopped their
swings immediately and obeyed without protesting. The

perambulator gave its familiar groan as she dumped the Twins and Annabel into it. Jane and Michael walked quietly beside her. The earth was still swaying beneath their feet. They were happy and calm and silent.

Creak, creak! went the perambulator along the path.

Trip, trip, went Mary Poppins' shoes.

Michael glanced up as the last light fell on the faint green leaves of the Cherry-Trees.

"I believe," he said dreamily to Jane, "that Nellie Rubina's been here!"

"Here today and gone tomorrow — that's me!" cried a tinkling voice.

They turned to find Nellie Rubina herself rolling along on her wooden disc. And behind her came the wheeling shape of old Uncle Dodger.

"What a roll I've had!" cried Nellie Rubina. "I've looked for you everywhere!" she panted. "How are you all? Doing nicely, I hope! I wanted to see you, dear Miss Poppins, to give you a —— "

"And also," said Uncle Dodger eagerly, "to wish you a very good —— "

"Uncle Dodger!" said Nellie Rubina, with a warning glint in her eye.

"Oh, excuse me! Begging your pardon, my dear!" the old man answered quickly.

"Just a Little Something to remember us by," Nellie Rubina went on. Then, thrusting out her wooden arm, she popped a small white object into Mary Poppins' hand.

The children crowded to look at it.

"It's a Conversation!" Michael exclaimed.

Jane peered at the letters in the fading light. " 'Fare Thee Well, my Fairy Fay!' " she read out. "Are you going away, then, Nellie Rubina?"

"Oh, dear me, yes! Tonight's the night!" Nellie Rubina gave a tinkling laugh as she glanced at Mary Poppins.

"You can keep it to eat on the way, Miss Poppins!" Uncle Dodger nodded at the Conversation.

"Uncle Dodger!" cried Nellie Rubina.

"Oh, my! Oh, my! Out of turn again! I'm too old, that's what it is, my dear. And begging your pardon, of course."

"Well, it's very kind of you both, I'm sure," said Mary Poppins politely. You could see she was pleased by the way she smiled. Then she tucked the Conversation into her pocket and gave the pram a push.

"Oh, do wait a minute, Mary Poppins!" cried a breathless voice behind them. A patter of steps came along the path and the children turned quickly.

"Why, it's Mr. and Mrs. Turvy!" cried Michael, as a tall, thin shape and a round, fat one came forward, hand in hand.

"We now call ourselves the Topsy-Turvies. We think it sounds better." Mr. Turvy looked down at them over his glasses as his wife shook hands all round.

"Well, Mary," he went on, in his gloomy voice, "we thought we'd drop in, just for a moment — to say So Long, you know."

"And not *too* long, we hope, dear Mary!" added Mrs. Turvy, smiling. Her round, fat face shook like a jelly and she looked extremely happy.

"Oh, thank you kindly, Cousin Arthur! And you, too, Topsy!" said Mary Poppins, as she shook them both by the hand.

"What does it mean — So Long?" asked Jane, as she leant against Mary Poppins. Something — perhaps it was the darkness — made her suddenly want to be very close to that warm and comforting figure.

"It means my daughters!" a small voice screeched, as a shape emerged from the shadows. "So long, so wide, so huge, so stupid — the great Gallumping Giraffes."

And there on the path stood Mrs. Corry with her coat all covered with threepenny-bits. And behind her, Fannie and Annie stalked, like a pair of mournful giants.

"Well, here we are again!" shrieked Mrs. Corry, as she grinned at the staring children. "H'm! Growing up fast, aren't they, Mary Poppins? I can see that they won't need *you* much longer!"

Mary Poppins gave a nod of agreement as Michael, with a cry of protest, rushed to her side.

"We'll always need her — always!" he cried, hugging Mary Poppins' waist so tightly that he felt her strong hard bones.

She glared at him like an angry panther.

"Kindly do not crush me, Michael! I am not a Sardine in a Tin!"

"Well, I just came to have a word with you," Mrs. Corry cackled on. "An old word, Mary, and one that is best said quickly. As I used to tell Solomon when he was making that fuss about the Queen of Sheba — if you've got to say it sometime, why not now?" Mrs. Corry looked searchingly at Mary Poppins. Then she added softly, "Good-bye, my dear!"

"Are you going away, too?" Michael demanded, as he stared at Mrs. Corry.

She gave a merry shriek of laughter. "Well — yes, I am, in a manner of speaking! Once one goes they all go — that's the way of it. Now, Fannie and Annie ——" she glanced around, "what have you idiots done with those presents?"

"Here, Mother!" the sisters answered nervously. And the huge hands dropped into Mary Poppins' palm two tiny pieces of gingerbread. One was shaped like a heart and the other like a star.

Mary Poppins gave a cry of delight.

"Why, Mrs. Corry! *What* a surprise! This is a Treat as well as a Pleasure!"

"Oh, it's nothing. Just a Souvenir." Mrs. Corry airily waved her hand, and her little elastic-sided boots danced along beside the perambulator.

"All your friends seem to be here tonight!" remarked Michael to Mary Poppins.

"Well, what do you think I am — a Hermit? I suppose I can see my friends when I like!"

"I was only remarking ——" he began, when a glad shriek interrupted him.

"Why, Albert — if it isn't you!" cried Mrs. Corry gaily. And she ran to meet a roly-poly figure that was hurrying towards them. The children gave a shout of joy as they recognized Mr. Wigg.

"Well, Bless my Boots. It's Clara Corry!" cried Mr. Wigg, shaking her hand affectionately.

"I didn't know you knew each other!" exclaimed Jane, looking very surprised.

"What *you* don't know would fill a Dictionary," Mary Poppins broke in with a snort.

"Know each other? Why, we were children together — weren't we, Albert?" cried Mrs. Corry.

Mr. Wigg chuckled. "Ah, the good old days!" he answered cheerily. "Well, how are you, Mary, my girl?"

"Nicely, thank you, Uncle Albert. Mustn't complain," replied Mary Poppins.

"I thought I'd step up for One Last Word. Pleasant trip and all that. It's a nice night for it." Mr. Wigg glanced round at the clear blue dusk that was creeping through the Park.

"A nice night for what?" demanded Michael. He hoped Mary Poppins would not be lonely with her friends going off like this. But, after all, he thought to himself — she's still got me and what more could she want?

"A nice night to go sailing — that's what it's for!" roared Admiral Boom in his rollicking voice. He was striding through the trees towards them, singing as he came:

> "Sailing, sailing, over the Bounding Main,
>   And many a stormy Wind shall blow
>   Till we come home again!
>   Sailing, sailing — "

"Ahoy there, lubbers! Hoist the mainsail! Up with the anchor and let her go. For away I'm bound to go — oho! — 'cross the wide Missouri!" He blew his nose with a sound like a foghorn and looked at Mary Poppins.

"All aboard?" he enquired gruffly, putting a hand on her shoulder.

"All aboard, Sir," she answered primly, and she gave him a curious look.

"Hrrrrrrrrmph! Well ——

"I'll be true to my love,
    If my Love will be tru-ue to me!"

he sang, in a voice that was almost gentle. "Here —— " he broke off. "Port and Starboard! Cockles and Whelks! You can't do that to a Sailor!"

"Balloons *and* Balloons!" cried a high-pitched voice as a little shape went whizzing past and knocked off the Admiral's hat.

It was the Balloon Woman. One small balloon flew from her hand. It bounced her upon the end of its string and swept her away through the shadows.

"Good-bye *and* Good-bye, my Dearie Duck!" she called as she disappeared.

"There she goes — off like a streak of lightning!" cried Jane, gazing after her.

"Well, she's certainly not a creeping Snail, like *some*

people I could mention! Kindly walk up!" said Mary Poppins. "I haven't all night to waste!"

"I should think not!" Mrs. Corry said, grinning.

They walked up. For once they were eager to do anything she told them. They put their hands on the perambulator beside her black-gloved fingers. And the blue dusk lapped them round like a river as they hurried along with the chattering group.

They were nearly at the Park Gates now. The Lane stretched darkly in front of them and from it came a strain of music. Jane and Michael looked at each other. What could it be? said their upraised brows. Then their curiosity got the better of them. They wanted to stay with Mary Poppins but they also wanted to see what was happening. They gave one glance at her dark blue figure and then began to run.

"Oh, look!" cried Jane, as she reached the Gate. "It's Mr. Twigley with a Hurdy-gurdy!"

And Mr. Twigley it was indeed, drawing a sweet wild tune from the box as he busily turned the handle. Beside him stood a small bright figure that was vaguely familiar.

"And all of them made of the Finest Sugar," it was saying gaily to Mr. Twigley as the children crossed the road. Then, of course, they knew who it was.

> "Stare, stare,
> Like a Bear,

Then you'll know me
Everywhere!"

chanted Miss Calico cheerfully, as she waved her hand towards them.

"Could you move your feet a bit, please, kids! You're standing on one of my roses!"

Bert, the Matchman, crouched on the pavement, right at their own front gate. He was drawing a large bouquet of flowers in coloured chalks on the asphalt. Ellen and the Policeman were watching him. And Miss Lark and her dogs were listening to the music as they stood outside Next Door.

"Wait a minute," she cried to Mr. Twigley, "while I run in and get you a shilling!"

Mr. Twigley smiled his twinkly smile and shook his head gently.

"Don't bother, ma'am," he advised Miss Lark. "A shilling would be no use to me. I'm doing it All for Love." And the children saw him lift his eyes and exchange a look with Mary Poppins as she strode out of the Park. He wound the handle with all his might and the tune grew louder and quicker.

"One Forget-me-not — and then it's finished," the Matchman murmured to himself as he added a flower to the bunch.

"That's dainty, Bert!" said Mary Poppins admiringly.

She had pushed the perambulator up behind him and was gazing at the picture. He sprang to his feet with a little cry and, plucking the bouquet from the pavement, he pressed it into her hand.

"They're yours, Mary," he told her shyly. "I drew them all for you!"

"Did you really, Bert?" she said with a smile. "Well, I just don't know how to thank you!" She hid her blushing face in the flowers and the children could smell the scent of roses.

The Matchman looked at her glowing eyes and smiled a loving smile.

"It's tonight — isn't it, Mary?" he said.

"Yes, Bert," she said, nodding, as she gave him her hand. The Matchman looked at it sadly for a moment. Then he bent his head and kissed it.

"Good-bye, then, Mary!" they heard him whisper.

And she answered softly, "Good-bye, Bert!"

"What is all this about tonight?" demanded Michael, inquisitively.

"Tonight is the happiest night of my life!" said Miss Lark as she listened to the Hurdy-gurdy. "I never heard such beautiful music. It makes my feet simply twinkle!"

"Well, let 'em twinkle with mine!" roared the Admiral. And he snatched Miss Lark away from her gate and polka-ed along the Lane.

"Oh, Admiral!" they heard her cry, as he swung her round and round.

"Lovey-dovey-cat's-eyes!" cooed Mrs. Turvy. And Mr.

Turvy, looking very embarrassed, allowed her to dance him round.

"Wot about it — eh?" the Policeman smirked, and before Ellen had time to blow her nose, he had whirled her into the dance.

One, two, three! One, two, three! High and sweet, the music flowed from the Hurdy-gurdy. The street lamps blazed with sudden brightness and speckled the Lane with light and shadow. One, two, three, went Miss Calico's feet, as she danced alone beside Mr. Twigley. It was such a wild and merry tune that Jane and Michael could stand still no longer. Off they darted and one, two, three, their feet went tapping on the echoing road.

" 'Ere! Wot's all this? Observe the Rules! We can't 'ave dancing in Public Places! Move on, now, don't obstruct the traffic!" The Park Keeper, goggling as usual, came threading his way through the Lane.

"Mercy me and a Jumping Bean! You're just the man I want!" shrieked Miss Calico. And before the Park Keeper knew where he was, she had swung him into the mazy dance where he gulped and gaped and twirled.

"Round we go, Clara!" cried Mr. Wigg, swinging past with Mrs. Corry.

"I used to do this with Henry the Eighth — and oh, what a time we had!" she shrieked. "Get along, clumsies! Keep your feet to yourselves!" she added, in a different voice, to Fannie and Annie who were dancing together like a pair of gloomy elephants.

"I've never been so happy before!" came Miss Lark's excited cry.

"You should go to sea, my dear Lucinda! Everyone's happy at sea!" roared the Admiral, as he polka-ed madly along.

"I do believe I will," she replied.

And her two dogs looked at each other aghast and hoped she would change her mind.

Deeper and deeper grew the dusk as the dancers whirled in a ring. And there in the centre stood Mary Poppins with her flowers clasped in her hands. She rocked the perambulator gently and her foot beat time with the music. The Matchman watched her from the pavement.

Straight and stiff she stood there, smiling, and her eyes went roving from one to the other — Miss Lark and the Admiral, the Topsy-Turvies; the two Noahs rolling around on their discs; Miss Calico clutching the Park Keeper; Mrs. Corry in the arms of Mr. Wigg; and Mrs. Corry's big daughters. Then her bright glance fell on the two young children who were dancing round in the ring. She looked at them for a long, long moment, watching their bright enchanted faces and their arms going out to each other.

And suddenly, as though they felt that look upon them, they stopped in the middle of their dance and ran to her, laughing and breathless.

"Mary Poppins!" they both cried, pressing against her.

And there in the centre stood Mary Poppins

Then they found they had nothing else to say. Her name seemed to be enough.

She put her arms about their shoulders and looked into their eyes. It was a long, deep, searching look that plunged right down to their very hearts and saw what was there. Then she smiled to herself and turned away. She took her parrot-headed umbrella from the perambulator and gathered Annabel into her arms.

"I must go in now, Jane and Michael! You two can bring the Twins later."

They nodded, still panting from the dance.

"Now, be good children!" she said quietly. "And remember all I have told you."

They smiled at her reassuringly. What a funny thing to say, they thought. As if they would dare forget!

She gave the Twins' curls a gentle rumple; she buttoned up Michael's coat at the neck and straightened Jane's collar.

"Now, spit-spot and away we go!" she cried gaily to Annabel.

Then off she tripped through the garden-gate, with the baby, the flowers and the parrot umbrella held lightly in her arms. Up the steps went the prim, trim figure, walking with a jaunty air as though she was thoroughly pleased with herself.

"Farewell, Mary Poppins!" the dancers cried, as she paused at the Front Door.

She glanced back over her shoulder and nodded. Then the Hurdy-gurdy gave a loud sweet peal and the Front Door closed behind her.

Jane shivered as the music ceased. Perhaps it was the frost in the air that made her feel so lonely.

"We'll wait till all the people leave and then we'll go in," she said.

She glanced around at the group of dancers. They were standing still upon the pavement and seemed to be waiting for something. For every face was gazing upwards at Number Seventeen.

"What can they be looking at?" said Michael, as he craned his own head backwards.

Then a glow appeared at the Nursery windows and a dark shape moved across it. The children knew it was Mary Poppins, lighting the evening fire. And presently the flames sprang up. They sparkled on the window-panes and shone through the darkening garden. Higher and higher leapt the blaze, brighter and brighter the windows gleamed. Then suddenly they saw the Nursery reflected upon Miss Lark's side wall. There it gleamed, high above the garden, with its sparkling fire and the mantelpiece and the old armchair and ——

"The Door! The Door!" A breathless cry went up from the crowd in the Lane.

What door? Jane and Michael stared at each other. And suddenly — they knew!

"Oh, Michael! It isn't her friends who are going away!" cried Jane in an anguished voice. "It's — oh, hurry, hurry! We must go and find her!"

With trembling hands they hauled out the Twins and dragged them through the gate. They tore at the Front Door, rushed upstairs and burst into the Nursery.

Their faces fell as they stared at the room, for everything in it was as quiet and peaceful as it had always been. The fire was crackling behind its bars and, cosily tucked inside her cot, Annabel was softly cooing. The bricks they had used for the morning's Castle were neatly piled in a corner. And beside them lay the precious box of Mary Poppins' dominoes.

"Oh!" they panted, surprised and puzzled to find everything just the same.

Everything? No! There was one thing missing.

"The camp bed!" Michael cried. "It's gone! Then — where is Mary Poppins?"

He ran to the bathroom and out on the landing and back to the Nursery again.

"Mary Poppins! Mary Poppins! Mary Poppins!"

Then Jane glanced up from the fire to the window and gave a little cry.

"Oh, Michael, Michael! There she is! And there is the Other Door!"

He followed the line of her pointing finger and his mouth opened wide.

For there, on the outer side of the window, another Nursery glimmered. It stretched from Number Seventeen to the wall of Miss Lark's house; and everything in the real Nursery was reflected in that shining room. There was Annabel's gleaming cot and the table made of light. There was the fire, leaping up in mid-air; and there, at last, was the Other Door, exactly the same as the one behind them. It shimmered like a panel of light at the other side of the garden. Beside it stood their own reflections and towards it, along the airy floor, tripped the figure of Mary Poppins. She carried the carpet bag in her hand; and the Matchman's flowers and the parrot umbrella were tucked beneath her arm. Away she stalked through the Nursery's reflection, away through the shimmering likenesses of the old familiar things. And as she went, the daisies nodded on the crown of her black straw hat.

A loud cry burst from Michael's mouth as he rushed towards the window.

"Mary Poppins!" he cried. "Come back! Come back!"

Behind him the Twins began to grizzle.

"Oh, please, Mary Poppins, come back to us!" called Jane, from the window-seat.

But Mary Poppins took no notice. She strode on swiftly towards the Door that shimmered in the air.

"She won't get anywhere that way!" said Michael. "It will only lead to Miss Lark's wall."

But even as he spoke, Mary Poppins reached the Other

Away she stalked through the Nursery's reflection

Door and pulled it wide open. A gasp of surprise went up from the children. For the wall they had expected to see had entirely disappeared. Beyond Mary Poppins' straight blue figure there was nothing but field on field of sky, and the dark spreading night.

"Come back, Mary Poppins!" they cried together, in a last despairing wail.

And as though she had heard them, she paused for a minute, with one foot on the threshold. The starfish sparkled on her collar as she glanced back swiftly towards the Nursery. She smiled at the four sad watching faces and waved her bouquet of flowers. Then she snapped the parrot umbrella open and stepped out into the night.

The umbrella wobbled for a moment and the light from the fire shone full upon it as it swayed in the air. Then, with a bound, as though glad to be free, it soared away through the sky. Up, up went Mary Poppins with it, tightly holding the parrot handle as she cleared the tops of the trees. And as she went, the Hurdy-gurdy broke out with a peal of music, as loud and proud and triumphant as any wedding march.

Back in the Nursery the great blaze faded and sank into crimson coals. The flames went down and with them went the shining other room. Soon there was nothing to be seen but the Cherry-Trees waving through the air and the blank brick wall of Miss Lark's house.

But above the roof a bright form rose, flying higher

every minute. It seemed to have gathered into itself the sparkle and flame of the fire. For it glowed like a little core of light in the black frosty sky.

Leaning upon the window-seat, the four children watched it. Their cheeks lay heavily in their hands and their hearts were heavy within their breasts. They did not try to explain it to themselves, for they knew there were things about Mary Poppins that could never be explained. Where she had come from nobody knew, and where she was going they could not guess. They were certain only of one thing — that she had kept her promise. She had stayed with them till the Door opened and then she had left them. And they could not tell if they would ever see that trim shape again.

Michael reached out for the box of dominoes. He put it on the sill beside Jane. And together they held it as they watched the umbrella go sailing through the sky.

Presently Mrs. Banks came in.

"What — sitting all alone, my darlings?" she cried as she snapped on the light. "Where's Mary Poppins?" she enquired, with a glance round the room.

"Gone, ma'am," said a resentful voice, as Mrs. Brill appeared on the landing.

Mrs. Banks' face had a startled look.

"What do you mean?" she demanded anxiously.

"Well, it's this way," Mrs. Brill replied. "I was listenin' to a Nurdy-gurdy that's down in the Lane, when I sees the

empty perambulator and the Match-man wheelin' it up
to the door. " 'Ullo!' I says, 'where's that Mary Poppins?'
And 'e tells me she's gone again. Lock, stock and barrer
gone. Not even a note on 'er pincushion!"

"Oh, what shall I do?" wailed Mrs. Banks, sitting down
on the old armchair.

"Do? You can come and dance with me!" cried Mr.
Banks' voice, as he raced upstairs.

"Oh, don't be so silly, George! Something's happened.
Mary Poppins has gone again!" Mrs. Banks' face was

a tragedy. "George! George! Please listen to me!" she begged.

For Mr. Banks had taken no notice. He was waltzing round and round the room, holding out his coattails.

"I can't! There's a Hurdy-gurdy down in the Lane and it's playing the *Blue Danube*. Ta-rum pom-pom-pom — de-di, de-dum!"

And, pulling Mrs. Banks from the chair, he waltzed her round, singing lustily. Then they both collapsed on the window-seat among the watching children.

"But, George — this is serious!" Mrs. Banks protested, half-laughing, half-crying, as she pinned up her hair.

"I see something much more serious!" he exclaimed, as he glanced through the Nursery window. "A shooting star! Look at it! Wish on it, children!"

Away through the sky streaked the shining spark, cleaving a path through the darkness. And as they watched it, every heart was filled with sudden sweetness. Down in the Lane the music ceased and the dancers stood gazing, hand in hand.

"My dear Love!" Mr. Banks said tenderly, as he touched Mrs. Banks' cheek. And they put their arms around each other and wished on the star.

Jane and Michael held their breath as the sweetness brimmed up within them. And the thing they wished was that all their lives they might remember Mary Poppins. Where and How and When and Why — had nothing to do with them. They knew that as far as she was concerned those questions had no answers. The bright shape speeding through the air above them would forever keep its secret. But in the summer days to come and the long nights of winter, they would remember Mary Poppins and think of all she had told them. The rain and the sun would remind them of her, and the birds and the beasts and the changing seasons. Mary Poppins herself had flown away, but the gifts she had brought would remain for always.

"We'll never forget you, Mary Poppins!" they breathed, looking up at the sky.

Her bright shape paused in its flight for a moment and gave an answering wave. Then darkness folded its wing about her and hid her from their eyes.

"It's gone!" said Mr. Banks, with a sigh, looking out at the starless night.

Then he pulled the curtains across the window and drew them all to the fire. . . .

Sussex, England,
New York, U.S.A.

GLORIA IN EXCELSIS DEO

Sitting bolt upright against the tree

MARY
POPPINS
IN THE
PARK

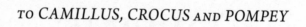

TO CAMILLUS, CROCUS AND POMPEY

CONTENTS

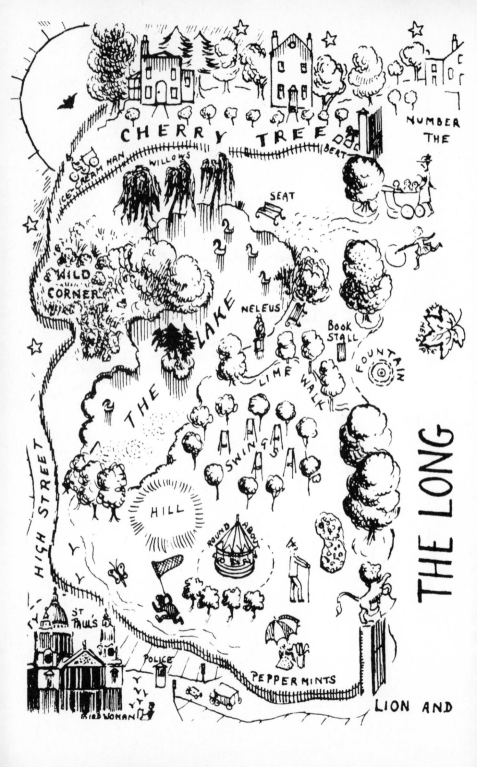

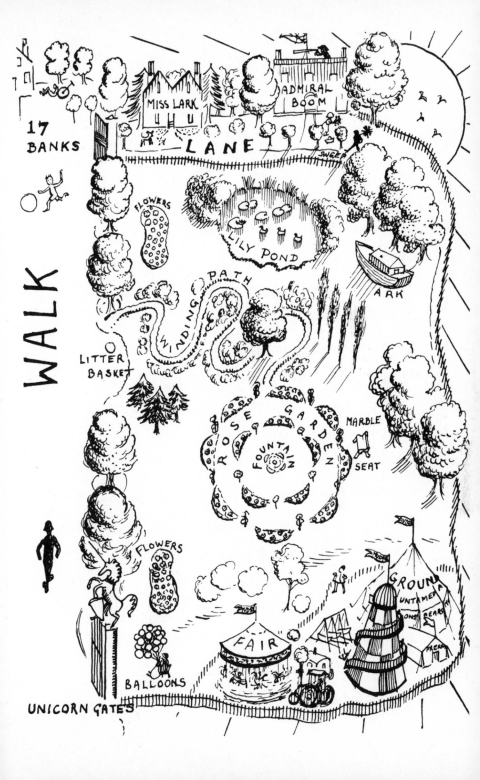

ILLUSTRATIONS

Also insets and tailpieces

The adventures in this book should be understood to have happened during any of the three visits of Mary Poppins to the Banks family. This is a word of warning to anybody who may be expecting they are in for a fourth visit. She cannot forever arrive and depart. And, apart from that, it should be remembered that three is a lucky number.

Those who already know Mary Poppins will also be familiar with many of the other characters who appear here. And those who don't — if they want to know them more intimately — can find them in the earlier volumes.

P. L. T.

CHAPTER
ONE

EVERY GOOSE A SWAN

The summer day was hot and still. The cherry-trees that bordered the Lane could feel their cherries ripening — the green slowly turning to yellow and the yellow blushing red.

The houses dozed in the dusty gardens with their shutters over their eyes. "Do not disturb us!" they seemed to say. "We rest in the afternoon."

And the starlings hid themselves in the chimneys with their heads under their wings.

Over the Park lay a cloud of sunlight as thick and as golden as syrup. No wind stirred the heavy leaves. The flowers stood up, very still and shiny, as though they were made of metal.

Down by the Lake the benches were empty. The people who usually sat there had gone home out of the heat. Neleus, the little marble statue, looked down at the placid water. No goldfish flirted a scarlet tail. They were all sitting under the lily-leaves — using them as umbrellas.

The Lawns spread out like a green carpet, motionless in the sunlight. Except for a single, rhythmic movement, you might have thought that the whole Park was only a painted picture. To and fro, by the big magnolia, the Park Keeper was spearing up rubbish and putting it into a litter-basket.

He stopped his work and looked up as two dogs trotted by.

They had come from Cherry-Tree Lane, he knew, for Miss Lark was calling from behind her shutters.

"Andrew! Willoughby! Please come back! Don't go swimming in that dirty Lake! I'll make you some Iced Tea!"

Andrew and Willoughby looked at each other, winked, and trotted on. But as they passed the big magnolia, they started and pulled up sharply. Down they flopped on the grass, panting — with their pink tongues lolling out.

Mary Poppins, neat and prim in her blue skirt and a new hat trimmed with a crimson tulip, looked at them over her knitting. She was sitting bolt upright against the tree, with a plaid rug spread on the lawn around her. Her hand-bag sat tidily by her side. And above her, from a flowering branch, the parrot umbrella dangled.

She glanced at the two thumping tails and gave a little sniff.

"Put in your tongues and sit up straight! You are not a pair of wolves."

The two dogs sprang at once to attention. And Jane, lying on the lawn, could see they were doing their very best to put their tongues in their cheeks.

"And remember, if you're going swimming," Mary Poppins continued, "to shake yourselves when you come out. Don't come sprinkling *us!*"

Andrew and Willoughby looked reproachful.

"As though, Mary Poppins," they seemed to say, "we would dream of such a thing!"

"All right, then. Be off with you!" And they sped away like shots from a gun.

"Come back!" Miss Lark cried anxiously.

But nobody took any notice.

"Why can't *I* swim in the Park Lake?" asked Michael in a smothered voice. He was lying face downwards in the grass watching a family of ants.

"You're not a dog!" Mary Poppins reminded him.

"I know, Mary Poppins. But if I were —— " Was she smiling or not? — he couldn't be sure, with his nose pressed into the earth.

"Well — what would you do?" she enquired, with a sniff.

He wanted to say that if *he* were a dog he would do just as he liked — swim or not, as the mood took him, without asking leave of anyone. But what if her face was looking fierce! Silence was best, he decided.

"Nothing!" he said in a meek voice. "It's too hot to argue, Mary Poppins!"

"Out of nothing comes nothing!" She tossed her head in its tulip hat. "And I'm not arguing, I'm talking!" She was having the last word, as usual.

The sunlight caught her knitting-needles as it shone through the broad magnolia leaves on the little group below. John and Barbara, leaning their heads on each other's shoulders, were dozing and waking, waking and dozing. Annabel was fast asleep in Mary Poppins' shadow. Light and darkness dappled them all and splotched the face of the Park Keeper as he dived at a piece of newspaper.

"All litter to be placed in the baskets! Obey the rules!" he said sternly.

Mary Poppins looked him up and down. Her glance would have withered an oak-tree.

"That's not my litter," she retorted.

"Oh?" he said disbelievingly.

"No!" she replied, with a virtuous snort.

"Well, *someone* must 'ave put it there. It doesn't grow — like roses!"

He pushed his cap to the back of his head and mopped behind his ears. What with the heat, and her tone of voice, he was feeling quite depressed.

" 'Ot weather we're 'avin'!" he remarked, eyeing her nervously. He looked like an eager, lonely dog.

"That's what we expect in the middle of summer!" Her knitting-needles clicked.

The Park Keeper sighed and tried again.

"I see you brought yer parrot!" he said, glancing up at the black silk shape that hung among the leaves.

"You mean my *parrot-headed umbrella*," she haughtily corrected him.

He gave a little anxious laugh. "You don't think it's goin' to rain, do you? With all this sun about?"

"I don't think, I *know*," she told him calmly. "And if I," she went on, "were a Park Keeper, I wouldn't be wasting half the day like *some* people I could mention! There's a piece of orange peel over there — why don't you pick it up?"

She pointed with her knitting-needle and kept it pointed accusingly while he speared up the offending litter and tossed it into a basket.

"If *she* was me," he said to himself, "there'd be no Park at all. Only a nice tidy desert!" He fanned his face with his cap.

"And anyway," he said aloud, "it's no fault of mine I'm a Park Keeper. I should 'ave been a Nexplorer by rights, away in foreign parts. If I'd 'ad me way I wouldn't be 'ere. I'd be sittin' on a piece of ice along with a Polar Bear!"

He sighed and leaned upon his stick, falling into a daydream.

"Humph!" said Mary Poppins loudly. And a startled dove in the tree above her ruffled its wing in surprise.

A feather came slowly drifting down. Jane stretched out her hand and caught it.

"How deliciously it tickles!" she murmured, running the grey edge over her nose. Then she tucked the feather above her brow and bound her ribbon round it.

"I'm the daughter of an Indian Chief. Minnehaha, Laughing Water, gliding along the river."

"Oh, no, you're not," contradicted Michael. "You're Jane Caroline Banks."

"That's only my outside," she insisted. "Inside I'm somebody quite different. It's a very funny feeling."

"You should have eaten a bigger lunch. Then you wouldn't have funny feelings. And Daddy's not an Indian Chief, so you can't be Minnehaha!"

He gave a sudden start as he spoke and peered more closely into the grass.

"There he goes!" he shouted wildly, wriggling forward on his stomach and thumping with his toes.

"I'll thank you, Michael," said Mary Poppins, "to stop kicking my shins. What are you — a Performing Horse?"

"Not a horse, a hunter, Mary Poppins! I'm tracking in the jungle!"

"Jungles!" scoffed the Park Keeper. "My vote is for snowy wastes!"

"If you're not careful, Michael Banks, you'll be tracking home to bed. I never knew such a silly pair. And you're the third," snapped Mary Poppins, eyeing the Park Keeper. "Always wanting to be something else instead of what you are. If it's not Miss Minnie-what's-her-name, it's this or that or the other. You're as bad as the Goose-girl and the Swineherd!"

"But it isn't geese or swine I'm after. It's a lion, Mary Poppins. He may be only an ant on the outside but inside — ah, at last, I've got him! — inside he's a man-eater!"

Michael rolled over, red in the face, holding something small and black between his finger and thumb.

"Jane," he began in an eager voice. But the sentence was never finished. For Jane was making signs to him, and as he turned to Mary Poppins he understood their meaning.

Her knitting had fallen on to the rug and her hands lay folded in her lap. She was looking at something far away, beyond the Lane, beyond the Park, perhaps beyond the horizon.

Carefully, so as not to disturb her, the children crept to her side. The Park Keeper plumped himself down on the rug and stared at her, goggle-eyed.

"Yes, Mary Poppins?" prompted Jane. "The Goose-girl — tell us about her!"

Michael pressed against her skirt and waited expectantly. He could feel her legs, bony and strong, beneath the cool blue linen.

From under the shadow of her hat she glanced at them for a short moment, and looked away again.

"Well, there she sat —— " she began gravely, speaking in the soft accents that were so unlike her usual voice.

"There she sat, day after day, amid her flock of geese, braiding her hair and unbraiding it for lack of something to do. Sometimes she would pick a fern and wave it before her like a fan, the way the Lord Chancellor's wife might do, or even the Queen, maybe.

"Or again, she would weave a necklace of flowers and go to the brook to admire it. And every time she did that she noticed that her eyes were blue — bluer than any periwinkle — and her cheeks like the breast of the robin. As for her mouth — not to mention her nose! — her opinion of these was so high she had no words fit to describe them."

"She sounds like you, Mary Poppins," said Michael. "So terribly pleased with herself!"

Her glance came darting from the horizon and flickered at him fiercely.

"I mean, Mary Poppins —— " he began to stammer. Had he broken the thread of the story?

"I mean," he went on flatteringly, "*you've* got pink cheeks and blue eyes, too. Like lollipops and bluebells."

A slow smile of satisfaction melted her angry look, and Michael gave a sigh of relief as she took up the tale again.

Well, she went on, there was the brook, and there was the Goose-girl's reflection. And each time she looked at it, she was sorry for everyone in the world who was missing such a spectacle. And she pitied in particular the handsome Swineherd who herded his flock on the other side of the stream.

"If only," she thought, lamentingly, "I were not the person I am! If I were merely what I seem, I could then invite him over. But since I am something more than a goose-girl, it would not be right or proper."

And reluctantly she turned her back and looked in the other direction.

She would have been surprised, perhaps, had she known what the Swineherd was thinking.

He, too, for lack of a looking-glass, made use of the little river. And when it reflected his dark curls, and the curve of his chin and his well-shaped ears, he grieved for the whole human race, thinking of all it was missing. And especially he grieved for the Goose-girl.

"Undoubtedly," he told himself, "she is dying of loneliness — sitting there in her shabby dress, braiding her yellow hair. It is very pretty hair, too, and — but for the fact that I am *who* I am — I would willingly speak a word to her and while away the time."

And reluctantly he turned his back and looked in the other direction.

What a coincidence, you will say! But there's more to the story than that. Not only the Goose-girl and the Swineherd, but every creature in that place was thinking the same thoughts.

The geese, as they nibbled the buttercups and flattened the grass into star-like shapes, were convinced — and they made no secret of it — they were something more than geese.

And the swine would have laughed at any suggestion that they were merely pigs.

And so it was with the grey Ass who pulled the Swineherd's cart to market; and the Toad who lived beside the stream, under one of the stepping-stones; and the barefoot Boy with the Toy Monkey who played on the bridge every day.

Each believed that his real self was infinitely greater and grander than the one to be seen with the naked eye.

Around his little shaggy body, the Ass was confident, a lordlier, finer, sleeker shape kicked its hooves in the daisies.

To the Toad, however, *his* true self was smaller than his outward shape, and very gay and green. He would gaze for hours at his reflection but, ugly as it truly was, the sight never depressed him.

"That's only my outside," he would say, nodding at his wrinkled skin and yellow bulging eyes. But he kept his outside out of sight when the Boy was on the bridge. For he dreaded the curses that greeted him if he showed as much as a toe.

"Heave to!" the ferocious voice would cry. "Enemy sighted to starboard! A bottle of rum and a new dagger to the man who rips him apart!"

For the Boy was something more than a boy — as you'll probably have guessed. Inside, he knew the Straits of Magellan as you know the nose on your face. Honest mariners paled at his fame, his deeds were a byword in seven seas. He could sack a dozen ships in a morning and bury the treasure so cleverly that even he could not find it.

To a passer-by it might have seemed that the Boy had two good eyes. But in his own private opinion, he was only possessed of one. He had lost the other in a hand-to-hand fight somewhere off Gibraltar. His everyday name always made him smile when people called him by it. "If they knew who I really am," he would say, "they wouldn't look so cheerful!"

As for the Monkey, *he* believed he was nothing like a monkey.

"This old fur coat," he assured himself, "is simply to keep me warm. And I swing by my tail for the fun of it, not because I must."

Well, there they all were, one afternoon, full of their fine ideas. The sun spread over them like a fan, very warm and cosy. The meadow flowers hung on their stems, bright as newly-washed china. Up in the sky the larks were singing — on and on, song without end, as though they were all wound up.

The Goose-girl sat among her geese, the Swineherd with his swine. The Ass in his field, and the Toad in his hole, were nodding sleepily. And the Boy and his Monkey lolled on the bridge discussing their further plans for bloodshed.

Suddenly the Ass snorted and his ear gave a questioning twitch. Larks were above and the brook beneath, but he heard among these daily sounds the echo of a footstep.

Along the path that led to the stream a ragged man was lounging. His tattered clothes were so old that you couldn't find one bit of them that wasn't tied with string. The brim of his hat framed a face that was rosy and mild in the sunlight, and through the brim his hair stuck up in tufts of grey and silver. His steps were alternately light and heavy, for one foot wore an old boot and the other a bedroom slipper. You would have to look for a long time to find a shabbier man.

But his shabbiness seemed not to trouble him — indeed, he appeared to enjoy it. For he wandered along contentedly, eating a crust and a pickled onion and whistling between mouthfuls. Then he spied the group in the meadow, and stared, and his tune broke off in the middle.

"A beautiful day!" he said politely, plucking the hat-brim from his head and bowing to the Goose-girl.

She gave him a haughty, tossing glance, but the Tramp did not seem to notice it.

"You two been quarrelling?" he asked, jerking his head at the Swineherd.

The Goose-girl laughed indignantly. "Quarrelling? What a silly remark! Why, I do not even know him!"

"Well," said the Tramp, with a cheerful smile, would you like me to introduce you?"

"Certainly not!" She flung up her head. "How could I associate with a swineherd? I'm a princess in disguise."

"Indeed?" said the Tramp, looking very surprised. "If that is the case, I must not detain you. I expect you want to be back at the Palace, getting on with your work."

"Work? What work?" The Goose-girl stared.

It was now her turn to look surprised. Surely princesses sat upon cushions, with slaves to perform their least command.

"Why, spinning and weaving. And etiquette! Practising patience and cheerfulness while unsuitable suitors beg for your hand. Trying to look as if you liked it when you hear, for the hundred-thousandth time, the King's three silly riddles! Not many princesses — as you must know — have leisure to sit all day in the sun among a handful of geese!"

"But what about wearing a pearly crown? And dancing till dawn with the Sultan's son?"

"Dancing? Pearls? Oh, my! Oh, my!" A burst of laughter broke from the Tramp, as he took from his sleeve a piece of sausage.

"Those crowns are as heavy as lead or iron. You'd have a ridge in your head in no time. And a princess's duty — surely you know? — is to dance with her father's old friends first. Then the Lord Chamberlain. Then the Lord Chancellor. And, of course, the Keeper of the Seal. By the time you get round to the Sultan's son, it's late and he's had to go home."

The Goose-girl pondered the Tramp's words. Could he really be speaking the truth? All the goose-girls in all the stories were princesses in disguise. But, oh, how difficult it sounded! What did one say to Lord Chamberlains? "Come here!" "Go there!" as one would to a goose? Spinning and weaving! Etiquette!

Perhaps, taking everything into account, it might be better, the Goose-girl thought, simply to be a goose-girl.

"Well, away to the Palace!" the Tramp advised her. "You're wasting your time sitting here, you know! Don't you agree?" he called to the Swineherd, who was listening from his side of the stream.

"Agree with what?" said the Swineherd quickly, as though he hadn't heard a word. "I never concern myself with goose-girls," he added untruthfully. "It would not be fitting or suitable. I am a prince in disguise!"

"You are?" cried the Tramp, admiringly. "Then you're occupying your time, I suppose, in getting up muscle to fight the Dragon."

The Swineherd's damask cheek grew pale. "What dragon?" he asked in a stifled voice.

"Oh, any that you chance to meet. All princes, as you

yourself must know, have to fight at least one dragon. That is what princes are for."

"Two-headed?" enquired the Swineherd, gulping.

"Two?" cried the Tramp. "Seven, you mean! Two-headed dragons are quite out of date."

The Swineherd felt his heart thump. Suppose, in spite of all the stories, instead of the prince killing the monster, the monster should kill the prince? He was not, you understand, afraid. But he wondered whether, after all, he were not a simple swineherd.

"A fine lot of porkers you've got there!" The Tramp glanced appreciatively from the swine to his piece of sausage.

A snort of disgust went up from the herd. A raggedy tramp to be calling them porkers!

"Perhaps you are not aware," they grunted, "that we are sheep in disguise!"

"Oh, dear!" said the Tramp, with a doleful air. "I'm sorry for you, my friends!"

"Why should you be sorry?" demanded the swine, sticking their snouts in the air.

"Why? Surely you know that the people here are extremely partial to mutton! If they knew there was a flock of sheep — however disguised — in this meadow —— " He broke off, shaking his head and sighing. Then he searched among his tattered rags, discovered a piece of plum cake and munched it sombrely.

The swine, aghast, looked at each other. Mutton—what a frightful word! They had thought of themselves as graceful lambs prancing for ever in fields of flowers—never as legs of mutton. Would it not be wiser, they cogitated, to decide to be merely pigs?

"Here, goosey-ganders!" chirruped the Tramp. He tossed his crumbs to the Goose-girl's flock.

The geese, as one bird, raised their heads and let out a snake-like hiss.

"We're swans!" they cackled in high-pitched chorus. And then, as he did not seem to believe them, they added the word, "Disguised!"

"Well, if that's the case," the Tramp remarked, "you won't be here very long. All swans, as you know, belong to the King. Dear me, what lucky birds you are! You will swim on the ornamental lake, and courtiers with golden scissors will clip your flying-feathers. Strawberry jam on silver plates will be given you every morning. And not a care in the world will you have—not even the trouble of hatching your eggs, for these His Majesty eats for breakfast."

"What!" cried the geese. "No grubs? No goslings?"

"Certainly not! But think of the honour!" The Tramp chuckled and turned away, bumping into a shaggy shape that was standing among the daisies.

The geese stood rigid in the grass, staring at each other.

Strawberry jam! Clipped wings! No hatching season! Could they have made a mistake, they wondered? Were they not, after all, just geese?

From something that once had been a pocket the Tramp extracted an apple.

"Pardon, friend!" he said to the Ass, as he took a juicy bite. "I'd offer you half — but you don't need it. You've all this buttercup field."

The Ass surveyed the scene with distaste. "It may be all very well for donkeys, but don't imagine," he remarked, "that I'm such an ass as I look. As you may be interested to know, I'm an Arab steed in disguise!"

"Indeed?" The Tramp looked very impressed. "How you must long, if that is so, for the country of your birth. Sandstorms! Mirages! Waterless deserts!"

"Waterless?" The Ass looked anxious.

"Well, practically. But that's nothing to you. The way you Arab animals can live for weeks on nothing — nothing to eat, nothing to drink, nowhere to sleep — it's wonderful!"

"But what about all those oases? Surely grass grows there?"

"Few and far between," said the Tramp. "But what of that, my friend? The less you eat the faster you go! The less you drink the lighter you are! It only takes you half a jiffy to fling yourself down and shelter your master when his enemies attack!"

"But," cried the Ass, "in that case, *I* should be shot at first!"

"Naturally," the Tramp replied. "That's why one admires you so — you noble Arab steeds. You're ready to die at any moment!"

The Ass rubbed his forehead against his leg. Was he ready to die at any moment? He could not honestly answer Yes. Weeks and weeks with nothing to eat! And here the buttercups and daisies were enough for a dozen asses. He might indeed be an Arab steed — but then again, he mightn't. Up and down went his shaggy head as he pondered the difficult problem.

"That's for you, old Natterjack!" The Tramp tossed the core of his apple under the stepping-stone.

"Don't call me Natterjack!" snapped the Toad.

"Puddocky, then, if you prefer it!"

"Those are the names one gives to toads. *I* am a frog in disguise."

"Oh, happy creature!" the Tramp exclaimed. "Sitting on lily-leaves all night, singing a song to the moon."

"All night? I'd take my death of cold!"

"Catching spiders and dragonflies for the lady-frog of your choice!"

"None for myself?" the Toad enquired.

"A frog that would a-wooing go — and you are certainly such a one! — wouldn't want to catch for himself!"

The Toad was, however, not so sure. He liked a juicy

spider. He was just deciding, after all, that he might as well be a toad, when — plop! — went a pebble right beside him and he hurriedly popped in his head.

"Who threw that?" said the Tramp quickly.

"I did," came the answer from the bridge. "Not to hit him! Just to make him jump!"

"Good boy!" The Tramp looked up with a smile. "A fine, friendly lad like you wouldn't hurt a toad!"

"Of course I wouldn't. Or anything else. But don't you call me boy or lad. I'm really a ——— "

"Wait! Don't tell me! Let me guess! An Indian? No — a pirate!"

"That's right!" said the Boy, with a curt nod, showing all the gaps in his teeth in a terrible pirate smile. "If you want to know my name," he snarled, "just call me One-eyed Corambo!"

"Got your cutlass?" the Tramp enquired. "Your skull-and-crossbones? Your black silk mask? Well, I shouldn't hang about here any longer! Landlubbers aren't worth robbing! Set your course away from the North. Make for Tierra del Fuego."

"Been there," the Boy said loftily.

"Well, any other place you like — no pirate lingers long on land. Have you been ——— " the Tramp lowered his voice, "have you been to *Dead Man's Drop?*"

The Boy smiled and shook his head.

"That's the place for me," he cried, reaching for his

Monkey "I'll just go and say good-bye to my mother and——"

"Your mother! Did I hear aright? One-eyed Corambo hopping off to say good-bye to his mother! A pirate captain wasting time by running home—well, really!" The Tramp was overcome with amusement.

The Boy looked at him doubtfully. Where, he wondered, *was* Dead Man's Drop? How long would it take him to go and come? His mother would be anxious. And apart from that—as he'd reason to know—she was making pancakes for supper. It might be better, just for today, to be his outer self. Corambo could wait until tomorrow, Corambo was always there.

"Taking your monkey along as a mascot?" The Tramp looked quizzically at the toy.

He was answered by an angry squeal. "Don't you call me a monkey!" it jabbered. "I'm a little boy in disguise!"

"A boy!" cried the Tramp. "And not at school?"

"School?" said the Monkey nervously. "'Two and two make five,' you mean, and all that sort of thing?"

"Exactly," said the Tramp gravely. "You'd better hurry along now before they find you're missing. Here!" He scrabbled among his rags, drew two chocolates from under his collar, and offered one to the Monkey.

But the little creature turned its back. School—he hadn't bargained for that. Better, any day of the week, to be a moth-eaten monkey. He felt a sudden rush of love for his old fur coat and his glass eyes and his wrinkled jungle tail.

"You take it, Corambo!" The Tramp grinned. "Pirates are always hungry." He handed one chocolate to the Boy and ate the other himself.

"Well," he said, licking his lips. "Time flies and so must I!" He glanced round at the little group and gave a cheerful nod.

"So long!" He smiled at them rosily. And thrusting his hands among his rags he brought out a piece of bread and butter and sauntered away across the bridge.

The Boy gazed after him thoughtfully, with a line across his brow. Then suddenly he threw up his hand.

"Hey!" he cried.

The Tramp paused.

"What is your name? You never told us! Who are *you*?" said the Boy.

"Yes, indeed!" came a score of voices. "Who are *you*?" the Goose-girl asked; and the Swineherd, the geese, the swine and the Ass echoed the eager question. Even the Toad put out his head and demanded: "Who are *you*?"

"Me?" cried the Tramp, with an innocent smile. "If you really want to know," he said, "I'm an angel in disguise."

He bowed to them amid his tatters and waved as he turned away.

"Ha, ha, ha! A jolly good joke!"

The Boy burst into a peal of laughter. Jug-jug-jug! in his throat it went. That tattered old thing an angel!

But suddenly the laugh ceased. The Boy stared, screwed up his eyes, looked again and stared.

The Tramp was skipping along the road, hopping for joy, it seemed. Each time he skipped his feet went higher and the earth — could it really be true, the Boy wondered? — was falling away beneath him. Now he was skimming the tops of the daisies and presently he was over the hedge, skipping higher and higher. Up, up he went and cleared the woodland, plumbing the depths of the sky. Then he spread himself on the sunny air and stretched his arms and legs.

And as he did so the tattered rags fluttered along his back. Something, the watchers clearly saw, was pushing them aside.

Then, feather by feather, from under each shoulder, a broad grey pinion showed. Out and out the big plumes stretched, on either side of the Tramp, until he was only a tattered scrap between his lifting wings. They flapped for a moment above the trees, balancing strongly against the air, then with a sweeping sea-gull movement they bore him up and away.

"Oh, dear! Oh, dear!" the Goose-girl sighed, knitting her brows in a frown. For the Tramp had put her in an awkward predicament. She was almost — if not quite — convinced she was not the daughter of a King, and now — well look at him! All those feathers under his rags! If he was an angel, what was she? A goose-girl — or something grander?

Up, up he went, plumbing the depths of the sky

Her mind was whirling. Which was true? Shaking her head in bewilderment, she glanced across the stream at the Swineherd, and the sight of him made her burst out laughing. Really, she couldn't help it.

There he sat, gazing up at the sky, with his curls standing on end with surprise, and his eyes as round as soup-plates.

"Ahem!" She gave a delicate cough. "Perhaps it will not be necessary to fight the Dragon now!"

He turned to her with a startled look. Then he saw that she was smiling gently and his face suddenly cleared. He laughed and leapt across the stream.

"You shall have your golden crown," he cried. "I'll make it for you myself!"

"Gold is too heavy," she said demurely, behind her ferny fan.

"Not my kind of gold." The Swineherd smiled. He gathered a handful of buttercups, wove them into a little wreath and set it on her head.

And from that moment the question which was once so grave — were they goose-girl and swineherd, or prince and princess? — seemed to them not to matter. They sat there gazing at each other, forgetting everything else.

The geese, who were also quite amazed, glanced from the fading speck in the sky to their neighbours in the meadow.

"Poor pigs!" they murmured mockingly. "Roast mutton with onion sauce!"

"You'll look pretty foolish," the swine retorted, "on an ornamental lake!"

But though they spoke harshly to each other, they could not help feeling, privately, that the Tramp had put them in a very tight corner.

Then an old goose gave a high-pitched giggle.

"What does it matter?" he cackled gaily. "Whatever we are within ourselves, at least we *look* like geese!"

"True!" agreed an elderly pig. "And *we* have the shape of swine!"

And at that, as though released from a burden, they all began to laugh. The field rang with their mingled cries and the larks looked down in wonder.

"What does it matter — cackle, cackle! What does it matter — ker-onk, ker-onk!"

"Hee-haw!" said the Ass, as he flung up his head and joined in the merry noise.

"Thinking about your fine oasis?" the Toad enquired sarcastically.

"Hee-haw! Hee-haw! I am indeed! What an ass I was, not to see it before. I've only just realised, Natterjack, that my oasis is not in the desert. Heehaw! Hee-haw! It's under my hoof — here in this very field."

"Then you're not an Arab steed after all?" the Toad enquired, with a jeer.

"Ah," said the Ass, "I wouldn't say that. But now" — he glanced at the flying figure — "I'm content with my disguise!"

He snatched at a buttercup hungrily as though he had galloped a long distance through a leafless, sandy land.

The Toad looked up with a wondering eye.

"Could *I* be content with *my* disguise?" He pondered the question gravely. And as he did so a hazel nut fell from a branch above him. It hit his head and bounced off lightly, bobbing away on the stream.

"That would have stunned a frog," thought the Toad, "but I, in my horny coat, felt nothing." A gratified smile, very large and toothy, split his face in the middle. He thrust out his head and craned it upwards.

"Come on with your pebbles, boy!" he croaked. "I've got my armour on!"

But the Boy did not hear the puddocky challenge. He was leaning back against the bridge, watching the Tramp on his broad wings flying into the sunset. Not with surprise — perhaps he was not yet old enough to be surprised at things — but his eyes had a look of lively interest.

He watched and watched till the sky grew dusky and the first stars twinkled out. And when the little flying speck was no longer even a speck, he drew a long, contented sigh and turned again to the earth.

That he was Corambo, he did not doubt. He had never doubted it. But now he knew he was other things, as well as a one-eyed pirate. And far above all — he rejoiced at it — he was just a bare-foot boy. And, moreover, a boy who was feeling peckish and ready for his supper.

"Come on!" he called to the Toy Monkey. He tucked it

comfortably under his arm, with its tail around his wrist. And the two of them kept each other warm as they wandered home together.

The long day fell away behind him to join his other days. All he could think of now was the night. He could sense already the warmth of the kitchen, the sizzling pancakes on the stove and his mother bending above them. Her face, framed in its ring of curls, would be ruddy and weary — like the sun. For, indeed, as he had many times told her, the sun has a mother's face.

And presently, there he was on the doorstep and there was she as he had pictured her. He leaned against her checked apron and broke off a piece of pancake.

"Well, what have you been doing?" she smiled.

"Nothing," he murmured contentedly.

For he knew — and perhaps she knew it too — that nothing is a useful word. It can mean exactly what you like — anything — everything. . . .

The end of the story died away.

Mary Poppins sat still and silent.

Around her lay the motionless children, making never a sound. Her gaze, coming back from the far horizon, flickered across their quiet faces and over the head of the Park Keeper, as it nodded dreamily.

"Humph!" she remarked, with a haughty sniff. "I recount a chapter of history and you all fall fast asleep!"

"I'm not asleep," Jane reassured her. "I'm thinking about the story."

"I heard every word," said Michael, yawning.

The Park Keeper rocked, as if in a trance. "A Nexplorer in disguise," he murmured, "sittin' in the midnight sun and climbin' the North Pole!"

"Ouch!" cried Michael, starting up. "I felt a drop on my nose!"

"And I felt one on my chin," said Jane.

They rubbed their eyes and looked about them. The

syrupy sun had disappeared and a cloud was creeping over the Park. Plop! Plop! Patter, patter! The big drops drummed on the leaves.

The Park Keeper opened his eyes and stared.

"It's rainin'!" he cried in astonishment. "And me with no umbrella!"

He glanced at the dangling shape on the bough and darted towards the parrot.

"Oh, no, you don't!" said Mary Poppins. Quick as a needle, she grasped the handle.

"I've a long way to go and me chest is bad and I oughtn't to wet me feet!" The Park Keeper gave her a pleading glance.

"Then you'd better not go to the North Pole!" She snapped the parrot umbrella open and gathered up Annabel. "The Equator — that's the place for you!" She turned away with a snort of contempt.

"Wake up, John and Barbara, please! Jane and Michael, take the rug and wrap it round yourselves and the Twins."

Raindrops bigger than sugar-plums were tumbling all about them. They drummed and thumped on the children's heads as they wrapped themselves in the rug.

"We're a parcel!" cried Michael excitedly. "Tie us up with string, Mary Poppins, and send us through the post!"

"Run!" she commanded, taking no notice. And away they hurried, stumbling and tumbling, over the rainy grass.

The dogs came barking along beside them and, forgetting their promise to Mary Poppins, shook themselves over her skirt.

"All that sun and all this rain! One after another! Who'd 'ave thought it?"

The Park Keeper shook his head in bewilderment. He could still hardly believe it.

"An explorer would!" snapped Mary Poppins. She gave her head a satisfied toss. "And so would I — so there!"

"Too big for your boots — that's what you are!" The Park Keeper's words were worse than they sounded. For he whispered them into his coat-collar in case she should overhear. But, even so, perhaps she guessed them, for she flung at him a smile of conceit and triumph as she hurried after the children.

Off she tripped through the streaming Park, picking her way among the puddles. Neat and trim as a fashion-plate she crossed Cherry-Tree Lane and flitted up the garden path of Number Seventeen. . . .

Jane emerged from the plaid bundle and patted her soaking hair.

"Oh, bother!" she said. "I've lost my feather."

"That settles it, then," said Michael calmly. "You can't be Minnehaha!"

He unwound himself and felt in his pocket. "Ah, here's my ant! I've got him safely!"

"Oh, I don't mean Minnehaha, really — but some-body," persisted Jane, "somebody else inside me. I know. I always have the feeling."

The black ant hurried across the table.

"I don't," Michael said, as he gazed at it. "I don't feel anything inside me but my dinner and Michael Banks."

But Jane was thinking her own thoughts.

"And Mary Poppins," she went on. "She's somebody in disguise, too. Everybody is."

"Oh, no, she's not!" said Michael stoutly. "I'm absolute-ly certain!"

A light step sounded on the landing.

"Who's not what?" enquired a voice.

"You, Mary Poppins!" Michael cried. "Jane says you're somebody in disguise. And *I* say you aren't. You're no-body!"

Her head went up with a quick jerk and her eyes had a hint of danger.

"I hope," she said, with awful calmness, "that I did not hear what I *think* I heard. Did you say I was nobody, Michael?"

"Yes! I mean — no!" He tried again. "I really meant to say, Mary Poppins, that you're not really *anybody!*"

"Oh, indeed?" Her eyes were now as black as a boot-button. "If I'm not anybody, Michael, who *am* I — I'd like to know!"

"Oh, dear!" he wailed. "I'm all muddled. You're not *somebody,* Mary Poppins — that's what I'm trying to say."

Not somebody in her tulip hat! Not somebody in her fine blue skirt! Her reflection gazed at her from the mirror, assuring her that she and it were an elegant pair of somebodies.

"Well!" She drew a deep breath and seemed to grow taller as she spoke. "You have often insulted me, Michael Banks. But I never thought I would see the day when you'd tell me I wasn't somebody. What am I, then, a painted portrait?"

She took a step towards him.

"I m-m-mean —— " he stammered, clutching at Jane. Her hand was warm and reassuring and the words he was looking for leapt to his lips.

"I don't mean somebody, Mary Poppins! I mean not somebody *else!* You're Mary Poppins through and through! Inside and outside. And round about. All of you is Mary Poppins. That is how I like you!"

"Humph!" she said, disbelievingly. But the fierceness faded away from her face.

With a laugh of relief he sprang towards her, embracing her wet blue skirt.

"Don't grab me like that, Michael Banks. I am not a Dutch Doll, thank you!"

"You are!" he shouted. "No, you're not! You only look like one. Oh, Mary Poppins, tell me truly! You aren't anybody in disguise? I want you just as you are!"

A faint, pleased smile puckered her mouth. Her head gave a prideful toss.

"Me! Disguised! Certainly not!"

With a loud sniff at the mere idea, she disengaged his hands.

"But, Mary Poppins ——" Jane persisted. "Supposing you weren't Mary Poppins, who would you choose to be?"

The blue eyes under the tulip hat turned to her in surprise.

There was only one answer to such a question.

"Mary Poppins!" she said.

CHAPTER TWO

THE FAITHFUL FRIENDS

"Faster, please!" said Mary Poppins, tapping on the glass panel with the beak of her parrot-headed umbrella.

Jane and Michael had spent the morning at the Barber's shop, and the Dentist's, and because it was late, as a great treat, they were taking a taxi home.

The Taxi Man stared straight before him and gave his head a shake.

"If I go any faster," he shouted, "it'll make me late for me dinner."

"Why?" demanded Jane, through the window. It seemed such a silly thing to say. Surely, the quicker a Taxi Man drove the earlier he would arrive!

"Why?" echoed the Taxi Man, keeping his eye on the wheel. "A Naccident — that's why! If I go any faster, I'll run into something — and that'll be a Naccident. And a Naccident — it's plain enough! — will make me late for me dinner. Oh, dear!" he exclaimed, as he put on the brake. "Red again, I see!"

He turned and put his head through the window. His bulgy eyes and drooping whiskers made him look like a seal.

"There's always trouble at these 'ere signals!" He waved his hand at the stream of cars all waiting for the lights to change.

And now it was Michael who asked him why.

"Don't you know *nothing?*" the Taxi Man cried. "It's because of the chap on duty!"

He pointed to the signal-box, where a helmeted figure, with his head on his hand, was gazing into the distance.

"Absent-minded — that's what 'e is. Always staring and moping. And 'alf the time 'e forgets the lights. I've known them stay red for a whole morning. If it's goin' to be like that today I'll never get me dinner. You 'aven't got a sangwidge on you?" He looked at Michael, hopefully.

"No? Nor yet a chocolate drop?" Jane smiled and shook her head.

The Taxi Man sighed despondently.

"Nobody thinks of nobody these days."

"*I'm* thinking of someone!" said Mary Poppins. And she looked so stern and disapproving that he turned away in dismay.

"They're green!" he cried, as he looked at the lights. And, huddling nervously over the wheel, he drove along Park Avenue as though pursued by wolves.

Bump! Bump! Rattle! Rattle! The three of them jolted and bounced on their seats.

"Sit up straight!" said Mary Poppins, sliding into a corner. "You are not a couple of Jack-in-the-boxes!"

"I know I'm not," said Michael, gasping. "But I feel like one and my bones are shaking —— " He gulped quickly and bit his tongue and left the sentence unfinished. For the taxi had stopped with a frightful jerk and flung them all to the floor.

"Mary Poppins," said Jane in a muffled voice, "I think you're *sitting* on me!"

"My foot! My foot! It's caught in something!"

"I'll thank you, Michael," said Mary Poppins, "to take it out of my hat!"

She rose majestically from the floor, and seizing her parrot-headed umbrella sprang out on to the pavement.

"Well, you said to go faster," the Taxi Man muttered, as she thrust the fare into his hand. She glared at him in offended silence. And in order to escape that look he shrank himself down inside his collar so that nothing was left but his whiskers.

"Don't bother about a tip," he begged. "It's really been a p-p-pleasure."

"I had no intention of bothering!" She opened the gate of Number Seventeen with an angry flick of her hand.

The Taxi Man started up his engine and jerked away down the Lane. "She's upset me, that's what she's done!" he murmured. "If I do get home in time for me dinner I shan't be able to eat it!"

Mary Poppins tripped up the path, followed by Jane and Michael.

Mrs. Banks stood in the front hall, looking up at the stairs.

"Oh, do be careful, Robertson Ay!" she was saying anxiously. He was carrying a cardboard box and lurching slowly from stair to stair as though he were almost asleep.

"Never a moment's peace!" he muttered. "First it's one thing, then another. There!" He gave a sleepy heave, thrust the package into the nursery and fell in a snoring heap on the landing.

Jane dashed upstairs to took at the label.

"What's in it — a present?" shouted Michael.

The Twins, bursting with curiosity, were jumping up

and down. And Annabel peered through her cot railings and banged her rattle loudly.

"Is this a nursery or a bear-pit?" Mary Poppins stepped over Robertson Ay as she hurried into the room.

"A bear-pit!" Michael longed to answer. But he caught her eye and refrained.

"Really!" Mrs. Banks protested, as she stumbled over Robertson Ay. "He chooses such inconvenient places! Oh, gently, children! Do be careful! That box belongs to Miss Andrew!"

Miss Andrew! Their faces fell.

"Then it isn't presents!" said Michael blankly. He gave the box a push.

"It's probably full of medicine bottles!" said Jane, in a bitter voice.

"It's not," insisted Mrs. Banks. "Miss Andrew has sent us all her treasures. And I thought, Mary Poppins" — she glanced at the stiff white shape beside her — "I thought, perhaps, you could keep them here!" She nodded towards the mantelpiece.

Mary Poppins regarded her in silence. If a pin had fallen you could have heard it.

"Am I an octopus?" she enquired, finding her voice at last.

"An octopus?" cried Mrs. Banks. Had she ever suggested such a thing? "Of course you're not, Mary Poppins."

"Exactly!" Mary Poppins retorted. "I have only one pair of hands."

Mrs. Banks nodded uneasily. She had never expected her to have more.

"And that one pair has enough to do without dusting *anyone's* treasures."

"But Mary Poppins, I never dreamed——" Mrs. Banks was getting more and more flustered. "Ellen is here to do the dusting. And it's only until Miss Andrew comes back — if, of course, she ever does. She behaved so strangely when she was here. Why are you giggling, Jane?"

But Jane only snickered and shook her head. She remembered that strange behaviour!

"Where has she gone to?" Michael asked.

"She seems to have had some sort of a shock — what are you laughing at, children? — and the doctor has ordered a long voyage, away to the South Seas. She says —— " Mrs. Banks fished into her pocket and brought out a crumpled letter. "And while I am away," she read out,

"I shall leave my valuables with you. Be sure they are put in a safe place where nothing can happen to them. I shall expect, on my return, to find everything exactly as it is — nothing broken, nothing mended. Tell George to wear his overcoat. This weather is changeable."

"So you see, Mary Poppins," said Mrs. Banks, looking up with a flattering smile, "the nursery does seem the best place. Anything left in *your* charge is always perfectly safe!"

"There's safety *and* safety!" sniffed Mary Poppins. "And I hope I see further than my nose!" It was tilted upwards, as she spoke, even more than usual.

"Oh, I am sure you do!" murmured Mrs. Banks, wondering, for the hundredth time, why Mary Poppins — no matter what the situation — was always so pleased with herself.

"Well, now I think I must go and —— " But without saying what she was going to do, she ran out of the nursery, jumped over Robertson Ay's legs and bustled away down the stairs.

"Allow me, Michael, if you please!" Mary Poppins seized his wrist, as he pulled the lid off the box. "Remember what curiosity did — it killed the cat, you know!"

Her quick hands darted among the papers, and briskly unwrapped a little bundle. Out came a bird with a chipped nose and a Chelsea china lamb.

"Funny sort of treasures," said Michael. "I could mend this bird with a piece of putty. But I mustn't — so Miss Andrew said. They're to stay exactly as they are."

"Nothing does that," said Mary Poppins, with a priggish look on her face.

"You do!" he insisted, gallantly.

She sniffed, and glanced at the nursery mirror. Her reflection gave a similar sort of sniff and glanced at Mary Poppins. Each of them, it was easy to see, highly approved of the other.

"I wonder why she kept this?" Jane took an old cracked tile from the box. The picture showed a boatload of people rowing towards an island.

"To remind her of her youth," said Michael.

"To give more trouble," snapped Mary Poppins, shaking the dust from another wrapping.

Back and forth the children ran, collecting and setting up the treasures — a cottage in a snowstorm, with *Home Sweet Home* on the glass globe; a pottery hen on a yellow nest; a red-and-white china clown; a winged horse of celluloid, prancing on its hind legs; a flower vase in the shape of a swan; a little red fox of carved wood; an egg-shaped piece of polished granite; a painted apple with a boy and a girl playing together inside it; and a roughly made, full-rigged ship in a jam-jar.

"I hope that's all," grumbled Michael. "The mantelpiece is crowded."

"Only one more," said Mary Poppins, as she drew out a knobbly bundle. A couple of china ornaments came forth from the paper wrapper. Her eyebrows went up as she looked at them and she gave a little shrug. Then she handed one each to Jane and Michael.

Weary of running back and forth, they set the ornaments hurriedly at either end of the mantelpiece. Then Jane looked at hers and blinked her eyes.

A china lion, with his paw on the chest of a china huntsman, was reclining beneath a banana tree which, of course, was also china. The man and the animal leaned together, smiling blissfully. Never, thought Jane, in all her life, had she seen two happier creatures.

"He reminds me of somebody!" she exclaimed, as she gazed at the smiling huntsman. Such a manly figure he looked, too, in his spruce blue jacket and black top-boots.

"Yes," agreed Michael. "Who can it be?"

He frowned as he tried to recall the name. Then he looked at his half of the china pair and gave a cry of dismay.

"Oh! Jane! *What* a pity! My lion has lost his huntsman!"

It was true. There stood another banana-tree, there

sat another painted lion. But in the other huntsman's
place there was only a gap of roughened china. All that
remained of his manly shape was one black shiny boot.

"Poor lion!" said Michael. "He looks so sad!"

And, indeed, there was no denying it. Jane's lion was
wreathed in smiles, but his brother had such a dejected
look that he seemed to be almost in tears.

"*You'll* be looking sad in a minute — unless you get
ready for lunch!"

Mary Poppins' face was so like her voice that they ran to obey her without a word.

But they caught a glimpse, as they rushed away, of her starched white figure standing there, with its arms full of crumpled paper. She was gazing with a reflective smile at Miss Andrew's broken treasure — and it seemed to them that her lips moved.

Michael gave Jane a fleeting grin.

"I expect she's only saying 'Humph!'"

But Jane was not so sure. . . .

"Let's go to the swings," suggested Michael, as they hurried across the Lane after lunch.

"Oh, no! The Lake. I'm tired of swinging."

"Neither swings nor lakes," said Mary Poppins. "We are taking the Long Walk!"

"Oh, Mary Poppins," grumbled Jane, "the Long Walk's far too long!"

"I can't walk all that way," said Michael. "I've eaten much too much."

The Long Walk stretched across the Park from the Lane to the Far Gate, linking the little countrified road to the busy streets they had travelled that morning. It was wide and straight and uncompromising — not like the narrow, curly paths that led to the Lake and the Playground. Trees and fountains bordered it, but it always seemed to Jane and Michael at least ten miles in length.

"The Long Walk — or the short walk home! Take your choice!" Mary Poppins warned them.

Michael was just about to say he would go home, when Jane ran on ahead.

"I'll race you," she cried, "to the first tree!"

Michael could never bear to be beaten. "That's not fair! You had a good start!" And off he dashed at her heels.

"Don't expect *me* to keep up with you! I am not a centipede!"

Mary Poppins sauntered along, enjoying the balmy air, and assuring herself that the balmy air was enjoying Mary Poppins. How could it do otherwise, she thought, when under her arm was the parrot umbrella and over her wrist a new black hand-bag?

The perambulator creaked and groaned. In it, the Twins and Annabel, packed as close as birds in a nest, were playing with the blue duck.

"That's cheating, Michael!" grumbled Jane. For accidentally on purpose, he had pushed her aside and was running past.

From tree to tree they raced along, first one ahead and then the other, each of them trying to win. The Long Walk streamed away behind them and Mary Poppins and the perambulator were only specks in the distance.

"Next time you push me I'll give you a punch!" said Michael, red in the face.

"If you bump into me again I'll pull your hair, Michael!"

"Now, now!" the Park Keeper warned them sternly. "Observe the rules! No argle-bargling!"

He was meant to be sweeping up the twigs but, instead, he was chatting with the Policeman, who was leaning against a maple-tree, whiling away his time.

Jane and Michael stopped in their tracks. Their race, they were both surprised to find, had brought them right across the Park and near to the Far Gate.

The Park Keeper looked at them severely. "Always argufying!" he said. "I never did that when *I* was a boy. But then I was a Nonly child, just me and me poor old mother. I never 'ad nobody to play with. You two don't know when you're lucky!"

"Well, I dunno!" the Policeman said. "Depends on how you look at it. I had someone to play with, you might say, but it never did *me* any good!"

"Brothers or sisters?" Jane enquired, all her crossness vanishing. She liked the Policeman very much. And to-day he seemed to remind her of someone, but she couldn't think who it was.

"Brothers!" the Policeman informed her, without enthusiasm.

"Older or younger?" Michael asked. Where, he wondered to himself, had he seen another face like that?

"Same age," replied the Policeman flatly.

"Then you must have been twins, like John and Barbara!"

"I was triplets," the Policeman said.

"How lovely!" cried Jane, with a sigh of envy.

"Well, it wasn't so lovely, not to *my* mind. The opposite, I'd say. 'Egbert,' my mother was always asking, 'why don't you play with Herbert and Albert?' But it wasn't me — it was *them* that wouldn't. All they wanted was to go to the Zoo, and when they came back they'd be animals — tigers tearing about the house and letting on it was Timbuctoo or around the Gobi Desert. *I* never wanted to be a tiger. I liked playing bus-conductors and keeping things neat and tidy."

"Like 'er!" The Park Keeper waved to a distant fountain where Mary Poppins was leaning over to admire the set of her hat.

"Like her," agreed the Policeman, nodding. "Or," he said, grinning, "that nice Miss Ellen."

"Ellen's not neat," protested Michael. "Her hair straggles and her feet are too big."

"And when they grew up," demanded Jane, "what did Herbert and Albert do?" She liked to hear the end of a story.

"Do?" said the Policeman, very surprised. "What one triplet does, the others do. They joined the police, of course!"

"But I thought you were all so different!"

"We were and we are!" the Policeman argued. "Seeing as how I stayed in London and they went off to distant lands. Wanted to be near the jungle, they said, and mix with giraffes and leopards. One of 'em — Herbert — he never came back. Just sent a note saying not to worry. 'I'm happy,' he said, 'and I feel at home!' And after that, never a word — not even a card at Christmas."

"And what about Albert?" the children prompted.

"Ah — Albert — yes! He did come back. After he met with his accident."

"What accident?" they wanted to know. They were burning with curiosity.

"Lorst his foot," the Policeman answered. "Wouldn't say how, or why or where. Just got himself a wooden one and never smiled again. Now he works on the traffic signals. Sits in his box and pines away. And sometimes —— " The Policeman lowered his voice. "Sometimes he *forgets* the lights. Leaves them at red for a whole day till London's at a standstill!"

Michael gave an excited skip. "He must be the one we passed this morning, in the box by the Far Gate!"

"That's him all right!" The Policeman nodded.

"But what is he pining for?" asked Jane. She wanted every detail.

"For the jungle, he keeps on telling me. He says he's got a friend there!"

"A funny place to 'ave a friend!" The Park Keeper glanced around the Park to see that all was in order.

"T'chah!" he exclaimed disgustedly. "That's Willerby up to 'is tricks again! Look at 'im sittin' up there on the wall! Come down out of that! Remember the bye-laws! No dogs allowed on the Park Wall. I shall 'ave to speak to Miss Lark," he muttered, "feedin' 'im all that dainty food! 'E's twice the size he was yesterday!"

"That's not Willoughby!" said Michael. "It's a much, much larger dog."

"It isn't a dog at all!" cried Jane. "It's a —— "

"Lumme! You're right!" The Policeman stared. "It's not a dog — it's a lion!"

"Oh, what shall I do?" wailed the Park Keeper. "Nothing like this ever 'appened before, not even when I was a boy!"

"Go and get someone from the Zoo — it must have escaped from there! Here, you two ——" the Policeman cried. He caught the children and swung them up to the top of a near-by fountain. "You stay there while I head him off!"

"Observe the rules!" shrieked the Park Keeper. "No lions allowed in the Park!" He gave one look at the tawny shape and ran in the opposite direction.

The Lion swung his head about, glancing along Cherry-Tree Lane and then across the lawns. Then he leapt from the wall with a swift movement and made for the Long Walk. His curly mane blew out in the breeze like a large lacy collar.

"Take care!" cried Jane to the Policeman, as he darted forward with arms outspread. It would be sad indeed, she felt, if that manly figure were gobbled up.

"Gurrrr!" the Policeman shouted fiercely.

His voice was so loud and full of warning that everyone in the Park was startled.

Miss Lark, who was knitting by the Lake, came hurrying to the Long Walk with her dogs in close attendance.

"Such a commotion!" she twittered shrilly. "Whatever is the matter? Oh!" she cried, running round in a circle. "What shall I do? It's a wild beast! Send for the Prime Minister!"

"Get up a tree!" the Policeman yelled, shaking his fist at the Lion.

"Which tree? Oh, how undignified!"

"That one!" screamed Michael, waving his hand.

Gulping and panting, Miss Lark climbed up, her hair catching in every twig and her knitting wool winding around her legs.

"Andrew and Willoughby, come up, please!" she called down, anxiously. But the dogs were not going to lose their heads. They composed themselves at the foot of the tree and waited to see what would happen.

By this time everyone in the Park had become aware of the Lion. Terrified shouts rang through the air as people swung themselves into the branches or hid behind seats or statues.

"Call out the Firemen!" they all cried. "Tell the Lord Mayor! Send for a rope!"

But the Lion noticed none of them. He crossed the lawn in enormous leaps, making direct for the blue serge shape of the Officer of the Law.

"Gurrrr, I said!" the Policeman roared, taking out his baton.

The Lion merely tossed his head and flung himself into a crouching position. A ripple ran through all his muscles as he made ready to spring.

"Oh, save him, somebody!" cried Jane, with an anxious glance at the manly figure.

"Help!" screamed a voice from every tree.

"Prime Minister!" cried Miss Lark again.

And then the Lion sprang. He sped like an arrow through the air and landed beside the big black boots.

"Be off, I say!" the Policeman shouted, in a last protesting cry.

But as he spoke a strange thing happened. The Lion rolled over on his back and waved his legs in the air.

"Just like a kitten," whispered Michael. But he held Jane's hand a little tighter.

"Away with you!" the Policeman bellowed, waving his baton again.

But as though the words were as sweet as music, the Lion put out a long red tongue and licked the Policeman's boots.

"Stop it, I tell you! Get along off!"

But the Lion only wagged its tail and, springing up on its hind legs, it clasped the blue serge jacket.

"Help! Oh, help!" the Policeman gasped.

"Coming!" croaked a hoarse voice, as the Park Keeper crawled to the edge of the Walk with an empty litter-basket over his head.

Beside him crept a small thin man with a butterfly net in his hand.

"I brought the Keeper of the Zoological Gardens!" the Park Keeper hissed at the Policeman. "Go on!" he urged the little man. "It's your property — take it away!"

The Keeper of the Zoological Gardens darted behind a fountain. He took a careful look at the Lion as it hugged the dark blue waist.

"Not one of ours!" He shook his head. "It's far too red

and curly. Seems to know *you!*" he called to the Policeman. "What are you — a lion tamer?"

"Never saw him before in my life!" The head in the helmet turned aside.

"Oh, wurra! wurra!" the Lion growled, in a voice that held a note of reproach.

"Will nobody send for the Prime Minister?" Miss Lark's voice shrilled from her maple bough.

"I have been sent for, my dear madam!" a voice observed from the next tree. An elderly gentleman in striped trousers was scrambling into the branches.

"Then *do* something!" ordered Miss Lark, in a frenzy.

"Shoo!" said the Prime Minister earnestly, waving his hat at the Lion.

But the Lion bared its teeth in a grin as it hugged the Policeman closer.

"Now, what's the trouble? Who sent for me?" cried a loud impatient voice.

The Lord Mayor hurried along the Walk with his Aldermen at his heels.

"Good gracious! What are you doing, Smith?" He stared in disgust at the Park Keeper. "Come out of that basket and stand up straight! It is there to be used for litter, Smith, and not some foolish game."

"I'm usin' it for armour, your Worship! There's a lion in the Park!"

"A lion, Smith? What nonsense you talk! The lions are in the Zoo!"

The Lion ... clasped the blue serge jacket

"A lion?" echoed the Aldermen. "Ha, ha! What a silly story!"

"It's true!" yelled Jane and Michael at once. "Look out! He's just behind you!"

The three portly figures turned, and their faces grew pale as marble.

The Lord Mayor waved a feeble hand at the trembling Aldermen.

"Get me water! Wine! Hot milk!" he moaned.

But for once the Aldermen disobeyed. Hot milk, indeed! they seemed to say as they dragged him to the Prime Minister's tree and pushed him into the branches.

"Police! Police!" the Lord Mayor cried, catching hold of a bough.

"I'm here, your Honour!" the Policeman panted, pushing away a tawny paw.

But the Lion took this for a mark of affection.

"Gurrrrumph!" he said in a husky voice, as he clasped the Policeman tighter.

"Oh, dear! Oh, dear!" Miss Lark wailed. "Has nobody got a gun?"

"A dagger! A sword! A crowbar!" cried the voices from every tree.

The Park was ringing with shouts and screams. The Park Keeper rattled his stick on the litter-basket. "Yoohoo!" cried the Keeper of the Zoological Gardens to distract the Lion's attention. The Lion was growling.

The Policeman was yelling. The Lord Mayor and the Aldermen were still crying "Police!"

Then suddenly a silence fell. And a neat, trim figure appeared on the path. Straight on she came, as a ship into port, with the perambulator wheeling before her and the tulip standing up stiff on her hat.

Creak went the wheels.

Tap went her shoes.

And the watching faces grew pale with horror as she tripped towards the Lion.

"Go back, Mary Poppins!" screamed Miss Lark, breaking the awful silence. "Save yourself and the little ones! There's a wild beast down on the path!"

Mary Poppins looked up at Miss Lark's face as it hung like a fruit among the leaves.

"Go back? When I've only just come out?" She smiled a superior smile.

"Away! Away!" The Prime Minister warned her. "Take care of those children, woman!"

Mary Poppins gave him a glance so icy that he felt himself freeze to the bough.

"I *am* taking care of these children, thank you. And as for the wild beasts ——" She gave a sniff. "They seem to be all in the trees!"

"It's a lion, Mary Poppins, look!" Michael pointed a trembling finger — and she turned and beheld the two locked figures.

The Policeman now was ducking sideways to prevent the Lion licking his cheek. His helmet was off and his face was pale, but he still had a plucky look in his eye.

"I might have known it!" said Mary Poppins, as she stared at the curious pair. "Rover!" she called in exasperation. "What do you think you're doing?"

From under his lacy, flopping mane the Lion pricked up an ear.

"Rover!" she called again. "Down, I say!"

The Lion gave one look at her and dropped with a thud to the ground. Then he gave a little throaty growl and bounded away towards her.

"Oh, the Twins! He'll eat them! Help!" cried Jane.

But the Lion hardly looked at the Twins. He was fawning at Mary Poppins. He rolled his eyes and wagged his tail and arched himself against her skirt. Then away he rushed to the Policeman, seized the blue trousers between his teeth and tugged them towards the perambulator.

"Don't be so silly!" said Mary Poppins. "Do as I tell you! Let him go! You've got the wrong one."

The Lion loosed the trouser-leg and rolled his eyes in surprise.

"Do you mean," the Prime Minister called from his bough, "he's to eat *another* Policeman?"

Mary Poppins made no reply. Instead, she fished inside her hand-bag and brought out a silver whistle. Then, setting it daintily to her lips, she puffed out her cheeks and blew.

"Why — *I* could have blown *my* whistle" — the Policeman stared at the silver shape — "if only I'd thought of it."

She turned upon him a look of scorn. "The trouble with you is that you don't think. Neither do you!" she snapped at the Lion.

He hung his head between his paws and looked very hurt and foolish.

"You don't listen, either," she added severely. "In at one ear and out of the next. There was no need to make such a foolish mistake."

The Lion's tail crept between his legs.

"You're careless, thoughtless and inattentive. You ought to be thoroughly ashamed of yourself."

The Lion gave a humble snuffle as though he agreed with her.

"Who whistled?" called a voice from the Gate. "Who summoned an Officer of the Law?"

Along the Walk came another policeman, limping unevenly. His face had a melancholy look, as though he possessed a secret sorrow.

"I can't stay long whatever it is," he said, as he reached the group. "I left the lights when I heard the whistle and I must get back to them. Why, Egbert!" he said to the First Policeman, "what's the matter with you?"

"Oh, nothing to complain of, Albert! I've just been attacked by a lion!"

"Lion?" The sad face grew a shade more cheerful as

the Second Policeman glanced about him. "Oh, what a beauty!" he exclaimed, limping towards the tawny shape at Mary Poppins' side.

Jane turned to whisper in Michael's ear.

"He must be the Policeman's brother — the one with the wooden foot!"

"Nice lion! Pretty lion!" said the Second Policeman softly.

And the Lion, at the sound of his voice, leapt to his feet with a roar.

"Now gently, gently! Be a good lion. He's an elegant fellow, so he is!" the Second Policeman crooned.

Then he put back the mane from the Lion's brow and met the golden eyes. A shudder of joy ran through his frame.

"Rover! My dear old friend! It's you!" He flung out his arms with a loving gesture and the Lion rushed into them.

"Oh, Rover! After all these years!" the Second Policeman sobbed.

"Wurra, wurra!" the Lion growled, licking the tears away.

And for a whole minute it was nothing but Rover — Wurra, Rover — Wurra, while they hugged and kissed each other.

"But how did you get here? How did you find me?" demanded the Second Policeman.

"Woof! Burrrum!" replied the Lion, nodding towards the perambulator.

"No! You don't say! How very kind! We must always be grateful, Rover! And if I can do you a good turn, Miss Poppins ——"

"Oh, get along, do — the pair of you!" said Mary Poppins snappily. For the Lion had rushed to lick her hand and darted back to his friend.

"Woof? Wurra-woof?" he said in a growl.

"Will I come with you? What do you think? As if I could ever leave you again!" And flinging his arm round the Lion's shoulders, the Second Policeman turned.

"Hey!" cried the First Policeman sternly. "Where are you going to, may I ask? And where are you taking that animal?"

"He's taking *me!*" cried the Second Policeman. "And

we're going where we belong!" His gloomy face had quite changed. It was now rosy and gay.

"But what about the traffic lights? Who's going to look after those?"

"They're all at green!" said the Second Policeman. "No more signals for me, Egbert! The traffic can do what it likes!"

He looked at the Lion and roared with laughter, and the two of them turned away. Over the lawns they sauntered, chatting — the Lion on its hind legs and the Policeman limping a little. When they came to the Lane Gate they paused for a moment and waved. Then through they went and shut it behind them, and the watchers saw them no more.

The Keeper of the Zoological Gardens gathered up his net.

"I hope they're not making for the Zoo. We haven't a cage to spare!"

"Well, as long as he's out of the public Park —— " The Prime Minister clambered out of the tree.

"Haven't we met before?" he enquired, as he took off his hat to Mary Poppins. "I'm afraid I've forgotten where it was!"

"Up in the air! On a red balloon!" She bowed in a lady-like manner.

"Ah, yes! Hurrrmph!" He seemed rather embarrassed. "Well — I must be off and make some more laws!"

And, glancing round to make sure the Lion was not coming back, he made for the Far Gate.

"Constable!" cried the Lord Mayor, as he swung himself down from his branch. "You must go at once to the signal box and switch the lights to red. The traffic can do as it likes, indeed! Whoever heard of such a thing!"

The Policeman, mopping up his scratches, gallantly sprang to attention.

"Very good, Your Honour!" he said smartly, and marched away down the Walk.

"As for you, Smith, this is all your fault. Your duty is to look after the Park! But what do I find when I pass this way? Wild animals running all over it. You disappoint me again and again. I must mention it to the King."

The Park Keeper fell on his knees with a groan.

"Oh, *please* don't mention it, Your Honour! Think of me poor old mother!"

"You should have thought of her yourself before you let that lion in!"

"But I never let 'im in, Your Worship! It wasn't my fault 'e came over the wall. If anyone's to blame, it's —— " The Park Keeper broke off nervously, but he looked in Mary Poppins' direction.

So did the Lord Mayor.

"Aha!" he exclaimed, with a gracious smile. "Charmed to meet you again, Miss — er —— ?"

"Poppins," said Mary Poppins politely.

"Poppins — ah, yes! A charming name! Now, if Smith were only *you*, Miss Poppins, these things would never occur!"

With a bow, the Lord Mayor turned away and billowed down the Walk. The two Aldermen also bowed, and billowed along behind him.

"That's all *you* know!" said the Park Keeper, as he watched them disappear. "If I was 'er — ha, ha, that's funny! — *anything* could happen!"

"If I were *you*, I'd straighten my tie," said Mary Poppins primly. "Get down from that fountain, Jane and Michael!" She glanced at their grimy knees and faces. "You look like a couple of Blackamoors!"

"We can't all be like you, you know!" the Park Keeper said sarcastically.

"No," she agreed. "And more's the pity!" She pushed the perambulator forward.

"But, Mary Poppins —— " Michael burst out. He was longing to ask her about the Lion.

"Butting's for goats — not human beings! Best foot forward, please!"

"It's no use, Michael," whispered Jane. "You know she never explains."

But Michael was too excited to heed.

"Well, if I can't talk about the Lion, will you let me blow your whistle?"

"Certainly not!" She sauntered on.

"I wonder, Mary Poppins," he cried, "if you'll ever let me do *anything!*"

"I wonder!" she said, with a mocking smile.

Twilight was falling over the Park. People were scrambling out of the trees and hurrying home to safety.

From the Far Gate came a frightful din. And looking through it the children saw a motionless block of traffic. The lights were red, the horns were hooting and the drivers were shaking their fists.

The Policeman was calmly surveying the scene. He had been given an order and he was obeying it.

"Has your brother Albert gone for good?" cried Jane, as he waved to them.

"No idea," he replied calmly. "And it's no affair of mine!"

Then round the perambulator swung and they all went back by the Long Walk. The Twins and Annabel, weary of playing with the blue duck, let it drop over the side. Nobody noticed. Jane and Michael were far too busy thinking about the day's adventure. And Mary Poppins was far too busy thinking about Mary Poppins.

"I wonder where Albert's gone?" murmured Michael, as he strolled along beside her.

"How should *I* know?" she answered, shrugging.

"I thought you knew everything!" he retorted. "I meant it politely, Mary Poppins!"

Her face, which was just about to be fierce, took on a conceited expression.

"Maybe I do," she said smugly, as she hurried them across the Lane and in through the front gate. . . .

"Oh, Ellen!" Mrs. Banks was saying, as they all came into the hall. "Would you dust the mantelpiece while you're there? Well, darlings?" She greeted the children gaily.

Ellen, half-way up the stairs, replied with a loud sneeze. "A-tishoo!" She had Hay Fever. She was carrying mugs of milk on a tray and they rattled each time she sneezed.

"Oh, go on, Ellen! You're so *slow!*" said Michael impatiently.

"You hard-hearted — a-tishoo!" she cried, as she dumped the tray on the nursery table.

Helter-skelter they all ran in, as Ellen took a cloth from her pocket and began to dust Miss Andrew's treasures.

"Rock cakes for supper! I'll have the biggest!" cried Michael greedily.

Mary Poppins was buttoning on her apron. "Michael Banks —— " she began in a warning voice. But the sentence was never finished.

"Oh, help!" A wild scream rent the air and Ellen fell backwards against the table.

Bang! went the milk mugs on to the floor.

"It's *him!*" shrieked Ellen. "Oh, what shall I do?" She stood in a running stream of milk and pointed to the mantelpiece.

"What's him? Who's him?" cried Jane and Michael. "Whatever's the matter, Ellen?"

"There! Under that banana bush! His very self! A-tishoo!"

She was pointing straight at Miss Andrew's huntsman as he smiled in the arms of his Lion.

"Why, of course!" cried Jane, as she looked at the huntsman. "He's exactly like Egbert — our Policeman!"

"The only one I ever loved, and now a wild beast's got him!"

Ellen flung out a frenzied arm and knocked the teapot over. "A-tishoo!" she sneezed, distractedly, as she hurried sobbing from the room and thundered down the stairs.

"What a silly she is!" said Michael, laughing. "As if he'd have turned into china! Besides, we saw him a moment ago, away by the Far Gate!"

"Yes, she's a silly," Jane agreed. "But he's very like the huntsman, Michael —— " She smiled at the smiling china face. "And both such manly figures . . ."

"Well, Constable?" said Mr. Banks, as he came up the garden path that evening. He wondered if he had broken a bye-law when he saw the policeman at the door.

"It's about the duck!" The Policeman smiled.

"We don't keep ducks," said Mr. Banks. "Good heavens! What have you done to your face?"

The Policeman patted his bruised cheek. "Just a scratch," he murmured modestly. "But now, that there blue duck —— "

"Whoever heard of a blue duck? Go and ask Admiral Boom!"

The Policeman gave a patient sigh and handed over a dingy object.

"Oh, that thing!" Mr. Banks exclaimed. "I suppose the children dropped it!" He stuffed the blue duck into his pocket and opened the front door.

It was at this moment that Ellen, her face hidden in her duster, hurled herself down the front stairs and straight into his arms.

"A-tishoo!" She sneezed so violently that Mr. Banks' bowler hat fell off.

"Why, Ellen! What on earth's the matter?" Mr. Banks staggered beneath her weight.

"He's gone right into that bit of china!" Her shoulders heaved as she sobbed out the news.

"You're going to China?" said Mr. Banks. "Well, don't be so depressed about it! My dear," he remarked to Mrs. Banks, who was hurrying up the kitchen stairs. "Ellen is feeling upset, she says, because she is going to China!"

"China?" cried Mrs. Banks, raising her eyebrows.

"No! It's *him* that's gorn!" insisted Ellen. "Under a banana in the African jungle!"

"Africa!" Mr. Banks exclaimed, catching only a word here and there. "I made a mistake," he said to Mrs. Banks. "She's going to Africa!"

Mrs. Banks seemed quite stupefied.

"I'm not! I'm not!" shrieked Ellen wildly.

"Well, wherever you're going, do make up your mind!" Mr. Banks thrust her towards a chair.

"Allow me, sir!" the Policeman murmured, stepping into the hall.

Ellen looked up at the sound of his voice and gave a strangled sob.

"*Egbert.* But I thought you were up on the mantelpiece — and a wild beast going to eat you!" She flung out her arm towards the nursery.

"Mantelpiece?" Mr. Banks exclaimed.

"A wild beast?" murmured Mrs. Banks. Could they — they wondered — believe their ears?

"Leave it to me," the Policeman said. "I'll take her a turn along the path. Perhaps it will clear her head."

He heaved Ellen out of the chair and led her, still gaping, through the door.

Mr. Banks mopped his beaded brow. "Neither China, nor Africa," he murmured. "Merely to the front gate with the Policeman. I never knew that his name was Egbert! Well, I'll just go and say goodnight to the children. . . . All well, Mary Poppins?" he asked gaily, as he sauntered into the nursery.

She gave a conceited toss of her head. Could all be anything but well while *she* was about the house?

Mr. Banks glanced contentedly at the roomful of rosy children. Then his eye fell on the mantelpiece and he gave a start of surprise.

"Hullo!" he exclaimed. "Where did those things come from?"

"Miss Andrew!" all the children answered.

"Quick — let me escape!" Mr. Banks turned pale. "Tell her I've run away! Gone to the moon!"

"She's not here, Daddy," they reassured him. "She's far away in the South Seas. And these are all her treasures."

"Well, I hope she stays there — right at the bottom! *Her* treasures, you say! Well this one isn't!" Mr. Banks marched to the mantelpiece and picked up the celulloid horse. "I won him myself at an Easter Fair when I was a little boy. Ah, there's my friend, the soapstone bird! A thousand years old, she said it was. And, look, *I* made that little ship. Aren't you proud of your father?"

Mr. Banks smiled at his cleverness as he glanced along the mantelpiece.

"I feel like a boy again," he said. "These things all come from my old schoolroom. That hen used to warm my breakfast egg. And the fox and the clown and *Home Sweet Home* — how well I remember them! And there — bless their hearts! — are the Lion and Huntsman. I always called them the Faithful Friends. Used to be a pair of these fellows, but they weren't complete, I remember. The second huntsman was broken off, nothing left of him but his boot. Ah! *There's* the other — the broken one. Good gracious!" He gave a start of surprise. "*Both* the huntsmen are here!"

They looked at the broken ornament and blinked with astonishment.

For there, where the blank white gap had been, was a second smiling figure. Beneath the banana-tree he sat, leaning — like his unbroken brother — against a shaggy shape. A paw lay lovingly on his breast and his lion — only this morning so sad and tearful — was now showing all his teeth in a grin.

The two ornaments were exactly alike — the two trees bore the same fruit, the two lions were equally happy and the two huntsmen smiled. Exactly alike — but for one exception. For the second hunts-man had a crack in his leg just above his boot — the sort of crack you always find when two pieces of broken china are carefully fitted together.

A smile swept over Jane's face as she realised what had happened. She gently touched the crack with her fingers.

"It's Albert, Michael! Albert and Rover! And the oth-er" — she touched the unbroken pair — "the other must be Herbert!"

Michael's head nodded backwards and forwards like the head of a mandarin.

The questions rose in them like bubbles and they turned to Mary Poppins.

But just as the words leapt to their tongues she silenced them with a look.

"Extraordinary thing," Mr. Banks was saying. "I could have sworn one figure was missing. It just goes to show — I'm getting older. Losing my memory, I'm afraid. Well, what are you two so amused about?"

"Nothing!" they gurgled, as they flung back their heads and burst into peals of laughter. How could they assure him that his memory was as good as ever it was? How explain the afternoon's adventure, or tell him that they knew now where the Second Policeman had gone? Some things there are that are past telling. And it's no use trying — as they knew very well — to say what cannot be said.

"It's a long time," grumbled Mr. Banks, "since *I* could laugh at nothing!"

But he looked quite cheerful as he kissed them and went downstairs to dinner.

"Let's put them side by side," said Jane, setting the little cracked huntsman next to his crackless brother. "Now they're *both* at home!"

Michael looked up at the mantelpiece and gave a contented chuckle.

"But what will Miss Andrew say, I wonder? Everything was to be kept safe — nothing broken, nothing mended. You don't think she'll separate them, Jane?"

"Just let her try!" said a voice behind them. "Safe she said they were to be, and safe they are going to stay!"

Mary Poppins was standing on the hearth-rug with the teapot in her hand. And her manner was so belligerent that for half a second Jane and Michael felt sorry for Miss Andrew.

She looked from them to the mantelpiece, glancing from their living faces to the smiling china figures.

"One and one makes two," she declared. "And two halves make a whole. And Faithful Friends should be together, never kept apart. But, of course, if you don't approve, Michael — — " for his face had assumed a thoughtful expression. "If you think they'd be safer somewhere else —— If you'd like to go to the South Seas and ask Miss Andrew's permission —— "

"You know I approve, Mary Poppins!" he cried. "And I don't want to go to the South Seas. I was only thinking —— " He hesitated. "Well — if *you* hadn't been there, Mary Poppins, do you think they'd have found each other?"

She stood there like a pillar of starch. He was almost sorry he had spoken, she looked so stern and priggish.

"Ifs and whys and buts and hows — you want too much," she said. But her blue eyes gave a sudden sparkle, and a pleased smile — very like those on the huntsmen's face — trembled about her lips.

At the sight of it Michael forgot his question. Only that sparkle mattered.

"Oh, be my lion, Mary Poppins! Put your paw around me!"

"And me!" cried Jane as she turned to join them.

Her arms came lightly across their shoulders as she drew them close to the starched apron. And there they were, the three of them, embracing under the nursery lamplight as though beneath a banana-tree.

With a little push, Michael spun them round. And again a push. And again a spin. And soon they were all revolving gently in the middle of the room.

"Michael," said Mary Poppins severely, "I am not a merry-go-round!"

But he only laughed and hugged her tighter.

"The Faithful Friends are together," he cried. "*All* the Faithful Friends!"

CHAPTER THREE

LUCKY THURSDAY

I't's dod fair!" grumbled Michael.

He pressed his nose to the window-pane and sniffed a tear away. And, as if to taunt him, a gust of rain rattled against the glass.

All day the storm had raged. And Michael, because he had a cold, was not allowed to go out. Jane and the Twins had put on gum-boots and gone to play in the Park. Even Annabel, wrapped in a mackintosh, had sailed off under the parrot umbrella, looking as proud as a queen.

Oh, how lonely Michael felt! It was Ellen's Day Out. His mother had gone shopping. Mrs. Brill was down in the kitchen. And Robertson Ay, up in the attic, was asleep in a cabin trunk.

"Get up and play in your dressing-gown. But don't put a toe outside the nursery!" Mary Poppins had warned him.

So there he was, all by himself, with nothing to do but grumble. He built a castle with his blocks, but it tumbled down when he blew his nose. He tried cutting his hair with his penknife, but the blade was far too blunt. And at last there was nothing left to do but breathe on the rainy window-pane and draw a picture there.

The nursery clock ticked the day away. The weather grew wetter and Michael grew crosser.

But then, at sunset, the clouds lifted and a line of crimson shone from the West. Everything glittered in rain and sun. Rat-tat-tat — on the black umbrellas, the cherry-trees dropped their weight of water. The shouts of Jane and John and Barbara floated up to the window. They were playing leapfrog over the gutters on their way home from the Park.

Admiral Boom came splashing past, looking like a shiny sunflower in his big yellow sou'wester.

The Ice Cream Man trundled along the lane, with a waterproof cape spread over his tricycle. And in front of it the notice said:

DON'T STOP ME

I WANT MY TEA

He glanced at Number Seventeen and waved his hand to the window. Michael, on any other day, would gladly have answered back. But today he deliberately took no notice. He huddled on the window-seat, glumly watching the sunset, and looking over Miss Lark's roof at the first faint star in the sky.

"The others ged all the fud," he sniffed. "I wish *I* could
have sobe luck!"

Then footsteps clattered on the stairs. The door burst
open and Jane ran in.

"Oh, Michael, it was lovely!" she cried. "We were up to
our knees in water."

"Thed I hobe you catch a code!" he snapped. He gave a
guilty glance round to see if Mary Poppins had heard. She
was busy unwrapping Annabel and shaking the rain from
her parrot umbrella.

"Don't be cross. We all missed you," said Jane in a coaxing voice.

But Michael did not want to be coaxed. He wanted to be
as cross as he liked. Nobody, if he could help it, was going
to alter his bad mood. Indeed, he was almost enjoying it.

"Dode touch be, Jade. You're all wet!" he said in a sulky voice.

"So are we!" chirped John and Barbara, running across to hug him.

"Oh, go away!" he cried angrily, turning back to the window. "I dode want to talk to any of you. I wish you'd all leave be alode!"

"Miss Lark's roof is made of gold!" Jane gazed out at the sunset. "And there's the first star — wish on it! How does the tune go, Michael?"

He shook his head and wouldn't tell, so she sang the song herself.

> "Star light
> Star bright,
> First star I've seen tonight,
> Wish I may
> Wish I might
> That the wish may come true
> That I wish tonight."

She finished the song and looked at the star.

"I've wished," she whispered, smiling.

"It's easy for *you* to sbile, Jade — you hawed got a code!" He blew his nose for the hundredth time and gave a gloomy sniff. "I wish I was biles frob everywhere! Sobewhere *I* could have sobe fud. Hullo, whad's that?"

he said, staring, as a small dark shape leapt on to the sill.

"What's what?" she murmured dreamily.

"John! Barbara! And you too, Jane! Take off your coats at once. I will not have supper with Three Drowned Rats!" said Mary Poppins sharply.

They slithered off the window-seat and hurried to obey her. When Mary Poppins looked like that it was always best to obey.

The dark shape crept along the sill and a speckled face peeped in. Could it be — yes, it was! — a cat. A tortoise-shell cat with yellow eyes and a collar made of gold.

Michael pressed his nose to the pane. And the cat pressed its nose to the other side and looked at him thoughtfully. Then it smiled a most mysterious smile and, whisking off the window-sill, it sprang across Miss Lark's garden and disappeared over the roof.

"Who owns it, I wonder?" Michael murmured, as he gazed at the spot where the cat had vanished. He knew it couldn't belong to Miss Lark. She only cared for dogs.

"What are you looking at?" called Jane, as she dried her hair by the fire.

"Dothing!" he said in a horrid voice. He was not going to share the cat with her. She had had enough fun in the Park.

"I only asked," she protested mildly.

He knew she was trying to be kind and something inside him wanted to melt. But his crossness would not let it.

"Ad I odly adswered!" he retorted.

Mary Poppins looked at him. He knew that look and he guessed what was coming, but he felt too tired to care.

"You," she remarked in a chilly voice, "can answer questions in bed. Spit-spot and in you go — and kindly close the door!"

Her eyes bored into him like gimlets as he stalked away to the night nursery and kicked the door to with a bang.

The steam-kettle bubbled beside his bed, sending out fragrant whiffs of balsam. But he turned his nose away on purpose and put his head under the blankets.

"Dothing dice ever happeds to be," he grumbled to his pillow.

But it offered its cool white cheek in silence as if it had not heard.

He gave it a couple of furious thumps, burrowed in like an angry rabbit, and immediately fell asleep.

A moment later — or so it seemed — he woke to find the morning sun streaming in upon him.

"What day is today, Mary Poppins?" he shouted.

"Thursday," she called from the next room. Her voice, he thought, was strangely polite.

The camp-bed groaned as she sprang out. He could always tell what she was doing simply by the sound — the clip-clip of hooks and eyes, the swish of the hairbrush, the thump of her shoes and the rattle of the starched apron as she buttoned it round her waist. Then came a moment of solemn silence as she glanced approvingly at the mirror. And after that a hurricane as she whisked the others out of bed.

"May I get up, too, Mary Poppins?"

She answered "Yes!", to his surprise, and he scrambled out like lightning in case she should change her mind.

His new sweater — navy blue with three red fir-trees — was lying on the chair. And for fear she would stop him wearing it, he dragged it quickly over his head and swaggered in to breakfast.

Jane was buttering her toast.

"How's your cold?" she enquired.

He gave an experimental sniff.

"Gone!" He seized the milk jug.

"I knew it would go," she said, smiling. "That's what I wished on the star last night."

"Just as well you did," he remarked. "Now you've got me to play with."

"There are always the Twins," she reminded him.

"Not the same thing at all," he said. "May I have some more sugar, Mary Poppins?"

He fully expected her to say "No!" But, instead, she smiled serenely.

"If you want it, Michael," she replied, with the lady-like nod she reserved for strangers.

Could he believe his ears, he wondered? He hurriedly emptied the sugar bowl in case they had made a mistake.

"The post has come!" cried Mrs. Banks, bustling in with a package. "Nothing for anyone but Michael!"

He tore apart the paper and string. Aunt Flossie had sent him a cake of chocolate!

"Nut milk — my favourite!" he exclaimed, and was just about to take a bite when there came a knock at the door.

Robertson Ay shuffled slowly in.

"Message from Mrs. Brill," he yawned. "She's mixed a sponge cake, she says, and would like him to scrape the bowl!" He pointed a weary finger at Michael.

Scrape the cake-bowl! What a treat! And as rare as unexpected!

"I'm coming right away!" he shouted, stuffing the chocolate into his pocket. And, feeling rather bold and daring, he decided to slide down the banisters.

"The very chap I wanted to see!" cried Mr. Banks, as Michael landed. He fumbled in his waistcoat pocket and handed his son a shilling.

"What's that for?" demanded Michael. He had never had a shilling before.

"To spend," said Mr. Banks solemnly, as he took his bowler hat and bag and hurried down the path.

Michael felt very proud and important. He puffed out his chest in a lordly way and clattered down to the kitchen.

"Good — is it, dearie?" said Mrs. Brill, as he tasted the sticky substance.

"Delicious," he said, smacking his lips.

But before he had time for another spoonful a well-known voice floated in from the Lane.

"All hands on deck! Up with the anchor! For I'm bound for the Rio Grande!"

It was Admiral Boom, setting out for a walk.

Upon his head was a black hat, painted with skull-and-crossbones — the one he had taken from a pirate chief in a desperate fight off Falmouth.

Away through the garden Michael dashed to get a look at it. For his dearest hope was that some day he, too, would have such a hat.

"Heave her over!" the Admiral roared, leaning against the front gate and lazily mopping his brow.

The autumn day was warm and misty. The sun was drawing into the sky the rain that had fallen last night.

"Blast my gizzard!" cried Admiral Boom, fanning himself with his hat. "Tropical weather that's what it is — it oughtn't to be allowed. The Admiral's hat is too hot for the Admiral. You take it, messmate, till I come back. For away I'm bound to go — oho! — 'cross the wide Missouri!"

And spreading his handkerchief over his head, he thrust the pirate's hat at Michael and stamped away, singing.

Michael clasped the skull-and-crossbones. His heart hammered with excitement as he put the hat on his head.

"I'll just go down the Lane," he said, hoping that everybody in it would see him wearing the treasure. It banged against his brow as he walked and wobbled whenever he looked up. But nevertheless, behind each curtain — he was sure — there lurked an admiring eye.

It was not until he was nearly home that he noticed Miss Lark's dogs. They had thrust their heads through the garden fence and were looking at him in astonishment. Andrew's tail gave a well-bred wag, but Willoughby merely stared.

"Luncheon!" trilled Miss Lark's voice.

And as Willoughby rose to answer the summons he winked at Andrew and sniggered.

"Can he be laughing at me?" thought Michael. But he put the idea aside as ridiculous and sauntered up to the nursery.

"Do I have to wash my hands, Mary Poppins? They're quite clean," he assured her.

"Well, the others, of course, have washed theirs — but you do as *you* think best!"

At last she realised, he thought, that Michael Banks was no ordinary boy. He could wash or not, as *he* thought best, and she hadn't even told him to take off his hat! He decided to go straight in to luncheon.

"Now, away to the Park," said Mary Poppins, as soon as the meal was over. "If that is convenient for *you*, Michael?" She waited for his approval.

"Oh, perfickly convenient!" He gave a lordly wave of his hand. "I think I shall go to the swings."

"Not to the Lake?" protested Jane. She wanted to look at Neleus.

"Certainly not!" said Mary Poppins. "We shall do what Michael wishes!"

And she stood aside respectfully as he strutted before her through the gate.

The soft bright mist still rose from the grass, blurring the shapes of seats and fountains. Bushes and trees seemed to float in the air. Nothing was like its real self until you were close upon it.

Mary Poppins sat down on a bench, settled the perambulator beside her and began to read a book. The children dashed away to the playground.

Up and down on the swings went Michael, with the pirate's hat bumping against his eyes. Then he took a ride on the spinning-jenny and after that, the loop. He couldn't turn somersaults, like Jane, for fear of dropping the hat.

"What next?" he thought, feeling rather bored. Everything possible, he felt, had happened to him this morning. Now there was nothing left to do.

He wandered back through the weaving mist and sat beside Mary Poppins. She gave him a small, preoccupied smile, as though she had never seen him before, and went on reading her book. It was called *Everything a Lady Should Know.*

Michael sighed, to attract her attention.

But she did not seem to hear.

He kicked a hole in the rainy grass.

Mary Poppins read on.

Then his eye fell on her open hand-bag which was lying on the seat. Inside it was a handkerchief, and beneath the handkerchief a mirror and beside the mirror her silver whistle.

He gazed at it with envious eyes. Then he glanced at Mary Poppins. There she was, still deep in her book. Should he ask her again for a loan of the whistle? She seemed to be in the best of humours — not a cross word the whole day long.

But was the humour to be relied on? Suppose he asked and she said no!

He decided not to risk asking, but just to take the whistle. It was only borrowing, after all. He could put it back in a minute.

Quick as a fish his hand darted, and the whistle was in his trouser-pocket.

Round behind the bench he hurried, feeling the silver shape against him. He was just about to take it out when something small and bright ran past him.

"I believe that's the cat I saw last night!" said Michael to himself.

And, indeed, it was one and the same. The same black-and-yellow coat shone in the sunny mist, more like dapples of light and shadow than ordinary fur. And about its neck was the same gold collar.

The cat glanced up invitingly, smiling the same mysterious smile, and padded lightly on.

Michael darted after it, in and out of the patches of mist that seemed to grow thicker as he ran.

Something fell with a chink at his feet.

"My shilling!" he cried, as he bent to retrieve it. He searched among the steaming grasses, turning over the wet blades, feeling under the clover. Not here! Not there! Where could it have gone?

"Come on!" said a soft, inviting voice. He looked round quickly. To his surprise there was nobody near — except the smiling cat.

"Hurry!" cried the voice again.

It was the cat who had spoken.

Michael sprang up. It was no use hunting, the shilling had gone. He hurried after the voice.

The cat smiled and rubbed against his legs as he caught it up. The steaming vapour rose up from the earth, wrapping them both around. And before them stood a wall of mist almost as thick as a cloud.

"Take hold of my collar," the cat advised. Its voice was no more than a soft mew, but it held a note of command.

Michael felt a twinge of excitement. Something new was happening! He bent down obediently and clasped the band of gold.

"Now, jump!" the cat ordered. "Lift your feet!"

And holding the golden collar tightly, Michael sprang into the mist.

"Whee — ee — ee!" cried a rushing wind in his ears. The sunny cloud was sweeping past him and all around him was empty space. The only solid things in the world were the shining band round the cat's neck and the hat on his own head.

"Where on earth are we going?" Michael gasped.

At the same moment the mist cleared. His feet touched something firm and shiny. And he saw that he stood on the steps of a palace — a palace made of gold.

"Nowhere on earth," replied the cat, pressing a bell with its paw.

The doors of the palace opened slowly. Sweet music came to Michael's ears and the sight he beheld quite dazzled him.

Before him lay a great gold hall, blazing with plumes

of light. Never, in his richest dreams, had Michael imagined such splendour. But the grandeur of the palace was as nothing compared to the brilliance of its inhabitants. For the hall was full of cats.

There were cats playing fiddles, cats playing flutes, cats on trapezes, cats in hammocks; cats juggling with golden hoops, cats dancing on the tips of their toes; cats turning somersaults; cats chasing tails and cats merely lolling about daintily licking their paws.

Moreover, they were tortoiseshell cats, all of them dappled with yellow and black; and the light in the hall seemed to come from their coats, for each cat shone with its own brightness.

In the centre, before a golden curtain, lay a pair of golden cushions. And on these reclined two dazzling creatures, each wearing a crown of gold. They leaned together, paw in paw, majestically surveying the scene.

"They must be the King and Queen," thought Michael.

To one side of this lordly pair stood three very young cats. Their fur was as smooth and bright as sunlight, and each had a chaplet of yellow flowers perched between the ears. Round about them were other cats who looked like courtiers — for all were wearing golden collars and ceremoniously standing on their hind legs.

One of these turned and beckoned to Michael.

"Here he is, Your Majesty!" He bowed obsequiously.

"Ah," said the King, with a stately nod. "So glad you've

turned up at last! The Queen and I and our three daughters" — he waved his paw at the three young cats — "have been expecting you!"

Expecting him! How flattering! But, of course, no more than his due.

"May we offer you a little refreshment?" asked the Queen, with a gracious smile.

"Yes, please!" said Michael eagerly. In such a graceful environment there would surely be nothing less than jelly — and probably ice cream!

Immediately three courtier cats presented three golden platters. On one lay a dead mouse, on the second a bat, and the third held a small raw fish.

Michael felt his face fall. "Oh no! thank you!" he said, with a shudder.

"First Yes Please and then No Thank You! Which do you mean?" the King demanded.

"Well, I don't like mice!" protested Michael. "And I never eat bats or raw fish either."

"Don't like mice?" cried a hundred voices, as the cats all stared at each other.

"Fancy!" exclaimed the three Princesses.

"Then perhaps you would care for a little milk?" said the Queen, with a queenly smile.

At once a courtier stood before him with milk in a golden saucer.

Michael put out his hands to take it.

"Oh, not with your paws!" the Queen implored him. "Let him hold it while you lap!"

"But I *can't* lap!" Michael protested. "I haven't got that kind of tongue."

"Can't lap!" Again the cats regarded each other. They seemed quite scandalised.

"Fancy!" the three Princesses mewed.

"Well," said the Queen hospitably, "a little rest after your journey!"

"Oh, it wasn't much of a journey," said Michael. "Just a big jump and here we were! It's funny," he went on, thoughtfully, "I've never seen this palace before — and I'm always in the Park! It must have been hidden behind the trees."

"In the Park?"

The King and Queen raised their eyebrows. So did all the courtiers. And the three Princesses were so overcome that they took three golden fans from their pockets and hid their smiles behind them.

"You're not in the Park now, I assure you. Far from it!" the King informed him.

"Well, it can't be *very* far," said Michael. "It only took me a minute to get here."

"Ah!" said the King. "But how long is a minute?"

"Sixty seconds!" Michael replied. Surely, he thought, a King should know that!

"*Your* minutes may be sixty seconds, but ours are about two hundred years."

Michael smiled at him amiably. A King, he thought, must have his joke.

"Now tell me," continued the King blandly, "did you ever hear of the Dog Star?"

"Yes," said Michael, very surprised. What had the Dog Star to do with it? "His other name is Sirius."

"Well, this," said the King, "is the Cat Star. And its other name is a secret. A secret, may I further add, that is only known to cats."

"But how did I get here?" Michael enquired. He was feeling more and more pleased with himself. Think of it — visiting a star! That didn't happen to everyone.

"You wished," replied the King calmly.

"Did I?" He couldn't remember it.

"Of course you did!" the King retorted.

"Last night!" the Queen reminded him.

"Looking at the first star!" the courtiers added firmly.

"Which happened," said the King, "to be ours. Read the Report, Lord Chamberlain!"

An elderly cat, in spectacles and a long gold wig, stepped forward with an enormous book.

"Last night," he read out pompously, "Michael Banks, of Number Seventeen, Cherry-Tree Lane — a little house on the planet Earth — gave expression to three wishes."

"Three?" cried Michael. "I never did!"

"Shush!" warned the King. "Don't interrupt."

"Wish Number One," the Lord Chamberlain read, "was that *he* could have some luck!"

An elderly cat stepped forward

A memory stirred in Michael's mind. He saw himself on the window-seat, gazing up at the sky.

"Oh, now I remember!" he agreed. "But it wasn't very important."

"All wishes are important!" The Lord Chamberlain looked at him severely.

"Well — and what happened?" the King enquired. "I presume the wish came true?"

Michael reflected. It had been a most unusual day, full of all kinds of luck.

"Yes, it did!" he admitted cheerfully.

"In what way?" asked the King. "Do tell us!"

"Well," began Michael, "I scraped the cakebowl —— "

"Scraped the cake-bowl?" the cats repeated. They stared as though he were out of his wits.

"Fancy!" the three Princesses purred.

The King wrinkled his nose in disgust. "Some people have strange ideas of luck! But do continue, please!"

Michael straightened his shoulders proudly. "And then — because it was hot, you know — the Admiral let me borrow this hat!" What would they say to that? he wondered. They would surely be green with envy.

But the cats merely flicked their tails and silently gazed at the skull-and-crossbones.

"Well, everyone to his own taste," said the King after a pause. "The question is — is it comfortable?"

"Er — not exactly," Michael admitted. For the hat did not fit him anywhere. "It's rather heavy," he added.

"H'm!" the King murmured. "Well, please go on!"

"Then Daddy gave me a shilling this morning. But I lost it in the grass."

"How much use is a lost shilling?" The way the King put the question, it sounded like a conundrum.

Michael wished he had been more careful.

"Not much," he said. Then he brightened up.

"Oh — and Aunt Flossie sent me a bar of chocolate."

He felt for it in his trouser pocket and realised, as he fished it out, that he must have been sitting on it. For now it was only a flattened mass with bits of fluff all over it and a nail embedded among the nuts.

The cats eyed the object fastidiously.

"If you ask me," said the King, looking squeamish, "I much prefer a bat to that!"

Michael also stared at the chocolate. How quickly all his luck had vanished! There was nothing left to show for it.

"Read on, Lord Chamberlain!" ordered the King.

The old cat gave his wig a pat.

"The second wish was" — he turned the page — "that the others would leave him alone."

"It wasn't!" cried Michael uncomfortably.

But he saw himself, even as he spoke, pushing the Twins away.

"Well," he said lamely, "perhaps it was. But I didn't really mean it!"

The King straightened up on his golden cushion.

"You made a wish that you didn't mean? Wasn't that rather dangerous?"

"And *did* they leave you alone?" asked the Queen. Her eyes were very inquisitive.

Michael considered. Now that he came to think of it, in spite of his luck, the day had been lonely. Jane had played her own games. The Twins had hardly been near him. And Mary Poppins, although she had treated him most politely, had certainly left him alone.

"Yes," he admitted unwillingly.

"Of course they did!" the King declared. "If you wish on the first star it always comes true, especially" — he twirled his whiskers — "if it happens to be ours. Well, what about the third wish?"

The Lord Chamberlain adjusted his glasses.

"He wished to be miles from everybody and somewhere where *he* could have all the fun."

"But that was only a sort of joke! I didn't even realise I was looking at a star. And I never thought of it coming true."

"Exactly so! You never thought! That's what all of them say." The King regarded him quizzically.

"All?" echoed Michael. "Who else said it?"

"Dear me!" The King gave a dainty yawn. "You don't think you're the only child who has wished to be miles away! I assure you, it's quite a common request. And one — when it's wished on *our* star — that *we* find very useful. *Very useful indeed!*" he repeated. "Malkin!" He waved to a courtier. "Be good enough to draw the curtain!"

A young cat, whom Michael recognised as the one that had accompanied him from the Park, sprang to the back of the hall.

The golden curtain swung aside, disclosing the palace kitchens.

"Now, come along!" cried Malkin sternly. "Hurry up, all! No dawdling!"

"Yes, Malkin!"

"No, Malkin!"

"Coming, Malkin!"

A chorus of treble voices answered. And Michael saw, to his surprise, that the kitchen was full of children.

There were boys and girls of every size, all of them working frantically at different domestic tasks.

Some were washing up golden plates, others were shining the cats' gold collars. One boy was skinning mice, another was boning bats, and two more were down on their knees busily scrubbing the floor. Two little girls in party dresses were sweeping up fishbones and sardine tins and putting them into a golden dustbin. Another was sitting under a table winding a skein of golden wool. They all looked very forlorn and harassed, and the child beneath the table was weeping.

The Lord Chamberlain looked at her and gave an impatient growl.

"Be quick with that wool, now, Arabella! The Princesses want to play cat's-cradle!"

The Queen stretched out her hind leg to a boy in a sailor suit.

"Come, Robert," she said in a fretful voice. "It's time to polish my claws."

"I'm hungry!" whined the eldest Princess.

"Matilda! Matilda!" Malkin thundered. "A haddock for Princess Tiger-Lily! And Princess Marigold's sugared milk! And a rat for the Princess Crocus!"

A girl in plaits and a pinafore appeared with three golden bowls. The Princesses nibbled a morsel each and

tossed the rest to the floor. And several children ran in and began to sweep up the scraps.

The King glanced slyly across at Michael and smiled at his astonishment.

"Our servants are very well trained, don't you think? Malkin insists on them toeing the line. They keep the palace like a new pin. And they cost us practically nothing."

"But—— " began Michael in a very small voice. "Do the children do all the work?"

"Who else?" said the King, with the lift of an eyebrow. "You could hardly expect a cat to do it! Cats have other and better occupations. A cat in the kitchen — what an idea! Our duty is to be wise and handsome — isn't that enough?"

Michael's face was full of pity as he gazed at the luckless children.

"But how did they get here?" he wanted to know.

"Exactly as you did," the King replied. "They wished they were miles from everywhere. So here they are, you see."

"But that wasn't what they really wanted!"

"I'm afraid that's no affair of ours. All we can do is to grant their wishes. I'll introduce you in a moment. They're always glad to see a new face. And so are we, for that matter." The King's face wore an expressive smile. "Many hands make light work, you know!"

"But *I'm* not going to work!" cried Michael. "That wasn't what I wished for."

"Ah! Then you should have been more careful. Wishes are tricky things. You must ask for *exactly* what you want or you never know where they will land you. Well, never mind. You'll soon settle down."

"Settle down?" echoed Michael uneasily.

"Certainly. Just as the others have done. Malkin will show you your duties presently, when you've had the rest of your wish. We mustn't be forgetting that. There are still the riddles, you know."

"Riddles? I never mentioned riddles!" Michael was beginning to wonder if he were really enjoying this adventure.

"Didn't you wish to have all the fun? Well, what is more

fun than a riddle? Especially," purred the King, "to a cat!
Tell him the rules, Lord Chamberlain!"

The old cat peered over his glasses.

"It has always been our custom here, when any child
wishes for all the fun, to let him have three guesses. If he
answers them all — correctly, of course — he wins a third
of the Cats' kingdom and the hand of one of the Princesses
in marriage."

"And if he fails," the King added, "we find him *some
other occupation*." He glanced significantly at the labour-
ing children.

"I need hardly add," he continued blandly, exchanging a smile with his three daughters, "that no one has
guessed the riddles yet. Let the curtain be drawn for
the — ahem! — time being. Silence in the hall, please!
Lord Chamberlain, begin!"

Immediately, the music ceased. The dancers stood on
the tips of their paws and the hoops hung motionless in
the air.

Michael's spirits rose again. Now that the children
were out of sight, he felt a good deal better. Besides, he
loved a guessing game.

The Lord Chamberlain opened his book and read:

> *Round as a marble, blue as the sea,*
> *Unless I am brown or grey, maybe!*
> *Smile, and I shine my window-pane,*

Frown at me and down comes my rain.
I see all things but nothing I hear,
Sing me to sleep and I disappear.

Michael frowned. The cats were all watching him as if he were a mouse.

"A bit of a poser, I'm afraid!" The King leaned back on his cushion.

"No, it isn't!" cried Michael suddenly. "I've got it! An Eye!"

The cats glanced cornerwise at each other. The King's wide gaze grew narrower.

"H'm," he murmured. "Not bad, not bad! Well, now for the second riddle."

"A-hurrrrrum!" The Lord Chamberlain cleared his throat.

Deep within me is a bird
And in that bird another me,
And in that me a bird again —
Now, what am I, in letters three?

"That's easy!" Michael gave a shout. "The answer's an Egg, of course!"

Again the cats swivelled their eyes.

"You are right," said the King unwillingly. He seemed to be only faintly pleased. "But I wonder" — he arched his dappled back — "I wonder what you will make of the third!"

"Silence!" commanded the Lord Chamberlain, though there wasn't a sound in the hall.

> *Elegant the jungle beast*
> *That lives in field and fold.*
> *He's like the sun when he is young*
> *And like the moon when old.*
> *He sees no clock, he hears no chime*
> *And yet he always knows the time.*

"This is more difficult," Michael murmured. "The third is always the worst. H'm, let me see — a jungle beast — he's elegant and he knows the time. Oh, dear, it's on the tip of my tongue. I've got it! Dandelion!"

"He's guessed it!" cried the King, rising.

And at once the cats all leapt to life. They surrounded Michael with fur and whiskers and arched themselves against him.

"You are cleverer than I thought," said the King. "Almost as clever as a cat. Well, now I must go and divide the kingdom. And as to a bride — the Princess Crocus, it seems to me, would be the most suitable choice."

"Oh, thank you," said Michael cheerfully — he was feeling quite himself again — "but I must be getting home now."

"Home!" cried the King in astonishment.

"Home?" the Queen echoed, raising her eyebrows.

"Well, I have to be back for tea," explained Michael.

"Tea?" repeated the courtiers, gaping.

"Fancy!" the three Princesses tittered.

"Are you so certain you still have a home?" said the King in a curious voice.

"Of course I am," said Michael, staring. "What could have happened to it? From the Park to — er — here, it was just a jump. And it only took me a minute."

"You've forgotten, I think," said the King smoothly, "that our minutes last for two hundred years. And as you've been here at least half an hour —— "

"Two hundred?" Michael's cheek paled. So it hadn't been a joke after all!

"It stands to reason," the King continued, "that many changes must have occurred since you were on the Earth. Number Seventeen Applebush Avenue —— "

"Cherry-Tree Lane," the Lord Chamberlain muttered.

"Well, whatever its name, you may be sure it isn't the same as it was. I dare say it's overgrown with brambles —— "

"Briars!" added the Queen, purring.

"Nettles," suggested the courtiers.

"Blackberries," murmured the three Princesses.

"Oh, I'm sure it isn't!" Michael gulped. He was feeling such a longing for home that the thought of it made him choke.

"However," the King went blandly on. "If you're certain you can find your way — I'm afraid we can't spare Malkin again — by all means set out!" He waved his paw towards the door.

Michael ran to the entrance. "Of course I'm certain!" he cried stoutly. But his courage ebbed as he looked out.

There were the shining steps of the palace, but below them, as far as he could see, there was nothing but wreathing mist. What if he jumped? he thought to himself. And if he jumped, where would he land?

He bit his lip and turned back to the hall. The cats were softly creeping towards him, gazing at him mockingly from black-and-yellow eyes.

"You see!" said the King of the Cats, smiling — and not a kindly smile either. "In spite of being so clever at guessing, you do not know the way back! You wished to be miles from everywhere, but you foolishly neglected to add that you would also like to return home. Well! Well! Everyone makes mistakes at times — unless, of course, they are cats! And think how fortunate you are! No kitchen work — you have solved the riddles. Plenty of rats and bats and spiders. And you can settle down with the Princess Crocus and live happily ever after."

"But I don't *want* to marry the Princess Crocus! I only want to go home!"

A low growl came from every throat. Every whisker bristled.

"You . . . don't . . . want . . . to . . . marry . . . the . . . Princess . . . Crocus?"

Word by word the King came nearer, growing larger at every step.

"No I don't!" declared Michael. "She's only a cat!"

"*Only* a cat!" the cats squealed, swelling and rearing with rage.

Black-and-yellow shapes swarmed round him. "*Only* a cat!" They spat out the words.

"Oh, what shall I do?" He backed away, shielding his eyes from their gaze.

"You wissshed!" they hissed at him, padding closer. "You sssought our ssstar! You mussst take the consssequencesss!"

"Oh, where shall I go?" cried Michael wildly.

"You will ssstay bessside usss," the King whispered with a terrible cat-like softness. "You guesssed our riddlesss, you ssstole our sssecretsss. Do you think we would let you go?"

A wall of cats was all about him. He flung out an arm to thrust it away. But their arching backs were too much for him. His hand dropped limply to his side and fell upon the rigid shape of Mary Poppins' whistle.

With a cry, he snatched it from his pocket and blew it with all his might.

A shrill peal sounded through the Hall.

"Sssilence him! Ssseize him! He mussstn't essscape!" The furious cats pressed closer.

In desperation he blew again.

A whining caterwaul answered the blast as a wave of cats rolled forward.

He felt himself enveloped in fur — fur in his nose, fur in his eyes. Oh, which of them had leapt at him — or was it all the cats together? With their screeches echoing in his ears, he felt himself borne upwards. A fur-covered arm, or perhaps a leg, was clasped about his waist. And his face was crushed to a furry something — a breast or a back, he could not tell.

Wind was blowing everywhere, sweeping him wildly on, with cat to the right of him, cat to the left of him, cat above him and cat below. He was wrapped in a cocoon of cats and the long furry arm that held him was as strong as an iron band.

With an effort he wrenched his head sideways and blew the whistle so violently that his hat fell off his head.

The strong arm drew him closer still.

"Whee — ee!" cried the wind, with a hollow voice.

And now it seemed that he and the cats were falling through the air. Down, down, down in a furry mass. Oh, where were they taking him?

Again and again he blew the whistle, struggling madly against the fur and kicking in all directions.

"Oo's making all that dreadful rumpus? Mind what you're doin'! You knocked off me cap!"

A wonderfully familiar voice sounded in Michael's ears.

Cautiously he opened an eye and saw that he was drift-ing down past the top of a chestnut-tree.

The next minute his feet touched the dewy grass of the Park and there, on the lawn, was the Park Keeper, looking as though he had seen a ghost.

"Now, now! Wot's all this. Wot 'ave you two been up to?"

You *two!* The words had a cheerful ring. He was held, it seemed, by only one cat and not, after all, by the whole tribe. Was it the Lord Chamberlain? Or, perhaps, the Princess Crocus!

Michael glanced from the Park Keeper to the furry arm around him. It ended, to his great surprise, not in a paw — but a hand. And on the hand was a neat glove — black, not tortoiseshell.

He turned his head enquiringly and his cheek encoun-tered a bone button that was nestling in the fur. Surely he knew that piece of bone! Oh, was it possible —— ? Could it be —— ?

His glance slid upwards past the button till it came to a neat fur collar. And above the collar was a circle of straw topped with a crimson flower.

He gave a long-drawn sigh of relief. Cats, he was glad to realise, do not wear tulip hats on their heads, nor kid gloves over their claws.

"It's you!" he cried exultantly, pressing his face to her rabbit-skin jacket. "Oh, Mary Poppins — I was up in the star — and all the cats came snarling at me — and I

The next minute his feet touched the dewy grass

thought I'd never find the way home — and I blew the whistle and —— "

Suddenly he began to stammer, for her face, beneath the brim of her hat, was cold and very haughty.

"And here I am —— " he concluded lamely.

Mary Poppins said never a word. She bowed to him in a distant manner as though she had never met him before. Then in silence she held out her hand.

He hung his head guiltily and put the whistle into it.

"So *that's* the reason for the hullabaloo!" The Park Keepers spluttered with disapproval. "I warn you, this is your last chance. Blow that whistle once again and I'll resign — I promise!"

"A pie-crust promise!" scoffed Mary Poppins, as she pocketed the whistle.

The Park Keeper shook his head in despair.

"You ought to know the rules by now. All litter to be placed in the baskets. No climbin' of trees in the Park!"

"Litter yourself!" said Mary Poppins. "And I never climbed a tree in my life!"

"Well, might I enquire where you came from, then? Droppin' down from the sky like that and knockin' off me cap?"

"There's not a law against enquiring, so far as I am aware!"

"Been up in the Milky Way, I suppose!" The Park Keeper snorted sarcastically.

"Exactly," she said, with a smile of triumph.

"Huh! You can't expect me — a respectable man — to believe that tarradiddle!" And yet, he thought uneasily, she had certainly come from somewhere.

"I don't expect anything," she retorted. "And I'll thank you to let me pass!"

Still holding Michael close to her side, she gave her head a disdainful toss, pushed the Park Keeper out of the way and tripped towards the Gate.

An outraged cry sounded behind them as the Park Keeper wildly waved his stick.

"You've broken the rules! You've disturbed the peace! And you don't even say you're sorry!"

"I'm not!" she called back airily, as she whisked across the Lane.

Speechless at so many broken bye-laws, the Park Keeper bent to pick up his cap. There it lay on the rainy grass. And beside it sprawled a strange dark object on which was painted, in gleaming white, a design of skull-and-crossbones.

"When will they learn," he sighed to himself, "what to do with their litter?"

And because he was so upset and flustered, he mistakenly put his cap in the basket and walked home wearing the pirate's hat. . . .

Michael glanced eagerly at Number Seventeen as they hurried across the Lane. It was easy to see — for the mist had cleared — that there wasn't a bramble near it. The cats had not been right, after all.

The hall light flooded him with welcome and the stairs seemed to run away beneath him as he bounded up to the nursery.

"Oh, there you are," cried Jane gaily. "Wherever have you been?"

He had not the words to answer her. He could only gaze at the well-known room, as though he had been away for years. How could he explain, even to Jane, how precious it seemed to him?

The Twins ran in with open arms. He bent and hugged them lovingly and, putting out his hand to Jane, he drew her into the hug.

A light footstep made him glance up. Mary Poppins came tripping in, buttoning on her apron. Everything about her tonight — the darting movements, the stern glance, even the way her nose turned up — was deliciously familiar.

"What would you like me to do, Mary Poppins?" He hoped she would ask for something tremendous.

"Whatever *you* like," she answered calmly, with the same extravagant courtesy she had shown him all day long.

"Don't, Mary Poppins! Don't!" he pleaded.

"Don't what?" she enquired, with annoying calm.

"Don't speak to me in that elegant way. I can't bear any more luck!"

"But luck," she said brightly, "was what you wanted!"

"It was. But it isn't. I've had enough. Oh, don't be polite and kind."

The cool smile faded from her face.

"And am I not usually polite? Have you ever known me to be unkind? What do you take me for — a hyena?"

"No, not a hyena, Mary Poppins. And you *are* polite and you *are* kind! But today I like you best when you're angry. It makes me feel much safer."

"Indeed? And when am I angry, I'd like to know?"

She looked, as she spoke, very angry indeed. Her eyes flashed, her cheeks were scarlet. And for once, the sight delighted him. Now that her chilly smile was gone, he didn't mind what happened. She was her own familiar self and he no longer a stranger.

"And when you sniff — that's when I like you!" he added with stupendous daring.

"Sniff?" she said, sniffing. "What an idea!"

"And when you say 'Humph' — like a camel!"

"Like a what?" She looked quite petrified. Then she bristled wrathfully. She reminded him of the wave of cats as she crossed the nursery like an oncoming storm.

"You dare to stand there," she accused him sternly, taking a step with every word, just as the King had done, "and tell me I'm a dromedary? Four legs and a tail and a hump or two?"

"But, Mary Poppins, I only meant —— "

"That is enough from you, Michael. One more piece of impertinence and you'll go to bed, spit-spot."

"I'm in it already, Mary Poppins," he said in a quavering voice. For by now she had backed him through the nursery and into his room.

"First a hyena and then a camel. I suppose I'll be a gorilla next!"

"But——"

"Not another word!" she spluttered, giving her head a proud toss as she stalked out of the room.

He knew he had insulted her, but he couldn't really be sorry. She was so exactly like herself that all he could feel was gladness.

Off went his clothes and in he dived, hugging his pillow to him. Its cheek was warm and friendly now as it pressed against his own.

The shadows crept slowly across his bed as he listened to the familiar sounds — bath-water running, the Twins' chatter and the rattle and clink of nursery supper.

The sounds grew fainter . . . the pillow grew softer . . .

But, suddenly, a delicious something — a scent or a flavour — filled the room, and made him sit up with a start.

A cup of chocolate hovered above him. Its fragrance came sweetly to his nose and mingled with the fresh-toast scent of Mary Poppins' apron. There she stood, like a starched statue, gazing calmly down.

He met her glance contentedly, feeling it plunging into

him and seeing what was there. He knew that she knew that he knew she was not a camel. The day was over, his adventure behind him. The Cat Star was far away in the sky. And it seemed to him, as he stirred his chocolate, he had everything he wanted.

"I do believe, Mary Poppins," he said, "that I've nothing left to wish for."

She smiled a superior, sceptical smile.

"Humph!" she remarked. "That's lucky!"

CHAPTER FOUR

THE CHILDREN IN THE STORY

Rattle! Rattle! Rattle!

Clank! Clank! Clank!

Up and down went the lawn-mower, leaving stripes of newly-cut grass in its wake.

Behind it panted the Park Keeper, pushing with all his might. At the end of each stripe he paused for a moment to glance round the Park and make sure that everybody was observing the rules.

Suddenly, out of the comer of his eye, he spied a large net waving backwards and forwards behind the laurels.

"Benjamin!" he called warningly. "Benjamin Winkle, remember the bye-laws!"

The Keeper of the Zoological Gardens thrust his head round a clump of leaves and put his finger to his lips. He was a small, nervous-looking man, with a beard like a ham-frill fringing his face.

"Sh!" he whispered. "I'm after an Admiral!"

"A n'Admiral? Well, you won't find 'im in a laurel bush. 'E's over there, at the end of the Lane. Big 'ouse, with a telescope on the flagpole."

"I mean a *Red* Admiral!" hissed the Keeper of the Zoological Gardens.

"Well, *'e's* red enough for anything. Got a face like a stormy sunset!"

"It's not a man I'm after, Fred." The Keeper of the Zoological Gardens gave the Park Keeper a look of solemn reproach. "I'm catching butterflies for the Insect House and all I've got" — he glanced dejectedly into his net — "is one Cabbage White."

"Cabbage?" cried the Park Keeper, rattling off down the lawn. "If you want a cabbage, I've some in my garden. H'artichokes, too. And turnips! Fine day, Egbert!" he called to the Policeman, who was taking a short-cut through the Park, in the course of his daily duties.

"Might be worse," the Policeman agreed, glancing up at the windows of Number Seventeen, in the hope of catching a glimpse of Ellen.

He sighed. "And might be better!" he added glumly. For Ellen was nowhere to be seen.

Rattle, rattle. Clank, clank.

The sunlight spangled the stripy lawn and spread like a fan over Park and Lane. It even went so far as to shine on the Fair Ground, and the swinging-boats and the merry-go-round and the big blue banner with MUDGE'S FAIR printed on it in gold.

The Park Keeper paused at the end of a stripe and sent a hawk-like glance about him.

A fat man with a face like a poppy was sauntering through the little gate that led from the Fair. He had a bowler hat on the back of his head and a large cigar in his mouth.

"Keep Off the Grass!" the Park Keeper called to him.

"I wasn't on it!" retorted the fat man, with a look of injured innocence.

"Well, I'm just givin' you a Word of Warnin'. All litter to be placed in the baskets — especially, Mr. Mudge, in the Fair Ground!"

"Mr. Smith," said the fat man in a fat confident voice. "If you find so much as a postage stamp when the Fair's over, I'll — well, I'll be surprised. You'll be able to eat your dinner off that Fair Ground or my name's not Willie Mudge."

And he stuck his thumbs into the armholes of his jacket and swaggered off, looking very important.

"Last year," the Park Keeper shouted after him, "I swept up sacks of postage stamps! And I don't eat me dinner there. I go 'ome for it!"

He turned to his work again with a sigh and the lawnmower went up and down with a steady, sleepy drone. At the last stripe, where the lawn ended in the Rose Garden, he glanced cautiously round. Now was the moment, he felt, if there was nobody about to report him to the Lord Mayor, to take a little rest.

The Rose Garden was a ring of rose-beds enclosing

a little green space. In the middle was a pool and in the pool stood a fountain of white marble shaped like an open rose.

The Park Keeper peered through the flowering bushes. There, by the fountain, lay Jane and Michael. And just beyond the Rose Garden, on a marble seat, sat an elderly gentleman. He seemed to have forgotten his hat, for his bald head was sheltered from the sun by a peaked cap made of newspaper. His nose was deep in an enormous book, which he was reading with the aid of a magnifying-glass. He muttered to himself as he turned the pages.

Jane and Michael, too, had a book. And Jane's voice mingled with the sound of the fountain as she read aloud to Michael. It was a peaceful scene.

"Quiet for once," the Park Keeper murmured. "I shall just snatch Forty Winks!" And he lay down cautiously among the bushes hoping that if anyone passed they would mistake him for a rose.

Had he looked in the other direction he might have thought better of behaving so recklessly. For, away under the wistarias, pushing the perambulator backwards and forwards in a rhythmic, soothing movement, was Mary Poppins.

Creak, creak, went the wheels.

Whimper, whimper, went Annabel, who was cutting her first tooth.

"Shoo now! Shoo now!" murmured Mary Poppins, in an absent-minded voice.

She was thinking about her new pink blouse, with the lace-edged handkerchief stuck in the pocket. How nicely it harmonised, she thought, with the tulip in her hat. And she could not help wishing there were more people in the Park to appreciate the spectacle. On every bench and under every tree there should have been an admiring onlooker. "There's that charming Miss Poppins," she imagined them saying, "always so neat and respectable!"

But there were only a few scattered strangers hurrying along the paths and taking no notice of anybody.

She could see the Policeman forlornly gazing up at the windows of Number Seventeen. And the fat man with the large cigar who, in spite of all the Park Keeper's warnings, was walking on the grass. She prinked a little as Bert, the Match Man, biting into a rosy apple, came sauntering through the Gate. Perhaps he was looking for her, she thought, smoothing her neat black gloves.

She could also see Miss Lark, whose two dogs were taking her for an afternoon run. They rushed down the Long Walk laughing and barking, while Miss Lark, with the two leads in her hands, came tumbling behind. Her hat was over one ear and her scarf flapped about like a flag in the breeze. Gloves and spectacles scattered from her, and her necklaces and beads and bracelets were swinging in all directions.

Mary Poppins sniffed. Miss Lark, she thought, was not so tidy as *somebody* she could mention! She smiled a small self-satisfied smile and went on rocking Annabel.

Now that the lawn-mower was silent there was hardly a sound in the Park. Only the music of the fountain and Jane's voice coming to the end of a story.

"So that," she concluded, "was the end of the Witch. And the King and the Maiden were married next day and lived happily ever after."

Michael sighed contentedly and nibbled a leaf of clover.

Away beyond the Rose Garden, the elderly gentleman took off his glasses, spread his handkerchief over his face and dozed on the marble seat.

"Go on, Jane. Don't stop!" urged Michael. "Read another one."

Jane turned the pages of *The Silver Fairy Book*. It was worn and faded, for its life had been long and busy. Once it had belonged to Mrs. Banks, and before that it had been given to her mother by *her* mother. Many of the pictures had disappeared and the drawings had all been coloured with crayons, either by Jane and Michael or by their mother. Perhaps, even, by their Grandmother, too.

"It's so hard to choose," Jane murmured, for she loved every one of the stories.

"Well, read wherever it falls open — the way you always do!"

She closed the book, held it between her hands for a second, and then let it go. With a little thud it fell on the grass and opened right in the middle.

"Hooray!" said Michael. "It's *The Three Princes.*" And he settled himself to listen.

"Once upon a time," read Jane, "there lived a King who had three sons. The eldest was Prince Florimond, the second Prince Veritain, and the third Prince Amor. Now, it so happened that — — "

"Let me see the picture!" interrupted Michael.

It was a drawing he particularly liked, for he and Jane had coloured it one rainy afternoon. The Princes were standing at the edge of a forest and the branches that spread above their heads bore fruit and flowers together. A saddled Unicorn stood beside them, with its rein looped round the arm of the eldest.

Prince Florimond was in green crayon with a purple cap. Prince Veritain had an orange jerkin and his cap was scarlet. And little Prince Amor was all in blue, with

a golden dagger stuck in his belt. Chrome-coloured ringlets fell about the shoulders of the two elder brothers. And
the youngest, who was bareheaded, had a yellow circlet of
short curls, rather like a crown.

As for the Unicorn, he was silvery white from mane to
tail — except for his eyes, which were the colour of forget-
me-nots; and his horn, which was striped with red and
black.

Jane and Michael gazed down at the page and smiled
at the pictured children. And the three Princes smiled up
from the book and seemed to lean forward from the forest.

Michael sighed. "If only I had a dagger like Amor's. It would just be about my size."

A breeze rustled the trees of the Park and the coloured drawing seemed to tremble.

"I never can choose between Florimond and Veritain," Jane murmured. "They are both so beautiful."

The fountain gave a laughing ripple and an echo of laughter seemed to come from the book.

"I'll lend it to you!" said the youngest Prince, whipping the dagger from his belt.

"Why not choose us both?" cried the two eldest, stepping forward on to the lawn.

Jane and Michael caught their breath. What had happened? Had the painted forest come to the Park? Or was it that the Rose Garden had gone into the picture? Are we there? Are they here? Which is which? they asked themselves, and could not give an answer.

"Don't you know us, Jane?" asked Florimond, smiling.

"Yes, of course!" she gasped. "But — how did you get here?"

"Didn't you see?" asked Veritain. "You smiled at us and we smiled at you. And the picture looked so shiny and bright — you and Michael and the painted roses — — "

"So we jumped right into the story!" Amor concluded gaily.

"Out of it, you mean!" cried Michael. "We're not a story. We're real people. It's you who are the pictures!"

The Princes tossed their curls and laughed.

"Touch me!" said Florimond.

"Take my hand!" urged Veritain.

"Here's my dagger!" cried Amor.

Michael took the golden weapon. It was sharp and solid and warm from Amor's body.

"Who's real now?" Amor demanded. "Tuck it into your belt," he said, smiling at Michael's astonished face.

"You see — I was right!" said Florimond, as Jane put one hand on his sleeve and the other in Veritain's outstretched palm. She felt the warmth of both and nodded.

"But — —" she protested. "How can it be? You are in Once Upon a Time. And that is long ago."

"Oh, no!" said Veritain. "It's always. Do you remember your great-great-great-great-grandmother?"

"Of course not. I am much too young."

"We do," said Florimond, with a smile. "And what about your great-great-great-great-granddaughter? Will you ever see her, do you think?"

Jane shook her head a little wistfully. That charming far-away little girl — how much she would like to know her!

"We shall," said Veritain confidently.

"But how? You're the children in the story!"

Florimond laughed and shook his head.

"*You* are the children in the story! We've read about you so often, Jane, and looked at the picture and longed to know you. So today — when the book fell open — we simply walked in. We come once into everyone's story — the grandparents and the grandchildren are all the same to us. But most people take no notice." He sighed. "Or if they do, they forget very quickly. Only a few remember."

Jane's hand tightened on his sleeve. She felt *she* would never forget him, not if she lived to be forty.

"Oh, don't waste time explaining," begged Amor. "We want to explore the picture!"

"We'll lead the way!" cried Michael eagerly, as he seized Amor by the hand. He hardly cared whether he was a real boy or a boy in a story, so long as the golden dagger lay snugly in his belt.

"We'll follow!" cried Veritain, running behind them.

Florimond gave a piercing whistle and tugged at the rein on his arm.

Immediately, as if from nowhere, the Unicorn appeared at his side. Florimond patted the silky neck and, moving off beside Jane, he glanced about him eagerly.

"Look, brothers — over there is the Lake! Do you see Neleus with his Dolphin? And that must be Number Seventeen. We never could see it clearly before," he explained to Jane and Michael. "In the picture it's hidden behind the trees."

"H'm — a very small house," said Amor, gazing.

"But it's solid and friendly," said Veritain kindly.

"And the grounds are very extensive." Florimond made a sweeping gesture and bent to sniff at a rose.

"Now, now! Wot are you doin'!" The Park Keeper, roused from his Forty Winks, sat up and rubbed his eyes.

"Observe the rules," he grumbled, stretching. "No pickin' of flowers allowed."

"I wasn't picking. I was just smelling. Though, of course," said Florimond politely, "I would like to have a rose from Jane's garden. As a souvenir, you know!"

"*Jane's* garden?" The Park Keeper stared. "This is no garden. It's a Public Park. And it don't belong to Jane. Souveneer, indeed!" he spluttered. " 'Oo do you think you are?"

"Oh, I don't think — I know!" the Prince replied. "I am Florimond, the King's eldest son. These are my brothers — don't you remember? And our task is to fight the Dragon."

The Park Keeper's eyes nearly dropped from his head.

"King's eldest —— ? Dragon? No dragons allowed in the Public Parks. And no horses, neither!" he added, as his eyes fell on the silvery hooves that were lightly pawing the lawn.

A peal of laughter burst from Amor.

Jane and Michael giggled.

"That's not a horse," Veritain protested. "Can't you see? He's a Unicorn!"

"Now, now!" The Park Keeper heaved to his feet. "I

ought to know a Norse when I see one and that's a Norse or I'm a —— Lumme!"

The milk-white creature raised its head.

"It is! It *is* a Unycorn! 'Orn and all — just like a picture. I never saw such a thing before — at least —— " The Park Keeper wrinkled up his brow as though he were trying to remember something. "No, no," he murmured, "I couldn't have! Not even when I was a boy. A Unycorn! I must make a report. Winkle, where are you? 'Ere, you boys —— " He turned to the astonished Princes. "You 'old 'im quiet till I get back. Don't let 'im go wotever you do!"

And off he went, leaping over the flower-beds. " 'Orn and all!" they heard him shouting, as he darted among the laurels.

The Princes, their eyes round with surprise, gazed after his disappearing figure.

"Your gardener seems very excitable," said Florimond to Jane.

She was just about to explain that the Park Keeper was not their gardener, when a shrill voice interrupted her.

"Wait! Wait! Not so fast! My arms are nearly out of their sockets. Oh, what shall I do? There goes my scarf!"

Into the Rose Garden plunged Miss Lark, with the two dogs straining at their leads. Her hat was wobbling dangerously and her hair hung in wisps around her face.

"Oh, goodness! There they go again! Andrew! Willoughby! Do come back!"

But the dogs merely laughed. They tugged the leathers from her hands and, bounding gaily towards the Princes, they leapt up at Amor.

"Oh, Jane! Oh, Michael!" Miss Lark panted. "Do help me, please, to catch the dogs. I don't like them talking to strangers. Look at that queer boy kissing Andrew! He may have a cold and the dogs will catch it. Who *are* these children? What very odd clothes! And their hair is much too long!"

"This is Florimond," said Jane politely.

"This is Veritain," added Michael.

"And this is Amor!" said Amor, laughing, as he kissed Willoughby's nose.

"Peculiar names!" exclaimed Miss Lark. "And yet —— " Her face had a puzzled expression. "I seem to have heard them before. Where can it have been? In a pantomime?"

She peered at the Princes and shook her head. "They're foreigners, without a doubt. And what have they got there — a donkey? Gracious!" She gave a shriek of surprise. "It can't be! Yes! No! Yes — it is! A Unicorn — how *wonderful!*"

She clasped her hands in ecstasy and trilled away like a lark. "Horn and all! A Unicorn! But why isn't somebody looking after it?"

"We are looking after him," said Florimond calmly.

"Nonsense! Ridiculous! Absurd! He should be in

charge of responsible people. I shall go myself to the British Museum and find the Chief Professor. Andrew and Willoughby, leave that boy and come along with Mother! Quickly, quickly!" She seized the leads. "We must go at once for help!"

The two dogs exchanged a wink and dashed away at full speed.

"Oh, not so quickly as that," cried Miss Lark. "You will have me head-over-heels. Oh, dear, oh, dear — there goes my bracelet! Never mind!" she called over her shoulder, as Veritain stooped to pick it up. "Keep it! I've no time to waste!"

And off she stumbled behind the dogs with her hair and necklaces flying.

"Officer!" they heard her calling to the Policeman. "There's a Unicorn in the Rose Garden. Be sure you don't let him escape!"

"Escape?" said Amor. "But why should he want to! He'd never be happy away from us."

He smiled lovingly at Michael as the Unicorn thrust his head between them and tickled their cheeks with his mane.

"A Unicorn!" The Policeman stared. "Miss Lark's gettin' queerer and queerer!" he muttered, as he watched her fluttering down the path. " 'Ere! Look where you're going, Mr. Mudge! You can't do that to the Law."

For a large fat man had bumped into him and was

breathlessly hurrying by. The Policeman seized him by the arm.

"A Unicorn, the old girl said!" Mr. Mudge panted heavily.

"A Unicorn?" cried the passing strangers. "We don't believe it! We must write to *The Times!*"

"Of course, I know there's no sich thing. Somebody's having a bit of a joke." Mr. Mudge mopped his poppy cheeks. "But I thought as I'd go and see."

"Well, you go quietly," the Policeman advised him. "And treat the Law with respect."

He released Mr. Mudge's arm and strode on ahead of him.

"Come, let us go deeper into the picture," Florimond was saying. He took Jane gently by the hand and Veritain came to her other side.

"Hurry up, Michael! Let's try the swings. And then we can paddle in the Lake." Amor gave a tug to Michael's hand. "But who are all these people?"

The five children glanced about them. The Park, which had been so quiet before, was now filled with flying figures, all racing towards the Rose Garden and shouting as they came. The Policeman stalked along before them with big important strides.

As the children turned to leave the garden, his large blue body barred the way.

He gave one glance at the Unicorn and his eyebrows went up to the edge of his helmet.

"Miss Lark was right, after all," he muttered. Then he eyed the Princes sternly.

"Might I h'ask what you think you're up to — disturbing the peace in a public place? And I'd like to know how you three tinkers got hold of that there animal!"

"They're not tinkers!" protested Michael. He was shocked at the Policeman's words. Couldn't he *see* who they were?

"Gypsies, then. You can tell by their clothes. Too gaudy for respectable people."

"But don't you remember them?" cried Jane. She was fond of the Policeman and wanted him not to make a mistake.

"Never saw them before in my life." He took out his notebook and pencil. "Now, I want a few pertickelers. Honesty's the best policy, lads, so speak up clearly and state the facts. First of all, where do you come from?"

"Nowhere!" giggled Amor.

"Everywhere!" said Veritain.

"East of the Sun and West of the Moon," Florimond added gravely.

"Now, now! This won't do. I asked a plain question and I want a plain answer. Where do you live? What place on the map?"

"Oh, it's not on the map," said Florimond. "But it's easy to find if you really want to. You only have to wish."

"No fixed address," the Policeman murmured, writing in his notebook. "You see! They're gypsies — just

like I said. Now then, young man — your father's
name!"

"Fidelio," answered Florimond.

"Mother's name?" The Law gave his pencil a careful
lick.

"Esperanza," Veritain told him. "With a 'Z'," he added
helpfully, for the Policeman, it seemed, was not a good
speller.

"Aunts?" enquired the Policeman again, laboriously
writing.

"Oh, we have hundreds." Amor grinned. "Cinderella,
Snow White, Badroulbador, the White Cat, Little-Two-
Eyes, Baba Yaga — and, of course, the Sleeping Beauty."

"Sleeping Beauty —— " the Policeman murmured.

Then he looked at the words he had written and
glanced up angrily.

"You're making a mock of the Law!" he cried. "The
Sleeping Beauty wasn't nobody's aunt. She was somebody
in a book. Now, see here! Since you boys refuse to give me
h'information in h'accordance with the h'regulations, it is
my duty to take that animal in charge."

He stepped forward resolutely.

The Unicorn gave an angry snort and flung up his hind
legs.

"'Ands off! 'Ands off!" yelled the Park Keeper, as he
flung himself across the roses and pushed the Policeman
aside.

"There 'e is, Ben!" he cried in triumph, as the Keeper

THE CHILDREN IN THE STORY

of the Zoological Gardens, nervously waving his butterfly net, came tip-toeing into the Rose Garden.

"'Orn and all — just like I told yer!" The Park Keeper reached for the silver bridle and immediately turned a back somersault.

For the Unicorn had lowered his head and swung his horn against him.

"E-e-eh! Oh! O-o-o-h!" The Keeper of the Zoological Gardens, with a frightened yelp, took refuge behind the Policeman.

"Dear me, is he dangerous? Does he bite? That horn looks very sharp!"

"It's sharp *and* solid, Benjamin!" The Park Keeper ruefully rubbed his stomach.

"He's gentle and good," Florimond protested. "But he isn't used to strangers."

"H'm. Well, you'd better bring him along to the Zoo and settle him down in a cage."

"A cage! Oh, no," cried Jane and Michael, angrily stamping their feet.

And the Unicorn, as though in agreement, drummed with his hooves on the lawn.

"But what would he do in a cage?" asked Amor, his eyes wide with interest.

"Do?" echoed the Keeper of the Zoological Gardens. "He'd do what the other animals do — just stand there to be looked at!"

"Oh, he wouldn't like that," put in Veritain quickly.

"He's used to being quite free. Besides," he added, smiling politely, "he belongs to us, you know!"

"Free!" The Policeman shook his fist. "Nobody's free to kick at the Law!"

"Whoa there!" cried the Keeper of the Zoological Gardens.

"I *won't* whoa there!" the Policeman shouted. "I'm only doing what's right!"

"I was talking to *him*," murmured Mr. Winkle. And he pointed to the Unicorn who was dancing madly on all four feet.

"Now then," he cooed, "be a good little Dobbin. And we'll get him some hay and a nice clean house next door to the Hippopotamus!"

The Unicorn gave his tail a twitch and lashed it at Mr. Winkle. It was quite clear that he had no intention of living anywhere near a hippopotamus.

"Don't coax 'im, Benjamin, just take 'im!" The Park Keeper gave his friend a push.

"Oh, no! Not yet! Wait just one minute!"

Miss Lark's voice sounded shriller than ever as she hurried back to the scene. In one hand she held up her tattered skirt and with the other she dragged along an elderly gentleman in a newspaper hat. He was carrying a large book and a magnifying-glass and looking very bewildered.

"So fortunate!" Miss Lark panted. "I found the Professor asleep on a bench. There now, Professor——"

She flung out her hand. "Do you still say you don't believe me?"

"Don't believe what?" the Professor mumbled.

"Tch! Tch! I've told you a dozen times. I've found a Unicorn!"

"Indeed?" The Professor fumbled in his pockets till at length he found his spectacles and fixed them on his nose.

"Er — what was it, dear lady, I had to look at?" He seemed to have quite forgotten what he wanted his spectacles for.

Miss Lark sighed.

"The Unicorn!" she answered patiently.

The Professor blinked and turned his head.

"Well, well! Er — hum! Extraordinary!"

He leaned forward for a closer look and the Unicorn made a thrust with his head and prodded the Professor with the end of his horn.

"You're right!" The Professor toppled backwards. "It *is* — ah — hum — a Unicorn!"

"Of course it is!" scoffed the Park Keeper. "We don't need nobody in a paper 'at to tell us that bit o' news."

The Professor took not the slightest notice. He was turning the pages of his book and waving the magnifying-glass.

"O.P.Q.R.S.T.U. Ah, here it is! Yes. A fabulous beast. Rarely — if ever! — seen by man. Reputed to be worth a city — — "

"A city!" exclaimed the Policeman, staring. "A horse with a bit o' bone on his head!"

"Distinguishing marks — — " the Professor gabbled. "White body, tail of similar hue, and a broad brow from which a horn — — "

"Yes, yes, Professor," Miss Lark broke in. "We know what he looks like. You needn't tell us. The question is — what shall we do with him?"

"Do?" The Professor looked over the top of his glasses. "There's only one thing to be done, madam. We must arrange to — ah — have him stuffed!"

"Stuffed?" Miss Lark gave a little gasp. She glanced uneasily at the Unicorn and he gave her a long, reproachful stare.

"Stuffed!" cried Jane in a horrified voice.

"Stuffed!" echoed Michael, squeakily. He could hardly bear to think of it.

The Princes shook their golden heads. Their eyes as they gazed at the Professor were grave and full of pity.

"Stuffed? Stuff and nonsense!" said a raucous voice, as Mr. Mudge, looking redder than ever, came lumbering into the Rose Garden. "Nobody's going to stuff an animal that might be of use to Mudge. Where is it?" he demanded loudly.

His bulgy eyes grew bulgier still as they fell on the silver shape.

"Well, I never!" He whistled softly. "Cleverest dodge I ever saw. Somebody's glued a horn on a horse! My word — what a sideshow this will make! Who's in charge of the beast?"

"We are," said Florimond, Veritain and Amor.

Mr. Mudge turned and surveyed the Princes.

"Out of the Circus, I see!" He grinned. "What are you — acrobats?"

The Princes smiled and shook their heads.

"Well, you can come along with the nag. Those velvet jackets are just the thing. Three meals a day and oats for the horse. And I'll bill you as Mudge's Unicorn and his

Three Servants. Hey, back up, Neddy — look what you're doing!"

Mr. Mudge jumped sideways just in time to escape a nip from the Unicorn's teeth.

"Here, tighten that rein!" he shouted sharply. "Take care! He's got a nasty temper!"

"Oh, no he hasn't," said Florimond quickly. "But he doesn't care to be part of a sideshow."

"And we're not his servants," said Veritain.

"It's the other way round!" Amor added.

"Now, I want no sauciness, my lads! Just bring him along and behave yourselves. We've got to get him settled down before the Fair opens."

The Unicorn tossed his silver mane.

"Begging your pardon, Mr. Mudge! But that Unicorn belongs to the Zoo!"

Thump! went the Unicorn's horn on the lawn.

"Nonsense — er — hum!" the Professor exclaimed. "He must go with me to the British Museum. And stand — ah — hum — on a pedestal for all the world to see."

"The world can see him in his cage," said Mr. Winkle stubbornly.

"At the Fair, you mean!" Mr. Mudge insisted. "The Only Unicorn in the World! Money back if not satisfied. Roll up! Roll up! Sixpence a look!"

"He belongs to the Princes!" shouted Michael.

But nobody took any notice.

The Park was ringing with many voices. People came running from all directions, all giving different advice.

"Get him a halter! Hobble his legs! Bind him! Hold him! Put him in chains!"

And the Unicorn lashed out with his hooves and swung his horn around like a sword and kept them all at a distance.

"He belongs to the Law!" the Policeman roared, taking out his baton.

"To Mudge's Fair!" cried Mr. Mudge. "Children Half-Price! Babies Free!"

"To the Zoo!" squeaked the Keeper of the Zoological Gardens, waving his net in the air.

"What's going on — an accident?" Bert, the Match Man, pushed through the crowd and sauntered into the Rose Garden.

At the sight of his calm and cheerful face, Jane gave a sigh of relief.

"Oh, help us, please!" She ran to him. "They're trying to take the Unicorn."

"The *what?*" said the Match Man, very surprised. He glanced at the little group by the fountain and gave a sudden start. A look of joy spread over his face as he sprang across the lawn.

"Gently, boy, gently! Easy does it!" He seized the Unicorn by the mane and held out the apple he was

munching. The Unicorn lowered his tossing head, sniffed
enquiringly at the outstretched hand and then, with a sigh
of satisfaction, he gobbled up the core.

The Match Man gave him a friendly slap. Then he
turned to the Princes with a loving look and, falling upon
one knee, kissed Florimond's hand.

There was a sudden silence in the Rose Garden.
Everybody stared.

"What's the matter with Bert?" the Park Keeper muttered. " 'E must 'ave gorn mad!"

For the Match Man had turned to Veritain and Amor
and was kissing their hands, too.

"Welcome, my Princes!" he said softly. "I am happy to
see you again!"

"Princes, indeed!" the Policeman exploded. "A set of
rascals, that's what they are. I found them loitering in the
Park in wrongful possession of a fabbilous animal. And
I'm taking it in charge!"

"What, *that?*" The Match Man glanced at the Unicorn
and laughed as he shook his head. "You wouldn't be able
to catch him, Egbert. He isn't your sort of animal. And
what's a Unicorn, anyway, compared with the three of
them?"

He turned to the Princes with outstretched arms.

"They've forgotten us, Bert," said Florimond sadly.

"Well, you won't forget *me* in a hurry," the Policeman
put in grimly. "Move away, Bert, you're obstructing the

Law. Now, bring that Unicorn along and follow me, all three!"

"Don't you go, lads," urged Mr. Mudge. "Just slip along to the Fair Ground and you and horsie will be treated proper."

"Oh, come with me, boys!" begged Mr. Winkle. "If I let that Unicorn slip through my fingers, the Head Keeper will never forgive me."

"No!" said Veritain.

"No!" said Amor.

"I am sorry," said Florimond, shaking his head. "But we cannot go with any of you."

"You'll come, if I have to carry you!" The Policeman strode towards the Princes with an angry gleam in his eye.

"Oh, please don't touch them!" Jane cried wildly, flinging herself in his way.

"You leave them alone!" screamed Michael, as he seized the Policeman by the leg.

"'Ooligans!" exclaimed Mr. Mudge. "*I* never behaved like that!"

"Let me go, Michael!" the Policeman yelled.

"What shocking conduct! How badly brought up!" cried voices in the crowd.

"Professor, Professor, please do something!" Miss Lark's voice rose above the din.

"Such goings on!" murmured Mr. Winkle. "It's worse than the Lion House!"

He turned in terror from the scene and knocked against a moving object that was entering the Rose Garden. A creaking wheel passed over his foot and his net became entangled with a large crimson flower.

"Out of my way!" said Mary Poppins, as she disengaged the net from her hat. "And I'll thank you to remember," she added, "that I'm not a butterfly!"

"I can see that," said the Keeper of the Zoological Gardens, as he dragged his foot from under the wheel.

Mary Poppins gave him an icy glare as she thrust him calmly out of her way and tripped towards the fountain.

At the sight of her neat and dignified figure there was a moment's silence. The crowd gave her a respectful stare. The Match Man took off his cap.

"Good-afternoon, Bert!" she said, with a bow. But the lady-like smile froze on her lips as her glance fell upon the children.

"May I ask what you think you're doing, Jane? And you, too, Michael! Let go that Policeman! Is this a garden or a Cannibal Island?"

"A Cannibal Island!" cried the youngest Prince, laughing with joy as he ran towards her. "At last! At last, Mary Poppins!" he murmured, as he flung his arms round her waist.

"Mary Poppins! Mary Poppins!" cried the elder brothers as they leapt together over the fountain and seized her kid-gloved hands.

Michael seized the Policeman by the leg

"Whin-n-n-e-e-e-h-o-o-o!" The Unicorn gave a happy neigh and, trotting daintily towards her, he touched his horn to her black-buttoned shoe.

Mary Poppins' eyes darkened.

"Florimond! Veritain! Amor! What are you doing here?"

"Well, the book fell open ——"

"At Jane and Michael's story ——"

"So we just jumped into the picture ——"

The three Princes hung their heads as they all answered together.

"Then you'd better jump out of it — spit-spot! You're very naughty boys!"

Amor gave her a loving smile.

"And you're a naughty girl!" he retorted. "Going away and leaving us with never a Word of Warning!"

Michael stared. He loosed his hold on the Policeman's leg and ran to Amor.

"Do you know Mary Poppins?" he demanded. "And did she do that to you, too?" He felt rather jealous of his friend. Would *he* ever be so brave, he wondered, as to call her a naughty girl?

"Of course we know her. And she's always doing it — coming and going without a word. Oh, don't be cross with us, Mary Poppins!" Amor looked up with an impish grin. "I see you've got a new hat!"

A ghost of a smile crept round her mouth, but she changed it into a sniff.

"Your face is dirty, Amor, as usual!"

And whipping out her lace-edged handkerchief she dabbed it quickly against his tongue, gave his cheek a vigorous rub and tucked the handkerchief into his pocket.

"H'm. That's more like it," she said tartly. "Florimond, put your cap on straight. It was always on one side, I remember. And, Veritain, will you never learn? If I've told you once, I've told you twice, to tie your laces with *double* knots. Just look at your slippers!"

Veritain stooped to his velvet shoes and tied the straggling cords.

"Yes — *you* remember, Mary Poppins!" Florimond straightened the set of his cap. "But, except for Jane and

Michael and Bert, you are the only one. All *they* want is the Unicorn —— " He pointed to the watching crowd. "And they can't even agree about him."

The Unicorn nodded his silver head and his blue eye blazed with wrath.

"Pooh!" Mary Poppins turned up her nose. "What else could you expect — from them? It's their misfortune, Florimond. No fault of yours!"

The Policeman blushed as red as a beetroot beneath her scornful gaze.

"I remember my duty!" he said doggedly.

"I remember the public's entertainment!" Mr. Mudge bristled.

"I remember the Head Keeper!" whispered the Keeper of the Zoological Gardens.

"Wait! I remember something else!" The Park Keeper clapped his hand to his brow.

"'Arf a minute — it's comin' back. I can see me old mother readin' aloud. A silver book. And the cat by the fire. And them —— " He flung out a hand to the Princes.

"And them and me goin' 'and in 'and. There was flower and fruit on the same branch and a Unycorn trottin' through the forest. Oh, what 'as 'appened?" he cried aloud. "Me 'eart is beatin' the way it used to! I feel like I felt when I was a boy. No litter, no bye-laws, no Lord Mayor, and sausages for supper. Oh, now I remember you, Mister — er — Prince —— "

The Park Keeper turned to Florimond. His sombre face had quite changed. It was gleaming with happiness.

"A sooveneer!" he shouted gaily. "Something for you to remember me by!"

And recklessly he dashed at the flower-beds and snapped off three of the largest roses.

"I shall get into trouble, but what do I care? I'm doin' it for you!" With a shy and humble gesture, he thrust the flowers at Florimond.

Grave and glad were Florimond's eyes as he touched the Park Keeper's cheek.

"Thank you." He smiled. "I shall keep them always."

"Aw!" The Park Keeper gave an embarrassed laugh. "You can't do that. They'll fade, you know!"

"Oh, no, they won't!" cried Miss Lark suddenly. "In their country, dear Park Keeper, the roses bloom for ever."

She turned to the Princes eagerly, with her hands against her heart.

"Oh, how could I have forgotten?" she murmured. "It was yesterday — or the day before! I was wearing a pinafore tied at the back ——"

"And button-boots," put in Veritain.

"And yellow curls with a blue ribbon," said Amor helpfully. "She does remember!" he cried to his brothers, smiling at Miss Lark.

"And you were everywhere!" she whispered. "Playing beside me in the sunlight, swinging with me on the garden gate. The birds in the tree were you disguised. I stepped over every ant and beetle for fear it might be one of my princes. I meant to marry a King — I remember — or at least a Caliph's younger son. And you three were to be always near me. And then — oh, what happened? How did I lose you? Was it really only yesterday? Where are my curls, my yellow curls? Why am I all alone in the world, except for two little dogs?"

Andrew and Willoughby glanced up indignantly. "Except, indeed!" they seemed to say.

"Yes, yes, I'm getting old," said Miss Lark, as she peered through her wisps of hair. "I'll forget you again, my darling Princes! But, oh, do not forget me! What shall I give you to remember me by? I have lost" — she scrabbled in her pockets — "so many of my possessions!"

"We will never forget you," said Veritain gently. "And you've given us something already."

He drew his velvet sleeve aside and showed her the glitter at his wrist.

"My bracelet! But it's only glass!"

"No!" cried Veritain. "Rubies! Sapphires!"

He raised his hand above his head and the bracelet shone so bright in the sunset that it dazzled every eye.

"Golly!" the Policeman muttered. "He's stolen the Crown Jewels!"

"Oh!" breathed Miss Lark, as she clasped her hands and gazed at the shining stones.

"I understand," she murmured softly. "Professor, Professor, do you see?"

But the Professor put his hand to his eyes and turned his head away.

"I have seen too much," he said sadly. "I have seen how foolish I am! Books!" he cried, tossing the volume from him. "Magnifying-glasses!" He flung the glass among the roses. "Alas, alas! I have wasted my time. Florimond, Veritain, Amor — I recognise you now!" He turned his tearful face to the Princes.

"Oh, Beauty, Truth and Love," he whispered. "To think that I knew you when I was a lad! To think that I could forget! All day long you ran at my side. And your voices called to me in the dusk — Follow! Follow! Follow! I see it now — I've been looking for wisdom. But wisdom was there and I turned my back. I've been running away from it ever since, trying to find it in books. So far away" — the Professor hid his face in his arm — "that when I met a Unicorn, I imagined I could have him stuffed! Oh, how can I make up for that? I have no rose, no jewels, nothing."

He glanced about him doubtfully and put his hand to his forehead. And as he did so his face cleared. A happy thought had struck him.

"Take this, my child!" he said to Amor, as he plucked the newspaper hat from his brow. "Your way is long and the night will be chilly and you've nothing on your head!"

"Thank you, Professor!" Amor smiled and set the hat

at a jaunty angle over his crown of curls. "I hope you will
not be cold without it."

"Cold?" the Professor murmured vaguely, as his gaze
slipped past the Princes to the snow-white creature on the
lawn. He put out an aged trembling hand and the Unicorn
rose from the dewy grass and calmly came to his side.

"Forgive me!" the Professor whispered. "It was not
I that would have stuffed you. A madman wearing my
skin — not I! No, no! I'll never be cold again. I have
stroked a Unicorn!"

His fingers touched the milky neck. The Unicorn
stood mild and still. His blue eyes did not flicker.

"That's right, Professor!" said the Policeman cheerfully. "No good trying to stuff a h'animal that by rights
belongs to the Law!"

"He belongs to the Law," the Professor murmured. "But not the Law you know —— "

"The Fair!" insisted Mr. Mudge, elbowing past the Policeman.

"Yes! All is fair where he comes from." The Professor stroked the Unicorn's nose.

"He'll be among the stars of the Zoo," the Zoo Keeper promised breathlessly.

"He'll be among the stars," said the Professor, touching the tip of the Unicorn's horn, "but far, far from the Zoo."

"Exactly, Professor! You're a sensible chap! Now, I've no more time for h'argument. The boys and the beast are under arrest and I'm taking them off to the Police Station!"

The Policeman put out a determined hand and seized the Unicorn's bridle.

"Quick, Florimond!" warned Mary Poppins.

And Florimond, with a single bound, leapt on the Unicorn's back.

Up went Veritain behind him.

"Good-bye, Michael," whispered Amor, hugging him round the waist. Then with a graceful, running leap he landed behind his brothers.

"Oh, do not leave me!" cried Miss Lark. "I may forget again!"

"I won't forget!" said Michael stoutly, waving his hand to Amor.

"Nor I! Oh, never!" echoed Jane, with a long look at Florimond and Veritain. She felt that their faces were in her heart for ever.

"If you remember, we'll come again!" Florimond promised, smiling. "Are you ready, my brothers? We must go!"

"Ready!" the younger Princes cried.

Then one by one they leant sideways and kissed Mary Poppins.

"We'll be waiting for you," said Florimond.

"Do not be long!" urged Veritain.

"Come back to us," said Amor, laughing, "with a tulip in your hat!"

She tried to look stern, but she simply couldn't. Her

firm lips trembled into a smile as she gazed at their shining faces.

"Get along with you — and behave yourselves!" she said with surprising softness.

Then she raised her parrot-headed umbrella and touched the Unicorn's flank.

At once he lifted his silver head and pointed his horn at the sky.

"Remember!" cried Florimond, waving his roses.

Veritain held his hand aloft and set the bracelet sparkling.

Amor flourished the handkerchief.

"Remember! Remember!" they cried together, as the Unicorn bounded into the air.

The Park seemed to tremble in the fading light as his hooves flashed over the fountain. A streak of colour shone above the spray, a shimmer of velvet and gold. A single moment of moving brightness and after that — nothing. Princes and Unicorn were gone. Only a far faint echo — "Remember!" — came back to the silent watchers. And the pages of the book on the lawn stirred in the evening breeze.

"After them!" the Policeman shouted. "Robbers! Desperadoes!"

He blew his whistle vigorously and dashed across the Rose Garden.

"A trick! A trick!" yelled Mr. Mudge. "The Invisible Horse and his Three Riders! Why, it's better than Sawing a Lady in Half! Come back, my lads, and I'll buy your secret! Was it this way? That way? Where did they go?"

And off he went, dodging among the trees, in his search for the lost Princes.

"Oh, dear," moaned the Keeper of the Zoological Gardens. "Here today and gone tomorrow! Just like the butterflies!"

He gave Mary Poppins a nervous look and hurried away to the Zoo.

For a moment the only sound in the garden was the music of the fountain. Then Miss Lark sighed and broke the silence.

"Why, goodness me — how late it is! Now, I wonder where I left my gloves! And what did I do with my scarf? I seem to have lost my spectacles. Gracious, yes — and my bracelet, too!"

Her eyes widened and she yawned a little as though she were coming out of a dream.

"You gave it to Veritain!" Jane reminded her.

"Veritain? Veritain? Who can that be? It sounds like something out of a story. I expect you are dreaming, Jane, as usual! Andrew and Willoughby — come along! Oh, Chief Professor! How nice to see you! But what are you doing here?"

The Professor gave her a puzzled glance and he, too, yawned a little.

"I — I'm not quite sure," he answered vaguely.

"And without a hat — you must be cold! Come home with me, Professor, do! And we'll all have muffins for tea."

"Muffins? Er — hum. I used to like muffins when I was a lad, but I haven't had one since. And I had a hat this afternoon. Now, what have I done with it?"

"Amor is wearing it!" cried Michael.

"Amor? Is that a friend of yours? He's welcome! It was only paper. But I'm not a bit cold, Miss Lark — er — hum! I have never felt so warm in my life."

The Professor smiled a contented smile.

"And I," said Miss Lark with a trill of laughter, "have never felt so happy. I can't think why — but there it is. Come, dearest dogs! This way, Professor!"

And, taking the Professor by the hand, she led him out of the Rose Garden.

Jane and Michael stared after them.

"What is your other — er — hum! — name?" they heard him vaguely asking.

"Lucinda Emily," she replied, as she drew him towards the Gate.

"Eee — ow — oo! I was 'arf asleep!" The Park Keeper yawned and stretched his arms and glanced around the garden.

" 'Ere! Wot's all this?" he demanded loudly. "Someone's been pickin' the flowers!"

"You did it yourself," said Jane, laughing.

"Don't you remember?" Michael reminded him. "You gave them to Florimond."

"What? Me pick a rose? I wouldn't dare! And yet——" The Park Keeper frowned in perplexity. "It's funny. I'm feeling quite brave tonight. If the Lord Mayor himself were to come along I wouldn't so much as tremble. And why shouldn't Florrie Wat's-a-name 'ave them, instead of them dyin' on the bush? Well, I must be gettin' 'ome to me mother. Tch! Tch! Tch! Remember the bye-laws!" The Park Keeper pounced on two dark objects.

"All litter to be placed in the baskets!" he cried, as he bore away the Professor's book and magnifying-glass and dumped them into a litter-basket.

Jane sighed. "They've forgotten already, all of them. Miss Lark, the Professor and now the Park Keeper."

"Yes," agreed Michael, shaking his head.

"And what have *you* forgotten, pray?" Mary Poppins' eyes were bright in the sunset and she seemed to come back to the Rose Garden from very far away.

"Oh, nothing, Mary Poppins, nothing!" With the happy assurance they ran to her side. As if they could ever forget the Princes and the strange and wonderful visit!

"Then what is that book doing there?" She pointed her black-gloved finger at *The Silver Fairy Book*.

"Oh, that!" Michael darted to get it.

"Wait for me, Mary Poppins!" he cried, pushing his way through the watching crowd that was still staring up at the sky.

The Match Man took the perambulator and sent it creaking out of the garden. Mary Poppins stood still in the entrance with her parrot umbrella under her arm and her hand-bag hanging from her wrist.

"I remember *everything*," said Michael, as he hurried back to her side. "And so does Jane — don't you, Jane? And you do, too, Mary Poppins!" The three of us, he thought to himself, we all remember together.

Mary Poppins quickened her steps and they caught up with the perambulator.

"I remember that I want my tea, if that's what you mean!" she said.

"I wonder if Amor drinks tea!" mused Michael, running beside her.

"Tea!" cried the Match Man, thirstily. "Hot and strong, that's how I like it. And at least three lumps of sugar!"

"Do you think they're nearly home, Mary Poppins? How long is it from here to there?" Michael was thinking about the Princes. He could not get them out of his head.

"*I'm* nearly home, that's all I know," she replied conceitedly.

"They'll come again, they said they would!" He skipped with joy at the thought. Then he remembered something else and stood stock-still with dismay.

"But you won't go back to them, Mary Poppins?" He seized her arm and shook it. "We need you more than the Princes do. They've got the Unicorn — that's enough. Oh, p-p-please, Mary P-pop-pins —— " He was now so anxious he could hardly speak. "P-p-promise me you won't go back with a t-t-tulip in your hat!"

She stared at him in angry astonishment.

"Princes with tulips in their hats? Me on the back of a Unicorn? If you're so good at remembering, I'll thank you to remember *me!* Am I the kind of person that would gallop around on a —— "

"No, no! You're mixing it all up. You don't understand, Mary Poppins!"

"I understand that you're behaving like a Hottentot. Me on a Unicorn, indeed! Let me go, Michael, if you please. I hope I can walk without assistance. And you can do the same!"

"Oh! Oh! She's forgotten already!" he wailed, turning to Jane for comfort.

"But the Match Man remembers, don't you, Bert?" Impulsively Jane ran to him and looked for his reassuring smile.

The Match Man took no notice. He was pushing the perambulator on a zigzag course and gazing at Mary Poppins. You would have thought she was the only person in the world, the way he looked at her.

"You see! He's forgotten, too," said Michael. "But it must have happened, mustn't it, Jane? After all, I've got the dagger!"

He felt for the dagger in his belt, but his hand closed on nothing.

"It's gone!" He stared at her mournfully. "He must have taken it when he hugged me good-bye. Or else it wasn't true at all. Do you think we only dreamed it?"

"Perhaps," she answered uncertainly, glancing from the empty belt to the calm and unexcited faces of the Match Man and Mary Poppins. "But, oh" — she thought of Florimond's smiling eyes — "I was so sure they were real!"

They took each other's hands for comfort and leaning their heads on each other's shoulders they walked along together, thinking of the three bright figures and the gentle fairy steed.

Dusk fell about them as they went. The trees like shadows bent above them. And as they came to the big gate they stepped into a pool of light from the newly-lit lamp in the Lane.

"Let's look at them once again," said Jane. Sad it would be, but also sweet, to see their pictured faces. She took the book from Michael's hand and opened it at the well-known page.

"Yes! The dagger's in his belt," she murmured. "Just as it always was." Then her eyes roved over the rest of the picture and she gave a quick, glad cry.

"Oh, Michael, look! It was not a dream. I knew, I *knew* it was true!"

"Where? Where? Show me quickly!" He followed her pointing finger.

"Oh!" he cried, drawing in his breath. And "Oh!" he said. And again "Oh!" There was nothing else to say.

For the picture was not as it had been. The fruits and flowers still shone on the tree and there on the grass the Princes stood with the Unicorn beside them.

But now in the crook of Florimond's arm there lay a bunch of roses; a little circlet of coloured stones gleamed on Veritain's wrist; Amor was wearing a paper hat perched on the back of his head and from the pocket of his jerkin there peeped a lace-edged handkerchief.

Jane and Michael smiled down on the page. And the three Princes smiled up from the book and their eyes seemed to twinkle in the lamplight.

"They remember us!" declared Jane in triumph.

"And we remember them!" crowed Michael. "Even if Mary Poppins doesn't."

"Oh, indeed?" her voice enquired behind them.

They glanced up quickly and there she stood, a pink-cheeked Dutch Doll figure, as neat as a new pin.

"And what have I forgotten, pray?"

She smiled as she spoke, but not at them. Her eyes were fixed on the three Princes. She nodded complacently at the picture and then at the Match Man who nodded back.

And suddenly Michael understood. He knew that she remembered. How could he and Jane have dared to imagine that she would ever forget!

He turned and hid his face in her skirt.

"You've forgotten nothing, Mary Poppins. It was just my little mistake."

"Little!" She gave an outraged sniff.

"But tell me, Mary Poppins," begged Jane, as she looked from the coloured picture-book to the confident face above her. "Which are the children in the story — the Princes, or Jane and Michael?"

Mary Poppins was silent for a moment. She glanced at the children on the printed page and back to the living children before her. Her eyes were as blue as the Unicorn's, as she took Jane's hand in hers.

They waited breathlessly for her answer.

It seemed to tremble on her lips. The words were on the tip of her tongue. And then — she changed her mind.

Perhaps she remembered that Mary Poppins never told anyone anything.

She smiled a tantalising smile.

"I wonder!" she said.

CHAPTER FIVE

THE PARK IN THE PARK

nother sandwich, please!" said Michael, sprawling across Mary Poppins' legs as he reached for the picnic basket.

It was Ellen's Day Out and Mrs. Brill had gone to see her cousin's niece's new baby. So the children were having tea in the Park, away by the Wild Corner.

This was the only place in the Park that was never mown or weeded. Clover, daisies, buttercups, bluebells, grew as high as the children's waists. Nettles and dandelions flaunted their blossoms, for they knew very well that the Park Keeper would never have time to root them out. None of them observed the rules. They scattered their seeds across the lawns, jostled each other for the best places, and crowded together so closely that their stems were always in shadowy darkness.

Mary Poppins, in a sprigged cotton dress, sat bolt upright in a clump of bluebells.

She was thinking, as she darned the socks, that pretty though the Wild Corner was, she knew of something prettier. If it came to a choice between, say, a bunch of clover and herself, it would not be the clover she would choose.

The four children were scattered about her.

Annabel bounced in the perambulator.

And not far off, among the nettles, the Park Keeper was making a daisy-chain.

Birds were piping on every bough, and the Ice Cream Man sang cheerfully as he trundled his barrow along.

The notice on the front said:

THE DAY IS HOT

BUT ICE CREAM'S NOT

"I wonder if he's coming here," Jane murmured to herself.

She was lying face downwards in the grass, making little plasticine figures.

"Where *have* those sandwiches gone?" cried Michael, scrabbling in the basket.

"Be so kind, Michael, as to get off my legs. I am not a Turkey carpet! The sandwiches have all been eaten. You had the last yourself."

Mary Poppins heaved him on to the grass and took up her darning needle. Beside her, a mug of warm tea, sprinkled with grass seed and nettle flowers, sent up a delicious fragrance.

"But, Mary Poppins, I've only had six!"

"That's three too many," she retorted. "You've eaten your share and Barbara's."

"Takin' the food from 'is sister's mouth — what next?" said the Park Keeper.

He sniffed the air and licked his lips, just like a thirsty dog.

"Nothin' to beat a 'ot cup o' tea!" he remarked to Mary Poppins.

With dignified calm she took up the mug. "Nothing," she answered, sipping.

"Exactly what a person needs at the 'eight of the h'afternoon!" He gave the teapot a wistful glance.

"Exactly," she agreed serenely, as she poured herself another cup.

The Park Keeper sighed and plucked a daisy. The pot, he knew, was now empty.

"Well — another sponge cake, then, Mary Poppins!"

"The cakes are finished, too, Michael. What are you, pray — a boy or a crocodile?"

He would have liked to say he was a crocodile, but a glance at her face was enough to forbid it.

"John!" he coaxed, with a crocodile smile. "Would you like me to eat your crusts?"

"No!" said John, as he gobbled them up.

"Shall I help you with your biscuit, Barbara?"

"No!" she protested through the crumbs.

Michael shook his head in reproach and turned to Annabel.

There she sat, like a queen in her carriage, clutching her little mug. The perambulator groaned loudly as she bounced up and down. It was looking more battered than ever today. For Robertson Ay, after doing nothing all the morning, had leaned against it to take a rest and broken the wooden handle.

"Oh, dear! Oh, dear!" Mrs. Banks had cried. "Why couldn't he lean on something stronger? Mary Poppins, what shall we do? We can't afford a new one!"

"I'll take it to my cousin, ma'am. He'll make it as good as new."

"Well — if you think he really can ——" Mrs. Banks cast a doubtful eye on the bar of splintered wood.

Mary Poppins drew herself up.

"A member of *my* family, ma'am ——" Her voice seemed to come from the North Pole.

"Oh, yes! Indeed! Quite so! Exactly!" Mrs. Banks nervously backed away.

"But why," she silently asked herself, "is her family so superior? She is far too vain and self-satisfied. I shall tell her so some day."

But, looking at that stern face and listening to those reproving sniffs, she knew she would never dare.

Michael rolled over among the daisies, hungrily chewing a blade of grass.

"When are you going to take the perambulator to your cousin, Mary Poppins?"

"Everything comes to him who waits. All in my own good time!"

"Oh! Well, Annabel isn't taking her milk. Would you like me to drink it for her?"

But at that moment Annabel lifted her mug and drained the last drop.

"Mary Poppins!" he wailed. "I'll starve to death — just like Robinson Crusoe."

"He didn't starve to death," said Jane. She was busily clearing a space in the weeds.

"Well, the Swiss Family Robinson, then," said Michael.

"The Swiss Family always had plenty to eat. But I'm not hungry, Michael. You can have my cake if you like."

"Dear, kind, sensible Jane!" he thought, as he took the cake.

"What are you making?" he enquired, flinging himself on the grass beside her.

"A Park for Poor People," she replied. "Everyone is happy there. And nobody ever quarrels."

She tossed aside a handful of leaves and he saw, amid the wildweed, a tidy square of green. It was threaded with little pebbled paths as wide as a finger-nail. And beside them were tiny flower-beds made of petals massed together. A summer-house of nettle twigs nestled on the lawn; flowers were stuck in the earth for trees; and in their shade stood twig benches, very neat and inviting.

On one of these sat a plasticine man, no more than an inch high. His face was round, his body was round and so were his arms and legs. The only pointed thing about him was his little turned-up nose. He was reading a plasticine newspaper and a plasticine tool-bag lay at his feet.

"Who's that?" asked Michael. "He reminds me of someone. But I can't think who it is!"

Jane thought for a moment.

"His name is Mr. Mo," she decided. "He is resting after his morning labours. He had a wife sitting next to him, but her hat went wrong, so I crumbled her up. I'll try again with the last of the plasticine —— " She glanced at the shapeless, coloured lump that lay behind the summer-house.

"And that?" He pointed to a feminine figure that stood by one of the flower-beds.

"That's Mrs. Hickory," said Jane. "She's going to have a house, too. And after that I shall build a Fun Fair."

He gazed at the plump little plasticine woman and admired the way her hair curled and the two large dimples in her cheeks.

"Do she and Mr. Mo know each other?"

"Oh, yes. They meet on the way to the Lake."

And she showed him a little pebbly hollow where, when Mary Poppins' head was turned, she had poured her mug of milk. At the end of the lake a plasticine statue reminded Michael of Neleus.

"Or down by the swing——" She pointed to two upright sticks from which an even smaller stick hung on a strand of darning wool.

Michael touched the swing with his finger-tip and it swayed backwards and forwards.

"And what's that under the buttercup?"

A scrap of cardboard from the lid of the cake-box had been bent to form a table. Around it stood several cardboard stools and upon it was spread a meal so tempting that a king might have envied it.

In the centre stood a two-tiered cake and around it were bowls piled high with fruit — peaches, cherries, bananas, oranges. One end of the table bore an apple-pie and the other a chicken with a pink frill. There were sausages,

and currant buns, and a pat of butter on a little green plat-
ter. Each place was set with a plate and a mug and a bottle
of ginger wine.

The buttercup-tree spread over the feast. Jane had
set two plasticine doves in its branches and a bumblebee
buzzed among its flowers.

"Go away, greedy fly!" cried Michael, as a small black
shape settled on the chicken. "Oh, dear! How hungry it
makes me feel!"

Jane gazed with pride at her handiwork. "Don't drop
your crumbs on the lawn, Michael. They make it look untidy."

"I don't see any litter-baskets. All I can see is an ant in
the grass." He swept his eyes round the tiny Park, so neat
amid the wildweed.

"There is never any litter," said Jane. "Mr. Mo lights the fire with his paper. And he saves his orange peel for Christmas puddings. Oh, Michael, don't bend down so close, you're keeping the sun away!"

His shadow lay over the Park like a cloud.

"Sorry!" he said, as he bent sideways. And the sunlight glinted down again as Jane lifted Mr. Mo and his tool-bag and set them beside the table.

"Is it his dinner-time?" asked Michael.

"Well — no!" said a little scratchy voice. "As a matter of fact, it's breakfast!"

"How clever Jane is!" thought Michael admiringly. "She can not only make a little old man, she can talk like one as well."

But her eyes, as he met them, were full of questions.

"Did *you* speak, Michael, in that squeaky way?"

"Of course he didn't," said the voice again.

And, turning, they saw that Mr. Mo was waving his hat in greeting. His rosy face was wreathed in smiles and his turned-up nose had a cheerful look.

"It isn't what you call the meal. It's how it tastes that matters. Help yourself!" he cried to Michael. "A growing lad is always hungry. Take a piece of pie!"

"I'm having a beautiful dream," thought Michael, hurriedly helping himself.

"Don't eat it, Michael. It's plasticine!"

"It's not! It's apple!" he cried, with his mouth full.

"But I know! I made it myself!" Jane turned to Mr. Mo.

"You did?" Mr. Mo seemed very surprised. "I suppose you mean you *helped* to make it. Well, I'm very glad you did, my girl. Too many cooks make delicious broth!"

"They spoil it, you mean," corrected Jane.

"Oh, no, no! Not in my opinion. One puts one thing, one another — oatmeal, cucumber, pepper, tripe. The merrier the more, you know!"

"The more of what?" asked Michael, staring.

"Everything!" Mr. Mo replied. "There's more of everything when one's merry. Take a peach!" He turned to Jane. "It matches your complexion."

From sheer politeness — for she could not disappoint that smiling face — Jane took the fruit and tasted. Refreshing juice ran over her chin, the peach-stone grated against her teeth.

"Delicious!" she cried in astonishment.

"Of course it is!" crowed Mr. Mo. "As my dear wife always used to say — 'You can't go by the look of a thing, it's what's inside that matters.'"

"What happened to her?" asked Michael politely, as he helped himself to an orange. He had quite forgotten, in the joy of finding more to eat, that Jane had crumbled her up.

"I lost her," murmured Mr. Mo. He gave his head a sorrowful shake as he popped the orange peel into his pocket.

Jane felt herself blushing.

"Well — her hat wouldn't sit on straight," she faltered. But now it seemed to her that this was hardly a good enough reason for getting rid of the hat's owner.

"I know, I know! She was always rather an awkward shape. Nothing seemed to fit her. If it wasn't her hat it was her boots. Even so — I was fond of her." Mr. Mo heaved a heavy sigh. "However," he went on gloomily, "I've found another one!"

"Another wife?" cried Jane in surprise. She knew she had not made two Mrs. Mo's. "But you haven't had time for that!"

"No time? Why, I've all the time in the world. Look at those dandelions!" He waved his chubby hand round the Park. "And I had to have someone to care for the children. Can't do everything myself. So — I troubled trouble before it troubled me and got myself married just now. This feast here is our wedding-breakfast. But, alas——" He glanced around him nervously. "Every silver lining has a cloud. I'm afraid I made a bad choice."

"Coo-roo! Coo-roo!
We told you so!"

cried the plasticine doves from their branch.

"Children?" said Jane, with a puzzled frown. She was sure she had made no children.

"Three fine boys," Mr. Mo said proudly. "Surely you two have heard of them! Hi!" he shouted, cupping his hands. "Eenie, Meenie, Mynie — where are you?"

Jane and Michael stared at each other and then at Mr. Mo.

"Oh, of course we've heard of them," agreed Michael.

"Eenie, Meenie, Mynie, Mo,
Catch an Indian by the ——

But I thought they were only words in a game."

Mr. Mo smiled a teasing smile.

"Take my advice, my dear young friend, and don't do too much thinking. Bad for the appetite. Bad for the brain. The more you think, the less you know, as my dear — er — first wife used to say. But I can't spend all day chattering, much as I enjoy it!" He plucked a dandelion ball and blew the seeds on the air.

"Goodness, yes, it's four o'clock. And I've got a job to do."

He took from his tool-bag a piece of wood and began to polish it with his apron.

"What kind of work do you do?" asked Michael.

"Can't you read?" cried the chubby man, waving towards the summer-house.

They turned to Jane's little shelter of twigs and saw to their surprise that it had grown larger. The sticks were solid logs of wood and instead of the airy space between them there were now white walls and curtained windows. Above them rose a new thatched roof, and a sturdy chimney puffed forth smoke. The entrance was closed by a red front door bearing a white placard.

S. MO (it said)

BUILDER

AND

CARPENTER

"But I didn't build the house like that! Who altered it?" Jane demanded.

"I did, of course." Mr. Mo grinned. "Couldn't live in it as it was — far too damp and draughty. What did you say — *you* built my house?" He chuckled at the mere idea. "A little wisp of a lass like you, not as high as my elbow!"

This was really too much for Jane.

"It's you who are little," she protested. "I made you of straw and plasticine! You're not as big as my thumb!"

"Ha, ha! That's a good one. Made me of hay while the sun shone — is that what you're telling me? Straw, indeed!" laughed Mr. Mo. "You're just like my children — always dreaming. And wonderful dreams they are!"

He gave her head a little pat. And as he did so she realised that she was not, indeed, as high as his elbow. Beneath the branch of yellow blossoms Mr. Mo towered above her.

The lawns that she herself had plucked now stretched to a distant woodland. And beyond that nothing could she see. The big Park had entirely disappeared, as the world outside disappears when we cross the threshold of home.

She looked up. The bumble-bee seemed like a moving cloud. The shimmering fly that darted past was about the size of a starling and the ant that gave her a bright black stare was nearly as high as her ankle.

What had happened? Had Mr. Mo grown taller or was it that she herself had dwindled? It was Michael who answered the question.

"Jane! Jane!" he cried. "We're in your Park. I thought it was just a tiny patch, but now it's as big as the world!"

"Well, I wouldn't say that," Mr. Mo observed. "It only stretches as far as the forest, but it's big enough for us."

Michael turned, at his words, towards the woodland. It was dense and wild and mysterious, and some of the trees had giant blooms.

"Daisies the size of umbrellas!" he gasped. "And bluebells large enough to bathe in!"

"Yes, it's a wonderful wood," Mr. Mo agreed, eyeing the forest with a carpenter's eye. "My — er — second wife wants me to cut it down and sell it to make my fortune. But this is a Park for Poor People. What would I do with a fortune? My own idea — but that was before the wedding, of course — was to build a little Fun Fair —— "

"I thought of that, too," Jane broke in, smiling.

"Well, happy minds think alike, you know! What do you say to a merry-go-round? A coconut-shy, and some swinging-boats? And free to all, friends and strangers alike? Hurrah, I knew you'd agree with me!" He clapped his hands excitedly. But suddenly the eager look died away from his face.

"Oh, it's no good planning," he went on sadly. "*She* doesn't approve of Fun Fairs — too frivolous and no money in them. What a terrible mistake I've made — married in haste to repent at leisure! But it's no good crying over spilt milk!"

Mr. Mo's eyes brimmed up with tears, and Jane was just about to offer him her handkerchief, when a clatter of feet sounded on the lawn and his face suddenly brightened.

"Papa!" cried a trio of squeaky voices. And three little figures sprang over the path and flung themselves into his arms. They were all alike, as peas in a pod; and the image of their father.

"Papa, we caught an Indian! We caught him by the toe, papa! But he hollered, papa, so we let him go!"

"Quite right, my lads!" smiled Mr. Mo. "He'll be happier in the forest."

"Indians?" Michael's eyes widened. "Among those daisy trees?"

"He was looking for a squaw, papa, to take care of his wigwam!"

"Well, I hope he finds one," said Mr. Mo. "Oh, yes, of course there are Indians! And goodness only knows what else. Quite like a jungle, you might say. We never go very far in, you know. Much too dangerous. But — let me introduce my sons. This is Eenie, this is Meenie, and this is Mynie!"

Three pairs of blue eyes twinkled, three pointed noses turned up to the sky and three round faces grinned.

"And these ——" said Mr. Mo, turning. Then he chuckled and flung up his hands. "Well! Here we are, old friends already, and I don't even know your names!"

They told him, shaking hands with his children.

"Banks? Not the Banks of Cherry-Tree Lane? Why, I'm doing a job for you!" Mr. Mo rummaged in his tool-bag.

"What kind of job?" demanded Michael.

"It's a new — ah, there you are, Mrs. Hickory!"

Mr. Mo turned and waved a greeting as a dumpy little feminine figure came hurrying towards them. Two dimples twinkled in her cheeks, two rosy babies bounced in her arms and she carried in her looped-up apron a large bulky object.

"But she had no children!" said Jane to herself, as she stared at the two fat babies.

"We've brought you a present, Mr. Mo!" Mrs. Hickory blushed and opened her apron. "I found this lovely loaf on the lawn — somebody dropped it, I expect. My twins — this is Dickory, this is Dock," she explained to the astonished children — "are far too young to eat fresh bread. So here it is for the breakfast!"

"That's not a loaf, it's a sponge-cake crumb. I dropped it myself," said Michael. But he could not help feeling that the crumb was a good deal larger than he remembered it.

"Tee-hee!"

Mrs. Hickory giggled shyly and her dimples went in and out. You could see she thought he was joking and that she liked being joked with.

"A neighbourly thought!" said Mr. Mo. "Let's cut it in two and have half each. Half a loaf's better than no bread! And, in return, Mrs. Hickory, may I give you a speck of butter?"

"Indeed you may NOT!" said a furious voice. And the door of Mr. Mo's house burst open.

Jane and Michael fell back a pace. For there stood the largest and ugliest woman they had ever seen in their lives. She seemed to be made of a series of knobs, rather like a potato. A knob of a nose, a knob of hair, knobbly hands, knobbly feet, and her mouth had only two teeth.

She was more like a lump of clay than a human being and Jane was reminded of the scrap of plasticine that had lain behind the summer-house. A dingy pinafore covered her body and in one of her large knobbly hands she held a rolling-pin.

"May I ask what you think you're doing, Samuel? Giving away *my* butter?"

She stepped forward angrily and flourished the rolling-pin.

"I—I thought we could spare it, my—er—dear!" Mr. Mo quailed beneath her gaze.

"Not unless she pays for it! Spare, spare and your back will go bare!"

"Oh, no, my dear, you've got it wrong! Spare, spare and you'll know no care. Poor people must share and share alike—that's what makes them happy!"

"Nobody's going to share anything that belongs to Matilda Mo! Or spare either, if it comes to that. Last week you spared a footstool for your cousin, Mrs. Corry! And what have you got to show for it?"

"A lucky threepenny-piece from her coat!"

"Tush! And you mended a table for the Turvys —— "

"Well, Topsy gave me a charming smile!" Mr. Mo beamed at the sweet recollection.

"Smiles won't fill a sack with gold! And the week before that it was Albert Wigg who wanted his ceiling raised."

"Well, he needed more room to bounce about in. And it gave me so much pleasure, Matilda!"

"Pleasure? Where's the profit in that? In future you can get your pleasure by giving things to *me*. And you, too!" added Mrs. Mo, shaking her fist at the boys.

"Alas, alas!" muttered Mr. Mo. "No rose without a thorn! No joy without annoy!"

"Eenie!" Mrs. Mo shouted. "Get me a wedding-wreath this instant! Look at me — a blushing bride — and nothing on my head."

"Oh, no!" breathed Jane. "You'll spoil my garden!"

But Eenie, with a look of alarm, had already darted to the flower-beds and plucked a crown of flowers.

"Not good enough, but better than nothing!" Mrs. Mo grunted ungraciously as she planted the garland on her knobbly head.

"Coo, Coo!" laughed the doves on the buttercup branch.

> "They don't suit you.
> Oo-hoo! Oo-hoo!"

"Meenie!" cried Mrs. Mo in a rage. "Up with you quickly and catch those birds! I'll make them into a pigeon pie!"

But the doves merely ruffled their wings and flew away, giggling.

"Two birds in the bush are worth one in the hand," said Mr. Mo, gazing after them. "I mean," he added nervously, "they sing more sweetly when they're free! Don't you agree, Matilda?"

"I never agree," snapped Mrs. Mo. "And I'll have no singing here. Mynie! Tell that man to be quiet!"

For a lusty voice was filling the air with the words of a well-known song.

> "I'll sing you one-o,
>   Green grow the rushes-o!"

It was the Ice Cream Man, cycling along the path.

Jane and Michael had no time to wonder how he had managed to get into the little Park, for Eenie, Meenie and Mynie were shouting.

"Papa! Papa! A penny, please!"

"No ices!" bellowed Mrs. Mo. "We haven't the money to spare!"

"Matilda!" Mr. Mo entreated. "There's my lucky three-penny-piece."

"That is for a rainy day. Not for mere enjoyment."

"Oh, it's not going to rain, I'm sure, Matilda!"

"Of course it will rain. And, anyway, it's *my* threepenny-piece. From today, Samuel, what's yours is mine. Get along," she yelled to the Ice Cream Man, "and don't come here making foolish noises."

"It's not a noise, it's a song," he retorted. "And I'll sing it as much as I like."

And away he wheeled, singing

> "I'll sing you two-o"

as loudly as he could.

"Out of sight," sighed Mr. Mo, as the barrow disappeared among the trees, "but not, alas, out of mind! Well, we mustn't grumble, boys!" He brightened. "We still have the wedding-feast. Now, Mrs. Hickory, where will you sit?"

Mrs. Hickory's dimples twinkled gaily.

"She won't sit anywhere, Samuel. She has not received an invitation."

The dimples disappeared again.

"Oh, but, Matilda —— !" cried Mr. Mo, with a crest-fallen look on his rosy face.

"But me no buts!" Mrs. Mo retorted, advancing towards the table. "What's this?" she demanded. "Something's missing! A peach and an orange have disappeared. And who has been eating my apple-pie?"

"I h-have," said Michael nervously. "B-but only a very small slice."

"And I took a peach," Jane said in a whisper. She found it hard to make the confession, Mrs. Mo looked so large and fierce.

"Oh, indeed?" The knobbly woman turned to the children. "And who invited *you*?"

"Well, you see," began Jane, "I was making a Park. And suddenly I found myself— 1 mean, it happened — I mean — I — well —— " However could she explain?

"Don't hum and haw, Jane, if you please. Speak when you're spoken to. Come when you're called. And, Michael, do not gape like that. The wind may change and where will you be?"

A voice that was welcome as Nuts in May sounded in their ears.

"Mary Poppins!" cried Michael in glad surprise, staring — in spite of the changing wind — from her to Mr. Mo.

For there, beneath the buttercup, was the crowded perambulator. And beside it stood a tidy shape with buttoned-shoes, tulip-trimmed hat and parrot-headed umbrella.

"Oh, Mary! At last! Better late than never! How are you?" cried Mr. Mo. He darted round the end of the table and kissed her black-gloved hand.

"I knew he reminded me of someone!" said Michael in a careful whisper. "Look, Jane! Their noses are just the same!"

"Nicely, thank you, Cousin Sam! My goodness, how the boys have grown!" With a lady-like air she offered her cheek to Eenie, Meenie and Mynie.

Mr. Mo looked on with a fond smile. But it faded as he turned to his wife.

"And this," he said sadly, "is Matilda!"

Mary Poppins regarded Mrs. Mo with a long and searching look. Then she smiled, to the children's great surprise, and made a dainty bow.

"I hope," she said, in a well-bred voice, "that we are not intruding? I wanted Sam — with your permission, of course, Matilda" — she bowed again to Mrs. Mo — "to make me a new —— "

"It's ready, Mary!" cried Mr. Mo, as he seized his piece of polished wood. "All it wants is —— " He flew to the perambulator. "A nail *here* and a nail *there* and another one and it's finished!"

The brand-new handle gleamed in its place and John and Barbara clapped their hands.

"Don't think you're going to get it free!" Mrs. Mo shook the rolling-pin. "From now on, everything's got to be paid for. Nothing for nothing — that's my motto!"

"Oh, I'll certainly pay him," said Mary Poppins, with her best society simper. "Everyone gets what he deserves — that's my motto, Matilda!"

"Well, the quicker the better, please, Miss Poppins. I've no intention of waiting!"

"You won't have to wait, I promise you!" Mary Poppins gave a twirl to her hand-bag and Jane and Michael watched with interest as she glanced round the little Park. They had never seen her behave like this — such elegant tact, such polished manners.

"What a charming little place you have!" She waved the parrot-headed umbrella towards the summer-house.

Mrs. Mo gave a snort of disgust.

"Charming, you call it? I call it a hovel. If Samuel thinks I can live in that, he'll have to change his mind. He's not going to knock *me* down with a feather!"

"Oh, I wouldn't dream of it, Matilda! I don't possess such a thing."

"A castle is what I want, Samuel. You owe it to your handsome bride!"

"Handsome is as handsome does!" said Mr. Mo in a whisper.

But Mary Poppins' smile grew brighter.

"Handsome indeed," she agreed admiringly. "And you're wearing such a lovely wreath!"

"Pooh," Mrs. Mo remarked, with contempt. "Two or three flowers twisted together. A crown of gold would be more to my liking — and I'll have it, too, before I'm finished!"

"Kind hearts are more than coronets," said Mr. Mo meekly.

"Not to me!" snapped Mrs. Mo. "I'll have a beaded band of gold! You mark my words, Miss Mary Poppins, I'll be queen of the forest yet!"

"I do not doubt it," said Mary Poppins. And her manner was so correct and respectful that Mrs. Mo smiled a mollified smile and displayed her two front teeth.

"Well," she said grudgingly, "now that you're here, you'd better stay and be useful. You may pass round the food at the wedding-feast. And then you can wash up the dishes."

The children clapped their hands to their lips and glanced at Mary Poppins. What would she say to *that,* they wondered.

Mr. Mo gave a gasp of horror. "But, Matilda — don't you realise? Don't you know who she is?"

"That will do, Sam," said Mary Poppins. She waved him aside with the parrot umbrella. Her blue eyes had grown a shade more blue but, to Jane's and Michael's astonishment, her smile was broader than ever.

"So pleased to be of use, Matilda. And where do you plan to build your castle?"

"Well, I thought" — Mrs. Mo fell back a step and swung the rolling-pin — "we'd have the entrance gates here. And here" — she took another large stride backwards — "the main door and the marble stairs."

"But we can't dwell in marble halls, Matilda! They're far too grand for us."

"For you, perhaps, Samuel. Nothing can be too grand for me. And then" — Mrs. Mo fell back again — "a large and lofty reception room where I shall receive my guests."

"Splendid!" said Mary Poppins brightly, pushing the perambulator before her, as she followed step by step.

And behind her marched Mr. Mo and the children, followed by Eenie, Meenie and Mynie, and Mrs. Hickory and her babies — all of them gazing, as if in a trance, at the two figures before them.

"The ballroom here!" shouted Mrs. Mo, sweeping the rolling-pin about her.

"Ballroom!" Mr. Mo groaned. "But who is going to use it?"

"I am," said Mrs. Mo, smirking. "And you'll please let *me* do the talking, Samuel!"

"Silence is golden, Matilda, remember!" Mr. Mo warned her.

"Oh, pray go on!" urged Mary Poppins, advancing another foot.

"Drawing-room! Dining-room! Pantry! Kitchen!"

Chamber by chamber the castle grew, invisible but imposing. With every word Mrs. Mo fell backwards. With every word Mary Poppins stepped forward. And the rest of the party followed. They were almost across the Park now — for Mrs. Mo's rooms were large and airy — and nearing the edge of the woodland.

"My bedroom will be here!" she declared, swinging her arms in a wide circle. "And next to it" — the rolling-pin wheeled again through the air — "I shall have a spacious nursery."

"That will be nice for the boys, Matilda!" Mr. Mo brightened at the thought.

Mrs. Mo gave him a scornful glance.

"Eenie, Meenie and Mynie," she said, "can fend for themselves in the attic. The nursery will be for my *own* children. And — if she brings me a reference, saying she is honest and reliable — Mary Poppins may come and look after them!"

"But she's looking after us!" cried Michael. He seized a fold of the sprigged skirt and pulled her to his side.

"It's kind of you, I'm sure, Matilda. But I never give references."

Mary Poppins' eyes had a curious glint as she thrust the perambulator forward.

"Then you're no use to me!" declared Mrs. Mo, strutting backwards through her invisible mansion.

"Oh, indeed?" Mary Poppins' balmy tones had now an icy edge.

"Yes, indeed!" retorted Mrs. Mo. "I won't have people in my castle who are likely to steal the silver! And don't look at me like that!" she added. There was now a note of alarm in her voice, as though there was something frightening in the smiling face that pursued her.

"Like what?" said Mary Poppins softly. And she gave the perambulator another push.

Mrs. Mo retreated again and raised her rolling-pin.

"Away with you! Be off!" she cried. "You're an uninvited guest!" Her face was the colour of her apron and her large body trembled.

"Oh no, I'm not!" said Mary Poppins, moving forward, like an oncoming storm. "You told me to stay and wash the dishes!"

"Well — I take it back!" quavered Mrs. Mo. "You pay us what you owe and be gone. I won't have you in my Park!" The rolling-pin shivered in her hand as she stumbled back into the forest shade.

"*Your* Park, did you say?" murmured Mary Poppins, advancing with ever quicker steps.

"Yes, mine! Oh, Samuel, do something — can't you? I

won't have her smiling at me like that! Ow! Let me go! Oh, what has caught me! I'm stuck, I can't get free! What is it?"

As she spoke, an arm went round her waist and strong hands gripped her by the wrist.

Behind her stood a stalwart figure smiling triumphantly. A head-dress of feathers was on his brow, a bow and some arrows hung from one shoulder and the other was draped with a striped blanket.

"At last! At last I find my squaw!" He grasped his wriggling captive closer.

"Let me go, you savage!" shrieked Mrs. Mo, as she turned and beheld his face.

"Let go? Not I! What I find I keep. You shall come with me to my wigwam."

"I won't! Unhand me! Samuel! Tell him to set me free!"

"Oh, I wouldn't dare — he's far too strong. And the best of friends must part, Matilda!"

"Free? Nay, nay, you shall be my slave. There!" said the Indian cheerfully, as he strung some yellow beads round her head and stuck a feather in the knob of her hair. "This I give as a great honour. Now you're Indian, too!"

"I'm not! I won't! Oh, help! Oh, Sam!"

"Well, you wanted a crown of beaded gold and you seem to have got it, my dear!"

"Wash in the stream, cook over twigs!" The Indian wrinkled his nose at her. "All the wide greenwood for your house and sky above for your roof!"

"Let me go, you savage!"

"That's larger than the largest castle." Mr. Mo gave her a beaming glance.

"Nay, struggle not," said the Indian, as Mrs. Mo tried to wriggle away. "A good squaw obeys her master. And a queen must do the same!"

"Queen?" cried Mrs. Mo, wildly kicking.

The Indian tossed his head proudly. "Did you not know I was King of the Forest?"

"Matilda, how splendid! Just what you wanted!"

"I didn't, I didn't! Not in this way!"

"There are more ways than one of being a queen," said Mary Poppins primly.

Mrs. Mo turned on her in a fury. She drummed with her feet on the Indian's shins and brandished the rolling-pin.

"This is *your* doing — you wolf in sheep's clothing! Things were going so nicely until you came. Oh, Samuel, why did you let her in?" Mrs. Mo burst into angry tears.

"Nicely for you!" said Mary Poppins. "But not for anyone else!"

"A wolf? A lamb, you mean, Matilda! I didn't let her in — she came. As if I could keep *that* wolf from the door!" Mr. Mo laughed at his little joke.

"Oh, help me, Samuel! Set me free and I'll lend you the threepenny-piece. And the boys can have a slice of pie every second Friday!" Mrs. Mo, with an imploring gesture, flung out her knobbly arms.

"What?" she cried, glaring at each in turn. "Does *no-body* want me back?"

There was silence in the little group. Mr. Mo glanced at his three sons and then at Mary Poppins. One by one all shook their heads.

> "Coo-roo! Coo-roo!
> They don't want you!"

cooed the doves as they fluttered past.

"Oh, what shall I do?" wailed Mrs. Mo.

"*I* want you, Mahtildah!" the Indian cried. "I need you, Mahtildah, to boil the pot! Sweep the wigwam! Sew the moccasins! Make the arrows! Fill the pipe! And — on every second Monday, Mahtildah,

> "You shall sit on the blanket beneath a
>   moonbeam
> And feed on wild strawberries, snakes and
>   nut cream!"

"Snakes? Moonbeams? Let me go! I eat nothing but mutton chops. Oh, help! Murder! Ambulance! Fire!"

Her voice rose to an anguished scream as the Indian flung her over his shoulder and stepped back into the woodland. Clasping his struggling burden tightly, he glanced at the three little boys.

"They let me go when I hollered," he said. "So — one good turn deserves another!"

And, smiling broadly at Mr. Mo, he bore the protesting Mrs. Mo into the depths of the forest.

"Police! Police!" they heard her shriek, as she and the Indian and the rolling-pin disappeared from view.

Mr. Mo gave a sigh of relief.

"Well, it certainly is an ill wind that blows nobody any good! I hope Matilda will settle down and enjoy being a queen. Mary, you've paid me well for that handle. I shall always be in your debt."

"She said she would do it in her own good time — and she has," said Michael proudly.

"Ah!" said Mr. Mo, shaking his head. "She does everything in her own time — it's a very special kind."

"You owe me nothing, Cousin Sam!" Mary Poppins turned away from the forest with a conquering shine in her eye. "Except, of course," she added severely, "not to be so foolish in future."

"Out of the frying-pan into the fire? Oh, I'll never marry again, Mary! Once bitten, twice shy. The boys must manage somehow."

"Perhaps, Mr. Mo," Mrs. Hickory dimpled, "you would let *me* wash and mend for them. It would be no trouble at all."

"What a beautiful thought!" cried Mr. Mo. "All's well that ends well, Mary, you see! And I in return, Mrs.

Hickory, will build you a nice little house. Oh, I've lost sixpence and found a shilling! Look!" he said, pointing to the sunset. "Red sky at night is the shepherd's delight! My dears, we are all going to be so happy. I shall start on my Fun Fair at once!"

And away he dashed across the lawn, with the rest of the party at his heels.

"But what about the wedding-breakfast?" Michael panted after him.

"My goodness, I'd forgotten. Here — fruit, cake, sausages, buns!" He took a piece from every dish and thrust it into Michael's hands.

Mary Poppins looked on disapprovingly.

"Now, Michael, not another bite! You will have no room for your supper."

"Enough's as good as a feast, my lad!" Mr. Mo grinned at Michael as he watched the food disappearing.

"Enough is too much!" said Mary Poppins. "Come along, both of you!"

"Oh, I cannot bear to leave it!" cried Jane. Her little Park seemed brighter than ever, as it shone in the setting sun.

"You never will!" Mr. Mo declared. "As long as you remember it, you can always come and go. And I hope you're not going to tell me that you can't be in two places at once. A clever girl who makes parks and people surely knows how to do that!" He smiled his twinkling, teasing smile.

Mary Poppins stepped out from under the buttercup, with a homeward took in her eye.

"Say good-bye politely, Jane!" She sent the perambulator rolling along the pebbled path.

"Good-bye, Mr. Mo!" said Jane softly, as she stood on tip-toe and held out her arms.

"Oh, luck! Oh, joy!" He patted his cheek. "This is no Park for Poor People! I'm rich — she's given me a kiss! Share and share alike!" he cried, as he kissed Mrs. Hickory right on a dimple.

"Remember, Sam!" warned Mary Poppins. "Look before you leap!"

"Oh, I shan't do any leaping, Mary! A little dance and a hop or two — nothing more serious, I assure you!"

She gave a disbelieving sniff, but Mr. Mo did not hear it. He was skipping beside Mrs. Hickory and seizing her apron-strings.

"May I have the pleasure?" they heard him saying.

"Me, too!" cried Eeenie, Meenie and Mynie, as they flew to join their father.

And there they all were, prancing round the table, helping themselves to pie and wine and hanging the cherries behind their ears. Mrs. Hickory's dimples were twinkling gaily and her babies were bobbing about in her arms.

"It's a poor heart that never rejoices!" cried Mr. Mo, as he whirled her about. He seemed to have quite forgotten his guests in the gaiety of the moment.

"It's love that makes the world go round!" yelled Eenie, Meenie and Mynie.

And, indeed, the world did seem to be spinning, turning for joy upon its axis, as the little Park spun round its buttercup-tree. Round and round and round it went in a steady, stately movement.

The wedding-party was waltzing and singing, and the Ice Cream Man was singing, too, as he pedalled back along the path. A cluster of Fruit Bars was in his hand and he tossed them on to the table.

"Three for luck and free for luck!" he cried, as he trundled by.

"Step up, if you please," said Mary Poppins, hustling them along before her as a hen hustles her chicks. "And what are you doing, Jane and Michael, walking backwards like that?"

"I'b wadching the weddig-feast!" mumbled Michael, with his mouth full of his last cherry. He gave a long lugubrious sigh as each creak of the perambulator drew him farther from that wonderful meal.

"Taking one more look at my Park, Mary Poppins," said Jane, as she gazed at the happy scene.

"Well, you're not a pair of crabs! Turn round — and walk in the right direction."

The sunset dazzled their eyes as they turned. And the afternoon seemed to be turning with them, from two o'clock till five. Tick-tock! said every clock. Ding-dong! said the bells in the steeples.

Then the spinning world slowed down and was still, and they blinked as though coming out of a dream. Had it taken them seconds, minutes or hours to walk down that pebbly path? They looked about them curiously.

The blossoms of clover were now at their feet, instead of above their heads, and the grasses of the Wild Corner brushed against their knees. The bumblebee went buzzing by, no larger, it seemed, than usual. And the fly on a near-by bluebell was about the size of a fly. As for the ant — it was hiding under a grass-seed and was therefore invisible.

The big Park spread serenely round them, just the same as ever. The Ice Cream Man, who had come to the last verse of his song —

> "I'll sing you twelve-o
> Green grow the rushes-o,"

was wheeling away from the Wild Corner. And the Park Keeper, with the finished daisy-chain round his neck, was lumbering towards them.

They glanced down. Below them lay the little Park, hemmed in by its walls of weed. They blinked again and smiled at each other as they fell on their knees among the flowers.

The little lawns were now in shadow. Long patterns of daisy and bluebell lay black across the paths. The tiny flowers in Jane's garden were bending on their stems. By lake and swing the seats were deserted.

"They've eaten every bit of the feast. Look!" whispered Michael. "Empty plates!"

"And not a sign of anyone. I expect they've all gone home to bed." Jane sighed. She would like to have seen Mr. Mo again, and to measure herself against his elbow.

"They're lucky, then, 'ooever they are! Let's to bed, says Sleepy-'Ead — as they told me when I was a boy!" The Park Keeper stooped above them and surveyed Jane's handiwork.

"No Parks allowed in the Park!" he observed. Then he eyed the two rapt faces. "Well, you seem very preh'occupied! What are you lookin' for?"

Jane gave him an absent-minded glance.

"Mary Poppins' cousin," she murmured, as she searched through the little Park.

The Park Keeper's face was a sight to see.

"Cousin! Down there — among the weeds? You'll be tellin' me next 'e's a beetle!"

"*I'll* be telling you something in a minute!" said a wrathful voice beside him. Mary Poppins regarded him frostily. "Did I or didn't I hear you referring to me as an insect?"

"Well — not to you," the Park Keeper faltered. "But if your cousin's down in that grass, what can 'e be but a beetle?"

"Oh, indeed! And if he's a beetle, what am I?"

He looked at her uneasily and wished that something would strike him dumb.

"Hum," he said, fumbling for a word. "I may be as mad as a March Hatter ——"

"*May* be!" she gave a disdainful sniff.

"But I don't see 'ow you *can* 'ave a cousin sittin' under a buttercup!"

"I can have a cousin anywhere — and no business of yours!"

"You can't!" he cried. "T'isn't natural. I suppose," he added sarcastically, "you're related to the Man in the Moon!"

"My uncle!" said Mary Poppins calmly, as she turned the perambulator into the path that led from the Wild Corner.

The Park Keeper opened his mouth in surprise and shut it again with a snap.

"Ha, ha! You will 'ave your little joke. 'Owsum-ever, I don't believe it!"

"Nobody asked you to," she replied. "Come, Jane! Come, Michael! Quick march, please!"

Night had now come to the little Park. The wild-weed, thickly clustered about it, looked very like a forest. No light came through the trackless stems, it was dark as any jungle. With a last glance at the lonely lawns, they turned away regretfully and ran after the perambulator.

"Mary Poppins! They've all gone home," cried Michael. "There's nothing left on the plates."

"East, West, home's best. And who are 'they,' I'd like to know?"

"I meant your funny little cousin — and all his family!"

She pulled up sharply and looked at him with a calm that was worse than anger.

"Did you say 'funny'?" she enquired. "And what was so funny about him, pray?"

"Well — at first he wasn't as big as a beetle and then he stretched out to the usual s-s-size!" He trembled as he looked at her.

"Beetles again! Why not grasshoppers? Or perhaps you'd prefer a grub! Stretching, indeed! Are you trying to tell me, Michael Banks, that my cousin is made of elastic?"

"Well — no, not elastic. Plasticine!" There! It was out. He had said it at last.

She drew herself up. And now it seemed as if *she* were stretching, for her rage seemed to make her twice as tall.

"Well!" she began, in a voice that told him clearly she had never been so shocked in her life. "If anyone had ever warned me —— " But he interrupted wildly.

"Oh, don't be angry, *please,* Mary Poppins — not in your tulip hat! I didn't mean he was funny to laugh at, but funny in the nicest way. And I won't say another word — I promise!"

"Humph!" She subsided. "Silence is golden."

And as she stalked along beside him, with her heels going click-clack on the path, he wondered where he had heard that before.

He glanced at Jane carefully from the corner of his eye.

"But it happened, didn't it?" he whispered. "We did go into the little Park and join them at the feast? I'm sure it was true, because I'm not hungry. All I want for supper is a hard-boiled egg and a piece of buttered toast. And rice pudding and two tomatoes and perhaps a cup of milk!"

"Oh, yes, it was true." Jane sighed for joy as she gazed round the great familiar Park. Within it, she knew, lay another one. And perhaps ——

"Do you think, Mary Poppins ——" She hesitated. "Do you think that everything in the world is inside something else? My little Park inside the big one and the big one inside a larger one? Again and again? Away and away?" She waved her arm to take in the sky. "And to someone very far out there — do you think we would look like ants?"

"Ants and beetles! Grasshoppers! Grubs! What next, I'd like to know! I can't answer for you, Jane, but *I'm* not an ant to *anyone*, thank you!"

Mary Poppins gave a disgusted sniff.

"Of course you're not!" said a cheerful voice, as Mr. Banks — coming back from the City — caught up with the little group.

"You're more like a glow-worm, Mary Poppins, shining to show us the right way home!" He waited for the self-satisfied smile to spread across her face. "Here," he said, "take the evening paper and I'll wheel the perambulator. The exercise will do me good. I think I'm getting a cold."

The Twins and Annabel crowed with delight as Mr. Banks sent them skimming along.

"Dear me," he remarked. "What a fine new handle! That cousin of yours is a good workman. You must let me know what you paid for it."

"*I* know!" cried Michael eagerly. "She gave Mrs. Mo to the Indian!"

"A-tishoo! I didn't quite hear what you said, Michael. She gave Mr. Rowe two shillings?" Mr. Banks blew his nose with a flourish.

"No, no! She gave Mrs. Mo —— ! I mean —— " He never finished the sentence. For Mary Poppins' eye was on him and he thought it best to drop the subject.

"There will be no charge, sir!" she said politely. "My cousin was pleased to do it."

"That's uncommonly kind of him, Mary Poppins. Hey!" he broke off. "Do look where you're going! Observe the rules of the Park, Smith! You nearly upset the perambutator."

For the Park Keeper, bounding after them, had knocked into the little group and scattered it in all directions.

"Beg pardon all, I'm sure!" he panted. "Sorry, Mr. Banks, sir, but if you'll excuse me, it's *'er* I'm after."

He flung out a hand at Mary Poppins. The daisy-chain dangled from his wrist.

"Why, Mary Poppins, what have you done? Broken a bye-law or what?"

The Park Keeper gave a lonely groan.

"Bye-law? She's broken *all* the laws! Oh, it isn't natural — but it's true!" He turned to Mary Poppins.

"You said you could 'ave one anywhere! Well, 'e's down there under a dandelion. I 'eard 'im with me own ears — laughin' and singin' — just like a party. 'Ere, take it!" he cried in a broken voice, as he flung the daisy-chain over her head. "I meant it for me poor old Mother — but I feel I owe you somethin'."

"You do," said Mary Poppins calmly, as she straightened the daisy-chain.

The Park Keeper stared at her for a moment. Then he turned away with a sigh.

"I shall never h'understand," he muttered, knocking over a litter-basket as he tottered off down the path.

Mr. Banks gazed after him with a look of shocked surprise.

"Somebody under a dandelion? Having a party? What can he mean? Really, I sometimes wonder if Smith is right

in the head. Under a dandelion — laughing and singing!
Did you ever hear such a thing?"

"Never!" said Mary Poppins demurely, with a dainty
shake of her head.

And as she shook it a buttercup petal fell from the brim
of her hat.

The children watched it fluttering down and turned
and smiled at each other.

"There's one on your head, too, Michael!"

"Is there?" he said, with a happy sigh. "Bend down and
let me look at yours."

And sure enough Jane had a petal, too.

"I told you so!" She nodded wisely. And she held her
head very high and still so as not to disturb it.

Crowned with the gold of the buttercup-tree she
walked home under the maple boughs. All was quiet. The
sun had set. The shadows of the Long Walk were falling
all about her. And at the same time the brightness of the
little Park folded her closely round. The dark of one, the
light of the other — she felt them both together.

"I am in two places at once," she whispered, "just as he
said I would be!"

And she thought again of the little clearing among
the thronging weeds. The daisies would grow again, she
knew. Clover would hide the little lawns. Cardboard table
and swings would crumble. The forest would cover it all.

But somehow, somewhere, in spite of that, she knew

she would find it again — as neat and as gay and as happy as it had been today. She only had to remember it and there she would be once more. Time upon time she would return — hadn't Mr. Mo said so? — and stand at the edge of that patch of brightness and never see it fade. . . .

CHAPTER SIX
HALLOWE'EN

Mary Poppins!" called Michael. "Wait for us!"

"W-a-a-a-i-t!" the wind echoed, whining round him.

It was a dusky, gusty autumn evening. The clouds blew in and out of the sky. And in all the houses of Cherry-Tree Lane the curtains blew in and out of the windows. Swish-swish. Flap-flap.

The Park was tossing like a ship in a storm. Leaves and litter-paper turned head-over-heels in the air. The trees groaned and waved their arms, the spray of the fountain was blown and scattered. Benches shivered. Swings were creaking. The Lake water leapt into foamy waves. Nothing was still in the whole Park as it bowed and shuddered under the wind.

And through it all stalked Mary Poppins, with not a hair out of place. Her neat blue coat with its silver buttons was neither creased nor ruffled, and the tulip sat on her hat so firmly that it might have been made of marble.

Far behind her the children ran, splashing through drifts of leaves. They had been to Mr. Folly's stall for nuts and toffee-apples. And now they were trying to catch her up.

"Wait for us, Mary Poppins!"

In front of her, on the Long Walk, the perambulator trundled. The wind whistled through the wheels, and the Twins and Annabel clung together for fear of being blown overboard. Their tasselled caps were tossing wildly and the rug was flapping loose, like a flag.

"O-o-o-h!" they squeaked, like excited mice, as a sudden gust tore it free and carried it away.

Someone was coming down the path, bowling along like a tattered newspaper.

"Help!" shrilled a high, familiar voice. "Something has blown right over my hat! I can't see where I'm going."

It was Miss Lark, out for her evening walk. Her two dogs bounded on ahead and behind her the Professor straggled, with his hair standing on end.

"Is that you, Mary Poppins?" she cried, as she plucked the rug away from her face and flung it upon the perambulator. "What a dreadful night! Such a wild wind! I wonder you're not blown away!"

Mary Poppins raised her eyebrows and gave a superior sniff. If the wind blew anyone away, it would not be herself, she thought.

"What do you mean—a dreadful night?" Admiral Boom strode up behind them. His dachshund, Pompey, was at his heels, wearing a little sailor's jacket to keep him from catching cold.

"It's a perfect night, my dear lady, for a life on the ocean wave!

Sixteen men on a dead man's chest
Yo, ho, ho! And a bottle of rum.

You must sail the Seven Seas, Lucinda!"

"Oh — I couldn't sit on a dead man's chest!" Miss Lark seemed quite upset at the thought. "Nor drink rum, either, Admiral. Do keep up, Professor, please. There — my scarf has blown away! Oh, goodness, now the dogs have gone!"

"Perhaps they've blown away, too!" The Professor glanced up into a tree, looking for Andrew and Willoughby. Then he peered short-sightedly down the Walk.

"Ah, here they come!" he murmured vaguely. "How strange they look with only two legs!"

"Two legs!" said Miss Lark reproachfully. "How absent-minded you are, Professor. Those aren't my darling, precious dogs — they're only Jane and Michael."

The Admiral whipped out his telescope and clapped it to his eye.

"Ahoy, there, shipmates!" he roared to the children.

"Look!" shouted Michael, running up. "I put out my hand to hold my cap and the wind blew a leaf right into it!"

"And one into mine the same minute!" Jane panted behind him.

They stood there, laughing and glowing, with their packages held against their chests and the star-shaped maple leaves in their hands.

"Thank you," said Mary Poppins firmly, as she plucked the leaves from between their fingers, gave them a scrutinising glance and popped them into her pocket.

"Catch a leaf, a message brief!" Miss Lark's voice shrieked above the wind. "But, of course, it's only an old wives' tale. Ah, there you are, dear dogs — at last! Take my hand, Professor, please. We must hurry home to safety."

And she shooed them all along before her, with her skirts blowing out in every direction.

Michael hopped excitedly. "Was it a message, Mary Poppins?"

"That's as may be," said Mary Poppins, turning up her nose to the sky.

"But we caught them!" Jane protested.

"C. caught it. G. got it," she answered, with annoying calm.

"Will you show us when we get home?" screamed Michael, his voice floating away.

"Home is the sailor, home from the sea!" The Admiral took off his hat with a flourish. "Au revoir, messmates and Miss Poppins! Up with the anchor, Pompey!"

"Ay, ay, sir!" Pompey seemed to be saying, as he galloped after his master.

Michael rummaged in his package.

"Mary Poppins, why didn't you wait? I wanted to give you a toffee-apple."

"Time and tide wait for no man," she answered priggishly.

He was just about to ask what time and tide had to do with toffee-apples, when he caught her disapproving look.

"A pair of Golliwogs — that's what you are! Just look at your hair! Sweets to the sweet," she added conceitedly, as she took the sticky fruit he offered and nibbled it daintily.

"It's not our fault, it's the wind!" said Michael, tossing the hair from his brow.

"Well, the quicker you're into it the quicker you're out

of it!" She thrust the perambulator forward under the groaning trees.

"Look out! Be careful! What are you doin'?"

A howl of protest rent the air as a figure, clutching his tie and his cap, lurched sideways in the dusk.

"Remember the bye-laws! Look where you're goin'! You can't knock over the Park Keeper."

Mary Poppins gave him a haughty stare.

"I can if he's in my way," she retorted. "You'd no right to be there."

"I've a right to be anywhere in the Park. It's in the Regulations." He peered at her through the gathering dark and staggered back with a cry.

"Toffee-apples? And bags o' nuts? Then it must be 'Allowe'en! I might 'ave known it ——" His voice shook. "You don't get a wind like this for nothin'. O-o-ow!" He shuddered. "It gives me the 'Orrors. I'll leave the Park to look after itself. This is no night to be out."

"Why not?" Jane handed him a nut. "What happens at Hallowe'en?"

The Park Keeper's eyes grew as round as plates. He glanced nervously over his shoulder and leant towards the children.

"*Things,*" he said in a hoarse whisper, "come out and walk in the night. I don't know what they are quite — never 'avin' seen them — ghosts, perhaps, or h'apparitions. Anyway, it's spooky. Hey — what's that?" He clutched

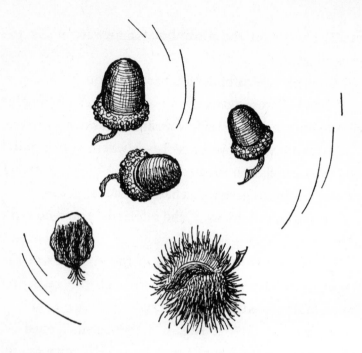

his stick. "Look! There's one of them up there — a white thing in the trees!"

A light was gleaming among the branches, turning their black to silver. The wind had blown the clouds away and a great bright globe rode through the sky.

"It's only the moon!" Jane and Michael laughed. "Don't you recognise it?"

"Ah——" The Park Keeper shook his head. "It *looks* like the moon and it *feels* like the moon. And it may be the moon — *but it may not.* You never can tell on 'Allowe'en!"

And he turned up his coat-collar and hurried away, not daring to look behind him.

"Of course it's the moon," said Michael stoutly. "There's moonlight on the grass!"

Jane gazed at the blowing, shining scene.

"The bushes are dancing in the wind. Look! There's one coming towards us — a small bush and two larger ones. Oh, Mary Poppins, perhaps they're ghosts?" She clutched a fold of the blue coat. "They're coming nearer, Mary Poppins! I'm sure they're apparitions!"

"I don't want to see them!" Michael screamed. He seized the end of the parrot umbrella as though it were an anchor.

"Apparitions, indeed!" shrieked the smallest bush. "Well, I've heard myself called many things — Charlemagne said I looked like a fairy and Boadicea called me a goblin — but nobody ever said to my face that I was an apparition. Though I dare say" — the bush gave a witchlike cackle — "that I often look like one!"

A skinny little pair of legs came capering towards them and a wizened face, like an old apple, peered out through wisps of hair.

Michael drew a long breath.

"It's only Mrs. Corry!" he said, loosing his hold on the parrot umbrella.

"And Miss Fannie and Miss Annie!" Jane waved in relief to the two large bushes.

"How de do?" said their mournful voices, as Mrs. Corry's enormous daughters caught up with their tiny mother.

"Well, here we are again, my dears — as I heard St. George remark to the Dragon. Just the kind of night for —— " Mrs. Corry looked at Mary Poppins and gave her a knowing grin. "For all sorts of things," she concluded. "You got a message, I hope!"

"Thank you kindly, Mrs. Corry. I have had a communication."

"What message?" asked Michael inquisitively. "Was it one on a leaf?"

Mrs. Corry cocked her head. And her coat — which was covered with threepenny-bits — twinkled in the moonlight.

"Ah," she murmured mysteriously. "There are so many kinds of communication! You look at me, I look at you, and something passes between us. John o' Groats could send me a message, simply by dropping an eyelid. And once — five hundred years ago — Mother Goose handed me a feather. I knew exactly what it meant — 'Come to dinner. Roast Duck'!"

"And a tasty dish it must have been! But, excuse me, Mrs. Corry, please — we must be getting home. This is no night for dawdling — as you will understand." Mary Poppins gave her a meaning look.

"Quite right, Miss Poppins! Early to bed, early to rise, makes a man healthy, wealthy and —— Now, who was it first told me that — Robert the Bruce? No, I've forgotten!"

"See you later," said Fannie and Annie, waving to Jane and Michael.

"Later?" said Jane. "But we're going to bed."

"There you go — you galumphing giraffes! Can't you ever open your mouths without putting your feet into them? They mean, my dears," said Mrs. Corry, "they'll be seeing you later in the *year!* November, perhaps, or after Christmas. Unless, of course" — her smile widened — "unless you are *very clever!* Well, good night and sleep well!"

She held out her little wrinkled hands and Jane and Michael both sprang forward.

"Look out! Look out!" she shrieked at them. "You're stepping on my shadow!"

"Oh — I'm sorry!" They both jumped back in alarm.

"Deary goodness — you gave me a turn!" Mrs. Corry clapped her hand to her heart. "Two of you standing right on its head — the poor thing *will* be distressed!"

They looked at her in astonishment and then at the little patch of black that lay on the windy grass.

"But I didn't think shadows could feel," said Jane.

"Not feel! What nonsense!" cried Mrs. Corry. "They feel twice as much as you do. I warn you, children, take care of your shadows or your shadows won't take care of you. How would you like to wake one morning and find they had run away? And what's a man without a shadow? Practically nothing, you might say!"

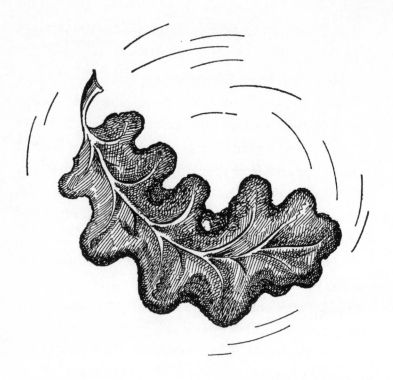

"I wouldn't like it at all," said Michael, glancing at his own shadow rippling in the wind. He realised, for the first time, how fond he was of it.

"Exactly!" Mrs. Corry snorted. "Ah, my love," she crooned to her shadow. "We've been through a lot together — haven't we? — you and I. And never a hair of your head hurt till these two went and stepped on it. All right, all right, don't look so glum!" She twinkled at Jane and Michael. "But remember what I say — take care! Fannie and Annie, stir your stumps. Look lively — if you possibly can!"

And off she trotted between her daughters, bending sideways now and again to blow a kiss to her shadow.

"Now, come along. No loitering," said Mary Poppins briskly.

"We're keeping an eye on our shadows!" said Jane. "We don't want anything to hurt them."

"You and your shadows," said Mary Poppins, "can go to bed — spit-spot!"

And sure enough that was what they did. In next to no time they had eaten their supper, undressed before the crackling fire and bounced under the blankets.

The nursery curtains blew in and out and the nightlight flickered on the ceiling.

"I see my shadow and my shadow sees me!" Jane looked at the neatly brushed head reflected on the wall. She nodded in a friendly way and her shadow nodded back.

"My shadow and I are two swans!" Michael held his arm in the air and snapped his fingers together. And upon the wall a long-necked bird opened and closed its beak.

"Swans!" said Mary Poppins, sniffing, as she laid her coat and tulip hat at the end of her camp-bed. "Geese more like it, I should say!"

The canvas creaked as she sprang in.

Michael craned his neck and called: "Why don't you hang up your coat, Mary Poppins, the way you always do?"

"My feet are cold, that's why! Now, not another word!"

He looked at Jane. Jane looked at him. They knew it was only half an answer. What was she up to tonight, they wondered. But Mary Poppins never explained. You might as well ask the Sphinx.

"Tick!" said the clock on the mantelpiece.

They were warm as toast inside their beds. And their beds were warm inside the nursery. And the nursery was warm inside the house. And the howling of the wind outside made it seem warmer still.

They leaned their cheeks upon their palms and let their eyelids fall.

"Tock!" said the clock on the mantelpiece.

But neither of them heard. . . .

"What is it?" Jane murmured sleepily. "Who's scratching my nose?"

"It's me!" said Michael in a whisper. He was standing at the side of her bed with a wrinkled leaf in his hand.

"I've been scratching it for ages, Jane! The front door banged and woke me up and I found this on my pillow. Look! There's one on yours, too. And Mary Poppins' bed is empty and her coat and hat have gone!"

Jane took the leaves and ran to the window.

"Michael," she cried, "there *was* a message. One leaf says 'Come' and the other 'Tonight.'"

"But where has she gone? I can't see her!" He craned his neck and looked out.

All was quiet. The wind had dropped. Every house was fast asleep. And the full moon filled the world with light.

"Jane! There are shadows in the garden — and not a single person!"

He pointed to two little dark shapes — one in pyjamas, one in a nightgown — that were floating down the front path and through the garden railings.

Jane glanced at the nursery walls and ceiling. The

night-light glowed like a bright eye. But in spite of that steady, watchful gleam there was not a single shadow!

"They're ours, Michael! Put something on. Quick — we must go and catch them!"

He seized a sweater and followed her, tip-toeing down the creaking stairs and out into the moonlight.

Cherry-Tree Lane was calm and still, but from the Park came strains of music and trills of high-pitched laughter.

The children, clutching their brown leaves, dashed through the Lane Gate. And something, light as snow or feathers, fell upon Michael's shoulder. Something gentler than air brushed against Jane's cheek.

"Touched you last!" two voices cried. And they turned and beheld their shadows.

"But why did you run away?" asked Jane, gazing at the transparent face that looked so like her own.

"We're guests at the Party." Her shadow smiled.

"What party?" Michael demanded.

"It's Hallowe'en," his shadow told him. "The night when every shadow is free. And this is a very special occasion. For one thing, there's a full moon — and it falls on the Birthday Eve. But come along, we mustn't be late!"

And away the two little shadows flitted, with the children solidly running behind them.

The music grew louder every second, and as they darted round the laurels they beheld a curious sight.

The whole playground was thronged with shadows,

each of them laughing and greeting the others and hopping about in the moonlight. And the strange thing was
that, instead of lying flat on the ground, they were all
standing upright. Long shadows, short shadows, thin
shadows, fat shadows, were bobbing, hobnobbing, bowing, kowtowing, and passing in and out of each other with
happy cries of welcome.

In one of the swings sat a helmeted shape, playing a
concertina. It smiled and waved a shadowy hand, and
Jane and Michael saw at once that it belonged to the
Policeman.

"Got your invitations?" he cried. "No human beings allowed in without a special pass!"

Jane and Michael held up their leaves.

"Good!" The Policeman's shadow nodded. "Bless
you!" he added, as a shape beside him was seized with a fit
of sneezing.

Could it be Ellen's shadow? Yes — and blowing a shadowy nose!

"Good-evening!" murmured a passing shape. "If any
evening's good!"

Its dreary voice and long face reminded Jane of the
Fishmonger. And surely the jovial shadow beside it belonged to the Family Butcher! A shadowy knife was in his
hand, a striped apron about his waist, and he led along an
airy figure with horns upon its head.

"Michael!" said Jane in a loud whisper. "I think that's
the Dancing Cow!"

But Michael was too absorbed to answer. He was chatting to a furry shape that was lazily trimming its whiskers.

"My other part," it said, miaowing, "is asleep on the mantelpiece. So, of course — this being Hallowe'en — I took the evening off!" It adjusted a shadowy wreath of flowers that was looped about its neck.

"The Cat that looked at the King!" exclaimed Jane. She put out a hand to stroke its head, but all she felt was the air.

"Well, don't let him come near me!" cried a voice. "I've quite enough troubles as it is, without having cats to deal with."

A plump, bird-like shape tripped past, nodding abstractedly at the children.

"Poor old Cock Robin — and his troubles!" The shadowy Cat gave a shadowy yawn. "He's never got over that funeral and all the fuss there was."

"Cock Robin? But he's a Nursery Rhyme. He doesn't exist!" said Jane.

"Doesn't exist? Then why am *I* here?" The phantom bird seemed quite annoyed. "You can have a substance without a shadow, but you can't have a shadow without a substance — anyone knows that! And what about them — don't *they* exist?"

It waved a dark transparent wing at a group of airy figures — a tall boy lifting a flute to his mouth, and a bulky shape, with a crown on its head, clasping a bowl and a pipe. Beside them stood three phantom fiddlers holding their bows aloft.

A peal of laughter burst from Michael. "That's the shadow of Old King Cole. It's exactly like the picture!"

"And Tom, the Piper's son, too!" Cock Robin glared at Jane. "If they're shadows, they must be shadows of *something* — deny it if you can!"

"Balloons *and* balloons, my deary ducks! No arguing tonight!" A cosy little feminine shape, with balloons bobbing about her bonnet, whizzed through the air above them.

"Have the goodness, please, to be more careful. You nearly went through my hat!"

A trumpeting voice that was somehow familiar sounded amid the laughter. The children peered through the weaving crowd. Could it be? — yes, it was — Miss Andrew! Or rather, Miss Andrew's shadow. The same beaked nose, the same small eyes, the grey veil over the felt hat and the coat of rabbit fur.

"I haven't come from the South Seas to have my head knocked off!"

Shaking its fist at the Balloon Woman, Miss Andrew's shadow protested loudly. "And who's that pulling my veil?" it cried, turning on two little dark shapes, who dashed away, screaming with terror.

Jane and Michael nudged each other. "Ours!" they whispered, giggling.

"Make way! Move on! The Prime Minister's comin'!"
A shadow in a peaked cap waved the children aside.

"Oh, it's you, is it? Well, remember the Bye-laws! Don't
get in anyone's way." The phantom face — moustache
and all — was exactly like the Park Keeper's.

"I thought you'd have been too frightened to come.
You said it was spooky!" Jane reminded him.

"Oh, I'm not frightened, Miss — it's 'im. My body, so
to speak. A very nervous chap 'e is — afraid of 'is own
shadow. Ha, ha! Excuse my little joke! Make room! Move
on! Observe the rules!"

The Prime Minister's shadow floated by, bowing to
right and left.

"Greeting, friends! What a wonderful night. Dear me!" He stared at Jane and Michael. "You're very thick and lumpish!"

"Hsssst!" The shadow of the Park Keeper muttered in his ear. "Invitation . . . special occasion . . . friends of . . . whisper, whisper."

"Ah! If that's the case, you're very welcome. But do be careful where you tread. We don't like to be stepped on."

"One of them's stepping on me, I think!" A nervous voice seemed to come from the grass.

Michael carefully shifted his feet as the shadow of the Keeper of the Zoological Gardens came crawling past on all fours.

"Any luck?" cried the crowd excitedly.

"Hundreds!" came the happy reply. "Red Admirals. Blue Admirals. Spotted Bermudas. Pink Amazons. Chinese Yellows!"

He waved the shadow of his net. It was full of butterfly shadows.

"Well, I know one you haven't got — and that's an Admiral Boom!" A shadow in a cocked hat, with a spectral dachshund at its heels, elbowed its way through the throng. "Very rare specimen indeed. Largest butterfly in the world! All hail, my hearties!"

"Yo, ho, ho! And a bottle of rum!" The shadows yelled in reply.

The Admiral's shadow turned to the children.

"Welcome aboard!" it said, winking. " 'Catch a leaf, a

message brief' — only an old wives' tale — hey? Ah, here she comes! Your servant, ma'am."

The cocked hat bowed to a broad shadow that was sailing through the see-saw. It was dressed in a shadowy swirl of skirts, and a swarm of little weightless shapes fluttered about its head.

"The Bird Woman!" whispered Jane to Michael.

"Who are you callin' an old wife? Feed the birds! Tuppence a bag!"

A cry of pleasure went up from the crowd as everyone greeted the new arrival. The children saw their own reflections running to kiss her cheeks, and as though — tonight — *they* were the shadows, they hurried after them.

The party was growing more and more lively. The whole Park was ringing with laughter. And above the voices, high and sweet, came the reedy note of the flute.

"Over the hills and far away!" played Tom, the Piper's son.

And in Cherry-Tree Lane the people lying in bed listened and huddled under the blankets.

"It's Hallowe'en!" each said to himself. "Of course I don't believe in ghosts — but listen to them shrieking!"

They would have been surprised, perhaps, had they dared to look out of the window.

Every second the crowd thickened. And it seemed to the children as they watched that everyone they had ever known had a shadow at the party. Was that Aunt Flossie's?

They could not tell. She was there and gone again. And surely those were John's and Barbara's flitting among the leaves!

"Well, lovies?" murmured the Bird Woman's shadow, as it smiled at the four young faces — a girl with her airy shape beside her and a boy arm-in-arm with his double.

"Quack-quack!" said a voice at the same moment.

"Oh, Goosey Gander, wait for us!" And away went the airy children.

The Bird Woman's shadow gathered its skirts and made room on the bench for Jane and Michael.

"My!" she exclaimed, as her arms went round them. "You're solid and no mistake!"

"That's because we're real," said Jane.

"Bones and toe-nails and hair and blood," Michael kindly informed her.

"Ah!" The Bird Woman's shadow nodded. "I expect you 'ad a Special Ticket. It isn't everyone gets the chance. But you're not tellin' me — are you, lovies? — that shadders isn't real?"

"Well — they go through things. And they're made of nothing ——" Jane tried to explain.

The Bird Woman shook her shadowy head.

"Nothin's made of nothin', lovey. And that's what they're for — to go through things. Through and out on the other side — it's the way they get to be wise. You take my word for it, my loves, when you know what your shadder knows — then you know a lot. Your shadder's the other part of you, the outside of your inside — if you understand what I mean."

"Don't explain! It's no use. *They* don't understand anything!"

The portly shadow of Cock Robin came tripping past the bench.

"They told me only a moment ago that Cock Robin never existed. Well, who was buried, I'd like to know! And why were the birds a-sighing and a-sobbing? Take care, Bo-peep! Do look where you're going. Those lambs of yours nearly knocked me over!"

A shadow carrying a crook was skimming through the crowd. And behind her a flock of curly shapes gambolled on the lawn.

"But I thought Bo-peep had *lost* her sheep!" cried Michael in surprise.

"That's right!" The Bird Woman's shadow chuckled. "But 'er shadder always finds them."

"We've been looking for you everywhere!" a trio of voices grunted. Three furry shadows scattered the sheep and bore Bo-peep away.

"Oh!" exclaimed Jane. "They're the Three Bears. I hope they'll do nothing to hurt her."

"Hurt her? Bless you, why should they? A shadder never did anyone harm — at least, not as I know of. See! The four of 'em — dancin' together as friendly as can be!"

The Bird Woman's shadow surveyed the scene, beating time to the Piper's flute. Then suddenly the music changed and she started up with a cry. "'Ere they are at last, lovies! Get up on the bench and look!"

"Who are here?" demanded Michael. But even as he spoke, he knew.

The music of the concertina had changed to a stately march. The shadows were clearing a path in their midst. And down between the waving lines came a pair of familiar figures.

One of them was small and old, with elastic-sided boots on her feet and threepenny-bits on her coat.

And the other — oh, how well they knew it — was carrying a parrot-headed umbrella and wearing a tulip-trimmed hat.

Tum! Tum! Tee-um, tum, tum! the concertina boomed.

On they came, the two figures, graciously bowing to all spectators and followed by the bulky forms of Fannie and Annie Corry. Solid flesh and bone they were amid the transparent shapes, and the children saw that their four shadows were firmly attached to their heels.

A shout of rapture rose from the throng.

And the sleepers in Cherry-Tree Lane shuddered and thrust their heads under their pillows.

"A Hallowe'en welcome, Mary Poppins! Three cheers for the Birthday Eve!"

The shadows were clearing a path in their midst

"'Ip, 'Ip, 'Ooray!" yelled the Bird Woman's shadow.

"Whose birthday is it?" Jane enquired. She was standing on tip-toe on the bench, trembling with excitement.

"It's 'ers — Miss Mary Poppins' — tomorrer! 'Allowe'en falls on the day before, so of course we make a night of it. Feed the Birds! Tuppence a bag!" she shouted to Mary Poppins.

The rosy face beneath the tulip smiled at her in acknowledgment. Then it glanced up at the two children and the smile disappeared.

"Why aren't you wearing a dressing-gown, Michael? And, Jane, where are your slippers? A fine pair of scarecrows you are — to come to an evening party!"

"Aha! You were cleverer than I thought! Taking care of your shadows, I hope!" Mrs. Corry grinned.

But before the children had time to reply, the music changed from a solemn march to a reeling, romping dance.

"Choose your partners! Time's running out! We must all be back on the stroke of twelve!" The voice of the Policeman's shadow rose above the laughter.

"Pray give me the pleasure, dearest friend!" The shadow of the Father Bear bowed to Mrs. Corry.

"A-a-way, you rolling river!" The Admiral's shadow grasped Miss Andrew's and whirled it through a litter-basket.

The Fishmonger's shadow raised its hat to another

that looked like Mrs. Brill; the shadow of the Mother Bear floated to Old King Cole. The Prime Minister's shadow and Aunt Flossie's jumped up and down in the fountain. And Cock Robin propelled a languid shape whose head hung down on its chest.

"Wake up, wake up, my good shadow! Who are you? Where do you live?"

The shadow gave a loud yawn and slumped against Cock Robin. "Mumble, mumble. Broom cupboard. Over across the Lane."

Jane and Michael glanced at each other.

"Robertson Ay!" they said.

Round and round went the swaying shapes, hand reaching out to hand. And the children's shadows were everywhere — darting after the Baby Bear or hugging the Dancing Cow.

"Really!" Mrs. Corry trilled. "I haven't had such an evening out since the days of Good Queen Bess!"

"How frivolous she is!" said her daughters, as they lumbered along together.

As for Mary Poppins, she was whirling like a spinning-top from one pair of arms to another. Now it would be the Admiral's shadow and next it would be Goosey Gander's turn. She danced a polka with Cock Robin's shadow and a waltz with the Park Keeper's. And when the transparent Butcher claimed her, they broke into a mad gallop, while her own shadow stuck to her shoes and capered after her.

Twining together and interlacing, the vaporous shapes went by. And Jane and Michael, watching the revels, began to feel quite giddy.

"I wonder why Mary Poppins' shadow isn't free — like the others? It's dancing beside her all the time. And so is Mrs. Corry's!" Jane turned with a frown to the Bird Woman's shadow.

"Ah, she's cunning — that Mrs. Corry! She's old and she's learnt a lot. Let 'er shadder escape — not she! Nor Fannie's and Annie's either. And as for Mary Poppins' shadder——" A chuckle shook the broad shape. "It wouldn't leave 'er if you paid it — not for a thousand pound!"

"My turn!" cried the shadow of Old King Cole, as he plucked Mary Poppins from the Butcher's arms and bore her off in triumph.

"Mine, too! Mine, too!" cried a score of voices. "Haste, haste, no time to waste!"

Faster and faster, the music played as the fateful hour drew nearer. The merriment was at its peak — when suddenly, above the din, came a shrill cry of distress.

And there, at the edge of the group of dancers, stood a small white-clad figure. It was Mrs. Boom, in her dressing-gown, with a lighted candle in her hand, looking like an anxious hen as she gazed at the lively scene.

"Oh, please——" she pleaded. "Will somebody help me? The Admiral's in such a state. He's threatening

to sink the ship because he's lost his shadow. Ah, there you are!" Her face brightened, as she spied the shape she sought. "He's ranting and roaring so dreadfully — won't you please come home?"

The Admiral's shadow heaved a sigh.

"I leave him for one night in the year — and he threatens to sink the ship! Now, that's a thing *I'd* never do. He's nothing but a spoiled child — no sense of responsibility. But I cannot disoblige you, ma'am ——— "

He waved his hand to his fellow-shadows and lightly blew a kiss each to Mary Poppins and Mrs. Corry.

"Farewell and Adieu to you, sweet Spanish ladies!" he sang as he turned away.

"So kind of you!" chirped Mrs. Boom, as she tripped

beside him with her candle. "Who's that?" she called, as they came to the Gate. "Surely it can't be you, Miss Lark?"

A nightgowned figure was rushing through it, wrapped in a tartan shawl. And beside her, two excited dogs snatched at the trailing fringes.

"It can! It is!" Miss Lark replied, as she dashed across the lawn. "Oh, dear!" she moaned, as she came to the swings. "I dreamed that my shadow had run away — and when I woke up it was true. Alas, alas, what shall I do? I can't get along without it!"

She turned her tearful eyes to the dancers and her eyebrows went up with a jerk.

"Goodgraciousme, Lucinda Emily! What are you doing here? Dancing? With strangers? In the Park? I wouldn't have thought it of you."

"Friends — not strangers!" a voice replied, as a shadow decked in scarves and beads fluttered out of the crowd. "I'm gayer than you think, Lucinda. And so are you, if you but knew it. Why are you always fussing and fretting instead of enjoying yourself? If you stood on your head occasionally, I'd never run away!"

"Well —— " Miss Lark said doubtfully. It seemed such a strange idea.

"Come home and let us try it together!" Her shadow took her by the hand.

"I will, I will!" Miss Lark declared. And her two dogs looked at each other in horror at the thought of such a thing. "We'll practise on the drawing-room hearth-rug. Professor! What are you doing out at night? Think of your rheumatism!"

The Lane Gate opened with a creak and the Professor ambled over the grass with his hand clasped to his brow.

"Alack!" he cried. "I've lost something. But I can't remember what it is."

"L-look for L-lost P-property in the l-litter-b-basket!" a trembling voice advised him. The Park Keeper, dodging from bush to bush, was edging towards the dancers.

"I 'ad to come." His teeth chattered. "I must do my duty to the Park no matter what goes on!"

From behind the big magnolia-tree he stared at the rollicking scene.

"Golly!" he muttered, reeling backwards. "It's enough to give you the shivers! Ow! Look out! There's one of 'em comin'!"

A shadow broke away from the rest and floated towards the Professor.

"Lost something, I heard you say. And can't think what it is? Now, that's a strange coincidence — I'm in the same plight!"

It peered short-sightedly at the Professor and a sudden smile of recognition spread across its face.

"My dear fellow — can it be? *It is.* We've lost each other!"

A pair of long, transparent arms enfolded the tweed jacket. The Professor gave a crow of delight.

"Lost and found!" He embraced his shadow. "How beautiful are those two words when one hears them both together! Oh, never let us part again! You will remember what I forget —— "

"And vice versa!" his shadow cried. And the two old men wandered off with their arms round each other.

"But I tell you it's against the Rules!" The Park Keeper pulled himself together. " 'Allowe'en ought to be forbidden. Get along off, you ghosts and shadows! No dancin' allowed in the Park!"

"You should talk!" jeered Mary Poppins, as she capered past with the Cat. She nodded her head towards the swings and the Park Keeper's face grew red with shame.

For there he beheld his own shadow dancing a Highland Fling!

Tee-um, turn. Tee-um, turn.
Tee-um, tee-um, tee-um.

"Stop! Whoa there! Have done!" he shouted. "You come along with me this minute. I'm ashamed of you — breakin' the rules like this. Lumme, what's 'appenin' to me legs?"

For his feet, as though they lived a life of their own, had begun to hop and skip. Off they went — tee-um, tee-um! And by the time he had reached his shadow he, too, was doing the Highland Fling.

"Now, you keep still!" he warned it sternly, as they both slowed down together. "Be'ave yourself like a 'uman bein'!"

"But shadows are so much nicer!" his shadow said with a giggle.

"Fred! Fred!" hissed an anxious voice, as a head in an old-fashioned nightcap came round the edge of a laurel.

"Benjamin!" the Park Keeper cried. "What do you think you're doin'?"

"Searching for my shadow, Fred," said the Keeper of the Zoological Gardens. "It ran away when I wasn't looking. And I dare not face the Head Keeper unless I have it with me! A-a-ah!" He made a swoop with his net.

"Got you!" he cried, triumphantly, as he scooped up a flying shape.

His shadow gave a ghostly laugh, clear and high and tinkling.

"You've got me, Benjamin!" it trilled. "But you haven't got my treasures. You shan't have *them* to put in a cage — they're going where they belong!"

Out of the net came an airy hand. And a cluster of tiny flitting shapes sped away through the sky. One alone fluttered over the dancers as though looking for something. Then it darted down towards the grass and settled on the left shoulder of Mary Poppins' shadow.

"A birthday gift!" piped a voice from the net, as the Keeper of the Zoological Gardens carried his shadow home.

"A butterfly for a birthday!" The friendly shadows whooped with delight.

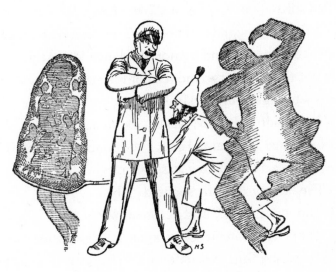

"That's all very well," said a cheerful voice. "Butterflies is all right in their place — but what about my birdies?"

Along the path came a buxom woman, with a tossing, cooing crowd of doves tumbling all about her. There was one on her hat, one on her shawl; a dove's bright eye peered out from her pocket and another from under her skirt.

"Mum!" said the Park Keeper, anxiously. "It's late for you to be out."

Keeping a firm hold of his shadow, he hurried to her side.

"I know it, lad. But I 'ad to come. I don't so much mind about my own — but my birdies 'ave lost their shadders!"

"Excuse me, lovies!" said the Bird Woman's shadow, as she smiled at Jane and Michael. "But I 'ave to go where I belong — that's the law, you know. Hey, old dear!" it called softly. "Lookin' for me, I wonder?"

"I shouldn't wonder if I was!" The Bird Woman gave her shadow a calm and humorous glance. "I got the birds, you got the shadders. And it's not for me to say which is best — but they ought to be together."

Her shadow lightly waved its hand and the Bird Woman gave a contented chuckle. For now, beneath each grey dove, a dark shadow was flying.

"Feed the birds!" she shouted gaily.

"Tuppence a bag!" said her shadow.

"Tuppence, fourpence, sixpence, eightpence — that makes twenty-four. No, it doesn't. What's the matter? I've forgotten how to add!"

Mr. Banks came slowly across the Park with his bathrobe over his shoulders. His arms were stretched out straight before him and he walked with his eyes closed.

"We're here, daddy!" cried Jane and Michael. But Mr. Banks took no notice.

"I've got my bag and the morning paper — and yet there's something missing —— "

"Take him home, someone!" the shadows cried. "He's walking in his sleep!"

And one of them — in a shadowy coat and bowler hat — sprang to Mr. Banks' side.

"There, old chap! I'll do the counting. Come along back to bed."

Mr. Banks turned obediently and his sleeping face lit up.

"I thought there was something missing," he murmured. "But it seems I was mistaken!" He took his shadow by the arm and sauntered away with it.

"Seeking's finding—eh, ducky?" The Bird Woman nudged her shadow. "Oh, beg pardon, Your Worship." She bobbed a curtsey. "I wasn't addressin' *you!*"

For the Lord Mayor and two Aldermen were advancing along the Walk. Their big cloaks billowed out behind them and their chains of office jingled.

"I 'ope I find Your Honour well?" the Bird Woman murmured politely.

"You do not, Mrs. Smith," the Lord Mayor grumbled. "I am feeling very upset."

"Upset, my boy?" shrieked Mrs. Corry, dancing past with the Cow. "Well, an apple a day keeps the doctor away, as I used to remind my great-great-grandson who was thrice Lord Mayor of London. Whittington, his name was. Perhaps you've heard of him?"

"Your great-great-grandfather you mean——" The Lord Mayor looked at her haughtily.

"Fiddlesticks! Indeed, I don't. Well, what's upsetting you?"

"A terrible misfortune, ma'am. I've lost——" He glanced around the Park and his eyes bulged in his head.

"That!" he cried, flinging out his hand. For there, indeed, was his portly shadow, doing its best to conceal itself behind Fannie and Annie.

"Oh, bother!" it wailed. "What a nuisance you are! Couldn't you let me have one night off? If you knew how weary I am of processions! And as for going to see the King——"

"Certainly not!" said the Lord Mayor, "I could never agree to appear in public without a suitable shadow. Such a suggestion is most improper and, what is more, undignified."

"Well, you needn't be so high and mighty. You're only a Lord Mayor, you know — not the Shah of Baghdad!"

"Hic-Hic!" The Park Keeper stifled a snigger and the Lord Mayor turned to him sternly.

"Smith," he declared, "this is your fault. You know the rules and you break them all. Giving a party in the Park! What next, I wonder? I'm afraid there's nothing for it, Smith, but to speak to the Lord High Chancellor!"

"It's not *my* party, Yer Worship — please! Give me another chance, Yer Honour. Think of me pore old——"

"Don't you worry about me, Fred!" The Bird Woman snapped her fingers sharply.

And at once the doves clapped their wings and swooped towards the Lord Mayor. They sat on his head, they sat on his nose, they tucked their tail-feathers down his neck and fluttered inside his cloak.

"Oh, don't! I'm a ticklish man! Hee, hee!" The Lord Mayor, quite against his will, burst into helpless laughter.

"Remove these birds at once, Smith! I won't be tickled — oh, ha, ha!"

He laughed, he crowed, he guffawed, he tittered, ducking and whirling among the dancers as he tried to escape the doves.

"Not under my chin! — Oh, oh! — Have mercy! Oof! There's one inside my sleeve. Oh, ha, ha, ha, ha, ha, ha, hee! Dear me! Is that you, Miss Mary Poppins? Well, that makes all the — tee-hee! — difference. You're so re — ho, ho! — spectable." The Lord Mayor writhed as the soft feathers rustled behind his ears.

"What a wonderful party you're having!" he shrieked. "Ha, ha! Ho, ho! I should have come sooner. Listen! I hear

my favourite tune — 'Over the hills and far away!' Hee, hee! Ha, ha! And far away!"

"Is there anything the matter, your honour?" The Policeman, with Ellen on his arm, strode towards the revels.

"There is!" The Lord Mayor giggled wildly. "I'm ticklish and I can't stop laughing. Everything seems so terribly funny — and you in particular. Do you realise you've lost your shadow? It's over there on a swing — hee, hee! — playing a concertina!"

"No shadow, sir? A concertina?" The Policeman gaped at the Lord Mayor as though he had lost his wits. "Nobody's got a shadow, your honour. And shadows don't play on concertinas — at least, not to my knowledge."

"Don't be so — tee-hee! — silly, man. Everyone's got a shadow!"

"Not at this moment they haven't, your worship! There's a cloud coming over the moon!"

"Alas! A cloud! It came too soon! When shall we meet again?"

A shadowy wailing filled the air. For even as the Policeman spoke, the bright moon veiled her face. Darkness dropped like a cloak on the scene and before the eyes of the watching children every shadow vanished. The merry music died away. And as silence fell upon the Park the steeples above the sleeping city rang their midnight chime.

"Our time is up!" cried the plaintive voices. "Hallowe'en's over! Away, away!"

Light as a breeze, past Jane and Michael, the invisible shadows swept.

"Farewell!" said one.

"Adieu!" another.

And a third at the edge of Jane's ear piped a note on his flute.

"Feed the birds, tuppence a bag!" The Bird Woman whistled softly. And the doves crept out of the Lord Mayor's sleeve and from under the brim of his hat.

Nine! Ten! Eleven! Twelve! The bells of midnight ceased.

"Farewell! Farewell!" called the fading voices.

"Over the hills and far away!" came the far-off fluting echo.

"Oh, Tom, the Piper's son," cried Jane. "When shall we see you again?"

Then something softer than air touched them, enfolded them and drew them away.

"Who are you?" they cried in the falling night. They seemed to be floating on wings of darkness, over the Park and home.

And the answer came from without and within them.

"Your other selves — your shadows . . ."

"Hrrrrumph!" The Lord Mayor gave himself a shake as though he were coming out of a dream.

"Farewell!" he murmured, waving his hand. "Though who — or what — I'm saying it to, I really do not know. I seemed to be part of a beautiful party. All so merry! But where have they gone?"

"I expect you're over-tired, your worship!" The Policeman, closely followed by Ellen, drew him away to the Long Walk and the gate that led to the City.

Behind them marched the Aldermen, solemn and disapproving.

"I expect I am," the Lord Mayor said. "But it didn't *feel* like that . . ."

The Park Keeper glanced around the Park and took his mother's arm. Darkness filled the sky like a tide. In all the world, as far as his watchful eyes could see, there were only two points of light.

"That there star," he said, pointing, "and the night-light in Number Seventeen — if you look at 'em long enough, mum, you can 'ardly tell which is which!"

The Bird Woman drew her doves about her and smiled at him comfortably.

"Well, one's the shadder of the other! Let's be goin', lad . . ."

Michael came slowly in to breakfast, looking back over his shoulder. And slowly, slowly, a dark shape followed him over the floor.

"My shadow's here — is yours, Jane?"

"Yes," she said, sipping her milk. She had been awake a long time, smiling at her shadow. And it seemed to her, as the sun shone in, that her shadow was smiling back.

"And where else would they be, pray? Take your porridge, please."

Mary Poppins, in a fresh white apron, crackled into the room. She was carrying her best blue coat and the hat with the crimson tulip.

"Well — sometimes they're in the Park," said Jane. She gave the white apron a cautious glance. What would it say to *that?* she wondered.

The coat went on to its hook with a jerk and the hat seemed to leap to its paper bag.

"In the Park — or the garden — or up a tree! A shadow goes wherever you go. Don't be silly, Jane."

"But sometimes they escape, Mary Poppins." Michael reached for the sugar. "Like ours, last night, at the Hallowe'en Party!"

"Hallowe'en Party?" she said, staring. And you would have thought, to look at her, she had never heard those words before.

"Yes," he said rashly, taking no notice. "But your shadow never runs away — does it, Mary Poppins?"

She glanced across at the nursery mirror and met her own reflection. The blue eyes glowed, the pink cheeks shone and the mouth wore a small complacent smile.

"Why should it want to?" she said, sniffing. Run away? The idea!

"Not for a thousand pounds!" cried Michael. And the memory of the night's adventure bubbled up inside him. "Oh, how I laughed at the Lord Mayor!" He spluttered at the very thought. "And Mrs. Corry! And Goosey Gander!"

"And you, Mary Poppins," giggled Jane. "Hopping about all over the Park — and the butterfly on your shadow's shoulder!"

Michael and Jane looked at each other and roared with mirth. They flung back their heads and held their sides and rolled around in their chairs.

"Oh, dear! I'm choking! How funny it was!"

"Indeed?"

A voice as sharp as an icicle brought them up with a jerk.

They stopped in the middle of a laugh and tried to compose their faces. For the bright blue eyes of Mary Poppins were wide with shocked surprise.

"Hopping about? With a butterfly? At night? In a public place? Do you sit there, Jane and Michael Banks, and call me a kangaroo?"

This, they could see, was the last straw. The camel's back was broken.

"Sitting on Goosey Gander's shoulder? Hopping and flying all over the Park — is that what you're trying to tell me?"

"Well, not like a kangaroo, Mary Poppins. But you *were* hopping, I *think* —— " Michael plunged for the right

word as she glared at him over the teapot. But the sight of
her face was too much for him. Out of the corner of his
eye he looked across at Jane.

"Help me!" he cried to her silently. "Surely we did not
dream it?"

But Jane, from the corner of *her* eye, was looking back
at him. "No, it was true!" she seemed to say. For she gave
her head a little shake and pointed towards the floor.

Michael looked down.

There lay Mary Poppins' shadow, neatly spread out
upon the carpet. Jane's shadow and his own were leaning
up against it, and upon its shoulder, black in the sun, was
a shadowy butterfly.

"Oh!" cried Michael joyfully, dropping his spoon with a clatter.

"Oh, what?" said Mary Poppins tartly, glancing down at the floor.

She looked from the butterfly to Michael and then from Michael to Jane. And the porridge grew cold on their three plates as they all gazed at each other. Nothing was said — there was nothing to say. There were things, they knew, that could not be told. And, anyway, what did it matter? The three linked shadows on the floor understood it all.

"It's your birthday, isn't it, Mary Poppins?" said Michael at last, with a grin.

"Many happy returns, Mary Poppins!" Jane gave her hand a pat.

A pleased smile crept about her mouth, but she pursed her lips to prevent it.

"Who told you that?" she enquired, sniffing. As if she didn't know!

But Michael was full of joy and courage. If Mary Poppins never explained, why, indeed, should he? He only shook his head and smiled.

"I wonder!" he said, in a priggish voice exactly like her own.

"Impudence!" She sprang at him. But he darted, laughing, away from the table, out of the nursery and down the stairs, with Jane close at his heels.

Along the garden path they ran, through the gate and over the Lane and into the waiting Park.

The morning air was bright and clear, the birds were singing their autumn songs, and the Park Keeper was coming towards them with a late rose stuck in his cap. . . .

Chelsea, London
March 1952

G. I. E. D.

P. L. TRAVERS (1899–1996) was a drama critic, travel essayist, reviewer, lecturer, and the creator of Mary Poppins. Travers wrote eight Mary Poppins books altogether, including *Mary Poppins* (1934), *Mary Poppins Comes Back* (1935), *Mary Poppins Opens the Door* (1943), and *Mary Poppins in the Park* (1952). Ms. Travers wrote several other children's books as well as adult books, but it is for the character of Mary Poppins that she is best remembered.

ON NOT WRITING FOR CHILDREN*

P. L. Travers

"On Not Writing for Children"—what an odd title for a lecture, you will say, especially from one whose books are largely read by children! But I hope they are also read by grownups, as you will see by what I'm going to say. I think that grownups are a very important part of children's literature, so called. I'm not sure that I believe in children's literature, but as I go on, you'll see why. Well, you know, I'm not writing for children. This seems to suggest that there exists some particular reason for the fact that I don't write for children, and that I am proposing to explain it: a sort of secret recipe that, with luck, can be divulged.

But if there is a secret, I am not going to divulge it, not because I will not, but because I cannot. I cannot tell you how it's done. There is something in me that hesitates to inquire too closely into this business of writing; fear perhaps that if one discovered the "how" of it, the way it's done, one might be tempted to make use of it and let it become mechanical. There is something in me that could go on writing and writing, book after book about Mary Poppins; and maybe I will do that, but if I know how to do it, I shan't be able to do it at all. To me it is a mystery, and I think it should remain a mystery. Some of you will know, perhaps, that one of the most annoying aspects of a character in a book of mine is that she never explains. There is a Chinese ideogram called *pai* that has, I am told, two different meanings, depending on the context. One is "explain," but the other is "in vain." How can I add anything to that? It is in vain to explain that the Chinese know better than we, even though they are doing all those terrible things to Confucius.

And yet I feel bound to clarify this feeling I have. No, it is stronger than a feeling—this conviction I have, that very few people write for children.

Not long ago, an American journalist, Clifton Fadiman, a well-known writer and collector of children's books, asked me for (and I quote) "your general ideas on literature for children, your aims and purposes and what led you to the field." Well, this flummoxed me. I hadn't any ideas, general or specific, on literature for children and I hadn't set out with aims or purposes. I couldn't say that anything I had done was intended or invented. It simply happened. Furthermore, I told him that I was not at all sure that I was in his field, even though many children throughout the world have been kind enough to read my books. I said it was a strong belief of mine that I didn't write for children at all, that the idea simply didn't enter my head. I am bound to assume, and I told him this, that there is such a field. I hear about it so often, but I wonder if it is a valid one or whether it has not been created less by writers than by publishers and booksellers—and perhaps indeed by people who teach Children's Literature. I am always astonished when I see books labeled "For from 5 to 7" or "From 9 to 12" because who is to know what child will be moved by what book and at what age? Who is to be the judge? I'm not one; I can't tell.

Nothing I had written before Mary Poppins had anything to do with children and I have always assumed, when I thought about it at all, that she had come out of the same well of nothingness (and by nothingness, I mean no-thing-ness) as the poetry, myth, and legend that had absorbed me all my writing life. If I had been told while I was working on the book that I was doing it for children, I think I would have been terrified. How would I have had the effrontery to attempt such a thing? For, if for children, the question immediately arises, "for what children?" That word "children" is a large blanket; it covers, as with grownups, every kind of being that exists. Was I writing for the children in Japan, where Mary Poppins is required reading in the English language schools and universities, telling a race of people who have no staircases in their homes about somebody who slid up the bannisters? For the children in Africa, who read it in Swahili, and who have never even seen an umbrella, much less used one? Or to come to those nearer my world, was I writing for the boy who wrote to me with such noble anger when he came to the end of the third book where Mary Poppins goes away forever, "Madum (he spelt it M-A-D-U-M), you have sent Mary Poppins away. Madum, I will never forgive you. You have made the children cry." Well, what a reproach! What a picture.

The children weeping in the world and I alone responsible! The labels "From 5 to 7" or "9 to 12" can have no relation to such a letter. It came straight out of the human heart, a heart that, no matter what age, was capable of pain. That boy had already begun to know what sorrow was and he reproached me for his knowledge.

. . .

And here it is worth while remembering, since we are discussing Not Writing for Children, that neither the Sleeping Beauty nor Rumpelstiltzkin was really written for children. In fact, none of the fundamental fairy stories was ever written at all. They all arose spontaneously from the folk and were transmitted orally from generation to generation to unlettered listeners of all ages. It was not until the nineteenth century, when the collectors set them down in print, that the children purloined them and made them their own. They were the perquisites of the grownups and the children simply took them. I remember a poem of Walter de la Mare's which begins, "I'll sing you a song of the world's little children magic has stolen away." Well, I could sing you a song of the world's magic the children have stolen away. For in the long run it is children themselves who decide what they want. They put out their hands and abstract a treasure from all sorts of likely and unlikely places, as I have tried to show. So, confronted with this hoard of stolen riches, the question of who writes or who does not write for children becomes small and, in fact, irrelevant. For every book is a message, and if children happen to receive and like it, they will appropriate it to themselves no matter what the author may say nor what label he gives himself. And those who, against all odds, and I'm one of them, protest that they do not write for children cannot help being aware of this fact and are, I assure you, grateful.

*Excerpt of transcription of a paper read by P. L. Travers at the University of Connecticut, March 26, 1974. Reprinted with permission of the Estate of P. L. Travers. All rights reserved.